CHASE BRANCH LIBRARY
17731 W. SEVEN MILE RD.
DETROIT, MI 48235
578-8002

"SUCH A SPLENDID TALE AND SUCH
A FANTISTORICAL! I READ MY EYES OUT."
—ANNE McCAFFREY

"MARTIN MAKES A TRIUMPHANT RETURN TO HIGH
FANTASY....[HIS] TROPHY CASE IS ALREADY STUFFED
WITH MAJOR PRIZES, INCLUDING HUGOS, NEBULAS,
LOCUS AWARDS AND A BRAM STOKER. HE'S PROBABLY
GOING TO HAVE TO ADD ANOTHER SHELF, AT LEAST."
—PUBLISHERS WEEKLY (STARRED REVIEW)

"IT IS PERHAPS THE BEST OF THE EPIC FANTASIES."
—MARION ZIMMER BRADLEY

"THE MAJOR FANTASY OF THE
DECADE...COMPULSIVELY READABLE."
—THE DENVER POST

"GEORGE R. R. MARTIN IS ONE OF OUR VERY
BEST SCIENCE FICTION WRITERS, AND THIS IS ONE
OF HIS VERY BEST BOOKS."
—RAYMOND E. FEIST

"WE HAVE BEEN INVITED TO A GRAND FEAST AND
PAGEANT: GEORGE R. R. MARTIN HAS UNVEILED FOR US
AN INTENSELY REALIZED, ROMANTIC BUT REALISTIC
WORLD....IF THE NEXT TWO VOLUMES ARE AS GOOD AS
THIS ONE, IT WILL BE A WONDERFUL FEAST INDEED."
—CHICAGO SUN-TIMES

"THE MAJOR FANTASY PUBLISHING EVENT OF 1996."
—SCIENCE FICTION CHRONICLE

BY GEORGE R. R. MARTIN

A SONG OF ICE AND FIRE
Book One: *A Game of Thrones*
Book Two: *A Clash of Kings*
Book Three: *A Storm of Swords*

Dying of the Light
Windhaven (with Lisa Tuttle)
Fevre Dream
The Armageddon Rag
Dead Man's Hand (with John J. Miller)

SHORT STORY COLLECTIONS
A Song for Lya and Other Stories
Songs of Stars and Shadows
Sandkings
Songs the Dead Men Sing
Nightflyers
Tuf Voyaging
Portraits of His Children

EDITED BY GEORGE R. R. MARTIN
New Voices in Science Fiction, Volumes 1–4
The Science Fiction Weight-Loss Book
(with Isaac Asimov and Martin Harry Greenberg)
The John W. Campbell Awards, Volume 5
Night Visions 3
Wild Cards I–XV

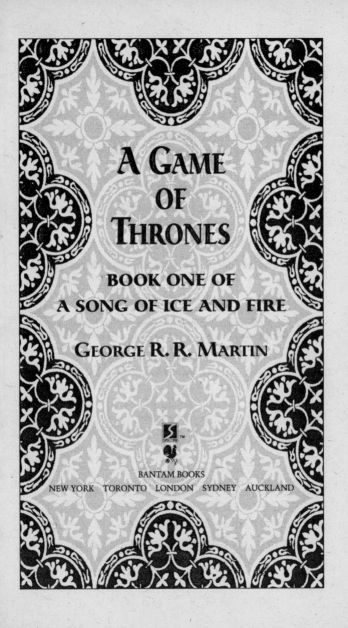

A GAME OF THRONES

BOOK ONE OF
A SONG OF ICE AND FIRE

GEORGE R. R. MARTIN

BANTAM BOOKS
NEW YORK TORONTO LONDON SYDNEY AUCKLAND

A GAME OF THRONES
A Bantam Spectra Book

PUBLISHING HISTORY
Bantam Spectra hardcover edition published September 1996
Bantam Spectra mass market reissue edition published September 1997
Bantam Spectra trade paperback edition published June 2002
Bantam Spectra mass market reissue edition / August 2005

Published by
Bantam Dell
A Division of Random House, Inc.
New York, New York

This is a work of fiction. Names, characters, places, and incidents
either are the product of the author's imagination or are used
fictitiously. Any resemblance to actual persons, living or dead,
events, or locales is entirely coincidental.

All rights reserved
Copyright © 1996 by George R. R. Martin
Cover art copyright © 2005 by Stephen Youll
Cover design copyright © 2005 by Jamie S. Warren Youll
Maps by James Sinclair
Heraldic crests by Virginia Norey
Library of Congress Catalog Number: 95-43936

If you purchased this book without a cover, you should be aware
that this book is stolen property. It was reported as "unsold and
destroyed" to the publisher, and neither the author nor the
publisher has received any payment for this "stripped book."

Bantam Books, the rooster colophon, Spectra, and the portrayal of
a boxed "s" are registered trademarks of Random House, Inc.

ISBN 0-553-58848-6

Manufactured in the United States of America
Published simultaneously in Canada

www.bantamdell.com

OPM   10   9   8   7   6   5   4   3   2   1

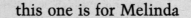
this one is for Melinda

PROLOGUE

"We should start back," Gared urged as the woods began to grow dark around them. "The wildlings are dead."

"Do the dead frighten you?" Ser Waymar Royce asked with just the hint of a smile.

Gared did not rise to the bait. He was an old man, past fifty, and he had seen the lordlings come and go. "Dead is dead," he said. "We have no business with the dead."

"Are they dead?" Royce asked softly. "What proof have we?"

"Will saw them," Gared said. "If he says they are dead, that's proof enough for me."

Will had known they would drag him into the quarrel sooner or later. He wished it had been later rather than sooner. "My mother told me that dead men sing no songs," he put in.

"My wet nurse said the same thing, Will," Royce replied. "Never believe anything you hear at a woman's tit. There are things to be learned even from the dead." His voice echoed, too loud in the twilit forest.

"We have a long ride before us," Gared pointed out. "Eight days, maybe nine. And night is falling."

Ser Waymar Royce glanced at the sky with disinterest. "It does that every day about this time. Are you unmanned by the dark, Gared?"

Will could see the tightness around Gared's mouth, the barely suppressed anger in his eyes under the thick black hood of his cloak. Gared had spent forty years in the Night's Watch, man and boy, and he was not accustomed to being made light of. Yet it was more than that. Under the wounded pride, Will could sense something else in the older man. You could taste it; a nervous tension that came perilous close to fear.

Will shared his unease. He had been four years on the Wall. The first time he had been sent beyond, all the old stories had come rushing back, and his bowels had turned to water. He had laughed about it afterward. He was a veteran of a hundred rangings by now, and the endless dark wilderness that the southron called the haunted forest had no more terrors for him.

Until tonight. Something was different tonight. There was an edge to this darkness that made his hackles rise. Nine days they had been riding, north and northwest and then north again, farther and farther from the Wall, hard on the track of a band of wildling raiders. Each day had been worse than the day that had come before it. Today was the worst of all. A cold wind was blowing out of the north, and it made the trees rustle like living things. All day, Will had felt as though something were watching him, something cold and implacable that loved him not. Gared had felt it too. Will wanted nothing so much as to ride hellbent for the safety of the Wall, but that was not a feeling to share with your commander.

Especially not a commander like this one.

Ser Waymar Royce was the youngest son of an ancient house with too many heirs. He was a handsome youth of eighteen, grey-eyed and graceful and slender as a knife. Mounted on his huge black destrier, the knight towered above Will and Gared on their smaller garrons. He wore black leather boots, black woolen pants, black moleskin gloves, and a fine supple coat of gleaming black ringmail over layers of black wool and boiled leather. Ser Waymar had been a Sworn Brother of the Night's Watch for less than half a year, but no one could say he had not prepared for his vocation. At least insofar as his wardrobe was concerned.

His cloak was his crowning glory; sable, thick and black and soft as sin. "Bet he killed them all himself, he did," Gared told the barracks over wine, "twisted their little heads off, our mighty warrior." They had all shared the laugh.

It is hard to take orders from a man you laughed at in your cups, Will reflected as he sat shivering atop his garron. Gared must have felt the same.

"Mormont said as we should track them, and we did," Gared said. "They're dead. They shan't trouble us no more. There's hard riding before us. I don't like this weather. If it snows, we could be a fortnight getting back, and snow's the best we can hope for. Ever seen an ice storm, my lord?"

The lordling seemed not to hear him. He studied the deepening twilight in that half-bored, half-distracted way he had. Will had ridden with the knight long enough to understand that it was best not to interrupt him when he looked like that. "Tell me again what you saw, Will. All the details. Leave nothing out."

Will had been a hunter before he joined the Night's Watch. Well, a poacher in truth. Mallister freeriders had caught him red-handed in the Mallisters' own woods, skinning one of the Mallisters' own bucks, and it had been a choice of putting on the black or losing a hand. No one could move through the woods as silent as Will, and it had not taken the black brothers long to discover his talent.

"The camp is two miles farther on, over that ridge, hard beside a stream," Will said. "I got close as I dared. There's eight of them, men and women both. No children I could see. They put up a lean-to against the rock. The snow's pretty well covered it now, but I could still make it out. No fire burning, but the firepit was still plain as day. No one moving. I watched a long time. No living man ever lay so still."

"Did you see any blood?"

"Well, no," Will admitted.

"Did you see any weapons?"

"Some swords, a few bows. One man had an axe.

Heavy-looking, double-bladed, a cruel piece of iron. It was on the ground beside him, right by his hand."

"Did you make note of the position of the bodies?"

Will shrugged. "A couple are sitting up against the rock. Most of them on the ground. Fallen, like."

"Or sleeping," Royce suggested.

"Fallen," Will insisted. "There's one woman up an ironwood, half-hid in the branches. A far-eyes." He smiled thinly. "I took care she never saw me. When I got closer, I saw that she wasn't moving neither." Despite himself, he shivered.

"You have a chill?" Royce asked.

"Some," Will muttered. "The wind, m'lord."

The young knight turned back to his grizzled man-at-arms. Frost-fallen leaves whispered past them, and Royce's destrier moved restlessly. "What do you think might have killed these men, Gared?" Ser Waymar asked casually. He adjusted the drape of his long sable cloak.

"It was the cold," Gared said with iron certainty. "I saw men freeze last winter, and the one before, when I was half a boy. Everyone talks about snows forty foot deep, and how the ice wind comes howling out of the north, but the real enemy is the cold. It steals up on you quieter than Will, and at first you shiver and your teeth chatter and you stamp your feet and dream of mulled wine and nice hot fires. It burns, it does. Nothing burns like the cold. But only for a while. Then it gets inside you and starts to fill you up, and after a while you don't have the strength to fight it. It's easier just to sit down or go to sleep. They say you don't feel any pain toward the end. First you go weak and drowsy, and everything starts to fade, and then it's like sinking into a sea of warm milk. Peaceful, like."

"Such eloquence, Gared," Ser Waymar observed. "I never suspected you had it in you."

"I've had the cold in me too, lordling." Gared pulled back his hood, giving Ser Waymar a good long look at the stumps where his ears had been. "Two ears, three toes, and the little finger off my left hand. I got off light. We found my brother frozen at his watch, with a smile on his face."

Ser Waymar shrugged. "You ought dress more warmly, Gared."

Gared glared at the lordling, the scars around his ear holes flushed red with anger where Maester Aemon had cut the ears away. "We'll see how warm you can dress when the winter comes." He pulled up his hood and hunched over his garron, silent and sullen.

"If Gared said it was the cold . . ." Will began.

"Have you drawn any watches this past week, Will?"

"Yes, m'lord." There never was a week when he did not draw a dozen bloody watches. What was the man driving at?

"And how did you find the Wall?"

"Weeping," Will said, frowning. He saw it clear enough, now that the lordling had pointed it out. "They couldn't have froze. Not if the Wall was weeping. It wasn't cold enough."

Royce nodded. "Bright lad. We've had a few light frosts this past week, and a quick flurry of snow now and then, but surely no cold fierce enough to kill eight grown men. Men clad in fur and leather, let me remind you, with shelter near at hand, and the means of making fire." The knight's smile was cocksure. "Will, lead us there. I would see these dead men for myself."

And then there was nothing to be done for it. The order had been given, and honor bound them to obey.

Will went in front, his shaggy little garron picking the way carefully through the undergrowth. A light snow had fallen the night before, and there were stones and roots and hidden sinks lying just under its crust, waiting for the careless and the unwary. Ser Waymar Royce came next, his great black destrier snorting impatiently. The warhorse was the wrong mount for ranging, but try and tell that to the lordling. Gared brought up the rear. The old man-at-arms muttered to himself as he rode.

Twilight deepened. The cloudless sky turned a deep purple, the color of an old bruise, then faded to black. The stars began to come out. A half-moon rose. Will was grateful for the light.

"We can make a better pace than this, surely," Royce said when the moon was full risen.

"Not with this horse," Will said. Fear had made him insolent. "Perhaps my lord would care to take the lead?"

Ser Waymar Royce did not deign to reply.

Somewhere off in the wood a wolf howled.

Will pulled his garron over beneath an ancient gnarled ironwood and dismounted.

"Why are you stopping?" Ser Waymar asked.

"Best go the rest of the way on foot, m'lord. It's just over that ridge."

Royce paused a moment, staring off into the distance, his face reflective. A cold wind whispered through the trees. His great sable cloak stirred behind like something half-alive.

"There's something wrong here," Gared muttered.

The young knight gave him a disdainful smile. "Is there?"

"Can't you feel it?" Gared asked. "Listen to the darkness."

Will could feel it. Four years in the Night's Watch, and he had never been so afraid. What was it?

"Wind. Trees rustling. A wolf. Which sound is it that unmans you so, Gared?" When Gared did not answer, Royce slid gracefully from his saddle. He tied the destrier securely to a low-hanging limb, well away from the other horses, and drew his longsword from its sheath. Jewels glittered in its hilt, and the moonlight ran down the shining steel. It was a splendid weapon, castle-forged, and new-made from the look of it. Will doubted it had ever been swung in anger.

"The trees press close here," Will warned. "That sword will tangle you up, m'lord. Better a knife."

"If I need instruction, I will ask for it," the young lord said. "Gared, stay here. Guard the horses."

Gared dismounted. "We need a fire. I'll see to it."

"How big a fool are you, old man? If there are enemies in this wood, a fire is the last thing we want."

"There's some enemies a fire will keep away," Gared said. "Bears and direwolves and . . . and other things . . ."

Ser Waymar's mouth became a hard line. "No fire."

Gared's hood shadowed his face, but Will could see the hard glitter in his eyes as he stared at the knight. For a moment he was afraid the older man would go for his sword. It was a short, ugly thing, its grip discolored by sweat, its edge nicked from hard use, but Will would not have given an iron bob for the lordling's life if Gared pulled it from its scabbard.

Finally Gared looked down. "No fire," he muttered, low under his breath.

Royce took it for acquiescence and turned away. "Lead on," he said to Will.

Will threaded their way through a thicket, then started up the slope to the low ridge where he had found his vantage point under a sentinel tree. Under the thin crust of snow, the ground was damp and muddy, slick footing, with rocks and hidden roots to trip you up. Will made no sound as he climbed. Behind him, he heard the soft metallic slither of the lordling's ringmail, the rustle of leaves, and muttered curses as reaching branches grabbed at his longsword and tugged on his splendid sable cloak.

The great sentinel was right there at the top of the ridge, where Will had known it would be, its lowest branches a bare foot off the ground. Will slid in underneath, flat on his belly in the snow and the mud, and looked down on the empty clearing below.

His heart stopped in his chest. For a moment he dared not breathe. Moonlight shone down on the clearing, the ashes of the firepit, the snow-covered lean-to, the great rock, the little half-frozen stream. Everything was just as it had been a few hours ago.

They were gone. All the bodies were gone.

"Gods!" he heard behind him. A sword slashed at a branch as Ser Waymar Royce gained the ridge. He stood there beside the sentinel, longsword in hand, his cloak billowing behind him as the wind came up, outlined nobly against the stars for all to see.

"Get *down!*" Will whispered urgently. "Something's wrong."

Royce did not move. He looked down at the empty clearing and laughed. "Your dead men seem to have moved camp, Will."

Will's voice abandoned him. He groped for words that did not come. It was not possible. His eyes swept back and forth over the abandoned campsite, stopped on the axe. A huge double-bladed battle-axe, still lying where he had seen it last, untouched. A valuable weapon . . .

"On your feet, Will," Ser Waymar commanded. "There's no one here. I won't have you hiding under a bush."

Reluctantly, Will obeyed.

Ser Waymar looked him over with open disapproval. "I am not going back to Castle Black a failure on my first ranging. We *will* find these men." He glanced around. "Up the tree. Be quick about it. Look for a fire."

Will turned away, wordless. There was no use to argue. The wind was moving. It cut right through him. He went to the tree, a vaulting grey-green sentinel, and began to climb. Soon his hands were sticky with sap, and he was lost among the needles. Fear filled his gut like a meal he could not digest. He whispered a prayer to the nameless gods of the wood, and slipped his dirk free of its sheath. He put it between his teeth to keep both hands free for climbing. The taste of cold iron in his mouth gave him comfort.

Down below, the lordling called out suddenly, "Who goes there?" Will heard uncertainty in the challenge. He stopped climbing; he listened; he watched.

The woods gave answer: the rustle of leaves, the icy rush of the stream, a distant hoot of a snow owl.

The Others made no sound.

Will saw movement from the corner of his eye. Pale shapes gliding through the wood. He turned his head, glimpsed a white shadow in the darkness. Then it was gone. Branches stirred gently in the wind, scratching at one another with wooden fingers. Will opened his mouth to call down a warning, and the words seemed to freeze in his throat. Perhaps he was wrong. Perhaps it had only been a bird, a reflection on the snow, some trick of the moonlight. What had he seen, after all?

"Will, where are you?" Ser Waymar called up. "Can you see anything?" He was turning in a slow circle, suddenly wary, his sword in hand. He must have felt them, as Will felt them. There was nothing to see. "Answer me! Why is it so cold?"

It *was* cold. Shivering, Will clung more tightly to his perch. His face pressed hard against the trunk of the sentinel. He could feel the sweet, sticky sap on his cheek.

A shadow emerged from the dark of the wood. It stood in front of Royce. Tall, it was, and gaunt and hard as old bones, with flesh pale as milk. Its armor seemed to change color as it moved; here it was white as new-fallen snow, there black as shadow, everywhere dappled with the deep grey-green of the trees. The patterns ran like moonlight on water with every step it took.

Will heard the breath go out of Ser Waymar Royce in a long hiss. "Come no farther," the lordling warned. His voice cracked like a boy's. He threw the long sable cloak back over his shoulders, to free his arms for battle, and took his sword in both hands. The wind had stopped. It was very cold.

The Other slid forward on silent feet. In its hand was a longsword like none that Will had ever seen. No human metal had gone into the forging of that blade. It was alive with moonlight, translucent, a shard of crystal so thin that it seemed almost to vanish when seen edge-on. There was a faint blue shimmer to the thing, a ghost-light that played around its edges, and somehow Will knew it was sharper than any razor.

Ser Waymar met him bravely. "Dance with me then." He lifted his sword high over his head, defiant. His hands trembled from the weight of it, or perhaps from the cold. Yet in that moment, Will thought, he was a boy no longer, but a man of the Night's Watch.

The Other halted. Will saw its eyes; blue, deeper and bluer than any human eyes, a blue that burned like ice. They fixed on the longsword trembling on high, watched the moonlight running cold along the metal. For a heart-beat he dared to hope.

They emerged silently from the shadows, twins to the first. Three of them . . . four . . . five . . . Ser Waymar may have felt the cold that came with them, but he never saw them, never heard them. Will had to call out. It was his duty. And his death, if he did. He shivered, and hugged the tree, and kept the silence.

The pale sword came shivering through the air.

Ser Waymar met it with steel. When the blades met, there was no ring of metal on metal; only a high, thin sound at the edge of hearing, like an animal screaming in pain. Royce checked a second blow, and a third, then fell back a step. Another flurry of blows, and he fell back again.

Behind him, to right, to left, all around him, the watchers stood patient, faceless, silent, the shifting patterns of their delicate armor making them all but invisible in the wood. Yet they made no move to interfere.

Again and again the swords met, until Will wanted to cover his ears against the strange anguished keening of their clash. Ser Waymar was panting from the effort now, his breath steaming in the moonlight. His blade was white with frost; the Other's danced with pale blue light.

Then Royce's parry came a beat too late. The pale sword bit through the ringmail beneath his arm. The young lord cried out in pain. Blood welled between the rings. It steamed in the cold, and the droplets seemed red as fire where they touched the snow. Ser Waymar's fingers brushed his side. His moleskin glove came away soaked with red.

The Other said something in a language that Will did not know; his voice was like the cracking of ice on a winter lake, and the words were mocking.

Ser Waymar Royce found his fury. "For Robert!" he shouted, and he came up snarling, lifting the frost-covered longsword with both hands and swinging it around in a flat sidearm slash with all his weight behind it. The Other's parry was almost lazy.

When the blades touched, the steel shattered.

A scream echoed through the forest night, and the longsword shivered into a hundred brittle pieces, the shards scattering like a rain of needles. Royce went to his knees, shrieking, and covered his eyes. Blood welled between his fingers.

The watchers moved forward together, as if some signal had been given. Swords rose and fell, all in a deathly silence. It was cold butchery. The pale blades sliced through ringmail as if it were silk. Will closed his eyes. Far beneath him, he heard their voices and laughter sharp as icicles.

When he found the courage to look again, a long time had passed, and the ridge below was empty.

He stayed in the tree, scarce daring to breathe, while the moon crept slowly across the black sky. Finally, his muscles cramping and his fingers numb with cold, he climbed down.

Royce's body lay facedown in the snow, one arm outflung. The thick sable cloak had been slashed in a dozen places. Lying dead like that, you saw how young he was. A boy.

He found what was left of the sword a few feet away,

the end splintered and twisted like a tree struck by lightning. Will knelt, looked around warily, and snatched it up. The broken sword would be his proof. Gared would know what to make of it, and if not him, then surely that old bear Mormont or Maester Aemon. Would Gared still be waiting with the horses? He had to hurry.

Will rose. Ser Waymar Royce stood over him.

His fine clothes were a tatter, his face a ruin. A shard from his sword transfixed the blind white pupil of his left eye.

The right eye was open. The pupil burned blue. It saw.

The broken sword fell from nerveless fingers. Will closed his eyes to pray. Long, elegant hands brushed his cheek, then tightened around his throat. They were gloved in the finest moleskin and sticky with blood, yet the touch was icy cold.

BRAN

The morning had dawned clear and cold, with a crispness that hinted at the end of summer. They set forth at daybreak to see a man beheaded, twenty in all, and Bran rode among them, nervous with excitement. This was the first time he had been deemed old enough to go with his lord father and his brothers to see the king's justice done. It was the ninth year of summer, and the seventh of Bran's life.

The man had been taken outside a small holdfast in the hills. Robb thought he was a wildling, his sword sworn to Mance Rayder, the King-beyond-the-Wall. It made Bran's skin prickle to think of it. He remembered the hearth tales Old Nan told them. The wildlings were cruel men, she said, slavers and slayers and thieves. They consorted with giants and ghouls, stole girl children in the dead of night, and drank blood from polished horns. And their women lay with the Others in the Long Night to sire terrible half-human children.

But the man they found bound hand and foot to the holdfast wall awaiting the king's justice was old and scrawny, not much taller than Robb. He had lost both ears and a finger to frostbite, and he dressed all in black, the same as a brother of the Night's Watch, except that his furs were ragged and greasy.

The breath of man and horse mingled, steaming, in the cold morning air as his lord father had the man cut down from the wall and dragged before them. Robb and Jon sat tall and still on their horses, with Bran between them on his pony, trying to seem older than seven, trying to pretend that he'd seen all this before. A faint wind blew through the holdfast gate. Over their heads flapped the banner of the Starks of Winterfell: a grey direwolf racing across an ice-white field.

Bran's father sat solemnly on his horse, long brown hair stirring in the wind. His closely trimmed beard was shot with white, making him look older than his thirty-five years. He had a grim cast to his grey eyes this day, and he seemed not at all the man who would sit before the fire in the evening and talk softly of the age of heroes and the children of the forest. He had taken off Father's face, Bran thought, and donned the face of Lord Stark of Winterfell.

There were questions asked and answers given there in the chill of morning, but afterward Bran could not recall much of what had been said. Finally his lord father gave a command, and two of his guardsmen dragged the ragged man to the ironwood stump in the center of the square. They forced his head down onto the hard black wood. Lord Eddard Stark dismounted and his ward Theon Greyjoy brought forth the sword. "Ice," that sword was called. It was as wide across as a man's hand, and taller even than Robb. The blade was Valyrian steel, spell-forged and dark as smoke. Nothing held an edge like Valyrian steel.

His father peeled off his gloves and handed them to Jory Cassel, the captain of his household guard. He took hold of Ice with both hands and said, "In the name of Robert of the House Baratheon, the First of his Name, King of the Andals and the Rhoynar and the First Men, Lord of the Seven Kingdoms and Protector of the Realm, by the word of Eddard of the House Stark, Lord of Winterfell and Warden of the North, I do sentence you to die." He lifted the greatsword high above his head.

Bran's bastard brother Jon Snow moved closer. "Keep

the pony well in hand," he whispered. "And don't look away. Father will know if you do."

Bran kept his pony well in hand, and did not look away.

His father took off the man's head with a single sure stroke. Blood sprayed out across the snow, as red as summerwine. One of the horses reared and had to be restrained to keep from bolting. Bran could not take his eyes off the blood. The snows around the stump drank it eagerly, reddening as he watched.

The head bounced off a thick root and rolled. It came up near Greyjoy's feet. Theon was a lean, dark youth of nineteen who found everything amusing. He laughed, put his boot on the head, and kicked it away.

"Ass," Jon muttered, low enough so Greyjoy did not hear. He put a hand on Bran's shoulder, and Bran looked over at his bastard brother. "You did well," Jon told him solemnly. Jon was fourteen, an old hand at justice.

It seemed colder on the long ride back to Winterfell, though the wind had died by then and the sun was higher in the sky. Bran rode with his brothers, well ahead of the main party, his pony struggling hard to keep up with their horses.

"The deserter died bravely," Robb said. He was big and broad and growing every day, with his mother's coloring, the fair skin, red-brown hair, and blue eyes of the Tullys of Riverrun. "He had courage, at the least."

"No," Jon Snow said quietly. "It was not courage. This one was dead of fear. You could see it in his eyes, Stark." Jon's eyes were a grey so dark they seemed almost black, but there was little they did not see. He was of an age with Robb, but they did not look alike. Jon was slender where Robb was muscular, dark where Robb was fair, graceful and quick where his half brother was strong and fast.

Robb was not impressed. "The Others take his eyes," he swore. "He died well. Race you to the bridge?"

"Done," Jon said, kicking his horse forward. Robb cursed and followed, and they galloped off down the trail, Robb laughing and hooting, Jon silent and intent. The hooves of their horses kicked up showers of snow as they went.

Bran did not try to follow. His pony could not keep up.

He had seen the ragged man's eyes, and he was thinking of them now. After a while, the sound of Robb's laughter receded, and the woods grew silent again.

So deep in thought was he that he never heard the rest of the party until his father moved up to ride beside him. "Are you well, Bran?" he asked, not unkindly.

"Yes, Father," Bran told him. He looked up. Wrapped in his furs and leathers, mounted on his great warhorse, his lord father loomed over him like a giant. "Robb says the man died bravely, but Jon says he was afraid."

"What do you think?" his father asked.

Bran thought about it. "Can a man still be brave if he's afraid?"

"That is the only time a man can be brave," his father told him. "Do you understand why I did it?"

"He was a wildling," Bran said. "They carry off women and sell them to the Others."

His lord father smiled. "Old Nan has been telling you stories again. In truth, the man was an oathbreaker, a deserter from the Night's Watch. No man is more dangerous. The deserter knows his life is forfeit if he is taken, so he will not flinch from any crime, no matter how vile. But you mistake me. The question was not why the man had to die, but why *I* must do it."

Bran had no answer for that. "King Robert has a headsman," he said, uncertainly.

"He does," his father admitted. "As did the Targaryen kings before him. Yet our way is the older way. The blood of the First Men still flows in the veins of the Starks, and we hold to the belief that the man who passes the sentence should swing the sword. If you would take a man's life, you owe it to him to look into his eyes and hear his final words. And if you cannot bear to do that, then perhaps the man does not deserve to die.

"One day, Bran, you will be Robb's bannerman, holding a keep of your own for your brother and your king, and justice will fall to you. When that day comes, you must take no pleasure in the task, but neither must you look away. A ruler who hides behind paid executioners soon forgets what death is."

That was when Jon reappeared on the crest of the hill before them. He waved and shouted down at them. *"Fa-*

ther, Bran, come quickly, see what Robb has found!"
Then he was gone again.

Jory rode up beside them. "Trouble, my lord?"

"Beyond a doubt," his lord father said. "Come, let us
see what mischief my sons have rooted out now." He sent
his horse into a trot. Jory and Bran and the rest came after.

They found Robb on the riverbank north of the bridge,
with Jon still mounted beside him. The late summer
snows had been heavy this moonturn. Robb stood knee-
deep in white, his hood pulled back so the sun shone in
his hair. He was cradling something in his arm, while the
boys talked in hushed, excited voices.

The riders picked their way carefully through the
drifts, groping for solid footing on the hidden, uneven
ground. Jory Cassel and Theon Greyjoy were the first to
reach the boys. Greyjoy was laughing and joking as
he rode. Bran heard the breath go out of him. "*Gods!*" he
exclaimed, struggling to keep control of his horse as he
reached for his sword.

Jory's sword was already out. "Robb, get away from
it!" he called as his horse reared under him.

Robb grinned and looked up from the bundle in his
arms. "She can't hurt you," he said. "She's dead, Jory."

Bran was afire with curiosity by then. He would have
spurred the pony faster, but his father made them dismount beside the bridge and approach on foot. Bran
jumped off and ran.

By then Jon, Jory, and Theon Greyjoy had all dismounted as well. "What in the seven hells is it?" Greyjoy
was saying.

"A wolf," Robb told him.

"A freak," Greyjoy said. "Look at the *size* of it."

Bran's heart was thumping in his chest as he pushed
through a waist-high drift to his brothers' side.

Half-buried in bloodstained snow, a huge dark shape
slumped in death. Ice had formed in its shaggy grey fur,
and the faint smell of corruption clung to it like a
woman's perfume. Bran glimpsed blind eyes crawling
with maggots, a wide mouth full of yellowed teeth. But it
was the size of it that made him gasp. It was bigger than
his pony, twice the size of the largest hound in his father's kennel.

"It's no freak," Jon said calmly. "That's a direwolf. They grow larger than the other kind."

Theon Greyjoy said, "There's not been a direwolf sighted south of the Wall in two hundred years."

"I see one now," Jon replied.

Bran tore his eyes away from the monster. That was when he noticed the bundle in Robb's arms. He gave a cry of delight and moved closer. The pup was a tiny ball of grey-black fur, its eyes still closed. It nuzzled blindly against Robb's chest as he cradled it, searching for milk among his leathers, making a sad little whimpery sound. Bran reached out hesitantly. "Go on," Robb told him. "You can touch him."

Bran gave the pup a quick nervous stroke, then turned as Jon said, "Here you go." His half brother put a second pup into his arms. "There are five of them." Bran sat down in the snow and hugged the wolf pup to his face. Its fur was soft and warm against his cheek.

"Direwolves loose in the realm, after so many years," muttered Hullen, the master of horse. "I like it not."

"It is a sign," Jory said.

Father frowned. "This is only a dead animal, Jory," he said. Yet he seemed troubled. Snow crunched under his boots as he moved around the body. "Do we know what killed her?"

"There's something in the throat," Robb told him, proud to have found the answer before his father even asked. "There, just under the jaw."

His father knelt and groped under the beast's head with his hand. He gave a yank and held it up for all to see. A foot of shattered antler, tines snapped off, all wet with blood.

A sudden silence descended over the party. The men looked at the antler uneasily, and no one dared to speak. Even Bran could sense their fear, though he did not understand.

His father tossed the antler to the side and cleansed his hands in the snow. "I'm surprised she lived long enough to whelp," he said. His voice broke the spell.

"Maybe she didn't," Jory said. "I've heard tales . . . maybe the bitch was already dead when the pups came."

"Born with the dead," another man put in. "Worse luck."

"No matter," said Hullen. "They be dead soon enough too."

Bran gave a wordless cry of dismay.

"The sooner the better," Theon Greyjoy agreed. He drew his sword. "Give the beast here, Bran."

The little thing squirmed against him, as if it heard and understood. *"No!"* Bran cried out fiercely. "It's mine."

"Put away your sword, Greyjoy," Robb said. For a moment he sounded as commanding as their father, like the lord he would someday be. "We will keep these pups."

"You cannot do that, boy," said Harwin, who was Hullen's son.

"It be a mercy to kill them," Hullen said.

Bran looked to his lord father for rescue, but got only a frown, a furrowed brow. "Hullen speaks truly, son. Better a swift death than a hard one from cold and starvation."

"No!" He could feel tears welling in his eyes, and he looked away. He did not want to cry in front of his father.

Robb resisted stubbornly. "Ser Rodrik's red bitch whelped again last week," he said. "It was a small litter, only two live pups. She'll have milk enough."

"She'll rip them apart when they try to nurse."

"Lord Stark," Jon said. It was strange to hear him call Father that, so formal. Bran looked at him with desperate hope. "There are five pups," he told Father. "Three male, two female."

"What of it, Jon?"

"You have five trueborn children," Jon said. "Three sons, two daughters. The direwolf is the sigil of your House. Your children were meant to have these pups, my lord."

Bran saw his father's face change, saw the other men exchange glances. He loved Jon with all his heart at that moment. Even at seven, Bran understood what his brother had done. The count had come right only because Jon had omitted himself. He had included the girls, included even Rickon, the baby, but not the bastard who bore the surname Snow, the name that custom decreed be given to all those in the north unlucky enough to be born with no name of their own.

Their father understood as well. "You want no pup for yourself, Jon?" he asked softly.

"The direwolf graces the banners of House Stark," Jon pointed out. "I am no Stark, Father."

Their lord father regarded Jon thoughtfully. Robb rushed into the silence he left. "I will nurse him myself, Father," he promised. "I will soak a towel with warm milk, and give him suck from that."

"Me too!" Bran echoed.

The lord weighed his sons long and carefully with his eyes. "Easy to say, and harder to do. I will not have you wasting the servants' time with this. If you want these pups, you will feed them yourselves. Is that understood?"

Bran nodded eagerly. The pup squirmed in his grasp, licked at his face with a warm tongue.

"You must train them as well," their father said. "*You* must train them. The kennelmaster will have nothing to do with these monsters, I promise you that. And the gods help you if you neglect them, or brutalize them, or train them badly. These are not dogs to beg for treats and slink off at a kick. A direwolf will rip a man's arm off his shoulder as easily as a dog will kill a rat. Are you sure you want this?"

"Yes, Father," Bran said.

"Yes," Robb agreed.

"The pups may die anyway, despite all you do."

"They won't die," Robb said. "We won't *let* them die."

"Keep them, then. Jory, Desmond, gather up the other pups. It's time we were back to Winterfell."

It was not until they were mounted and on their way that Bran allowed himself to taste the sweet air of victory. By then, his pup was snuggled inside his leathers, warm against him, safe for the long ride home. Bran was wondering what to name him.

Halfway across the bridge, Jon pulled up suddenly.

"What is it, Jon?" their lord father asked.

"Can't you hear it?"

Bran could hear the wind in the trees, the clatter of their hooves on the ironwood planks, the whimpering of his hungry pup, but Jon was listening to something else.

"There," Jon said. He swung his horse around and galloped back across the bridge. They watched him dismount where the direwolf lay dead in the snow, watched him kneel. A moment later he was riding back to them, smiling.

"He must have crawled away from the others," Jon said.

"Or been driven away," their father said, looking at the sixth pup. His fur was white, where the rest of the litter was grey. His eyes were as red as the blood of the ragged man who had died that morning. Bran thought it curious that this pup alone would have opened his eyes while the others were still blind.

"An albino," Theon Greyjoy said with wry amusement. "This one will die even faster than the others."

Jon Snow gave his father's ward a long, chilling look. "I think not, Greyjoy," he said. "This one belongs to me."

CATELYN

Catelyn had never liked this godswood.

She had been born a Tully, at Riverrun far to the south, on the Red Fork of the Trident. The godswood there was a garden, bright and airy, where tall redwoods spread dappled shadows across tinkling streams, birds sang from hidden nests, and the air was spicy with the scent of flowers.

The gods of Winterfell kept a different sort of wood. It was a dark, primal place, three acres of old forest untouched for ten thousand years as the gloomy castle rose around it. It smelled of moist earth and decay. No redwoods grew here. This was a wood of stubborn sentinel trees armored in grey-green needles, of mighty oaks, of ironwoods as old as the realm itself. Here thick black trunks crowded close together while twisted branches wove a dense canopy overhead and misshapen roots wrestled beneath the soil. This was a place of deep silence and brooding shadows, and the gods who lived here had no names.

But she knew she would find her husband here tonight. Whenever he took a man's life, afterward he would seek the quiet of the godswood.

Catelyn had been anointed with the seven oils and named in the rainbow of light that filled the sept of River-run. She was of the Faith, like her father and grandfather and his father before him. Her gods had names, and their faces were as familiar as the faces of her parents. Worship was a septon with a censer, the smell of incense, a seven-sided crystal alive with light, voices raised in song. The Tullys kept a godswood, as all the great houses did, but it was only a place to walk or read or lie in the sun. Worship was for the sept.

For her sake, Ned had built a small sept where she might sing to the seven faces of god, but the blood of the First Men still flowed in the veins of the Starks, and his own gods were the old ones, the nameless, faceless gods of the greenwood they shared with the vanished children of the forest.

At the center of the grove an ancient weirwood brooded over a small pool where the waters were black and cold. "The heart tree," Ned called it. The weirwood's bark was white as bone, its leaves dark red, like a thousand bloodstained hands. A face had been carved in the trunk of the great tree, its features long and melancholy, the deep-cut eyes red with dried sap and strangely watchful. They were old, those eyes; older than Winterfell itself. They had seen Brandon the Builder set the first stone, if the tales were true; they had watched the castle's granite walls rise around them. It was said that the children of the forest had carved the faces in the trees during the dawn centuries before the coming of the First Men across the narrow sea.

In the south the last weirwoods had been cut down or burned out a thousand years ago, except on the Isle of Faces where the green men kept their silent watch. Up here it was different. Here every castle had its godswood, and every godswood had its heart tree, and every heart tree its face.

Catelyn found her husband beneath the weirwood, seated on a moss-covered stone. The greatsword Ice was across his lap, and he was cleaning the blade in those waters black as night. A thousand years of humus lay thick upon the godswood floor, swallowing the sound of her feet, but the red eyes of the weirwood seemed to follow her as she came. "Ned," she called softly.

He lifted his head to look at her. "Catelyn," he said. His voice was distant and formal. "Where are the children?"

He would always ask her that. "In the kitchen, arguing about names for the wolf pups." She spread her cloak on the forest floor and sat beside the pool, her back to the weirwood. She could feel the eyes watching her, but she did her best to ignore them. "Arya is already in love, and Sansa is charmed and gracious, but Rickon is not quite sure."

"Is he afraid?" Ned asked.

"A little," she admitted. "He is only three."

Ned frowned. "He must learn to face his fears. He will not be three forever. And winter is coming."

"Yes," Catelyn agreed. The words gave her a chill, as they always did. The Stark words. Every noble house had its words. Family mottoes, touchstones, prayers of sorts, they boasted of honor and glory, promised loyalty and truth, swore faith and courage. All but the Starks. *Winter is coming,* said the Stark words. Not for the first time, she reflected on what a strange people these northerners were.

"The man died well, I'll give him that," Ned said. He had a swatch of oiled leather in one hand. He ran it lightly up the greatsword as he spoke, polishing the metal to a dark glow. "I was glad for Bran's sake. You would have been proud of Bran."

"I am always proud of Bran," Catelyn replied, watching the sword as he stroked it. She could see the rippling deep within the steel, where the metal had been folded back on itself a hundred times in the forging. Catelyn had no love for swords, but she could not deny that Ice had its own beauty. It had been forged in Valyria, before the Doom had come to the old Freehold, when the ironsmiths had worked their metal with spells as well as hammers. Four hundred years old it was, and as sharp as the day it was forged. The name it bore was older still, a legacy from the age of heroes, when the Starks were Kings in the North.

"He was the fourth this year," Ned said grimly. "The poor man was half-mad. Something had put a fear in him so deep that my words could not reach him." He sighed. "Ben writes that the strength of the Night's Watch is down below a thousand. It's not only desertions. They are losing men on rangings as well."

"Is it the wildlings?" she asked.

"Who else?" Ned lifted Ice, looked down the cool steel length of it. "And it will only grow worse. The day may come when I will have no choice but to call the banners and ride north to deal with this King-beyond-the-Wall for good and all."

"Beyond the Wall?" The thought made Catelyn shudder.

Ned saw the dread on her face. "Mance Rayder is nothing for us to fear."

"There are darker things beyond the Wall." She glanced behind her at the heart tree, the pale bark and red eyes, watching, listening, thinking its long slow thoughts.

His smile was gentle. "You listen to too many of Old Nan's stories. The Others are as dead as the children of the forest, gone eight thousand years. Maester Luwin will tell you they never lived at all. No living man has ever seen one."

"Until this morning, no living man had ever seen a direwolf either," Catelyn reminded him.

"I ought to know better than to argue with a Tully," he said with a rueful smile. He slid Ice back into its sheath. "You did not come here to tell me crib tales. I know how little you like this place. What is it, my lady?"

Catelyn took her husband's hand. "There was grievous news today, my lord. I did not wish to trouble you until you had cleansed yourself." There was no way to soften the blow, so she told him straight. "I am so sorry, my love. Jon Arryn is dead."

His eyes found hers, and she could see how hard it took him, as she had known it would. In his youth, Ned had fostered at the Eyrie, and the childless Lord Arryn had become a second father to him and his fellow ward, Robert Baratheon. When the Mad King Aerys II Targaryen had demanded their heads, the Lord of the Eyrie had raised his moon-and-falcon banners in revolt rather than give up those he had pledged to protect.

And one day fifteen years ago, this second father had become a brother as well, as he and Ned stood together in the sept at Riverrun to wed two sisters, the daughters of Lord Hoster Tully.

"Jon . . ." he said. "Is this news certain?"

"It was the king's seal, and the letter is in Robert's own hand. I saved it for you. He said Lord Arryn was taken quickly. Even Maester Pycelle was helpless, but he brought the milk of the poppy, so Jon did not linger long in pain."

"That is some small mercy, I suppose," he said. She could see the grief on his face, but even then he thought first of her. "Your sister," he said. "And Jon's boy. What word of them?"

"The message said only that they were well, and had returned to the Eyrie," Catelyn said. "I wish they had gone to Riverrun instead. The Eyrie is high and lonely, and it was ever her husband's place, not hers. Lord Jon's memory will haunt each stone. I know my sister. She needs the comfort of family and friends around her."

"Your uncle waits in the Vale, does he not? Jon named him Knight of the Gate, I'd heard."

Catelyn nodded. "Brynden will do what he can for her, and for the boy. That is some comfort, but still . . ."

"Go to her," Ned urged. "Take the children. Fill her halls with noise and shouts and laughter. That boy of hers needs other children about him, and Lysa should not be alone in her grief."

"Would that I could," Catelyn said. "The letter had other tidings. The king is riding to Winterfell to seek you out."

It took Ned a moment to comprehend her words, but when the understanding came, the darkness left his eyes. "Robert is coming here?" When she nodded, a smile broke across his face.

Catelyn wished she could share his joy. But she had heard the talk in the yards; a direwolf dead in the snow, a broken antler in its throat. Dread coiled within her like a snake, but she forced herself to smile at this man she loved, this man who put no faith in signs. "I knew that would please you," she said. "We should send word to your brother on the Wall."

"Yes, of course," he agreed. "Ben will want to be here. I shall tell Maester Luwin to send his swiftest bird." Ned rose and pulled her to her feet. "Damnation, how many years has it been? And he gives us no more notice than this? How many in his party, did the message say?"

"I should think a hundred knights, at the least, with all their retainers, and half again as many freeriders. Cersei and the children travel with them."

"Robert will keep an easy pace for their sakes," he said. "It is just as well. That will give us more time to prepare."

"The queen's brothers are also in the party," she told him.

Ned grimaced at that. There was small love between him and the queen's family, Catelyn knew. The Lannisters of Casterly Rock had come late to Robert's cause, when victory was all but certain, and he had never forgiven them. "Well, if the price for Robert's company is an infestation of Lannisters, so be it. It sounds as though Robert is bringing half his court."

"Where the king goes, the realm follows," she said.

"It will be good to see the children. The youngest was still sucking at the Lannister woman's teat the last time I saw him. He must be, what, five by now?"

"Prince Tommen is seven," she told him. "The same age as Bran. Please, Ned, guard your tongue. The Lannister woman is our queen, and her pride is said to grow with every passing year."

Ned squeezed her hand. "There must be a feast, of course, with singers, and Robert will want to hunt. I shall send Jory south with an honor guard to meet them on the kingsroad and escort them back. Gods, how are we going to feed them all? On his way already, you said? Damn the man. Damn his royal hide."

DAENERYS

Her brother held the gown up for her inspection. "This is beauty. Touch it. Go on. Caress the fabric."

Dany touched it. The cloth was so smooth that it seemed to run through her fingers like water. She could not remember ever wearing anything so soft. It frightened her. She pulled her hand away. "Is it really mine?"

"A gift from the Magister Illyrio," Viserys said, smiling. Her brother was in a high mood tonight. "The color will bring out the violet in your eyes. And you shall have gold as well, and jewels of all sorts. Illyrio has promised. Tonight you must look like a princess."

A princess, Dany thought. She had forgotten what that was like. Perhaps she had never really known. "Why does he give us so much?" she asked. "What does he want from us?" For nigh on half a year, they had lived in the magister's house, eating his food, pampered by his servants. Dany was thirteen, old enough to know that such gifts seldom come without their price, here in the free city of Pentos.

"Illyrio is no fool," Viserys said. He was a gaunt young man with nervous hands and a feverish look in his pale lilac eyes. "The magister knows that I will not forget my friends when I come into my throne."

Dany said nothing. Magister Illyrio was a dealer in spices, gemstones, dragonbone, and other, less savory things. He had friends in all of the Nine Free Cities, it was said, and even beyond, in Vaes Dothrak and the fabled lands beside the Jade Sea. It was also said that he'd never had a friend he wouldn't cheerfully sell for the right price. Dany listened to the talk in the streets, and she heard these things, but she knew better than to question her brother when he wove his webs of dream. His anger was a terrible thing when roused. Viserys called it "waking the dragon."

Her brother hung the gown beside the door. "Illyrio will send the slaves to bathe you. Be sure you wash off the stink of the stables. Khal Drogo has a thousand horses, tonight he looks for a different sort of mount." He studied her critically. "You still slouch. Straighten yourself." He pushed back her shoulders with his hands. "Let them see that you have a woman's shape now." His fingers brushed lightly over her budding breasts and tightened on a nipple. "You will not fail me tonight. If you do, it will go hard for you. You don't want to wake the dragon, do you?" His fingers twisted her, the pinch cruelly hard through the rough fabric of her tunic. *"Do you?"* he repeated.

"No," Dany said meekly.

Her brother smiled. "Good." He touched her hair, almost with affection. "When they write the history of my reign, sweet sister, they will say that it began tonight."

When he was gone, Dany went to her window and looked out wistfully on the waters of the bay. The square brick towers of Pentos were black silhouettes outlined against the setting sun. Dany could hear the singing of the red priests as they lit their night fires and the shouts of ragged children playing games beyond the walls of the estate. For a moment she wished she could be out there with them, barefoot and breathless and dressed in tatters, with no past and no future and no feast to attend at Khal Drogo's manse.

Somewhere beyond the sunset, across the narrow sea, lay a land of green hills and flowered plains and great rushing rivers, where towers of dark stone rose amidst magnificent blue-grey mountains, and armored knights rode to battle beneath the banners of their lords. The Dothraki called that land *Rhaesh Andahli*, the land of the Andals. In the Free Cities, they talked of Westeros and the Sunset Kingdoms. Her brother had a simpler name. "Our land," he called it. The words were like a prayer with him. If he said them enough, the gods were sure to hear. "Ours by blood right, taken from us by treachery, but ours still, ours forever. You do not steal from the dragon, oh, no. The dragon remembers."

And perhaps the dragon did remember, but Dany could not. She had never seen this land her brother said was theirs, this realm beyond the narrow sea. These places he talked of, Casterly Rock and the Eyrie, Highgarden and the Vale of Arryn, Dorne and the Isle of Faces, they were just words to her. Viserys had been a boy of eight when they fled King's Landing to escape the advancing armies of the Usurper, but Daenerys had been only a quickening in their mother's womb.

Yet sometimes Dany would picture the way it had been, so often had her brother told her the stories. The midnight flight to Dragonstone, moonlight shimmering on the ship's black sails. Her brother Rhaegar battling the Usurper in the bloody waters of the Trident and dying for the woman he loved. The sack of King's Landing by the ones Viserys called the Usurper's dogs, the lords Lannister and Stark. Princess Elia of Dorne pleading for mercy as Rhaegar's heir was ripped from her breast and murdered before her eyes. The polished skulls of the last dragons staring down sightlessly from the walls of the throne room while the Kingslayer opened Father's throat with a golden sword.

She had been born on Dragonstone nine moons after their flight, while a raging summer storm threatened to rip the island fastness apart. They said that storm was terrible. The Targaryen fleet was smashed while it lay at anchor, and huge stone blocks were ripped from the parapets and sent hurtling into the wild waters of the narrow sea. Her mother had died birthing her, and for that her brother Viserys had never forgiven her.

She did not remember Dragonstone either. They had run again, just before the Usurper's brother set sail with his new-built fleet. By then only Dragonstone itself, the ancient seat of their House, had remained of the Seven

Kingdoms that had once been theirs. It would not remain for long. The garrison had been prepared to sell them to the Usurper, but one night Ser Willem Darry and four loyal men had broken into the nursery and stolen them both, along with her wet nurse, and set sail under cover of darkness for the safety of the Braavosian coast.

She remembered Ser Willem dimly, a great grey bear of a man, half-blind, roaring and bellowing orders from his sickbed. The servants had lived in terror of him, but he had always been kind to Dany. He called her "Little Princess" and sometimes "My Lady," and his hands were soft as old leather. He never left his bed, though, and the smell of sickness clung to him day and night, a hot, moist, sickly sweet odor. That was when they lived in Braavos, in the big house with the red door. Dany had her own room there, with a lemon tree outside her window. After Ser Willem had died, the servants had stolen what little money they had left, and soon after they had been put out of the big house. Dany had cried when the red door closed behind them forever.

They had wandered since then, from Braavos to Myr, from Myr to Tyrosh, and on to Qohor and Volantis and Lys, never staying long in any one place. Her brother would not allow it. The Usurper's hired knives were close behind them, he insisted, though Dany had never seen one.

At first the magisters and archons and merchant princes were pleased to welcome the last Targaryens to their homes and tables, but as the years passed and the Usurper continued to sit upon the Iron Throne, doors closed and their lives grew meaner. Years past they had been forced to sell their last few treasures, and now even the coin they had gotten from Mother's crown had gone. In the alleys and wine sinks of Pentos, they called her brother "the beggar king." Dany did not want to know what they called her.

"We will have it all back someday, sweet sister," he would promise her. Sometimes his hands shook when he talked about it. "The jewels and the silks, Dragonstone and King's Landing, the Iron Throne and the Seven Kingdoms, all they have taken from us, we will have it back." Viserys lived for that day. All that Daenerys wanted back was the big house with the red door, the lemon tree outside her window, the childhood she had never known.

There came a soft knock on her door. "Come," Dany said, turning away from the window. Illyrio's servants entered, bowed, and set about their business. They were slaves, a gift from one of the magister's many Dothraki friends. There was no slavery in the free city of Pentos. Nonetheless, they were slaves. The old woman, small and grey as a mouse, never said a word, but the girl made up for it. She was Illyrio's favorite, a fair-haired, blue-eyed wench of sixteen who chattered constantly as she worked.

They filled her bath with hot water brought up from the kitchen and scented it with fragrant oils. The girl pulled the rough cotton tunic over Dany's head and helped her into the tub. The water was scalding hot, but Daenerys did not flinch or cry out. She liked the heat. It made her feel clean. Besides, her brother had often told her that it was never too hot for a Targaryen. "Ours is the house of the dragon," he would say. "The fire is in our blood."

The old woman washed her long, silver-pale hair and gently combed out the snags, all in silence. The girl scrubbed her back and her feet and told her how lucky she was. "Drogo is so rich that even his slaves wear golden collars. A hundred thousand men ride in his *khalasar,* and his palace in Vaes Dothrak has two hundred rooms and doors of solid silver." There was more like that, so much more, what a handsome man the *khal* was, so tall and fierce, fearless in battle, the best rider ever to mount a horse, a demon archer. Daenerys said nothing. She had always assumed that she would wed Viserys when she came of age. For centuries the Targaryens had married brother to sister, since Aegon the Conqueror had taken his sisters to bride. The line must be kept pure, Viserys had told her a thousand times; theirs was the kingsblood, the golden blood of old Valyria, the blood of the dragon. Dragons did not mate with the beasts of the field, and Targaryens did not mingle their blood with that of lesser men. Yet now Viserys schemed to sell her to a stranger, a barbarian.

When she was clean, the slaves helped her from the water and toweled her dry. The girl brushed her hair until it shone like molten silver, while the old woman anointed her with the spiceflower perfume of the Dothraki plains, a dab on each wrist, behind her ears, on the tips of her breasts, and one last one, cool on her lips, down there between her legs. They dressed her in the wisps that Magister Illyrio had sent up, and then the gown, a deep plum silk to bring out the violet in her eyes. The girl slid the gilded sandals onto her feet, while the old woman fixed the tiara in her hair, and slid golden bracelets crusted with amethysts around her wrists. Last of all came the collar, a heavy golden torc emblazoned with ancient Valyrian glyphs.

"Now you look all a princess," the girl said breathlessly when they were done. Dany glanced at her image in the silvered looking glass that Illyrio had so thoughtfully provided. *A princess*, she thought, but she remembered what the girl had said, how Khal Drogo was so rich even his slaves wore golden collars. She felt a sudden chill, and gooseflesh pimpled her bare arms.

Her brother was waiting in the cool of the entry hall, seated on the edge of the pool, his hand trailing in the water. He rose when she appeared and looked her over critically. "Stand there," he told her. "Turn around. Yes. Good. You look . . ."

"Regal," Magister Illyrio said, stepping through an archway. He moved with surprising delicacy for such a massive man. Beneath loose garments of flame-colored silk, rolls of fat jiggled as he walked. Gemstones glittered on every finger, and his man had oiled his forked yellow beard until it shone like real gold. "May the Lord of Light shower you with blessings on this most fortunate day, Princess Daenerys," the magister said as he took her hand. He bowed his head, showing a thin glimpse of crooked yellow teeth through the gold of his beard. "She is a vision, Your Grace, a vision," he told her brother. "Drogo will be enraptured."

"She's too skinny," Viserys said. His hair, the same silver-blond as hers, had been pulled back tightly behind his head and fastened with a dragonbone brooch. It was a severe look that emphasized the hard, gaunt lines of his face. He rested his hand on the hilt of the sword that Illyrio had lent him, and said, "Are you sure that Khal Drogo likes his women this young?"

"She has had her blood. She is old enough for the *khal*," Illyrio told him, not for the first time. "Look at her. That silver-gold hair, those purple eyes . . . she is the blood of old Valyria, no doubt, no doubt . . . and highborn, daughter of the old king, sister to the new, she cannot fail to entrance our Drogo." When he released her hand, Daenerys found herself trembling.

"I suppose," her brother said doubtfully. "The savages have queer tastes. Boys, horses, sheep . . ."

"Best not suggest this to Khal Drogo," Illyrio said.

Anger flashed in her brother's lilac eyes. "Do you take me for a fool?"

The magister bowed slightly. "I take you for a king. Kings lack the caution of common men. My apologies if I have given offense." He turned away and clapped his hands for his bearers.

The streets of Pentos were pitch-dark when they set out in Illyrio's elaborately carved palanquin. Two servants went ahead to light their way, carrying ornate oil lanterns with panes of pale blue glass, while a dozen strong men hoisted the poles to their shoulders. It was warm and close inside behind the curtains. Dany could smell the stench of Illyrio's pallid flesh through his heavy perfumes.

Her brother, sprawled out on his pillows beside her, never noticed. His mind was away across the narrow sea. "We won't need his whole *khalasar*," Viserys said. His fingers toyed with the hilt of his borrowed blade, though Dany knew he had never used a sword in earnest. "Ten thousand, that would be enough, I could sweep the Seven Kingdoms with ten thousand Dothraki screamers. The realm will rise for its rightful king. Tyrell, Redwyne, Darry, Greyjoy, they have no more love for the Usurper than I do. The Dornishmen burn to avenge Elia and her children. And the smallfolk will be with us. They cry out for their king." He looked at Illyrio anxiously. "They do, don't they?"

"They are your people, and they love you well," Magister Illyrio said amiably. "In holdfasts all across the realm, men lift secret toasts to your health while women sew dragon banners and hide them against the day of your return from across the water." He gave a massive shrug. "Or so my agents tell me."

Dany had no agents, no way of knowing what anyone was doing or thinking across the narrow sea, but she mistrusted Illyrio's sweet words as she mistrusted everything about Illyrio. Her brother was nodding eagerly, however. "I shall kill the Usurper myself," he promised, who had never killed anyone, "as he killed my brother Rhaegar. And Lannister too, the Kingslayer, for what he did to my father."

"That would be most fitting," Magister Illyrio said. Dany saw the smallest hint of a smile playing around his full lips, but her brother did not notice. Nodding, he pushed back a curtain and stared off into the night, and Dany knew he was fighting the Battle of the Trident once again.

The nine-towered manse of Khal Drogo sat beside the waters of the bay, its high brick walls overgrown with pale ivy. It had been given to the *khal* by the magisters of Pentos, Illyrio told them. The Free Cities were always generous with the horselords. "It is not that we fear these barbarians," Illyrio would explain with a smile. "The Lord of Light would hold our city walls against a million Dothraki, or so the red priests promise . . . yet why take chances, when their friendship comes so cheap?"

Their palanquin was stopped at the gate, the curtains pulled roughly back by one of the house guards. He had the copper skin and dark almond eyes of a Dothraki, but his face was hairless and he wore the spiked bronze cap of the Unsullied. He looked them over coldly. Magister Illyrio growled something to him in the rough Dothraki tongue; the guardsman replied in the same voice and waved them through the gates.

Dany noticed that her brother's hand was clenched tightly around the hilt of his borrowed sword. He looked almost as frightened as she felt. "Insolent eunuch," Viserys muttered as the palanquin lurched up toward the manse.

Magister Illyrio's words were honey. "Many important men will be at the feast tonight. Such men have enemies. The *khal* must protect his guests, yourself chief among them, Your Grace. No doubt the Usurper would pay well for your head."

"Oh, yes," Viserys said darkly. "He has tried, Illyrio, I promise you that. His hired knives follow us everywhere.

I am the last dragon, and he will not sleep easy while I live."

The palanquin slowed and stopped. The curtains were thrown back, and a slave offered a hand to help Daenerys out. His collar, she noted, was ordinary bronze. Her brother followed, one hand still clenched hard around his sword hilt. It took two strong men to get Magister Illyrio back on his feet.

Inside the manse, the air was heavy with the scent of spices, pinchfire and sweet lemon and cinnamon. They were escorted across the entry hall, where a mosaic of colored glass depicted the Doom of Valyria. Oil burned in black iron lanterns all along the walls. Beneath an arch of twining stone leaves, a eunuch sang their coming. "Viserys of the House Targaryen, the Third of his Name," he called in a high, sweet voice, "King of the Andals and the Rhoynar and the First Men, Lord of the Seven Kingdoms and Protector of the Realm. His sister, Daenerys Stormborn, Princess of Dragonstone. His honorable host, Illyrio Mopatis, Magister of the Free City of Pentos."

They stepped past the eunuch into a pillared courtyard overgrown in pale ivy. Moonlight painted the leaves in shades of bone and silver as the guests drifted among them. Many were Dothraki horselords, big men with red-brown skin, their drooping mustachios bound in metal rings, their black hair oiled and braided and hung with bells. Yet among them moved bravos and sellswords from Pentos and Myr and Tyrosh, a red priest even fatter than Illyrio, hairy men from the Port of Ibben, and lords from the Summer Isles with skin as black as ebony. Daenerys looked at them all in wonder . . . and realized, with a sudden start of fear, that she was the only woman there.

Illyrio whispered to them. "Those three are Drogo's bloodriders, there," he said. "By the pillar is Khal Moro, with his son Rhogoro. The man with the green beard is brother to the Archon of Tyrosh, and the man behind him is Ser Jorah Mormont."

The last name caught Daenerys. "A knight?"

"No less." Illyrio smiled through his beard. "Anointed with the seven oils by the High Septon himself."

"What is he doing here?" she blurted.

"The Usurper wanted his head," Illyrio told them. "Some trifling affront. He sold some poachers to a Tyroshi slaver instead of giving them to the Night's Watch. Absurd law. A man should be able to do as he likes with his own chattel."

"I shall wish to speak with Ser Jorah before the night is done," her brother said. Dany found herself looking at the knight curiously. He was an older man, past forty and balding, but still strong and fit. Instead of silks and cottons, he wore wool and leather. His tunic was a dark green, embroidered with the likeness of a black bear standing on two legs.

She was still looking at this strange man from the homeland she had never known when Magister Illyrio placed a moist hand on her bare shoulder. "Over there, sweet princess," he whispered, "there is the *khal* himself."

Dany wanted to run and hide, but her brother was looking at her, and if she displeased him she knew she would wake the dragon. Anxiously, she turned and looked at the man Viserys hoped would ask to wed her before the night was done.

The slave girl had not been far wrong, she thought. Khal Drogo was a head taller than the tallest man in the room, yet somehow light on his feet, as graceful as the panther in Illyrio's menagerie. He was younger than she'd thought, no more than thirty. His skin was the color of polished copper, his thick mustachios bound with gold and bronze rings.

"I must go and make my submissions," Magister Illyrio said. "Wait here. I shall bring him to you."

Her brother took her by the arm as Illyrio waddled over to the *khal*, his fingers squeezing so hard that they hurt. "Do you see his braid, sweet sister?"

Drogo's braid was black as midnight and heavy with scented oil, hung with tiny bells that rang softly as he moved. It swung well past his belt, below even his buttocks, the end of it brushing against the back of his thighs.

"You see how long it is?" Viserys said. "When Dothraki are defeated in combat, they cut off their braids in disgrace, so the world will know their shame. Khal Drogo has never lost a fight. He is Aegon the Dragonlord come again, and you will be his queen."

Dany looked at Khal Drogo. His face was hard and

cruel, his eyes as cold and dark as onyx. Her brother hurt her sometimes, when she woke the dragon, but he did not frighten her the way this man frightened her. "I don't want to be his queen," she heard herself say in a small, thin voice. "Please, *please*, Viserys, I don't want to, I want to go home."

"Home?" He kept his voice low, but she could hear the fury in his tone. "How are we to go home, sweet sister? They took our home from us!" He drew her into the shadows, out of sight, his fingers digging into her skin. *"How are we to go home?"* he repeated, meaning King's Landing, and Dragonstone, and all the realm they had lost.

Dany had only meant their rooms in Illyrio's estate, no true home surely, though all they had, but her brother did not want to hear that. There was no home there for him. Even the big house with the red door had not been home for him. His fingers dug hard into her arm, demanding an answer. "I don't know . . ." she said at last, her voice breaking. Tears welled in her eyes.

"I do," he said sharply. "We go home with an army, sweet sister. With Khal Drogo's army, that is how we go home. And if you must wed him and bed him for that, you will." He smiled at her. "I'd let his whole *khalasar* fuck you if need be, sweet sister, all forty thousand men, and their horses too if that was what it took to get my army. Be grateful it is only Drogo. In time you may even learn to like him. Now dry your eyes. Illyrio is bringing him over, and he will *not* see you crying."

Dany turned and saw that it was true. Magister Illyrio, all smiles and bows, was escorting Khal Drogo over to where they stood. She brushed away unfallen tears with the back of her hand.

"Smile," Viserys whispered nervously, his hand falling to the hilt of his sword. "And stand up straight. Let him see that you have breasts. Gods know, you have little enough as is."

Daenerys smiled, and stood up straight.

EDDARD

The visitors poured through the castle gates in a river of gold and silver and polished steel, three hundred strong, a pride of bannermen and knights, of sworn swords and freeriders. Over their heads a dozen golden banners whipped back and forth in the northern wind, emblazoned with the crowned stag of Baratheon.

Ned knew many of the riders. There came Ser Jaime Lannister with hair as bright as beaten gold, and there Sandor Clegane with his terrible burned face. The tall boy beside him could only be the crown prince, and that stunted little man behind them was surely the Imp, Tyrion Lannister.

Yet the huge man at the head of the column, flanked by two knights in the snow-white cloaks of the Kingsguard, seemed almost a stranger to Ned . . . until he vaulted off the back of his warhorse with a familiar roar, and crushed him in a bone-crunching hug. "*Ned!* Ah, but it is good to see that frozen face of yours." The king looked him over top to bottom, and laughed. "You have not changed at all."

Would that Ned had been able to say the same. Fifteen years past, when they had ridden forth to win a throne, the Lord of Storm's End had been clean-shaven, clear-eyed, and muscled like a maiden's fantasy. Six and a half feet tall, he towered over lesser men, and when he donned his armor and the great antlered helmet of his House, he became a veritable giant. He'd had a giant's strength too, his weapon of choice a spiked iron warhammer that Ned could scarcely lift. In those days, the smell of leather and blood had clung to him like perfume.

Now it was perfume that clung to him like perfume, and he had a girth to match his height. Ned had last seen the king nine years before during Balon Greyjoy's rebellion, when the stag and the direwolf had joined to end the pretensions of the self-proclaimed King of the Iron Islands. Since the night they had stood side by side in Greyjoy's fallen stronghold, where Robert had accepted the rebel lord's surrender and Ned had taken his son Theon as hostage and ward, the king had gained at least eight stone. A beard as coarse and black as iron wire covered his jaw to hide his double chin and the sag of the royal jowls, but nothing could hide his stomach or the dark circles under his eyes.

Yet Robert was Ned's king now, and not just a friend, so he said only, "Your Grace. Winterfell is yours."

By then the others were dismounting as well, and grooms were coming forward for their mounts. Robert's queen, Cersei Lannister, entered on foot with her younger children. The wheelhouse in which they had ridden, a huge double-decked carriage of oiled oak and gilded metal pulled by forty heavy draft horses, was too wide to pass through the castle gate. Ned knelt in the snow to kiss the queen's ring, while Robert embraced Catelyn like a long-lost sister. Then the children had been brought forward, introduced, and approved of by both sides.

No sooner had those formalities of greeting been completed than the king had said to his host, "Take me down to your crypt, Eddard. I would pay my respects."

Ned loved him for that, for remembering her still after all these years. He called for a lantern. No other words were needed. The queen had begun to protest. They had been riding since dawn, everyone was tired and cold, surely they should refresh themselves first. The dead would wait. She had said no more than that; Robert had looked at her, and her twin brother Jaime had taken her quietly by the arm, and she had said no more.

They went down to the crypt together, Ned and this king he scarcely recognized. The winding stone steps were narrow. Ned went first with the lantern. "I was starting to think we would never reach Winterfell," Robert complained as they descended. "In the south, the way they talk about my Seven Kingdoms, a man forgets that your part is as big as the other six combined."

"I trust you enjoyed the journey, Your Grace?"

Robert snorted. "Bogs and forests and fields, and scarcely a decent inn north of the Neck. I've never seen such a vast emptiness. Where are all your *people*?"

"Likely they were too shy to come out," Ned jested. He could feel the chill coming up the stairs, a cold breath from deep within the earth. "Kings are a rare sight in the north."

Robert snorted. "More likely they were hiding under the snow. *Snow*, Ned!" The king put one hand on the wall to steady himself as they descended.

"Late summer snows are common enough," Ned said. "I hope they did not trouble you. They are usually mild."

"The Others take your mild snows," Robert swore. "What will this place be like in winter? I shudder to think."

"The winters are hard," Ned admitted. "But the Starks will endure. We always have."

"You need to come south," Robert told him. "You need a taste of summer before it flees. In Highgarden there are fields of golden roses that stretch away as far as the eye can see. The fruits are so ripe they explode in your mouth—melons, peaches, fireplums, you've never tasted such sweetness. You'll see, I brought you some. Even at Storm's End, with that good wind off the bay, the days are so hot you can barely move. And you ought to see the towns, Ned! Flowers everywhere, the markets bursting with food, the summerwines so cheap and so good that you can get drunk just breathing the air. Everyone is fat and drunk and rich." He laughed and slapped his own ample stomach a thump. "And the *girls*, Ned!" he exclaimed, his eyes sparkling. "I swear, women lose all modesty in the heat. They swim naked in the river, right beneath the castle. Even in the streets, it's too damn hot for wool or fur, so they go around in these short gowns, silk if they have the silver and cotton if not, but it's all the same when they start sweating and the cloth sticks to their skin, they might as well be naked." The king laughed happily.

Robert Baratheon had always been a man of huge appetites, a man who knew how to take his pleasures. That was not a charge anyone could lay at the door of Eddard Stark. Yet Ned could not help but notice that those pleasures were taking a toll on the king. Robert was breathing heavily by the time they reached the bottom of the stairs, his face red in the lantern light as they stepped out into the darkness of the crypt.

"Your Grace," Ned said respectfully. He swept the lantern in a wide semicircle. Shadows moved and lurched. Flickering light touched the stones underfoot and brushed against a long procession of granite pillars that marched ahead, two by two, into the dark. Between the pillars, the dead sat on their stone thrones against the walls, backs against the sepulchres that contained their mortal remains. "She is down at the end, with Father and Brandon."

He led the way between the pillars and Robert followed wordlessly, shivering in the subterranean chill. It was always cold down here. Their footsteps rang off the stones and echoed in the vault overhead as they walked among the dead of House Stark. The Lords of Winterfell watched them pass. Their likenesses were carved into the stones that sealed the tombs. In long rows they sat, blind eyes staring out into eternal darkness, while great stone direwolves curled round their feet. The shifting shadows made the stone figures seem to stir as the living passed by.

By ancient custom an iron longsword had been laid across the lap of each who had been Lord of Winterfell, to keep the vengeful spirits in their crypts. The oldest had long ago rusted away to nothing, leaving only a few red stains where the metal had rested on stone. Ned wondered if that meant those ghosts were free to roam the castle now. He hoped not. The first Lords of Winterfell had been men hard as the land they ruled. In the centuries before the Dragonlords came over the sea, they had sworn allegiance to no man, styling themselves the Kings in the North.

Ned stopped at last and lifted the oil lantern. The crypt continued on into darkness ahead of them, but beyond this point the tombs were empty and unsealed; black holes waiting for their dead, waiting for him and his children. Ned did not like to think on that. "Here," he told his king.

Robert nodded silently, knelt, and bowed his head.

There were three tombs, side by side. Lord Rickard Stark, Ned's father, had a long, stern face. The stonemason had known him well. He sat with quiet dignity, stone fingers holding tight to the sword across his lap, but in life all swords had failed him. In two smaller sepulchres on either side were his children.

Brandon had been twenty when he died, strangled by order of the Mad King Aerys Targaryen only a few short days before he was to wed Catelyn Tully of Riverrun. His father had been forced to watch him die. He was the true heir, the eldest, born to rule.

Lyanna had only been sixteen, a child-woman of surpassing loveliness. Ned had loved her with all his heart. Robert had loved her even more. She was to have been his bride.

"She was more beautiful than that," the king said after a silence. His eyes lingered on Lyanna's face, as if he could will her back to life. Finally he rose, made awkward by his weight. "Ah, damn it, Ned, did you have to bury her in a place like *this*?" His voice was hoarse with remembered grief. "She deserved more than darkness . . ."

"She was a Stark of Winterfell," Ned said quietly. "This is her place."

"She should be on a hill somewhere, under a fruit tree, with the sun and clouds above her and the rain to wash her clean."

"I was with her when she died," Ned reminded the king. "She wanted to come home, to rest beside Brandon and Father." He could hear her still at times. *Promise me,* she had cried, in a room that smelled of blood and roses. *Promise me, Ned.* The fever had taken her strength and her voice had been faint as a whisper, but when he gave her his word, the fear had gone out of his sister's eyes. Ned remembered the way she had smiled then, how

tightly her fingers had clutched his as she gave up her
hold on life, the rose petals spilling from her palm, dead
and black. After that he remembered nothing. They had
found him still holding her body, silent with grief. The
little crannogman, Howland Reed, had taken her hand
from his. Ned could recall none of it. "I bring her flowers
when I can," he said. "Lyanna was . . . fond of flowers."

The king touched her cheek, his fingers brushing
across the rough stone as gently as if it were living flesh.
"I vowed to kill Rhaegar for what he did to her."

"You did," Ned reminded him.

"Only once," Robert said bitterly.

They had come together at the ford of the Trident
while the battle crashed around them, Robert with his
warhammer and his great antlered helm, the Targaryen
prince armored all in black. On his breastplate was the
three-headed dragon of his House, wrought all in rubies
that flashed like fire in the sunlight. The waters of the
Trident ran red around the hooves of their destriers as
they circled and clashed, again and again, until at last a
crushing blow from Robert's hammer stove in the dragon
and the chest beneath it. When Ned had finally come on
the scene, Rhaegar lay dead in the stream, while men of
both armies scrabbled in the swirling waters for rubies
knocked free of his armor.

"In my dreams, I kill him every night," Robert admitted. "A thousand deaths will still be less than he deserves."

There was nothing Ned could say to that. After a quiet,
he said, "We should return, Your Grace. Your wife will be
waiting."

"The Others take my wife," Robert muttered sourly,
but he started back the way they had come, his footsteps
falling heavily. "And if I hear 'Your Grace' once more, I'll
have your head on a spike. We are more to each other
than that."

"I had not forgotten," Ned replied quietly. When the
king did not answer, he said, "Tell me about Jon."

Robert shook his head. "I have never seen a man
sicken so quickly. We gave a tourney on my son's name
day. If you had seen Jon then, you would have sworn he
would live forever. A fortnight later he was dead. The
sickness was like a fire in his gut. It burned right through

him." He paused beside a pillar, before the tomb of a long-dead Stark. "I loved that old man."

"We both did." Ned paused a moment. "Catelyn fears for her sister. How does Lysa bear her grief?"

Robert's mouth gave a bitter twist. "Not well, in truth," he admitted. "I think losing Jon has driven the woman mad, Ned. She has taken the boy back to the Eyrie. Against my wishes. I had hoped to foster him with Tywin Lannister at Casterly Rock. Jon had no brothers, no other sons. Was I supposed to leave him to be raised by women?"

Ned would sooner entrust a child to a pit viper than to Lord Tywin, but he left his doubts unspoken. Some old wounds never truly heal, and bleed again at the slightest word. "The wife has lost the husband," he said carefully. "Perhaps the mother feared to lose the son. The boy is very young."

"Six, and sickly, and Lord of the Eyrie, gods have mercy," the king swore. "Lord Tywin had never taken a ward before. Lysa ought to have been honored. The Lannisters are a great and noble House. She refused to even hear of it. Then she left in the dead of night, without so much as a by-your-leave. Cersei was furious." He sighed deeply. "The boy is my namesake, did you know that? Robert Arryn. I am sworn to protect him. How can I do that if his mother steals him away?"

"I will take him as ward, if you wish," Ned said. "Lysa should consent to that. She and Catelyn were close as girls, and she would be welcome here as well."

"A generous offer, my friend," the king said, "but too late. Lord Tywin has already given his consent. Fostering the boy elsewhere would be a grievous affront to him."

"I have more concern for my nephew's welfare than I do for Lannister pride," Ned declared.

"That is because you do not sleep with a Lannister." Robert laughed, the sound rattling among the tombs and bouncing from the vaulted ceiling. His smile was a flash of white teeth in the thicket of the huge black beard. "Ah, Ned," he said, "you are still too serious." He put a massive arm around Ned's shoulders. "I had planned to wait a few days to speak to you, but I see now there's no need for it. Come, walk with me."

They started back down between the pillars. Blind

stone eyes seemed to follow them as they passed. The king kept his arm around Ned's shoulder. "You must have wondered why I finally came north to Winterfell, after so long."

Ned had his suspicions, but he did not give them voice. "For the joy of my company, surely," he said lightly. "And there is the Wall. You need to see it, Your Grace, to walk along its battlements and talk to those who man it. The Night's Watch is a shadow of what it once was. Benjen says—"

"No doubt I will hear what your brother says soon enough," Robert said. "The Wall has stood for what, eight thousand years? It can keep a few days more. I have more pressing concerns. These are difficult times. I need good men about me. Men like Jon Arryn. He served as Lord of the Eyrie, as Warden of the East, as the Hand of the King. He will not be easy to replace."

"His son . . ." Ned began.

"His son will succeed to the Eyrie and all its incomes," Robert said brusquely. "No more."

That took Ned by surprise. He stopped, startled, and turned to look at his king. The words came unbidden. "The Arryns have always been Wardens of the East. The title goes with the domain."

"Perhaps when he comes of age, the honor can be restored to him," Robert said. "I have this year to think of, and next. A six-year-old boy is no war leader, Ned."

"In peace, the title is only an honor. Let the boy keep it. For his father's sake if not his own. Surely you owe Jon that much for his service."

The king was not pleased. He took his arm from around Ned's shoulders. "Jon's service was the duty he owed his liege lord. I am not ungrateful, Ned. You of all men ought to know that. But the son is not the father. A mere boy cannot hold the east." Then his tone softened. "Enough of this. There is a more important office to discuss, and I would not argue with you." Robert grasped Ned by the elbow. "I have need of you, Ned."

"I am yours to command, Your Grace. Always." They were words he had to say, and so he said them, apprehensive about what might come next.

Robert scarcely seemed to hear him. "Those years we spent in the Eyrie . . . *gods*, those were good years. I want you at my side again, Ned. I want you down in King's Landing, not up here at the end of the world where you are no damned use to anybody." Robert looked off into the darkness, for a moment as melancholy as a Stark. "I swear to you, sitting a throne is a thousand times harder than winning one. Laws are a tedious business and counting coppers is worse. And the people . . . there is no end of them. I sit on that damnable iron chair and listen to them complain until my mind is numb and my ass is raw. They all want something, money or land or justice. The lies they tell . . . and my lords and ladies are no better. I am surrounded by flatterers and fools. It can drive a man to madness, Ned. Half of them don't dare tell me the truth, and the other half can't find it. There are nights I wish we had lost at the Trident. Ah, no, not truly, but . . ."

"I understand," Ned said softly.

Robert looked at him. "I think you do. If so, you are the only one, my old friend." He smiled. "Lord Eddard Stark, I would name you the Hand of the King."

Ned dropped to one knee. The offer did not surprise him; what other reason could Robert have had for coming so far? The Hand of the King was the second-most powerful man in the Seven Kingdoms. He spoke with the king's voice, commanded the king's armies, drafted the king's laws. At times he even sat upon the Iron Throne to dispense king's justice, when the king was absent, or sick, or otherwise indisposed. Robert was offering him a responsibility as large as the realm itself.

It was the last thing in the world he wanted.

"Your Grace," he said. "I am not worthy of the honor."

Robert groaned with good-humored impatience. "If I wanted to honor you, I'd let you retire. I am planning to make you run the kingdom and fight the wars while I eat and drink and wench myself into an early grave." He slapped his gut and grinned. "You know the saying, about the king and his Hand?"

Ned knew the saying. "What the king dreams," he said, "the Hand builds."

"I bedded a fishmaid once who told me the lowborn have a choicer way to put it. The king eats, they say, and the Hand takes the shit." He threw back his head and roared his laughter. The echoes rang through the darkness, and all around them the dead of Winterfell seemed to watch with cold and disapproving eyes.

Finally the laughter dwindled and stopped. Ned was still on one knee, his eyes upraised. "Damn it, Ned," the king complained. "You might at least humor me with a smile."

"They say it grows so cold up here in winter that a man's laughter freezes in his throat and chokes him to death," Ned said evenly. "Perhaps that is why the Starks have so little humor."

"Come south with me, and I'll teach you how to laugh again," the king promised. "You helped me win this damnable throne, now help me hold it. We were meant to rule together. If Lyanna had lived, we should have been brothers, bound by blood as well as affection. Well, it is not too late. I have a son. You have a daughter. My Joff and your Sansa shall join our houses, as Lyanna and I might once have done."

This offer *did* surprise him. "Sansa is only eleven."

Robert waved an impatient hand. "Old enough for betrothal. The marriage can wait a few years." The king smiled. "Now stand up and say yes, curse you."

"Nothing would give me greater pleasure, Your Grace," Ned answered. He hesitated. "These honors are all so unexpected. May I have some time to consider? I need to tell my wife . . ."

"Yes, yes, of course, tell Catelyn, sleep on it if you must." The king reached down, clasped Ned by the hand, and pulled him roughly to his feet. "Just don't keep me waiting too long. I am not the most patient of men."

For a moment Eddard Stark was filled with a terrible sense of foreboding. *This* was his place, here in the north. He looked at the stone figures all around them, breathed deep in the chill silence of the crypt. He could feel the eyes of the dead. They were all listening, he knew. And winter was coming.

JON

There were times—not many, but a few—when Jon Snow was glad he was a bastard. As he filled his wine cup once more from a passing flagon, it struck him that this might be one of them.

He settled back in his place on the bench among the younger squires and drank. The sweet, fruity taste of summerwine filled his mouth and brought a smile to his lips.

The Great Hall of Winterfell was hazy with smoke and heavy with the smell of roasted meat and fresh-baked bread. Its grey stone walls were draped with banners. White, gold, crimson: the direwolf of Stark, Baratheon's crowned stag, the lion of Lannister. A singer was playing the high harp and reciting a ballad, but down at this end of the hall his voice could scarcely be heard above the roar of the fire, the clangor of pewter plates and cups, and the low mutter of a hundred drunken conversations.

It was the fourth hour of the welcoming feast laid for the king. Jon's brothers and sisters had been seated with the royal children, beneath the raised platform where Lord and Lady Stark hosted the king and queen. In honor of the occasion, his lord father would doubtless permit each child a glass of wine, but no more than that. Down here on the benches, there was no one to stop Jon drinking as much as he had a thirst for.

And he was finding that he had a man's thirst, to the raucous delight of the youths around him, who urged him on every time he drained a glass. They were fine company, and Jon relished the stories they were telling, tales of battle and bedding and the hunt. He was certain that his companions were more entertaining than the king's offspring. He had sated his curiosity about the visitors when they made their entrance. The procession had passed not a foot from the place he had been given on the bench, and Jon had gotten a good long look at them all.

His lord father had come first, escorting the queen. She was as beautiful as men said. A jeweled tiara gleamed amidst her long golden hair, its emeralds a perfect match for the green of her eyes. His father helped her up the steps to the dais and led her to her seat, but the queen never so much as looked at him. Even at fourteen, Jon could see through her smile.

Next had come King Robert himself, with Lady Stark on his arm. The king was a great disappointment to Jon. His father had talked of him often: the peerless Robert Baratheon, demon of the Trident, the fiercest warrior of the realm, a giant among princes. Jon saw only a fat man, red-faced under his beard, sweating through his silks. He walked like a man half in his cups.

After them came the children. Little Rickon first, managing the long walk with all the dignity a three-year-old could muster. Jon had to urge him on when he stopped to visit. Close behind came Robb, in grey wool trimmed with white, the Stark colors. He had the Princess Myrcella on his arm. She was a wisp of a girl, not quite eight, her hair a cascade of golden curls under a jeweled net. Jon noticed the shy looks she gave Robb as they passed between the tables and the timid way she smiled at him. He decided she was insipid. Robb didn't even have the sense to realize how stupid she was; he was grinning like a fool.

His half sisters escorted the royal princes. Arya was paired with plump young Tommen, whose white-blond hair was longer than hers. Sansa, two years older, drew the crown prince, Joffrey Baratheon. He was twelve, younger than Jon or Robb, but taller than either, to Jon's vast dismay. Prince Joffrey had his sister's hair and his mother's deep green eyes. A thick tangle of blond curls dripped down past his golden choker and high velvet collar. Sansa looked radiant as she walked beside him, but Jon did not like Joffrey's pouty lips or the bored, disdainful way he looked at Winterfell's Great Hall.

He was more interested in the pair that came behind him: the queen's brothers, the Lannisters of Casterly Rock. The Lion and the Imp; there was no mistaking which was which. Ser Jaime Lannister was twin to Queen Cersei; tall and golden, with flashing green eyes and a smile that cut like a knife. He wore crimson silk, high black boots, a black satin cloak. On the breast of his tunic, the lion of his House was embroidered in gold thread, roaring its defiance. They called him the Lion of Lannister to his face and whispered "Kingslayer" behind his back.

Jon found it hard to look away from him. *This is what a king should look like,* he thought to himself as the man passed.

Then he saw the other one, waddling along half-hidden by his brother's side. Tyrion Lannister, the youngest of Lord Tywin's brood and by far the ugliest. All that the gods had given to Cersei and Jaime, they had denied Tyrion. He was a dwarf, half his brother's height, struggling to keep pace on stunted legs. His head was too large for his body, with a brute's squashed-in face beneath a swollen shelf of brow. One green eye and one black one peered out from under a lank fall of hair so blond it seemed white. Jon watched him with fascination.

The last of the high lords to enter were his uncle, Benjen Stark of the Night's Watch, and his father's ward, young Theon Greyjoy. Benjen gave Jon a warm smile as he went by. Theon ignored him utterly, but there was nothing new in that. After all had been seated, toasts were made, thanks were given and returned, and then the feasting began.

Jon had started drinking then, and he had not stopped.

Something rubbed against his leg beneath the table. Jon saw red eyes staring up at him. "Hungry again?" he asked. There was still half a honeyed chicken in the center of the table. Jon reached out to tear off a leg, then had a better idea. He knifed the bird whole and let the carcass slide to the floor between his legs. Ghost ripped into it in savage silence. His brothers and sisters had not been permitted to bring their wolves to the banquet, but there were more curs than Jon could count at this end of the hall, and no one had said a word about his pup. He told himself he was fortunate in that too.

His eyes stung. Jon rubbed at them savagely, cursing the smoke. He swallowed another gulp of wine and watched his direwolf devour the chicken.

Dogs moved between the tables, trailing after the serving girls. One of them, a black mongrel bitch with long yellow eyes, caught a scent of the chicken. She stopped and edged under the bench to get a share. Jon watched the confrontation. The bitch growled low in her throat and moved closer. Ghost looked up, silent, and fixed the dog with those hot red eyes. The bitch snapped an angry challenge. She was three times the size of the direwolf pup. Ghost did not move. He stood over his prize and opened his mouth, baring his fangs. The bitch tensed, barked again, then thought better of this fight. She turned and slunk away, with one last defiant snap to save her pride. Ghost went back to his meal.

Jon grinned and reached under the table to ruffle the shaggy white fur. The direwolf looked up at him, nipped gently at his hand, then went back to eating.

"Is this one of the direwolves I've heard so much of?" a familiar voice asked close at hand.

Jon looked up happily as his uncle Ben put a hand on his head and ruffled his hair much as Jon had ruffled the wolf's. "Yes," he said. "His name is Ghost."

One of the squires interrupted the bawdy story he'd been telling to make room at the table for their lord's brother. Benjen Stark straddled the bench with long legs and took the wine cup out of Jon's hand. "Summerwine," he said after a taste. "Nothing so sweet. How many cups have you had, Jon?"

Jon smiled.

Ben Stark laughed. "As I feared. Ah, well. I believe I was younger than you the first time I got truly and sincerely drunk." He snagged a roasted onion, dripping brown with gravy, from a nearby trencher and bit into it. It crunched.

His uncle was sharp-featured and gaunt as a mountain crag, but there was always a hint of laughter in his blue-grey eyes. He dressed in black, as befitted a man of the Night's Watch. Tonight it was rich black velvet, with high leather boots and a wide belt with a silver buckle. A heavy silver chain was looped round his neck. Benjen watched Ghost with amusement as he ate his onion. "A very quiet wolf," he observed.

"He's not like the others," Jon said. "He never makes a sound. That's why I named him Ghost. That, and because he's white. The others are all dark, grey or black."

"There are still direwolves beyond the Wall. We hear them on our rangings." Benjen Stark gave Jon a long look. "Don't you usually eat at table with your brothers?"

"Most times," Jon answered in a flat voice. "But tonight Lady Stark thought it might give insult to the royal family to seat a bastard among them."

"I see." His uncle glanced over his shoulder at the raised table at the far end of the hall. "My brother does not seem very festive tonight."

Jon had noticed that too. A bastard had to learn to notice things, to read the truth that people hid behind their eyes. His father was observing all the courtesies, but there was tightness in him that Jon had seldom seen before. He said little, looking out over the hall with hooded eyes, seeing nothing. Two seats away, the king had been drinking heavily all night. His broad face was flushed behind his great black beard. He made many a toast, laughed loudly at every jest, and attacked each dish like a starving man, but beside him the queen seemed as cold as an ice sculpture. "The queen is angry too," Jon told his uncle in a low, quiet voice. "Father took the king down to the crypts this afternoon. The queen didn't want him to go."

Benjen gave Jon a careful, measuring look. "You don't miss much, do you, Jon? We could use a man like you on the Wall."

Jon swelled with pride. "Robb is a stronger lance than I am, but I'm the better sword, and Hullen says I sit a horse as well as anyone in the castle."

"Notable achievements."

"Take me with you when you go back to the Wall," Jon said in a sudden rush. "Father will give me leave to go if you ask him, I know he will."

Uncle Benjen studied his face carefully. "The Wall is a hard place for a boy, Jon."

"I am almost a man grown," Jon protested. "I will turn fifteen on my next name day, and Maester Luwin says bastards grow up faster than other children."

"That's true enough," Benjen said with a downward twist of his mouth. He took Jon's cup from the table, filled it fresh from a nearby pitcher, and drank down a long swallow.

"Daeren Targaryen was only fourteen when he conquered Dorne," Jon said. The Young Dragon was one of his heroes.

"A conquest that lasted a summer," his uncle pointed out. "Your Boy King lost ten thousand men taking the place, and another fifty trying to hold it. Someone should have told him that war isn't a game." He took another sip of wine. "Also," he said, wiping his mouth, "Daeren Targaryen was only eighteen when he died. Or have you forgotten that part?"

"I forget nothing," Jon boasted. The wine was making him bold. He tried to sit very straight, to make himself seem taller. "I want to serve in the Night's Watch, Uncle."

He had thought on it long and hard, lying abed at night while his brothers slept around him. Robb would someday inherit Winterfell, would command great armies as the Warden of the North. Bran and Rickon would be Robb's bannermen and rule holdfasts in his name. His sisters Arya and Sansa would marry the heirs of other great houses and go south as mistress of castles of their own. But what place could a bastard hope to earn?

"You don't know what you're asking, Jon. The Night's Watch is a sworn brotherhood. We have no families. None of us will ever father sons. Our wife is duty. Our mistress is honor."

"A bastard can have honor too," Jon said. "I am ready to swear your oath."

"You are a boy of fourteen," Benjen said. "Not a man, not yet. Until you have known a woman, you cannot understand what you would be giving up."

"I don't care about that!" Jon said hotly.

"You might, if you knew what it meant," Benjen said.

"If you knew what the oath would cost you, you might be less eager to pay the price, son."

Jon felt anger rise inside him. "I'm not your son!"

Benjen Stark stood up. "More's the pity." He put a hand on Jon's shoulder. "Come back to me after you've fathered a few bastards of your own, and we'll see how you feel."

Jon trembled. "I will never father a bastard," he said carefully. *"Never!"* He spat it out like venom.

Suddenly he realized that the table had fallen silent, and they were all looking at him. He felt the tears begin to well behind his eyes. He pushed himself to his feet.

"I must be excused," he said with the last of his dignity. He whirled and bolted before they could see him cry. He must have drunk more wine than he had realized. His feet got tangled under him as he tried to leave, and he lurched sideways into a serving girl and sent a flagon of spiced wine crashing to the floor. Laughter boomed all around him, and Jon felt hot tears on his cheeks. Someone tried to steady him. He wrenched free of their grip and ran, half-blind, for the door. Ghost followed close at his heels, out into the night.

The yard was quiet and empty. A lone sentry stood high on the battlements of the inner wall, his cloak pulled tight around him against the cold. He looked bored and miserable as he huddled there alone, but Jon would have traded places with him in an instant. Otherwise the castle was dark and deserted. Jon had seen an abandoned holdfast once, a drear place where nothing moved but the wind and the stones kept silent about whatever people had lived there. Winterfell reminded him of that tonight.

The sounds of music and song spilled through the open windows behind him. They were the last things Jon wanted to hear. He wiped away his tears on the sleeve of his shirt, furious that he had let them fall, and turned to go.

"Boy," a voice called out to him. Jon turned.

Tyrion Lannister was sitting on the ledge above the door to the Great Hall, looking for all the world like a gargoyle. The dwarf grinned down at him. "Is that animal a wolf?"

"A direwolf," Jon said. "His name is Ghost." He stared up at the little man, his disappointment suddenly forgotten. "What are you doing up there? Why aren't you at the feast?"

"Too hot, too noisy, and I'd drunk too much wine," the dwarf told him. "I learned long ago that it is considered rude to vomit on your brother. Might I have a closer look at your wolf?"

Jon hesitated, then nodded slowly. "Can you climb down, or shall I bring a ladder?"

"Oh, bleed that," the little man said. He pushed himself off the ledge into empty air. Jon gasped, then watched with awe as Tyrion Lannister spun around in a tight ball, landed lightly on his hands, then vaulted backward onto his legs.

Ghost backed away from him uncertainly.

The dwarf dusted himself off and laughed. "I believe I've frightened your wolf. My apologies."

"He's not scared," Jon said. He knelt and called out. "Ghost, come here. Come on. That's it."

The wolf pup padded closer and nuzzled at Jon's face, but he kept a wary eye on Tyrion Lannister, and when the dwarf reached out to pet him, he drew back and bared his fangs in a silent snarl. "Shy, isn't he?" Lannister observed.

"Sit, Ghost," Jon commanded. "That's it. Keep still." He looked up at the dwarf. "You can touch him now. He won't move until I tell him to. I've been training him."

"I see," Lannister said. He ruffled the snow-white fur between Ghost's ears and said, "Nice wolf."

"If I wasn't here, he'd tear out your throat," Jon said. It wasn't actually true yet, but it would be.

"In that case, you had best stay close," the dwarf said. He cocked his oversized head to one side and looked Jon over with his mismatched eyes. "I am Tyrion Lannister."

"I know," Jon said. He rose. Standing, he was taller than the dwarf. It made him feel strange.

"You're Ned Stark's bastard, aren't you?"

Jon felt a coldness pass right through him. He pressed his lips together and said nothing.

"Did I offend you?" Lannister said. "Sorry. Dwarfs don't have to be tactful. Generations of capering fools in motley have won me the right to dress badly and say any damn thing that comes into my head." He grinned. "You *are* the bastard, though."

"Lord Eddard Stark is my father," Jon admitted stiffly.

Lannister studied his face. "Yes," he said. "I can see it. You have more of the north in you than your brothers."

"Half brothers," Jon corrected. He was pleased by the dwarf's comment, but he tried not to let it show.

"Let me give you some counsel, bastard," Lannister said. "Never forget what you are, for surely the world will not. Make it your strength. Then it can never be your weakness. Armor yourself in it, and it will never be used to hurt you."

Jon was in no mood for anyone's counsel. "What do you know about being a bastard?"

"All dwarfs are bastards in their father's eyes."

"You are your mother's trueborn son of Lannister."

"Am I?" the dwarf replied, sardonic. "Do tell my lord father. My mother died birthing me, and he's never been sure."

"I don't even know who my mother was," Jon said.

"Some woman, no doubt. Most of them are." He favored Jon with a rueful grin. "Remember this, boy. All dwarfs may be bastards, yet not all bastards need be dwarfs." And with that he turned and sauntered back into the feast, whistling a tune. When he opened the door, the light from within threw his shadow clear across the yard, and for just a moment Tyrion Lannister stood tall as a king.

CATELYN

Of all the rooms in Winterfell's Great Keep, Catelyn's bedchambers were the hottest. She seldom had to light a fire. The castle had been built over natural hot springs, and the scalding waters rushed through its walls and chambers like blood through a man's body, driving the chill from the stone halls, filling the glass gardens with a moist warmth, keeping the earth from freezing. Open pools smoked day and night in a dozen small courtyards. That was a little thing, in summer; in winter, it was the difference between life and death.

Catelyn's bath was always hot and steaming, and her walls warm to the touch. The warmth reminded her of Riverrun, of days in the sun with Lysa and Edmure, but Ned could never abide the heat. The Starks were made for the cold, he would tell her, and she would laugh and tell him in that case they had certainly built their castle in the wrong place.

So when they had finished, Ned rolled off and climbed from her bed, as he had a thousand times before. He crossed the room, pulled back the heavy tapestries, and threw open the high narrow windows one by one, letting the night air into the chamber.

The wind swirled around him as he stood facing the dark, naked and empty-handed. Catelyn pulled the furs to her chin and watched him. He looked somehow smaller and more vulnerable, like the youth she had wed in the sept at Riverrun, fifteen long years gone. Her loins still ached from the urgency of his lovemaking. It was a good ache. She could feel his seed within her. She prayed that it might quicken there. It had been three years since Rickon. She was not too old. She could give him another son.

"I will refuse him," Ned said as he turned back to her. His eyes were haunted, his voice thick with doubt.

Catelyn sat up in the bed. "You cannot. You *must* not."

"My duties are here in the north. I have no wish to be Robert's Hand."

"He will not understand that. He is a king now, and kings are not like other men. If you refuse to serve him, he will wonder why, and sooner or later he will begin to suspect that you oppose him. Can't you see the danger that would put us in?"

Ned shook his head, refusing to believe. "Robert would never harm me or any of mine. We were closer than brothers. He loves me. If I refuse him, he will roar and curse and bluster, and in a week we will laugh about it together. I know the man!"

"You knew the man," she said. "The king is a stranger to you." Catelyn remembered the direwolf dead in the snow, the broken antler lodged deep in her throat. She had to make him see. "Pride is everything to a king, my lord. Robert came all this way to see you, to bring you these great honors, you cannot throw them back in his face."

"Honors?" Ned laughed bitterly.

"In his eyes, yes," she said.

"And in yours?"

"*And* in mine," she blazed, angry now. Why couldn't he see? "He offers his own son in marriage to our daughter, what else would you call that? Sansa might someday be queen. Her sons could rule from the Wall to the mountains of Dorne. What is so wrong with that?"

"Gods, Catelyn, Sansa is only *eleven*," Ned said. "And Joffrey . . . Joffrey is . . ."

She finished for him. ". . . crown prince, and heir to the Iron Throne. And I was only twelve when my father promised me to your brother Brandon."

That brought a bitter twist to Ned's mouth. "Brandon. Yes. Brandon would know what to do. He always did. It was all meant for Brandon. You, Winterfell, everything. He was born to be a King's Hand and a father to queens. I never asked for this cup to pass to me."

"Perhaps not," Catelyn said, "but Brandon is dead, and the cup has passed, and you must drink from it, like it or not."

Ned turned away from her, back to the night. He stood staring out in the darkness, watching the moon and the stars perhaps, or perhaps the sentries on the wall.

Catelyn softened then, to see his pain. Eddard Stark had married her in Brandon's place, as custom decreed, but the shadow of his dead brother still lay between them, as did the other, the shadow of the woman he would not name, the woman who had borne him his bastard son.

She was about to go to him when the knock came at the door, loud and unexpected. Ned turned, frowning. "What is it?"

Desmond's voice came through the door. "My lord, Maester Luwin is without and begs urgent audience."

"You told him I had left orders not to be disturbed?"

"Yes, my lord. He insists."

"Very well. Send him in."

Ned crossed to the wardrobe and slipped on a heavy robe. Catelyn realized suddenly how cold it had become. She sat up in bed and pulled the furs to her chin. "Perhaps we should close the windows," she suggested.

Ned nodded absently. Maester Luwin was shown in.

The maester was a small grey man. His eyes were grey, and quick, and saw much. His hair was grey, what little the years had left him. His robe was grey wool, trimmed with white fur, the Stark colors. Its great floppy sleeves had pockets hidden inside. Luwin was always tucking things into those sleeves and producing other things from them: books, messages, strange artifacts, toys for the children. With all he kept hidden in his sleeves, Catelyn was surprised that Maester Luwin could lift his arms at all.

The maester waited until the door had closed behind him before he spoke. "My lord," he said to Ned, "pardon for disturbing your rest. I have been left a message."

Ned looked irritated. "Been *left*? By whom? Has there been a rider? I was not told."

"There was no rider, my lord. Only a carved wooden box, left on a table in my observatory while I napped. My servants saw no one, but it must have been brought by someone in the king's party. We have had no other visitors from the south."

"A wooden box, you say?" Catelyn said.

"Inside was a fine new lens for the observatory, from Myr by the look of it. The lenscrafters of Myr are without equal."

Ned frowned. He had little patience for this sort of thing, Catelyn knew. "A lens," he said. "What has that to do with me?"

"I asked the same question," Maester Luwin said. "Clearly there was more to this than the seeming."

Under the heavy weight of her furs, Catelyn shivered. "A lens is an instrument to help us see."

"Indeed it is." He fingered the collar of his order; a heavy chain worn tight around the neck beneath his robe, each link forged from a different metal.

Catelyn could feel dread stirring inside her once again. "What is it that they would have us see more clearly?"

"The very thing I asked myself." Maester Luwin drew a tightly rolled paper out of his sleeve. "I found the true message concealed within a false bottom when I dismantled the box the lens had come in, but it is not for my eyes."

Ned held out his hand. "Let me have it, then."

Luwin did not stir. "Pardons, my lord. The message is not for you either. It is marked for the eyes of the Lady Catelyn, and her alone. May I approach?"

Catelyn nodded, not trusting to speak. The maester placed the paper on the table beside the bed. It was sealed with a small blob of blue wax. Luwin bowed and began to retreat.

"Stay," Ned commanded him. His voice was grave. He looked at Catelyn. "What is it? My lady, you're shaking."

"I'm afraid," she admitted. She reached out and took the letter in trembling hands. The furs dropped away from her nakedness, forgotten. In the blue wax was the moon-and-falcon seal of House Arryn. "It's from Lysa." Catelyn looked at her husband. "It will not make us glad," she told him. "There is grief in this message, Ned. I can feel it."

Ned frowned, his face darkening. "Open it."

Catelyn broke the seal.

Her eyes moved over the words. At first they made no sense to her. Then she remembered. "Lysa took no chances. When we were girls together, we had a private language, she and I."

"Can you read it?"

"Yes," Catelyn admitted.

"Then tell us."

"Perhaps I should withdraw," Maester Luwin said.

"No," Catelyn said. "We will need your counsel." She threw back the furs and climbed from the bed. The night air was as cold as the grave on her bare skin as she padded across the room.

Maester Luwin averted his eyes. Even Ned looked shocked. "What are you doing?" he asked.

"Lighting a fire," Catelyn told him. She found a dressing gown and shrugged into it, then knelt over the cold hearth.

"Maester Luwin—" Ned began.

"Maester Luwin has delivered all my children," Catelyn said. "This is no time for false modesty." She slid the paper in among the kindling and placed the heavier logs on top of it.

Ned crossed the room, took her by the arm, and pulled her to her feet. He held her there, his face inches from her. "My lady, tell me! What was this message?"

Catelyn stiffened in his grasp. "A warning," she said softly. "If we have the wits to hear."

His eyes searched her face. "Go on."

"Lysa says Jon Arryn was murdered."

His fingers tightened on her arm. "By whom?"

"The Lannisters," she told him. "The queen."

Ned released his hold on her arm. There were deep red marks on her skin. "Gods," he whispered. His voice was hoarse. "Your sister is sick with grief. She cannot know what she is saying."

"She knows," Catelyn said. "Lysa is impulsive, yes,

but this message was carefully planned, cleverly hidden. She knew it meant death if her letter fell into the wrong hands. To risk so much, she must have had more than mere suspicion." Catelyn looked to her husband. "Now we truly have no choice. You *must* be Robert's Hand. You must go south with him and learn the truth."

She saw at once that Ned had reached a very different conclusion. "The only truths I know are here. The south is a nest of adders I would do better to avoid."

Luwin plucked at his chain collar where it had chafed the soft skin of his throat. "The Hand of the King has great power, my lord. Power to find the truth of Lord Arryn's death, to bring his killers to the king's justice. Power to protect Lady Arryn and her son, if the worst be true."

Ned glanced helplessly around the bedchamber. Catelyn's heart went out to him, but she knew she could not take him in her arms just then. First the victory must be won, for her children's sake. "You say you love Robert like a brother. Would you leave your brother surrounded by Lannisters?"

"The Others take both of you," Ned muttered darkly. He turned away from them and went to the window. She did not speak, nor did the maester. They waited, quiet, while Eddard Stark said a silent farewell to the home he loved. When he turned away from the window at last, his voice was tired and full of melancholy, and moisture glittered faintly in the corners of his eyes. "My father went south once, to answer the summons of a king. He never came home again."

"A different time," Maester Luwin said. "A different king."

"Yes," Ned said dully. He seated himself in a chair by the hearth. "Catelyn, you shall stay here in Winterfell."

His words were like an icy draft through her heart. "No," she said, suddenly afraid. Was this to be her punishment? Never to see his face again, nor to feel his arms around her?

"Yes," Ned said, in words that would brook no argument. "You must govern the north in my stead, while I run Robert's errands. There must always be a Stark in Winterfell. Robb is fourteen. Soon enough, he will be a man grown. He must learn to rule, and I will not be here for him. Make him part of your councils. He must be ready when his time comes."

"Gods will, not for many years," Maester Luwin murmured.

"Maester Luwin, I trust you as I would my own blood. Give my wife your voice in all things great and small. Teach my son the things he needs to know. Winter is coming."

Maester Luwin nodded gravely. Then silence fell, until Catelyn found her courage and asked the question whose answer she most dreaded. "What of the other children?"

Ned stood, and took her in his arms, and held her face close to his. "Rickon is very young," he said gently. "He should stay here with you and Robb. The others I would take with me."

"I could not bear it," Catelyn said, trembling.

"You must," he said. "Sansa must wed Joffrey, that is clear now, we must give them no grounds to suspect our devotion. And it is past time that Arya learned the ways of a southron court. In a few years she will be of an age to marry too."

Sansa would shine in the south, Catelyn thought to herself, and the gods knew that Arya needed refinement. Reluctantly, she let go of them in her heart. But not Bran. Never Bran. "Yes," she said, "but please, Ned, for the love you bear me, let Bran remain here at Winterfell. He is only seven."

"I was eight when my father sent me to foster at the Eyrie," Ned said. "Ser Rodrik tells me there is bad feeling between Robb and Prince Joffrey. That is not healthy. Bran can bridge that distance. He is a sweet boy, quick to laugh, easy to love. Let him grow up with the young princes, let him become their friend as Robert became mine. Our House will be the safer for it."

He was right; Catelyn knew it. It did not make the pain any easier to bear. She would lose all four of them, then: Ned, and both girls, and her sweet, loving Bran. Only Robb and little Rickon would be left to her. She felt lonely already. Winterfell was such a vast place. "Keep him off the walls, then," she said bravely. "You know how Bran loves to climb."

Ned kissed the tears from her eyes before they could

fall. "Thank you, my lady," he whispered. "This is hard, I know."

"What of Jon Snow, my lord?" Maester Luwin asked.

Catelyn tensed at the mention of the name. Ned felt the anger in her, and pulled away.

Many men fathered bastards. Catelyn had grown up with that knowledge. It came as no surprise to her, in the first year of her marriage, to learn that Ned had fathered a child on some girl chance met on campaign. He had a man's needs, after all, and they had spent that year apart, Ned off at war in the south while she remained safe in her father's castle at Riverrun. Her thoughts were more of Robb, the infant at her breast, than of the husband she scarcely knew. He was welcome to whatever solace he might find between battles. And if his seed quickened, she expected he would see to the child's needs.

He did more than that. The Starks were not like other men. Ned brought his bastard home with him, and called him "son" for all the north to see. When the wars were over at last, and Catelyn rode to Winterfell, Jon and his wet nurse had already taken up residence.

That cut deep. Ned would not speak of the mother, not so much as a word, but a castle has no secrets, and Catelyn heard her maids repeating tales they heard from the lips of her husband's soldiers. They whispered of Ser Arthur Dayne, the Sword of the Morning, deadliest of the seven knights of Aerys's Kingsguard, and of how their young lord had slain him in single combat. And they told how afterward Ned had carried Ser Arthur's sword back to the beautiful young sister who awaited him in a castle called Starfall on the shores of the Summer Sea. The Lady Ashara Dayne, tall and fair, with haunting violet eyes. It had taken her a fortnight to marshal her courage, but finally, in bed one night, Catelyn had asked her husband the truth of it, asked him to his face.

That was the only time in all their years that Ned had ever frightened her. "Never ask me about Jon," he said, cold as ice. "He is my blood, and that is all you need to know. And now I will learn where you heard that name, my lady." She had pledged to obey; she told him; and from that day on, the whispering had stopped, and Ashara Dayne's name was never heard in Winterfell again.

Whoever Jon's mother had been, Ned must have loved

her fiercely, for nothing Catelyn said would persuade him to send the boy away. It was the one thing she could never forgive him. She had come to love her husband with all her heart, but she had never found it in her to love Jon. She might have overlooked a dozen bastards for Ned's sake, so long as they were out of sight. Jon was never out of sight, and as he grew, he looked more like Ned than any of the trueborn sons she bore him. Somehow that made it worse. "Jon must go," she said now.

"He and Robb are close," Ned said. "I had hoped . . ."

"He cannot stay here," Catelyn said, cutting him off. "He is your son, not mine. I will not have him." It was hard, she knew, but no less the truth. Ned would do the boy no kindness by leaving him here at Winterfell.

The look Ned gave her was anguished. "You know I cannot take him south. There will be no place for him at court. A boy with a bastard's name . . . you know what they will say of him. He will be shunned."

Catelyn armored her heart against the mute appeal in her husband's eyes. "They say your friend Robert has fathered a dozen bastards himself."

"And none of them has ever been seen at court!" Ned blazed. "The Lannister woman has seen to that. How can you be so damnably cruel, Catelyn? He is only a boy. He—"

His fury was on him. He might have said more, and worse, but Maester Luwin cut in. "Another solution presents itself," he said, his voice quiet. "Your brother Benjen came to me about Jon a few days ago. It seems the boy aspires to take the black."

Ned looked shocked. "He asked to join the Night's Watch?"

Catelyn said nothing. Let Ned work it out in his own mind; her voice would not be welcome now. Yet gladly would she have kissed the maester just then. His was the perfect solution. Benjen Stark was a Sworn Brother. Jon would be a son to him, the child he would never have. And in time the boy would take the oath as well. He would father no sons who might someday contest with Catelyn's own grandchildren for Winterfell.

Maester Luwin said, "There is great honor in service on the Wall, my lord."

"And even a bastard may rise high in the Night's

Watch," Ned reflected. Still, his voice was troubled. "Jon is so young. If he asked this when he was a man grown, that would be one thing, but a boy of fourteen . . ."

"A hard sacrifice," Maester Luwin agreed. "Yet these are hard times, my lord. His road is no crueler than yours or your lady's."

Catelyn thought of the three children she must lose. It was not easy keeping silent then.

Ned turned away from them to gaze out the window, his long face silent and thoughtful. Finally he sighed, and turned back. "Very well," he said to Maester Luwin. "I suppose it is for the best. I will speak to Ben."

"When shall we tell Jon?" the maester asked.

"When I must. Preparations must be made. It will be a fortnight before we are ready to depart. I would sooner let Jon enjoy these last few days. Summer will end soon enough, and childhood as well. When the time comes, I will tell him myself."

ARYA

Arya's stitches were crooked again.

She frowned down at them with dismay and glanced over to where her sister Sansa sat among the other girls. Sansa's needlework was exquisite. Everyone said so. "Sansa's work is as pretty as she is," Septa Mordane told their lady mother once. "She has such fine, delicate hands." When Lady Catelyn had asked about Arya, the septa had sniffed. "Arya has the hands of a blacksmith."

Arya glanced furtively across the room, worried that Septa Mordane might have read her thoughts, but the septa was paying her no attention today. She was sitting with the Princess Myrcella, all smiles and admiration. It was not often that the septa was privileged to instruct a royal princess in the womanly arts, as she had said when the queen brought Myrcella to join them. Arya thought that Myrcella's stitches looked a little crooked too, but you would never know it from the way Septa Mordane was cooing.

She studied her own work again, looking for some way to salvage it, then sighed and put down the needle. She looked glumly at her sister. Sansa was chatting away happily as she worked. Beth Cassel, Ser Rodrik's little girl, was sitting by her feet, listening to every word she said, and Jeyne Poole was leaning over to whisper something in her ear.

"What are you talking about?" Arya asked suddenly.

Jeyne gave her a startled look, then giggled. Sansa looked abashed. Beth blushed. No one answered.

"Tell me," Arya said.

Jeyne glanced over to make certain that Septa Mordane was not listening. Myrcella said something then, and the septa laughed along with the rest of the ladies.

"We were talking about the prince," Sansa said, her voice soft as a kiss.

Arya knew which prince she meant: Joffrey, of course. The tall, handsome one. Sansa got to sit with him at the feast. Arya had to sit with the little fat one. Naturally.

"Joffrey likes your sister," Jeyne whispered, proud as if she had something to do with it. She was the daughter of Winterfell's steward and Sansa's dearest friend. "He told her she was very beautiful."

"He's going to marry her," little Beth said dreamily, hugging herself. "Then Sansa will be queen of all the realm."

Sansa had the grace to blush. She blushed prettily. She did everything prettily, Arya thought with dull resentment. "Beth, you shouldn't make up stories," Sansa corrected the younger girl, gently stroking her hair to take the harshness out of her words. She looked at Arya. "What did you think of Prince Joff, sister? He's very gallant, don't you think?"

"Jon says he looks like a girl," Arya said.

Sansa sighed as she stitched. "Poor Jon," she said. "He gets jealous because he's a bastard."

"He's our brother," Arya said, much too loudly. Her voice cut through the afternoon quiet of the tower room.

Septa Mordane raised her eyes. She had a bony face, sharp eyes, and a thin lipless mouth made for frowning. It was frowning now. "What are you talking about, children?"

"Our half brother," Sansa corrected, soft and precise. She smiled for the septa. "Arya and I were remarking on how pleased we were to have the princess with us today," she said.

Septa Mordane nodded. "Indeed. A great honor for us all." Princess Myrcella smiled uncertainly at the compliment. "Arya, why aren't you at work?" the septa asked. She rose to her feet, starched skirts rustling as she started across the room. "Let me see your stitches."

Arya wanted to scream. It was just like Sansa to go and attract the septa's attention. "Here," she said, surrendering up her work.

The septa examined the fabric. "Arya, Arya, Arya," she said. "This will not do. This will not do at all."

Everyone was looking at her. It was too much. Sansa was too well bred to smile at her sister's disgrace, but Jeyne was smirking on her behalf. Even Princess Myrcella looked sorry for her. Arya felt tears filling her eyes. She pushed herself out of her chair and bolted for the door.

Septa Mordane called after her. "Arya, come back here! Don't you take another step! Your lady mother will hear of this. In front of our royal princess too! You'll shame us all!"

Arya stopped at the door and turned back, biting her lip. The tears were running down her cheeks now. She managed a stiff little bow to Myrcella. "By your leave, my lady."

Myrcella blinked at her and looked to her ladies for guidance. But if she was uncertain, Septa Mordane was not. "Just where do you think you are going, Arya?" the septa demanded.

Arya glared at her. "I have to go shoe a horse," she said sweetly, taking a brief satisfaction in the shock on the septa's face. Then she whirled and made her exit, running down the steps as fast as her feet would take her.

It wasn't fair. Sansa had everything. Sansa was two years older; maybe by the time Arya had been born, there had been nothing left. Often it felt that way. Sansa could sew and dance and sing. She wrote poetry. She knew how to dress. She played the high harp *and* the bells. Worse, she was beautiful. Sansa had gotten their mother's fine high cheekbones and the thick auburn hair of the Tullys. Arya took after their lord father. Her hair was a lusterless brown, and her face was long and solemn. Jeyne used to call her Arya Horseface, and neigh whenever she came near. It hurt that the one thing Arya could do better than her sister was ride a horse. Well, that and manage a household. Sansa had never had much of a head for figures. If she did marry Prince Joff, Arya hoped for his sake that he had a good steward.

Nymeria was waiting for her in the guardroom at the base of the stairs. She bounded to her feet as soon as she caught sight of Arya. Arya grinned. The wolf pup loved her, even if no one else did. They went everywhere together, and Nymeria slept in her room, at the foot of her bed. If Mother had not forbidden it, Arya would gladly have taken the wolf with her to needlework. Let Septa Mordane complain about her stitches *then*.

Nymeria nipped eagerly at her hand as Arya untied her. She had yellow eyes. When they caught the sunlight, they gleamed like two golden coins. Arya had named her after the warrior queen of the Rhoyne, who had led her people across the narrow sea. That had been a great scandal too. Sansa, of course, had named her pup "Lady." Arya made a face and hugged the wolfling tight. Nymeria licked her ear, and she giggled.

By now Septa Mordane would certainly have sent word to her lady mother. If she went to her room, they would find her. Arya did not care to be found. She had a better notion. The boys were at practice in the yard. She wanted to see Robb put gallant Prince Joffrey flat on his back. "Come," she whispered to Nymeria. She got up and ran, the wolf coming hard at her heels.

There was a window in the covered bridge between the armory and the Great Keep where you had a view of the whole yard. That was where they headed.

They arrived, flushed and breathless, to find Jon seated on the sill, one leg drawn up languidly to his chin. He was watching the action, so absorbed that he seemed unaware of her approach until his white wolf moved to meet them. Nymeria stalked closer on wary feet. Ghost, already larger than his litter mates, smelled her, gave her ear a careful nip, and settled back down.

Jon gave her a curious look. "Shouldn't you be working on your stitches, little sister?"

Arya made a face at him. "I wanted to see them fight."

He smiled. "Come here, then."

Arya climbed up on the window and sat beside him, to a chorus of thuds and grunts from the yard below.

To her disappointment, it was the younger boys drilling. Bran was so heavily padded he looked as though he had belted on a featherbed, and Prince Tommen, who was plump to begin with, seemed positively round. They were huffing and puffing and hitting at each other with padded wooden swords under the watchful eye of old Ser Rodrik Cassel, the master-at-arms, a great stout keg of a man with magnificent white cheek whiskers. A dozen spectators, man and boy, were calling out encouragement, Robb's voice the loudest among them. She spotted Theon Greyjoy beside him, his black doublet emblazoned with the golden kraken of his House, a look of wry contempt on his face. Both of the combatants were staggering. Arya judged that they had been at it awhile.

"A shade more exhausting than needlework," Jon observed.

"A shade more fun than needlework," Arya gave back at him. Jon grinned, reached over, and messed up her hair. Arya flushed. They had always been close. Jon had their father's face, as she did. They were the only ones. Robb and Sansa and Bran and even little Rickon all took after the Tullys, with easy smiles and fire in their hair. When Arya had been little, she had been afraid that meant that she was a bastard too. It had been Jon she had gone to in her fear, and Jon who had reassured her.

"Why aren't you down in the yard?" Arya asked him.

He gave her a half smile. "Bastards are not allowed to damage young princes," he said. "Any bruises they take in the practice yard must come from trueborn swords."

"Oh." Arya felt abashed. She should have realized. For the second time today, Arya reflected that life was not fair.

She watched her little brother whack at Tommen. "I could do just as good as Bran," she said. "He's only seven. I'm nine."

Jon looked her over with all his fourteen-year-old wisdom. "You're too skinny," he said. He took her arm to feel her muscle. Then he sighed and shook his head. "I doubt you could even lift a longsword, little sister, never mind swing one."

Arya snatched back her arm and glared at him. Jon messed up her hair again. They watched Bran and Tommen circle each other.

"You see Prince Joffrey?" Jon asked.

She hadn't, not at first glance, but when she looked again she found him to the back, under the shade of the high stone wall. He was surrounded by men she did not recognize, young squires in the livery of Lannister and Baratheon, strangers all. There were a few older men among them; knights, she surmised.

"Look at the arms on his surcoat," Jon suggested.

Arya looked. An ornate shield had been embroidered on the prince's padded surcoat. No doubt the needlework was exquisite. The arms were divided down the middle; on one side was the crowned stag of the royal House, on the other the lion of Lannister.

"The Lannisters are proud," Jon observed. "You'd think the royal sigil would be sufficient, but no. He makes his mother's House equal in honor to the king's."

"The woman is important too!" Arya protested.

Jon chuckled. "Perhaps you should do the same thing, little sister. Wed Tully to Stark in your arms."

"A wolf with a fish in its mouth?" It made her laugh. "That would look silly. Besides, if a girl can't fight, why should she have a coat of arms?"

Jon shrugged. "Girls get the arms but not the swords. Bastards get the swords but not the arms. I did not make the rules, little sister."

There was a shout from the courtyard below. Prince Tommen was rolling in the dust, trying to get up and failing. All the padding made him look like a turtle on its back. Bran was standing over him with upraised wooden sword, ready to whack him again once he regained his feet. The men began to laugh.

"Enough!" Ser Rodrik called out. He gave the prince a hand and yanked him back to his feet. "Well fought. Lew, Donnis, help them out of their armor." He looked around. "Prince Joffrey, Robb, will you go another round?"

Robb, already sweaty from a previous bout, moved forward eagerly. "Gladly."

Joffrey moved into the sunlight in response to Rodrik's summons. His hair shone like spun gold. He looked bored. "This is a game for children, Ser Rodrik."

Theon Greyjoy gave a sudden bark of laughter. "You are children," he said derisively.

"Robb may be a child," Joffrey said. "I am a prince. And I grow tired of swatting at Starks with a play sword."

"You got more swats than you gave, Joff," Robb said. "Are you afraid?"

Prince Joffrey looked at him. "Oh, terrified," he said. "You're so much older." Some of the Lannister men laughed.

Jon looked down on the scene with a frown. "Joffrey is truly a little shit," he told Arya.

Ser Rodrik tugged thoughtfully at his white whiskers. "What are you suggesting?" he asked the prince.

"Live steel."

"Done," Robb shot back. "You'll be sorry!"

The master-at-arms put a hand on Robb's shoulder to quiet him. "Live steel is too dangerous. I will permit you tourney swords, with blunted edges."

Joffrey said nothing, but a man strange to Arya, a tall knight with black hair and burn scars on his face, pushed forward in front of the prince. "This is your prince. Who are you to tell him he may not have an edge on his sword, *ser?*"

"Master-at-arms of Winterfell, Clegane, and you would do well not to forget it."

"Are you training women here?" the burned man wanted to know. He was muscled like a bull.

"I am training *knights,*" Ser Rodrik said pointedly. "They will have steel when they are ready. When they are of an age."

The burned man looked at Robb. "How old are you, boy?"

"Fourteen," Robb said.

"I killed a man at twelve. You can be sure it was not with a blunt sword."

Arya could see Robb bristle. His pride was wounded. He turned on Ser Rodrik. "Let me do it. I can beat him."

"Beat him with a tourney blade, then," Ser Rodrik said.

Joffrey shrugged. "Come and see me when you're older, Stark. If you're not *too* old." There was laughter from the Lannister men.

Robb's curses rang through the yard. Arya covered her mouth in shock. Theon Greyjoy seized Robb's arm to keep him away from the prince. Ser Rodrik tugged at his whiskers in dismay.

Joffrey feigned a yawn and turned to his younger

brother. "Come, Tommen," he said. "The hour of play is done. Leave the children to their frolics."

That brought more laughter from the Lannisters, more curses from Robb. Ser Rodrik's face was beet-red with fury under the white of his whiskers. Theon kept Robb locked in an iron grip until the princes and their party were safely away.

Jon watched them leave, and Arya watched Jon. His face had grown as still as the pool at the heart of the godswood. Finally he climbed down off the window. "The show is done," he said. He bent to scratch Ghost behind the ears. The white wolf rose and rubbed against him. "You had best run back to your room, little sister. Septa Mordane will surely be lurking. The longer you hide, the sterner the penance. You'll be sewing all through winter. When the spring thaw comes, they will find your body with a needle still locked tight between your frozen fingers."

Arya didn't think it was funny. "I hate needlework!" she said with passion. "It's not fair!"

"Nothing is fair," Jon said. He messed up her hair again and walked away from her, Ghost moving silently beside him. Nymeria started to follow too, then stopped and came back when she saw that Arya was not coming.

Reluctantly she turned in the other direction.

It was worse than Jon had thought. It wasn't Septa Mordane waiting in her room. It was Septa Mordane *and* her mother.

BRAN

The hunt left at dawn. The king wanted wild boar at the feast tonight. Prince Joffrey rode with his father, so Robb had been allowed to join the hunters as well. Uncle Benjen, Jory, Theon Greyjoy, Ser Rodrik, and even the queen's funny little brother had all ridden out with them. It was the last hunt, after all. On the morrow they left for the south.

Bran had been left behind with Jon and the girls and Rickon. But Rickon was only a baby and the girls were only girls and Jon and his wolf were nowhere to be found. Bran did not look for him very hard. He thought Jon was angry at him. Jon seemed to be angry at everyone these days. Bran did not know why. He was going with Uncle Ben to the Wall, to join the Night's Watch. That was almost as good as going south with the king. Robb was the one they were leaving behind, not Jon.

For days, Bran could scarcely wait to be off. He was going to ride the kingsroad on a horse of his own, not a pony but a real horse. His father would be the Hand of the King, and they were going to live in the red castle at King's Landing, the castle the Dragonlords had built. Old Nan said there were ghosts there, and dungeons where terrible things had been done, and dragon heads on the walls. It gave Bran a shiver just to think of it, but he was not afraid. How could he be afraid? His father would be with him, and the king with all his knights and sworn swords.

Bran was going to be a knight himself someday, one of the Kingsguard. Old Nan said they were the finest swords in all the realm. There were only seven of them, and they wore white armor and had no wives or children, but lived only to serve the king. Bran knew all the stories. Their names were like music to him. Serwyn of the Mirror Shield. Ser Ryam Redwyne. Prince Aemon the Dragonknight. The twins Ser Erryk and Ser Arryk, who had died on one another's swords hundreds of years ago, when brother fought sister in the war the singers called the Dance of the Dragons. The White Bull, Gerold Hightower. Ser Arthur Dayne, the Sword of the Morning. Barristan the Bold.

Two of the Kingsguard had come north with King Robert. Bran had watched them with fascination, never quite daring to speak to them. Ser Boros was a bald man with a jowly face, and Ser Meryn had droopy eyes and a beard the color of rust. Ser Jaime Lannister looked more like the knights in the stories, and he was of the Kingsguard too, but Robb said he had killed the old mad king and shouldn't count anymore. The greatest living knight was Ser Barristan Selmy, Barristan the Bold, the Lord Commander of the Kingsguard. Father had promised that they would meet Ser Barristan when they reached King's Landing, and Bran had been marking the days on his wall, eager to depart, to see a world he had only dreamed of and begin a life he could scarcely imagine.

Yet now that the last day was at hand, suddenly Bran felt lost. Winterfell had been the only home he had ever known. His father had told him that he ought to say his farewells today, and he had tried. After the hunt had ridden out, he wandered through the castle with his wolf at his side, intending to visit the ones who would be left behind, Old Nan and Gage the cook, Mikken in his smithy, Hodor the stableboy who smiled so much and took care of his pony and never said anything but "Hodor," the man in the glass gardens who gave him a blackberry when he came to visit . . .

But it was no good. He had gone to the stable first, and seen his pony there in its stall, except it wasn't *his* pony anymore, he was getting a real horse and leaving the pony behind, and all of a sudden Bran just wanted to sit down and cry. He turned and ran off before Hodor and the other stableboys could see the tears in his eyes. That was the end of his farewells. Instead Bran spent the morning alone in the godswood, trying to teach his wolf to fetch a stick, and failing. The wolfling was smarter than any of the hounds in his father's kennel and Bran would have sworn he understood every word that was said to him, but he showed very little interest in chasing sticks.

He was still trying to decide on a name. Robb was calling his Grey Wind, because he ran so fast. Sansa had named hers Lady, and Arya named hers after some old witch queen in the songs, and little Rickon called his Shaggydog, which Bran thought was a pretty stupid name for a direwolf. Jon's wolf, the white one, was Ghost. Bran wished he had thought of that first, even though his wolf wasn't white. He had tried a hundred names in the last fortnight, but none of them sounded right.

Finally he got tired of the stick game and decided to go climbing. He hadn't been up to the broken tower for weeks with everything that had happened, and this might be his last chance.

He raced across the godswood, taking the long way around to avoid the pool where the heart tree grew. The heart tree had always frightened him; trees ought not have eyes, Bran thought, or leaves that looked like hands. His wolf came sprinting at his heels. "You stay here," he told him at the base of the sentinel tree near the armory wall. "Lie down. That's right. Now *stay*."

The wolf did as he was told. Bran scratched him behind the ears, then turned away, jumped, grabbed a low branch, and pulled himself up. He was halfway up the tree, moving easily from limb to limb, when the wolf got to his feet and began to howl.

Bran looked back down. His wolf fell silent, staring up at him through slitted yellow eyes. A strange chill went through him. He began to climb again. Once more the wolf howled. "Quiet," he yelled. "Sit down. Stay. You're worse than Mother." The howling chased him all the way up the tree, until finally he jumped off onto the armory roof and out of sight.

The rooftops of Winterfell were Bran's second home. His mother often said that Bran could climb before he could walk. Bran could not remember when he first learned to walk, but he could not remember when he started to climb either, so he supposed it must be true.

To a boy, Winterfell was a grey stone labyrinth of walls and towers and courtyards and tunnels spreading out in all directions. In the older parts of the castle, the halls slanted up and down so that you couldn't even be sure what floor you were on. The place had grown over the centuries like some monstrous stone tree, Maester Luwin told him once, and its branches were gnarled and thick and twisted, its roots sunk deep into the earth.

When he got out from under it and scrambled up near the sky, Bran could see all of Winterfell in a glance. He liked the way it looked, spread out beneath him, only birds wheeling over his head while all the life of the castle went on below. Bran could perch for hours among the shapeless, rain-worn gargoyles that brooded over the First Keep, watching it all: the men drilling with wood and steel in the yard, the cooks tending their vegetables in the glass garden, restless dogs running back and forth in the kennels, the silence of the godswood, the girls gossiping beside the washing well. It made him feel like he was lord of the castle, in a way even Robb would never know.

It taught him Winterfell's secrets too. The builders had not even leveled the earth; there were hills and valleys behind the walls of Winterfell. There was a covered bridge that went from the fourth floor of the bell tower across to the second floor of the rookery. Bran knew about that. And he knew you could get inside the inner wall by the south gate, climb three floors and run all the way around Winterfell through a narrow tunnel in the stone, and then come out *on ground level* at the north gate, with a hundred feet of wall looming over you. Even Maester Luwin didn't know *that*, Bran was convinced.

His mother was terrified that one day Bran would slip off a wall and kill himself. He told her that he wouldn't, but she never believed him. Once she made him promise that he would stay on the ground. He had managed to keep that promise for almost a fortnight, miserable every day, until one night he had gone out the window of his bedroom when his brothers were fast asleep.

He confessed his crime the next day in a fit of guilt. Lord Eddard ordered him to the godswood to cleanse himself. Guards were posted to see that Bran remained there alone all night to reflect on his disobedience. The next morning Bran was nowhere to be seen. They finally found him fast asleep in the upper branches of the tallest sentinel in the grove.

As angry as he was, his father could not help but laugh. "You're not my son," he told Bran when they fetched him down, "you're a squirrel. So be it. If you must climb, then climb, but try not to let your mother see you."

Bran did his best, although he did not think he ever really fooled her. Since his father would not forbid it, she turned to others. Old Nan told him a story about a bad little boy who climbed too high and was struck down by lightning, and how afterward the crows came to peck out his eyes. Bran was not impressed. There were crows' nests atop the broken tower, where no one ever went but him, and sometimes he filled his pockets with corn before he climbed up there and the crows ate it right out of his hand. None of them had ever shown the slightest bit of interest in pecking out his eyes.

Later, Maester Luwin built a little pottery boy and dressed him in Bran's clothes and flung him off the wall into the yard below, to demonstrate what would happen to Bran if he fell. That had been fun, but afterward Bran just looked at the maester and said, "I'm not made of clay. And anyhow, I never fall."

Then for a while the guards would chase him whenever they saw him on the roofs, and try to haul him down. That was the best time of all. It was like playing a game with his brothers, except that Bran always won. None of the guards could climb half so well as Bran, not even Jory. Most of the time they never saw him anyway. People never looked up. That was another thing he liked about climbing; it was almost like being invisible.

He liked how it felt too, pulling himself up a wall stone by stone, fingers and toes digging hard into the small crevices between. He always took off his boots and went barefoot when he climbed; it made him feel as if he had four hands instead of two. He liked the deep, sweet ache it left in the muscles afterward. He liked the way the air tasted way up high, sweet and cold as a winter peach. He liked the birds: the crows in the broken tower, the tiny little sparrows that nested in cracks between the stones, the ancient owl that slept in the dusty loft above the old armory. Bran knew them all.

Most of all, he liked going places that no one else could go, and seeing the grey sprawl of Winterfell in a way that no one else ever saw it. It made the whole castle Bran's secret place.

His favorite haunt was the broken tower. Once it had been a watchtower, the tallest in Winterfell. A long time ago, a hundred years before even his father had been born, a lightning strike had set it afire. The top third of the structure had collapsed inward, and the tower had never been rebuilt. Sometimes his father sent ratters into the base of the tower, to clean out the nests they always found among the jumble of fallen stones and charred and rotten beams. But no one ever got up to the jagged top of the structure now except for Bran and the crows.

He knew two ways to get there. You could climb straight up the side of the tower itself, but the stones were loose, the mortar that held them together long gone to ash, and Bran never liked to put his full weight on them.

The *best* way was to start from the godswood, shinny up the tall sentinel, and cross over the armory and the guards hall, leaping roof to roof, barefoot so the guards wouldn't hear you overhead. That brought you up to the blind side of the First Keep, the oldest part of the castle, a squat round fortress that was taller than it looked. Only rats and spiders lived there now but the old stones still made for good climbing. You could go straight up to where the gargoyles leaned out blindly over empty space, and swing from gargoyle to gargoyle, hand over hand, around to the north side. From there, if you really stretched, you could reach out and pull yourself over to the broken tower where it leaned close. The last part was the scramble up the blackened stones to the eyrie, no more than ten feet, and then the crows would come round to see if you'd brought any corn.

Bran was moving from gargoyle to gargoyle with the ease of long practice when he heard the voices. He was so startled he almost lost his grip. The First Keep had been empty all his life.

"I do not like it," a woman was saying. There was a row of windows beneath him, and the voice was drifting out of the last window on this side. "*You* should be the Hand."

"Gods forbid," a man's voice replied lazily. "It's not an honor I'd want. There's far too much work involved."

Bran hung, listening, suddenly afraid to go on. They might glimpse his feet if he tried to swing by.

"Don't you see the danger this puts us in?" the woman said. "Robert loves the man like a brother."

"Robert can barely stomach his brothers. Not that I blame him. Stannis would be enough to give anyone indigestion."

"Don't play the fool. Stannis and Renly are one thing, and Eddard Stark is quite another. Robert will *listen* to Stark. Damn them both. I should have *insisted* that he name you, but I was certain Stark would refuse him."

"We ought to count ourselves fortunate," the man said. "The king might as easily have named one of his brothers, or even Littlefinger, gods help us. Give me honorable enemies rather than ambitious ones, and I'll sleep more easily by night."

They were talking about Father, Bran realized. He wanted to hear more. A few more feet . . . but they would see him if he swung out in front of the window.

"We will have to watch him carefully," the woman said.

"I would sooner watch you," the man said. He sounded bored. "Come back here."

"Lord Eddard has never taken any interest in anything that happened south of the Neck," the woman said. "Never. I tell you, he means to move against us. Why else would he leave the seat of his power?"

"A hundred reasons. Duty. Honor. He yearns to write his name large across the book of history, to get away from his wife, or both. Perhaps he just wants to be warm for once in his life."

"His wife is Lady Arryn's sister. It's a wonder Lysa was not here to greet us with her accusations."

Bran looked down. There was a narrow ledge beneath

the window, only a few inches wide. He tried to lower himself toward it. Too far. He would never reach.

"You fret too much. Lysa Arryn is a frightened cow."

"That frightened cow shared Jon Arryn's bed."

"If she knew anything, she would have gone to Robert before she fled King's Landing."

"When he had already agreed to foster that weakling son of hers at Casterly Rock? I think not. She knew the boy's life would be hostage to her silence. She may grow bolder now that he's safe atop the Eyrie."

"Mothers." The man made the word sound like a curse. "I think birthing does something to your minds. You are all mad." He laughed. It was a bitter sound. "Let Lady Arryn grow as bold as she likes. Whatever she knows, whatever she thinks she knows, she has no proof." He paused a moment. "Or does she?"

"Do you think the king will require proof?" the woman said. "I tell you, he loves me not."

"And whose fault is that, sweet sister?"

Bran studied the ledge. He could drop down. It was too narrow to land on, but if he could catch hold as he fell past, pull himself up . . . except that might make a noise, draw them to the window. He was not sure what he was hearing, but he knew it was not meant for his ears.

"You are as blind as Robert," the woman was saying.

"If you mean I see the same thing, yes," the man said. "I see a man who would sooner die than betray his king."

"He betrayed one already, or have you forgotten?" the woman said. "Oh, I don't deny he's loyal to Robert, that's obvious. What happens when Robert dies and Joff takes the throne? And the sooner *that* comes to pass, the safer we'll all be. My husband grows more restless every day. Having Stark beside him will only make him worse. He's still in love with the sister, the insipid little dead sixteen-year-old. How long till he decides to put me aside for some new Lyanna?"

Bran was suddenly very frightened. He wanted nothing so much as to go back the way he had come, to find his brothers. Only what would he tell them? He had to get closer, Bran realized. He had to see who was talking.

The man sighed. "You should think less about the future and more about the pleasures at hand."

"Stop that!" the woman said. Bran heard the sudden slap of flesh on flesh, then the man's laughter.

Bran pulled himself up, climbed over the gargoyle, crawled out onto the roof. This was the easy way. He moved across the roof to the next gargoyle, right above the window of the room where they were talking.

"All this talk is getting very tiresome, sister," the man said. "Come here and be quiet."

Bran sat astride the gargoyle, tightened his legs around it, and swung himself around, upside down. He hung by his legs and slowly stretched his head down toward the window. The world looked strange upside down. A courtyard swam dizzily below him, its stones still wet with melted snow.

Bran looked in the window.

Inside the room, a man and a woman were wrestling. They were both naked. Bran could not tell who they were. The man's back was to him, and his body screened the woman from view as he pushed her up against a wall.

There were soft, wet sounds. Bran realized they were kissing. He watched, wide-eyed and frightened, his breath tight in his throat. The man had a hand down between her legs, and he must have been hurting her there, because the woman started to moan, low in her throat. "Stop it," she said, "stop it, stop it. Oh, *please* . . ." But her voice was low and weak, and she did not push him away. Her hands buried themselves in his hair, his tangled golden hair, and pulled his face down to her breast.

Bran saw her face. Her eyes were closed and her mouth was open, moaning. Her golden hair swung from side to side as her head moved back and forth, but still he recognized the queen.

He must have made a noise. Suddenly her eyes opened, and she was staring right at him. She screamed.

Everything happened at once then. The woman pushed the man away wildly, shouting and pointing. Bran tried to pull himself up, bending double as he reached for the gargoyle. He was in too much of a hurry. His hand scraped uselessly across smooth stone, and in his panic his legs slipped, and suddenly he was falling. There was an instant of vertigo, a sickening lurch as the window flashed past. He shot out a hand, grabbed for the ledge, lost it, caught it again with his other hand. He swung against the building, hard. The impact took the breath out of him. Bran dangled, one-handed, panting.

Faces appeared in the window above him.

The queen. And now Bran recognized the man beside her. They looked as much alike as reflections in a mirror.

"He *saw* us," the woman said shrilly.

"So he did," the man said.

Bran's fingers started to slip. He grabbed the ledge with his other hand. Fingernails dug into unyielding stone. The man reached down. "Take my hand," he said. "Before you fall."

Bran seized his arm and held on tight with all his strength. The man yanked him up to the ledge. "What are you doing?" the woman demanded.

The man ignored her. He was very strong. He stood Bran up on the sill. "How old are you, boy?"

"Seven," Bran said, shaking with relief. His fingers had dug deep gouges in the man's forearm. He let go sheepishly.

The man looked over at the woman. "The things I do for love," he said with loathing. He gave Bran a shove.

Screaming, Bran went backward out the window into empty air. There was nothing to grab on to. The courtyard rushed up to meet him.

Somewhere off in the distance, a wolf was howling. Crows circled the broken tower, waiting for corn.

TYRION

Somewhere in the great stone maze of Winterfell, a wolf howled. The sound hung over the castle like a flag of mourning.

Tyrion Lannister looked up from his books and shivered, though the library was snug and warm. Something about the howling of a wolf took a man right out of his here and now and left him in a dark forest of the mind, running naked before the pack.

When the direwolf howled again, Tyrion shut the heavy leather-bound cover on the book he was reading, a hundred-year-old discourse on the changing of the seasons by a long-dead maester. He covered a yawn with the back of his hand. His reading lamp was flickering, its oil all but gone, as dawn light leaked through the high windows. He had been at it all night, but that was nothing new. Tyrion Lannister was not much a one for sleeping.

His legs were stiff and sore as he eased down off the bench. He massaged some life back into them and limped heavily to the table where the septon was snoring softly, his head pillowed on an open book in front of him. Tyrion glanced at the title. A life of the Grand Maester Aethelmure, no wonder. "Chayle," he said softly. The young man jerked up, blinking, confused, the crystal of his order swinging wildly on its silver chain. "I'm off to break my fast. See that you return the books to the shelves. Be gentle with the Valyrian scrolls, the parchment is very dry. Ayrmidon's *Engines of War* is quite rare, and yours is the only complete copy I've ever seen." Chayle gaped at him, still half-asleep. Patiently, Tyrion repeated his instructions, then clapped the septon on the shoulder and left him to his tasks.

Outside, Tyrion swallowed a lungful of the cold morning air and began his laborious descent of the steep stone steps that corkscrewed around the exterior of the library tower. It was slow going; the steps were cut high and narrow, while his legs were short and twisted. The rising sun had not yet cleared the walls of Winterfell, but the men were already hard at it in the yard below. Sandor Clegane's rasping voice drifted up to him. "The boy is a long time dying. I wish he would be quicker about it."

Tyrion glanced down and saw the Hound standing with young Joffrey as squires swarmed around them. "At least he dies quietly," the prince replied. "It's the wolf that makes the noise. I could scarce sleep last night."

Clegane cast a long shadow across the hard-packed earth as his squire lowered the black helm over his head. "I could silence the creature, if it please you," he said through his open visor. His boy placed a longsword in his hand. He tested the weight of it, slicing at the cold morning air. Behind him, the yard rang to the clangor of steel on steel.

The notion seemed to delight the prince. "Send a dog to kill a dog!" he exclaimed. "Winterfell is so infested with wolves, the Starks would never miss one."

Tyrion hopped off the last step onto the yard. "I beg to differ, nephew," he said. "The Starks can count past six. Unlike some princes I might name."

Joffrey had the grace at least to blush.

"A voice from nowhere," Sandor said. He peered through his helm, looking this way and that. "Spirits of the air!"

The prince laughed, as he always laughed when his bodyguard did this mummer's farce. Tyrion was used to it. "Down here."

The tall man peered down at the ground, and pretended to notice him. "The little lord Tyrion," he said. "My pardons. I did not see you standing there."

"I am in no mood for your insolence today." Tyrion turned to his nephew. "Joffrey, it is past time you called on Lord Eddard and his lady, to offer them your comfort."

Joffrey looked as petulant as only a boy prince can look. "What good will my comfort do them?"

"None," Tyrion said. "Yet it is expected of you. Your absence has been noted."

"The Stark boy is nothing to me," Joffrey said. "I cannot abide the wailing of women."

Tyrion Lannister reached up and slapped his nephew hard across the face. The boy's cheek began to redden.

"One word," Tyrion said, "and I will hit you again."

"I'm going to tell Mother!" Joffrey exclaimed.

Tyrion hit him again. Now both cheeks flamed.

"You tell your mother," Tyrion told him. "But first you get yourself to Lord and Lady Stark, and you fall to your knees in front of them, and you tell them how very sorry you are, and that you are at their service if there is the slightest thing you can do for them or theirs in this desperate hour, and that all your prayers go with them. Do you understand? *Do you?*"

The boy looked as though he was going to cry. Instead, he managed a weak nod. Then he turned and fled headlong from the yard, holding his cheek. Tyrion watched him run.

A shadow fell across his face. He turned to find Clegane looming overhead like a cliff. His soot-dark armor seemed to blot out the sun. He had lowered the visor on his helm. It was fashioned in the likeness of a snarling black hound, fearsome to behold, but Tyrion had always thought it a great improvement over Clegane's hideously burned face.

"The prince will remember that, little lord," the Hound warned him. The helm turned his laugh into a hollow rumble.

"I pray he does," Tyrion Lannister replied. "If he forgets, be a good dog and remind him." He glanced around the courtyard. "Do you know where I might find my brother?"

"Breaking fast with the queen."

"Ah," Tyrion said. He gave Sandor Clegane a perfunctory nod and walked away as briskly as his stunted legs would carry him, whistling. He pitied the first knight to try the Hound today. The man did have a temper.

A cold, cheerless meal had been laid out in the morning room of the Guest House. Jaime sat at table with Cersei and the children, talking in low, hushed voices.

"Is Robert still abed?" Tyrion asked as he seated himself, uninvited, at the table.

His sister peered at him with the same expression of faint distaste she had worn since the day he was born. "The king has not slept at all," she told him. "He is with Lord Eddard. He has taken their sorrow deeply to heart."

"He has a large heart, our Robert," Jaime said with a lazy smile. There was very little that Jaime took seriously. Tyrion knew that about his brother, and forgave it. During all the terrible long years of his childhood, only Jaime had ever shown him the smallest measure of affection or respect, and for that Tyrion was willing to forgive him most anything.

A servant approached. "Bread," Tyrion told him, "and two of those little fish, and a mug of that good dark beer to wash them down. Oh, and some bacon. Burn it until it turns black." The man bowed and moved off. Tyrion turned back to his siblings. Twins, male and female. They looked very much the part this morning. Both had chosen a deep green that matched their eyes. Their blond curls were all a fashionable tumble, and gold ornaments shone at wrists and fingers and throats.

Tyrion wondered what it would be like to have a twin, and decided that he would rather not know. Bad enough to face himself in a looking glass every day. Another him was a thought too dreadful to contemplate.

Prince Tommen spoke up. "Do you have news of Bran, Uncle?"

"I stopped by the sickroom last night," Tyrion announced. "There was no change. The maester thought that a hopeful sign."

"I don't want Brandon to die," Tommen said timorously. He was a sweet boy. Not like his brother, but then Jaime and Tyrion were somewhat less than peas in a pod themselves.

"Lord Eddard had a brother named Brandon as well,"

Jaime mused. "One of the hostages murdered by Targaryen. It seems to be an unlucky name."

"Oh, not so unlucky as all that, surely," Tyrion said. The servant brought his plate. He ripped off a chunk of black bread.

Cersei was studying him warily. "What do you mean?"

Tyrion gave her a crooked smile. "Why, only that Tommen may get his wish. The maester thinks the boy may yet live." He took a sip of beer.

Myrcella gave a happy gasp, and Tommen smiled nervously, but it was not the children Tyrion was watching. The glance that passed between Jaime and Cersei lasted no more than a second, but he did not miss it. Then his sister dropped her gaze to the table. "That is no mercy. These northern gods are cruel to let the child linger in such pain."

"What were the maester's words?" Jaime asked.

The bacon crunched when he bit into it. Tyrion chewed thoughtfully for a moment and said, "He thinks that if the boy were going to die, he would have done so already. It has been four days with no change."

"Will Bran get better, Uncle?" little Myrcella asked. She had all of her mother's beauty, and none of her nature.

"His back is broken, little one," Tyrion told her. "The fall shattered his legs as well. They keep him alive with honey and water, or he would starve to death. Perhaps, if he wakes, he will be able to eat real food, but he will never walk again."

"If he wakes," Cersei repeated. "Is that likely?"

"The gods alone know," Tyrion told her. "The maester only hopes." He chewed some more bread. "I would swear that wolf of his is keeping the boy alive. The creature is outside his window day and night, howling. Every time they chase it away, it returns. The maester said they closed the window once, to shut out the noise, and Bran seemed to weaken. When they opened it again, his heart beat stronger."

The queen shuddered. "There is something unnatural about those animals," she said. "They are dangerous. I will *not* have any of them coming south with us."

Jaime said, "You'll have a hard time stopping them, sister. They follow those girls everywhere."

Tyrion started on his fish. "Are you leaving soon, then?"

"Not near soon enough," Cersei said. Then she frowned. "Are *we* leaving?" she echoed. "What about you? Gods, don't tell me you are staying *here*?"

Tyrion shrugged. "Benjen Stark is returning to the Night's Watch with his brother's bastard. I have a mind to go with them and see this Wall we have all heard so much of."

Jaime smiled. "I hope you're not thinking of taking the black on us, sweet brother."

Tyrion laughed. "What, me, celibate? The whores would go begging from Dorne to Casterly Rock. No, I just want to stand on top of the Wall and piss off the edge of the world."

Cersei stood abruptly. "The children don't need to hear this filth. Tommen, Myrcella, come." She strode briskly from the morning room, her train and her pups trailing behind her.

Jaime Lannister regarded his brother thoughtfully with those cool green eyes. "Stark will never consent to leave Winterfell with his son lingering in the shadow of death."

"He will if Robert commands it," Tyrion said. "And Robert *will* command it. There is nothing Lord Eddard can do for the boy in any case."

"He could end his torment," Jaime said. "I would, if it were my son. It would be a mercy."

"I advise against putting that suggestion to Lord Eddard, sweet brother," Tyrion said. "He would not take it kindly."

"Even if the boy does live, he will be a cripple. Worse than a cripple. A grotesque. Give me a good clean death."

Tyrion replied with a shrug that accentuated the twist of his shoulders. "Speaking for the grotesques," he said, "I beg to differ. Death is so terribly final, while life is full of possibilities."

Jaime smiled. "You are a perverse little imp, aren't you?"

"Oh, yes," Tyrion admitted. "I hope the boy does wake. I would be most interested to hear what he might have to say."

His brother's smile curdled like sour milk. "Tyrion,

my sweet brother," he said darkly, "there are times when you give me cause to wonder whose side you are on."

Tyrion's mouth was full of bread and fish. He took a swallow of strong black beer to wash it all down, and grinned up wolfishly at Jaime. "Why, Jaime, my sweet brother," he said, "you wound me. You know how much I love my family."

JON

Jon climbed the steps slowly, trying not to think that this might be the last time ever. Ghost padded silently beside him. Outside, snow swirled through the castle gates, and the yard was all noise and chaos, but inside the thick stone walls it was still warm and quiet. Too quiet for Jon's liking.

He reached the landing and stood for a long moment, afraid. Ghost nuzzled at his hand. He took courage from that. He straightened, and entered the room.

Lady Stark was there beside his bed. She had been there, day and night, for close on a fortnight. Not for a moment had she left Bran's side. She had her meals brought to her there, and chamber pots as well, and a small hard bed to sleep on, though it was said she had scarcely slept at all. She fed him herself, the honey and water and herb mixture that sustained life. Not once did she leave the room. So Jon had stayed away.

But now there was no more time.

He stood in the door for a moment, afraid to speak, afraid to come closer. The window was open. Below, a wolf howled. Ghost heard and lifted his head.

Lady Stark looked over. For a moment she did not

seem to recognize him. Finally she blinked. "What are *you* doing here?" she asked in a voice strangely flat and emotionless.

"I came to see Bran," Jon said. "To say good-bye."

Her face did not change. Her long auburn hair was dull and tangled. She looked as though she had aged twenty years. "You've said it. Now go away."

Part of him wanted only to flee, but he knew that if he did he might never see Bran again. He took a nervous step into the room. "Please," he said.

Something cold moved in her eyes. "I told you to leave," she said. "We don't want you here."

Once that would have sent him running. Once that might even have made him cry. Now it only made him angry. He would be a Sworn Brother of the Night's Watch soon, and face worse dangers than Catelyn Tully Stark. "He's my brother," he said.

"Shall I call the guards?"

"Call them," Jon said, defiant. "You can't stop me from seeing him." He crossed the room, keeping the bed between them, and looked down on Bran where he lay.

She was holding one of his hands. It looked like a claw. This was not the Bran he remembered. The flesh had all gone from him. His skin stretched tight over bones like sticks. Under the blanket, his legs bent in ways that made Jon sick. His eyes were sunken deep into black pits; open, but they saw nothing. The fall had shrunken him somehow. He looked half a leaf, as if the first strong wind would carry him off to his grave.

Yet under the frail cage of those shattered ribs, his chest rose and fell with each shallow breath.

"Bran," he said, "I'm sorry I didn't come before. I was afraid." He could feel the tears rolling down his cheeks. Jon no longer cared. "Don't die, Bran. Please. We're all waiting for you to wake up. Me and Robb and the girls, everyone . . ."

Lady Stark was watching. She had not raised a cry. Jon took that for acceptance. Outside the window, the direwolf howled again. The wolf that Bran had not had time to name.

"I have to go now," Jon said. "Uncle Benjen is waiting. I'm to go north to the Wall. We have to leave today, before the snows come." He remembered how excited Bran had been at the prospect of the journey. It was more than he could bear, the thought of leaving him behind like this. Jon brushed away his tears, leaned over, and kissed his brother lightly on the lips.

"I wanted him to stay here with me," Lady Stark said softly.

Jon watched her, wary. She was not even looking at him. She was talking to him, but for a part of her, it was as though he were not even in the room.

"I prayed for it," she said dully. "He was my special boy. I went to the sept and prayed seven times to the seven faces of god that Ned would change his mind and leave him here with me. Sometimes prayers are answered."

Jon did not know what to say. "It wasn't your fault," he managed after an awkward silence.

Her eyes found him. They were full of poison. "I need none of your absolution, bastard."

Jon lowered his eyes. She was cradling one of Bran's hands. He took the other, squeezed it. Fingers like the bones of birds. "Good-bye," he said.

He was at the door when she called out to him. "Jon," she said. He should have kept going, but she had never called him by his name before. He turned to find her looking at his face, as if she were seeing it for the first time.

"Yes?" he said.

"It should have been you," she told him. Then she turned back to Bran and began to weep, her whole body shaking with the sobs. Jon had never seen her cry before.

It was a long walk down to the yard.

Outside, everything was noise and confusion. Wagons were being loaded, men were shouting, horses were being harnessed and saddled and led from the stables. A light snow had begun to fall, and everyone was in an uproar to be off.

Robb was in the middle of it, shouting commands with the best of them. He seemed to have grown of late, as if Bran's fall and his mother's collapse had somehow made him stronger. Grey Wind was at his side.

"Uncle Benjen is looking for you," he told Jon. "He wanted to be gone an hour ago."

"I know," Jon said. "Soon." He looked around at all

the noise and confusion. "Leaving is harder than I thought."

"For me too," Robb said. He had snow in his hair, melting from the heat of his body. "Did you see him?"

Jon nodded, not trusting himself to speak.

"He's not going to die," Robb said. "I know it."

"You Starks are hard to kill," Jon agreed. His voice was flat and tired. The visit had taken all the strength from him.

Robb knew something was wrong. "My mother . . ."

"She was . . . very kind," Jon told him.

Robb looked relieved. "Good." He smiled. "The next time I see you, you'll be all in black."

Jon forced himself to smile back. "It was always my color. How long do you think it will be?"

"Soon enough," Robb promised. He pulled Jon to him and embraced him fiercely. "Farewell, Snow."

Jon hugged him back. "And you, Stark. Take care of Bran."

"I will." They broke apart and looked at each other awkwardly. "Uncle Benjen said to send you to the stables if I saw you," Robb finally said.

"I have one more farewell to make," Jon told him.

"Then I haven't seen you," Robb replied. Jon left him standing there in the snow, surrounded by wagons and wolves and horses. It was a short walk to the armory. He picked up his package and took the covered bridge across to the Keep.

Arya was in her room, packing a polished ironwood chest that was bigger than she was. Nymeria was helping. Arya would only have to point, and the wolf would bound across the room, snatch up some wisp of silk in her jaws, and fetch it back. But when she smelled Ghost, she sat down on her haunches and yelped at them.

Arya glanced behind her, saw Jon, and jumped to her feet. She threw her skinny arms tight around his neck. "I was afraid you were gone," she said, her breath catching in her throat. "They wouldn't let me out to say goodbye."

"What did you do now?" Jon was amused.

Arya disentangled herself from him and made a face. "Nothing. I was all packed and everything." She gestured at the huge chest, no more than a third full, and at the clothes that were scattered all over the room. "Septa Mordane says I have to do it all over. My things weren't properly folded, she says. A proper southron lady doesn't ·just throw her clothes inside her chest like old rags, she says."

"Is that what you did, little sister?"

"Well, they're going to get all messed up anyway," she said. "Who cares how they're folded?"

"Septa Mordane," Jon told her. "I don't think she'd like Nymeria helping, either." The she-wolf regarded him silently with her dark golden eyes. "It's just as well. I have something for you to take with you, and it has to be packed very carefully."

Her face lit up. "A present?"

"You could call it that. Close the door."

Wary but excited, Arya checked the hall. "Nymeria, here. Guard." She left the wolf out there to warn of intruders and closed the door. By then Jon had pulled off the rags he'd wrapped it in. He held it out to her.

Arya's eyes went wide. Dark eyes, like his. "A sword," she said in a small, hushed breath.

The scabbard was soft grey leather, supple as sin. Jon drew out the blade slowly, so she could see the deep blue sheen of the steel. "This is no toy," he told her. "Be careful you don't cut yourself. The edges are sharp enough to shave with."

"Girls don't shave," Arya said.

"Maybe they should. Have you ever seen the septa's legs?"

She giggled at him. "It's so skinny."

"So are you," Jon told her. "I had Mikken make this special. The bravos use swords like this in Pentos and Myr and the other Free Cities. It won't hack a man's head off, but it can poke him full of holes if you're fast enough."

"I can be fast," Arya said.

"You'll have to work at it every day." He put the sword in her hands, showed her how to hold it, and stepped back. "How does it feel? Do you like the balance?"

"I think so," Arya said.

"First lesson," Jon said. "Stick them with the pointy end."

Arya gave him a *whap* on the arm with the flat of her

blade. The blow stung, but Jon found himself grinning like an idiot. "I know which end to use," Arya said. A doubtful look crossed her face. "Septa Mordane will take it away from me."

"Not if she doesn't know you have it," Jon said.

"Who will I practice with?"

"You'll find someone," Jon promised her. "King's Landing is a true city, a thousand times the size of Winterfell. Until you find a partner, watch how they fight in the yard. Run, and ride, make yourself strong. And whatever you do . . ."

Arya knew what was coming next. They said it together.

". . . don't . . . tell . . . Sansa!"

Jon messed up her hair. "I will miss you, little sister."

Suddenly she looked like she was going to cry. "I wish you were coming with us."

"Different roads sometimes lead to the same castle. Who knows?" He was feeling better now. He was not going to let himself be sad. "I better go. I'll spend my first year on the Wall emptying chamber pots if I keep Uncle Ben waiting any longer."

Arya ran to him for a last hug. "Put down the sword first," Jon warned her, laughing. She set it aside almost shyly and showered him with kisses.

When he turned back at the door, she was holding it again, trying it for balance. "I almost forgot," he told her. "All the best swords have names."

"Like Ice," she said. She looked at the blade in her hand. "Does this have a name? Oh, tell me."

"Can't you guess?" Jon teased. "Your very favorite thing."

Arya seemed puzzled at first. Then it came to her. She was that quick. They said it together:

"Needle!"

The memory of her laughter warmed him on the long ride north.

DAENERYS

Daenerys Targaryen wed Khal Drogo with fear and barbaric splendor in a field beyond the walls of Pentos, for the Dothraki believed that all things of importance in a man's life must be done beneath the open sky.

Drogo had called his *khalasar* to attend him and they had come, forty thousand Dothraki warriors and uncounted numbers of women, children, and slaves. Outside the city walls they camped with their vast herds, raising palaces of woven grass, eating everything in sight, and making the good folk of Pentos more anxious with every passing day.

"My fellow magisters have doubled the size of the city guard," Illyrio told them over platters of honey duck and orange snap peppers one night at the manse that had been Drogo's. The *khal* had joined his *khalasar*, his estate given over to Daenerys and her brother until the wedding.

"Best we get Princess Daenerys wedded quickly before they hand half the wealth of Pentos away to sellswords and bravos," Ser Jorah Mormont jested. The exile had offered her brother his sword the night Dany had been sold to Khal Drogo; Viserys had accepted eagerly. Mormont had been their constant companion ever since.

Magister Illyrio laughed lightly through his forked beard, but Viserys did not so much as smile. "He can have her tomorrow, if he likes," her brother said. He glanced over at Dany, and she lowered her eyes. "So long as he pays the price."

Illyrio waved a languid hand in the air, rings glittering on his fat fingers. "I have told you, all is settled. Trust me. The *khal* has promised you a crown, and you shall have it."

"Yes, but when?"

"When the *khal* chooses," Illyrio said. "He will have the girl first, and after they are wed he must make his procession across the plains and present her to the *dosh khaleen* at Vaes Dothrak. After that, perhaps. If the omens favor war."

Viserys seethed with impatience. "I piss on Dothraki omens. The Usurper sits on my father's throne. How long must I wait?"

Illyrio gave a massive shrug. "You have waited most of your life, great king. What is another few months, another few years?"

Ser Jorah, who had traveled as far east as Vaes Dothrak, nodded in agreement. "I counsel you to be patient, Your Grace. The Dothraki are true to their word, but they do things in their own time. A lesser man may beg a favor from the *khal*, but must never presume to berate him."

Viserys bristled. "Guard your tongue, Mormont, or I'll have it out. I am no lesser man, I am the rightful Lord of the Seven Kingdoms. The dragon does not beg."

Ser Jorah lowered his eyes respectfully. Illyrio smiled enigmatically and tore a wing from the duck. Honey and grease ran over his fingers and dripped down into his beard as he nibbled at the tender meat. *There are no more dragons,* Dany thought, staring at her brother, though she did not dare say it aloud.

Yet that night she dreamt of one. Viserys was hitting her, hurting her. She was naked, clumsy with fear. She ran from him, but her body seemed thick and ungainly. He struck her again. She stumbled and fell. "You woke the dragon," he screamed as he kicked her. "You woke the dragon, you woke the dragon." Her thighs were slick with blood. She closed her eyes and whimpered. As if in answer, there was a hideous *ripping* sound and the crackling of some great fire. When she looked again, Viserys was gone, great columns of flame rose all around, and in the midst of them was the dragon. It turned its great head slowly. When its molten eyes found hers, she woke, shaking and covered with a fine sheen of sweat. She had never been so afraid . . .

. . . until the day of her wedding came at last.

The ceremony began at dawn and continued until dusk, an endless day of drinking and feasting and fighting. A mighty earthen ramp had been raised amid the grass palaces, and there Dany was seated beside Khal Drogo, above the seething sea of Dothraki. She had never seen so many people in one place, nor people so strange and frightening. The horselords might put on rich fabrics and sweet perfumes when they visited the Free Cities, but out under the open sky they kept the old ways. Men and women alike wore painted leather vests over bare chests and horsehair leggings cinched by bronze medallion belts, and the warriors greased their long braids with fat from the rendering pits. They gorged themselves on horseflesh roasted with honey and peppers, drank themselves blind on fermented mare's milk and Illyrio's fine wines, and spat jests at each other across the fires, their voices harsh and alien in Dany's ears.

Viserys was seated just below her, splendid in a new black wool tunic with a scarlet dragon on the chest. Illyrio and Ser Jorah sat beside him. Theirs was a place of high honor, just below the *khal*'s own bloodriders, but Dany could see the anger in her brother's lilac eyes. He did not like sitting beneath her, and he fumed when the slaves offered each dish first to the *khal* and his bride, and served him from the portions they refused. He could do nothing but nurse his resentment, so nurse it he did, his mood growing blacker by the hour at each insult to his person.

Dany had never felt so alone as she did seated in the midst of that vast horde. Her brother had told her to smile, and so she smiled until her face ached and the tears came unbidden to her eyes. She did her best to hide them, knowing how angry Viserys would be if he saw her crying, terrified of how Khal Drogo might react. Food was brought to her, steaming joints of meat and thick black sausages and Dothraki blood pies, and later fruits and sweetgrass stews and delicate pastries from the kitchens of Pentos, but she waved it all away. Her stomach was a roil, and she knew she could keep none of it down.

There was no one to talk to. Khal Drogo shouted commands and jests down to his bloodriders, and laughed at their replies, but he scarcely glanced at Dany beside him. They had no common language. Dothraki was incomprehensible to her, and the *khal* knew only a few words of the bastard Valyrian of the Free Cities, and none at all of the Common Tongue of the Seven Kingdoms. She would even have welcomed the conversation of Illyrio and her brother, but they were too far below to hear her.

So she sat in her wedding silks, nursing a cup of honeyed wine, afraid to eat, talking silently to herself. *I am blood of the dragon*, she told herself. *I am Daenerys Stormborn, Princess of Dragonstone, of the blood and seed of Aegon the Conqueror.*

The sun was only a quarter of the way up the sky when she saw her first man die. Drums were beating as some of the women danced for the *khal*. Drogo watched without expression, but his eyes followed their movements, and from time to time he would toss down a bronze medallion for the women to fight over.

The warriors were watching too. One of them finally stepped into the circle, grabbed a dancer by the arm, pushed her down to the ground, and mounted her right there, as a stallion mounts a mare. Illyrio had told her that might happen. "The Dothraki mate like the animals in their herds. There is no privacy in a *khalasar*, and they do not understand sin or shame as we do."

Dany looked away from the coupling, frightened when she realized what was happening, but a second warrior stepped forward, and a third, and soon there was no way to avert her eyes. Then two men seized the same woman. She heard a shout, saw a shove, and in the blink of an eye the *arakhs* were out, long razor-sharp blades, half sword and half scythe. A dance of death began as the warriors circled and slashed, leaping toward each other, whirling the blades around their heads, shrieking insults at each clash. No one made a move to interfere.

It ended as quickly as it began. The *arakhs* shivered

together faster than Dany could follow, one man missed a step, the other swung his blade in a flat arc. Steel bit into flesh just above the Dothraki's waist, and opened him from backbone to belly button, spilling his entrails into the dust. As the loser died, the winner took hold of the nearest woman—not even the one they had been quarreling over—and had her there and then. Slaves carried off the body, and the dancing resumed.

Magister Illyrio had warned Dany about this too. "A Dothraki wedding without at least three deaths is deemed a dull affair," he had said. Her wedding must have been especially blessed; before the day was over, a dozen men had died.

As the hours passed, the terror grew in Dany, until it was all she could do not to scream. She was afraid of the Dothraki, whose ways seemed alien and monstrous, as if they were beasts in human skins and not true men at all. She was afraid of her brother, of what he might do if she failed him. Most of all, she was afraid of what would happen tonight under the stars, when her brother gave her up to the hulking giant who sat drinking beside her with a face as still and cruel as a bronze mask.

I am the blood of the dragon, she told herself again.

When at last the sun was low in the sky, Khal Drogo clapped his hands together, and the drums and the shouting and feasting came to a sudden halt. Drogo stood and pulled Dany to her feet beside him. It was time for her bride gifts.

And after the gifts, she knew, after the sun had gone down, it would be time for the first ride and the consummation of her marriage. Dany tried to put the thought aside, but it would not leave her. She hugged herself to try to keep from shaking.

Her brother Viserys gifted her with three handmaids. Dany knew they had cost him nothing; Illyrio no doubt had provided the girls. Irri and Jhiqui were copper-skinned Dothraki with black hair and almond-shaped eyes, Doreah a fair-haired, blue-eyed Lysene girl. "These are no common servants, sweet sister," her brother told her as they were brought forward one by one. "Illyrio and I selected them personally for you. Irri will teach you riding, Jhiqui the Dothraki tongue, and Doreah will instruct you in the womanly arts of love." He smiled thinly. "She's very good, Illyrio and I can both swear to that."

Ser Jorah Mormont apologized for his gift. "It is a small thing, my princess, but all a poor exile could afford," he said as he laid a small stack of old books before her. They were histories and songs of the Seven Kingdoms, she saw, written in the Common Tongue. She thanked him with all her heart.

Magister Illyrio murmured a command, and four burly slaves hurried forward, bearing between them a great cedar chest bound in bronze. When she opened it, she found piles of the finest velvets and damasks the Free Cities could produce . . . and resting on top, nestled in the soft cloth, three huge eggs. Dany gasped. They were the most beautiful things she had ever seen, each different than the others, patterned in such rich colors that at first she thought they were crusted with jewels, and so large it took both of her hands to hold one. She lifted it delicately, expecting that it would be made of some fine porcelain or delicate enamel, or even blown glass, but it was much heavier than that, as if it were all of solid stone. The surface of the shell was covered with tiny scales, and as she turned the egg between her fingers, they shimmered like polished metal in the light of the setting sun. One egg was a deep green, with burnished bronze flecks that came and went depending on how Dany turned it. Another was pale cream streaked with gold. The last was black, as black as a midnight sea, yet alive with scarlet ripples and swirls. "What are they?" she asked, her voice hushed and full of wonder.

"Dragon's eggs, from the Shadow Lands beyond Asshai," said Magister Illyrio. "The eons have turned them to stone, yet still they burn bright with beauty."

"I shall treasure them always." Dany had heard tales of such eggs, but she had never seen one, nor thought to see one. It was a truly magnificent gift, though she knew that Illyrio could afford to be lavish. He had collected a fortune in horses and slaves for his part in selling her to Khal Drogo.

The *khal*'s bloodriders offered her the traditional three weapons, and splendid weapons they were. Haggo gave her a great leather whip with a silver handle, Cohollo a magnificent *arakh* chased in gold, and Qotho a double-curved dragonbone bow taller than she was. Magister Illyrio and Ser Jorah had taught her the traditional refusals for these offerings. "This is a gift worthy of a great warrior, O blood of my blood, and I am but a woman. Let my lord husband bear these in my stead." And so Khal Drogo too received his "bride gifts."

Other gifts she was given in plenty by other Dothraki: slippers and jewels and silver rings for her hair, medallion belts and painted vests and soft furs, sandsilks and jars of scent, needles and feathers and tiny bottles of purple glass, and a gown made from the skin of a thousand mice. "A handsome gift, *Khaleesi*," Magister Illyrio said of the last, after he had told her what it was. "Most lucky." The gifts mounted up around her in great piles, more gifts than she could possibly imagine, more gifts than she could want or use.

And last of all, Khal Drogo brought forth his own bride gift to her. An expectant hush rippled out from the center of the camp as he left her side, growing until it had swallowed the whole *khalasar*. When he returned, the dense press of Dothraki gift-givers parted before him, and he led the horse to her.

She was a young filly, spirited and splendid. Dany knew just enough about horses to know that this was no ordinary animal. There was something about her that took the breath away. She was grey as the winter sea, with a mane like silver smoke.

Hesitantly she reached out and stroked the horse's neck, ran her fingers through the silver of her mane. Khal Drogo said something in Dothraki and Magister Illyrio translated. "Silver for the silver of your hair, the *khal* says."

"She's beautiful," Dany murmured.

"She is the pride of the *khalasar*," Illyrio said. "Custom decrees that the *khaleesi* must ride a mount worthy of her place by the side of the *khal*."

Drogo stepped forward and put his hands on her waist. He lifted her up as easily as if she were a child and set her on the thin Dothraki saddle, so much smaller than the ones she was used to. Dany sat there uncertain for a moment. No one had told her about this part. "What should I do?" she asked Illyrio.

It was Ser Jorah Mormont who answered. "Take the reins and ride. You need not go far."

Nervously Dany gathered the reins in her hands and slid her feet into the short stirrups. She was only a fair rider; she had spent far more time traveling by ship and wagon and palanquin than by horseback. Praying that she would not fall off and disgrace herself, she gave the filly the lightest and most timid touch with her knees.

And for the first time in hours, she forgot to be afraid. Or perhaps it was for the first time ever.

The silver-grey filly moved with a smooth and silken gait, and the crowd parted for her, every eye upon them. Dany found herself moving faster than she had intended, yet somehow it was exciting rather than terrifying. The horse broke into a trot, and she smiled. Dothraki scrambled to clear a path. The slightest pressure with her legs, the lightest touch on the reins, and the filly responded. She sent it into a gallop, and now the Dothraki were hooting and laughing and shouting at her as they jumped out of her way. As she turned to ride back, a firepit loomed ahead, directly in her path. They were hemmed in on either side, with no room to stop. A daring she had never known filled Daenerys then, and she gave the filly her head.

The silver horse leapt the flames as if she had wings.

When she pulled up before Magister Illyrio, she said, "Tell Khal Drogo that he has given me the wind." The fat Pentoshi stroked his yellow beard as he repeated her words in Dothraki, and Dany saw her new husband smile for the first time.

The last sliver of sun vanished behind the high walls of Pentos to the west just then. Dany had lost all track of time. Khal Drogo commanded his bloodriders to bring forth his own horse, a lean red stallion. As the *khal* was saddling the horse, Viserys slid close to Dany on her silver, dug his fingers into her leg, and said, "Please him, sweet sister, or I swear, you will see the dragon wake as it has never woken before."

The fear came back to her then, with her brother's words. She felt like a child once more, only thirteen and all alone, not ready for what was about to happen to her.

They rode out together as the stars came out, leaving the *khalasar* and the grass palaces behind. Khal Drogo spoke no word to her, but drove his stallion at a hard trot through the gathering dusk. The tiny silver bells in his long braid rang softly as he rode. "I am the blood of the dragon," she whispered aloud as she followed, trying to keep her courage up. "I am the blood of the dragon. I am the blood of the dragon." The dragon was never afraid.

Afterward she could not say how far or how long they had ridden, but it was full dark when they stopped at a grassy place beside a small stream. Drogo swung off his horse and lifted her down from hers. She felt as fragile as glass in his hands, her limbs as weak as water. She stood there helpless and trembling in her wedding silks while he secured the horses, and when he turned to look at her, she began to cry.

Khal Drogo stared at her tears, his face strangely empty of expression. "No," he said. He lifted his hand and rubbed away the tears roughly with a callused thumb.

"You speak the Common Tongue," Dany said in wonder.

"No," he said again.

Perhaps he had only that word, she thought, but it was one word more than she had known he had, and somehow it made her feel a little better. Drogo touched her hair lightly, sliding the silver-blond strands between his fingers and murmuring softly in Dothraki. Dany did not understand the words, yet there was warmth in the tone, a tenderness she had never expected from this man.

He put his finger under her chin and lifted her head, so she was looking up into his eyes. Drogo towered over her as he towered over everyone. Taking her lightly under the arms, he lifted her and seated her on a rounded rock beside the stream. Then he sat on the ground facing her, legs crossed beneath him, their faces finally at a height. "No," he said.

"Is that the only word you know?" she asked him.

Drogo did not reply. His long heavy braid was coiled in the dirt beside him. He pulled it over his right shoulder and began to remove the bells from his hair, one by one. After a moment Dany leaned forward to help. When they were done, Drogo gestured. She understood. Slowly, carefully, she began to undo his braid.

It took a long time. All the while he sat there silently, watching her. When she was done, he shook his head, and his hair spread out behind him like a river of darkness, oiled and gleaming. She had never seen hair so long, so black, so thick.

Then it was his turn. He began to undress her.

His fingers were deft and strangely tender. He removed her silks one by one, carefully, while Dany sat unmoving, silent, looking at his eyes. When he bared her small breasts, she could not help herself. She averted her eyes and covered herself with her hands. "No," Drogo said. He pulled her hands away from her breasts, gently but firmly, then lifted her face again to make her look at him. "No," he repeated.

"No," she echoed back at him.

He stood her up then and pulled her close to remove the last of her silks. The night air was chilly on her bare skin. She shivered, and gooseflesh covered her arms and legs. She was afraid of what would come next, but for a while nothing happened. Khal Drogo sat with his legs crossed, looking at her, drinking in her body with his eyes.

After a while he began to touch her. Lightly at first, then harder. She could sense the fierce strength in his hands, but he never hurt her. He held her hand in his own and brushed her fingers, one by one. He ran a hand gently down her leg. He stroked her face, tracing the curve of her ears, running a finger gently around her mouth. He put both hands in her hair and combed it with his fingers. He turned her around, massaged her shoulders, slid a knuckle down the path of her spine.

It seemed as if hours passed before his hands finally went to her breasts. He stroked the soft skin underneath until it tingled. He circled her nipples with his thumbs, pinched them between thumb and forefinger, then began to pull at her, very lightly at first, then more insistently, until her nipples stiffened and began to ache.

He stopped then, and drew her down onto his lap. Dany was flushed and breathless, her heart fluttering in her chest. He cupped her face in his huge hands and she looked into his eyes. "No?" he said, and she knew it was a question.

She took his hand and moved it down to the wetness between her thighs. "Yes," she whispered as she put his finger inside her.

EDDARD

The summons came in the hour before the dawn, when the world was still and grey.

Alyn shook him roughly from his dreams and Ned stumbled into the predawn chill, groggy from sleep, to find his horse saddled and the king already mounted. Robert wore thick brown gloves and a heavy fur cloak with a hood that covered his ears, and looked for all the world like a bear sitting a horse. "Up, Stark!" he roared. "Up, up! We have matters of state to discuss."

"By all means," Ned said. "Come inside, Your Grace." Alyn lifted the flap of the tent.

"No, no, *no*," Robert said. His breath steamed with every word. "The camp is full of ears. Besides, I want to ride out and taste this country of yours." Ser Boros and Ser Meryn waited behind him with a dozen guardsmen, Ned saw. There was nothing to do but rub the sleep from his eyes, dress, and mount up.

Robert set the pace, driving his huge black destrier hard as Ned galloped along beside him, trying to keep up. He called out a question as they rode, but the wind blew his words away, and the king did not hear him. After that Ned rode in silence. They soon left the kingsroad and took off across rolling plains dark with mist. By then the guard had fallen back a small distance, safely out of ear-shot, but still Robert would not slow.

Dawn broke as they crested a low ridge, and finally the king pulled up. By then they were miles south of the main party. Robert was flushed and exhilarated as Ned reined up beside him. "Gods," he swore, laughing, "it feels good to get out and *ride* the way a man was meant to ride! I swear, Ned, this creeping along is enough to drive a man mad." He had never been a patient man, Robert Baratheon. "That damnable wheelhouse, the way it creaks and groans, climbing every bump in the road as if it were a mountain . . . I promise you, if that wretched thing breaks another axle, I'm going to burn it, and Cersei can walk!"

Ned laughed. "I will gladly light the torch for you."

"Good man!" The king clapped him on the shoulder. "I've half a mind to leave them all behind and just keep going."

A smile touched Ned's lips. "I do believe you mean it."

"I do, I do," the king said. "What do you say, Ned? Just you and me, two vagabond knights on the kingsroad, our swords at our sides and the gods know what in front of us, and maybe a farmer's daughter or a tavern wench to warm our beds tonight."

"Would that we could," Ned said, "but we have duties now, my liege . . . to the realm, to our children, I to my lady wife and you to your queen. We are not the boys we were."

"You were never the boy you were," Robert grumbled. "More's the pity. And yet there was that one time . . . what was her name, that common girl of yours? Becca? No, she was one of mine, gods love her, black hair and these sweet big eyes, you could drown in them. Yours was . . . Aleena? No. You told me once. Was it Merryl? You know the one I mean, your bastard's mother?"

"Her name was Wylla," Ned replied with cool cour-tesy, "and I would sooner not speak of her."

"Wylla. Yes." The king grinned. "She must have been a rare wench if she could make Lord Eddard Stark forget his honor, even for an hour. You never told me what she looked like . . ."

Ned's mouth tightened in anger. "Nor will I. Leave it

be, Robert, for the love you say you bear me. I dishonored myself and I dishonored Catelyn, in the sight of gods and men."

"Gods have mercy, you scarcely *knew* Catelyn."

"I had taken her to wife. She was carrying my child."

"You are too hard on yourself, Ned. You always were. Damn it, no woman wants Baelor the Blessed in her bed." He slapped a hand on his knee. "Well, I'll not press you if you feel so strong about it, though I swear, at times you're so prickly you ought to take the hedgehog as your sigil."

The rising sun sent fingers of light through the pale white mists of dawn. A wide plain spread out beneath them, bare and brown, its flatness here and there relieved by long, low hummocks. Ned pointed them out to his king. "The barrows of the First Men."

Robert frowned. "Have we ridden onto a graveyard?"

"There are barrows everywhere in the north, Your Grace," Ned told him. "This land is old."

"And cold," Robert grumbled, pulling his cloak more tightly around himself. The guard had reined up well behind them, at the bottom of the ridge. "Well, I did not bring you out here to talk of graves or bicker about your bastard. There was a rider in the night, from Lord Varys in King's Landing. Here." The king pulled a paper from his belt and handed it to Ned.

Varys the eunuch was the king's master of whisperers. He served Robert now as he had once served Aerys Targaryen. Ned unrolled the paper with trepidation, thinking of Lysa and her terrible accusation, but the message did not concern Lady Arryn. "What is the source for this information?"

"Do you remember Ser Jorah Mormont?"

"Would that I might forget him," Ned said bluntly. The Mormonts of Bear Island were an old house, proud and honorable, but their lands were cold and distant and poor. Ser Jorah had tried to swell the family coffers by selling some poachers to a Tyroshi slaver. As the Mormonts were bannermen to the Starks, his crime had dishonored the north. Ned had made the long journey west to Bear Island, only to find when he arrived that Jorah had taken ship beyond the reach of Ice and the king's justice. Five years had passed since then.

"Ser Jorah is now in Pentos, anxious to earn a royal

pardon that would allow him to return from exile," Robert explained. "Lord Varys makes good use of him."

"So the slaver has become a spy," Ned said with distaste. He handed the letter back. "I would rather he become a corpse."

"Varys tells me that spies are more useful than corpses," Robert said. "Jorah aside, what do you make of his report?"

"Daenerys Targaryen has wed some Dothraki horselord. What of it? Shall we send her a wedding gift?"

The king frowned. "A knife, perhaps. A good sharp one, and a bold man to wield it."

Ned did not feign surprise; Robert's hatred of the Targaryens was a madness in him. He remembered the angry words they had exchanged when Tywin Lannister had presented Robert with the corpses of Rhaegar's wife and children as a token of fealty. Ned had named that murder; Robert called it war. When he had protested that the young prince and princess were no more than babes, his new-made king had replied, "I see no babes. Only dragonspawn." Not even Jon Arryn had been able to calm that storm. Eddard Stark had ridden out that very day in a cold rage, to fight the last battles of the war alone in the south. It had taken another death to reconcile them; Lyanna's death, and the grief they had shared over her passing.

This time, Ned resolved to keep his temper. "Your Grace, the girl is scarcely more than a child. You are no Tywin Lannister, to slaughter innocents." It was said that Rhaegar's little girl had cried as they dragged her from beneath her bed to face the swords. The boy had been no more than a babe in arms, yet Lord Tywin's soldiers had torn him from his mother's breast and dashed his head against a wall.

"And how long will this one remain an innocent?" Robert's mouth grew hard. "This *child* will soon enough spread her legs and start breeding more dragonspawn to plague me."

"Nonetheless," Ned said, "the murder of children . . . it would be vile . . . unspeakable . . ."

"*Unspeakable?*" the king roared. "What Aerys did to your brother Brandon was unspeakable. The way your lord father died, that was unspeakable. And Rhaegar . . . how many times do you think he raped your sister? How many *hundreds* of times?" His voice had grown so loud that his horse whinnied nervously beneath him. The king jerked the reins hard, quieting the animal, and pointed an angry finger at Ned. "I will kill every Targaryen I can get my hands on, until they are as dead as their dragons, and then I will piss on their graves."

Ned knew better than to defy him when the wrath was on him. If the years had not quenched Robert's thirst for revenge, no words of his would help. "You can't get your hands on this one, can you?" he said quietly.

The king's mouth twisted in a bitter grimace. "No, gods be cursed. Some pox-ridden Pentoshi cheesemonger had her brother and her walled up on his estate with pointy-hatted eunuchs all around them, and now he's handed them over to the Dothraki. I should have had them both killed years ago, when it was easy to get at them, but Jon was as bad as you. More fool I, I listened to him."

"Jon Arryn was a wise man and a good Hand."

Robert snorted. The anger was leaving him as suddenly as it had come. "This Khal Drogo is said to have a hundred thousand men in his horde. What would Jon say to *that*?"

"He would say that even a million Dothraki are no threat to the realm, so long as they remain on the other side of the narrow sea," Ned replied calmly. "The barbarians have no *ships*. They hate and fear the open sea."

The king shifted uncomfortably in his saddle. "Perhaps. There are ships to be had in the Free Cities, though. I tell you, Ned, I do not like this marriage. There are still those in the Seven Kingdoms who call me Usurper. Do you forget how many houses fought for Targaryen in the war? They bide their time for now, but give them half a chance, they will murder me in my bed, and my sons with me. If the beggar king crosses with a Dothraki horde at his back, the traitors will join him."

"He will not cross," Ned promised. "And if by some mischance he does, we will throw him back into the sea. Once you choose a new Warden of the East—"

The king groaned. "For the last time, I will not name the Arryn boy Warden. I know the boy is your nephew, but with Targaryens climbing in bed with Dothraki, I would be mad to rest one quarter of the realm on the shoulders of a sickly child."

Ned was ready for that. "Yet we still must have a Warden of the East. If Robert Arryn will not do, name one of your brothers. Stannis proved himself at the siege of Storm's End, surely."

He let the name hang there for a moment. The king frowned and said nothing. He looked uncomfortable.

"That is," Ned finished quietly, watching, "unless you have already promised the honor to another."

For a moment Robert had the grace to look startled. Just as quickly, the look became annoyance. "What if I have?"

"It's Jaime Lannister, is it not?"

Robert kicked his horse back into motion and started down the ridge toward the barrows. Ned kept pace with him. The king rode on, eyes straight ahead. "Yes," he said at last. A single hard word to end the matter.

"Kingslayer," Ned said. The rumors were true, then. He rode on dangerous ground now, he knew. "An able and courageous man, no doubt," he said carefully, "but his father is Warden of the West, Robert. In time Ser Jaime will succeed to that honor. No one man should hold both East and West." He left unsaid his real concern; that the appointment would put half the armies of the realm into the hands of Lannisters.

"I will fight that battle when the enemy appears on the field," the king said stubbornly. "At the moment, Lord Tywin looms eternal as Casterly Rock, so I doubt that Jaime will be succeeding anytime soon. Don't vex me about this, Ned, the stone has been set."

"Your Grace, may I speak frankly?"

"I seem unable to stop you," Robert grumbled. They rode through tall brown grasses.

"Can you trust Jaime Lannister?"

"He is my wife's twin, a Sworn Brother of the Kingsguard, his life and fortune and honor all bound to mine."

"As they were bound to Aerys Targaryen's," Ned pointed out.

"Why should I mistrust him? He has done everything I have ever asked of him. His sword helped win the throne I sit on."

His sword helped taint the throne you sit on, Ned

thought, but he did not permit the words to pass his lips. "He swore a vow to protect his king's life with his own. Then he opened that king's throat with a sword."

"Seven hells, *someone* had to kill Aerys!" Robert said, reining his mount to a sudden halt beside an ancient barrow. "If Jaime hadn't done it, it would have been left for you or me."

"We were not Sworn Brothers of the Kingsguard," Ned said. The time had come for Robert to hear the whole truth, he decided then and there. "Do you remember the Trident, Your Grace?"

"I won my crown there. How should I forget it?"

"You took a wound from Rhaegar," Ned reminded him. "So when the Targaryen host broke and ran, you gave the pursuit into my hands. The remnants of Rhaegar's army fled back to King's Landing. We followed. Aerys was in the Red Keep with several thousand loyalists. I expected to find the gates closed to us."

Robert gave an impatient shake of his head. "Instead you found that our men had already taken the city. What of it?"

"Not our men," Ned said patiently. "Lannister men. The lion of Lannister flew over the ramparts, not the crowned stag. And they had taken the city by treachery."

The war had raged for close to a year. Lords great and small had flocked to Robert's banners; others had remained loyal to Targaryen. The mighty Lannisters of Casterly Rock, the Wardens of the West, had remained aloof from the struggle, ignoring calls to arms from both rebels and royalists. Aerys Targaryen must have thought that his gods had answered his prayers when Lord Tywin Lannister appeared before the gates of King's Landing with an army twelve thousand strong, professing loyalty. So the mad king had ordered his last mad act. He had opened his city to the lions at the gate.

"Treachery was a coin the Targaryens knew well," Robert said. The anger was building in him again. "Lannister paid them back in kind. It was no less than they deserved. I shall not trouble my sleep over it."

"You were not there," Ned said, bitterness in his voice. Troubled sleep was no stranger to him. He had lived his lies for fourteen years, yet they still haunted him at night. "There was no honor in that conquest."

"The Others take your honor!" Robert swore. "What did any Targaryen ever know of honor? Go down into your crypt and ask Lyanna about the dragon's honor!"

"You avenged Lyanna at the Trident," Ned said, halting beside the king. *Promise me, Ned,* she had whispered.

"That did not bring her back." Robert looked away, off into the grey distance. "The gods be damned. It was a hollow victory they gave me. A crown . . . it was the *girl* I prayed them for. Your sister, safe . . . and mine again, as she was meant to be. I ask you, Ned, what good is it to wear a crown? The gods mock the prayers of kings and cowherds alike."

"I cannot answer for the gods, Your Grace . . . only for what I found when I rode into the throne room that day," Ned said. "Aerys was dead on the floor, drowned in his own blood. His dragon skulls stared down from the walls. Lannister's men were everywhere. Jaime wore the white cloak of the Kingsguard over his golden armor. I can see him still. Even his sword was gilded. He was seated on the Iron Throne, high above his knights, wearing a helm fashioned in the shape of a lion's head. How he glittered!"

"This is well known," the king complained.

"I was still mounted. I rode the length of the hall in silence, between the long rows of dragon skulls. It felt as though they were watching me, somehow. I stopped in front of the throne, looking up at him. His golden sword was across his legs, its edge red with a king's blood. My men were filling the room behind me. Lannister's men drew back. I never said a word. I looked at him seated there on the throne, and I waited. At last Jaime laughed and got up. He took off his helm, and he said to me, 'Have no fear, Stark. I was only keeping it warm for our friend Robert. It's not a very comfortable seat, I'm afraid.'"

The king threw back his head and roared. His laughter startled a flight of crows from the tall brown grass. They took to the air in a wild beating of wings. "You think I should mistrust Lannister because he sat on my throne for a few moments?" He shook with laughter again. "Jaime was all of seventeen, Ned. Scarce more than a boy."

"Boy or man, he had no right to that throne."

"Perhaps he was tired," Robert suggested. "Killing

kings is weary work. Gods know, there's no place else to rest your ass in that damnable room. And he spoke truly, it *is* a monstrous uncomfortable chair. In more ways than one." The king shook his head. "Well, now I know Jaime's dark sin, and the matter can be forgotten. I am heartily sick of secrets and squabbles and matters of state, Ned. It's all as tedious as counting coppers. Come, let's ride, you used to know how. I want to feel the wind in my hair again." He kicked his horse back into motion and galloped up over the barrow, raining earth down behind him.

For a moment Ned did not follow. He had run out of words, and he was filled with a vast sense of helplessness. Not for the first time, he wondered what he was doing here and why he had come. He was no Jon Arryn, to curb the wildness of his king and teach him wisdom. Robert would do what he pleased, as he always had, and nothing Ned could say or do would change that. He belonged in Winterfell. He belonged with Catelyn in her grief, and with Bran.

A man could not always be where he belonged, though. Resigned, Eddard Stark put his boots into his horse and set off after the king.

TYRION

The north went on forever.

Tyrion Lannister knew the maps as well as anyone, but a fortnight on the wild track that passed for the kingsroad up here had brought home the lesson that the map was one thing and the land quite another.

They had left Winterfell on the same day as the king, amidst all the commotion of the royal departure, riding out to the sound of men shouting and horses snorting, to the rattle of wagons and the groaning of the queen's huge wheelhouse, as a light snow flurried about them. The kingsroad was just beyond the sprawl of castle and town. There the banners and the wagons and the columns of knights and freeriders turned south, taking the tumult with them, while Tyrion turned north with Benjen Stark and his nephew.

It had grown colder after that, and far more quiet.

West of the road were flint hills, grey and rugged, with tall watchtowers on their stony summits. To the east the land was lower, the ground flattening to a rolling plain that stretched away as far as the eye could see. Stone bridges spanned swift, narrow rivers, while small farms spread in rings around holdfasts walled in wood and stone. The road was well trafficked, and at night for their comfort there were rude inns to be found.

Three days ride from Winterfell, however, the farmland gave way to dense wood, and the kingsroad grew lonely. The flint hills rose higher and wilder with each passing mile, until by the fifth day they had turned into mountains, cold blue-grey giants with jagged promontories and snow on their shoulders. When the wind blew from the north, long plumes of ice crystals flew from the high peaks like banners.

With the mountains a wall to the west, the road veered north by northeast through the wood, a forest of oak and evergreen and black brier that seemed older and darker than any Tyrion had ever seen. "The wolfswood," Benjen Stark called it, and indeed their nights came alive with the howls of distant packs, and some not so distant. Jon Snow's albino direwolf pricked up his ears at the nightly howling, but never raised his own voice in reply. There was something very unsettling about that animal, Tyrion thought.

There were eight in the party by then, not counting the wolf. Tyrion traveled with two of his own men, as befit a Lannister. Benjen Stark had only his bastard nephew and some fresh mounts for the Night's Watch, but at the edge of the wolfswood they stayed a night behind the wooden walls of a forest holdfast, and there joined up with another of the black brothers, one Yoren. Yoren was stooped and sinister, his features hidden behind a beard as black as his clothing, but he seemed as tough as an old root and as hard as stone. With him were a pair of ragged peasant boys from the Fingers. "Rapers," Yoren said with a cold look at his charges. Tyrion understood. Life on the Wall was said to be hard, but no doubt it was preferable to castration.

Five men, three boys, a direwolf, twenty horses, and a cage of ravens given over to Benjen Stark by Maester Luwin. No doubt they made a curious fellowship for the kingsroad, or any road.

Tyrion noticed Jon Snow watching Yoren and his sullen companions, with an odd cast to his face that looked uncomfortably like dismay. Yoren had a twisted shoulder and a sour smell, his hair and beard were matted and greasy and full of lice, his clothing old, patched, and seldom washed. His two young recruits smelled even worse, and seemed as stupid as they were cruel.

No doubt the boy had made the mistake of thinking that the Night's Watch was made up of men like his uncle. If so, Yoren and his companions were a rude awakening. Tyrion felt sorry for the boy. He had chosen a hard life . . . or perhaps he should say that a hard life had been chosen for him.

He had rather less sympathy for the uncle. Benjen Stark seemed to share his brother's distaste for Lannisters, and he had not been pleased when Tyrion had told him of his intentions. "I warn you, Lannister, you'll find no inns at the Wall," he had said, looking down on him.

"No doubt you'll find some place to put me," Tyrion had replied. "As you might have noticed, I'm small."

One did not say no to the queen's brother, of course, so that had settled the matter, but Stark had not been happy. "You will not like the ride, I promise you that," he'd said curtly, and since the moment they set out, he had done all he could to live up to that promise.

By the end of the first week, Tyrion's thighs were raw from hard riding, his legs were cramping badly, and he was chilled to the bone. He did not complain. He was damned if he would give Benjen Stark that satisfaction.

He took a small revenge in the matter of his riding fur, a tattered bearskin, old and musty-smelling. Stark had offered it to him in an excess of Night's Watch gallantry, no doubt expecting him to graciously decline. Tyrion had accepted with a smile. He had brought his warmest clothing with him when they rode out of Winterfell, and soon discovered that it was nowhere near warm enough. It was *cold* up here, and growing colder. The nights were well below freezing now, and when the wind blew it was like a knife cutting right through his warmest woolens. By now Stark was no doubt regretting his chivalrous impulse. Perhaps he had learned a lesson. The Lannisters never declined, graciously or otherwise. The Lannisters took what was offered.

Farms and holdfasts grew scarcer and smaller as they pressed northward, ever deeper into the darkness of the wolfswood, until finally there were no more roofs to shelter under, and they were thrown back on their own resources.

Tyrion was never much use in making a camp or breaking one. Too small, too hobbled, too in-the-way. So while Stark and Yoren and the other men erected rude shelters, tended the horses, and built a fire, it became his custom to take his fur and a wineskin and go off by himself to read.

On the eighteenth night of their journey, the wine was a rare sweet amber from the Summer Isles that he had brought all the way north from Casterly Rock, and the book a rumination on the history and properties of dragons. With Lord Eddard Stark's permission, Tyrion had borrowed a few rare volumes from the Winterfell library and packed them for the ride north.

He found a comfortable spot just beyond the noise of the camp, beside a swift-running stream with waters clear and cold as ice. A grotesquely ancient oak provided shelter from the biting wind. Tyrion curled up in his fur with his back against the trunk, took a sip of the wine, and began to read about the properties of dragonbone. *Dragonbone is black because of its high iron content,* the book told him. *It is strong as steel, yet lighter and far more flexible, and of course utterly impervious to fire. Dragonbone bows are greatly prized by the Dothraki, and small wonder. An archer so armed can outrange any wooden bow.*

Tyrion had a morbid fascination with dragons. When he had first come to King's Landing for his sister's wedding to Robert Baratheon, he had made it a point to seek out the dragon skulls that had hung on the walls of Targaryen's throne room. King Robert had replaced them with banners and tapestries, but Tyrion had persisted until he found the skulls in the dank cellar where they had been stored.

He had expected to find them impressive, perhaps even frightening. He had not thought to find them beautiful. Yet they were. As black as onyx, polished smooth, so the bone seemed to shimmer in the light of his torch. They liked the fire, he sensed. He'd thrust the torch into the mouth of one of the larger skulls and made the shadows leap and dance on the wall behind him. The teeth were long, curving knives of black diamond. The flame of the torch was nothing to them; they had bathed in the heat of far greater fires. When he had moved away, Tyrion could have sworn that the beast's empty eye sockets had watched him go.

There were nineteen skulls. The oldest was more than three thousand years old; the youngest a mere century and a half. The most recent were also the smallest; a matched pair no bigger than mastiff's skulls, and oddly misshapen, all that remained of the last two hatchlings born on Dragonstone. They were the last of the Targaryen dragons, perhaps the last dragons anywhere, and they had not lived very long.

From there the skulls ranged upward in size to the three great monsters of song and story, the dragons that Aegon Targaryen and his sisters had unleashed on the Seven Kingdoms of old. The singers had given them the names of gods: Balerion, Meraxes, Vhaghar. Tyrion had stood between their gaping jaws, wordless and awed. You could have ridden a horse down Vhaghar's gullet, although you would not have ridden it out again. Meraxes was even bigger. And the greatest of them, Balerion, the Black Dread, could have swallowed an aurochs whole, or even one of the hairy mammoths said to roam the cold wastes beyond the Port of Ibben.

Tyrion stood in that dank cellar for a long time, staring at Balerion's huge, empty-eyed skull until his torch burned low, trying to grasp the size of the living animal, to imagine how it must have looked when it spread its great black wings and swept across the skies, breathing fire.

His own remote ancestor, King Loren of the Rock, had tried to stand against the fire when he joined with King Mern of the Reach to oppose the Targaryen conquest. That was close on three hundred years ago, when the Seven Kingdoms *were* kingdoms, and not mere provinces of a greater realm. Between them, the Two Kings had six hundred banners flying, five thousand mounted knights, and ten times as many freeriders and men-at-arms. Aegon Dragonlord had perhaps a fifth that number, the chroniclers said, and most of those were conscripts from the ranks of the last king he had slain, their loyalties uncertain.

The hosts met on the broad plains of the Reach, amidst golden fields of wheat ripe for harvest. When the Two Kings charged, the Targaryen army shivered and shattered and began to run. For a few moments, the chroniclers wrote, the conquest was at an end . . . but only for those few moments, before Aegon Targaryen and his sisters joined the battle.

It was the only time that Vhaghar, Meraxes, and Balerion were all unleashed at once. The singers called it the Field of Fire.

Near four thousand men had burned that day, among them King Mern of the Reach. King Loren had escaped, and lived long enough to surrender, pledge his fealty to the Targaryens, and beget a son, for which Tyrion was duly grateful.

"Why do you read so much?"

Tyrion looked up at the sound of the voice. Jon Snow was standing a few feet away, regarding him curiously. He closed the book on a finger and said, "Look at me and tell me what you see."

The boy looked at him suspiciously. "Is this some kind of trick? I see you. Tyrion Lannister."

Tyrion sighed. "You are remarkably polite for a bastard, Snow. What you see is a dwarf. You are what, twelve?"

"Fourteen," the boy said.

"Fourteen, and you're taller than I will ever be. My legs are short and twisted, and I walk with difficulty. I require a special saddle to keep from falling off my horse. A saddle of my own design, you may be interested to know. It was either that or ride a pony. My arms are strong enough, but again, too short. I will never make a swordsman. Had I been born a peasant, they might have left me out to die, or sold me to some slaver's grotesquerie. Alas, I was born a Lannister of Casterly Rock, and the grotesqueries are all the poorer. Things are expected of me. My father was the Hand of the King for twenty years. My brother later killed that very same king, as it turns out, but life is full of these little ironies. My sister married the new king and my repulsive nephew will be king after him. I must do my part for the honor of my House, wouldn't you agree? Yet how? Well, my legs may be too small for my body, but my head is too large, although I prefer to think it is just large enough for my mind. I have a realistic grasp of my own strengths and weaknesses. My mind is my weapon. My brother has his sword, King Robert has his warhammer, and I have my mind . . . and a mind needs books as a sword needs a whetstone, if it is to keep its edge." Tyrion tapped the leather cover of the book. "That's why I read so much, Jon Snow."

The boy absorbed that all in silence. He had the Stark face if not the name: long, solemn, guarded, a face that gave nothing away. Whoever his mother had been, she had left little of herself in her son. "What are you reading about?" he asked.

"Dragons," Tyrion told him.

"What good is that? There are no more dragons," the boy said with the easy certainty of youth.

"So they say," Tyrion replied. "Sad, isn't it? When I was your age, I used to dream of having a dragon of my own."

"You did?" the boy said suspiciously. Perhaps he thought Tyrion was making fun of him.

"Oh, yes. Even a stunted, twisted, ugly little boy can look down over the world when he's seated on a dragon's back." Tyrion pushed the bearskin aside and climbed to his feet. "I used to start fires in the bowels of Casterly Rock and stare at the flames for hours, pretending they were dragonfire. Sometimes I'd imagine my father burning. At other times, my sister." Jon Snow was staring at him, a look equal parts horror and fascination. Tyrion guffawed. "Don't look at me that way, bastard. I know your secret. You've dreamt the same kind of dreams."

"No," Jon Snow said, horrified. "I wouldn't . . ."

"No? Never?" Tyrion raised an eyebrow. "Well, no doubt the Starks have been terribly good to you. I'm certain Lady Stark treats you as if you were one of her own. And your brother Robb, he's always been kind, and why not? He gets Winterfell and you get the Wall. And your father . . . he must have good reasons for packing you off to the Night's Watch . . ."

"Stop it," Jon Snow said, his face dark with anger. "The Night's Watch is a noble calling!"

Tyrion laughed. "You're too smart to believe that. The Night's Watch is a midden heap for all the misfits of the realm. I've seen you looking at Yoren and his boys. Those are your new brothers, Jon Snow, how do you like them? Sullen peasants, debtors, poachers, rapers, thieves, and bastards like you all wind up on the Wall, watching for grumkins and snarks and all the other monsters your wet nurse warned you about. The good part is there are no grumkins or snarks, so it's scarcely dangerous work. The bad part is you freeze your balls off, but since you're not allowed to breed anyway, I don't suppose that matters."

"Stop it!" the boy screamed. He took a step forward, his hands coiling into fists, close to tears.

Suddenly, absurdly, Tyrion felt guilty. He took a step forward, intending to give the boy a reassuring pat on the shoulder or mutter some word of apology.

He never saw the wolf, where it was or how it came at him. One moment he was walking toward Snow and the next he was flat on his back on the hard rocky ground, the book spinning away from him as he fell, the breath going out of him at the sudden impact, his mouth full of dirt and blood and rotting leaves. As he tried to get up, his back spasmed painfully. He must have wrenched it in the fall. He ground his teeth in frustration, grabbed a root, and pulled himself back to a sitting position. "Help me," he said to the boy, reaching up a hand.

And suddenly the wolf was between them. He did not growl. The damned thing never made a sound. He only looked at him with those bright red eyes, and showed him his teeth, and that was more than enough. Tyrion sagged back to the ground with a grunt. "Don't help me, then. I'll sit right here until you leave."

Jon Snow stroked Ghost's thick white fur, smiling now. "Ask me nicely."

Tyrion Lannister felt the anger coiling inside him, and crushed it out with a will. It was not the first time in his life he had been humiliated, and it would not be the last. Perhaps he even deserved this. "I should be very grateful for your kind assistance, Jon," he said mildly.

"Down, Ghost," the boy said. The direwolf sat on his haunches. Those red eyes never left Tyrion. Jon came around behind him, slid his hands under his arms, and lifted him easily to his feet. Then he picked up the book and handed it back.

"Why did he attack me?" Tyrion asked with a sidelong glance at the direwolf. He wiped blood and dirt from his mouth with the back of his hand.

"Maybe he thought you were a grumkin."

Tyrion glanced at him sharply. Then he laughed, a raw

snort of amusement that came bursting out through his nose entirely without his permission. "Oh, gods," he said, choking on his laughter and shaking his head, "I suppose I do rather look like a grumkin. What does he do to snarks?"

"You don't want to know." Jon picked up the wineskin and handed it to Tyrion.

Tyrion pulled out the stopper, tilted his head, and squeezed a long stream into his mouth. The wine was cool fire as it trickled down his throat and warmed his belly. He held out the skin to Jon Snow. "Want some?"

The boy took the skin and tried a cautious swallow. "It's true, isn't it?" he said when he was done. "What you said about the Night's Watch."

Tyrion nodded.

Jon Snow set his mouth in a grim line. "If that's what it is, that's what it is."

Tyrion grinned at him. "That's good, bastard. Most men would rather deny a hard truth than face it."

"Most men," the boy said. "But not you."

"No," Tyrion admitted, "not me. I seldom even dream of dragons anymore. There are no dragons." He scooped up the fallen bearskin. "Come, we had better return to camp before your uncle calls the banners."

The walk was short, but the ground was rough underfoot and his legs were cramping badly by the time they got back. Jon Snow offered a hand to help him over a thick tangle of roots, but Tyrion shook him off. He would make his own way, as he had all his life. Still, the camp was a welcome sight. The shelters had been thrown up against the tumbledown wall of a long-abandoned holdfast, a shield against the wind. The horses had been fed and a fire had been laid. Yoren sat on a stone, skinning a squirrel. The savory smell of stew filled Tyrion's nostrils. He dragged himself over to where his man Morrec was tending the stewpot. Wordlessly, Morrec handed him the ladle. Tyrion tasted and handed it back. "More pepper," he said.

Benjen Stark emerged from the shelter he shared with his nephew. "There you are. Jon, damn it, don't go off like that by yourself. I thought the Others had gotten you."

"It was the grumkins," Tyrion told him, laughing. Jon Snow smiled. Stark shot a baffled look at Yoren. The old man grunted, shrugged, and went back to his bloody work.

The squirrel gave some body to the stew, and they ate it with black bread and hard cheese that night around their fire. Tyrion shared around his skin of wine until even Yoren grew mellow. One by one the company drifted off to their shelters and to sleep, all but Jon Snow, who had drawn the night's first watch.

Tyrion was the last to retire, as always. As he stepped into the shelter his men had built for him, he paused and looked back at Jon Snow. The boy stood near the fire, his face still and hard, looking deep into the flames.

Tyrion Lannister smiled sadly and went to bed.

CATELYN

N ed and the girls were eight days gone when Maester Luwin came to her one night in Bran's sickroom, carrying a reading lamp and the books of account. "It is past time that we reviewed the figures, my lady," he said. "You'll want to know how much this royal visit cost us."

Catelyn looked at Bran in his sickbed and brushed his hair back off his forehead. It had grown very long, she realized. She would have to cut it soon. "I have no need to look at figures, Maester Luwin," she told him, never taking her eyes from Bran. "I know what the visit cost us. Take the books away."

"My lady, the king's party had healthy appetites. We must replenish our stores before—"

She cut him off. "I said, take the books away. The steward will attend to our needs."

"We have no steward," Maester Luwin reminded her. Like a little grey rat, she thought, he would not let go. "Poole went south to establish Lord Eddard's household at King's Landing."

Catelyn nodded absently. "Oh, yes. I remember." Bran looked so pale. She wondered whether they might move his bed under the window, so he could get the morning sun.

Maester Luwin set the lamp in a niche by the door and fiddled with its wick. "There are several appointments that require your immediate attention, my lady. Besides the steward, we need a captain of the guards to fill Jory's place, a new master of horse—"

Her eyes snapped around and found him. "A master of *horse*?" Her voice was a whip.

The maester was shaken. "Yes, my lady. Hullen rode south with Lord Eddard, so—"

"My son lies here broken and dying, Luwin, and you wish to discuss a new master of *horse*? Do you think I care what happens in the stables? Do you think it matters to me one whit? I would gladly butcher every horse in Winterfell with my own hands if it would open Bran's eyes, do you understand that? *Do you?*"

He bowed his head. "Yes, my lady, but the appointments—"

"I'll make the appointments," Robb said.

Catelyn had not heard him enter, but there he stood in the doorway, looking at her. She had been shouting, she realized with a sudden flush of shame. What was happening to her? She was so tired, and her head hurt all the time.

Maester Luwin looked from Catelyn to her son. "I have prepared a list of those we might wish to consider for the vacant offices," he said, offering Robb a paper plucked from his sleeve.

Her son glanced at the names. He had come from outside, Catelyn saw; his cheeks were red from the cold, his hair shaggy and windblown. "Good men," he said. "We'll talk about them tomorrow." He handed back the list of names.

"Very good, my lord." The paper vanished into his sleeve.

"Leave us now," Robb said. Maester Luwin bowed and departed. Robb closed the door behind him and turned to her. He was wearing a sword, she saw. "Mother, what are you doing?"

Catelyn had always thought Robb looked like her; like Bran and Rickon and Sansa, he had the Tully coloring, the auburn hair, the blue eyes. Yet now for the first time she saw something of Eddard Stark in his face, something as stern and hard as the north. "What am I doing?" she echoed, puzzled. "How can you ask that? What do you imagine I'm doing? I am taking care of your brother. I am taking care of Bran."

"Is that what you call it? You haven't left this room since Bran was hurt. You didn't even come to the gate when Father and the girls went south."

"I said my farewells to them here, and watched them ride out from that window." She had begged Ned not to go, not now, not after what had happened; everything had changed now, couldn't he see that? It was no use. He had no choice, he had told her, and then he left, choosing. "I can't leave him, even for a moment, not when any moment could be his last. I have to be with him, if . . . if . . ." She took her son's limp hand, sliding his fingers through her own. He was so frail and thin, with no strength left in his hand, but she could still feel the warmth of life through his skin.

Robb's voice softened. "He's not going to die, Mother. Maester Luwin says the time of greatest danger has passed."

"And what if Maester Luwin is wrong? What if Bran needs me and I'm not here?"

"*Rickon* needs you," Robb said sharply. "He's only three, he doesn't understand what's happening. He thinks everyone has deserted him, so he follows me around all day, clutching my leg and crying. I don't know what to do with him." He paused a moment, chewing on his lower lip the way he'd done when he was little. "Mother, *I* need you too. I'm trying but I can't . . . I can't do it all by myself." His voice broke with sudden emotion, and Catelyn remembered that he was only fourteen. She wanted to get up and go to him, but Bran was still holding her hand and she could not move.

Outside the tower, a wolf began to howl. Catelyn trembled, just for a second.

"Bran's." Robb opened the window and let the night air into the stuffy tower room. The howling grew louder. It was a cold and lonely sound, full of melancholy and despair.

"Don't," she told him. "Bran needs to stay warm."

"He needs to hear them sing," Robb said. Somewhere

out in Winterfell, a second wolf began to howl in chorus with the first. Then a third, closer. "Shaggydog and Grey Wind," Robb said as their voices rose and fell together. "You can tell them apart if you listen close."

Catelyn was shaking. It was the grief, the cold, the howling of the direwolves. Night after night, the howling and the cold wind and the grey empty castle, on and on they went, never changing, and her boy lying there broken, the sweetest of her children, the gentlest, Bran who loved to laugh and climb and dreamt of knighthood, all gone now, she would never hear him laugh again. Sobbing, she pulled her hand free of his and covered her ears against those terrible howls. "Make them stop!" she cried. "I can't stand it, make them stop, make them stop, kill them all if you must, just make them *stop*!"

She didn't remember falling to the floor, but there she was, and Robb was lifting her, holding her in strong arms. "Don't be afraid, Mother. They would never hurt him." He helped her to her narrow bed in the corner of the sickroom. "Close your eyes," he said gently. "Rest. Maester Luwin tells me you've hardly slept since Bran's fall."

"I *can't*," she wept. "Gods forgive me, Robb, I can't, what if he dies while I'm asleep, what if he dies, what if he dies . . ." The wolves were still howling. She screamed and held her ears again. "Oh, gods, close the window!"

"If you swear to me you'll sleep." Robb went to the window, but as he reached for the shutters another sound was added to the mournful howling of the direwolves. "Dogs," he said, listening. "All the dogs are barking. They've never done that before . . ." Catelyn heard his breath catch in his throat. When she looked up, his face was pale in the lamplight. *"Fire,"* he whispered.

Fire, she thought, and then, *Bran!* "Help me," she said urgently, sitting up. "Help me with Bran."

Robb did not seem to hear her. "The library tower's on fire," he said.

Catelyn could see the flickering reddish light through the open window now. She sagged with relief. Bran was safe. The library was across the bailey, there was no way the fire would reach them here. "Thank the gods," she whispered.

Robb looked at her as if she'd gone mad. "Mother, stay here. I'll come back as soon as the fire's out." He ran then. She heard him shout to the guards outside the room, heard them descending together in a wild rush, taking the stairs two and three at a time.

Outside, there were shouts of "Fire!" in the yard, screams, running footsteps, the whinny of frightened horses, and the frantic barking of the castle dogs. The howling was gone, she realized as she listened to the cacophony. The direwolves had fallen silent.

Catelyn said a silent prayer of thanks to the seven faces of god as she went to the window. Across the bailey, long tongues of flame shot from the windows of the library. She watched the smoke rise into the sky and thought sadly of all the books the Starks had gathered over the centuries. Then she closed the shutters.

When she turned away from the window, the man was in the room with her.

"You weren't s'posed to be here," he muttered sourly. "No one was s'posed to be here."

He was a small, dirty man in filthy brown clothing, and he stank of horses. Catelyn knew all the men who worked in their stables, and he was none of them. He was gaunt, with limp blond hair and pale eyes deep-sunk in a bony face, and there was a dagger in his hand.

Catelyn looked at the knife, then at Bran. "No," she said. The word stuck in her throat, the merest whisper.

He must have heard her. "It's a mercy," he said. "He's dead already."

"No," Catelyn said, louder now as she found her voice again. "No, you *can't*." She spun back toward the window to scream for help, but the man moved faster than she would have believed. One hand clamped down over her mouth and yanked back her head, the other brought the dagger up to her windpipe. The stench of him was overwhelming.

She reached up with both hands and grabbed the blade with all her strength, pulling it away from her throat. She heard him cursing into her ear. Her fingers were slippery with blood, but she would not let go of the dagger. The hand over her mouth clenched more tightly, shutting off her air. Catelyn twisted her head to the side and managed to get a piece of his flesh between her teeth. She bit down hard into his palm. The man grunted in pain. She ground her teeth together and tore at him, and all of a sudden he let go. The taste of his blood filled her mouth. She sucked in air and screamed, and he grabbed her hair and pulled her away from him, and she stumbled and went down, and then he was standing over her, breathing hard, shaking. The dagger was still clutched tightly in his right hand, slick with blood. "You weren't s'posed to be here," he repeated stupidly.

Catelyn saw the shadow slip through the open door behind him. There was a low rumble, less than a snarl, the merest whisper of a threat, but he must have heard something, because he started to turn just as the wolf made its leap. They went down together, half sprawled over Catelyn where she'd fallen. The wolf had him under the jaw. The man's shriek lasted less than a second before the beast wrenched back its head, taking out half his throat.

His blood felt like warm rain as it sprayed across her face.

The wolf was looking at her. Its jaws were red and wet and its eyes glowed golden in the dark room. It was Bran's wolf, she realized. Of course it was. "Thank you," Catelyn whispered, her voice faint and tiny. She lifted her hand, trembling. The wolf padded closer, sniffed at her fingers, then licked at the blood with a wet rough tongue. When it had cleaned all the blood off her hand, it turned away silently and jumped up on Bran's bed and lay down beside him. Catelyn began to laugh hysterically.

That was the way they found them, when Robb and Maester Luwin and Ser Rodrik burst in with half the guards in Winterfell. When the laughter finally died in her throat, they wrapped her in warm blankets and led her back to the Great Keep, to her own chambers. Old Nan undressed her and helped her into a scalding hot bath and washed the blood off her with a soft cloth.

Afterward Maester Luwin arrived to dress her wounds. The cuts in her fingers went deep, almost to the bone, and her scalp was raw and bleeding where he'd pulled out a handful of hair. The maester told her the pain was just starting now, and gave her milk of the poppy to help her sleep.

Finally she closed her eyes.

When she opened them again, they told her that she had slept four days. Catelyn nodded and sat up in bed. It all seemed like a nightmare to her now, everything since Bran's fall, a terrible dream of blood and grief, but she had the pain in her hands to remind her that it was real. She felt weak and light-headed, yet strangely resolute, as if a great weight had lifted from her.

"Bring me some bread and honey," she told her servants, "and take word to Maester Luwin that my bandages want changing." They looked at her in surprise and ran to do her bidding.

Catelyn remembered the way she had been before, and she was ashamed. She had let them all down, her children, her husband, her House. It would not happen again. She would show these northerners how strong a Tully of Riverrun could be.

Robb arrived before her food. Rodrik Cassel came with him, and her husband's ward Theon Greyjoy, and lastly Hallis Mollen, a muscular guardsman with a square brown beard. He was the new captain of the guard, Robb said. Her son was dressed in boiled leather and ringmail, she saw, and a sword hung at his waist.

"Who was he?" Catelyn asked them.

"No one knows his name," Hallis Mollen told her. "He was no man of Winterfell, m'lady, but some says they seen him here and about the castle these past few weeks."

"One of the king's men, then," she said, "or one of the Lannisters'. He could have waited behind when the others left."

"Maybe," Hal said. "With all these strangers filling up Winterfell of late, there's no way of saying who he belonged to."

"He'd been hiding in your stables," Greyjoy said. "You could smell it on him."

"And how could he go unnoticed?" she said sharply.

Hallis Mollen looked abashed. "Between the horses Lord Eddard took south and them we sent north to the Night's Watch, the stalls were half-empty. It were no great trick to hide from the stableboys. Could be Hodor saw him, the talk is that boy's been acting queer, but simple as he is . . ." Hal shook his head.

"We found where he'd been sleeping," Robb put in.

"He had ninety silver stags in a leather bag buried beneath the straw."

"It's good to know my son's life was not sold cheaply," Catelyn said bitterly.

Hallis Mollen looked at her, confused. "Begging your grace, m'lady, you saying he was out to kill your *boy*?"

Greyjoy was doubtful. "That's madness."

"He came for Bran," Catelyn said. "He kept muttering how I wasn't supposed to be there. He set the library fire thinking I would rush to put it out, taking any guards with me. If I hadn't been half-mad with grief, it would have worked."

"Why would anyone want to kill Bran?" Robb said. "Gods, he's only a little boy, helpless, sleeping . . ."

Catelyn gave her firstborn a challenging look. "If you are to rule in the north, you must think these things through, Robb. Answer your own question. Why would anyone want to kill a sleeping child?"

Before he could answer, the servants returned with a plate of food fresh from the kitchen. There was much more than she'd asked for: hot bread, butter and honey and blackberry preserves, a rasher of bacon and a softboiled egg, a wedge of cheese, a pot of mint tea. And with it came Maester Luwin.

"How is my son, Maester?" Catelyn looked at all the food and found she had no appetite.

Maester Luwin lowered his eyes. "Unchanged, my lady."

It was the reply she had expected, no more and no less. Her hands throbbed with pain, as if the blade were still in her, cutting deep. She sent the servants away and looked back to Robb. "Do you have the answer yet?"

"Someone is afraid Bran might wake up," Robb said, "afraid of what he might say or do, afraid of something he knows."

Catelyn was proud of him. "Very good." She turned to the new captain of the guard. "We must keep Bran safe. If there was one killer, there could be others."

"How many guards do you want, m'lady?" Hal asked.

"So long as Lord Eddard is away, my son is the master of Winterfell," she told him.

Robb stood a little taller. "Put one man in the sickroom, night and day, one outside the door, two at the bottom of the stairs. No one sees Bran without my warrant or my mother's."

"As you say, m'lord."

"Do it now," Catelyn suggested.

"And let his wolf stay in the room with him," Robb added.

"Yes," Catelyn said. And then again: "Yes."

Hallis Mollen bowed and left the room.

"Lady Stark," Ser Rodrik said when the guardsman had gone, "did you chance to notice the dagger the killer used?"

"The circumstances did not allow me to examine it closely, but I can vouch for its edge," Catelyn replied with a dry smile. "Why do you ask?"

"We found the knife still in the villain's grasp. It seemed to me that it was altogether too fine a weapon for such a man, so I looked at it long and hard. The blade is Valyrian steel, the hilt dragonbone. A weapon like that has no business being in the hands of such as him. Someone gave it to him."

Catelyn nodded, thoughtful. "Robb, close the door."

He looked at her strangely, but did as she told him.

"What I am about to tell you must not leave this room," she told them. "I want your oaths on that. If even part of what I suspect is true, Ned and my girls have ridden into deadly danger, and a word in the wrong ears could mean their lives."

"Lord Eddard is a second father to me," said Theon Greyjoy. "I do so swear."

"You have my oath," Maester Luwin said.

"And mine, my lady," echoed Ser Rodrik.

She looked at her son. "And you, Robb?"

He nodded his consent.

"My sister Lysa believes the Lannisters murdered her husband, Lord Arryn, the Hand of the King," Catelyn told them. "It comes to me that Jaime Lannister did not join the hunt the day Bran fell. He remained here in the castle." The room was deathly quiet. "I do not think Bran fell from that tower," she said into the stillness. "I think he was thrown."

The shock was plain on their faces. "My lady, that is a monstrous suggestion," said Rodrik Cassel. "Even the

Kingslayer would flinch at the murder of an innocent child."

"Oh, would he?" Theon Greyjoy asked. "I wonder."

"There is no limit to Lannister pride or Lannister ambition," Catelyn said.

"The boy had always been surehanded in the past," Maester Luwin said thoughtfully. "He knew every stone in Winterfell."

"*Gods,*" Robb swore, his young face dark with anger. "If this is true, he will pay for it." He drew his sword and waved it in the air. "I'll kill him myself!"

Ser Rodrik bristled at him. "Put that away! The Lannisters are a hundred leagues away. *Never* draw your sword unless you mean to use it. How many times must I tell you, foolish boy?"

Abashed, Robb sheathed his sword, suddenly a child again. Catelyn said to Ser Rodrik, "I see my son is wearing steel now."

The old master-at-arms said, "I thought it was time."

Robb was looking at her anxiously. "Past time," she said. "Winterfell may have need of all its swords soon, and they had best not be made of wood."

Theon Greyjoy put a hand on the hilt of his blade and said, "My lady, if it comes to that, my House owes yours a great debt."

Maester Luwin pulled at his chain collar where it chafed against his neck. "All we have is conjecture. This is the queen's beloved brother we mean to accuse. She will not take it kindly. We must have proof, or forever keep silent."

"Your proof is in the dagger," Ser Rodrik said. "A fine blade like that will not have gone unnoticed."

There was only one place to find the truth of it, Catelyn realized. "Someone must go to King's Landing."

"I'll go," Robb said.

"No," she told him. "Your place is here. There must always be a Stark in Winterfell." She looked at Ser Rodrik with his great white whiskers, at Maester Luwin in his grey robes, at young Greyjoy, lean and dark and impetuous. Who to send? Who would be believed? Then she knew. Catelyn struggled to push back the blankets, her bandaged fingers as stiff and unyielding as stone. She climbed out of bed. "I must go myself."

"My lady," said Maester Luwin, "is that wise? Surely the Lannisters would greet your arrival with suspicion."

"What about Bran?" Robb asked. The poor boy looked utterly confused now. "You can't mean to leave him."

"I have done everything I can for Bran," she said, laying a wounded hand on his arm. "His life is in the hands of the gods and Maester Luwin. As you reminded me yourself, Robb, I have other children to think of now."

"You will need a strong escort, my lady," Theon said.

"I'll send Hal with a squad of guardsmen," Robb said.

"No," Catelyn said. "A large party attracts unwelcome attention. I would not have the Lannisters know I am coming."

Ser Rodrik protested. "My lady, let me accompany you at least. The kingsroad can be perilous for a woman alone."

"I will not be taking the kingsroad," Catelyn replied. She thought for a moment, then nodded her consent. "Two riders can move as fast as one, and a good deal faster than a long column burdened by wagons and wheelhouses. I will welcome your company, Ser Rodrik. We will follow the White Knife down to the sea, and hire a ship at White Harbor. Strong horses and brisk winds should bring us to King's Landing well ahead of Ned and the Lannisters." *And then,* she thought, *we shall see what we shall see.*

SANSA

Eddard Stark had left before dawn, Septa Mordane informed Sansa as they broke their fast. "The king sent for him. Another hunt, I do believe. There are still wild aurochs in these lands, I am told."

"I've never seen an aurochs," Sansa said, feeding a piece of bacon to Lady under the table. The direwolf took it from her hand, as delicate as a queen.

Septa Mordane sniffed in disapproval. "A noble lady does not feed dogs at her table," she said, breaking off another piece of comb and letting the honey drip down onto her bread.

"She's not a dog, she's a direwolf," Sansa pointed out as Lady licked her fingers with a rough tongue. "Anyway, Father said we could keep them with us if we want."

The septa was not appeased. "You're a good girl, Sansa, but I do vow, when it comes to that creature you're as willful as your sister Arya." She scowled. "And where is Arya this morning?"

"She wasn't hungry," Sansa said, knowing full well that her sister had probably stolen down to the kitchen hours ago and wheedled a breakfast out of some cook's boy.

"Do remind her to dress nicely today. The grey velvet, perhaps. We are all invited to ride with the queen and Princess Myrcella in the royal wheelhouse, and we must look our best."

Sansa already looked her best. She had brushed out her long auburn hair until it shone, and picked her nicest blue silks. She had been looking forward to today for more than a week. It was a great honor to ride with the queen, and besides, Prince Joffrey might be there. Her betrothed. Just thinking it made her feel a strange fluttering inside, even though they were not to marry for years and years. Sansa did not really *know* Joffrey yet, but she was already in love with him. He was all she ever dreamt her prince should be, tall and handsome and strong, with hair like gold. She treasured every chance to spend time with him, few as they were. The only thing that scared her about today was Arya. Arya had a way of ruining everything. You never knew what she would do. "I'll tell her," Sansa said uncertainly, "but she'll dress the way she always does." She hoped it wouldn't be too embarrassing. "May I be excused?"

"You may." Septa Mordane helped herself to more bread and honey, and Sansa slid from the bench. Lady followed at her heels as she ran from the inn's common room.

Outside, she stood for a moment amidst the shouts and curses and the creak of wooden wheels as the men broke down the tents and pavilions and loaded the wagons for another day's march. The inn was a sprawling three-story structure of pale stone, the biggest that Sansa had ever seen, but even so, it had accommodations for less than a third of the king's party, which had swollen to more than four hundred with the addition of her father's household and the freeriders who had joined them on the road.

She found Arya on the banks of the Trident, trying to hold Nymeria still while she brushed dried mud from her fur. The direwolf was not enjoying the process. Arya was wearing the same riding leathers she had worn yesterday and the day before.

"You better put on something pretty," Sansa told her. "Septa Mordane said so. We're traveling in the queen's wheelhouse with Princess Myrcella today."

"I'm not," Arya said, trying to brush a tangle out of Nymeria's matted grey fur. "Mycah and I are going to ride upstream and look for rubies at the ford."

"Rubies," Sansa said, lost. "What rubies?"

Arya gave her a look like she was so stupid. "*Rhaegar's* rubies. This is where King Robert killed him and won the crown."

Sansa regarded her scrawny little sister in disbelief. "You can't look for rubies, the princess is expecting us. The queen invited us both."

"I don't care," Arya said. "The wheelhouse doesn't even have *windows*, you can't see a thing."

"What could you want to see?" Sansa said, annoyed. She had been thrilled by the invitation, and her stupid sister was going to ruin everything, just as she'd feared. "It's all just fields and farms and holdfasts."

"It is *not*," Arya said stubbornly. "If you came with us sometimes, you'd see."

"I *hate* riding," Sansa said fervently. "All it does is get you soiled and dusty and sore."

Arya shrugged. "Hold *still*," she snapped at Nymeria, "I'm not hurting you." Then to Sansa she said, "When we were crossing the Neck, I counted thirty-six flowers I never saw before, and Mycah showed me a lizard-lion."

Sansa shuddered. They had been twelve days crossing the Neck, rumbling down a crooked causeway through an endless black bog, and she had hated every moment of it. The air had been damp and clammy, the causeway so narrow they could not even make proper camp at night, they had to stop right on the kingsroad. Dense thickets of half-drowned trees pressed close around them, branches dripping with curtains of pale fungus. Huge flowers bloomed in the mud and floated on pools of stagnant water, but if you were stupid enough to leave the causeway to pluck them, there were quicksands waiting to suck you down, and snakes watching from the trees, and lizard-lions floating half-submerged in the water, like black logs with eyes and teeth.

None of which stopped Arya, of course. One day she came back grinning her horsey grin, her hair all tangled and her clothes covered in mud, clutching a raggedy bunch of purple and green flowers for Father. Sansa kept hoping he would tell Arya to behave herself and act like the highborn lady she was supposed to be, but he never did, he only hugged her and thanked her for the flowers. That just made her worse.

Then it turned out the purple flowers were called *poison kisses,* and Arya got a rash on her arms. Sansa would have thought that might have taught her a lesson, but Arya laughed about it, and the next day she rubbed *mud* all over her arms like some ignorant bog woman just because her friend Mycah told her it would stop the itching. She had bruises on her arms and shoulders too, dark purple welts and faded green-and-yellow splotches; Sansa had seen them when her sister undressed for sleep. How she had gotten *those* only the seven gods knew.

Arya was still going on, brushing out Nymeria's tangles and chattering about things she'd seen on the trek south. "Last week we found this haunted watchtower, and the day before we chased a herd of wild horses. You should have seen them run when they caught a scent of Nymeria." The wolf wriggled in her grasp and Arya scolded her. "Stop that, I have to do the other side, you're all muddy."

"You're not supposed to leave the column," Sansa reminded her. "Father said so."

Arya shrugged. "I didn't go far. Anyway, Nymeria was with me the whole time. I don't always go off, either. Sometimes it's fun just to ride along with the wagons and talk to people."

Sansa knew all about the sorts of people Arya liked to talk to: squires and grooms and serving girls, old men and naked children, rough-spoken freeriders of uncertain birth. Arya would make friends with *anybody.* This Mycah was the worst; a butcher's boy, thirteen and wild, he slept in the meat wagon and smelled of the slaughtering block. Just the sight of him was enough to make Sansa feel sick, but Arya seemed to prefer his company to hers.

Sansa was running out of patience now. "You have to come with me," she told her sister firmly. "You can't refuse the queen. Septa Mordane will expect you."

Arya ignored her. She gave a hard yank with the brush. Nymeria growled and spun away, affronted. "Come *back* here!"

"There's going to be lemon cakes and tea," Sansa went on, all adult and reasonable. Lady brushed against her leg.

Sansa scratched her ears the way she liked, and Lady sat beside her on her haunches, watching Arya chase Nymeria. "Why would you want to ride a smelly old horse and get all sore and sweaty when you could recline on feather pillows and eat cakes with the queen?"

"I don't like the queen," Arya said casually. Sansa sucked in her breath, shocked that even *Arya* would say such a thing, but her sister prattled on, heedless. "She won't even let me bring Nymeria." She thrust the brush under her belt and stalked her wolf. Nymeria watched her approach warily.

"A royal wheelhouse is no place for a *wolf*," Sansa said. "And Princess Myrcella is afraid of them, you know that."

"Myrcella is a little baby." Arya grabbed Nymeria around her neck, but the moment she pulled out the brush again the direwolf wriggled free and bounded off. Frustrated, Arya threw down the brush. "*Bad* wolf!" she shouted.

Sansa couldn't help but smile a little. The kennelmaster once told her that an animal takes after its master. She gave Lady a quick little hug. Lady licked her cheek. Sansa giggled. Arya heard and whirled around, glaring. "I don't care what you say, I'm going out riding." Her long horsey face got the stubborn look that meant she was going to do something willful.

"Gods be true, Arya, sometimes you act like such a *child*," Sansa said. "I'll go by myself then. It will be ever so much nicer that way. Lady and I will eat all the lemon cakes and just have the best time without you."

She turned to walk off, but Arya shouted after her, "They won't let you bring Lady either." She was gone before Sansa could think of a reply, chasing Nymeria along the river.

Alone and humiliated, Sansa took the long way back to the inn, where she knew Septa Mordane would be waiting. Lady padded quietly by her side. She was almost in tears. All she wanted was for things to be nice and pretty, the way they were in the songs. Why couldn't Arya be sweet and delicate and kind, like Princess Myrcella? She would have liked a sister like that.

Sansa could never understand how two sisters, born only two years apart, could be so different. It would have been easier if Arya had been a bastard, like their half brother Jon. She even *looked* like Jon, with the long face and brown hair of the Starks, and nothing of their lady mother in her face or her coloring. And Jon's mother had been *common*, or so people whispered. Once, when she was littler, Sansa had even asked Mother if perhaps there hadn't been some mistake. Perhaps the grumkins had stolen her *real* sister. But Mother had only laughed and said no, Arya was her daughter and Sansa's trueborn sister, blood of their blood. Sansa could not think why Mother would want to lie about it, so she supposed it had to be true.

As she neared the center of camp, her distress was quickly forgotten. A crowd had gathered around the queen's wheelhouse. Sansa heard excited voices buzzing like a hive of bees. The doors had been thrown open, she saw, and the queen stood at the top of the wooden steps, smiling down at someone. She heard her saying, "The council does us great honor, my good lords."

"What's happening?" she asked a squire she knew.

"The council sent riders from King's Landing to escort us the rest of the way," he told her. "An honor guard for the king."

Anxious to see, Sansa let Lady clear a path through the crowd. People moved aside hastily for the direwolf. When she got closer, she saw two knights kneeling before the queen, in armor so fine and gorgeous that it made her blink.

One knight wore an intricate suit of white enameled scales, brilliant as a field of new-fallen snow, with silver chasings and clasps that glittered in the sun. When he removed his helm, Sansa saw that he was an old man with hair as pale as his armor, yet he seemed strong and graceful for all that. From his shoulders hung the pure white cloak of the Kingsguard.

His companion was a man near twenty whose armor was steel plate of a deep forest-green. He was the handsomest man Sansa had ever set eyes upon; tall and powerfully made, with jet-black hair that fell to his shoulders and framed a clean-shaven face, and laughing green eyes to match his armor. Cradled under one arm was an antlered helm, its magnificent rack shimmering in gold.

At first Sansa did not notice the third stranger. He did

not kneel with the others. He stood to one side, beside their horses, a gaunt grim man who watched the proceedings in silence. His face was pockmarked and beardless, with deepset eyes and hollow cheeks. Though he was not an old man, only a few wisps of hair remained to him, sprouting above his ears, but those he had grown long as a woman's. His armor was iron-grey chainmail over layers of boiled leather, plain and unadorned, and it spoke of age and hard use. Above his right shoulder the stained leather hilt of the blade strapped to his back was visible; a two-handed greatsword, too long to be worn at his side.

"The king is gone hunting, but I know he will be pleased to see you when he returns," the queen was saying to the two knights who knelt before her, but Sansa could not take her eyes off the third man. He seemed to feel the weight of her gaze. Slowly he turned his head. Lady growled. A terror as overwhelming as anything Sansa Stark had ever felt filled her suddenly. She stepped backward and bumped into someone.

Strong hands grasped her by the shoulders, and for a moment Sansa thought it was her father, but when she turned, it was the burned face of Sandor Clegane looking down at her, his mouth twisted in a terrible mockery of a smile. "You are shaking, girl," he said, his voice rasping. "Do I frighten you so much?"

He did, and had since she had first laid eyes on the ruin that fire had made of his face, though it seemed to her now that he was not half so terrifying as the other. Still, Sansa wrenched away from him, and the Hound laughed, and Lady moved between them, rumbling a warning. Sansa dropped to her knees to wrap her arms around the wolf. They were all gathered around gaping, she could feel their eyes on her, and here and there she heard muttered comments and titters of laughter.

"A wolf," a man said, and someone else said, "Seven hells, that's a direwolf," and the first man said, "What's it doing in camp?" and the Hound's rasping voice replied, "The Starks use them for wet nurses," and Sansa realized that the two stranger knights were looking down on her and Lady, swords in their hands, and then she was frightened again, and ashamed. Tears filled her eyes.

She heard the queen say, "Joffrey, go to her."

And her prince was there.

"Leave her alone," Joffrey said. He stood over her, beautiful in blue wool and black leather, his golden curls shining in the sun like a crown. He gave her his hand, drew her to her feet. "What is it, sweet lady? Why are you afraid? No one will hurt you. Put away your swords, all of you. The wolf is her little pet, that's all." He looked at Sandor Clegane. "And you, dog, away with you, you're scaring my betrothed."

The Hound, ever faithful, bowed and slid away quietly through the press. Sansa struggled to steady herself. She felt like such a fool. She was a Stark of Winterfell, a noble lady, and someday she would be a queen. "It was not him, my sweet prince," she tried to explain. "It was the other one."

The two stranger knights exchanged a look. "Payne?" chuckled the young man in the green armor.

The older man in white spoke to Sansa gently. "Ofttimes Ser Ilyn frightens me as well, sweet lady. He has a fearsome aspect."

"As well he should." The queen had descended from the wheelhouse. The spectators parted to make way for her. "If the wicked do not fear the King's Justice, you have put the wrong man in the office."

Sansa finally found her words. "Then surely you have chosen the right one, Your Grace," she said, and a gale of laughter erupted all around her.

"Well spoken, child," said the old man in white. "As befits the daughter of Eddard Stark. I am honored to know you, however irregular the manner of our meeting. I am Ser Barristan Selmy, of the Kingsguard." He bowed.

Sansa knew the name, and now the courtesies that Septa Mordane had taught her over the years came back to her. "The Lord Commander of the Kingsguard," she said, "and councillor to Robert our king and to Aerys Targaryen before him. The honor is mine, good knight. Even in the far north, the singers praise the deeds of Barristan the Bold."

The green knight laughed again. "Barristan the Old, you mean. Don't flatter him too sweetly, child, he thinks overmuch of himself already." He smiled at her. "Now, wolf girl, if you can put a name to me as well, then I must concede that you are truly our Hand's daughter."

Joffrey stiffened beside her. "Have a care how you address my betrothed."

"I can answer," Sansa said quickly, to quell her prince's anger. She smiled at the green knight. "Your helmet bears golden antlers, my lord. The stag is the sigil of the royal House. King Robert has two brothers. By your extreme youth, you can only be Renly Baratheon, Lord of Storm's End and councillor to the king, and so I name you."

Ser Barristan chuckled. "By his extreme youth, he can only be a prancing jackanapes, and so *I* name him."

There was general laughter, led by Lord Renly himself. The tension of a few moments ago was gone, and Sansa was beginning to feel comfortable . . . until Ser Ilyn Payne shouldered two men aside, and stood before her, unsmiling. He did not say a word. Lady bared her teeth and began to growl, a low rumble full of menace, but this time Sansa silenced the wolf with a gentle hand to the head. "I am sorry if I offended you, Ser Ilyn," she said.

She waited for an answer, but none came. As the headsman looked at her, his pale colorless eyes seemed to strip the clothes away from her, and then the skin, leaving her soul naked before him. Still silent, he turned and walked away.

Sansa did not understand. She looked at her prince. "Did I say something wrong, Your Grace? Why will he not speak to me?"

"Ser Ilyn has not been feeling talkative these past fourteen years," Lord Renly commented with a sly smile.

Joffrey gave his uncle a look of pure loathing, then took Sansa's hands in his own. "Aerys Targaryen had his tongue ripped out with hot pincers."

"He speaks most eloquently with his sword, however," the queen said, "and his devotion to our realm is unquestioned." Then she smiled graciously and said, "Sansa, the good councillors and I must speak together until the king returns with your father. I fear we shall have to postpone your day with Myrcella. Please give your sweet sister my apologies. Joffrey, perhaps you would be so kind as to entertain our guest today."

"It would be my pleasure, Mother," Joffrey said very formally. He took her by the arm and led her away from the wheelhouse, and Sansa's spirits took flight. A whole day with her prince! She gazed at Joffrey worshipfully. He was so gallant, she thought. The way he had rescued her from Ser Ilyn and the Hound, why, it was almost like the songs, like the time Serwyn of the Mirror Shield saved the Princess Daeryssa from the giants, or Prince Aemon the Dragonknight championing Queen Naerys's honor against evil Ser Morgil's slanders.

The touch of Joffrey's hand on her sleeve made her heart beat faster. "What would you like to do?"

Be with you, Sansa thought, but she said, "Whatever you'd like to do, my prince."

Joffrey reflected a moment. "We could go riding."

"Oh, I *love* riding," Sansa said.

Joffrey glanced back at Lady, who was following at their heels. "Your wolf is liable to frighten the horses, and my dog seems to frighten you. Let us leave them both behind and set off on our own, what do you say?"

Sansa hesitated. "If you like," she said uncertainly. "I suppose I could tie Lady up." She did not quite understand, though. "I didn't know you had a dog . . ."

Joffrey laughed. "He's my mother's dog, in truth. She has set him to guard me, and so he does."

"You mean the Hound," she said. She wanted to hit herself for being so slow. Her prince would never love her if she seemed stupid. "Is it safe to leave him behind?"

Prince Joffrey looked annoyed that she would even ask. "Have no fear, lady. I am almost a man grown, and I don't fight with wood like your brothers. All I need is this." He drew his sword and showed it to her; a longsword adroitly shrunken to suit a boy of twelve, gleaming blue steel, castle-forged and double-edged, with a leather grip and a lion's-head pommel in gold. Sansa exclaimed over it admiringly, and Joffrey looked pleased. "I call it Lion's Tooth," he said.

And so they left her direwolf and his bodyguard behind them, while they ranged east along the north bank of the Trident with no company save Lion's Tooth.

It was a glorious day, a magical day. The air was warm and heavy with the scent of flowers, and the woods here had a gentle beauty that Sansa had never seen in the north. Prince Joffrey's mount was a blood bay courser, swift as the wind, and he rode it with reckless abandon, so fast that Sansa was hard-pressed to keep up on her mare. It was a day for adventures. They explored the caves by the riverbank, and tracked a shadowcat to its lair, and when they grew hungry, Joffrey found a holdfast by its smoke and told them to fetch food and wine for their prince and his lady. They dined on trout fresh from the river, and Sansa drank more wine than she had ever drunk before. "My father only lets us have one cup, and only at feasts," she confessed to her prince.

"My betrothed can drink as much as she wants," Joffrey said, refilling her cup.

They went more slowly after they had eaten. Joffrey sang for her as they rode, his voice high and sweet and pure. Sansa was a little dizzy from the wine. "Shouldn't we be starting back?" she asked.

"Soon," Joffrey said. "The battleground is right up ahead, where the river bends. That was where my father killed Rhaegar Targaryen, you know. He smashed in his chest, *crunch*, right through the armor." Joffrey swung an imaginary warhammer to show her how it was done. "Then my uncle Jaime killed old Aerys, and my father was king. What's that sound?"

Sansa heard it too, floating through the woods, a kind of wooden clattering, *snack snack snack*. "I don't know," she said. It made her nervous, though. "Joffrey, let's go back."

"I want to see what it is." Joffrey turned his horse in the direction of the sounds, and Sansa had no choice but to follow. The noises grew louder and more distinct, the *clack* of wood on wood, and as they grew closer they heard heavy breathing as well, and now and then a grunt.

"Someone's there," Sansa said anxiously. She found herself thinking of Lady, wishing the direwolf was with her.

"You're safe with me." Joffrey drew his Lion's Tooth from its sheath. The sound of steel on leather made her tremble. "This way," he said, riding through a stand of trees.

Beyond, in a clearing overlooking the river, they came upon a boy and a girl playing at knights. Their swords were wooden sticks, broom handles from the look of them, and they were rushing across the grass, swinging at each other lustily. The boy was years older, a head taller, and much stronger, and he was pressing the attack. The girl, a scrawny thing in soiled leathers, was dodging and managing to get her stick in the way of most of the boy's blows, but not all. When she tried to lunge at him, he caught her stick with his own, swept it aside, and slid his wood down hard on her fingers. She cried out and lost her weapon.

Prince Joffrey laughed. The boy looked around, wide-eyed and startled, and dropped his stick in the grass. The girl glared at them, sucking on her knuckles to take the sting out, and Sansa was horrified. *"Arya?"* she called out incredulously.

"Go away," Arya shouted back at them, angry tears in her eyes. "What are you doing here? Leave us alone."

Joffrey glanced from Arya to Sansa and back again. "Your sister?" She nodded, blushing. Joffrey examined the boy, an ungainly lad with a coarse, freckled face and thick red hair. "And who are you, boy?" he asked in a commanding tone that took no notice of the fact that the other was a year his senior.

"Mycah," the boy muttered. He recognized the prince and averted his eyes. "M'lord."

"He's the butcher's boy," Sansa said.

"He's my friend," Arya said sharply. "You leave him alone."

"A butcher's boy who wants to be a knight, is it?" Joffrey swung down from his mount, sword in hand. "Pick up your sword, butcher's boy," he said, his eyes bright with amusement. "Let us see how good you are."

Mycah stood there, frozen with fear.

Joffrey walked toward him. "Go on, pick it up. Or do you only fight little girls?"

"She ast me to, m'lord," Mycah said. "She *ast* me to."

Sansa had only to glance at Arya and see the flush on her sister's face to know the boy was telling the truth, but Joffrey was in no mood to listen. The wine had made him wild. "Are you going to pick up your sword?"

Mycah shook his head. "It's only a stick, m'lord. It's not no sword, it's only a stick."

"And you're only a butcher's boy, and no knight." Joffrey lifted Lion's Tooth and laid its point on Mycah's cheek below the eye, as the butcher's boy stood trembling. "That was my lady's sister you were hitting, do you know that?" A bright bud of blood blossomed where his sword pressed into Mycah's flesh, and a slow red line trickled down the boy's cheek.

"*Stop it!*" Arya screamed. She grabbed up her fallen stick.

Sansa was afraid. "Arya, you stay out of this."

"I won't hurt him . . . much," Prince Joffrey told Arya, never taking his eyes off the butcher's boy.

Arya went for him.

Sansa slid off her mare, but she was too slow. Arya swung with both hands. There was a loud *crack* as the wood split against the back of the prince's head, and then everything happened at once before Sansa's horrified eyes. Joffrey staggered and whirled around, roaring curses. Mycah ran for the trees as fast as his legs would take him. Arya swung at the prince again, but this time Joffrey caught the blow on Lion's Tooth and sent her broken stick flying from her hands. The back of his head was all bloody and his eyes were on fire. Sansa was shrieking, "No, no, stop it, stop it, both of you, you're spoiling it," but no one was listening. Arya scooped up a rock and hurled it at Joffrey's head. She hit his horse instead, and the blood bay reared and went galloping off after Mycah. "*Stop it, don't, stop it!*" Sansa screamed. Joffrey slashed at Arya with his sword, screaming obscenities, terrible words, filthy words. Arya darted back, frightened now, but Joffrey followed, hounding her toward the woods, backing her up against a tree. Sansa didn't know what to do. She watched helplessly, almost blind from her tears.

Then a grey blur flashed past her, and suddenly Nymeria was there, leaping, jaws closing around Joffrey's sword arm. The steel fell from his fingers as the wolf knocked him off his feet, and they rolled in the grass, the wolf snarling and ripping at him, the prince shrieking in pain. "Get it *off*," he screamed. "Get it *off!*"

Arya's voice cracked like a whip. "*Nymeria!*"

The direwolf let go of Joffrey and moved to Arya's side. The prince lay in the grass, whimpering, cradling his mangled arm. His shirt was soaked in blood. Arya said, "She didn't hurt you . . . much." She picked up Lion's Tooth where it had fallen, and stood over him, holding the sword with both hands.

Joffrey made a scared whimpery sound as he looked up

at her. "No," he said, "don't hurt me. I'll tell my mother."

"You leave him alone!" Sansa screamed at her sister.

Arya whirled and heaved the sword into the air, putting her whole body into the throw. The blue steel flashed in the sun as the sword spun out over the river. It hit the water and vanished with a splash. Joffrey moaned. Arya ran off to her horse, Nymeria loping at her heels.

After they had gone, Sansa went to Prince Joffrey. His eyes were closed in pain, his breath ragged. Sansa knelt beside him. "Joffrey," she sobbed. "Oh, look what they did, look what they did. My poor prince. Don't be afraid. I'll ride to the holdfast and bring help for you." Tenderly she reached out and brushed back his soft blond hair.

His eyes snapped open and looked at her, and there was nothing but loathing there, nothing but the vilest contempt. "Then *go,*" he spit at her. "And *don't touch me.*"

EDDARD

"They've found her, my lord."

Ned rose quickly. "Our men or Lannister's?"

"It was Jory," his steward Vayon Poole replied. "She's not been harmed."

"Thank the gods," Ned said. His men had been searching for Arya for four days now, but the queen's men had been out hunting as well. "Where is she? Tell Jory to bring her here at once."

"I am sorry, my lord," Poole told him. "The guards on the gate were Lannister men, and they informed the queen when Jory brought her in. She's being taken directly before the king . . ."

"*Damn* that woman!" Ned said, striding to the door. "Find Sansa and bring her to the audience chamber. Her voice may be needed." He descended the tower steps in a red rage. He had led searches himself for the first three days, and had scarcely slept an hour since Arya had disappeared. This morning he had been so heartsick and weary he could scarcely stand, but now his fury was on him, filling him with strength.

Men called out to him as he crossed the castle yard, but Ned ignored them in his haste. He would have run, but he was still the King's Hand, and a Hand must keep his dignity. He was aware of the eyes that followed him, of the muttered voices wondering what he would do.

The castle was a modest holding a half day's ride south of the Trident. The royal party had made themselves the uninvited guests of its lord, Ser Raymun Darry, while the hunt for Arya and the butcher's boy was conducted on both sides of the river. They were not welcome visitors. Ser Raymun lived under the king's peace, but his family had fought beneath Rhaegar's dragon banners at the Trident, and his three older brothers had died there, a truth neither Robert nor Ser Raymun had forgotten. With king's men, Darry men, Lannister men, and Stark men all crammed into a castle far too small for them, tensions burned hot and heavy.

The king had appropriated Ser Raymun's audience chamber, and that was where Ned found them. The room was crowded when he burst in. Too crowded, he thought; left alone, he and Robert might have been able to settle the matter amicably.

Robert was slumped in Darry's high seat at the far end of the room, his face closed and sullen. Cersei Lannister and her son stood beside him. The queen had her hand on Joffrey's shoulder. Thick silken bandages still covered the boy's arm.

Arya stood in the center of the room, alone but for Jory Cassel, every eye upon her. "Arya," Ned called loudly. He went to her, his boots ringing on the stone floor. When she saw him, she cried out and began to sob.

Ned went to one knee and took her in his arms. She was shaking. "I'm sorry," she sobbed, "I'm sorry, I'm sorry."

"I know," he said. She felt so tiny in his arms, nothing but a scrawny little girl. It was hard to see how she had caused so much trouble. "Are you hurt?"

"No." Her face was dirty, and her tears left pink tracks down her cheeks. "Hungry some. I ate some berries, but there was nothing else."

"We'll feed you soon enough," Ned promised. He rose to face the king. "What is the meaning of this?" His eyes swept the room, searching for friendly faces. But for his own men, they were few enough. Ser Raymun Darry guarded his look well. Lord Renly wore a half smile that might mean anything, and old Ser Barristan was grave; the rest were Lannister men, and hostile. Their only good fortune was that both Jaime Lannister and Sandor Clegane were missing, leading searches north of the Trident. "Why was I not told that my daughter had been found?" Ned demanded, his voice ringing. "Why was she not brought to me at once?"

He spoke to Robert, but it was Cersei Lannister who answered. "How *dare* you speak to your king in that manner!"

At that, the king stirred. "Quiet, woman," he snapped. He straightened in his seat. "I am sorry, Ned. I never meant to frighten the girl. It seemed best to bring her here and get the business done with quickly."

"And what business is that?" Ned put ice in his voice.

The queen stepped forward. "You know full well, Stark. This girl of yours attacked my son. Her and her butcher's boy. That animal of hers tried to tear his arm off."

"That's not true," Arya said loudly. "She just bit him a little. He was hurting Mycah."

"Joff told us what happened," the queen said. "You and the butcher boy beat him with clubs while you set your wolf on him."

"That's not how it was," Arya said, close to tears again. Ned put a hand on her shoulder.

"Yes it is!" Prince Joffrey insisted. "They all attacked me, and she threw Lion's Tooth in the river!" Ned noticed that he did not so much as glance at Arya as he spoke.

"Liar!" Arya yelled.

"Shut up!" the prince yelled back.

"Enough!" the king roared, rising from his seat, his voice thick with irritation. Silence fell. He glowered at Arya through his thick beard. "Now, child, you will tell me what happened. Tell it all, and tell it true. It is a great crime to lie to a king." Then he looked over at his son. "When she is done, you will have your turn. Until then, hold your tongue."

As Arya began her story, Ned heard the door open behind him. He glanced back and saw Vayon Poole enter with Sansa. They stood quietly at the back of the hall as Arya spoke. When she got to the part where she threw Joffrey's sword into the middle of the Trident, Renly

Baratheon began to laugh. The king bristled. "Ser Barristan, escort my brother from the hall before he chokes."

Lord Renly stifled his laughter. "My brother is too kind. I can find the door myself." He bowed to Joffrey. "Perchance later you'll tell me how a nine-year-old girl the size of a wet rat managed to disarm you with a broom handle and throw your sword in the river." As the door swung shut behind him, Ned heard him say, "Lion's Tooth," and guffaw once more.

Prince Joffrey was pale as he began his very different version of events. When his son was done talking, the king rose heavily from his seat, looking like a man who wanted to be anywhere but here. "What in all the seven hells am I supposed to make of this? He says one thing, she says another."

"They were not the only ones present," Ned said. "Sansa, come here." Ned had heard her version of the story the night Arya had vanished. He knew the truth. "Tell us what happened."

His eldest daughter stepped forward hesitantly. She was dressed in blue velvets trimmed with white, a silver chain around her neck. Her thick auburn hair had been brushed until it shone. She blinked at her sister, then at the young prince. "I don't know," she said tearfully, looking as though she wanted to bolt. "I don't remember. Everything happened so fast, I didn't see . . ."

"*You rotten!*" Arya shrieked. She flew at her sister like an arrow, knocking Sansa down to the ground, pummeling her. "Liar, liar, liar, liar."

"Arya, *stop it!*" Ned shouted. Jory pulled her off her sister, kicking. Sansa was pale and shaking as Ned lifted her back to her feet. "Are you hurt?" he asked, but she was staring at Arya, and she did not seem to hear.

"The girl is as wild as that filthy animal of hers," Cersei Lannister said. "Robert, I want her punished."

"Seven hells," Robert swore. "Cersei, look at her. She's a child. What would you have me do, whip her through the streets? Damn it, children fight. It's over. No lasting harm was done."

The queen was furious. "Joff will carry those scars for the rest of his life."

Robert Baratheon looked at his eldest son. "So he will.

Perhaps they will teach him a lesson. Ned, see that your daughter is disciplined. I will do the same with my son."

"Gladly, Your Grace," Ned said with vast relief.

Robert started to walk away, but the queen was not done. "And what of the direwolf?" she called after him. "What of the beast that savaged your son?"

The king stopped, turned back, frowned. "I'd forgotten about the damned wolf."

Ned could see Arya tense in Jory's arms. Jory spoke up quickly. "We found no trace of the direwolf, Your Grace."

Robert did not look unhappy. "No? So be it."

The queen raised her voice. "A hundred golden dragons to the man who brings me its skin!"

"A costly pelt," Robert grumbled. "I want no part of this, woman. You can damn well buy your furs with Lannister gold."

The queen regarded him coolly. "I had not thought you so niggardly. The king I'd thought to wed would have laid a wolfskin across my bed before the sun went down."

Robert's face darkened with anger. "That would be a fine trick, without a wolf."

"We have a wolf," Cersei Lannister said. Her voice was very quiet, but her green eyes shone with triumph.

It took them all a moment to comprehend her words, but when they did, the king shrugged irritably. "As you will. Have Ser Ilyn see to it."

"Robert, you cannot mean this," Ned protested.

The king was in no mood for more argument. "Enough, Ned, I will hear no more. A direwolf is a savage beast. Sooner or later it would have turned on your girl the same way the other did on my son. Get her a dog, she'll be happier for it."

That was when Sansa finally seemed to comprehend. Her eyes were frightened as they went to her father. "He doesn't mean Lady, does he?" She saw the truth on his face. "No," she said. "No, not Lady, Lady didn't bite anybody, she's good . . ."

"Lady wasn't there," Arya shouted angrily. "You leave her alone!"

"Stop them," Sansa pleaded, "don't let them do it, please, please, it wasn't Lady, it was Nymeria, Arya did it, you can't, it wasn't Lady, don't let them hurt Lady, I'll make her be good, I promise, I promise . . ." She started to cry.

All Ned could do was take her in his arms and hold her while she wept. He looked across the room at Robert. His old friend, closer than any brother. "Please, Robert. For the love you bear me. For the love you bore my sister. Please."

The king looked at them for a long moment, then turned his eyes on his wife. "Damn you, Cersei," he said with loathing.

Ned stood, gently disengaging himself from Sansa's grasp. All the weariness of the past four days had returned to him. "Do it yourself then, Robert," he said in a voice cold and sharp as steel. "At least have the courage to do it yourself."

Robert looked at Ned with flat, dead eyes and left without a word, his footsteps heavy as lead. Silence filled the hall.

"Where is the direwolf?" Cersei Lannister asked when her husband was gone. Beside her, Prince Joffrey was smiling.

"The beast is chained up outside the gatehouse, Your Grace," Ser Barristan Selmy answered reluctantly.

"Send for Ilyn Payne."

"No," Ned said. "Jory, take the girls back to their rooms and bring me Ice." The words tasted of bile in his throat, but he forced them out. "If it must be done, I will do it."

Cersei Lannister regarded him suspiciously. "You, Stark? Is this some trick? Why would you do such a thing?"

They were all staring at him, but it was Sansa's look that cut. "She is of the north. She deserves better than a butcher."

He left the room with his eyes burning and his daughter's wails echoing in his ears, and found the direwolf pup where they chained her. Ned sat beside her for a while. "Lady," he said, tasting the name. He had never paid much attention to the names the children had picked, but looking at her now, he knew that Sansa had chosen well. She was the smallest of the litter, the prettiest, the most gentle and trusting. She looked at him with bright golden eyes, and he ruffled her thick grey fur.

Shortly, Jory brought him Ice.

When it was over, he said, "Choose four men and have them take the body north. Bury her at Winterfell."

"All that way?" Jory said, astonished.

"All that way," Ned affirmed. "The Lannister woman shall never have *this* skin."

He was walking back to the tower to give himself up to sleep at last when Sandor Clegane and his riders came pounding through the castle gate, back from their hunt.

There was something slung over the back of his destrier, a heavy shape wrapped in a bloody cloak. "No sign of your daughter, Hand," the Hound rasped down, "but the day was not wholly wasted. We got her little pet." He reached back and shoved the burden off, and it fell with a thump in front of Ned.

Bending, Ned pulled back the cloak, dreading the words he would have to find for Arya, but it was not Nymeria after all. It was the butcher's boy, Mycah, his body covered in dried blood. He had been cut almost in half from shoulder to waist by some terrible blow struck from above.

"You rode him down," Ned said.

The Hound's eyes seemed to glitter through the steel of that hideous dog's-head helm. "He ran." He looked at Ned's face and laughed. "But not very fast."

BRAN

It seemed as though he had been falling for years.

Fly, a voice whispered in the darkness, but Bran did not know how to fly, so all he could do was fall.

Maester Luwin made a little boy of clay, baked him till he was hard and brittle, dressed him in Bran's clothes, and flung him off a roof. Bran remembered the way he shattered. "But I never fall," he said, falling.

The ground was so far below him he could barely make it out through the grey mists that whirled around him, but he could feel how fast he was falling, and he knew what was waiting for him down there. Even in dreams, you could not fall forever. He would wake up in the instant before he hit the ground, he knew. You always woke up in the instant before you hit the ground.

And if you don't? the voice asked.

The ground was closer now, still far far away, a thousand miles away, but closer than it had been. It was cold here in the darkness. There was no sun, no stars, only the ground below coming up to smash him, and the grey mists, and the whispering voice. He wanted to cry.

Not cry. Fly.

"I can't fly," Bran said. "I can't, I can't . . ."

How do you know? Have you ever tried?

The voice was high and thin. Bran looked around to see where it was coming from. A crow was spiraling down with him, just out of reach, following him as he fell. "Help me," he said.

I'm trying, the crow replied. *Say, got any corn?*

Bran reached into his pocket as the darkness spun dizzily around him. When he pulled his hand out, golden kernels slid from between his fingers into the air. They fell with him.

The crow landed on his hand and began to eat.

"Are you really a crow?" Bran asked.

Are you really falling? the crow asked back.

"It's just a dream," Bran said.

Is it? asked the crow.

"I'll wake up when I hit the ground," Bran told the bird.

You'll die when you hit the ground, the crow said. It went back to eating corn.

Bran looked down. He could see mountains now, their peaks white with snow, and the silver thread of rivers in dark woods. He closed his eyes and began to cry.

That won't do any good, the crow said. *I told you, the answer is flying, not crying. How hard can it be? I'm doing it.* The crow took to the air and flapped around Bran's hand.

"You have wings," Bran pointed out.

Maybe you do too.

Bran felt along his shoulders, groping for feathers.

There are different kinds of wings, the crow said.

Bran was staring at his arms, his legs. He was so skinny, just skin stretched taut over bones. Had he always been so thin? He tried to remember. A face swam up at him out of the grey mist, shining with light, golden. "The things I do for love," it said.

Bran screamed.

The crow took to the air, cawing. *Not that,* it shrieked at him. *Forget that, you do not need it now, put it aside, put it away.* It landed on Bran's shoulder, and pecked at him, and the shining golden face was gone.

Bran was falling faster than ever. The grey mists howled around him as he plunged toward the earth below. "What are you doing to me?" he asked the crow, tearful.

Teaching you how to fly.

"I can't fly!"

You're flying right now.

"I'm *falling!*"

Every flight begins with a fall, the crow said. *Look down.*

"I'm afraid . . ."

LOOK DOWN!

Bran looked down, and felt his insides turn to water. The ground was rushing up at him now. The whole world was spread out below him, a tapestry of white and brown and green. He could see everything so clearly that for a moment he forgot to be afraid. He could see the whole realm, and everyone in it.

He saw Winterfell as the eagles see it, the tall towers looking squat and stubby from above, the castle walls just lines in the dirt. He saw Maester Luwin on his balcony, studying the sky through a polished bronze tube and frowning as he made notes in a book. He saw his brother Robb, taller and stronger than he remembered him, practicing swordplay in the yard with real steel in his hand. He saw Hodor, the simple giant from the stables, carrying an anvil to Mikken's forge, hefting it onto his shoulder as easily as another man might heft a bale of hay. At the heart of the godswood, the great white weirwood brooded over its reflection in the black pool, its leaves rustling in a chill wind. When it felt Bran watching, it lifted its eyes from the still waters and stared back at him knowingly.

He looked east, and saw a galley racing across the waters of the Bite. He saw his mother sitting alone in a cabin, looking at a bloodstained knife on a table in front of her, as the rowers pulled at their oars and Ser Rodrik leaned across a rail, shaking and heaving. A storm was gathering ahead of them, a vast dark roaring lashed by lightning, but somehow they could not see it.

He looked south, and saw the great blue-green rush of the Trident. He saw his father pleading with the king, his face etched with grief. He saw Sansa crying herself to sleep at night, and he saw Arya watching in silence and holding her secrets hard in her heart. There were shadows all around them. One shadow was dark as ash, with the terrible face of a hound. Another was armored like the sun, golden and beautiful. Over them both loomed a giant in armor made of stone, but when he opened his visor, there was nothing inside but darkness and thick black blood.

He lifted his eyes and saw clear across the narrow sea, to the Free Cities and the green Dothraki sea and beyond, to Vaes Dothrak under its mountain, to the fabled lands of the Jade Sea, to Asshai by the Shadow, where dragons stirred beneath the sunrise.

Finally he looked north. He saw the Wall shining like blue crystal, and his bastard brother Jon sleeping alone in a cold bed, his skin growing pale and hard as the memory of all warmth fled from him. And he looked past the Wall, past endless forests cloaked in snow, past the frozen shore and the great blue-white rivers of ice and the dead plains where nothing grew or lived. North and north and north he looked, to the curtain of light at the end of the world, and then beyond that curtain. He looked deep into the heart of winter, and then he cried out, afraid, and the heat of his tears burned on his cheeks.

Now you know, the crow whispered as it sat on his shoulder. *Now you know why you must live.*

"Why?" Bran said, not understanding, falling, falling.

Because winter is coming.

Bran looked at the crow on his shoulder, and the crow looked back. It had three eyes, and the third eye was full of a terrible knowledge. Bran looked down. There was nothing below him now but snow and cold and death, a frozen wasteland where jagged blue-white spires of ice waited to embrace him. They flew up at him like spears. He saw the bones of a thousand other dreamers impaled upon their points. He was desperately afraid.

"Can a man still be brave if he's afraid?" he heard his own voice saying, small and far away.

And his father's voice replied to him. "That is the only time a man can be brave."

Now, Bran, the crow urged. *Choose. Fly or die.*

Death reached for him, screaming.

Bran spread his arms and flew.

Wings unseen drank the wind and filled and pulled him upward. The terrible needles of ice receded below him. The sky opened up above. Bran soared. It was better than climbing. It was better than anything. The world grew small beneath him.

"I'm flying!" he cried out in delight.

I've noticed, said the three-eyed crow. It took to the air, flapping its wings in his face, slowing him, blinding him. He faltered in the air as its pinions beat against his cheeks. Its beak stabbed at him fiercely, and Bran felt a sudden blinding pain in the middle of his forehead, between his eyes.

"What are you doing?" he shrieked.

The crow opened its beak and cawed at him, a shrill scream of fear, and the grey mists shuddered and swirled around him and ripped away like a veil, and he saw that the crow was really a woman, a serving woman with long black hair, and he knew her from somewhere, from Winterfell, yes, that was it, he remembered her now, and then he realized that he was in Winterfell, in a bed high in some chilly tower room, and the black-haired woman dropped a basin of water to shatter on the floor and ran down the steps, shouting, "He's awake, he's awake, he's awake."

Bran touched his forehead, between his eyes. The place where the crow had pecked him was still burning, but there was nothing there, no blood, no wound. He felt weak and dizzy. He tried to get out of bed, but nothing happened.

And then there was movement beside the bed, and something landed lightly on his legs. He felt nothing. A pair of yellow eyes looked into his own, shining like the sun. The window was open and it was cold in the room, but the warmth that came off the wolf enfolded him like a hot bath. His pup, Bran realized . . . or was it? He was so *big* now. He reached out to pet him, his hand trembling like a leaf.

When his brother Robb burst into the room, breathless from his dash up the tower steps, the direwolf was licking Bran's face. Bran looked up calmly. "His name is Summer," he said.

CATELYN

"**W**e will make King's Landing within the hour."

Catelyn turned away from the rail and forced herself to smile. "Your oarmen have done well by us, Captain. Each one of them shall have a silver stag, as a token of my gratitude."

Captain Moreo Tumitis favored her with a half bow. "You are far too generous, Lady Stark. The honor of carrying a great lady like yourself is all the reward they need."

"But they'll take the silver anyway."

Moreo smiled. "As you say." He spoke the Common Tongue fluently, with only the slightest hint of a Tyroshi accent. He'd been plying the narrow sea for thirty years, he'd told her, as oarman, quartermaster, and finally captain of his own trading galleys. The *Storm Dancer* was his fourth ship, and his fastest, a two-masted galley of sixty oars.

She had certainly been the fastest of the ships available in White Harbor when Catelyn and Ser Rodrik Cassel had arrived after their headlong gallop downriver. The Tyroshi were notorious for their avarice, and Ser Rodrik had argued for hiring a fishing sloop out of the Three Sisters, but

Catelyn had insisted on the galley. It was good that she had. The winds had been against them much of the voyage, and without the galley's oars they'd still be beating their way past the Fingers, instead of skimming toward King's Landing and journey's end.

So close, she thought. Beneath the linen bandages, her fingers still throbbed where the dagger had bitten. The pain was her scourge, Catelyn felt, lest she forget. She could not bend the last two fingers on her left hand, and the others would never again be dexterous. Yet that was a small enough price to pay for Bran's life.

Ser Rodrik chose that moment to appear on deck. "My good friend," said Moreo through his forked green beard. The Tyroshi loved bright colors, even in their facial hair. "It is so fine to see you looking better."

"Yes," Ser Rodrik agreed. "I haven't wanted to die for almost two days now." He bowed to Catelyn. "My lady."

He *was* looking better. A shade thinner than he had been when they set out from White Harbor, but almost himself again. The strong winds in the Bite and the roughness of the narrow sea had not agreed with him, and he'd almost gone over the side when the storm seized them unexpectedly off Dragonstone, yet somehow he had clung to a rope until three of Moreo's men could rescue him and carry him safely below decks.

"The captain was just telling me that our voyage is almost at an end," she said.

Ser Rodrik managed a wry smile. "So soon?" He looked odd without his great white side whiskers; smaller somehow, less fierce, and ten years older. Yet back on the Bite it had seemed prudent to submit to a crewman's razor, after his whiskers had become hopelessly befouled for the third time while he leaned over the rail and retched into the swirling winds.

"I will leave you to discuss your business," Captain Moreo said. He bowed and took his leave of them.

The galley skimmed the water like a dragonfly, her oars rising and falling in perfect time. Ser Rodrik held the rail and looked out over the passing shore. "I have not been the most valiant of protectors."

Catelyn touched his arm. "We are here, Ser Rodrik, and safely. That is all that truly matters." Her hand groped beneath her cloak, her fingers stiff and fumbling.

The dagger was still at her side. She found she had to touch it now and then, to reassure herself. "Now we must reach the king's master-at-arms, and pray that he can be trusted."

"Ser Aron Santagar is a vain man, but an honest one." Ser Rodrik's hand went to his face to stroke his whiskers and discovered once again that they were gone. He looked nonplussed. "He may know the blade, yes . . . but, my lady, the moment we go ashore we are at risk. And there are those at court who will know you on sight."

Catelyn's mouth grew tight. "Littlefinger," she murmured. His face swam up before her; a boy's face, though he was a boy no longer. His father had died several years before, so he was Lord Baelish now, yet still they called him Littlefinger. Her brother Edmure had given him that name, long ago at Riverrun. His family's modest holdings were on the smallest of the Fingers, and Petyr had been slight and short for his age.

Ser Rodrik cleared his throat. "Lord Baelish once, ah . . ." His thought trailed off uncertainly in search of the polite word.

Catelyn was past delicacy. "He was my father's ward. We grew up together in Riverrun. I thought of him as a brother, but his feelings for me were . . . more than brotherly. When it was announced that I was to wed Brandon Stark, Petyr challenged for the right to my hand. It was madness. Brandon was twenty, Petyr scarcely fifteen. I had to beg Brandon to spare Petyr's life. He let him off with a scar. Afterward my father sent him away. I have not seen him since." She lifted her face to the spray, as if the brisk wind could blow the memories away. "He wrote to me at Riverrun after Brandon was killed, but I burned the letter unread. By then I knew that Ned would marry me in his brother's place."

Ser Rodrik's fingers fumbled once again for nonexistent whiskers. "Littlefinger sits on the small council now."

"I knew he would rise high," Catelyn said. "He was always clever, even as a boy, but it is one thing to be clever and another to be wise. I wonder what the years have done to him."

High overhead, the far-eyes sang out from the rigging. Captain Moreo came scrambling across the deck, giving orders, and all around them the *Storm Dancer* burst into frenetic activity as King's Landing slid into view atop its three high hills.

Three hundred years ago, Catelyn knew, those heights had been covered with forest, and only a handful of fisherfolk had lived on the north shore of the Blackwater Rush where that deep, swift river flowed into the sea. Then Aegon the Conqueror had sailed from Dragonstone. It was here that his army had put ashore, and there on the highest hill that he built his first crude redoubt of wood and earth.

Now the city covered the shore as far as Catelyn could see; manses and arbors and granaries, brick storehouses and timbered inns and merchant's stalls, taverns and graveyards and brothels, all piled one on another. She could hear the clamor of the fish market even at this distance. Between the buildings were broad roads lined with trees, wandering crookback streets, and alleys so narrow that two men could not walk abreast. Visenya's hill was crowned by the Great Sept of Baelor with its seven crystal towers. Across the city on the hill of Rhaenys stood the blackened walls of the Dragonpit, its huge dome collapsing into ruin, its bronze doors closed now for a century. The Street of the Sisters ran between them, straight as an arrow. The city walls rose in the distance, high and strong.

A hundred quays lined the waterfront, and the harbor was crowded with ships. Deepwater fishing boats and river runners came and went, ferrymen poled back and forth across the Blackwater Rush, trading galleys unloaded goods from Braavos and Pentos and Lys. Catelyn spied the queen's ornate barge, tied up beside a fat-bellied whaler from the Port of Ibben, its hull black with tar, while upriver a dozen lean golden warships rested in their cribs, sails furled and cruel iron rams lapping at the water.

And above it all, frowning down from Aegon's high hill, was the Red Keep; seven huge drum-towers crowned with iron ramparts, an immense grim barbican, vaulted halls and covered bridges, barracks and dungeons and granaries, massive curtain walls studded with archers' nests, all fashioned of pale red stone. Aegon the Conqueror had commanded it built. His son Maegor the Cruel had seen it completed. Afterward he had taken the heads of every stonemason, woodworker, and builder who had labored on it. Only the blood of the dragon would ever know the secrets of the fortress the Dragonlords had built, he vowed.

Yet now the banners that flew from its battlements were golden, not black, and where the three-headed dragon had once breathed fire, now pranced the crowned stag of House Baratheon.

A high-masted swan ship from the Summer Isles was beating out from port, its white sails huge with wind. The *Storm Dancer* moved past it, pulling steadily for shore.

"My lady," Ser Rodrik said, "I have thought on how best to proceed while I lay abed. You must not enter the castle. I will go in your stead and bring Ser Aron to you in some safe place."

She studied the old knight as the galley drew near to a pier. Moreo was shouting in the vulgar Valyrian of the Free Cities. "You would be as much at risk as I would."

Ser Rodrik smiled. "I think not. I looked at my reflection in the water earlier and scarcely recognized myself. My mother was the last person to see me without whiskers, and she is forty years dead. I believe I am safe enough, my lady."

Moreo bellowed a command. As one, sixty oars lifted from the river, then reversed and backed water. The galley slowed. Another shout. The oars slid back inside the hull. As they thumped against the dock, Tyroshi seamen leapt down to tie up. Moreo came bustling up, all smiles. "King's Landing, my lady, as you did command, and never has a ship made a swifter or surer passage. Will you be needing assistance to carry your things to the castle?"

"We shall not be going to the castle. Perhaps you can suggest an inn, someplace clean and comfortable and not too far from the river."

The Tyroshi fingered his forked green beard. "Just so. I know of several establishments that might suit your needs. Yet first, if I may be so bold, there is the matter of the second half of the payment we agreed upon. And of course the extra silver you were so kind as to promise. Sixty stags, I believe it was."

"For the oarmen," Catelyn reminded him.

"Oh, of a certainty," said Moreo. "Though perhaps I should hold it for them until we return to Tyrosh. For the sake of their wives and children. If you give them the silver here, my lady, they will dice it away or spend it all for a night's pleasure."

"There are worse things to spend money on," Ser Rodrik put in. "Winter is coming."

"A man must make his own choices," Catelyn said. "They earned the silver. How they spend it is no concern of mine."

"As you say, my lady," Moreo replied, bowing and smiling.

Just to be sure, Catelyn paid the oarmen herself, a stag to each man, and a copper to the two men who carried their chests halfway up Visenya's hill to the inn that Moreo had suggested. It was a rambling old place on Eel Alley. The woman who owned it was a sour crone with a wandering eye who looked them over suspiciously and bit the coin that Catelyn offered her to make sure it was real. Her rooms were large and airy, though, and Moreo swore that her fish stew was the most savory in all the Seven Kingdoms. Best of all, she had no interest in their names.

"I think it best if you stay away from the common room," Ser Rodrik said, after they had settled in. "Even in a place like this, one never knows who may be watching." He wore ringmail, dagger, and longsword under a dark cloak with a hood he could pull up over his head. "I will be back before nightfall, with Ser Aron," he promised. "Rest now, my lady."

Catelyn *was* tired. The voyage had been long and fatiguing, and she was no longer as young as she had been. Her windows opened on the alley and rooftops, with a view of the Blackwater beyond. She watched Ser Rodrik set off, striding briskly through the busy streets until he was lost in the crowds, then decided to take his advice. The bedding was stuffed with straw instead of feathers, but she had no trouble falling asleep.

She woke to a pounding on her door.

Catelyn sat up sharply. Outside the window, the rooftops of King's Landing were red in the light of the setting sun. She had slept longer than she intended. A fist hammered at her door again, and a voice called out, "Open, in the name of the king."

"A moment," she called out. She wrapped herself in her cloak. The dagger was on the bedside table. She snatched it up before she unlatched the heavy wooden door.

The men who pushed into the room wore the black ringmail and golden cloaks of the City Watch. Their leader smiled at the dagger in her hand and said, "No need for that, m'lady. We're to escort you to the castle."

"By whose authority?" she said.

He showed her a ribbon. Catelyn felt her breath catch in her throat. The seal was a mockingbird, in grey wax. "Petyr," she said. So soon. Something must have happened to Ser Rodrik. She looked at the head guardsman. "Do you know who I am?"

"No, m'lady," he said. "M'lord Littlefinger said only to bring you to him, and see that you were not mistreated."

Catelyn nodded. "You may wait outside while I dress."

She bathed her hands in the basin and wrapped them in clean linen. Her fingers were thick and awkward as she struggled to lace up her bodice and knot a drab brown cloak about her neck. How could Littlefinger have known she was here? Ser Rodrik would never have told him. Old he might be, but he was stubborn, and loyal to a fault. Were they too late, had the Lannisters reached King's Landing before her? No, if that were true, Ned would be here too, and surely he would have come to her. How . . . ?

Then she thought, *Moreo*. The Tyroshi knew who they were and where they were, damn him. She hoped he'd gotten a good price for the information.

They had brought a horse for her. The lamps were being lit along the streets as they set out, and Catelyn felt the eyes of the city on her as she rode, surrounded by the guard in their golden cloaks. When they reached the Red Keep, the portcullis was down and the great gates sealed for the night, but the castle windows were alive with flickering lights. The guardsmen left their mounts outside the walls and escorted her through a narrow postern door, then up endless steps to a tower.

He was alone in the room, seated at a heavy wooden table, an oil lamp beside him as he wrote. When they ushered her inside, he set down his pen and looked at her. "Cat," he said quietly.

"Why have I been brought here in this fashion?"

He rose and gestured brusquely to the guards. "Leave

us." The men departed. "You were not mistreated, I trust," he said after they had gone. "I gave firm instructions." He noticed her bandages. "Your hands . . ."

Catelyn ignored the implied question. "I am not accustomed to being summoned like a serving wench," she said icily. "As a boy, you still knew the meaning of courtesy."

"I've angered you, my lady. That was never my intent." He looked contrite. The look brought back vivid memories for Catelyn. He had been a sly child, but after his mischiefs he always looked contrite; it was a gift he had. The years had not changed him much. Petyr had been a small boy, and he had grown into a small man, an inch or two shorter than Catelyn, slender and quick, with the sharp features she remembered and the same laughing grey-green eyes. He had a little pointed chin beard now, and threads of silver in his dark hair, though he was still shy of thirty. They went well with the silver mockingbird that fastened his cloak. Even as a child, he had always loved his silver.

"How did you know I was in the city?" she asked him.

"Lord Varys knows all," Petyr said with a sly smile. "He will be joining us shortly, but I wanted to see you alone first. It has been too long, Cat. How many years?"

Catelyn ignored his familiarity. There were more important questions. "So it was the King's Spider who found me."

Littlefinger winced. "You don't want to call him that. He's very sensitive. Comes of being an eunuch, I imagine. Nothing happens in this city without Varys knowing. Ofttimes he knows about it *before* it happens. He has informants everywhere. His little birds, he calls them. One of his little birds heard about your visit. Thankfully, Varys came to me first."

"Why you?"

He shrugged. "Why not me? I am master of coin, the king's own councillor. Selmy and Lord Renly rode north to meet Robert, and Lord Stannis is gone to Dragonstone, leaving only Maester Pycelle and me. I was the obvious choice. I was ever a friend to your sister Lysa, Varys knows that."

"Does Varys know about . . ."

"Lord Varys knows everything . . . except why you are here." He lifted an eyebrow. "Why *are* you here?"

"A wife is allowed to yearn for her husband, and if a mother needs her daughters close, who can tell her no?"

Littlefinger laughed. "Oh, very good, my lady, but please don't expect me to believe that. I know you too well. What were the Tully words again?"

Her throat was dry. *"Family, Duty, Honor,"* she recited stiffly. He did know her too well.

"Family, Duty, Honor," he echoed. "All of which required you to remain in Winterfell, where our Hand left you. No, my lady, something has happened. This sudden trip of yours bespeaks a certain urgency. I beg of you, let me help. Old sweet friends should never hesitate to rely upon each other." There was a soft knock on the door. "Enter," Littlefinger called out.

The man who stepped through the door was plump, perfumed, powdered, and as hairless as an egg. He wore a vest of woven gold thread over a loose gown of purple silk, and on his feet were pointed slippers of soft velvet. "Lady Stark," he said, taking her hand in both of his, "to see you again after so many years is such a joy." His flesh was soft and moist, and his breath smelled of lilacs. "Oh, your poor hands. Have you burned yourself, sweet lady? The fingers are so delicate . . . Our good Maester Pycelle makes a marvelous salve, shall I send for a jar?"

Catelyn slid her fingers from his grasp. "I thank you, my lord, but my own Maester Luwin has already seen to my hurts."

Varys bobbed his head. "I was grievous sad to hear about your son. And him so young. The gods are cruel."

"On that we agree, Lord Varys," she said. The title was but a courtesy due him as a council member; Varys was lord of nothing but the spiderweb, the master of none but his whisperers.

The eunuch spread his soft hands. "On more than that, I hope, sweet lady. I have great esteem for your husband, our new Hand, and I know we do both love King Robert."

"Yes," she was forced to say. "For a certainty."

"Never has a king been so beloved as our Robert," quipped Little finger. He smiled slyly. "At least in Lord Varys's hearing."

"Good lady," Varys said with great solicitude. "There

are men in the Free Cities with wondrous healing powers. Say only the word, and I will send for one for your dear Bran."

"Maester Luwin is doing all that can be done for Bran," she told him. She would not speak of Bran, not here, not with these men. She trusted Littlefinger only a little, and Varys not at all. She would not let them see her grief. "Lord Baelish tells me that I have you to thank for bringing me here."

Varys giggled like a little girl. "Oh, yes. I suppose I am guilty. I hope you forgive me, kind lady." He eased himself down into a seat and put his hands together. "I wonder if we might trouble you to show us the dagger?"

Catelyn Stark stared at the eunuch in stunned disbelief. He *was* a spider, she thought wildly, an enchanter or worse. He knew things no one could possibly know, unless . . . "What have you done to Ser Rodrik?" she demanded.

Littlefinger was lost. "I feel rather like the knight who arrives at the battle without his lance. What dagger are we talking about? Who is Ser Rodrik?"

"Ser Rodrik Cassel is master-at-arms at Winterfell," Varys informed him. "I assure you, Lady Stark, nothing at all has been done to the good knight. He did call here early this afternoon. He visited with Ser Aron Santagar in the armory, and they talked of a certain dagger. About sunset, they left the castle together and walked to that dreadful hovel where you were staying. They are still there, drinking in the common room, waiting for your return. Ser Rodrik was very distressed to find you gone."

"How could you know all that?"

"The whisperings of little birds," Varys said, smiling. "I know things, sweet lady. That is the nature of my service." He shrugged. "You *do* have the dagger with you, yes?"

Catelyn pulled it out from beneath her cloak and threw it down on the table in front of him. "Here. Perhaps your little birds will whisper the name of the man it belongs to."

Varys lifted the knife with exaggerated delicacy and ran a thumb along its edge. Blood welled, and he let out a squeal and dropped the dagger back on the table.

"Careful," Catelyn told him, "it's sharp."

"Nothing holds an edge like Valyrian steel," Littlefinger said as Varys sucked at his bleeding thumb and looked at Catelyn with sullen admonition. Littlefinger hefted the knife lightly in his hand, testing the grip. He flipped it in the air, caught it again with his other hand. "Such sweet balance. You want to find the owner, is that the reason for this visit? You have no need of Ser Aron for that, my lady. You should have come to me."

"And if I had," she said, "what would you have told me?"

"I would have told you that there was only one knife like this at King's Landing." He grasped the blade between thumb and forefinger, drew it back over his shoulder, and threw it across the room with a practiced flick of his wrist. It struck the door and buried itself deep in the oak, quivering. "It's mine."

"Yours?" It made no sense. Petyr had not been at Winterfell.

"Until the tourney on Prince Joffrey's name day," he said, crossing the room to wrench the dagger from the wood. "I backed Ser Jaime in the jousting, along with half the court." Petyr's sheepish grin made him look half a boy again. "When Loras Tyrell unhorsed him, many of us became a trifle poorer. Ser Jaime lost a hundred golden dragons, the queen lost an emerald pendant, and I lost my knife. Her Grace got the emerald back, but the winner kept the rest."

"Who?" Catelyn demanded, her mouth dry with fear. Her fingers ached with remembered pain.

"The Imp," said Littlefinger as Lord Varys watched her face. "Tyrion Lannister."

JON

The courtyard rang to the song of swords.

Under black wool, boiled leather, and mail, sweat trickled icily down Jon's chest as he pressed the attack. Grenn stumbled backward, defending himself clumsily. When he raised his sword, Jon went underneath it with a sweeping blow that crunched against the back of the other boy's leg and sent him staggering. Grenn's downcut was answered by an overhand that dented his helm. When he tried a sideswing, Jon swept aside his blade and slammed a mailed forearm into his chest. Grenn lost his footing and sat down hard in the snow. Jon knocked his sword from his fingers with a slash to his wrist that brought a cry of pain.

"Enough!" Ser Alliser Thorne had a voice with an edge like Valyrian steel.

Grenn cradled his hand. "The bastard broke my wrist."

"The bastard hamstrung you, opened your empty skull, and cut off your hand. Or would have, if these blades had an edge. It's fortunate for you that the Watch needs stableboys as well as rangers." Ser Alliser gestured at Jeren and Toad. "Get the Aurochs on his feet, he has funeral arrangements to make."

Jon took off his helm as the other boys were pulling Grenn to his feet. The frosty morning air felt good on his face. He leaned on his sword, drew a deep breath, and allowed himself a moment to savor the victory.

"That is a longsword, not an old man's cane," Ser Alliser said sharply. "Are your legs hurting, Lord Snow?"

Jon hated that name, a mockery that Ser Alliser had hung on him the first day he came to practice. The boys had picked it up, and now he heard it everywhere. He slid the longsword back into its scabbard. "No," he replied.

Thorne strode toward him, crisp black leathers whispering faintly as he moved. He was a compact man of fifty years, spare and hard, with grey in his black hair and eyes like chips of onyx. "The truth now," he commanded.

"I'm tired," Jon admitted. His arm burned from the weight of the longsword, and he was starting to feel his bruises now that the fight was done.

"What you are is weak."

"I won."

"No. The Aurochs lost."

One of the other boys sniggered. Jon knew better than to reply. He had beaten everyone that Ser Alliser had sent against him, yet it gained him nothing. The master-at-arms served up only derision. Thorne hated him, Jon had decided; of course, he hated the other boys even worse.

"That will be all," Thorne told them. "I can only stomach so much ineptitude in any one day. If the Others ever come for us, I pray they have archers, because you lot are fit for nothing more than arrow fodder."

Jon followed the rest back to the armory, walking alone. He often walked alone here. There were almost twenty in the group he trained with, yet not one he could call a friend. Most were two or three years his senior, yet not one was half the fighter Robb had been at fourteen. Dareon was quick but afraid of being hit. Pyp used his sword like a dagger, Jeren was weak as a girl, Grenn slow and clumsy. Halder's blows were brutally hard but he ran right into your attacks. The more time he spent with them, the more Jon despised them.

Inside, Jon hung sword and scabbard from a hook in the stone wall, ignoring the others around him. Methodically, he began to strip off his mail, leather, and sweat-soaked woolens. Chunks of coal burned in iron braziers at either end of the long room, but Jon found himself shivering. The chill was always with him here. In a few years he would forget what it felt like to be warm.

The weariness came on him suddenly, as he donned the roughspun blacks that were their everyday wear. He sat on a bench, his fingers fumbling with the fastenings on his cloak. *So cold,* he thought, remembering the warm halls of Winterfell, where the hot waters ran through the walls like blood through a man's body. There was scant warmth to be found in Castle Black; the walls were cold here, and the people colder.

No one had told him the Night's Watch would be like this; no one except Tyrion Lannister. The dwarf had given him the truth on the road north, but by then it had been too late. Jon wondered if his father had known what the Wall would be like. He must have, he thought; that only made it hurt the worse.

Even his uncle had abandoned him in this cold place at the end of the world. Up here, the genial Benjen Stark he had known became a different person. He was First Ranger, and he spent his days and nights with Lord Commander Mormont and Maester Aemon and the other high officers, while Jon was given over to the less than tender charge of Ser Alliser Thorne.

Three days after their arrival, Jon had heard that Benjen Stark was to lead a half-dozen men on a ranging into the haunted forest. That night he sought out his uncle in the great timbered common hall and pleaded to go with him. Benjen refused him curtly. "This is not Winterfell," he told him as he cut his meat with fork and dagger. "On the Wall, a man gets only what he earns. You're no ranger, Jon, only a green boy with the smell of summer still on you."

Stupidly, Jon argued. "I'll be fifteen on my name day," he said. "Almost a man grown."

Benjen Stark frowned. "A boy you are, and a boy you'll remain until Ser Alliser says you are fit to be a man of the Night's Watch. If you thought your Stark blood would win you easy favors, you were wrong. We put aside our old families when we swear our vows. Your father will always have a place in my heart, but *these* are my brothers now." He gestured with his dagger at the men around them, all the hard cold men in black.

Jon rose at dawn the next day to watch his uncle leave. One of his rangers, a big ugly man, sang a bawdy song as he saddled his garron, his breath steaming in the cold morning air. Ben Stark smiled at that, but he had no smile for his nephew. "How often must I tell you no, Jon? We'll speak when I return."

As he watched his uncle lead his horse into the tunnel, Jon had remembered the things that Tyrion Lannister told him on the kingsroad, and in his mind's eye he saw Ben Stark lying dead, his blood red on the snow. The thought made him sick. What was he becoming? Afterward he sought out Ghost in the loneliness of his cell, and buried his face in his thick white fur.

If he must be alone, he would make solitude his armor. Castle Black had no godswood, only a small sept and a drunken septon, but Jon could not find it in him to pray to any gods, old or new. If they were real, he thought, they were as cruel and implacable as winter.

He missed his true brothers: little Rickon, bright eyes shining as he begged for a sweet; Robb, his rival and best friend and constant companion; Bran, stubborn and curious, always wanting to follow and join in whatever Jon and Robb were doing. He missed the girls too, even Sansa, who never called him anything but "my half brother" since she was old enough to understand what *bastard* meant. And Arya . . . he missed her even more than Robb, skinny little thing that she was, all scraped knees and tangled hair and torn clothes, so fierce and willful. Arya never seemed to fit, no more than he had . . . yet she could always make Jon smile. He would give anything to be with her now, to muss up her hair once more and watch her make a face, to hear her finish a sentence with him.

"You broke my wrist, bastard boy."

Jon lifted his eyes at the sullen voice. Grenn loomed over him, thick of neck and red of face, with three of his friends behind him. He knew Todder, a short ugly boy with an unpleasant voice. The recruits all called him Toad. The other two were the ones Yoren had brought north with them, Jon remembered, rapers taken down in the Fingers. He'd forgotten their names. He hardly ever spoke to them, if he could help it. They were brutes and bullies, without a thimble of honor between them.

Jon stood up. "I'll break the other one for you if you ask nicely." Grenn was sixteen and a head taller than Jon. All four of them were bigger than he was, but they did not scare him. He'd beaten every one of them in the yard.

"Maybe we'll break you," one of the rapers said.

"Try." Jon reached back for his sword, but one of them grabbed his arm and twisted it behind his back.

"You make us look bad," complained Toad.

"You looked bad before I ever met you," Jon told him. The boy who had his arm jerked upward on him, hard. Pain lanced through him, but Jon would not cry out.

Toad stepped close. "The little lordling has a mouth on him," he said. He had pig eyes, small and shiny. "Is that your mommy's mouth, bastard? What was she, some whore? Tell us her name. Maybe I had her a time or two." He laughed.

Jon twisted like an eel and slammed a heel down across the instep of the boy holding him. There was a sudden cry of pain, and he was free. He flew at Toad, knocked him backward over a bench, and landed on his chest with both hands on his throat, slamming his head against the packed earth.

The two from the Fingers pulled him off, throwing him roughly to the ground. Grenn began to kick at him. Jon was rolling away from the blows when a booming voice cut through the gloom of the armory. "STOP THIS! NOW!"

Jon pulled himself to his feet. Donal Noye stood glowering at them. "The yard is for fighting," the armorer said. "Keep your quarrels out of my armory, or I'll make them *my* quarrels. You won't like that."

Toad sat on the floor, gingerly feeling the back of his head. His fingers came away bloody. "He tried to kill me."

" 'S true. I saw it," one of the rapers put in.

"He broke my wrist," Grenn said again, holding it out to Noye for inspection.

The armorer gave the offered wrist the briefest of glances. "A bruise. Perhaps a sprain. Maestor Aemon will give you a salve. Go with him, Todder, that head wants looking after. The rest of you, return to your cells. Not you, Snow. You stay."

Jon sat heavily on the long wooden bench as the others

left, oblivious to the looks they gave him, the silent promises of future retribution. His arm was throbbing.

"The Watch has need of every man it can get," Donal Noye said when they were alone. "Even men like Toad. You won't win any honors killing him."

Jon's anger flared. "He said my mother was—"

"—a whore. I heard him. What of it?"

"Lord Eddard Stark was not a man to sleep with whores," Jon said icily. "His honor—"

"—did not prevent him from fathering a bastard. Did it?"

Jon was cold with rage. "Can I go?"

"You go when I tell you to go."

Jon stared sullenly at the smoke rising from the brazier, until Noye took him under the chin, thick fingers twisting his head around. "Look at me when I'm talking to you, boy."

Jon looked. The armorer had a chest like a keg of ale and a gut to match. His nose was flat and broad, and he always seemed in need of a shave. The left sleeve of his black wool tunic was fastened at the shoulder with a silver pin in the shape of a longsword. "Words won't make your mother a whore. She was what she was, and nothing Toad says can change that. You know, we have men on the Wall whose mothers *were* whores."

Not my mother, Jon thought stubbornly. He knew nothing of his mother; Eddard Stark would not talk of her. Yet he dreamed of her at times, so often that he could almost see her face. In his dreams, she was beautiful, and highborn, and her eyes were kind.

"You think you had it hard, being a high lord's bastard?" the armorer went on. "That boy Jeren is a septon's get, and Cotter Pyke is the baseborn son of a tavern wench. Now he commands Eastwatch by the Sea."

"I don't care," Jon said. "I don't care about them and I don't care about you or Thorne or Benjen Stark or any of it. I hate it here. It's too . . . it's cold."

"Yes. Cold and hard and mean, that's the Wall, and the men who walk it. Not like the stories your wet nurse told you. Well, piss on the stories and piss on your wet nurse. This is the way it is, and you're here for life, same as the rest of us."

"Life," Jon repeated bitterly. The armorer could talk

about life. He'd had one. He'd only taken the black after he'd lost an arm at the siege of Storm's End. Before that he'd smithed for Stannis Baratheon, the king's brother. He'd seen the Seven Kingdoms from one end to the other; he'd feasted and wenched and fought in a hundred battles. They said it was Donal Noye who'd forged King Robert's warhammer, the one that crushed the life from Rhaegar Targaryen on the Trident. He'd done all the things that Jon would never do, and then when he was old, well past thirty, he'd taken a glancing blow from an axe and the wound had festered until the whole arm had to come off. Only then, crippled, had Donal Noye come to the Wall, when his life was all but over.

"Yes, life," Noye said. "A long life or a short one, it's up to you, Snow. The road you're walking, one of your brothers will slit your throat for you one night."

"They're not my brothers," Jon snapped. "They hate me because I'm better than they are."

"No. They hate you because you act like you're better than they are. They look at you and see a castle-bred bastard who thinks he's a lordling." The armorer leaned close. "You're no lordling. Remember that. You're a Snow, not a Stark. You're a bastard and a bully."

"A *bully?*" Jon almost choked on the word. The accusation was so unjust it took his breath away. "They were the ones who came after me. Four of them."

"Four that you've humiliated in the yard. Four who are probably afraid of you. I've watched you fight. It's not training with you. Put a good edge on your sword, and they'd be dead meat; you know it, I know it, they know it. You leave them nothing. You shame them. Does that make you proud?"

Jon hesitated. He did feel proud when he won. Why shouldn't he? But the armorer was taking that away too, making it sound as if he were doing something wrong. "They're all older than me," he said defensively.

"Older and bigger and stronger, that's the truth. I'll wager your master-at-arms taught you how to fight bigger men at Winterfell, though. Who was he, some old knight?"

"Ser Rodrik Cassel," Jon said warily. There was a trap here. He felt it closing around him.

Donal Noye leaned forward, into Jon's face. "Now

think on this, boy. None of these others have ever had a master-at-arms until Ser Alliser. Their fathers were farmers and wagonmen and poachers, smiths and miners and oars on a trading galley. What they know of fighting they learned between decks, in the alleys of Oldtown and Lannisport, in wayside brothels and taverns on the kingsroad. They may have clacked a few sticks together before they came here, but I promise you, not one in twenty was ever rich enough to own a real sword." His look was grim. "So how do you like the taste of your victories now, Lord Snow?"

"Don't call me that!" Jon said sharply, but the force had gone out of his anger. Suddenly he felt ashamed and guilty. "I never . . . I didn't think . . ."

"Best you start thinking," Noye warned him. "That, or sleep with a dagger by your bed. Now go."

By the time Jon left the armory, it was almost midday. The sun had broken through the clouds. He turned his back on it and lifted his eyes to the Wall, blazing blue and crystalline in the sunlight. Even after all these weeks, the sight of it still gave him the shivers. Centuries of wind-blown dirt had pocked and scoured it, covering it like a film, and it often seemed a pale grey, the color of an overcast sky . . . but when the sun caught it fair on a bright day, it *shone*, alive with light, a colossal blue-white cliff that filled up half the sky.

The largest structure ever built by the hands of man, Benjen Stark had told Jon on the kingsroad when they had first caught sight of the Wall in the distance. "And beyond a doubt the most useless," Tyrion Lannister had added with a grin, but even the Imp grew silent as they rode closer. You could see it from miles off, a pale blue line across the northern horizon, stretching away to the east and west and vanishing in the far distance, immense and unbroken. *This is the end of the world*, it seemed to say.

When they finally spied Castle Black, its timbered keeps and stone towers looked like nothing more than a handful of toy blocks scattered on the snow, beneath the vast wall of ice. The ancient stronghold of the black brothers was no Winterfell, no true castle at all. Lacking walls, it could not be defended, not from the south, or east, or west; but it was only the north that concerned the

Night's Watch, and to the north loomed the Wall. Almost seven hundred feet high it stood, three times the height of the tallest tower in the stronghold it sheltered. His uncle said the top was wide enough for a dozen armored knights to ride abreast. The gaunt outlines of huge catapults and monstrous wooden cranes stood sentry up there, like the skeletons of great birds, and among them walked men in black as small as ants.

As he stood outside the armory looking up, Jon felt almost as overwhelmed as he had that day on the kingsroad, when he'd seen it for the first time. The Wall was like that. Sometimes he could almost forget that it was there, the way you forgot about the sky or the earth underfoot, but there were other times when it seemed as if there was nothing else in the world. It was older than the Seven Kingdoms, and when he stood beneath it and looked up, it made Jon dizzy. He could feel the great weight of all that ice pressing down on him, as if it were about to topple, and somehow Jon knew that if it fell, the world fell with it.

"Makes you wonder what lies beyond," a familiar voice said.

Jon looked around. "Lannister. I didn't see—I mean, I thought I was alone."

Tyrion Lannister was bundled in furs so thickly he looked like a very small bear. "There's much to be said for taking people unawares. You never know what you might learn."

"You won't learn anything from me," Jon told him. He had seen little of the dwarf since their journey ended. As the queen's own brother, Tyrion Lannister had been an honored guest of the Night's Watch. The Lord Commander had given him rooms in the King's Tower—so-called, though no king had visited it for a hundred years—and Lannister dined at Mormont's own table and spent his days riding the Wall and his nights dicing and drinking with Ser Alliser and Bowen Marsh and the other high officers.

"Oh, I learn things everywhere I go." The little man gestured up at the Wall with a gnarled black walking stick. "As I was saying . . . why is it that when one man builds a wall, the next man immediately needs to know what's on the other side?" He cocked his head and looked at Jon with his curious mismatched eyes. "You *do* want to know what's on the other side, don't you?"

"It's nothing special," Jon said. He wanted to ride with Benjen Stark on his rangings, deep into the mysteries of the haunted forest, wanted to fight Mance Rayder's wildlings and ward the realm against the Others, but it was better not to speak of the things you wanted. "The rangers say it's just woods and mountains and frozen lakes, with lots of snow and ice."

"And the grumkins and the snarks," Tyrion said. "Let us not forget them, Lord Snow, or else what's that big thing for?"

"Don't call me Lord Snow."

The dwarf lifted an eyebrow. "Would you rather be called the Imp? Let them see that their words can cut you, and you'll never be free of the mockery. If they want to give you a name, take it, make it your own. Then they can't hurt you with it anymore." He gestured with his stick. "Come, walk with me. They'll be serving some vile stew in the common hall by now, and I could do with a bowl of something hot."

Jon was hungry too, so he fell in beside Lannister and slowed his pace to match the dwarf's awkward, waddling steps. The wind was rising, and they could hear the old wooden buildings creaking around them, and in the distance a heavy shutter banging, over and over, forgotten. Once there was a muffled *thump* as a blanket of snow slid from a roof and landed near them.

"I don't see your wolf," Lannister said as they walked.

"I chain him up in the old stables when we're training. They board all the horses in the east stables now, so no one bothers him. The rest of the time he stays with me. My sleeping cell is in Hardin's Tower."

"That's the one with the broken battlement, no? Shattered stone in the yard below, and a lean to it like our noble king Robert after a long night's drinking? I thought all those buildings had been abandoned."

Jon shrugged. "No one cares where you sleep. Most of the old keeps are empty, you can pick any cell you want." Once Castle Black had housed five thousand fighting men with all their horses and servants and weapons. Now it was home to a tenth that number, and parts of it were falling into ruin.

Tyrion Lannister's laughter steamed in the cold air. "I'll be sure to tell your father to arrest more stonemasons, before your tower collapses."

Jon could taste the mockery there, but there was no denying the truth. The Watch had built nineteen great strongholds along the Wall, but only three were still occupied: Eastwatch on its grey windswept shore, the Shadow Tower hard by the mountains where the Wall ended, and Castle Black between them, at the end of the kingsroad. The other keeps, long deserted, were lonely, haunted places, where cold winds whistled through black windows and the spirits of the dead manned the parapets.

"It's better that I'm by myself," Jon said stubbornly. "The rest of them are scared of Ghost."

"Wise boys," Lannister said. Then he changed the subject. "The talk is, your uncle is too long away."

Jon remembered the wish he'd wished in his anger, the vision of Benjen Stark dead in the snow, and he looked away quickly. The dwarf had a way of sensing things, and Jon did not want him to see the guilt in his eyes. "He said he'd be back by my name day," he admitted. His name day had come and gone, unremarked, a fortnight past. "They were looking for Ser Waymar Royce, his father is bannerman to Lord Arryn. Uncle Benjen said they might search as far as the Shadow Tower. That's all the way up in the mountains."

"I hear that a good many rangers have vanished of late," Lannister said as they mounted the steps to the common hall. He grinned and pulled open the door. "Perhaps the grumkins are hungry this year."

Inside, the hall was immense and drafty, even with a fire roaring in its great hearth. Crows nested in the timbers of its lofty ceiling. Jon heard their cries overhead as he accepted a bowl of stew and a heel of black bread from the day's cooks. Grenn and Toad and some of the others were seated at the bench nearest the warmth, laughing and cursing each other in rough voices. Jon eyed them thoughtfully for a moment. Then he chose a spot at the far end of the hall, well away from the other diners.

Tyrion Lannister sat across from him, sniffing at the stew suspiciously. "Barley, onion, carrot," he muttered. "Someone should tell the cooks that turnip isn't a meat."

"It's mutton stew." Jon pulled off his gloves and

warmed his hands in the steam rising from the bowl. The smell made his mouth water.

"Snow."

Jon knew Alliser Thorne's voice, but there was a curious note in it that he had not heard before. He turned.

"The Lord Commander wants to see you. Now."

For a moment Jon was too frightened to move. Why would the Lord Commander want to see him? They had heard something about Benjen, he thought wildly, he was dead, the vision had come true. "Is it my uncle?" he blurted. "Is he returned safe?"

"The Lord Commander is not accustomed to waiting," was Ser Alliser's reply. "And I am not accustomed to having my commands questioned by bastards."

Tyrion Lannister swung off the bench and rose. "Stop it, Thorne. You're frightening the boy."

"Keep out of matters that don't concern you, Lannister. You have no place here."

"I have a place at court, though," the dwarf said, smiling. "A word in the right ear, and you'll die a sour old man before you get another boy to train. Now tell Snow why the Old Bear needs to see him. Is there news of his uncle?"

"No," Ser Alliser said. "This is another matter entirely. A bird arrived this morning from Winterfell, with a message that concerns his brother." He corrected himself. "His half brother."

"Bran," Jon breathed, scrambling to his feet. "Something's happened to Bran."

Tyrion Lannister laid a hand on his arm. "Jon," he said. "I am truly sorry."

Jon scarcely heard him. He brushed off Tyrion's hand and strode across the hall. He was running by the time he hit the doors. He raced to the Commander's Keep, dashing through drifts of old snow. When the guards passed him, he took the tower steps two at a time. By the time he burst into the presence of the Lord Commander, his boots were soaked and Jon was wild-eyed and panting. "Bran," he said. "What does it say about Bran?"

Jeor Mormont, Lord Commander of the Night's Watch, was a gruff old man with an immense bald head and a shaggy grey beard. He had a raven on his arm, and he was feeding it kernels of corn. "I am told you can read." He shook the raven off, and it flapped its wings and flew to the window, where it sat watching as Mormont drew a roll of paper from his belt and handed it to Jon. *"Corn,"* it muttered in a raucous voice. *"Corn, corn."*

Jon's finger traced the outline of the direwolf in the white wax of the broken seal. He recognized Robb's hand, but the letters seemed to blur and run as he tried to read them. He realized he was crying. And then, through the tears, he found the sense in the words, and raised his head. "He woke up," he said. "The gods gave him back."

"Crippled," Mormont said. "I'm sorry, boy. Read the rest of the letter."

He looked at the words, but they didn't matter. Nothing mattered. Bran was going to live. "My brother is going to live," he told Mormont. The Lord Commander shook his head, gathered up a fistful of corn, and whistled. The raven flew to his shoulder, crying, *"Live! Live!"*

Jon ran down the stairs, a smile on his face and Robb's letter in his hand. "My brother is going to live," he told the guards. They exchanged a look. He ran back to the common hall, where he found Tyrion Lannister just finishing his meal. He grabbed the little man under the arms, hoisted him up in the air, and spun him around in a circle. *"Bran is going to live!"* he whooped. Lannister looked startled. Jon put him down and thrust the paper into his hands. "Here, read it," he said.

Others were gathering around and looking at him curiously. Jon noticed Grenn a few feet away. A thick woolen bandage was wrapped around one hand. He looked anxious and uncomfortable, not menacing at all. Jon went to him. Grenn edged backward and put up his hands. "Stay away from me now, you bastard."

Jon smiled at him. "I'm sorry about your wrist. Robb used the same move on me once, only with a wooden blade. It hurt like seven hells, but yours must be worse. Look, if you want, I can show you how to defend that."

Alliser Thorne overheard him. "Lord Snow wants to take my place now." He sneered. "I'd have an easier time teaching a wolf to juggle than you will training this aurochs."

"I'll take that wager, Ser Alliser," Jon said. "I'd love to see Ghost juggle."

Jon heard Grenn suck in his breath, shocked. Silence fell.

Then Tyrion Lannister guffawed. Three of the black brothers joined in from a nearby table. The laughter spread up and down the benches, until even the cooks joined in. The birds stirred in the rafters, and finally even Grenn began to chuckle.

Ser Alliser never took his eyes from Jon. As the laughter rolled around him, his face darkened, and his sword hand curled into a fist. "That was a grievous error, Lord Snow," he said at last in the acid tones of an enemy.

EDDARD

Eddard Stark rode through the towering bronze doors of the Red Keep sore, tired, hungry, and irritable. He was still ahorse, dreaming of a long hot soak, a roast fowl, and a featherbed, when the king's steward told him that Grand Maester Pycelle had convened an urgent meeting of the small council. The honor of the Hand's presence was requested as soon as it was convenient. "It will be convenient on the morrow," Ned snapped as he dismounted.

The steward bowed very low. "I shall give the councillors your regrets, my lord."

"No, damn it," Ned said. It would not do to offend the council before he had even begun. "I will see them. Pray give me a few moments to change into something more presentable."

"Yes, my lord," the steward said. "We have given you Lord Arryn's former chambers in the Tower of the Hand, if it please you. I shall have your things taken there."

"My thanks," Ned said as he ripped off his riding gloves and tucked them into his belt. The rest of his household was coming through the gate behind him. Ned saw Vayon Poole, his own steward, and called out. "It seems the council has urgent need of me. See that my daughters find their bedchambers, and tell Jory to keep them there. Arya is not to go exploring." Poole bowed. Ned turned back to the royal steward. "My wagons are still straggling through the city. I shall need appropriate garments."

"It will be my great pleasure," the steward said.

And so Ned had come striding into the council chambers, bone-tired and dressed in borrowed clothing, to find four members of the small council waiting for him.

The chamber was richly furnished. Myrish carpets covered the floor instead of rushes, and in one corner a hundred fabulous beasts cavorted in bright paints on a carved screen from the Summer Isles. The walls were hung with tapestries from Norvos and Qohor and Lys, and a pair of Valyrian sphinxes flanked the door, eyes of polished garnet smoldering in black marble faces.

The councillor Ned liked least, the eunuch Varys, accosted him the moment he entered. "Lord Stark, I was grievous sad to hear about your troubles on the kingsroad. We have all been visiting the sept to light candles for Prince Joffrey. I pray for his recovery." His hand left powder stains on Ned's sleeve, and he smelled as foul and sweet as flowers on a grave.

"Your gods have heard you," Ned replied, cool yet polite. "The prince grows stronger every day." He disentangled himself from the eunuch's grip and crossed the room to where Lord Renly stood by the screen, talking quietly with a short man who could only be Littlefinger. Renly had been a boy of eight when Robert won the throne, but he had grown into a man so like his brother that Ned found it disconcerting. Whenever he saw him, it was as if the years had slipped away and Robert stood before him, fresh from his victory on the Trident.

"I see you have arrived safely, Lord Stark," Renly said.

"And you as well," Ned replied. "You must forgive me, but sometimes you look the very image of your brother Robert."

"A poor copy," Renly said with a shrug.

"Though much better dressed," Littlefinger quipped. "Lord Renly spends more on clothing than half the ladies of the court."

It was true enough. Lord Renly was in dark green velvet, with a dozen golden stags embroidered on his doublet. A cloth-of-gold half cape was draped casually across one shoulder, fastened with an emerald brooch. "There are worse crimes," Renly said with a laugh. "The way *you* dress, for one."

Littlefinger ignored the jibe. He eyed Ned with a smile on his lips that bordered on insolence. "I have hoped to meet you for some years, Lord Stark. No doubt Lady Catelyn has mentioned me to you."

"She has," Ned replied with a chill in his voice. The sly arrogance of the comment rankled him. "I understand you knew my brother Brandon as well."

Renly Baratheon laughed. Varys shuffled over to listen.

"Rather too well," Littlefinger said. "I still carry a token of his esteem. Did Brandon speak of me too?"

"Often, and with some heat," Ned said, hoping that would end it. He had no patience with this game they played, this dueling with words.

"I should have thought that heat ill suits you Starks," Littlefinger said. "Here in the south, they say you are all made of ice, and melt when you ride below the Neck."

"I do not plan on melting soon, Lord Baelish. You may count on it." Ned moved to the council table and said, "Maester Pycelle, I trust you are well."

The Grand Maester smiled gently from his tall chair at the foot of the table. "Well enough for a man of my years, my lord," he replied, "yet I do tire easily, I fear." Wispy strands of white hair fringed the broad bald dome of his forehead above a kindly face. His maester's collar was no simple metal choker such as Luwin wore, but two dozen heavy chains wound together into a ponderous metal necklace that covered him from throat to breast. The links were forged of every metal known to man: black iron and red gold, bright copper and dull lead, steel and tin and pale silver, brass and bronze and platinum. Garnets and amethysts and black pearls adorned the metalwork, and here and there an emerald or ruby. "Perhaps we might begin soon," the Grand Maester said, hands knitting together atop his broad stomach. "I fear I shall fall asleep if we wait much longer."

"As you will." The king's seat sat empty at the head of the table, the crowned stag of Baratheon embroidered in gold thread on its pillows. Ned took the chair beside it, as the right hand of his king. "My lords," he said formally, "I am sorry to have kept you waiting."

"You are the King's Hand," Varys said. "We serve at your pleasure, Lord Stark."

As the others took their accustomed seats, it struck Eddard Stark forcefully that he did not belong here, in this room, with these men. He remembered what Robert had told him in the crypts below Winterfell. *I am surrounded by flatterers and fools,* the king had insisted. Ned looked down the council table and wondered which were the flatterers and which the fools. He thought he knew already. "We are but five," he pointed out.

"Lord Stannis took himself to Dragonstone not long after the king went north," Varys said, "and our gallant Ser Barristan no doubt rides beside the king as he makes his way through the city, as befits the Lord Commander of the Kingsguard."

"Perhaps we had best wait for Ser Barristan and the king to join us," Ned suggested.

Renly Baratheon laughed aloud. "If we wait for my brother to grace us with his royal presence, it could be a long sit."

"Our good King Robert has many cares," Varys said. "He entrusts some small matters to us, to lighten his load."

"What Lord Varys means is that all this business of coin and crops and justice bores my royal brother to tears," Lord Renly said, "so it falls to us to govern the realm. He does send us a command from time to time." He drew a tightly rolled paper from his sleeve and laid it on the table. "This morning he commanded me to ride ahead with all haste and ask Grand Maester Pycelle to convene this council at once. He has an urgent task for us."

Littlefinger smiled and handed the paper to Ned. It bore the royal seal. Ned broke the wax with his thumb and flattened the letter to consider the king's urgent command, reading the words with mounting disbelief. Was there no end to Robert's folly? And to do this in *his* name, that was salt in the wound. "Gods be good," he swore.

"What Lord Eddard means to say," Lord Renly announced, "is that His Grace instructs us to stage a great tournament in honor of his appointment as the Hand of the King."

"How much?" asked Littlefinger, mildly.

Ned read the answer off the letter. "Forty thousand golden dragons to the champion. Twenty thousand to the man who comes second, another twenty to the winner of the melee, and ten thousand to the victor of the archery competition."

"Ninety thousand gold pieces," Littlefinger sighed. "And we must not neglect the other costs. Robert will want a prodigious feast. That means cooks, carpenters, serving girls, singers, jugglers, fools . . ."

"Fools we have in plenty," Lord Renly said.

Grand Maester Pycelle looked to Littlefinger and asked, "Will the treasury bear the expense?"

"What treasury is that?" Littlefinger replied with a twist of his mouth. "Spare me the foolishness, Maester. You know as well as I that the treasury has been empty for years. I shall have to borrow the money. No doubt the Lannisters will be accommodating. We owe Lord Tywin some three million dragons at present, what matter another hundred thousand?"

Ned was stunned. "Are you claiming that the Crown is *three million* gold pieces in debt?"

"The Crown is more than *six* million gold pieces in debt, Lord Stark. The Lannisters are the biggest part of it, but we have also borrowed from Lord Tyrell, the Iron Bank of Braavos, and several Tyroshi trading cartels. Of late I've had to turn to the Faith. The High Septon haggles worse than a Dornish fishmonger."

Ned was aghast. "Aerys Targaryen left a treasury flowing with gold. How could you let this happen?"

Littlefinger gave a shrug. "The master of coin finds the money. The king and the Hand spend it."

"I will not believe that Jon Arryn allowed Robert to beggar the realm," Ned said hotly.

Grand Maester Pycelle shook his great bald head, his chains clinking softly. "Lord Arryn was a prudent man, but I fear that His Grace does not always listen to wise counsel."

"My royal brother loves tournaments and feasts," Renly Baratheon said, "and he loathes what he calls 'counting coppers.'"

"I will speak with His Grace," Ned said. "This tourney is an extravagance the realm cannot afford."

"Speak to him as you will," Lord Renly said, "we had still best make our plans."

"Another day," Ned said. Perhaps too sharply, from the looks they gave him. He would have to remember that he was no longer in Winterfell, where only the king stood higher; here, he was but first among equals. "Forgive me, my lords," he said in a softer tone. "I am tired. Let us call a halt for today and resume when we are fresher." He did not ask for their consent, but stood abruptly, nodded at them all, and made for the door.

Outside, wagons and riders were still pouring through the castle gates, and the yard was a chaos of mud and horseflesh and shouting men. The king had not yet arrived, he was told. Since the ugliness on the Trident, the Starks and their household had ridden well ahead of the main column, the better to separate themselves from the Lannisters and the growing tension. Robert had hardly been seen; the talk was he was traveling in the huge wheelhouse, drunk as often as not. If so, he might be hours behind, but he would still be here too soon for Ned's liking. He had only to look at Sansa's face to feel the rage twisting inside him once again. The last fortnight of their journey had been a misery. Sansa blamed Arya and told her that it should have been Nymeria who died. And Arya was lost after she heard what had happened to her butcher's boy. Sansa cried herself to sleep, Arya brooded silently all day long, and Eddard Stark dreamed of a frozen hell reserved for the Starks of Winterfell.

He crossed the outer yard, passed under a portcullis into the inner bailey, and was walking toward what he thought was the Tower of the Hand when Littlefinger appeared in front of him. "You're going the wrong way, Stark. Come with me."

Hesitantly, Ned followed. Littlefinger led him into a tower, down a stair, across a small sunken courtyard, and along a deserted corridor where empty suits of armor stood sentinel along the walls. They were relics of the Targaryens, black steel with dragon scales cresting their helms, now dusty and forgotten. "This is not the way to my chambers," Ned said.

"Did I say it was? I'm leading you to the dungeons to

slit your throat and seal your corpse up behind a wall," Littlefinger replied, his voice dripping with sarcasm. "We have no time for this, Stark. Your wife awaits."

"What game are you playing, Littlefinger? Catelyn is at Winterfell, hundreds of leagues from here."

"Oh?" Littlefinger's grey-green eyes glittered with amusement. "Then it appears someone has managed an astonishing impersonation. For the last time, come. Or don't come, and I'll keep her for myself." He hurried down the steps.

Ned followed him warily, wondering if this day would ever end. He had no taste for these intrigues, but he was beginning to realize that they were meat and mead to a man like Littlefinger.

At the foot of the steps was a heavy door of oak and iron. Petyr Baelish lifted the crossbar and gestured Ned through. They stepped out into the ruddy glow of dusk, on a rocky bluff high above the river. "We're outside the castle," Ned said.

"You are a hard man to fool, Stark," Littlefinger said with a smirk. "Was it the sun that gave it away, or the sky? Follow me. There are niches cut in the rock. Try not to fall to your death, Catelyn would never understand." With that, he was over the side of the cliff, descending as quick as a monkey.

Ned studied the rocky face of the bluff for a moment, then followed more slowly. The niches were there, as Littlefinger had promised, shallow cuts that would be invisible from below, unless you knew just where to look for them. The river was a long, dizzying distance below. Ned kept his face pressed to the rock and tried not to look down any more often than he had to.

When at last he reached the bottom, a narrow, muddy trail along the water's edge, Littlefinger was lazing against a rock and eating an apple. He was almost down to the core. "You are growing old and slow, Stark," he said, flipping the apple casually into the rushing water. "No matter, we ride the rest of the way." He had two horses waiting. Ned mounted up and trotted behind him, down the trail and into the city.

Finally Baelish drew rein in front of a ramshackle building, three stories, timbered, its windows bright with lamplight in the gathering dusk. The sounds of music and raucous laughter drifted out and floated over the water. Beside the door swung an ornate oil lamp on a heavy chain, with a globe of leaded red glass.

Ned Stark dismounted in a fury. "A brothel," he said as he seized Littlefinger by the shoulder and spun him around. "You've brought me all this way to take me to a brothel."

"Your wife is inside," Littlefinger said.

It was the final insult. "Brandon was too kind to you," Ned said as he slammed the small man back against a wall and shoved his dagger up under the little pointed chin beard.

"My lord, *no*," an urgent voice called out. "He speaks the truth." There were footsteps behind him.

Ned spun, knife in hand, as an old white-haired man hurried toward them. He was dressed in brown rough-spun, and the soft flesh under his chin wobbled as he ran. "This is no business of yours," Ned began; then, suddenly, the recognition came. He lowered the dagger, astonished. *"Ser Rodrik?"*

Rodrik Cassel nodded. "Your lady awaits you upstairs."

Ned was lost. "Catelyn is truly here? This is not some strange jape of Littlefinger's?" He sheathed his blade.

"Would that it were, Stark," Littlefinger said. "Follow me, and try to look a shade more lecherous and a shade less like the King's Hand. It would not do to have you recognized. Perhaps you could fondle a breast or two, just in passing."

They went inside, through a crowded common room where a fat woman was singing bawdy songs while pretty young girls in linen shifts and wisps of colored silk pressed themselves against their lovers and dandled on their laps. No one paid Ned the least bit of attention. Ser Rodrik waited below while Littlefinger led him up to the third floor, along a corridor, and through a door.

Inside, Catelyn was waiting. She cried out when she saw him, ran to him, and embraced him fiercely.

"My lady," Ned whispered in wonderment.

"Oh, very good," said Littlefinger, closing the door. "You recognized her."

"I feared you'd never come, my lord," she whispered against his chest. "Petyr has been bringing me reports. He told me of your troubles with Arya and the young prince. How are my girls?"

"Both in mourning, and full of anger," he told her. "Cat, I do not understand. What are you doing in King's Landing? What's happened?" Ned asked his wife. "Is it Bran? Is he . . ." *Dead* was the word that came to his lips, but he could not say it.

"It is Bran, but not as you think," Catelyn said.

Ned was lost. "Then how? Why are you here, my love? What is this place?"

"Just what it appears," Littlefinger said, easing himself onto a window seat. "A brothel. Can you think of a less likely place to find a Catelyn Tully?" He smiled. "As it chances, I own this particular establishment, so arrangements were easily made. I am most anxious to keep the Lannisters from learning that Cat is here in King's Landing."

"Why?" Ned asked. He saw her hands then, the awkward way she held them, the raw red scars, the stiffness of the last two fingers on her left. "You've been hurt." He took her hands in his own, turned them over. "Gods. Those are deep cuts . . . a gash from a sword or . . . how did this happen, my lady?"

Catelyn slid a dagger out from under her cloak and placed it in his hand. "This blade was sent to open Bran's throat and spill his life's blood."

Ned's head jerked up. "But . . . who . . . why would . . ."

She put a finger to his lips. "Let me tell it all, my love. It will go faster that way. Listen."

So he listened, and she told it all, from the fire in the library tower to Varys and the guardsmen and Littlefinger. And when she was done, Eddard Stark sat dazed beside the table, the dagger in his hand. Bran's wolf had saved the boy's life, he thought dully. What was it that Jon had said when they found the pups in the snow? *Your children were meant to have these pups, my lord.* And he had killed Sansa's, and for what? Was it guilt he was feeling? Or fear? If the gods had sent these wolves, what folly had he done?

Painfully, Ned forced his thoughts back to the dagger and what it meant. "The Imp's dagger," he repeated. It made no sense. His hand curled around the smooth dragonbone hilt, and he slammed the blade into the table, felt it bite into the wood. It stood mocking him. "Why should Tyrion Lannister want Bran dead? The boy has never done him harm."

"Do you Starks have nought but snow between your ears?" Littlefinger asked. "The Imp would never have acted alone."

Ned rose and paced the length of the room. "If the queen had a role in this or, gods forbid, the king himself . . . no, I will not believe that." Yet even as he said the words, he remembered that chill morning on the barrowlands, and Robert's talk of sending hired knives after the Targaryen princess. He remembered Rhaegar's infant son, the red ruin of his skull, and the way the king had turned away, as he had turned away in Darry's audience hall not so long ago. He could still hear Sansa pleading, as Lyanna had pleaded once.

"Most likely the king did *not* know," Littlefinger said. "It would not be the first time. Our good Robert is practiced at closing his eyes to things he would rather not see."

Ned had no reply for that. The face of the butcher's boy swam up before his eyes, cloven almost in two, and afterward the king had said not a word. His head was pounding.

Littlefinger sauntered over to the table, wrenched the knife from the wood. "The accusation is treason either way. Accuse the king and you will dance with Ilyn Payne before the words are out of your mouth. The queen . . . *if* you can find proof, and *if* you can make Robert listen, then perhaps . . ."

"We have proof," Ned said. "We have the dagger."

"This?" Littlefinger flipped the knife casually end over end. "A sweet piece of steel, but it cuts two ways, my lord. The Imp will no doubt swear the blade was lost or stolen while he was at Winterfell, and with his hireling dead, who is there to give him the lie?" He tossed the knife lightly to Ned. "My counsel is to drop that in the river and forget that it was ever forged."

Ned regarded him coldly. "Lord Baelish, I am a Stark of Winterfell. My son lies crippled, perhaps dying. He would be dead, and Catelyn with him, but for a wolf pup we found in the snow. If you truly believe I could forget that, you are as big a fool now as when you took up sword against my brother."

"A fool I may be, Stark . . . yet I'm still here, while your brother has been moldering in his frozen grave for some fourteen years now. If you are so eager to molder beside him, far be it from me to dissuade you, but I would rather not be included in the party, thank you very much."

"You would be the last man I would willingly include in any party, Lord Baelish."

"You wound me deeply." Littlefinger placed a hand over his heart. "For my part, I always found you Starks a tiresome lot, but Cat seems to have become attached to you, for reasons I cannot comprehend. I shall try to keep you alive for her sake. A fool's task, admittedly, but I could never refuse your wife anything."

"I told Petyr our suspicions about Jon Arryn's death," Catelyn said. "He has promised to help you find the truth."

That was not news that Eddard Stark welcomed, but it was true enough that they needed help, and Littlefinger had been almost a brother to Cat once. It would not be the first time that Ned had been forced to make common cause with a man he despised. "Very well," he said, thrusting the dagger into his belt. "You spoke of Varys. Does the eunuch know all of it?"

"Not from my lips," Catelyn said. "You did not wed a fool, Eddard Stark. But Varys has ways of learning things that no man could know. He has some dark art, Ned, I swear it."

"He has spies, that is well known," Ned said, dismissive.

"It is more than that," Catelyn insisted. "Ser Rodrik spoke to Ser Aron Santagar in all secrecy, yet somehow the Spider knew of their conversation. I fear that man."

Littlefinger smiled. "Leave Lord Varys to me, sweet lady. If you will permit me a small obscenity—and where better for it than here—I hold the man's balls in the palm of my hand." He cupped his fingers, smiling. "Or would, if he were a man, or had any balls. You see, if the pie is opened, the birds begin to sing, and Varys would not like that. Were I you, I would worry more about the Lannisters and less about the eunuch."

Ned did not need Littlefinger to tell him that. He was thinking back to the day Arya had been found, to the look on the queen's face when she said, *We have a wolf*, so soft and quiet. He was thinking of the boy Mycah, of Jon Arryn's sudden death, of Bran's fall, of old mad Aerys Targaryen dying on the floor of his throne room while his life's blood dried on a gilded blade. "My lady," he said, turning to Catelyn, "there is nothing more you can do here. I want you to return to Winterfell at once. If there was one assassin, there could be others. Whoever ordered Bran's death will learn soon enough that the boy still lives."

"I had hoped to see the girls . . ." Catelyn said.

"That would be most unwise," Littlefinger put in. "The Red Keep is full of curious eyes, and children talk."

"He speaks truly, my love," Ned told her. He embraced her. "Take Ser Rodrik and ride for Winterfell. I will watch over the girls. Go home to our sons and keep them safe."

"As you say, my lord." Catelyn lifted her face, and Ned kissed her. Her maimed fingers clutched against his back with a desperate strength, as if to hold him safe forever in the shelter of her arms.

"Would the lord and lady like the use of a bedchamber?" asked Littlefinger. "I should warn you, Stark, we usually charge for that sort of thing around here."

"A moment alone, that's all I ask," Catelyn said.

"Very well." Littlefinger strolled to the door. "Don't be too long. It is past time the Hand and I returned to the castle, before our absence is noted."

Catelyn went to him and took his hands in her own. "I will not forget the help you gave me, Petyr. When your men came for me, I did not know whether they were taking me to a friend or an enemy. I have found you more than a friend. I have found a brother I'd thought lost."

Petyr Baelish smiled. "I am desperately sentimental, sweet lady. Best not tell anyone. I have spent years convincing the court that I am wicked and cruel, and I should hate to see all that hard work go for naught."

Ned believed not a word of that, but he kept his voice polite as he said, "You have my thanks as well, Lord Baelish."

"Oh, now *there's* a treasure," Littlefinger said, exiting.

When the door had closed behind him, Ned turned back to his wife. "Once you are home, send word to Helman Tallhart and Galbart Glover under my seal. They are to raise a hundred bowmen each and fortify Moat Cailin. Two hundred determined archers can hold the Neck against an army. Instruct Lord Manderly that he is to strengthen and repair all his defenses at White Harbor, and see that they are well manned. And from this day on, I want a careful watch kept over Theon Greyjoy. If there is war, we shall have sore need of his father's fleet."

"War?" The fear was plain on Catelyn's face.

"It will not come to that," Ned promised her, praying it was true. He took her in his arms again. "The Lannisters are merciless in the face of weakness, as Aerys Targaryen learned to his sorrow, but they would not dare attack the north without all the power of the realm behind them, and that they shall not have. I must play out this fool's masquerade as if nothing is amiss. Remember why I came here, my love. If I find proof that the Lannisters murdered Jon Arryn . . ."

He felt Catelyn tremble in his arms. Her scarred hands clung to him. "If," she said, "what then, my love?"

That was the most dangerous part, Ned knew. "All justice flows from the king," he told her. "When I know the truth, I must go to Robert." *And pray that he is the man I think he is,* he finished silently, *and not the man I fear he has become.*

TYRION

"Are you certain that you must leave us so soon?" the Lord Commander asked him.

"Past certain, Lord Mormont," Tyrion replied. "My brother Jaime will be wondering what has become of me. He may decide that you have convinced me to take the black."

"Would that I could." Mormont picked up a crab claw and cracked it in his fist. Old as he was, the Lord Commander still had the strength of a bear. "You're a cunning man, Tyrion. We have need of men of your sort on the Wall."

Tyrion grinned. "Then I shall scour the Seven Kingdoms for dwarfs and ship them all to you, Lord Mormont." As they laughed, he sucked the meat from a crab leg and reached for another. The crabs had arrived from Eastwatch only this morning, packed in a barrel of snow, and they were succulent.

Ser Alliser Thorne was the only man at table who did not so much as crack a smile. "Lannister mocks us."

"Only you, Ser Alliser," Tyrion said. This time the laughter round the table had a nervous, uncertain quality to it.

Thorne's black eyes fixed on Tyrion with loathing. "You have a bold tongue for someone who is less than half a man. Perhaps you and I should visit the yard together."

"Why?" asked Tyrion. "The crabs are here."

The remark brought more guffaws from the others. Ser Alliser stood up, his mouth a tight line. "Come and make your japes with steel in your hand."

Tyrion looked pointedly at his right hand. "Why, I *have* steel in my hand, Ser Alliser, although it appears to be a crab fork. Shall we duel?" He hopped up on his chair and began poking at Thorne's chest with the tiny fork. Roars of laughter filled the tower room. Bits of crab flew from the Lord Commander's mouth as he began to gasp and choke. Even his raven joined in, cawing loudly from above the window. *"Duel! Duel! Duel!"*

Ser Alliser Thorne walked from the room so stiffly it looked as though he had a dagger up his butt.

Mormont was still gasping for breath. Tyrion pounded him on the back. "To the victor goes the spoils," he called out. "I claim Thorne's share of the crabs."

Finally the Lord Commander recovered himself. "You are a wicked man, to provoke our Ser Alliser so," he scolded.

Tyrion seated himself and took a sip of wine. "If a man paints a target on his chest, he should expect that sooner or later someone will loose an arrow at him. I have seen dead men with more humor than your Ser Alliser."

"Not so," objected the Lord Steward, Bowen Marsh, a man as round and red as a pomegranate. "You ought to hear the droll names he gives the lads he trains."

Tyrion had heard a few of those droll names. "I'll wager the lads have a few names for him as well," he said. "Chip the ice off your eyes, my good lords. Ser Alliser Thorne should be mucking out your stables, not drilling your young warriors."

"The Watch has no shortage of stableboys," Lord Mormont grumbled. "That seems to be all they send us these days. Stableboys and sneak thieves and rapers. Ser Alliser is an anointed knight, one of the few to take the black since I have been Lord Commander. He fought bravely at King's Landing."

"On the wrong side," Ser Jeremy Rykker commented

dryly. "I ought to know, I was there on the battlements beside him. Tywin Lannister gave us a splendid choice. Take the black, or see our heads on spikes before evenfall. No offense intended, Tyrion."

"None taken, Ser Jaremy. My father is very fond of spiked heads, especially those of people who have annoyed him in some fashion. And a face as noble as yours, well, no doubt he saw you decorating the city wall above the King's Gate. I think you would have looked very striking up there."

"Thank you," Ser Jaremy replied with a sardonic smile.

Lord Commander Mormont cleared his throat. "Sometimes I fear Ser Alliser saw you true, Tyrion. You *do* mock us and our noble purpose here."

Tyrion shrugged. "We all need to be mocked from time to time, Lord Mormont, lest we start to take ourselves too seriously. More wine, please." He held out his cup.

As Rykker filled it for him, Bowen Marsh said, "You have a great thirst for a small man."

"Oh, I think that Lord Tyrion is quite a large man," Maester Aemon said from the far end of the table. He spoke softly, yet the high officers of the Night's Watch all fell quiet, the better to hear what the ancient had to say. "I think he is a giant come among us, here at the end of the world."

Tyrion answered gently, "I've been called many things, my lord, but *giant* is seldom one of them."

"Nonetheless," Maester Aemon said as his clouded, milk-white eyes moved to Tyrion's face, "I think it is true."

For once, Tyrion Lannister found himself at a loss for words. He could only bow his head politely and say, "You are too kind, Maester Aemon."

The blind man smiled. He was a tiny thing, wrinkled and hairless, shrunken beneath the weight of a hundred years so his maester's collar with its links of many metals hung loose about his throat. "I have been called many things, my lord," he said, "but *kind* is seldom one of them." This time Tyrion himself led the laughter.

Much later, when the serious business of eating was done and the others had left, Mormont offered Tyrion a chair beside the fire and a cup of mulled spirits so strong they brought tears to his eyes. "The kingsroad can be perilous this far north," the Lord Commander told him as they drank.

"I have Jyck and Morrec," Tyrion said, "and Yoren is riding south again."

"Yoren is only one man. The Watch shall escort you as far as Winterfell," Mormont announced in a tone that brooked no argument. "Three men should be sufficient."

"If you insist, my lord," Tyrion said. "You might send young Snow. He would be glad for a chance to see his brothers."

Mormont frowned through his thick grey beard. "Snow? Oh, the Stark bastard. I think not. The young ones need to forget the lives they left behind them, the brothers and mothers and all that. A visit home would only stir up feelings best left alone. I know these things. My own blood kin . . . my sister Maege rules Bear Island now, since my son's dishonor. I have nieces I have never seen." He took a swallow. "Besides, Jon Snow is only a boy. You shall have three strong swords, to keep you safe."

"I am touched by your concern, Lord Mormont." The strong drink was making Tyrion light-headed, but not so drunk that he did not realize that the Old Bear wanted something from him. "I hope I can repay your kindness."

"You can," Mormont said bluntly. "Your sister sits beside the king. Your brother is a great knight, and your father the most powerful lord in the Seven Kingdoms. Speak to them for us. Tell them of our need here. You have seen for yourself, my lord. The Night's Watch is dying. Our strength is less than a thousand now. Six hundred here, two hundred in the Shadow Tower, even fewer at Eastwatch, and a scant third of those fighting men. The Wall is a hundred leagues long. Think on that. Should an attack come, I have three men to defend each mile of wall."

"Three and a third," Tyrion said with a yawn.

Mormont scarcely seemed to hear him. The old man warmed his hands before the fire. "I sent Benjen Stark to search after Yohn Royce's son, lost on his first ranging. The Royce boy was green as summer grass, yet he insisted on the honor of his own command, saying it was his due as a knight. I did not wish to offend his lord father, so I yielded. I sent him out with two men I deemed as good as any in the Watch. More fool I."

"*Fool,*" the raven agreed. Tyrion glanced up. The bird peered down at him with those beady black eyes, ruffling its wings. "*Fool,*" it called again. Doubtless old Mormont would take it amiss if he throttled the creature. A pity.

The Lord Commander took no notice of the irritating bird. "Gared was near as old as I am and longer on the Wall," he went on, "yet it would seem he forswore himself and fled. I should never have believed it, not of him, but Lord Eddard sent me his head from Winterfell. Of Royce, there is no word. One deserter and two men lost, and now Ben Stark too has gone missing." He sighed deeply. "Who am I to send searching after *him*? In two years I will be seventy. Too old and too weary for the burden I bear, yet if I set it down, who will pick it up? Alliser Thorne? Bowen Marsh? I would have to be as blind as Maester Aemon not to see what *they* are. The Night's Watch has become an army of sullen boys and tired old men. Apart from the men at my table tonight, I have perhaps twenty who can read, and even fewer who can think, or plan, or *lead*. Once the Watch spent its summers building, and each Lord Commander raised the Wall higher than he found it. Now it is all we can do to stay alive."

He was in deadly earnest, Tyrion realized. He felt faintly embarrassed for the old man. Lord Mormont had spent a good part of his life on the Wall, and he needed to believe if those years were to have any meaning. "I promise, the king will hear of your need," Tyrion said gravely, "and I will speak to my father and my brother Jaime as well." And he would. Tyrion Lannister was as good as his word. He left the rest unsaid; that King Robert would ignore him, Lord Tywin would ask if he had taken leave of his senses, and Jaime would only laugh.

"You are a young man, Tyrion," Mormont said. "How many winters have you seen?"

He shrugged. "Eight, nine. I misremember."

"And all of them short."

"As you say, my lord." He had been born in the dead of winter, a terrible cruel one that the maesters said had lasted near three years, but Tyrion's earliest memories were of spring.

"When I was a boy, it was said that a long summer always meant a long winter to come. This summer has lasted *nine years*, Tyrion, and a tenth will soon be upon us. Think on that."

"When *I* was a boy," Tyrion replied, "my wet nurse told me that one day, if men were good, the gods would give the world a summer without ending. Perhaps we've been better than we thought, and the Great Summer is finally at hand." He grinned.

The Lord Commander did not seem amused. "You are not fool enough to believe that, my lord. Already the days grow shorter. There can be no mistake, Aemon has had letters from the Citadel, findings in accord with his own. The end of summer stares us in the face." Mormont reached out and clutched Tyrion tightly by the hand. "You must *make* them understand. I tell you, my lord, the darkness is coming. There are wild things in the woods, direwolves and mammoths and snow bears the size of aurochs, and I have seen darker shapes in my dreams."

"In your dreams," Tyrion echoed, thinking how badly he needed another strong drink.

Mormont was deaf to the edge in his voice. "The fisherfolk near Eastwatch have glimpsed white walkers on the shore."

This time Tyrion could not hold his tongue. "The fisherfolk of Lannisport often glimpse merlings."

"Denys Mallister writes that the mountain people are moving south, slipping past the Shadow Tower in numbers greater than ever before. They are running, my lord . . . but running from *what*?" Lord Mormont moved to the window and stared out into the night. "These are old bones, Lannister, but they have never felt a chill like this. Tell the king what I say, I pray you. Winter *is* coming, and when the Long Night falls, only the Night's Watch will stand between the realm and the darkness that sweeps from the north. The gods help us all if we are not ready."

"The gods help *me* if I do not get some sleep tonight. Yoren is determined to ride at first light." Tyrion got to his feet, sleepy from wine and tired of doom. "I thank you for all the courtesies you have done me, Lord Mormont."

"Tell them, Tyrion. Tell them and make them believe. That is all the thanks I need." He whistled, and his raven flew to him and perched on his shoulder. Mormont smiled and gave the bird some corn from his pocket, and that was how Tyrion left him.

It was bitter cold outside. Bundled thickly in his furs, Tyrion Lannister pulled on his gloves and nodded to the poor frozen wretches standing sentry outside the Commander's Keep. He set off across the yard for his own chambers in the King's Tower, walking as briskly as his legs could manage. Patches of snow crunched beneath his feet as his boots broke the night's crust, and his breath steamed before him like a banner. He shoved his hands into his armpits and walked faster, praying that Morrec had remembered to warm his bed with hot bricks from the fire.

Behind the King's Tower, the Wall glimmered in the light of the moon, immense and mysterious. Tyrion stopped for a moment to look up at it. His legs ached of cold and haste.

Suddenly a strange madness took hold of him, a yearning to look once more off the end of the world. It would be his last chance, he thought; tomorrow he would ride south, and he could not imagine why he would ever want to return to this frozen desolation. The King's Tower was before him, with its promise of warmth and a soft bed, yet Tyrion found himself walking past it, toward the vast pale palisade of the Wall.

A wooden stair ascended the south face, anchored on huge rough-hewn beams sunk deep into the ice and frozen in place. Back and forth it switched, clawing its way upward as crooked as a bolt of lightning. The black brothers assured him that it was much stronger than it looked, but Tyrion's legs were cramping too badly for him to even contemplate the ascent. He went instead to the iron cage beside the well, clambered inside, and yanked hard on the bell rope, three quick pulls.

He had to wait what seemed an eternity, standing there inside the bars with the Wall to his back. Long enough for Tyrion to begin to wonder why he was doing this. He had just about decided to forget his sudden whim and go to bed when the cage gave a jerk and began to ascend.

He moved upward slowly, by fits and starts at first, then more smoothly. The ground fell away beneath him, the cage swung, and Tyrion wrapped his hands around the iron bars. He could feel the cold of the metal even through his gloves. Morrec had a fire burning in his room, he noted with approval, but the Lord Commander's tower was dark. The Old Bear had more sense than he did, it seemed.

Then he was above the towers, still inching his way upward. Castle Black lay below him, etched in moonlight. You could see how stark and empty it was from up here; windowless keeps, crumbling walls, courtyards choked with broken stone. Farther off, he could see the lights of Mole's Town, the little village half a league south along the kingsroad, and here and there the bright glitter of moonlight on water where icy streams descended from the mountain heights to cut across the plains. The rest of the world was a bleak emptiness of windswept hills and rocky fields spotted with snow.

Finally a thick voice behind him said, "Seven hells, it's the dwarf," and the cage jerked to a sudden stop and hung there, swinging slowly back and forth, the ropes creaking.

"Bring him in, damn it." There was a grunt and a loud groaning of wood as the cage slid sideways and then the Wall was beneath him. Tyrion waited until the swinging had stopped before he pushed open the cage door and hopped down onto the ice. A heavy figure in black was leaning on the winch, while a second held the cage with a gloved hand. Their faces were muffled in woolen scarves so only their eyes showed, and they were plump with layers of wool and leather, black on black. "And what will you be wanting, this time of night?" the one by the winch asked.

"A last look."

The men exchanged sour glances. "Look all you want," the other one said. "Just have a care you don't fall off, little man. The Old Bear would have our hides." A small wooden shack stood under the great crane, and Tyrion saw the dull glow of a brazier and felt a brief gust of warmth when the winch men opened the door and went back inside. And then he was alone.

It was bitingly cold up here, and the wind pulled at his clothes like an insistent lover. The top of the Wall was wider than the kingsroad often was, so Tyrion had no fear of falling, although the footing was slicker than he would have liked. The brothers spread crushed stone across the walkways, but the weight of countless footsteps would melt the Wall beneath, so the ice would seem to grow around the gravel, swallowing it, until the path was bare again and it was time to crush more stone.

Still, it was nothing that Tyrion could not manage. He looked off to the east and west, at the Wall stretching before him, a vast white road with no beginning and no end and a dark abyss on either side. West, he decided, for no special reason, and he began to walk that way, following the pathway nearest the north edge, where the gravel looked freshest.

His bare cheeks were ruddy with the cold, and his legs complained more loudly with every step, but Tyrion ignored them. The wind swirled around him, gravel crunched beneath his boots, while ahead the white ribbon followed the lines of the hills, rising higher and higher, until it was lost beyond the western horizon. He passed a massive catapult, as tall as a city wall, its base sunk deep into the Wall. The throwing arm had been taken off for repairs and then forgotten; it lay there like a broken toy, half-embedded in the ice.

On the far side of the catapult, a muffled voice called out a challenge. "Who goes there? Halt!"

Tyrion stopped. "If I halt too long I'll freeze in place, Jon," he said as a shaggy pale shape slid toward him silently and sniffed at his furs. "Hello, Ghost."

Jon Snow moved closer. He looked bigger and heavier in his layers of fur and leather, the hood of his cloak pulled down over his face. "Lannister," he said, yanking loose the scarf to uncover his mouth. "This is the last place I would have expected to see you." He carried a heavy spear tipped in iron, taller than he was, and a sword hung at his side in a leather sheath. Across his chest was a gleaming black warhorn, banded with silver.

"This is the last place I would have expected to be seen," Tyrion admitted. "I was captured by a whim. If I touch Ghost, will he chew my hand off?"

"Not with me here," Jon promised.

Tyrion scratched the white wolf behind the ears. The red eyes watched him impassively. The beast came up as high as his chest now. Another year, and Tyrion had the gloomy feeling he'd be looking *up* at him. "What are *you* doing up here tonight?" he asked. "Besides freezing your manhood off . . ."

"I have drawn night guard," Jon said. "Again. Ser Alliser has kindly arranged for the watch commander to take a special interest in me. He seems to think that if they keep me awake half the night, I'll fall asleep during morning drill. So far I have disappointed him."

Tyrion grinned. "And has Ghost learned to juggle yet?"

"No," said Jon, smiling, "but Grenn held his own against Halder this morning, and Pyp is no longer dropping his sword quite so often as he did."

"Pyp?"

"Pypar is his real name. The small boy with the large ears. He saw me working with Grenn and asked for help. Thorne had never even shown him the proper way to grip a sword." He turned to look north. "I have a mile of Wall to guard. Will you walk with me?"

"If you walk slowly," Tyrion said.

"The watch commander tells me I must walk, to keep my blood from freezing, but he never said how fast."

They walked, with Ghost pacing along beside Jon like a white shadow. "I leave on the morrow," Tyrion said.

"I know." Jon sounded strangely sad.

"I plan to stop at Winterfell on the way south. If there is any message that you would like me to deliver . . ."

"Tell Robb that I'm going to command the Night's Watch and keep him safe, so he might as well take up needlework with the girls and have Mikken melt down his sword for horseshoes."

"Your brother is bigger than me," Tyrion said with a laugh. "I decline to deliver any message that might get me killed."

"Rickon will ask when I'm coming home. Try to explain where I've gone, if you can. Tell him he can have all my things while I'm away, he'll like that."

People seemed to be asking a great deal of him today, Tyrion Lannister thought. "You could put all this in a letter, you know."

"Rickon can't read yet. Bran . . ." He stopped suddenly. "I don't know what message to send to Bran. Help him, Tyrion."

"What help could I give him? I am no maester, to ease his pain. I have no spells to give him back his legs."

"You gave me help when I needed it," Jon Snow said.

"I gave you nothing," Tyrion said. "Words."

"Then give your words to Bran too."

"You're asking a lame man to teach a cripple how to dance," Tyrion said. "However sincere the lesson, the result is likely to be grotesque. Still, I know what it is to love a brother, Lord Snow. I will give Bran whatever small help is in my power."

"Thank you, my lord of Lannister." He pulled off his glove and offered his bare hand. "Friend."

Tyrion found himself oddly touched. "Most of my kin are bastards," he said with a wry smile, "but you're the first I've had to friend." He pulled a glove off with his teeth and clasped Snow by the hand, flesh against flesh. The boy's grip was firm and strong.

When he had donned his glove again, Jon Snow turned abruptly and walked to the low, icy northern parapet. Beyond him the Wall fell away sharply; beyond him there was only the darkness and the wild. Tyrion followed him, and side by side they stood upon the edge of the world.

The Night's Watch permitted the forest to come no closer than half a mile of the north face of the Wall. The thickets of ironwood and sentinel and oak that had once grown there had been harvested centuries ago, to create a broad swath of open ground through which no enemy could hope to pass unseen. Tyrion had heard that elsewhere along the Wall, between the three fortresses, the wildwood had come creeping back over the decades, that there were places where grey-green sentinels and pale white weirwoods had taken root in the shadow of the Wall itself, but Castle Black had a prodigious appetite for firewood, and here the forest was still kept at bay by the axes of the black brothers.

It was never far, though. From up here Tyrion could see it, the dark trees looming beyond the stretch of open ground, like a second wall built parallel to the first, a wall of night. Few axes had ever swung in *that* black wood, where even the moonlight could not penetrate the ancient tangle of root and thorn and grasping limb. Out there the trees grew huge, and the rangers said they seemed to brood and knew not men. It was small wonder the Night's Watch named it the haunted forest.

As he stood there and looked at all that darkness with

no fires burning anywhere, with the wind blowing and the cold like a spear in his guts, Tyrion Lannister felt as though he could almost believe the talk of the Others, the enemy in the night. His jokes of grumkins and snarks no longer seemed quite so droll.

"My uncle is out there," Jon Snow said softly, leaning on his spear as he stared off into the darkness. "The first night they sent me up here, I thought, Uncle Benjen will ride back tonight, and I'll see him first and blow the horn. He never came, though. Not that night and not any night."

"Give him time," Tyrion said.

Far off to the north, a wolf began to howl. Another voice picked up the call, then another. Ghost cocked his head and listened. "If he doesn't come back," Jon Snow promised, "Ghost and I will go find him." He put his hand on the direwolf's head.

"I believe you," Tyrion said, but what he thought was, *And who will go find you?* He shivered.

ARYA

Her father had been fighting with the council again. Arya could see it on his face when he came to table, late again, as he had been so often. The first course, a thick sweet soup made with pumpkins, had already been taken away when Ned Stark strode into the Small Hall. They called it that to set it apart from the Great Hall, where the king could feast a thousand, but it was a long room with a high vaulted ceiling and bench space for two hundred at its trestle tables.

"My lord," Jory said when Father entered. He rose to his feet, and the rest of the guard rose with him. Each man wore a new cloak, heavy grey wool with a white satin border. A hand of beaten silver clutched the woolen folds of each cloak and marked their wearers as men of the Hand's household guard. There were only fifty of them, so most of the benches were empty.

"Be seated," Eddard Stark said. "I see you have started without me. I am pleased to know there are still some men of sense in this city." He signaled for the meal to resume. The servants began bringing out platters of ribs, roasted in a crust of garlic and herbs.

"The talk in the yard is we shall have a tourney, my

lord," Jory said as he resumed his seat. "They say that knights will come from all over the realm to joust and feast in honor of your appointment as Hand of the King."

Arya could see that her father was not very happy about that. "Do they also say this is the last thing in the world I would have wished?"

Sansa's eyes had grown wide as the plates. "A *tourney*," she breathed. She was seated between Septa Mordane and Jeyne Poole, as far from Arya as she could get without drawing a reproach from Father. "Will we be permitted to go, Father?"

"You know my feelings, Sansa. It seems I must arrange Robert's games and pretend to be honored for his sake. That does not mean I must subject my daughters to this folly."

"Oh, *please*," Sansa said. "I want to see."

Septa Mordane spoke up. "Princess Myrcella will be there, my lord, and her younger than Lady Sansa. All the ladies of the court will be expected at a grand event like this, and as the tourney is in your honor, it would look queer if your family did not attend."

Father looked pained. "I suppose so. Very well, I shall arrange a place for you, Sansa." He saw Arya. "For both of you."

"I don't care about their stupid tourney," Arya said. She knew Prince Joffrey would be there, and she hated Prince Joffrey.

Sansa lifted her head. "It will be a *splendid* event. You shan't be wanted."

Anger flashed across Father's face. "*Enough*, Sansa. More of that and you will change my mind. I am weary unto death of this endless war you two are fighting. You are sisters. I expect you to behave like sisters, is that understood?"

Sansa bit her lip and nodded. Arya lowered her face to stare sullenly at her plate. She could feel tears stinging her eyes. She rubbed them away angrily, determined not to cry.

The only sound was the clatter of knives and forks. "Pray excuse me," her father announced to the table. "I find I have small appetite tonight." He walked from the hall.

After he was gone, Sansa exchanged excited whispers

with Jeyne Poole. Down the table Jory laughed at a joke, and Hullen started in about horseflesh. "Your warhorse, now, he may not be the best one for the joust. Not the same thing, oh, no, not the same at all." The men had heard it all before; Desmond, Jacks, and Hullen's son Harwin shouted him down together, and Porther called for more wine.

No one talked to Arya. She didn't care. She liked it that way. She would have eaten her meals alone in her bedchamber if they let her. Sometimes they did, when Father had to dine with the king or some lord or the envoys from this place or that place. The rest of the time, they ate in his solar, just him and her and Sansa. That was when Arya missed her brothers most. She wanted to tease Bran and play with baby Rickon and have Robb smile at her. She wanted Jon to muss up her hair and call her "little sister" and finish her sentences with her. But all of them were gone. She had no one left but Sansa, and Sansa wouldn't even talk to her unless Father made her.

Back at Winterfell, they had eaten in the Great Hall almost half the time. Her father used to say that a lord needed to eat with his men, if he hoped to keep them. "Know the men who follow you," she heard him tell Robb once, "and let them know you. Don't ask your men to die for a stranger." At Winterfell, he always had an extra seat set at his own table, and every day a different man would be asked to join him. One night it would be Vayon Poole, and the talk would be coppers and bread stores and servants. The next time it would be Mikken, and her father would listen to him go on about armor and swords and how hot a forge should be and the best way to temper steel. Another day it might be Hullen with his endless horse talk, or Septon Chayle from the library, or Jory, or Ser Rodrik, or even Old Nan with her stories.

Arya had loved nothing better than to sit at her father's table and listen to them talk. She had loved listening to the men on the benches too; to freeriders tough as leather, courtly knights and bold young squires, grizzled old men-at-arms. She used to throw snowballs at them and help them steal pies from the kitchen. Their wives gave her scones and she invented names for their babies and played monsters-and-maidens and hide-the-treasure and come-into-my-castle with their children. Fat Tom used to call her "Arya Underfoot," because he said that was where she always was. She'd liked that a lot better than "Arya Horseface."

Only that was Winterfell, a world away, and now everything was changed. This was the first time they had supped with the men since arriving in King's Landing. Arya hated it. She hated the sounds of their voices now, the way they laughed, the stories they told. They'd been her friends, she'd felt safe around them, but now she knew that was a lie. They'd let the queen kill Lady, that was horrible enough, but then the Hound found Mycah. Jeyne Poole had told Arya that he'd cut him up in so many pieces that they'd given him back to the butcher in a bag, and at first the poor man had thought it was a pig they'd slaughtered. And no one had raised a voice or drawn a blade or *anything*, not Harwin who always talked so bold, or Alyn who was going to be a knight, or Jory who was captain of the guard. Not even her father.

"He was my *friend*," Arya whispered into her plate, so low that no one could hear. Her ribs sat there untouched, grown cold now, a thin film of grease congealing beneath them on the plate. Arya looked at them and felt ill. She pushed away from the table.

"Pray, where do you think you are going, young lady?" Septa Mordane asked.

"I'm not hungry." Arya found it an effort to remember her courtesies. "May I be excused, please?" she recited stiffly.

"You may not," the septa said. "You have scarcely touched your food. You will sit down and clean your plate."

"You clean it!" Before anyone could stop her, Arya bolted for the door as the men laughed and Septa Mordane called loudly after her, her voice rising higher and higher.

Fat Tom was at his post, guarding the door to the Tower of the Hand. He blinked when he saw Arya rushing toward him and heard the septa's shouts. "Here now, little one, hold on," he started to say, reaching, but Arya slid between his legs and then she was running up the winding tower steps, her feet hammering on the stone while Fat Tom huffed and puffed behind her.

Her bedchamber was the only place that Arya liked in all of King's Landing, and the thing she liked best about it was the door, a massive slab of dark oak with black iron bands. When she slammed that door and dropped the heavy crossbar, nobody could get into her room, not Septa Mordane or Fat Tom or Sansa or Jory or the Hound, *nobody!* She slammed it now.

When the bar was down, Arya finally felt safe enough to cry.

She went to the window seat and sat there, sniffling, hating them all, and herself most of all. It was all her fault, everything bad that had happened. Sansa said so, and Jeyne too.

Fat Tom was knocking on her door. "Arya girl, what's wrong?" he called out. "You in there?"

"No!" she shouted. The knocking stopped. A moment later she heard him going away. Fat Tom was always easy to fool.

Arya went to the chest at the foot of her bed. She knelt, opened the lid, and began pulling her clothes out with both hands, grabbing handfuls of silk and satin and velvet and wool and tossing them on the floor. It was there at the bottom of the chest, where she'd hidden it. Arya lifted it out almost tenderly and drew the slender blade from its sheath.

Needle.

She thought of Mycah again and her eyes filled with tears. Her fault, her fault, her fault. If she had never asked him to play at swords with her . . .

There was a pounding at her door, louder than before. *"Arya Stark, you open this door at once, do you hear me?"*

Arya spun around, with Needle in her hand. "You better not come in here!" she warned. She slashed at the air savagely.

"The Hand will hear of this!" Septa Mordane raged.

"I don't care," Arya screamed. "Go away."

"You will rue this insolent behavior, young lady, I promise you that." Arya listened at the door until she heard the sound of the septa's receding footsteps.

She went back to the window, Needle in hand, and looked down into the courtyard below. If only she could climb like Bran, she thought; she would go out the window and down the tower, run away from this horrible place, away from Sansa and Septa Mordane and Prince

Joffrey, from all of them. Steal some food from the kitchens, take Needle and her good boots and a warm cloak. She could find Nymeria in the wild woods below the Trident, and together they'd return to Winterfell, or run to Jon on the Wall. She found herself wishing that Jon was here with her now. Then maybe she wouldn't feel so alone.

A soft knock at the door behind her turned Arya away from the window and her dreams of escape. "Arya," her father's voice called out. "Open the door. We need to talk."

Arya crossed the room and lifted the crossbar. Father was alone. He seemed more sad than angry. That made Arya feel even worse. "May I come in?" Arya nodded, then dropped her eyes, ashamed. Father closed the door. "Whose sword is that?"

"Mine." Arya had almost forgotten Needle, in her hand.

"Give it to me."

Reluctantly Arya surrendered her sword, wondering if she would ever hold it again. Her father turned it in the light, examining both sides of the blade. He tested the point with his thumb. "A bravo's blade," he said. "Yet it seems to me that I know this maker's mark. This is Mikken's work."

Arya could not lie to him. She lowered her eyes.

Lord Eddard Stark sighed. "My nine-year-old daughter is being armed from my own forge, and I know nothing of it. The Hand of the King is expected to rule the Seven Kingdoms, yet it seems I cannot even rule my own household. How is it that you come to own a sword, Arya? Where did you get this?"

Arya chewed her lip and said nothing. She would not betray Jon, not even to their father.

After a while, Father said, "I don't suppose it matters, truly." He looked down gravely at the sword in his hands. "This is no toy for children, least of all for a girl. What would Septa Mordane say if she knew you were playing with swords?"

"I wasn't *playing*," Arya insisted. "I hate Septa Mordane."

"That's enough." Her father's voice was curt and hard. "The septa is doing no more than is her duty, though gods know you have made it a struggle for the poor woman. Your mother and I have charged her with the impossible task of making you a lady."

"I don't *want* to be a lady!" Arya flared.

"I ought to snap this toy across my knee here and now, and put an end to this nonsense."

"Needle wouldn't break," Arya said defiantly, but her voice betrayed her words.

"It has a name, does it?" Her father sighed. "Ah, Arya. You have a wildness in you, child. 'The wolf blood,' my father used to call it. Lyanna had a touch of it, and my brother Brandon more than a touch. It brought them both to an early grave." Arya heard sadness in his voice; he did not often speak of his father, or of the brother and sister who had died before she was born. "Lyanna might have carried a sword, if my lord father had allowed it. You remind me of her sometimes. You even look like her."

"Lyanna was beautiful," Arya said, startled. Everybody said so. It was not a thing that was ever said of Arya.

"She was," Eddard Stark agreed, "beautiful, and willful, and dead before her time." He lifted the sword, held it out between them. "Arya, what did you think to do with this . . . Needle? Who did you hope to skewer? Your sister? Septa Mordane? Do you know the first thing about sword fighting?"

All she could think of was the lesson Jon had given her. "Stick them with the pointy end," she blurted out.

Her father snorted back laughter. "That *is* the essence of it, I suppose."

Arya desperately wanted to explain, to make him see. "I was trying to learn, but . . ." Her eyes filled with tears. "I asked Mycah to practice with me." The grief came on her all at once. She turned away, shaking. "I *asked* him," she cried. "It was my fault, it was me . . ."

Suddenly her father's arms were around her. He held her gently as she turned to him and sobbed against his chest. "No, sweet one," he murmured. "Grieve for your friend, but never blame yourself. You did not kill the butcher's boy. That murder lies at the Hound's door, him and the cruel woman he serves."

"I hate them," Arya confided, red-faced, sniffling. "The Hound and the queen and the king and Prince Joffrey. I hate all of them. Joffrey *lied*, it wasn't the way he said. I hate Sansa too. She *did* remember, she just lied so Joffrey would like her."

"We all lie," her father said. "Or did you truly think I'd believe that Nymeria ran off?"

Arya blushed guiltily. "Jory promised not to tell."

"Jory kept his word," her father said with a smile. "There are some things I do not need to be told. Even a blind man could see that wolf would never have left you willingly."

"We had to throw rocks," she said miserably. "I *told* her to run, to go be free, that I didn't want her anymore. There were other wolves for her to play with, we heard them howling, and Jory said the woods were full of game, so she'd have deer to hunt. Only she kept following, and finally we had to throw rocks. I hit her twice. She whined and looked at me and I felt so 'shamed, but it was right, wasn't it? The queen would have killed her."

"It was right," her father said. "And even the lie was . . . not without honor." He'd put Needle aside when he went to Arya to embrace her. Now he took the blade up again and walked to the window, where he stood for a moment, looking out across the courtyard. When he turned back, his eyes were thoughtful. He seated himself on the window seat, Needle across his lap. "Arya, sit down. I need to try and explain some things to you."

She perched anxiously on the edge of her bed. "You are too young to be burdened with all my cares," he told her, "but you are also a Stark of Winterfell. You know our words."

"Winter is coming," Arya whispered.

"The hard cruel times," her father said. "We tasted them on the Trident, child, and when Bran fell. You were born in the long summer, sweet one, you've never known anything else, but now the winter is truly coming. Remember the sigil of our House, Arya."

"The direwolf," she said, thinking of Nymeria. She hugged her knees against her chest, suddenly afraid.

"Let me tell you something about wolves, child. When the snows fall and the white winds blow, the lone wolf dies, but the pack survives. Summer is the time for squabbles. In winter, we must protect one another, keep each other warm, share our strengths. So if you must hate, Arya, hate those who would truly do us harm. Septa

Mordane is a good woman, and Sansa . . . Sansa is your sister. You may be as different as the sun and the moon, but the same blood flows through both your hearts. You need her, as she needs you . . . and I need both of you, gods help me."

He sounded so tired that it made Arya sad. "I don't hate Sansa," she told him. "Not truly." It was only half a lie.

"I do not mean to frighten you, but neither will I lie to you. We have come to a dark dangerous place, child. This is not Winterfell. We have enemies who mean us ill. We cannot fight a war among ourselves. This willfulness of yours, the running off, the angry words, the disobedience . . . at home, these were only the summer games of a child. Here and now, with winter soon upon us, that is a different matter. It is time to begin growing up."

"I will," Arya vowed. She had never loved him so much as she did in that instant. "I can be strong too. I can be as strong as Robb."

He held Needle out to her, hilt first. "Here."

She looked at the sword with wonder in her eyes. For a moment she was afraid to touch it, afraid that if she reached for it it would be snatched away again, but then her father said, "Go on, it's yours," and she took it in her hand.

"I can keep it?" she said. "For true?"

"For true." He smiled. "If I took it away, no doubt I'd find a morningstar hidden under your pillow within the fortnight. Try not to stab your sister, whatever the provocation."

"I won't. I promise." Arya clutched Needle tightly to her chest as her father took his leave.

The next morning, as they broke their fast, she apologized to Septa Mordane and asked for her pardon. The septa peered at her suspiciously, but Father nodded.

Three days later, at midday, her father's steward Vayon Poole sent Arya to the Small Hall. The trestle tables had been dismantled and the benches shoved against the walls. The hall seemed empty, until an unfamiliar voice said, "You are late, boy." A slight man with a bald head and a great beak of a nose stepped out of the shadows, holding a pair of slender wooden swords. "Tomorrow you will be here at midday." He had an accent, the lilt of the Free Cities, Braavos perhaps, or Myr.

"Who are you?" Arya asked.

"I am your dancing master." He tossed her one of the wooden blades. She grabbed for it, missed, and heard it clatter to the floor. "Tomorrow you will catch it. Now pick it up."

It was not just a stick, but a true wooden sword complete with grip and guard and pommel. Arya picked it up and clutched it nervously with both hands, holding it out in front of her. It was heavier than it looked, much heavier than Needle.

The bald man clicked his teeth together. "That is not the way, boy. This is not a greatsword that is needing two hands to swing it. You will take the blade in one hand."

"It's too heavy," Arya said.

"It is heavy as it needs to be to make you strong, and for the balancing. A hollow inside is filled with lead, just so. One hand now is all that is needing."

Arya took her right hand off the grip and wiped her sweaty palm on her pants. She held the sword in her left hand. He seemed to approve. "The left is good. All is reversed, it will make your enemies more awkward. Now you are standing wrong. Turn your body sideface, yes, so. You are skinny as the shaft of a spear, do you know. That is good too, the target is smaller. Now the grip. Let me see." He moved closer and peered at her hand, prying her fingers apart, rearranging them. "Just so, yes. Do not squeeze it so tight, no, the grip must be deft, delicate."

"What if I drop it?" Arya said.

"The steel must be part of your arm," the bald man told her. "Can you drop part of your arm? No. Nine years Syrio Forel was first sword to the Sealord of Braavos, he knows these things. Listen to him, boy."

It was the third time he had called her "boy." "I'm a girl," Arya objected.

"Boy, girl," Syrio Forel said. "You are a sword, that is all." He clicked his teeth together. "Just so, that is the grip. You are not holding a battle-axe, you are holding a—"

"—*needle*," Arya finished for him, fiercely.

"Just so. Now we will begin the dance. Remember, child, this is not the iron dance of Westeros we are learning, the knight's dance, hacking and hammering, no. This is the bravo's dance, the water dance, swift and sudden. All men are made of water, do you know this? When you pierce them, the water leaks out and they die." He took a step backward, raised his own wooden blade. "Now you will try to strike me."

Arya tried to strike him. She tried for four hours, until every muscle in her body was sore and aching, while Syrio Forel clicked his teeth together and told her what to do.

The next day their real work began.

DAENERYS

"The Dothraki sea," Ser Jorah Mormont said as he reined to a halt beside her on the top of the ridge. Beneath them, the plain stretched out immense and empty, a vast flat expanse that reached to the distant horizon and beyond. It *was* a sea, Dany thought. Past here, there were no hills, no mountains, no trees nor cities nor roads, only the endless grasses, the tall blades rippling like waves when the winds blew. "It's so green," she said.

"Here and now," Ser Jorah agreed. "You ought to see it when it blooms, all dark red flowers from horizon to horizon, like a sea of blood. Come the dry season, and the world turns the color of old bronze. And this is only *hranna*, child. There are a hundred kinds of grass out there, grasses as yellow as lemon and as dark as indigo, blue grasses and orange grasses and grasses like rainbows. Down in the Shadow Lands beyond Asshai, they say there are oceans of ghost grass, taller than a man on horseback with stalks as pale as milkglass. It murders all other grass and glows in the dark with the spirits of the damned. The Dothraki claim that someday ghost grass will cover the entire world, and then all life will end."

That thought gave Dany the shivers. "I don't want to talk about that now," she said. "It's so beautiful here, I don't want to think about everything dying."

"As you will, *Khaleesi*," Ser Jorah said respectfully.

She heard the sound of voices and turned to look behind her. She and Mormont had outdistanced the rest of their party, and now the others were climbing the ridge below them. Her handmaid Irri and the young archers of her *khas* were fluid as centaurs, but Viserys still struggled with the short stirrups and the flat saddle. Her brother was miserable out here. He ought never have come. Magister Illyrio had urged him to wait in Pentos, had offered him the hospitality of his manse, but Viserys would have none of it. He would stay with Drogo until the debt had been paid, until he had the crown he had been promised. "And if he tries to cheat me, he will learn to his sorrow what it means to wake the dragon," Viserys had vowed, laying a hand on his borrowed sword. Illyrio had blinked at that and wished him good fortune.

Dany realized that she did not want to listen to any of her brother's complaints right now. The day was too perfect. The sky was a deep blue, and high above them a hunting hawk circled. The grass sea swayed and sighed with each breath of wind, the air was warm on her face, and Dany felt at peace. She would not let Viserys spoil it.

"Wait here," Dany told Ser Jorah. "Tell them all to stay. Tell them I command it."

The knight smiled. Ser Jorah was not a handsome man. He had a neck and shoulders like a bull, and coarse black hair covered his arms and chest so thickly that there was none left for his head. Yet his smiles gave Dany comfort. "You are learning to talk like a queen, Daenerys."

"Not a queen," said Dany. "A *khaleesi*." She wheeled her horse about and galloped down the ridge alone.

The descent was steep and rocky, but Dany rode fearlessly, and the joy and the danger of it were a song in her heart. All her life Viserys had told her she was a princess, but not until she rode her silver had Daenerys Targaryen ever felt like one.

At first it had not come easy. The *khalasar* had broken camp the morning after her wedding, moving east toward Vaes Dothrak, and by the third day Dany thought she was going to die. Saddle sores opened on her bottom, hideous and bloody. Her thighs were chafed raw, her hands blistered from the reins, the muscles of her legs and back so wracked with pain that she could scarcely sit. By the time dusk fell, her handmaids would need to help her down from her mount.

Even the nights brought no relief. Khal Drogo ignored her when they rode, even as he had ignored her during their wedding, and spent his evenings drinking with his warriors and bloodriders, racing his prize horses, watching women dance and men die. Dany had no place in these parts of his life. She was left to sup alone, or with Ser Jorah and her brother, and afterward to cry herself to sleep. Yet every night, some time before the dawn, Drogo would come to her tent and wake her in the dark, to ride her as relentlessly as he rode his stallion. He always took her from behind, Dothraki fashion, for which Dany was grateful; that way her lord husband could not see the tears that wet her face, and she could use her pillow to muffle her cries of pain. When he was done, he would close his eyes and begin to snore softly and Dany would lie beside him, her body bruised and sore, hurting too much for sleep.

Day followed day, and night followed night, until Dany knew she could not endure a moment longer. She would kill herself rather than go on, she decided one night . . .

Yet when she slept that night, she dreamt the dragon dream again. Viserys was not in it this time. There was only her and the dragon. Its scales were black as night, wet and slick with blood. *Her* blood, Dany sensed. Its eyes were pools of molten magma, and when it opened its mouth, the flame came roaring out in a hot jet. She could hear it singing to her. She opened her arms to the fire, embraced it, let it swallow her whole, let it cleanse her and temper her and scour her clean. She could feel her flesh sear and blacken and slough away, could feel her blood boil and turn to steam, and yet there was no pain. She felt strong and new and fierce.

And the next day, strangely, she did not seem to hurt quite so much. It was as if the gods had heard her and taken pity. Even her handmaids noticed the change. *"Khaleesi,"* Jhiqui said, "what is wrong? Are you sick?"

"I was," she answered, standing over the dragon's eggs

that Illyrio had given her when she wed. She touched one, the largest of the three, running her hand lightly over the shell. *Black-and-scarlet,* she thought, *like the dragon in my dream.* The stone felt strangely warm beneath her fingers . . . or was she still dreaming? She pulled her hand back nervously.

From that hour onward, each day was easier than the one before it. Her legs grew stronger, her blisters burst and her hands grew callused; her soft thighs toughened, supple as leather.

The *khal* had commanded the handmaid Irri to teach Dany to ride in the Dothraki fashion, but it was the filly who was her real teacher. The horse seemed to know her moods, as if they shared a single mind. With every passing day, Dany felt surer in her seat. The Dothraki were a hard and unsentimental people, and it was not their custom to name their animals, so Dany thought of her only as the silver. She had never loved anything so much.

As the riding became less an ordeal, Dany began to notice the beauties of the land around her. She rode at the head of the *khalasar* with Drogo and his bloodriders, so she came to each country fresh and unspoiled. Behind them the great horde might tear the earth and muddy the rivers and send up clouds of choking dust, but the fields ahead of them were always green and verdant.

They crossed the rolling hills of Norvos, past terraced farms and small villages where the townsfolk watched anxiously from atop white stucco walls. They forded three wide placid rivers and a fourth that was swift and narrow and treacherous, camped beside a high blue waterfall, skirted the tumbled ruins of a vast dead city where ghosts were said to moan among blackened marble columns. They raced down Valyrian roads a thousand years old and straight as a Dothraki arrow. For half a moon, they rode through the Forest of Qohor, where the leaves made a golden canopy high above them, and the trunks of the trees were as wide as city gates. There were great elk in that wood, and spotted tigers, and lemurs with silver fur and huge purple eyes, but all fled before the approach of the *khalasar* and Dany got no glimpse of them.

By then her agony was a fading memory. She still ached after a long day's riding, yet somehow the pain had a sweetness to it now, and each morning she came will-

ingly to her saddle, eager to know what wonders waited
for her in the lands ahead. She began to find pleasure even
in her nights, and if she still cried out when Drogo took
her, it was not always in pain.

At the bottom of the ridge, the grasses rose around her,
tall and supple. Dany slowed to a trot and rode out onto
the plain, losing herself in the green, blessedly alone. In
the *khalasar* she was never alone. Khal Drogo came to her
only after the sun went down, but her handmaids fed her
and bathed her and slept by the door of her tent, Drogo's
bloodriders and the men of her *khas* were never far, and
her brother was an unwelcome shadow, day and night.
Dany could hear him on the top of the ridge, his voice
shrill with anger as he shouted at Ser Jorah. She rode on,
submerging herself deeper in the Dothraki sea.

The green swallowed her up. The air was rich with the
scents of earth and grass, mixed with the smell of horseflesh and Dany's sweat and the oil in her hair. Dothraki
smells. They seemed to belong here. Dany breathed it all
in, laughing. She had a sudden urge to feel the ground
beneath her, to curl her toes in that thick black soil.
Swinging down from her saddle, she let the silver graze
while she pulled off her high boots.

Viserys came upon her as sudden as a summer storm,
his horse rearing beneath him as he reined up too hard.
"You *dare!*" he screamed at her. "You give commands to
me? *To me!*" He vaulted off the horse, stumbling as he
landed. His face was flushed as he struggled back to his
feet. He grabbed her, shook her. "Have you forgotten who
you are? Look at you. *Look at you!*"

Dany did not need to look. She was barefoot, with
oiled hair, wearing Dothraki riding leathers and a painted
vest given her as a bride gift. She looked as though she
belonged here. Viserys was soiled and stained in city silks
and ringmail.

He was still screaming. "You do *not* command the
dragon. Do you understand? I am the Lord of the Seven
Kingdoms, I will not hear orders from some horselord's
slut, do you hear me?" His hand went under her vest, his
fingers digging painfully into her breast. *"Do you hear
me?"*

Dany shoved him away, hard.

Viserys stared at her, his lilac eyes incredulous. She

had never defied him. Never fought back. Rage twisted his features. He would hurt her now, and badly, she knew that.

Crack.

The whip made a sound like thunder. The coil took Viserys around the throat and yanked him backward. He went sprawling in the grass, stunned and choking. The Dothraki riders hooted at him as he struggled to free himself. The one with the whip, young Jhogo, rasped a question. Dany did not understand his words, but by then Irri was there, and Ser Jorah, and the rest of her *khas*. "Jhogo asks if you would have him dead, *Khaleesi*," Irri said.

"No," Dany replied. "No."

Jhogo understood that. One of the others barked out a comment, and the Dothraki laughed. Irri told her, "Quaro thinks you should take an ear to teach him respect."

Her brother was on his knees, his fingers digging under the leather coils, crying incoherently, struggling for breath. The whip was tight around his windpipe.

"Tell them I do not wish him harmed," Dany said.

Irri repeated her words in Dothraki. Jhogo gave a pull on the whip, yanking Viserys around like a puppet on a string. He went sprawling again, freed from the leather embrace, a thin line of blood under his chin where the whip had cut deep.

"I warned him what would happen, my lady," Ser Jorah Mormont said. "I told him to stay on the ridge, as you commanded."

"I know you did," Dany replied, watching Viserys. He lay on the ground, sucking in air noisily, red-faced and sobbing. He was a pitiful thing. He had always been a pitiful thing. Why had she never seen that before? There was a hollow place inside her where her fear had been.

"Take his horse," Dany commanded Ser Jorah. Viserys gaped at her. He could not believe what he was hearing; nor could Dany quite believe what she was saying. Yet the words came. "Let my brother walk behind us back to the *khalasar*." Among the Dothraki, the man who does not ride was no man at all, the lowest of the low, without honor or pride. "Let everyone see him as he is."

"*No!*" Viserys screamed. He turned to Ser Jorah, pleading in the Common Tongue with words the horsemen would not understand. "Hit her, Mormont. Hurt her.

Your king commands it. Kill these Dothraki dogs and teach her.''

The exile knight looked from Dany to her brother; she barefoot, with dirt between her toes and oil in her hair, he with his silks and steel. Dany could see the decision on his face. ''He shall walk, *Khaleesi*,'' he said. He took her brother's horse in hand while Dany remounted her silver.

Viserys gaped at him, and sat down in the dirt. He kept his silence, but he would not move, and his eyes were full of poison as they rode away. Soon he was lost in the tall grass. When they could not see him anymore, Dany grew afraid. ''Will he find his way back?'' she asked Ser Jorah as they rode.

''Even a man as blind as your brother should be able to follow our trail,'' he replied.

''He is proud. He may be too shamed to come back.''

Jorah laughed. ''Where else should he go? If he cannot find the *khalasar*, the *khalasar* will most surely find him. It is hard to drown in the Dothraki sea, child.''

Dany saw the truth of that. The *khalasar* was like a city on the march, but it did not march blindly. Always scouts ranged far ahead of the main column, alert for any sign of game or prey or enemies, while outriders guarded their flanks. They missed nothing, not here, in this land, the place where they had come from. These plains were a part of them . . . and of her, now.

''I hit him,'' she said, wonder in her voice. Now that it was over, it seemed like some strange dream that she had dreamed. ''Ser Jorah, do you think . . . he'll be so angry when he gets back . . .'' She shivered. ''I woke the dragon, didn't I?''

Ser Jorah snorted. ''Can you wake the dead, girl? Your brother Rhaegar was the last dragon, and he died on the Trident. Viserys is less than the shadow of a snake.''

His blunt words startled her. It seemed as though all the things she had always believed were suddenly called into question. ''You . . . you swore him your sword . . .''

''That I did, girl,'' Ser Jorah said. ''And if your brother is the shadow of a snake, what does that make his servants?'' His voice was bitter.

''He is still the true king. He is . . .''

Jorah pulled up his horse and looked at her. "Truth now. Would you want to see Viserys sit a throne?"

Dany thought about that. "He would not be a very good king, would he?"

"There have been worse . . . but not many." The knight gave his heels to his mount and started off again.

Dany rode close beside him. "Still," she said, "the common people are waiting for him. Magister Illyrio says they are sewing dragon banners and praying for Viserys to return from across the narrow sea to free them."

"The common people pray for rain, healthy children, and a summer that never ends," Ser Jorah told her. "It is no matter to them if the high lords play their game of thrones, so long as they are left in peace." He gave a shrug. "They never are."

Dany rode along quietly for a time, working his words like a puzzle box. It went against everything that Viserys had ever told her to think that the people could care so little whether a true king or a usurper reigned over them. Yet the more she thought on Jorah's words, the more they rang of truth.

"What do *you* pray for, Ser Jorah?" she asked him.

"Home," he said. His voice was thick with longing.

"I pray for home too," she told him, believing it.

Ser Jorah laughed. "Look around you then, *Khaleesi.*"

But it was not the plains Dany saw then. It was King's Landing and the great Red Keep that Aegon the Conqueror had built. It was Dragonstone where she had been born. In her mind's eye they burned with a thousand lights, a fire blazing in every window. In her mind's eye, all the doors were red.

"My brother will never take back the Seven Kingdoms," Dany said. She had known that for a long time, she realized. She had known it all her life. Only she had never let herself say the words, even in a whisper, but now she said them for Jorah Mormont and all the world to hear.

Ser Jorah gave her a measuring look. "You think not."

"He could not lead an army even if my lord husband gave him one," Dany said. "He has no coin and the only knight who follows him reviles him as less than a snake. The Dothraki make mock of his weakness. He will never take us home."

"Wise child." The knight smiled.

"I am no child," she told him fiercely. Her heels pressed into the sides of her mount, rousing the silver to a gallop. Faster and faster she raced, leaving Jorah and Irri and the others far behind, the warm wind in her hair and the setting sun red on her face. By the time she reached the *khalasar*, it was dusk.

The slaves had erected her tent by the shore of a spring-fed pool. She could hear rough voices from the woven grass palace on the hill. Soon there would be laughter, when the men of her *khas* told the story of what had happened in the grasses today. By the time Viserys came limping back among them, every man, woman, and child in the camp would know him for a walker. There were no secrets in the *khalasar*.

Dany gave the silver over to the slaves for grooming and entered her tent. It was cool and dim beneath the silk. As she let the door flap close behind her, Dany saw a finger of dusty red light reach out to touch her dragon's eggs across the tent. For an instant a thousand droplets of scarlet flame swam before her eyes. She blinked, and they were gone.

Stone, she told herself. *They are only stone, even Illyrio said so, the dragons are all dead.* She put her palm against the black egg, fingers spread gently across the curve of the shell. The stone was warm. Almost hot. "The sun," Dany whispered. "The sun warmed them as they rode."

She commanded her handmaids to prepare her a bath. Doreah built a fire outside the tent, while Irri and Jhiqui fetched the big copper tub—another bride gift—from the packhorses and carried water from the pool. When the bath was steaming, Irri helped her into it and climbed in after her.

"Have you ever seen a dragon?" she asked as Irri scrubbed her back and Jhiqui sluiced sand from her hair. She had heard that the first dragons had come from the east, from the Shadow Lands beyond Asshai and the islands of the Jade Sea. Perhaps some were still living there, in realms strange and wild.

"Dragons are gone, *Khaleesi*," Irri said.

"Dead," agreed Jhiqui. "Long and long ago."

Viserys had told her that the last Targaryen dragons

had died no more than a century and a half ago, during the reign of Aegon III, who was called the Dragonbane. That did not seem so long ago to Dany. "Everywhere?" she said, disappointed. "Even in the east?" Magic had died in the west when the Doom fell on Valyria and the Lands of the Long Summer, and neither spell-forged steel nor stormsingers nor dragons could hold it back, but Dany had always heard that the east was different. It was said that manticores prowled the islands of the Jade Sea, that basilisks infested the jungles of Yi Ti, that spellsingers, warlocks, and aeromancers practiced their arts openly in Asshai, while shadowbinders and bloodmages worked terrible sorceries in the black of night. Why shouldn't there be dragons too?

"No dragon," Irri said. "Brave men kill them, for dragon terrible evil beasts. It is known."

"It is known," agreed Jhiqui.

"A trader from Qarth once told me that dragons came from the moon," blond Doreah said as she warmed a towel over the fire. Jhiqui and Irri were of an age with Dany, Dothraki girls taken as slaves when Drogo destroyed their father's *khalasar*. Doreah was older, almost twenty. Magister Illyrio had found her in a pleasure house in Lys.

Silvery-wet hair tumbled across her eyes as Dany turned her head, curious. "The moon?"

"He told me the moon was an egg, *Khaleesi*," the Lysene girl said. "Once there were two moons in the sky, but one wandered too close to the sun and cracked from the heat. A thousand thousand dragons poured forth, and drank the fire of the sun. That is why dragons breathe flame. One day the other moon will kiss the sun too, and then it will crack and the dragons will return."

The two Dothraki girls giggled and laughed. "You are foolish strawhead slave," Irri said. "Moon is no egg. Moon is god, woman wife of sun. It is known."

"It is known," Jhiqui agreed.

Dany's skin was flushed and pink when she climbed from the tub. Jhiqui laid her down to oil her body and scrape the dirt from her pores. Afterward Irri sprinkled her with spiceflower and cinnamon. While Doreah brushed her hair until it shone like spun silver, she thought about the moon, and eggs, and dragons.

Her supper was a simple meal of fruit and cheese and fry bread, with a jug of honeyed wine to wash it down. "Doreah, stay and eat with me," Dany commanded when she sent her other handmaids away. The Lysene girl had hair the color of honey, and eyes like the summer sky.

She lowered those eyes when they were alone. "You honor me, *Khaleesi*," she said, but it was no honor, only service. Long after the moon had risen, they sat together, talking.

That night, when Khal Drogo came, Dany was waiting for him. He stood in the door of her tent and looked at her with surprise. She rose slowly and opened her sleeping silks and let them fall to the ground. "This night we must go outside, my lord," she told him, for the Dothraki believed that all things of importance in a man's life must be done beneath the open sky.

Khal Drogo followed her out into the moonlight, the bells in his hair tinkling softly. A few yards from her tent was a bed of soft grass, and it was there that Dany drew him down. When he tried to turn her over, she put a hand on his chest. "No," she said. "This night I would look on your face."

There is no privacy in the heart of the *khalasar*. Dany felt the eyes on her as she undressed him, heard the soft voices as she did the things that Doreah had told her to do. It was nothing to her. Was she not *khaleesi*? His were the only eyes that mattered, and when she mounted him she saw something there that she had never seen before. She rode him as fiercely as ever she had ridden her silver, and when the moment of his pleasure came, Khal Drogo called out her name.

They were on the far side of the Dothraki sea when Jhiqui brushed the soft swell of Dany's stomach with her fingers and said, "*Khaleesi*, you are with child."

"I know," Dany told her.

It was her fourteenth name day.

BRAN

In the yard below, Rickon ran with the wolves.

Bran watched from his window seat. Wherever the boy went, Grey Wind was there first, loping ahead to cut him off, until Rickon saw him, screamed in delight, and went pelting off in another direction. Shaggydog ran at his heels, spinning and snapping if the other wolves came too close. His fur had darkened until he was all black, and his eyes were green fire. Bran's Summer came last. He was silver and smoke, with eyes of yellow gold that saw all there was to see. Smaller than Grey Wind, and more wary. Bran thought he was the smartest of the litter. He could hear his brother's breathless laughter as Rickon dashed across the hard-packed earth on little baby legs.

His eyes stung. He wanted to be down there, laughing and running. Angry at the thought, Bran knuckled away the tears before they could fall. His eighth name day had come and gone. He was almost a man grown now, too old to cry.

"It was just a lie," he said bitterly, remembering the crow from his dream. "I can't fly. I can't even run."

"Crows are all liars," Old Nan agreed, from the chair

where she sat doing her needlework. "I know a story about a crow."

"I don't want any more stories," Bran snapped, his voice petulant. He had liked Old Nan and her stories once. Before. But it was different now. They left her with him all day now, to watch over him and clean him and keep him from being lonely, but she just made it worse. "I hate your stupid stories."

The old woman smiled at him toothlessly. "My stories? No, my little lord, not mine. The stories *are*, before me and after me, before you too."

She was a very ugly old woman, Bran thought spitefully, shrunken and wrinkled, almost blind, too weak to climb stairs, with only a few wisps of white hair left to cover a mottled pink scalp. No one really knew how old she was, but his father said she'd been called Old Nan even when he was a boy. She was the oldest person in Winterfell for certain, maybe the oldest person in the Seven Kingdoms. Nan had come to the castle as a wet nurse for a Brandon Stark whose mother had died birthing him. He had been an older brother of Lord Rickard, Bran's grandfather, or perhaps a younger brother, or a brother to *Lord Rickard's* father. Sometimes Old Nan told it one way and sometimes another. In all the stories the little boy died at three of a summer chill, but Old Nan stayed on at Winterfell with her own children. She had lost both her sons to the war when King Robert won the throne, and her grandson was killed on the walls of Pyke during Balon Greyjoy's rebellion. Her daughters had long ago married and moved away and died. All that was left of her own blood was Hodor, the simpleminded giant who worked in the stables, but Old Nan just lived on and on, doing her needlework and telling her stories.

"I don't care whose stories they are," Bran told her, "I hate them." He didn't want stories and he didn't want Old Nan. He wanted his mother and father. He wanted to go running with Summer loping beside him. He wanted to climb the broken tower and feed corn to the crows. He wanted to ride his pony again with his brothers. He wanted it to be the way it had been before.

"I know a story about a boy who hated stories," Old Nan said with her stupid little smile, her needles moving all the while, *click click click*, until Bran was ready to scream at her.

It would never be the way it had been, he knew. The crow had tricked him into flying, but when he woke up he was broken and the world was changed. They had all left him, his father and his mother and his sisters and even his bastard brother Jon. His father had promised he would ride a real horse to King's Landing, but they'd gone without him. Maester Luwin had sent a bird after Lord Eddard with a message, and another to Mother and a third to Jon on the Wall, but there had been no answers. "Ofttimes the birds are lost, child," the maester had told him. "There's many a mile and many a hawk between here and King's Landing, the message may not have reached them." Yet to Bran it felt as if they had all died while he had slept . . . or perhaps Bran had died, and they had forgotten him. Jory and Ser Rodrik and Vayon Poole had gone too, and Hullen and Harwin and Fat Tom and a quarter of the guard.

Only Robb and baby Rickon were still here, and Robb was changed. He was Robb the Lord now, or trying to be. He wore a real sword and never smiled. His days were spent drilling the guard and practicing his swordplay, making the yard ring with the sound of steel as Bran watched forlornly from his window. At night he closeted himself with Maester Luwin, talking or going over account books. Sometimes he would ride out with Hallis Mollen and be gone for days at a time, visiting distant holdfasts. Whenever he was away more than a day, Rickon would cry and ask Bran if Robb was ever coming back. Even when he was home at Winterfell, Robb the Lord seemed to have more time for Hallis Mollen and Theon Greyjoy than he ever did for his brothers.

"I could tell you the story about Brandon the Builder," Old Nan said. "That was always your favorite."

Thousands and thousands of years ago, Brandon the Builder had raised Winterfell, and some said the Wall. Bran knew the story, but it had never been his favorite. Maybe one of the other Brandons had liked that story. Sometimes Nan would talk to him as if he were *her* Brandon, the baby she had nursed all those years ago, and sometimes she confused him with his uncle Brandon, who was killed by the Mad King before Bran was even born. She had lived so long, Mother had told him once, that all the Brandon Starks had become one person in her head.

"That's not my favorite," he said. "My favorites were the scary ones." He heard some sort of commotion outside and turned back to the window. Rickon was running across the yard toward the gatehouse, the wolves following him, but the tower faced the wrong way for Bran to see what was happening. He smashed a fist on his thigh in frustration and felt nothing.

"Oh, my sweet summer child," Old Nan said quietly, "what do *you* know of fear? Fear is for the winter, my little lord, when the snows fall a hundred feet deep and the ice wind comes howling out of the north. Fear is for the long night, when the sun hides its face for years at a time, and little children are born and live and die all in darkness while the direwolves grow gaunt and hungry, and the white walkers move through the woods."

"You mean the Others," Bran said querulously.

"The Others," Old Nan agreed. "Thousands and thousands of years ago, a winter fell that was cold and hard and endless beyond all memory of man. There came a night that lasted a generation, and kings shivered and died in their castles even as the swineherds in their hovels. Women smothered their children rather than see them starve, and cried, and felt their tears freeze on their cheeks." Her voice and her needles fell silent, and she glanced up at Bran with pale, filmy eyes and asked, "So, child. This is the sort of story you like?"

"Well," Bran said reluctantly, "yes, only . . ."

Old Nan nodded. "In that darkness, the Others came for the first time," she said as her needles went *click click click*. "They were cold things, dead things, that hated iron and fire and the touch of the sun, and every creature with hot blood in its veins. They swept over holdfasts and cities and kingdoms, felled heroes and armies by the score, riding their pale dead horses and leading hosts of the slain. All the swords of men could not stay their advance, and even maidens and suckling babes found no pity in them. They hunted the maids through frozen forests, and fed their dead servants on the flesh of human children."

Her voice had dropped very low, almost to a whisper, and Bran found himself leaning forward to listen.

"Now these were the days before the Andals came, and long before the women fled across the narrow sea from the cities of the Rhoyne, and the hundred kingdoms of those times were the kingdoms of the First Men, who had taken these lands from the children of the forest. Yet here and there in the fastness of the woods the children still lived in their wooden cities and hollow hills, and the faces in the trees kept watch. So as cold and death filled the earth, the last hero determined to seek out the children, in the hopes that their ancient magics could win back what the armies of men had lost. He set out into the dead lands with a sword, a horse, a dog, and a dozen companions. For years he searched, until he despaired of ever finding the children of the forest in their secret cities. One by one his friends died, and his horse, and finally even his dog, and his sword froze so hard the blade snapped when he tried to use it. And the Others smelled the hot blood in him, and came silent on his trail, stalking him with packs of pale white spiders big as hounds—"

The door opened with a *bang*, and Bran's heart leapt up into his mouth in sudden fear, but it was only Maester Luwin, with Hodor looming in the stairway behind him. "Hodor!" the stableboy announced, as was his custom, smiling hugely at them all.

Maester Luwin was not smiling. "We have visitors," he announced, "and your presence is required, Bran."

"I'm listening to a story now," Bran complained.

"Stories wait, my little lord, and when you come back to them, why, there they are," Old Nan said. "Visitors are not so patient, and ofttimes they bring stories of their own."

"Who is it?" Bran asked Maester Luwin.

"Tyrion Lannister, and some men of the Night's Watch, with word from your brother Jon. Robb is meeting with them now. Hodor, will you help Bran down to the hall?"

"Hodor!" Hodor agreed happily. He ducked to get his great shaggy head under the door. Hodor was nearly seven feet tall. It was hard to believe that he was the same blood as Old Nan. Bran wondered if he would shrivel up as small as his great-grandmother when he was old. It did not seem likely, even if Hodor lived to be a thousand.

Hodor lifted Bran as easy as if he were a bale of hay, and cradled him against his massive chest. He always smelled faintly of horses, but it was not a bad smell. His arms were thick with muscle and matted with brown hair. "Hodor," he said again. Theon Greyjoy had once commented that Hodor did not know much, but no one could doubt that he knew his name. Old Nan had cackled like a hen when Bran told her that, and confessed that Hodor's real name was Walder. No one knew where "Hodor" had come from, she said, but when he started saying it, they started calling him by it. It was the only word he had.

They left Old Nan in the tower room with her needles and her memories. Hodor hummed tunelessly as he carried Bran down the steps and through the gallery, with Maester Luwin following behind, hurrying to keep up with the stableboy's long strides.

Robb was seated in Father's high seat, wearing ringmail and boiled leather and the stern face of Robb the Lord. Theon Greyjoy and Hallis Mollen stood behind him. A dozen guardsmen lined the grey stone walls beneath tall narrow windows. In the center of the room the dwarf stood with his servants, and four strangers in the black of the Night's Watch. Bran could sense the anger in the hall the moment that Hodor carried him through the doors.

"Any man of the Night's Watch is welcome here at Winterfell for as long as he wishes to stay," Robb was saying with the voice of Robb the Lord. His sword was across his knees, the steel bare for all the world to see. Even Bran knew what it meant to greet a guest with an unsheathed sword.

"Any man of the Night's Watch," the dwarf repeated, "but not me, do I take your meaning, boy?"

Robb stood and pointed at the little man with his sword. "I am the lord here while my mother and father are away, Lannister. I am not your boy."

"If you are a lord, you might learn a lord's courtesy," the little man replied, ignoring the sword point in his face. "Your bastard brother has all your father's graces, it would seem."

"*Jon*," Bran gasped out from Hodor's arms.

The dwarf turned to look at him. "So it is true, the boy lives. I could scarce believe it. You Starks are hard to kill."

"You Lannisters had best remember that," Robb said, lowering his sword. "Hodor, bring my brother here."

"Hodor," Hodor said, and he trotted forward smiling and set Bran in the high seat of the Starks, where the Lords of Winterfell had sat since the days when they called themselves the Kings in the North. The seat was cold stone, polished smooth by countless bottoms; the carved heads of direwolves snarled on the ends of its massive arms. Bran clasped them as he sat, his useless legs dangling. The great seat made him feel half a baby.

Robb put a hand on his shoulder. "You said you had business with Bran. Well, here he is, Lannister."

Bran was uncomfortably aware of Tyrion Lannister's eyes. One was black and one was green, and both were looking at him, studying him, weighing him. "I am told you were quite the climber, Bran," the little man said at last. "Tell me, how is it you happened to fall that day?"

"I *never*," Bran insisted. He never fell, never never *never*.

"The child does not remember anything of the fall, or the climb that came before it," said Maester Luwin gently.

"Curious," said Tyrion Lannister.

"My brother is not here to answer questions, Lannister," Robb said curtly. "Do your business and be on your way."

"I have a gift for you," the dwarf said to Bran. "Do you like to ride, boy?"

Maester Luwin came forward. "My lord, the child has lost the use of his legs. He cannot sit a horse."

"Nonsense," said Lannister. "With the right horse and the right saddle, even a cripple can ride."

The word was a knife through Bran's heart. He felt tears come unbidden to his eyes. "I'm *not* a cripple!"

"Then I am not a dwarf," the dwarf said with a twist of his mouth. "My father will rejoice to hear it." Greyjoy laughed.

"What sort of horse and saddle are you suggesting?" Maester Luwin asked.

"A smart horse," Lannister replied. "The boy cannot

use his legs to command the animal, so you must shape the horse to the rider, teach it to respond to the reins, to the voice. I would begin with an unbroken yearling, with no old training to be unlearned." He drew a rolled paper from his belt. "Give this to your saddler. He will provide the rest."

Maester Luwin took the paper from the dwarf's hand, curious as a small grey squirrel. He unrolled it, studied it. "I see. You draw nicely, my lord. Yes, this ought to work. I should have thought of this myself."

"It came easier to me, Maester. It is not terribly unlike my own saddles."

"Will I truly be able to ride?" Bran asked. He wanted to believe them, but he was afraid. Perhaps it was just another lie. The crow had promised him that he could fly.

"You will," the dwarf told him. "And I swear to you, boy, on horseback you will be as tall as any of them."

Robb Stark seemed puzzled. "Is this some trap, Lannister? What's Bran to you? Why should you want to help him?"

"Your brother Jon asked it of me. And I have a tender spot in my heart for cripples and bastards and broken things." Tyrion Lannister placed a hand over his heart and grinned.

The door to the yard flew open. Sunlight came streaming across the hall as Rickon burst in, breathless. The direwolves were with him. The boy stopped by the door, wide-eyed, but the wolves came on. Their eyes found Lannister, or perhaps they caught his scent. Summer began to growl first. Grey Wind picked it up. They padded toward the little man, one from the right and one from the left.

"The wolves do not like your smell, Lannister," Theon Greyjoy commented.

"Perhaps it's time I took my leave," Tyrion said. He took a step backward . . . and Shaggydog came out of the shadows behind him, snarling. Lannister recoiled, and Summer lunged at him from the other side. He reeled away, unsteady on his feet, and Grey Wind snapped at his arm, teeth ripping at his sleeve and tearing loose a scrap of cloth.

"No!" Bran shouted from the high seat as Lannister's men reached for their steel. "Summer, *here.* Summer, to me!"

The direwolf heard the voice, glanced at Bran, and again at Lannister. He crept backward, away from the little man, and settled down below Bran's dangling feet.

Robb had been holding his breath. He let it out with a sigh and called, "Grey Wind." His direwolf moved to him, swift and silent. Now there was only Shaggydog, rumbling at the small man, his eyes burning like green fire.

"Rickon, call him," Bran shouted to his baby brother, and Rickon remembered himself and screamed, "Home, Shaggy, home now." The black wolf gave Lannister one final snarl and bounded off to Rickon, who hugged him tightly around the neck.

Tyrion Lannister undid his scarf, mopped at his brow, and said in a flat voice, "How interesting."

"Are you well, my lord?" asked one of his men, his sword in hand. He glanced nervously at the direwolves as he spoke.

"My sleeve is torn and my breeches are unaccountably damp, but nothing was harmed save my dignity."

Even Robb looked shaken. "The wolves . . . I don't know why they did that . . ."

"No doubt they mistook me for dinner." Lannister bowed stiffly to Bran. "I thank you for calling them off, young ser. I promise you, they would have found me quite indigestible. And now I *will* be leaving, truly."

"A moment, my lord," Maester Luwin said. He moved to Robb and they huddled close together, whispering. Bran tried to hear what they were saying, but their voices were too low.

Robb Stark finally sheathed his sword. "I . . . I may have been hasty with you," he said. "You've done Bran a kindness, and, well . . ." Robb composed himself with an effort. "The hospitality of Winterfell is yours if you wish it, Lannister."

"Spare me your false courtesies, boy. You do not love me and you do not want me here. I saw an inn outside your walls, in the winter town. I'll find a bed there, and both of us will sleep easier. For a few coppers I may even find a comely wench to warm the sheets for me." He spoke to one of the black brothers, an old man with a twisted back and a tangled beard. "Yoren, we go south at daybreak. You will find me on the road, no doubt." With that he made his exit, struggling across the hall on his short legs, past Rickon and out the door. His men followed.

The four of the Night's Watch remained. Robb turned to them uncertainly. "I have had rooms prepared, and you'll find no lack of hot water to wash off the dust of the road. I hope you will honor us at table tonight." He spoke the words so awkwardly that even Bran took note; it was a speech he had learned, not words from the heart, but the black brothers thanked him all the same.

Summer followed them up the tower steps as Hodor carried Bran back to his bed. Old Nan was asleep in her chair. Hodor said "Hodor," gathered up his great-grandmother, and carried her off, snoring softly, while Bran lay thinking. Robb had promised that he could feast with the Night's Watch in the Great Hall. "Summer," he called. The wolf bounded up on the bed. Bran hugged him so hard he could feel the hot breath on his cheek. "I can ride now," he whispered to his friend. "We can go hunting in the woods soon, wait and see." After a time he slept.

In his dream he was climbing again, pulling himself up an ancient windowless tower, his fingers forcing themselves between blackened stones, his feet scrabbling for purchase. Higher and higher he climbed, through the clouds and into the night sky, and still the tower rose before him. When he paused to look down, his head swam dizzily and he felt his fingers slipping. Bran cried out and clung for dear life. The earth was a thousand miles beneath him and he could not fly. *He could not fly.* He waited until his heart had stopped pounding, until he could breathe, and he began to climb again. There was no way to go but up. Far above him, outlined against a vast pale moon, he thought he could see the shapes of gargoyles. His arms were sore and aching, but he dared not rest. He forced himself to climb faster. The gargoyles watched him ascend. Their eyes glowed red as hot coals in a brazier. Perhaps once they had been lions, but now they were twisted and grotesque. Bran could hear them whispering to each other in soft stone voices terrible to hear. He must not listen, he told himself, he must not hear, so long as he did not hear them he was safe. But when the gargoyles pulled themselves loose from the stone and padded down the side of the tower to where Bran clung, he knew he was not safe after all. "I didn't hear," he wept as they came closer and closer, "I didn't, I didn't."

He woke gasping, lost in darkness, and saw a vast shadow looming over him. "I didn't hear," he whispered, trembling in fear, but then the shadow said "Hodor," and lit the candle by the bedside, and Bran sighed with relief.

Hodor washed the sweat from him with a warm, damp cloth and dressed him with deft and gentle hands. When it was time, he carried him down to the Great Hall, where a long trestle table had been set up near the fire. The lord's seat at the head of the table had been left empty, but Robb sat to the right of it, with Bran across from him. They ate suckling pig that night, and pigeon pie, and turnips soaking in butter, and afterward the cook had promised honeycombs. Summer snatched table scraps from Bran's hand, while Grey Wind and Shaggydog fought over a bone in the corner. Winterfell's dogs would not come near the hall now. Bran had found that strange at first, but he was growing used to it.

Yoren was senior among the black brothers, so the steward had seated him between Robb and Maester Luwin. The old man had a sour smell, as if he had not washed in a long time. He ripped at the meat with his teeth, cracked the ribs to suck out the marrow from the bones, and shrugged at the mention of Jon Snow. "Ser Alliser's bane," he grunted, and two of his companions shared a laugh that Bran did not understand. But when Robb asked for news of their uncle Benjen, the black brothers grew ominously quiet.

"What is it?" Bran asked.

Yoren wiped his fingers on his vest. "There's hard news, m'lords, and a cruel way to pay you for your meat and mead, but the man as asks the question must bear the answer. Stark's gone."

One of the other men said, "The Old Bear sent him out to look for Waymar Royce, and he's late returning, my lord."

"Too long," Yoren said. "Most like he's dead."

"My uncle is not dead," Robb Stark said loudly, anger in his tones. He rose from the bench and laid his hand on the hilt of his sword. "Do you hear me? *My uncle is not dead!*" His voice rang against the stone walls, and Bran was suddenly afraid.

Old sour-smelling Yoren looked up at Robb, unimpressed. "Whatever you say, m'lord," he said. He sucked at a piece of meat between his teeth.

The youngest of the black brothers shifted uncomfortably in his seat. "There's not a man on the Wall knows the haunted forest better than Benjen Stark. He'll find his way back."

"Well," said Yoren, "maybe he will and maybe he won't. Good men have gone into those woods before, and never come out."

All Bran could think of was Old Nan's story of the Others and the last hero, hounded through the white woods by dead men and spiders big as hounds. He was afraid for a moment, until he remembered how that story ended. "The children will help him," he blurted, "the children of the forest!"

Theon Greyjoy sniggered, and Maester Luwin said, "Bran, the children of the forest have been dead and gone for thousands of years. All that is left of them are the faces in the trees."

"Down here, might be that's true, Maester," Yoren said, "but up past the Wall, who's to say? Up there, a man can't always tell what's alive and what's dead."

That night, after the plates had been cleared, Robb carried Bran up to bed himself. Grey Wind led the way, and Summer came close behind. His brother was strong for his age, and Bran was as light as a bundle of rags, but the stairs were steep and dark, and Robb was breathing hard by the time they reached the top.

He put Bran into bed, covered him with blankets, and blew out the candle. For a time Robb sat beside him in the dark. Bran wanted to talk to him, but he did not know what to say. "We'll find a horse for you, I promise," Robb whispered at last.

"Are they ever coming back?" Bran asked him.

"Yes," Robb said with such hope in his voice that Bran knew he was hearing his brother and not just Robb the Lord. "Mother will be home soon. Maybe we can ride out to meet her when she comes. Wouldn't that surprise her, to see you ahorse?" Even in the dark room, Bran could feel his brother's smile. "And afterward, we'll ride north to see the Wall. We won't even tell Jon we're coming, we'll just be there one day, you and me. It will be an adventure."

"An adventure," Bran repeated wistfully. He heard his brother sob. The room was so dark he could not see the tears on Robb's face, so he reached out and found his hand. Their fingers twined together.

EDDARD

"Lord Arryn's death was a great sadness for all of us, my lord," Grand Maester Pycelle said. "I would be more than happy to tell you what I can of the manner of his passing. Do be seated. Would you care for refreshments? Some dates, perhaps? I have some very fine persimmons as well. Wine no longer agrees with my digestion, I fear, but I can offer you a cup of iced milk, sweetened with honey. I find it most refreshing in this heat."

There was no denying the heat; Ned could feel the silk tunic clinging to his chest. Thick, moist air covered the city like a damp woolen blanket, and the riverside had grown unruly as the poor fled their hot, airless warrens to jostle for sleeping places near the water, where the only breath of wind was to be found. "That would be most kind," Ned said, seating himself.

Pycelle lifted a tiny silver bell with thumb and forefinger and tinkled it gently. A slender young serving girl hurried into the solar. "Iced milk for the King's Hand and myself, if you would be so kind, child. Well sweetened."

As the girl went to fetch their drinks, the Grand Maester knotted his fingers together and rested his hands on his stomach. "The smallfolk say that the last year of summer is always the hottest. It is not so, yet ofttimes it feels that way, does it not? On days like this, I envy you northerners your summer snows." The heavy jeweled chain around the old man's neck chinked softly as he shifted in his seat. "To be sure, King Maekar's summer was hotter than this one, and near as long. There were fools, even in the Citadel, who took that to mean that the Great Summer had come at last, the summer that never ends, but in the seventh year it broke suddenly, and we had a short autumn and a terrible long winter. Still, the heat was fierce while it lasted. Oldtown steamed and sweltered by day and came alive only by night. We would walk in the gardens by the river and argue about the gods. I remember the *smells* of those nights, my lord—perfume and sweat, melons ripe to bursting, peaches and pomegranates, nightshade and moonbloom. I was a young man then, still forging my chain. The heat did not exhaust me as it does now." Pycelle's eyes were so heavily lidded he looked half-asleep. "My pardons, Lord Eddard. You did not come to hear foolish meanderings of a summer forgotten before your father was born. Forgive an old man his wanderings, if you would. Minds are like swords, I do fear. The old ones go to rust. Ah, and here is our milk." The serving girl placed the tray between them, and Pycelle gave her a smile. "Sweet child." He lifted a cup, tasted, nodded. "Thank you. You may go."

When the girl had taken her leave, Pycelle peered at Ned through pale, rheumy eyes. "Now where were we? Oh, yes. You asked about Lord Arryn . . ."

"I did." Ned sipped politely at the iced milk. It was pleasantly cold, but oversweet to his taste.

"If truth be told, the Hand had not seemed quite himself for some time," Pycelle said. "We had sat together on council many a year, he and I, and the signs were there to read, but I put them down to the great burdens he had borne so faithfully for so long. Those broad shoulders were weighed down by all the cares of the realm, and more besides. His son was ever sickly, and his lady wife so anxious that she would scarcely let the boy out of her sight. It was enough to weary even a strong man, and the Lord Jon was not young. Small wonder if he seemed melancholy and tired. Or so I thought at the time. Yet now I am less certain." He gave a ponderous shake of his head.

"What can you tell me of his final illness?"

The Grand Maester spread his hands in a gesture of helpless sorrow. "He came to me one day asking after a certain book, as hale and healthy as ever, though it did seem to me that something was troubling him deeply. The next morning he was twisted over in pain, too sick to rise from bed. Maester Colemon thought it was a chill on the stomach. The weather had been hot, and the Hand often iced his wine, which can upset the digestion. When Lord Jon continued to weaken, I went to him myself, but the gods did not grant me the power to save him."

"I have heard that you sent Maester Colemon away."

The Grand Maester's nod was as slow and deliberate as a glacier. "I did, and I fear the Lady Lysa will never forgive me that. Maybe I was wrong, but at the time I thought it best. Maester Colemon is like a son to me, and I yield to none in my esteem for his abilities, but he is young, and the young ofttimes do not comprehend the frailty of an older body. He was purging Lord Arryn with wasting potions and pepper juice, and I feared he might kill him."

"Did Lord Arryn say anything to you during his final hours?"

Pycelle wrinkled his brow. "In the last stage of his fever, the Hand called out the name *Robert* several times, but whether he was asking for his son or for the king I could not say. Lady Lysa would not permit the boy to enter the sickroom, for fear that he too might be taken ill. The king did come, and he sat beside the bed for hours, talking and joking of times long past in hopes of raising Lord Jon's spirits. His love was fierce to see."

"Was there nothing else? No final words?"

"When I saw that all hope had fled, I gave the Hand the milk of the poppy, so he should not suffer. Just before he closed his eyes for the last time, he whispered something to the king and his lady wife, a blessing for his son. *The seed is strong,* he said. At the end, his speech was too slurred to comprehend. Death did not come until the next morning, but Lord Jon was at peace after that. He never spoke again."

Ned took another swallow of milk, trying not to gag on

the sweetness of it. "Did it seem to you that there was anything unnatural about Lord Arryn's death?"

"Unnatural?" The aged maester's voice was thin as a whisper. "No, I could not say so. Sad, for a certainty. Yet in its own way, death is the most natural thing of all, Lord Eddard. Jon Arryn rests easy now, his burdens lifted at last."

"This illness that took him," said Ned. "Had you ever seen its like before, in other men?"

"Near forty years I have been Grand Maester of the Seven Kingdoms," Pycelle replied. "Under our good King Robert, and Aerys Targaryen before him, and his father Jaehaerys the Second before him, and even for a few short months under Jaehaerys's father, Aegon the Fortunate, the Fifth of His Name. I have seen more of illness than I care to remember, my lord. I will tell you this: Every case is different, and every case is alike. Lord Jon's death was no stranger than any other."

"His wife thought otherwise."

The Grand Maester nodded. "I recall now, the widow is sister to your own noble wife. If an old man may be forgiven his blunt speech, let me say that grief can derange even the strongest and most disciplined of minds, and the Lady Lysa was never that. Since her last stillbirth, she has seen enemies in every shadow, and the death of her lord husband left her shattered and lost."

"So you are quite certain that Jon Arryn died of a sudden illness?"

"I am," Pycelle replied gravely. "If not illness, my good lord, what else could it be?"

"Poison," Ned suggested quietly.

Pycelle's sleepy eyes flicked open. The aged maester shifted uncomfortably in his seat. "A disturbing thought. We are not the Free Cities, where such things are common. Grand Maester Aethelmure wrote that all men carry murder in their hearts, yet even so, the poisoner is beneath contempt." He fell silent for a moment, his eyes lost in thought. "What you suggest is possible, my lord, yet I do not think it likely. Every hedge maester knows the common poisons, and Lord Arryn displayed none of the signs. And the Hand was loved by all. What sort of monster in man's flesh would dare to murder such a noble lord?"

"I have heard it said that poison is a woman's weapon."

Pycelle stroked his beard thoughtfully. "It is said. Women, cravens . . . and eunuchs." He cleared his throat and spat a thick glob of phlegm onto the rushes. Above them, a raven cawed loudly in the rookery. "The Lord Varys was born a slave in Lys, did you know? Put not your trust in spiders, my lord."

That was scarcely anything Ned needed to be told; there was something about Varys that made his flesh crawl. "I will remember that, Maester. And I thank you for your help. I have taken enough of your time." He stood.

Grand Maester Pycelle pushed himself up from his chair slowly and escorted Ned to the door. "I hope I have helped in some small way to put your mind at ease. If there is any other service I might perform, you need only ask."

"One thing," Ned told him. "I should be curious to examine the book that you lent Jon the day before he fell ill."

"I fear you would find it of little interest," Pycelle said. "It was a ponderous tome by Grand Maester Malleon on the lineages of the great houses."

"Still, I should like to see it."

The old man opened the door. "As you wish. I have it here somewhere. When I find it, I shall have it sent to your chambers straightaway."

"You have been most courteous," Ned told him. Then, almost as an afterthought, he said, "One last question, if you would be so kind. You mentioned that the king was at Lord Arryn's bedside when he died. I wonder, was the queen with him?"

"Why, no," Pycelle said. "She and the children were making the journey to Casterly Rock, in company with her father. Lord Tywin had brought a retinue to the city for the tourney on Prince Joffrey's name day, no doubt hoping to see his son Jaime win the champion's crown. In that he was sadly disappointed. It fell to me to send the queen word of Lord Arryn's sudden death. Never have I sent off a bird with a heavier heart."

"Dark wings, dark words," Ned murmured. It was a proverb Old Nan had taught him as a boy.

"So the fishwives say," Grand Maester Pycelle agreed, "but we know it is not always so. When Maester Luwin's bird brought the word about your Bran, the message lifted every true heart in the castle, did it not?"

"As you say, Maester."

"The gods are merciful." Pycelle bowed his head. "Come to me as often as you like, Lord Eddard. I am here to serve."

Yes, Ned thought as the door swung shut, *but whom?*

On the way back to his chambers, he came upon his daughter Arya on the winding steps of the Tower of the Hand, windmilling her arms as she struggled to balance on one leg. The rough stone had scuffed her bare feet. Ned stopped and looked at her. "Arya, what are you doing?"

"Syrio says a water dancer can stand on one toe for hours." Her hands flailed at the air to steady herself.

Ned had to smile. "Which toe?" he teased.

"*Any* toe," Arya said, exasperated with the question. She hopped from her right leg to her left, swaying dangerously before she regained her balance.

"Must you do your standing here?" he asked. "It's a long hard fall down these steps."

"Syrio says a water dancer *never* falls." She lowered her leg to stand on two feet. "Father, will Bran come and live with us now?"

"Not for a long time, sweet one," he told her. "He needs to win his strength back."

Arya bit her lip. "What will Bran do when he's of age?"

Ned knelt beside her. "He has years to find that answer, Arya. For now, it is enough to know that he will live." The night the bird had come from Winterfell, Eddard Stark had taken the girls to the castle godswood, an acre of elm and alder and black cottonwood overlooking the river. The heart tree there was a great oak, its ancient limbs overgrown with smokeberry vines; they knelt before it to offer their thanksgiving, as if it had been a weirwood. Sansa drifted to sleep as the moon rose, Arya several hours later, curling up in the grass under Ned's cloak. All through the dark hours he kept his vigil alone. When dawn broke over the city, the dark red blooms of dragon's breath surrounded the girls where they lay. "I dreamed of Bran," Sansa had whispered to him. "I saw him smiling."

"He was going to be a knight," Arya was saying now. "A knight of the Kingsguard. Can he still be a knight?"

"No," Ned said. He saw no use in lying to her. "Yet someday he may be the lord of a great holdfast and sit on the king's council. He might raise castles like Brandon the Builder, or sail a ship across the Sunset Sea, or enter your mother's Faith and become the High Septon." *But he will never run beside his wolf again*, he thought with a sadness too deep for words, *or lie with a woman, or hold his own son in his arms.*

Arya cocked her head to one side. "Can I be a king's councillor and build castles and become the High Septon?"

"You," Ned said, kissing her lightly on the brow, "will marry a king and rule his castle, and your sons will be knights and princes and lords and, yes, perhaps even a High Septon."

Arya screwed up her face. "No," she said, "that's *Sansa.*" She folded up her right leg and resumed her balancing. Ned sighed and left her there.

Inside his chambers, he stripped off his sweat-stained silks and sluiced cold water over his head from the basin beside the bed. Alyn entered as he was drying his face. "My lord," he said, "Lord Baelish is without and begs audience."

"Escort him to my solar," Ned said, reaching for a fresh tunic, the lightest linen he could find. "I'll see him at once."

Littlefinger was perched on the window seat when Ned entered, watching the knights of the Kingsguard practice at swords in the yard below. "If only old Selmy's mind were as nimble as his blade," he said wistfully, "our council meetings would be a good deal livelier."

"Ser Barristan is as valiant and honorable as any man in King's Landing." Ned had come to have a deep respect for the aged, white-haired Lord Commander of the Kingsguard.

"And as tiresome," Littlefinger added, "though I daresay he should do well in the tourney. Last year he unhorsed the Hound, and it was only four years ago that he was champion."

The question of who might win the tourney interested Eddard Stark not in the least. "Is there a reason for this visit, Lord Petyr, or are you here simply to enjoy the view from my window?"

Littlefinger smiled. "I promised Cat I would help you in your inquiries, and so I have."

That took Ned aback. Promise or no promise, he could not find it in him to trust Lord Petyr Baelish, who struck him as too clever by half. "You have something for me?"

"Some*one*," Littlefinger corrected. "Four someones, if truth be told. Had you thought to question the Hand's servants?"

Ned frowned. "Would that I could. Lady Arryn took her household back to the Eyrie." Lysa had done him no favor in that regard. All those who had stood closest to her husband had gone with her when she fled: Jon's maester, his steward, the captain of his guard, his knights and retainers.

"*Most* of her household," Littlefinger said, "not all. A few remain. A pregnant kitchen girl hastily wed to one of Lord Renly's grooms, a stablehand who joined the City Watch, a potboy discharged from service for theft, and Lord Arryn's squire."

"His squire?" Ned was pleasantly surprised. A man's squire often knew a great deal of his comings and goings.

"Ser Hugh of the Vale," Littlefinger named him. "The king knighted the boy after Lord Arryn's death."

"I shall send for him," Ned said. "And the others."

Littlefinger winced. "My lord, step over here to the window, if you would be so kind."

"Why?"

"Come, and I'll show you, my lord."

Frowning, Ned crossed to the window. Petyr Baelish made a casual gesture. "There, across the yard, at the door of the armory, do you see the boy squatting by the steps honing a sword with an oilstone?"

"What of him?"

"He reports to Varys. The Spider has taken a great interest in you and all your doings." He shifted in the window seat. "Now glance at the wall. Farther west, above the stables. The guardsman leaning on the ramparts?"

Ned saw the man. "Another of the eunuch's whisperers?"

"No, this one belongs to the queen. Notice that he enjoys a fine view of the door to this tower, the better to note who calls on you. There are others, many unknown even to me. The Red Keep is full of eyes. Why do you think I hid Cat in a brothel?"

Eddard Stark had no taste for these intrigues. "Seven hells," he swore. It *did* seem as though the man on the walls was watching him. Suddenly uncomfortable, Ned moved away from the window. "Is everyone someone's informer in this cursed city?"

"Scarcely," said Littlefinger. He counted on the fingers on his hand. "Why, there's me, you, the king . . . although, come to think on it, the king tells the queen much too much, and I'm less than certain about you." He stood up. "Is there a man in your service that you trust utterly and completely?"

"Yes," said Ned.

"In that case, I have a delightful palace in Valyria that I would dearly love to sell you," Littlefinger said with a mocking smile. "The wiser answer was *no*, my lord, but be that as it may. Send this paragon of yours to Ser Hugh and the others. Your own comings and goings will be noted, but even Varys the Spider cannot watch every man in your service every hour of the day." He started for the door.

"Lord Petyr," Ned called after him. "I . . . am grateful for your help. Perhaps I was wrong to distrust you."

Littlefinger fingered his small pointed beard. "You are slow to learn, Lord Eddard. Distrusting me was the wisest thing you've done since you climbed down off your horse."

JON

on was showing Dareon how best to deliver a side-stroke when the new recruit entered the practice yard. "Your feet should be farther apart," he urged. "You don't want to lose your balance. That's good. Now pivot as you deliver the stroke, get all your weight behind the blade."

Dareon broke off and lifted his visor. "Seven gods," he murmured. "Would you look at this, Jon."

Jon turned. Through the eye slit of his helm, he beheld the fattest boy he had ever seen standing in the door of the armory. By the look of him, he must have weighed twenty stone. The fur collar of his embroidered surcoat was lost beneath his chins. Pale eyes moved nervously in a great round moon of a face, and plump sweaty fingers wiped themselves on the velvet of his doublet. "They . . . they told me I was to come here for . . . for training," he said to no one in particular.

"A lordling," Pyp observed to Jon. "Southron, most like near Highgarden." Pyp had traveled the Seven Kingdoms with a mummers' troupe, and bragged that he could tell what you were and where you'd been born just from the sound of his voice.

A striding huntsman had been worked in scarlet thread upon the breast of the fat boy's fur-trimmed surcoat. Jon did not recognize the sigil. Ser Alliser Thorne looked over his new charge and said, "It would seem they have run short of poachers and thieves down south. Now they send us pigs to man the Wall. Is fur and velvet your notion of armor, my Lord of Ham?"

It was soon revealed that the new recruit had brought his own armor with him; padded doublet, boiled leather, mail and plate and helm, even a great wood-and-leather shield blazoned with the same striding huntsman he wore on his surcoat. As none of it was black, however, Ser Alliser insisted that he reequip himself from the armory. That took half the morning. His girth required Donal Noye to take apart a mail hauberk and refit it with leather panels at the sides. To get a helm over his head the armorer had to detach the visor. His leathers bound so tightly around his legs and under his arms that he could scarcely move. Dressed for battle, the new boy looked like an overcooked sausage about to burst its skin. "Let us hope you are not as inept as you look," Ser Alliser said. "Halder, see what Ser Piggy can do."

Jon Snow winced. Halder had been born in a quarry and apprenticed as a stonemason. He was sixteen, tall and muscular, and his blows were as hard as any Jon had ever felt. "This will be uglier than a whore's ass," Pyp muttered, and it was.

The fight lasted less than a minute before the fat boy was on the ground, his whole body shaking as blood leaked through his shattered helm and between his pudgy fingers. "I yield," he shrilled. "No more, I yield, don't hit me." Rast and some of the other boys were laughing.

Even then, Ser Alliser would not call an end. "On your feet, Ser Piggy," he called. "Pick up your sword." When the boy continued to cling to the ground, Thorne gestured to Halder. "Hit him with the flat of your blade until he finds his feet." Halder delivered a tentative smack to his foe's upraised cheeks. "You can hit harder than that," Thorne taunted. Halder took hold of his longsword with both hands and brought it down so hard the blow split leather, even on the flat. The new boy screeched in pain.

Jon Snow took a step forward. Pyp laid a mailed hand

on his arm. "Jon, *no*," the small boy whispered with an anxious glance at Ser Alliser Thorne.

"On your feet," Thorne repeated. The fat boy struggled to rise, slipped, and fell heavily again. "Ser Piggy is starting to grasp the notion," Ser Alliser observed. "Again."

Halder lifted the sword for another blow. "Cut us off a ham!" Rast urged, laughing.

Jon shook off Pyp's hand. "Halder, *enough*."

Halder looked to Ser Alliser.

"The Bastard speaks and the peasants tremble," the master-at-arms said in that sharp, cold voice of his. "I remind you that I am the master-at-arms here, Lord Snow."

"Look at him, Halder," Jon urged, ignoring Thorne as best he could. "There's no honor in beating a fallen foe. He yielded." He knelt beside the fat boy.

Halder lowered his sword. "He yielded," he echoed.

Ser Alliser's onyx eyes were fixed on Jon Snow. "It would seem our Bastard is in love," he said as Jon helped the fat boy to his feet. "Show me your steel, Lord Snow."

Jon drew his longsword. He dared defy Ser Alliser only to a point, and he feared he was well beyond it now.

Thorne smiled. "The Bastard wishes to defend his lady love, so we shall make an exercise of it. Rat, Pimple, help our Stone Head here." Rast and Albett moved to join Halder. "Three of you ought to be sufficient to make Lady Piggy squeal. All you need do is get past the Bastard."

"Stay behind me," Jon said to the fat boy. Ser Alliser had often sent two foes against him, but never three. He knew he would likely go to sleep bruised and bloody tonight. He braced himself for the assault.

Suddenly Pyp was beside him. "Three to two will make for better sport," the small boy said cheerfully. He dropped his visor and slid out his sword. Before Jon could even think to protest, Grenn had stepped up to make a third.

The yard had grown deathly quiet. Jon could feel Ser Alliser's eyes. "Why are you waiting?" he asked Rast and the others in a voice gone deceptively soft, but it was Jon who moved first. Halder barely got his sword up in time.

Jon drove him backward, attacking with every blow, keeping the older boy on the heels. *Know your foe*, Ser Rodrik had taught him once; Jon knew Halder, brutally strong but short of patience, with no taste for defense. Frustrate him, and he would leave himself open, as certain as sunset.

The clang of steel echoed through the yard as the others joined battle around him. Jon blocked a savage cut at his head, the shock of impact running up his arm as the swords crashed together. He slammed a sidestroke into Halder's ribs, and was rewarded with a muffled grunt of pain. The counterstroke caught Jon on the shoulder. Chainmail crunched, and pain flared up his neck, but for an instant Halder was unbalanced. Jon cut his left leg from under him, and he fell with a curse and a crash.

Grenn was standing his ground as Jon had taught him, giving Albett more than he cared for, but Pyp was hard-pressed. Rast had two years and forty pounds on him. Jon stepped up behind him and rang the raper's helm like a bell. As Rast went reeling, Pyp slid in under his guard, knocked him down, and leveled a blade at his throat. By then Jon had moved on. Facing two swords, Albett backed away. "I yield," he shouted.

Ser Alliser Thorne surveyed the scene with disgust. "The mummer's farce has gone on long enough for today." He walked away. The session was at an end.

Dareon helped Halder to his feet. The quarryman's son wrenched off his helm and threw it across the yard. "For an instant, I thought I finally had you, Snow."

"For an instant, you did," Jon replied. Under his mail and leather, his shoulder was throbbing. He sheathed his sword and tried to remove his helm, but when he raised his arm, the pain made him grit his teeth.

"Let me," a voice said. Thick-fingered hands unfastened helm from gorget and lifted it off gently. "Did he hurt you?"

"I've been bruised before." He touched his shoulder and winced. The yard was emptying around them.

Blood matted the fat boy's hair where Halder had split his helm asunder. "My name is Samwell Tarly, of Horn . . ." He stopped and licked his lips. "I mean, I *was* of Horn Hill, until I . . . left. I've come to take the black. My father is Lord Randyll, a bannerman to the Tyrells of Highgarden. I used to be his heir, only . . ." His voice trailed off.

"I'm Jon Snow, Ned Stark's bastard, of Winterfell."

Samwell Tarly nodded. "I . . . if you want, you can call me Sam. My mother calls me Sam."

"You can call *him* Lord Snow," Pyp said as he came up to join them. "You don't want to know what his mother calls him."

"These two are Grenn and Pypar," Jon said.

"Grenn's the ugly one," Pyp said.

Grenn scowled. "You're uglier than me. At least I don't have ears like a bat."

"My thanks to all of you," the fat boy said gravely.

"Why didn't you get up and fight?" Grenn demanded.

"I wanted to, truly. I just . . . I couldn't. I didn't want him to hit me anymore." He looked at the ground. "I . . . I fear I'm a coward. My lord father always said so."

Grenn looked thunderstruck. Even Pyp had no words to say to that, and Pyp had words for everything. What sort of man would proclaim himself a coward?

Samwell Tarly must have read their thoughts on their faces. His eyes met Jon's and darted away, quick as frightened animals. "I . . . I'm sorry," he said. "I don't mean to . . . to be like I am." He walked heavily toward the armory.

Jon called after him. "You were hurt," he said. "Tomorrow you'll do better."

Sam looked mournfully back over one shoulder. "No I won't," he said, blinking back tears. "I never do better."

When he was gone, Grenn frowned. "Nobody likes cravens," he said uncomfortably. "I wish we hadn't helped him. What if they think we're craven too?"

"You're too stupid to be craven," Pyp told him.

"I am not," Grenn said.

"Yes you are. If a bear attacked you in the woods, you'd be too stupid to run away."

"I would not," Grenn insisted. "I'd run away faster than you." He stopped suddenly, scowling when he saw Pyp's grin and realized what he'd just said. His thick neck flushed a dark red. Jon left them there arguing as he returned to the armory, hung up his sword, and stripped off his battered armor.

Life at Castle Black followed certain patterns; the mornings were for swordplay, the afternoons for work. The black brothers set new recruits to many different tasks, to learn where their skills lay. Jon cherished the rare afternoons when he was sent out with Ghost ranging at his side to bring back game for the Lord Commander's table, but for every day spent hunting, he gave a dozen to Donal Noye in the armory, spinning the whetstone while the one-armed smith sharpened axes grown dull from use, or pumping the bellows as Noye hammered out a new sword. Other times he ran messages, stood at guard, mucked out stables, fletched arrows, assisted Maester Aemon with his birds or Bowen Marsh with his counts and inventories.

That afternoon, the watch commander sent him to the winch cage with four barrels of fresh-crushed stone, to scatter gravel over the icy footpaths atop the Wall. It was lonely and boring work, even with Ghost along for company, but Jon found he did not mind. On a clear day you could see half the world from the top of the Wall, and the air was always cold and bracing. He could think here, and he found himself thinking of Samwell Tarly . . . and, oddly, of Tyrion Lannister. He wondered what Tyrion would have made of the fat boy. *Most men would rather deny a hard truth than face it,* the dwarf had told him, grinning. The world was full of cravens who pretended to be heroes; it took a queer sort of courage to admit to cowardice as Samwell Tarly had.

His sore shoulder made the work go slowly. It was late afternoon before Jon finished graveling the paths. He lingered on high to watch the sun go down, turning the western sky the color of blood. Finally, as dusk was settling over the north, Jon rolled the empty barrels back into the cage and signaled the winch men to lower him.

The evening meal was almost done by the time he and Ghost reached the common hall. A group of the black brothers were dicing over mulled wine near the fire. His friends were at the bench nearest the west wall, laughing. Pyp was in the middle of a story. The mummer's boy with the big ears was a born liar with a hundred different voices, and he did not tell his tales so much as live them, playing all the parts as needed, a king one moment and a swineherd the next. When he turned into an alehouse girl or a virgin princess, he used a high falsetto voice that reduced them all to tears of helpless laughter, and his eunuchs were always eerily accurate caricatures of Ser Alliser. Jon took as much pleasure from Pyp's antics as anyone . . . yet that night he turned away and went instead to the end of the bench, where Samwell Tarly sat alone, as far from the others as he could get.

He was finishing the last of the pork pie the cooks had served up for supper when Jon sat down across from him. The fat boy's eyes widened at the sight of Ghost. "Is that a wolf?"

"A direwolf," Jon said. "His name is Ghost. The direwolf is the sigil of my father's House."

"Ours is a striding huntsman," Samwell Tarly said.

"Do you like to hunt?"

The fat boy shuddered. "I hate it." He looked as though he was going to cry again.

"What's wrong now?" Jon asked him. "Why are you always so frightened?"

Sam stared at the last of his pork pie and gave a feeble shake of his head, too scared even to talk. A burst of laughter filled the hall. Jon heard Pyp squeaking in a high voice. He stood. "Let's go outside."

The round fat face looked up at him, suspicious. "Why? What will we do outside?"

"Talk," Jon said. "Have you seen the Wall?"

"I'm fat, not blind," Samwell Tarly said. "Of course I saw it, it's seven hundred feet high." Yet he stood up all the same, wrapped a fur-lined cloak over his shoulders, and followed Jon from the common hall, still wary, as if he suspected some cruel trick was waiting for him in the night. Ghost padded along beside them. "I never thought it would be like this," Sam said as they walked, his words steaming in the cold air. Already he was huffing and puffing as he tried to keep up. "All the buildings are falling down, and it's so . . . so . . . ."

"Cold?" A hard frost was settling over the castle, and Jon could hear the soft crunch of grey weeds beneath his boots.

Sam nodded miserably. "I hate the cold," he said. "Last night I woke up in the dark and the fire had gone out and I was certain I was going to freeze to death by morning."

"It must have been warmer where you come from."

"I never saw snow until last month. We were crossing the barrowlands, me and the men my father sent to see me north, and this white stuff began to fall, like a soft rain. At first I thought it was so beautiful, like feathers drifting from the sky, but it kept on and on, until I was frozen to the bone. The men had crusts of snow in their beards and more on their shoulders, and still it kept coming. I was afraid it would never end."

Jon smiled.

The Wall loomed before them, glimmering palely in the light of the half moon. In the sky above, the stars burned clear and sharp. "Are they going to make me go up there?" Sam asked. His face curdled like old milk as he looked at the great wooden stairs. "I'll die if I have to climb that."

"There's a winch," Jon said, pointing. "They can draw you up in a cage."

Samwell Tarly sniffled. "I don't like high places."

It was too much. Jon frowned, incredulous. "Are you afraid of *everything*?" he asked. "I don't understand. If you are truly so craven, why are you here? Why would a coward want to join the Night's Watch?"

Samwell Tarly looked at him for a long moment, and his round face seemed to cave in on itself. He sat down on the frost-covered ground and began to cry, huge choking sobs that made his whole body shake. Jon Snow could only stand and watch. Like the snowfall on the barrowlands, it seemed the tears would never end.

It was Ghost who knew what to do. Silent as shadow, the pale direwolf moved closer and began to lick the warm tears off Samwell Tarly's face. The fat boy cried out, startled . . . and somehow, in a heartbeat, his sobs turned to laughter.

Jon Snow laughed with him. Afterward they sat on the frozen ground, huddled in their cloaks with Ghost between them. Jon told the story of how he and Robb had found the pups newborn in the late summer snows. It seemed a thousand years ago now. Before long he found himself talking of Winterfell.

"Sometimes I dream about it," he said. "I'm walking down this long empty hall. My voice echoes all around, but no one answers, so I walk faster, opening doors, shouting names. I don't even know who I'm looking for. Most nights it's my father, but sometimes it's Robb instead, or my little sister Arya, or my uncle." The thought of Benjen Stark saddened him; his uncle was still missing. The Old Bear had sent out rangers in search of him. Ser

Jaremy Rykker had led two sweeps, and Quorin Halfhand had gone forth from the Shadow Tower, but they'd found nothing aside from a few blazes in the trees that his uncle had left to mark his way. In the stony highlands to the northwest, the marks stopped abruptly and all trace of Ben Stark vanished.

"Do you ever find anyone in your dream?" Sam asked.

Jon shook his head. "No one. The castle is always empty." He had never told anyone of the dream, and he did not understand why he was telling Sam now, yet somehow it felt good to talk of it. "Even the ravens are gone from the rookery, and the stables are full of bones. That always scares me. I start to run then, throwing open doors, climbing the tower three steps at a time, screaming for someone, for anyone. And then I find myself in front of the door to the crypts. It's black inside, and I can see the steps spiraling down. Somehow I know I have to go down there, but I don't want to. I'm afraid of what might be waiting for me. The old Kings of Winter are down there, sitting on their thrones with stone wolves at their feet and iron swords across their laps, but it's not them I'm afraid of. I scream that I'm not a Stark, that this isn't my place, but it's no good, I have to go anyway, so I start down, feeling the walls as I descend, with no torch to light the way. It gets darker and darker, until I want to scream." He stopped, frowning, embarrassed. "That's when I always wake." His skin cold and clammy, shivering in the darkness of his cell. Ghost would leap up beside him, his warmth as comforting as daybreak. He would go back to sleep with his face pressed into the direwolf's shaggy white fur. "Do you dream of Horn Hill?" Jon asked.

"No." Sam's mouth grew tight and hard. "I hated it there." He scratched Ghost behind the ear, brooding, and Jon let the silence breathe. After a long while Samwell Tarly began to talk, and Jon Snow listened quietly, and learned how it was that a self-confessed coward found himself on the Wall.

The Tarlys were a family old in honor, bannermen to Mace Tyrell, Lord of Highgarden and Warden of the South. The eldest son of Lord Randyll Tarly, Samwell was born heir to rich lands, a strong keep, and a storied two-handed greatsword named Heartsbane, forged of Valyrian steel and passed down from father to son near five hundred years.

Whatever pride his lord father might have felt at Samwell's birth vanished as the boy grew up plump, soft, and awkward. Sam loved to listen to music and make his own songs, to wear soft velvets, to play in the castle kitchen beside the cooks, drinking in the rich smells as he snitched lemon cakes and blueberry tarts. His passions were books and kittens and dancing, clumsy as he was. But he grew ill at the sight of blood, and wept to see even a chicken slaughtered. A dozen masters-at-arms came and went at Horn Hill, trying to turn Samwell into the knight his father wanted. The boy was cursed and caned, slapped and starved. One man had him sleep in his chainmail to make him more martial. Another dressed him in his mother's clothing and paraded him through the bailey to shame him into valor. He only grew fatter and more frightened, until Lord Randyll's disappointment turned to anger and then to loathing. "One time," Sam confided, his voice dropping from a whisper, "two men came to the castle, warlocks from Qarth with white skin and blue lips. They slaughtered a bull aurochs and made me bathe in the hot blood, but it didn't make me brave as they'd promised. I got sick and retched. Father had them scourged."

Finally, after three girls in as many years, Lady Tarly gave her lord husband a second son. From that day, Lord Randyll ignored Sam, devoting all his time to the younger boy, a fierce, robust child more to his liking. Samwell had known several years of sweet peace with his music and his books.

Until the dawn of his fifteenth name day, when he had been awakened to find his horse saddled and ready. Three men-at-arms had escorted him into a wood near Horn Hill, where his father was skinning a deer. "You are almost a man grown now, and my heir," Lord Randyll Tarly had told his eldest son, his long knife laying bare the carcass as he spoke. "You have given me no cause to disown you, but neither will I allow you to inherit the land and title that should be Dickon's. Heartsbane must go to a man strong enough to wield her, and you are not worthy to touch her hilt. So I have decided that you shall this day announce that you wish to take the black. You will for-

sake all claim to your brother's inheritance and start
north before evenfall.

"If you do not, then on the morrow we shall have a
hunt, and somewhere in these woods your horse will
stumble, and you will be thrown from the saddle to
die . . . or so I will tell your mother. She has a woman's
heart and finds it in her to cherish even you, and I have no
wish to cause her pain. Please do not imagine that it will
truly be that easy, should you think to defy me. Nothing
would please me more than to hunt you down like the pig
you are." His arms were red to the elbow as he laid the
skinning knife aside. "So. There is your choice. The
Night's Watch"—he reached inside the deer, ripped out
its heart, and held it in his fist, red and dripping—"or
this."   •

Sam told the tale in a calm, dead voice, as if it were
something that had happened to someone else, not to
him. And strangely, Jon thought, he did not weep, not
even once. When he was done, they sat together and listened to the wind for a time. There was no other sound in
all the world.

Finally Jon said, "We should go back to the common
hall."

"Why?" Sam asked.

Jon shrugged. "There's hot cider to drink, or mulled
wine if you prefer. Some nights Dareon sings for us, if the
mood is on him. He was a singer, before . . . well, not
truly, but almost, an apprentice singer."

"How did he come here?" Sam asked.

"Lord Rowan of Goldengrove found him in bed with
his daughter. The girl was two years older, and Dareon
swears she helped him through her window, but under
her father's eye she named it rape, so here he is. When
Maester Aemon heard him sing, he said his voice was
honey poured over thunder." Jon smiled. "Toad sometimes sings too, if you call it singing. Drinking songs he
learned in his father's winesink. Pyp says his voice is piss
poured over a fart." They laughed at that together.

"I should like to hear them both," Sam admitted, "but
they would not want me there." His face was troubled.
"He's going to make me fight again on the morrow, isn't
he?"

"He is," Jon was forced to say.

Sam got awkwardly to his feet. "I had better try to sleep." He huddled down in his cloak and plodded off.

The others were still in the common room when Jon returned, alone but for Ghost. "Where have *you* been?" Pyp asked.

"Talking with Sam," he said.

"He truly is craven," said Grenn. "At supper, there were still places on the bench when he got his pie, but he was too scared to come sit with us."

"The Lord of Ham thinks he's too good to eat with the likes of us," suggested Jeren.

"I saw him eat a pork pie," Toad said, smirking. "Do you think it was a brother?" He began to make *oink*ing noises.

"*Stop it!*" Jon snapped angrily.

The other boys fell silent, taken aback by his sudden fury. "Listen to me," Jon said into the quiet, and he told them how it was going to be. Pyp backed him, as he'd known he would, but when Halder spoke up, it was a pleasant surprise. Grenn was anxious at the first, but Jon knew the words to move him. One by one the rest fell in line. Jon persuaded some, cajoled some, shamed the others, made threats where threats were required. At the end they had all agreed . . . all but Rast.

"You girls do as you please," Rast said, "but if Thorne sends me against Lady Piggy, I'm going to slice me off a rasher of bacon." He laughed in Jon's face and left them there.

Hours later, as the castle slept, three of them paid a call on his cell. Grenn held his arms while Pyp sat on his legs. Jon could hear Rast's rapid breathing as Ghost leapt onto his chest. The direwolf's eyes burned red as embers as his teeth nipped lightly at the soft skin of the boy's throat, just enough to draw blood. "Remember, we know where you sleep," Jon said softly.

The next morning Jon heard Rast tell Albett and Toad how his razor had slipped while he shaved.

From that day forth, neither Rast nor any of the others would hurt Samwell Tarly. When Ser Alliser matched them against him, they would stand their ground and swat aside his slow, clumsy strokes. If the master-at-arms screamed for an attack, they would dance in and tap Sam lightly on breastplate or helm or leg. Ser Alliser raged and threatened and called them all cravens and women and worse, yet Sam remained unhurt. A few nights later, at Jon's urging, he joined them for the evening meal, taking a place on the bench beside Halder. It was another fortnight before he found the nerve to join their talk, but in time he was laughing at Pyp's faces and teasing Grenn with the best of them.

Fat and awkward and frightened he might be, but Samwell Tarly was no fool. One night he visited Jon in his cell. "I don't know what you did," he said, "but I know you did it." He looked away shyly. "I've never had a friend before."

"We're not friends," Jon said. He put a hand on Sam's broad shoulder. "We're brothers."

And so they were, he thought to himself after Sam had taken his leave. Robb and Bran and Rickon were his father's sons, and he loved them still, yet Jon knew that he had never truly been one of them. Catelyn Stark had seen to that. The grey walls of Winterfell might still haunt his dreams, but Castle Black was his life now, and his brothers were Sam and Grenn and Halder and Pyp and the other cast-outs who wore the black of the Night's Watch.

"My uncle spoke truly," he whispered to Ghost. He wondered if he would ever see Benjen Stark again, to tell him.

EDDARD

"It's the Hand's tourney that's the cause of all the trouble, my lords," the Commander of the City Watch complained to the king's council.

"The king's tourney," Ned corrected, wincing. "I assure you, the Hand wants no part of it."

"Call it what you will, my lord. Knights have been arriving from all over the realm, and for every knight we get two freeriders, three craftsmen, six men-at-arms, a dozen merchants, two dozen whores, and more thieves than I dare guess. This cursed heat had half the city in a fever to start, and now with all these visitors . . . last night we had a drowning, a tavern riot, three knife fights, a rape, two fires, robberies beyond count, and a drunken horse race down the Street of the Sisters. The night before a woman's head was found in the Great Sept, floating in the rainbow pool. No one seems to know how it got there or who it belongs to."

"How dreadful," Varys said with a shudder.

Lord Renly Baratheon was less sympathetic. "If you cannot keep the king's peace, Janos, perhaps the City Watch should be commanded by someone who can."

Stout, jowly Janos Slynt puffed himself up like an angry frog, his bald pate reddening. "Aegon the Dragon himself could not keep the peace, Lord Renly. I need more men."

"How many?" Ned asked, leaning forward. As ever, Robert had not troubled himself to attend the council session, so it fell to his Hand to speak for him.

"As many as can be gotten, Lord Hand."

"Hire fifty new men," Ned told him. "Lord Baelish will see that you get the coin."

"I will?" Littlefinger said.

"You will. You found forty thousand golden dragons for a champion's purse, surely you can scrape together a few coppers to keep the king's peace." Ned turned back to Janos Slynt. "I will also give you twenty good swords from my own household guard, to serve with the Watch until the crowds have left."

"All thanks, Lord Hand," Slynt said, bowing. "I promise you, they shall be put to good use."

When the Commander had taken his leave, Eddard Stark turned to the rest of the council. "The sooner this folly is done with, the better I shall like it." As if the expense and trouble were not irksome enough, all and sundry insisted on salting Ned's wound by calling it "the Hand's tourney," as if he were the cause of it. And Robert honestly seemed to think he should feel honored!

"The realm prospers from such events, my lord," Grand Maester Pycelle said. "They bring the great the chance of glory, and the lowly a respite from their woes."

"And put coins in many a pocket," Littlefinger added. "Every inn in the city is full, and the whores are walking bowlegged and jingling with each step."

Lord Renly laughed. "We're fortunate my brother Stannis is not with us. Remember the time he proposed to outlaw brothels? The king asked him if perhaps he'd like to outlaw eating, shitting, and breathing while he was at it. If truth be told, I ofttimes wonder how Stannis ever got that ugly daughter of his. He goes to his marriage bed like a man marching to a battlefield, with a grim look in his eyes and a determination to do his duty."

Ned had not joined the laughter. "I wonder about your brother Stannis as well. I wonder when he intends to end his visit to Dragonstone and resume his seat on this council."

"No doubt as soon as we've scourged all those whores into the sea," Littlefinger replied, provoking more laughter.

"I have heard quite enough about whores for one day," Ned said, rising. "Until the morrow."

Harwin had the door when Ned returned to the Tower of the Hand. "Summon Jory to my chambers and tell your father to saddle my horse," Ned told him, too brusquely.

"As you say, my lord."

The Red Keep and the "Hand's tourney" were chafing him raw, Ned reflected as he climbed. He yearned for the comfort of Catelyn's arms, for the sounds of Robb and Jon crossing swords in the practice yard, for the cool days and cold nights of the north.

In his chambers he stripped off his council silks and sat for a moment with the book while he waited for Jory to arrive. *The Lineages and Histories of the Great Houses of the Seven Kingdoms, With Descriptions of Many High Lords and Noble Ladies and Their Children*, by Grand Maester Malleon. Pycelle had spoken truly; it made for ponderous reading. Yet Jon Arryn had asked for it, and Ned felt certain he had reasons. There was something here, some truth buried in these brittle yellow pages, if only he could see it. But *what?* The tome was over a century old. Scarcely a man now alive had yet been born when Malleon had compiled his dusty lists of weddings, births, and deaths.

He opened to the section on House Lannister once more, and turned the pages slowly, hoping against hope that something would leap out at him. The Lannisters were an old family, tracing their descent back to Lann the Clever, a trickster from the Age of Heroes who was no doubt as legendary as Bran the Builder, though far more beloved of singers and taletellers. In the songs, Lann was the fellow who winkled the Casterlys out of Casterly Rock with no weapon but his wits, and stole gold from the sun to brighten his curly hair. Ned wished he were here now, to winkle the truth out of this damnable book.

A sharp rap on the door heralded Jory Cassel. Ned closed Malleon's tome and bid him enter. "I've promised the City Watch twenty of my guard until the tourney is done," he told him. "I rely on you to make the choice. Give Alyn the command, and make certain the men understand that they are needed to stop fights, not start them." Rising, Ned opened a cedar chest and removed a light linen undertunic. "Did you find the stableboy?"

"The watchman, my lord," Jory said. "He vows he'll never touch another horse."

"What did he have to say?"

"He claims he knew Lord Arryn well. Fast friends, they were." Jory snorted. "The Hand always gave the lads a copper on their name days, he says. Had a way with horses. Never rode his mounts too hard, and brought them carrots and apples, so they were always pleased to see him."

"Carrots and apples," Ned repeated. It sounded as if this boy would be even less use than the others. And he was the last of the four Littlefinger had turned up. Jory had spoken to each of them in turn. Ser Hugh had been brusque and uninformative, and arrogant as only a new-made knight can be. If the Hand wished to talk to him, he should be pleased to receive him, but he would not be questioned by a mere captain of guards . . . even if said captain was ten years older and a hundred times the swordsman. The serving girl had at least been pleasant. She said Lord Jon had been reading more than was good for him, that he was troubled and melancholy over his young son's frailty, and gruff with his lady wife. The pot-boy, now cordwainer, had never exchanged so much as a word with Lord Jon, but he was full of oddments of kitchen gossip: the lord had been quarreling with the king, the lord only picked at his food, the lord was sending his boy to be fostered on Dragonstone, the lord had taken a great interest in the breeding of hunting hounds, the lord had visited a master armorer to commission a new suit of plate, wrought all in pale silver with a blue jasper falcon and a mother-of-pearl moon on the breast. The king's own brother had gone with him to help choose the design, the potboy said. No, not Lord Renly, the other one, Lord Stannis.

"Did our watchman recall anything else of note?"

"The lad swears Lord Jon was as strong as a man half his age. Often went riding with Lord Stannis, he says."

Stannis again, Ned thought. He found that curious. Jon Arryn and he had been cordial, but never friendly. And while Robert had been riding north to Winterfell, Stannis had removed himself to Dragonstone, the Targaryen island fastness he had conquered in his brother's name. He had given no word as to when he might return. "Where did they go on these rides?" Ned asked.

"The boy says that they visited a brothel."

"A brothel?" Ned said. "The Lord of the Eyrie and Hand of the King visited a brothel with *Stannis Baratheon*?" He shook his head, incredulous, wondering what Lord Renly would make of this tidbit. Robert's lusts were the subject of ribald drinking songs throughout the realm, but Stannis was a different sort of man; a bare year younger than the king, yet utterly unlike him, stern, humorless, unforgiving, grim in his sense of duty.

"The boy insists it's true. The Hand took three guardsmen with him, and the boy says they were joking of it when he took their horses afterward."

"Which brothel?" Ned asked.

"The boy did not know. The guards would."

"A pity Lysa carried them off to the Vale," Ned said dryly. "The gods are doing their best to vex us. Lady Lysa, Maester Colemon, Lord Stannis . . . everyone who might actually know the truth of what happened to Jon Arryn is a thousand leagues away."

"Will you summon Lord Stannis back from Dragonstone?"

"Not yet," Ned said. "Not until I have a better notion of what this is all about and where he stands." The matter nagged at him. Why did Stannis leave? Had he played some part in Jon Arryn's murder? Or was he afraid? Ned found it hard to imagine what could frighten Stannis Baratheon, who had once held Storm's End through a year of siege, surviving on rats and boot leather while the Lords Tyrell and Redwyne sat outside with their hosts, banqueting in sight of his walls.

"Bring me my doublet, if you would. The grey, with the direwolf sigil. I want this armorer to know who I am. It might make him more forthcoming."

Jory went to the wardrobe. "Lord Renly is brother to Lord Stannis as well as the king."

"Yet it seems that he was not invited on these rides." Ned was not sure what to make of Renly, with all his friendly ways and easy smiles. A few days past, he had taken Ned aside to show him an exquisite rose gold locklet. Inside was a miniature painted in the vivid Myrish style, of a lovely young girl with doe's eyes and a cascade of soft brown hair. Renly had seemed anxious to know if the girl reminded him of anyone, and when Ned had no answer but a shrug, he had seemed disappointed. The maid was Loras Tyrell's sister Margaery, he'd confessed, but there were those who said she looked like Lyanna. "No," Ned had told him, bemused. Could it be that Lord Renly, who looked so like a young Robert, had conceived a passion for a girl he fancied to be a young Lyanna? That struck him as more than passing queer.

Jory held out the doublet, and Ned slid his hands through the armholes. "Perhaps Lord Stannis will return for Robert's tourney," he said as Jory laced the garment up the back.

"That would be a stroke of fortune, my lord," Jory said.

Ned buckled on a longsword. "In other words, not bloody likely." His smile was grim.

Jory draped Ned's cloak across his shoulders and clasped it at the throat with the Hand's badge of office. "The armorer lives above his shop, in a large house at the top of the Street of Steel. Alyn knows the way, my lord."

Ned nodded. "The gods help this potboy if he's sent me off haring after shadows." It was a slim enough staff to lean on, but the Jon Arryn that Ned Stark had known was not one to wear jeweled and silvered plate. Steel was steel; it was meant for protection, not ornament. He might have changed his views, to be sure. He would scarcely have been the first man who came to look on things differently after a few years at court . . . but the change was marked enough to make Ned wonder.

"Is there any other service I might perform?"

"I suppose you'd best begin visiting whorehouses."

"Hard duty, my lord." Jory grinned. "The men will be glad to help. Porther has made a fair start already."

Ned's favorite horse was saddled and waiting in the yard. Varly and Jacks fell in beside him as he rode through the yard. Their steel caps and shirts of mail must have been sweltering, yet they said no word of complaint. As Lord Eddard passed beneath the King's Gate into the stink of the city, his grey and white cloak streaming from his shoulders, he saw eyes everywhere and kicked his mount into a trot. His guard followed.

He looked behind him frequently as they made their way through the crowded city streets. Tomard and Desmond had left the castle early this morning to take up positions on the route they must take, and watch for anyone following them, but even so, Ned was uncertain. The shadow of the King's Spider and his little birds had him fretting like a maiden on her wedding night.

The Street of Steel began at the market square beside the River Gate, as it was named on maps, or the Mud Gate, as it was commonly called. A mummer on stilts was striding through the throngs like some great insect, with a horde of barefoot children trailing behind him, hooting. Elsewhere, two ragged boys no older than Bran were dueling with sticks, to the loud encouragement of some and the furious curses of others. An old woman ended the contest by leaning out of her window and emptying a bucket of slops on the heads of the combatants. In the shadow of the wall, farmers stood beside their wagons, bellowing out, "Apples, the best apples, cheap at twice the price," and "Blood melons, sweet as honey," and "Turnips, onions, roots, here you go here, here you go, turnips, onions, roots, here you go here."

The Mud Gate was open, and a squad of City Watchmen stood under the portcullis in their golden cloaks, leaning on spears. When a column of riders appeared from the west, the guardsmen sprang into action, shouting commands and moving the carts and foot traffic aside to let the knight enter with his escort. The first rider through the gate carried a long black banner. The silk rippled in the wind like a living thing; across the fabric was blazoned a night sky slashed with purple lightning. "Make way for Lord Beric!" the rider shouted. "Make way for Lord Beric!" And close behind came the young lord himself, a dashing figure on a black courser, with red-gold hair and a black satin cloak dusted with stars. "Here to fight in the Hand's tourney, my lord?" a guardsman called out to him. "Here to win the Hand's tourney," Lord Beric shouted back as the crowd cheered.

Ned turned off the square where the Street of Steel began and followed its winding path up a long hill, past blacksmiths working at open forges, freeriders haggling over mail shirts, and grizzled ironmongers selling old blades and razors from their wagons. The farther they climbed, the larger the buildings grew. The man they wanted was all the way at the top of the hill, in a huge house of timber and plaster whose upper stories loomed over the narrow street. The double doors showed a hunting scene carved in ebony and weirwood. A pair of stone knights stood sentry at the entrance, armored in fanciful suits of polished red steel that transformed them into griffin and unicorn. Ned left his horse with Jacks and shouldered his way inside.

The slim young serving girl took quick note of Ned's badge and the sigil on his doublet, and the master came hurrying out, all smiles and bows. "Wine for the King's Hand," he told the girl, gesturing Ned to a couch. "I am Tobho Mott, my lord, please, please, put yourself at ease." He wore a black velvet coat with hammers embroidered on the sleeves in silver thread. Around his neck was a heavy silver chain and a sapphire as large as a pigeon's egg. "If you are in need of new arms for the Hand's tourney, you have come to the right shop." Ned did not bother to correct him. "My work is costly, and I make no apologies for that, my lord," he said as he filled two matching silver goblets. "You will not find craftsmanship equal to mine anywhere in the Seven Kingdoms, I promise you. Visit every forge in King's Landing if you like, and compare for yourself. Any village smith can hammer out a shirt of mail; my work is art."

Ned sipped his wine and let the man go on. The Knight of Flowers bought all his armor here, Tobho boasted, and many high lords, the ones who knew fine steel, and even Lord Renly, the king's own brother. Perhaps the Hand had seen Lord Renly's new armor, the green plate with the golden antlers? No other armorer in the city could get that deep a green; he knew the secret of putting color in the steel itself, paint and enamel were the crutches of a journeyman. Or mayhaps the Hand wanted a blade? Tobho had learned to work Valyrian steel at the forges of Qohor as a boy. Only a man who knew the spells could take old weapons and forge them anew. "The direwolf is the sigil of House Stark, is it not? I could fashion a direwolf helm so real that children will run from you in the street," he vowed.

Ned smiled. "Did you make a falcon helm for Lord Arryn?"

Tobho Mott paused a long moment and set aside his wine. "The Hand did call upon me, with Lord Stannis, the king's brother. I regret to say, they did not honor me with their patronage."

Ned looked at the man evenly, saying nothing, waiting. He had found over the years that silence sometimes yielded more than questions. And so it was this time.

"They asked to see the boy," the armorer said, "so I took them back to the forge."

"The boy," Ned echoed. He had no notion who the boy might be. "I should like to see the boy as well."

Tobho Mott gave him a cool, careful look. "As you wish, my lord," he said with no trace of his former friendliness. He led Ned out a rear door and across a narrow yard, back to the cavernous stone barn where the work was done. When the armorer opened the door, the blast of hot air that came through made Ned feel as though he were walking into a dragon's mouth. Inside, a forge blazed in each corner, and the air stank of smoke and sulfur. Journeymen armorers glanced up from their hammers and tongs just long enough to wipe the sweat from their brows, while bare-chested apprentice boys worked the bellows.

The master called over a tall lad about Robb's age, his arms and chest corded with muscle. "This is Lord Stark, the new Hand of the King," he told him as the boy looked at Ned through sullen blue eyes and pushed back sweat-soaked hair with his fingers. Thick hair, shaggy and unkempt and black as ink. The shadow of a new beard darkened his jaw. "This is Gendry. Strong for his age, and he works hard. Show the Hand that helmet you made, lad." Almost shyly, the boy led them to his bench, and a steel helm shaped like a bull's head, with two great curving horns.

Ned turned the helm over in his hands. It was raw steel, unpolished but expertly shaped. "This is fine work. I would be pleased if you would let me buy it."

The boy snatched it out of his hands. "It's not for sale."

Tobho Mott looked horror-struck. "Boy, this is the King's Hand. If his lordship wants this helm, make him a gift of it. He honors you by asking."

"I made it for me," the boy said stubbornly.

"A hundred pardons, my lord," his master said hurriedly to Ned. "The boy is crude as new steel, and like new steel would profit from some beating. That helm is journeyman's work at best. Forgive him and I promise I will craft you a helm like none you have ever seen."

"He's done nothing that requires my forgiveness. Gendry, when Lord Arryn came to see you, what did you talk about?"

"He asked me questions is all, m'lord."

"What sort of questions?"

The boy shrugged. "How was I, and was I well treated, and if I liked the work, and stuff about my mother. Who she was and what she looked like and all."

"What did you tell him?" Ned asked.

The boy shoved a fresh fall of black hair off his forehead. "She died when I was little. She had yellow hair, and sometimes she used to sing to me, I remember. She worked in an alehouse."

"Did Lord Stannis question you as well?"

"The bald one? No, not him. He never said no word, just glared at me, like I was some raper who done for his daughter."

"Mind your filthy tongue," the master said. "This is the King's own Hand." The boy lowered his eyes. "A smart boy, but stubborn. That helm . . . the others call him bullheaded, so he threw it in their teeth."

Ned touched the boy's head, fingering the thick black hair. "Look at me, Gendry." The apprentice lifted his face. Ned studied the shape of his jaw, the eyes like blue ice. *Yes,* he thought, *I see it.* "Go back to your work, lad. I'm sorry to have bothered you." He walked back to the house with the master. "Who paid the boy's apprentice fee?" he asked lightly.

Mott looked fretful. "You saw the boy. Such a strong boy. Those hands of his, those hands were made for hammers. He had such promise, I took him on without a fee."

"The truth now," Ned urged. "The streets are full of strong boys. The day you take on an apprentice without a fee will be the day the Wall comes down. Who paid for him?"

"A lord," the master said reluctantly. "He gave no name, and wore no sigil on his coat. He paid in gold, twice the customary sum, and said he was paying once for the boy, and once for my silence."

"Describe him."

"He was stout, round of shoulder, not so tall as you. Brown beard, but there was a bit of red in it, I'll swear. He wore a rich cloak, that I do remember, heavy purple velvet worked with silver threads, but the hood shadowed his face and I never did see him clear." He hesitated a moment. "My lord, I want no trouble."

"None of us wants trouble, but I fear these are troubled times, Master Mott," Ned said. "You know who the boy is."

"I am only an armorer, my lord. I know what I'm told."

"You know who the boy is," Ned repeated patiently. "That is not a question."

"The boy is my apprentice," the master said. He looked Ned in the eye, stubborn as old iron. "Who he was before he came to me, that's none of my concern."

Ned nodded. He decided that he liked Tobho Mott, master armorer. "If the day ever comes when Gendry would rather wield a sword than forge one, send him to me. He has the look of a warrior. Until then, you have my thanks, Master Mott, and my promise. Should I ever want a helm to frighten children, this will be the first place I visit."

His guard was waiting outside with the horses. "Did you find anything, my lord?" Jacks asked as Ned mounted up.

"I did," Ned told him, wondering. What had Jon Arryn wanted with a king's bastard, and why was it worth his life?

CATELYN

"**M**y lady, you ought cover your head," Ser Rodrik told her as their horses plodded north. "You will take a chill."

"It is only water, Ser Rodrik," Catelyn replied. Her hair hung wet and heavy, a loose strand stuck to her forehead, and she could imagine how ragged and wild she must look, but for once she did not care. The southern rain was soft and warm. Catelyn liked the feel of it on her face, gentle as a mother's kisses. It took her back to her childhood, to long grey days at Riverrun. She remembered the godswood, drooping branches heavy with moisture, and the sound of her brother's laughter as he chased her through piles of damp leaves. She remembered making mud pies with Lysa, the weight of them, the mud slick and brown between her fingers. They had served them to Littlefinger, giggling, and he'd eaten so much mud he was sick for a week. How young they all had been.

Catelyn had almost forgotten. In the north, the rain fell cold and hard, and sometimes at night it turned to ice. It was as likely to kill a crop as nurture it, and it sent grown men running for the nearest shelter. That was no rain for little girls to play in.

"I am soaked through," Ser Rodrik complained. "Even my bones are wet." The woods pressed close around them, and the steady pattering of rain on leaves was accompanied by the small sucking sounds their horses made as their hooves pulled free of the mud. "We will want a fire tonight, my lady, and a hot meal would serve us both."

"There is an inn at the crossroads up ahead," Catelyn told him. She had slept many a night there in her youth, traveling with her father. Lord Hoster Tully had been a restless man in his prime, always riding somewhere. She still remembered the innkeep, a fat woman named Masha Heddle who chewed sourleaf night and day and seemed to have an endless supply of smiles and sweet cakes for the children. The sweet cakes had been soaked with honey, rich and heavy on the tongue, but how Catelyn had dreaded those smiles. The sourleaf had stained Masha's teeth a dark red, and made her smile a bloody horror.

"An inn," Ser Rodrik repeated wistfully. "If only . . . but we dare not risk it. If we wish to remain unknown, I think it best we seek out some small holdfast . . ." He broke off as they heard sounds up the road; splashing water, the clink of mail, a horse's whinny. "Riders," he warned, his hand dropping to the hilt of his sword. Even on the kingsroad, it never hurt to be wary.

They followed the sounds around a lazy bend of the road and saw them; a column of armed men noisily fording a swollen stream. Catelyn reined up to let them pass. The banner in the hand of the foremost rider hung sodden and limp, but the guardsmen wore indigo cloaks and on their shoulders flew the silver eagle of Seagard. "Mallisters," Ser Rodrik whispered to her, as if she had not known. "My lady, best pull up your hood."

Catelyn made no move. Lord Jason Mallister himself rode with them, surrounded by his knights, his son Patrek by his side and their squires close behind. They were riding for King's Landing and the Hand's tourney, she knew. For the past week, the travelers had been thick as flies upon the kingsroad; knights and freeriders, singers with their harps and drums, heavy wagons laden with hops or corn or casks of honey, traders and craftsmen and whores, and all of them moving south.

She studied Lord Jason boldly. The last time she had

seen him he had been jesting with her uncle at her wedding feast; the Mallisters stood bannermen to the Tullys, and his gifts had been lavish. His brown hair was salted with white now, his face chiseled gaunt by time, yet the years had not touched his pride. He rode like a man who feared nothing. Catelyn envied him that; she had come to fear so much. As the riders passed, Lord Jason nodded a curt greeting, but it was only a high lord's courtesy to strangers chance met on the road. There was no recognition in those fierce eyes, and his son did not even waste a look.

"He did not know you," Ser Rodrik said after, wondering.

"He saw a pair of mud-spattered travelers by the side of the road, wet and tired. It would never occur to him to suspect that one of them was the daughter of his liege lord. I think we shall be safe enough at the inn, Ser Rodrik."

It was near dark when they reached it, at the crossroads north of the great confluence of the Trident. Masha Heddle was fatter and greyer than Catelyn remembered, still chewing her sourleaf, but she gave them only the most cursory of looks, with nary a hint of her ghastly red smile. "Two rooms at the top of the stair, that's all there is," she said, chewing all the while. "They're under the bell tower, you won't be missing meals, though there's some thinks it too noisy. Can't be helped. We're full up, or near as makes no matter. It's those rooms or the road."

It was those rooms, low, dusty garrets at the top of a cramped narrow staircase. "Leave your boots down here," Masha told them after she'd taken their coin. "The boy will clean them. I won't have you tracking mud up my stairs. Mind the bell. Those who come late to meals don't eat." There were no smiles, and no mention of sweet cakes.

When the supper bell rang, the sound was deafening. Catelyn had changed into dry clothes. She sat by the window, watching rain run down the pane. The glass was milky and full of bubbles, and a wet dusk was falling outside. Catelyn could just make out the muddy crossing where the two great roads met.

The crossroads gave her pause. If they turned west from here, it was an easy ride down to Riverrun. Her father had always given her wise counsel when she needed it most, and she yearned to talk to him, to warn him of the gathering storm. If Winterfell needed to brace for war, how much more so Riverrun, so much closer to King's Landing, with the power of Casterly Rock looming to the west like a shadow. If only her father had been stronger, she might have chanced it, but Hoster Tully had been bedridden these past two years, and Catelyn was loath to tax him now.

The eastern road was wilder and more dangerous, climbing through rocky foothills and thick forests into the Mountains of the Moon, past high passes and deep chasms to the Vale of Arryn and the stony Fingers beyond. Above the Vale, the Eyrie stood high and impregnable, its towers reaching for the sky. There she would find her sister . . . and, perhaps, some of the answers Ned sought. Surely Lysa knew more than she had dared to put in her letter. She might have the very proof that Ned needed to bring the Lannisters to ruin, and if it came to war, they would need the Arryns and the eastern lords who owed them service.

Yet the mountain road was perilous. Shadowcats prowled those passes, rock slides were common, and the mountain clans were lawless brigands, descending from the heights to rob and kill and melting away like snow whenever the knights rode out from the Vale in search of them. Even Jon Arryn, as great a lord as any the Eyrie had ever known, had always traveled in strength when he crossed the mountains. Catelyn's only strength was one elderly knight, armored in loyalty.

No, she thought, Riverrun and the Eyrie would have to wait. Her path ran north to Winterfell, where her sons and her duty were waiting for her. As soon as they were safely past the Neck, she could declare herself to one of Ned's bannermen, and send riders racing ahead with orders to mount a watch on the kingsroad.

The rain obscured the fields beyond the crossroads, but Catelyn saw the land clear enough in her memory. The marketplace was just across the way, and the village a mile farther on, half a hundred white cottages surrounding a small stone sept. There would be more now; the summer had been long and peaceful. North of here the kingsroad ran along the Green Fork of the Trident, through fertile valleys and green woodlands, past thriving towns and stout holdfasts and the castles of the river lords.

Catelyn knew them all: the Blackwoods and the Brackens, ever enemies, whose quarrels her father was obliged to settle; Lady Whent, last of her line, who dwelt with her ghosts in the cavernous vaults of Harrenhal; irascible Lord Frey, who had outlived seven wives and filled his twin castles with children, grandchildren, and great-grandchildren, and bastards and grandbastards as well. All of them were bannermen to the Tullys, their swords sworn to the service of Riverrun. Catelyn wondered if that would be enough, if it came to war. Her father was the staunchest man who'd ever lived, and she had no doubt that he would call his banners . . . but would the banners come? The Darrys and Rygers and Mootons had sworn oaths to Riverrun as well, yet they had fought with Rhaegar Targaryen on the Trident, while Lord Frey had arrived with his levies well after the battle was over, leaving some doubt as to which army he had planned to join (theirs, he had assured the victors solemnly in the aftermath, but ever after her father had called him the Late Lord Frey). It must *not* come to war, Catelyn thought fervently. They must not let it.

Ser Rodrik came for her just as the bell ceased its clangor. "We had best make haste if we hope to eat tonight, my lady."

"It might be safer if we were not knight and lady until we pass the Neck," she told him. "Common travelers attract less notice. A father and daughter taken to the road on some family business, say."

"As you say, my lady," Ser Rodrik agreed. It was only when she laughed that he realized what he'd done. "The old courtesies die hard, my—my daughter." He tried to tug on his missing whiskers, and sighed with exasperation.

Catelyn took his arm. "Come, Father," she said. "You'll find that Masha Heddle sets a good table, I think, but try not to praise her. You truly don't want to see her smile."

The common room was long and drafty, with a row of huge wooden kegs at one end and a fireplace at the other. A serving boy ran back and forth with skewers of meat while Masha drew beer from the kegs, chewing her sourleaf all the while.

The benches were crowded, townsfolk and farmers mingling freely with all manner of travelers. The crossroads made for odd companions; dyers with black and purple hands shared a bench with rivermen reeking of fish, an ironsmith thick with muscle squeezed in beside a wizened old septon, hard-bitten sellswords and soft plump merchants swapped news like boon companions.

The company included more swords than Catelyn would have liked. Three by the fire wore the red stallion badge of the Brackens, and there was a large party in blue steel ringmail and capes of a silvery grey. On their shoulder was another familiar sigil, the twin towers of House Frey. She studied their faces, but they were all too young to have known her. The senior among them would have been no older than Bran when she went north.

Ser Rodrik found them an empty place on the bench near the kitchen. Across the table a handsome youth was fingering a woodharp. "Seven blessings to you, goodfolk," he said as they sat. An empty wine cup stood on the table before him.

"And to you, singer," Catelyn returned. Ser Rodrik called for bread and meat and beer in a tone that meant *now*. The singer, a youth of some eighteen years, eyed them boldly and asked where they were going, and from whence they had come, and what news they had, letting the questions fly as quick as arrows and never pausing for an answer. "We left King's Landing a fortnight ago," Catelyn replied, answering the safest of his questions.

"That's where I'm bound," the youth said. As she had suspected, he was more interested in telling his own story than in hearing theirs. Singers loved nothing half so well as the sound of their own voices. "The Hand's tourney means rich lords with fat purses. The last time I came away with more silver than I could carry . . . or would have, if I hadn't lost it all betting on the Kingslayer to win the day."

"The gods frown on the gambler," Ser Rodrik said sternly. He was of the north, and shared the Stark views on tournaments.

"They frowned on me, for certain," the singer said.

"Your cruel gods and the Knight of Flowers altogether did me in."

"No doubt that was a lesson for you," Ser Rodrik said.

"It was. This time my coin will champion Ser Loras."

Ser Rodrik tried to tug at whiskers that were not there, but before he could frame a rebuke the serving boy came scurrying up. He laid trenchers of bread before them and filled them with chunks of browned meat off a skewer, dripping with hot juice. Another skewer held tiny onions, fire peppers, and fat mushrooms. Ser Rodrik set to lustily as the lad ran back to fetch them beer.

"My name is Marillion," the singer said, plucking a string on his woodharp. "Doubtless you've heard me play somewhere?"

His manner made Catelyn smile. Few wandering singers ever ventured as far north as Winterfell, but she knew his like from her girlhood in Riverrun. "I fear not," she told him.

He drew a plaintive chord from the woodharp. "That is your loss," he said. "Who was the finest singer you've ever heard?"

"Alia of Braavos," Ser Rodrik answered at once.

"Oh, I'm *much* better than that old stick," Marillion said. "If you have the silver for a song, I'll gladly show you."

"I might have a copper or two, but I'd sooner toss it down a well than pay for your howling," Ser Rodrik groused. His opinion of singers was well known; music was a lovely thing for girls, but he could not comprehend why any healthy boy would fill his hand with a harp when he might have had a sword.

"Your grandfather has a sour nature," Marillion said to Catelyn. "I meant to do you honor. An homage to your beauty. In truth, I was made to sing for kings and high lords."

"Oh, I can see that," Catelyn said. "Lord Tully is fond of song, I hear. No doubt you've been to Riverrun."

"A hundred times," the singer said airily. "They keep a chamber for me, and the young lord is like a brother."

Catelyn smiled, wondering what Edmure would think of that. Another singer had once bedded a girl her brother fancied; he had hated the breed ever since. "And Winterfell?" she asked him. "Have you traveled north?"

"Why would I?" Marillion asked. "It's all blizzards and bearskins up there, and the Starks know no music but the howling of wolves." Distantly, she was aware of the door banging open at the far end of the room.

"Innkeep," a servant's voice called out behind her, "we have horses that want stabling, and my lord of Lannister requires a room and a hot bath."

"Oh, gods," Ser Rodrik said before Catelyn reached out to silence him, her fingers tightening hard around his forearm.

Masha Heddle was bowing and smiling her hideous red smile. "I'm sorry, m'lord, truly, we're full up, every room."

There were four of them, Catelyn saw. An old man in the black of the Night's Watch, two servants . . . and him, standing there small and bold as life. "My men will sleep in your stable, and as for myself, well, I do not require a *large* room, as you can plainly see." He flashed a mocking grin. "So long as the fire's warm and the straw reasonably free of fleas, I am a happy man."

Masha Heddle was beside herself. "M'lord, there's nothing, it's the tourney, there's no help for it, oh . . ."

Tyrion Lannister pulled a coin from his purse and flicked it up over his head, caught it, tossed it again. Even across the room, where Catelyn sat, the wink of gold was unmistakable.

A freerider in a faded blue cloak lurched to his feet. "You're welcome to my room, m'lord."

"Now there's a clever man," Lannister said as he sent the coin spinning across the room. The freerider snatched it from the air. "And a nimble one to boot." The dwarf turned back to Masha Heddle. "You will be able to manage food, I trust?"

"Anything you like, m'lord, anything at all," the innkeep promised. *And may he choke on it,* Catelyn thought, but it was Bran she saw choking, drowning on his own blood.

Lannister glanced at the nearest tables. "My men will have whatever you're serving these people. Double portions, we've had a long hard ride. I'll take a roast fowl— chicken, duck, pigeon, it makes no matter. And send up a flagon of your best wine. Yoren, will you sup with me?"

"Aye, m'lord, I will," the black brother replied.

The dwarf had not so much as glanced toward the far end of the room, and Catelyn was thinking how grateful she was for the crowded benches between them when she suddenly Marillion bounded to his feet. *"My lord of Lannister!"* he called out. "I would be pleased to entertain you while you eat. Let me sing you the lay of your father's great victory at King's Landing!"

"Nothing would be more likely to ruin my supper," the dwarf said dryly. His mismatched eyes considered the singer briefly, started to move away . . . and found Catelyn. He looked at her for a moment, puzzled. She turned her face away, but too late. The dwarf was smiling. "Lady Stark, what an unexpected pleasure," he said. "I was sorry to miss you at Winterfell."

Marillion gaped at her, confusion giving way to chagrin as Catelyn rose slowly to her feet. She heard Ser Rodrik curse. If only the man had lingered at the Wall, she thought, if only . . .

"Lady . . . Stark?" Masha Heddle said thickly.

"I was still Catelyn Tully the last time I bedded here," she told the innkeep. She could hear the muttering, feel the eyes upon her. Catelyn glanced around the room, at the faces of the knights and sworn swords, and took a deep breath to slow the frantic beating of her heart. Did she dare take the risk? There was no time to think it through, only the moment and the sound of her own voice ringing in her ears. "You in the corner," she said to an older man she had not noticed until now. "Is that the black bat of Harrenhal I see embroidered on your surcoat, ser?"

The man got to his feet. "It is, my lady."

"And is Lady Whent a true and honest friend to my father, Lord Hoster Tully of Riverrun?"

"She is," the man replied stoutly.

Ser Rodrik rose quietly and loosened his sword in its scabbard. The dwarf was blinking at them, blank-faced, with puzzlement in his mismatched eyes.

"The red stallion was ever a welcome sight in Riverrun," she said to the trio by the fire. "My father counts Jonos Bracken among his oldest and most loyal bannermen."

The three men-at-arms exchanged uncertain looks.

"Our lord is honored by his trust," one of them said hesitantly.

"I envy your father all these fine friends," Lannister quipped, "but I do not quite see the purpose of this, Lady Stark."

She ignored him, turning to the large party in blue and grey. They were the heart of the matter; there were more than twenty of them. "I know your sigil as well: the twin towers of Frey. How fares your good lord, sers?"

Their captain rose. "Lord Walder is well, my lady. He plans to take a new wife on his ninetieth name day, and has asked your lord father to honor the wedding with his presence."

Tyrion Lannister sniggered. That was when Catelyn knew he was hers. "This man came a guest into my house, and there conspired to murder my son, a boy of seven," she proclaimed to the room at large, pointing. Ser Rodrik moved to her side, his sword in hand. "In the name of King Robert and the good lords you serve, I call upon you to seize him and help me return him to Winterfell to await the king's justice."

She did not know what was more satisfying: the sound of a dozen swords drawn as one or the look on Tyrion Lannister's face.

SANSA

Sansa rode to the Hand's tourney with Septa Mordane and Jeyne Poole, in a litter with curtains of yellow silk so fine she could see right through them. They turned the whole world gold. Beyond the city walls, a hundred pavilions had been raised beside the river, and the common folk came out in the thousands to watch the games. The splendor of it all took Sansa's breath away; the shining armor, the great chargers caparisoned in silver and gold, the shouts of the crowd, the banners snapping in the wind . . . and the knights themselves, the knights most of all.

"It is better than the songs," she whispered when they found the places that her father had promised her, among the high lords and ladies. Sansa was dressed beautifully that day, in a green gown that brought out the auburn of her hair, and she knew they were looking at her and smiling.

They watched the heroes of a hundred songs ride forth, each more fabulous than the last. The seven knights of the Kingsguard took the field, all but Jaime Lannister in scaled armor the color of milk, their cloaks as white as fresh-fallen snow. Ser Jaime wore the white cloak as well, but beneath it he was shining gold from head to foot, with a lion's-head helm and a golden sword. Ser Gregor Clegane, the Mountain That Rides, thundered past them like an avalanche. Sansa remembered Lord Yohn Royce, who had guested at Winterfell two years before. "His armor is bronze, thousands and thousands of years old, engraved with magic runes that ward him against harm," she whispered to Jeyne. Septa Mordane pointed out Lord Jason Mallister, in indigo chased with silver, the wings of an eagle on his helm. He had cut down three of Rhaegar's bannermen on the Trident. The girls giggled over the warrior priest Thoros of Myr, with his flapping red robes and shaven head, until the septa told them that he had once scaled the walls of Pyke with a flaming sword in hand.

Other riders Sansa did not know; hedge knights from the Fingers and Highgarden and the mountains of Dorne, unsung freeriders and new-made squires, the younger sons of high lords and the heirs of lesser houses. Younger men, most had done no great deeds as yet, but Sansa and Jeyne agreed that one day the Seven Kingdoms would resound to the sound of their names. Ser Balon Swann. Lord Bryce Caron of the Marches. Bronze Yohn's heir, Ser Andar Royce, and his younger brother Ser Robar, their silvered steel plate filigreed in bronze with the same ancient runes that warded their father. The twins Ser Horas and Ser Hobber, whose shields displayed the grape cluster sigil of the Redwynes, burgundy on blue. Patrek Mallister, Lord Jason's son. Six Freys of the Crossing: Ser Jared, Ser Hosteen, Ser Danwell, Ser Emmon, Ser Theo, Ser Perwyn, sons and grandsons of old Lord Walder Frey, and his bastard son Martyn Rivers as well.

Jeyne Poole confessed herself frightened by the look of Jalabhar Xho, an exile prince from the Summer Isles who wore a cape of green and scarlet feathers over skin as dark as night, but when she saw young Lord Beric Dondarrion, with his hair like red gold and his black shield slashed by lightning, she pronounced herself willing to marry him on the instant.

The Hound entered the lists as well, and so too the king's brother, handsome Lord Renly of Storm's End. Jory, Alyn, and Harwin rode for Winterfell and the north. "Jory looks a beggar among these others," Septa Mordane sniffed when he appeared. Sansa could only agree. Jory's armor was blue-grey plate without device or ornament, and a thin grey cloak hung from his shoulders like a soiled rag. Yet he acquitted himself well, unhorsing Horas Redwyne in his first joust and one of the Freys in his second. In his third match, he rode three passes at a free-rider named Lothor Brune whose armor was as drab as his own. Neither man lost his seat, but Brune's lance was steadier and his blows better placed, and the king gave him the victory. Alyn and Harwin fared less well; Harwin was unhorsed in his first tilt by Ser Meryn of the Kingsguard, while Alyn fell to Ser Balon Swann.

The jousting went all day and into the dusk, the hooves of the great warhorses pounding down the lists until the field was a ragged wasteland of torn earth. A dozen times Jeyne and Sansa cried out in unison as riders crashed together, lances exploding into splinters while the commons screamed for their favorites. Jeyne covered her eyes whenever a man fell, like a frightened little girl, but Sansa was made of sterner stuff. A great lady knew how to behave at tournaments. Even Septa Mordane noted her composure and nodded in approval.

The Kingslayer rode brilliantly. He overthrew Ser Andar Royce and the Marcher Lord Bryce Caron as easily as if he were riding at rings, and then took a hard-fought match from white-haired Barristan Selmy, who had won his first two tilts against men thirty and forty years his junior.

Sandor Clegane and his immense brother, Ser Gregor the Mountain, seemed unstoppable as well, riding down one foe after the next in ferocious style. The most terrifying moment of the day came during Ser Gregor's second joust, when his lance rode up and struck a young knight from the Vale under the gorget with such force that it drove through his throat, killing him instantly. The youth fell not ten feet from where Sansa was seated. The point of Ser Gregor's lance had snapped off in his neck, and his life's blood flowed out in slow pulses, each weaker than the one before. His armor was shiny new; a bright streak of fire ran down his outstretched arm, as the steel caught the light. Then the sun went behind a cloud, and it was gone. His cloak was blue, the color of the sky on a clear summer's day, trimmed with a border of crescent moons, but as his blood seeped into it, the cloth darkened and the moons turned red, one by one.

Jeyne Poole wept so hysterically that Septa Mordane finally took her off to regain her composure, but Sansa sat with her hands folded in her lap, watching with a strange fascination. She had never seen a man die before. She ought to be crying too, she thought, but the tears would not come. Perhaps she had used up all her tears for Lady and Bran. It would be different if it had been Jory or Ser Rodrik or Father, she told herself. The young knight in the blue cloak was nothing to her, some stranger from the Vale of Arryn whose name she had forgotten as soon as she heard it. And now the world would forget his name too, Sansa realized; there would be no songs sung for him. That was sad.

After they carried off the body, a boy with a spade ran onto the field and shoveled dirt over the spot where he had fallen, to cover up the blood. Then the jousts resumed.

Ser Balon Swann also fell to Gregor, and Lord Renly to the Hound. Renly was unhorsed so violently that he seemed to fly backward off his charger, legs in the air. His head hit the ground with an audible *crack* that made the crowd gasp, but it was just the golden antler on his helm. One of the tines had snapped off beneath him. When Lord Renly climbed to his feet, the commons cheered wildly, for King Robert's handsome young brother was a great favorite. He handed the broken tine to his conqueror with a gracious bow. The Hound snorted and tossed the broken antler into the crowd, where the commons began to punch and claw over the little bit of gold, until Lord Renly walked out among them and restored the peace. By then Septa Mordane had returned, alone. Jeyne had been feeling ill, she explained; she had helped her back to the castle. Sansa had almost forgotten about Jeyne.

Later a hedge knight in a checkered cloak disgraced himself by killing Beric Dondarrion's horse, and was declared forfeit. Lord Beric shifted his saddle to a new mount, only to be knocked right off it by Thoros of Myr. Ser Aron Santagar and Lothor Brune tilted thrice without result; Ser Aron fell afterward to Lord Jason Mallister, and Brune to Yohn Royce's younger son, Robar.

In the end it came down to four; the Hound and his

monstrous brother Gregor, Jaime Lannister the King-slayer, and Ser Loras Tyrell, the youth they called the Knight of Flowers.

Ser Loras was the youngest son of Mace Tyrell, the Lord of Highgarden and Warden of the South. At sixteen, he was the youngest rider on the field, yet he had un-horsed three knights of the Kingsguard that morning in his first three jousts. Sansa had never seen anyone so beautiful. His plate was intricately fashioned and enam-eled as a bouquet of a thousand different flowers, and his snow-white stallion was draped in a blanket of red and white roses. After each victory, Ser Loras would remove his helm and ride slowly round the fence, and finally pluck a single white rose from the blanket and toss it to some fair maiden in the crowd.

His last match of the day was against the younger Royce. Ser Robar's ancestral runes proved small protec-tion as Ser Loras split his shield and drove him from his saddle to crash with an awful clangor in the dirt. Robar lay moaning as the victor made his circuit of the field. Finally they called for a litter and carried him off to his tent, dazed and unmoving. Sansa never saw it. Her eyes were only for Ser Loras. When the white horse stopped in front of her, she thought her heart would burst.

To the other maidens he had given white roses, but the one he plucked for her was red. "Sweet lady," he said, "no victory is half so beautiful as you." Sansa took the flower timidly, struck dumb by his gallantry. His hair was a mass of lazy brown curls, his eyes like liquid gold. She inhaled the sweet fragrance of the rose and sat clutching it long after Ser Loras had ridden off.

When Sansa finally looked up, a man was standing over her, staring. He was short, with a pointed beard and a silver streak in his hair, almost as old as her father. "You must be one of her daughters," he said to her. He had grey-green eyes that did not smile when his mouth did. "You have the Tully look."

"I'm Sansa Stark," she said, ill at ease. The man wore a heavy cloak with a fur collar, fastened with a silver mock-ingbird, and he had the effortless manner of a high lord, but she did not know him. "I have not had the honor, my lord."

Septa Mordane quickly took a hand. "Sweet child, this is Lord Petyr Baelish, of the king's small council."

"Your mother was *my* queen of beauty once," the man said quietly. His breath smelled of mint. "You have her hair." His fingers brushed against her cheek as he stroked one auburn lock. Quite abruptly he turned and walked away.

By then, the moon was well up and the crowd was tired, so the king decreed that the last three matches would be fought the next morning, before the melee. While the commons began their walk home, talking of the day's jousts and the matches to come on the morrow, the court moved to the riverside to begin the feast. Six monstrous huge aurochs had been roasting for hours, turning slowly on wooden spits while kitchen boys basted them with butter and herbs until the meat crackled and spit. Tables and benches had been raised outside the pavilions, piled high with sweetgrass and strawberries and fresh-baked bread.

Sansa and Septa Mordane were given places of high honor, to the left of the raised dais where the king himself sat beside his queen. When Prince Joffrey seated himself to her right, she felt her throat tighten. He had not spoken a word to her since the awful thing had happened, and she had not dared to speak to him. At first she thought she hated him for what they'd done to Lady, but after Sansa had wept her eyes dry, she told herself that it had not been Joffrey's doing, not truly. The queen had done it; she was the one to hate, her and Arya. Nothing bad would have happened except for Arya.

She could not hate Joffrey tonight. He was too beautiful to hate. He wore a deep blue doublet studded with a double row of golden lion's heads, and around his brow a slim coronet made of gold and sapphires. His hair was as bright as the metal. Sansa looked at him and trembled, afraid that he might ignore her or, worse, turn hateful again and send her weeping from the table.

Instead Joffrey smiled and kissed her hand, handsome and gallant as any prince in the songs, and said, "Ser Loras has a keen eye for beauty, sweet lady."

"He was too kind," she demurred, trying to remain modest and calm, though her heart was singing. "Ser

Loras is a true knight. Do you think he will win tomorrow, my lord?"

"No," Joffrey said. "My dog will do for him, or perhaps my uncle Jaime. And in a few years, when I am old enough to enter the lists, I shall do for them all." He raised his hand to summon a servant with a flagon of iced summerwine, and poured her a cup. She looked anxiously at Septa Mordane, until Joffrey leaned over and filled the septa's cup as well, so she nodded and thanked him graciously and said not another word.

The servants kept the cups filled all night, yet afterward Sansa could not recall ever tasting the wine. She needed no wine. She was drunk on the magic of the night, giddy with glamour, swept away by beauties she had dreamt of all her life and never dared hope to know. Singers sat before the king's pavilion, filling the dusk with music. A juggler kept a cascade of burning clubs spinning through the air. The king's own fool, the pie-faced simpleton called Moon Boy, danced about on stilts, all in motley, making mock of everyone with such deft cruelty that Sansa wondered if he was simple after all. Even Septa Mordane was helpless before him; when he sang his little song about the High Septon, she laughed so hard she spilled wine on herself.

And Joffrey was the soul of courtesy. He talked to Sansa all night, showering her with compliments, making her laugh, sharing little bits of court gossip, explaining Moon Boy's japes. Sansa was so captivated that she quite forgot all her courtesies and ignored Septa Mordane, seated to her left.

All the while the courses came and went. A thick soup of barley and venison. Salads of sweetgrass and spinach and plums, sprinkled with crushed nuts. Snails in honey and garlic. Sansa had never eaten snails before; Joffrey showed her how to get the snail out of the shell, and fed her the first sweet morsel himself. Then came trout fresh from the river, baked in clay; her prince helped her crack open the hard casing to expose the flaky white flesh within. And when the meat course was brought out, he served her himself, slicing a queen's portion from the joint, smiling as he laid it on her plate. She could see from the way he moved that his right arm was still troubling him, yet he uttered not a word of complaint.

Later came sweetbreads and pigeon pie and baked apples fragrant with cinnamon and lemon cakes frosted in sugar, but by then Sansa was so stuffed that she could not manage more than two little lemon cakes, as much as she loved them. She was wondering whether she might attempt a third when the king began to shout.

King Robert had grown louder with each course. From time to time Sansa could hear him laughing or roaring a command over the music and the clangor of plates and cutlery, but they were too far away for her to make out his words.

Now everybody heard him. *"No,"* he thundered in a voice that drowned out all other speech. Sansa was shocked to see the king on his feet, red of face, reeling. He had a goblet of wine in one hand, and he was drunk as a man could be. "You do not tell me what to do, woman," he screamed at Queen Cersei. "I am king here, do you understand? I rule here, and if I say that I will fight tomorrow, *I will fight!*"

Everyone was staring. Sansa saw Ser Barristan, and the king's brother Renly, and the short man who had talked to her so oddly and touched her hair, but no one made a move to interfere. The queen's face was a mask, so bloodless that it might have been sculpted from snow. She rose from the table, gathered her skirts around her, and stormed off in silence, servants trailing behind.

Jaime Lannister put a hand on the king's shoulder, but the king shoved him away hard. Lannister stumbled and fell. The king guffawed. "The great knight. I can still knock you in the dirt. Remember that, Kingslayer." He slapped his chest with the jeweled goblet, splashing wine all over his satin tunic. "Give me my hammer and not a man in the realm can stand before me!"

Jaime Lannister rose and brushed himself off. "As you say, Your Grace." His voice was stiff.

Lord Renly came forward, smiling. "You've spilled your wine, Robert. Let me bring you a fresh goblet."

Sansa started as Joffrey laid his hand on her arm. "It grows late," the prince said. He had a queer look on his face, as if he were not seeing her at all. "Do you need an escort back to the castle?"

"No," Sansa began. She looked for Septa Mordane, and was startled to find her with her head on the table, snoring soft and ladylike snores. "I mean to say . . . yes, thank you, that would be most kind. I *am* tired, and the way is so dark. I should be glad for some protection."

Joffrey called out, *"Dog!"*

Sandor Clegane seemed to take form out of the night, so quickly did he appear. He had exchanged his armor for a red woolen tunic with a leather dog's head sewn on the front. The light of the torches made his burned face shine a dull red. "Yes, Your Grace?" he said.

"Take my betrothed back to the castle, and see that no harm befalls her," the prince told him brusquely. And without even a word of farewell, Joffrey strode off, leaving her there.

Sansa could *feel* the Hound watching her. "Did you think Joff was going to take you himself?" He laughed. He had a laugh like the snarling of dogs in a pit. "Small chance of that." He pulled her unresisting to her feet. "Come, you're not the only one needs sleep. I've drunk too much, and I may need to kill my brother tomorrow." He laughed again.

Suddenly terrified, Sansa pushed at Septa Mordane's shoulder, hoping to wake her, but she only snored the louder. King Robert had stumbled off and half the benches were suddenly empty. The feast was over, and the beautiful dream had ended with it.

The Hound snatched up a torch to light their way. Sansa followed close beside him. The ground was rocky and uneven; the flickering light made it seem to shift and move beneath her. She kept her eyes lowered, watching where she placed her feet. They walked among the pavilions, each with its banner and its armor hung outside, the silence weighing heavier with every step. Sansa could not bear the sight of him, he frightened her so, yet she had been raised in all the ways of courtesy. A true lady would not notice his face, she told herself. "You rode gallantly today, Ser Sandor," she made herself say.

Sandor Clegane snarled at her. "Spare me your empty little compliments, girl . . . and your *ser*'s. I am no knight. I spit on them and their vows. My brother is a knight. Did you see him ride today?"

"Yes," Sansa whispered, trembling. "He was . . ."

"Gallant?" the Hound finished.

He was mocking her, she realized. "No one could

withstand him," she managed at last, proud of herself. It was no lie.

Sandor Clegane stopped suddenly in the middle of a dark and empty field. She had no choice but to stop beside him. "Some septa trained you well. You're like one of those birds from the Summer Isles, aren't you? A pretty little talking bird, repeating all the pretty little words they taught you to recite."

"That's unkind." Sansa could feel her heart fluttering in her chest. "You're frightening me. I want to go now."

"No one could withstand him," the Hound rasped. "That's truth enough. No one could ever withstand Gregor. That boy today, his second joust, oh, that was a pretty bit of business. You saw that, did you? Fool boy, he had no business riding in this company. No money, no squire, no one to help him with that armor. That gorget wasn't fastened proper. You think Gregor didn't notice that? You think *Ser* Gregor's lance rode up by chance, do you? Pretty little talking girl, you believe that, you're empty-headed as a bird for true. Gregor's lance goes where Gregor wants it to go. Look at me. *Look at me!*" Sandor Clegane put a huge hand under her chin and forced her face up. He squatted in front of her, and moved the torch close. "There's a pretty for you. Take a good long stare. You know you want to. I've watched you turning away all the way down the kingsroad. Piss on that. Take your look."

His fingers held her jaw as hard as an iron trap. His eyes watched hers. Drunken eyes, sullen with anger. She had to look.

The right side of his face was gaunt, with sharp cheekbones and a grey eye beneath a heavy brow. His nose was large and hooked, his hair thin, dark. He wore it long and brushed it sideways, because no hair grew on the *other* side of that face.

The left side of his face was a ruin. His ear had been burned away; there was nothing left but a hole. His eye was still good, but all around it was a twisted mass of scar, slick black flesh hard as leather, pocked with craters and fissured by deep cracks that gleamed red and wet when he moved. Down by his jaw, you could see a hint of bone where the flesh had been seared away.

Sansa began to cry. He let go of her then, and snuffed

out the torch in the dirt. "No pretty words for that, girl? No little compliment the septa taught you?" When there was no answer, he continued. "Most of them, they think it was some battle. A siege, a burning tower, an enemy with a torch. One fool asked if it was dragonsbreath." His laugh was softer this time, but just as bitter. "I'll tell you what it was, girl," he said, a voice from the night, a shadow leaning so close now that she could smell the sour stench of wine on his breath. "I was younger than you, six, maybe seven. A woodcarver set up shop in the village under my father's keep, and to buy favor he sent us gifts. The old man made marvelous toys. I don't remember what I got, but it was Gregor's gift I wanted. A wooden knight, all painted up, every joint pegged separate and fixed with strings, so you could make him fight. Gregor is five years older than me, the toy was nothing to him, he was already a squire, near six foot tall and muscled like an ox. So I took his knight, but there was no joy to it, I tell you. I was scared all the while, and true enough, he found me. There was a brazier in the room. Gregor never said a word, just picked me up under his arm and shoved the side of my face down in the burning coals and held me there while I screamed and screamed. You saw how strong he is. Even then, it took three grown men to drag him off me. The septons preach about the seven hells. What do they know? Only a man who's been burned knows what hell is truly like.

"My father told everyone my bedding had caught fire, and our maester gave me ointments. *Ointments!* Gregor got his ointments too. Four years later, they anointed him with the seven oils and he recited his knightly vows and Rhaegar Targaryen tapped him on the shoulder and said, 'Arise, Ser Gregor.'"

The rasping voice trailed off. He squatted silently before her, a hulking black shape shrouded in the night, hidden from her eyes. Sansa could hear his ragged breathing. She was sad for him, she realized. Somehow, the fear had gone away.

The silence went on and on, so long that she began to grow afraid once more, but she was afraid for him now, not for herself. She found his massive shoulder with her hand. "He was no true knight," she whispered to him.

The Hound threw back his head and roared. Sansa

stumbled back, away from him, but he caught her arm. "No," he growled at her, "no, little bird, he was no true knight."

The rest of the way into the city, Sandor Clegane said not a word. He led her to where the carts were waiting, told a driver to take them back to the Red Keep, and climbed in after her. They rode in silence through the King's Gate and up torchlit city streets. He opened the postern door and led her into the castle, his burned face twitching and his eyes brooding, and he was one step behind her as they climbed the tower stairs. He took her safe all the way to the corridor outside her bedchamber.

"Thank you, my lord," Sansa said meekly.

The Hound caught her by the arm and leaned close. "The things I told you tonight," he said, his voice sounding even rougher than usual. "If you ever tell Joffrey . . . your sister, your father . . . any of them . . ."

"I won't," Sansa whispered. "I promise."

It was not enough. "If you ever tell *anyone*," he finished, "I'll kill you."

EDDARD

"I stood last vigil for him myself," Ser Barristan Selmy said as they looked down at the body in the back of the cart. "He had no one else. A mother in the Vale, I am told."

In the pale dawn light, the young knight looked as though he were sleeping. He had not been handsome, but death had smoothed his rough-hewn features and the silent sisters had dressed him in his best velvet tunic, with a high collar to cover the ruin the lance had made of his throat. Eddard Stark looked at his face, and wondered if it had been for his sake that the boy had died. Slain by a Lannister bannerman before Ned could speak to him; could that be mere happenstance? He supposed he would never know.

"Hugh was Jon Arryn's squire for four years," Selmy went on. "The king knighted him before he rode north, in Jon's memory. The lad wanted it desperately, yet I fear he was not ready."

Ned had slept badly last night and he felt tired beyond his years. "None of us is ever ready," he said.

"For knighthood?"

"For death." Gently Ned covered the boy with his

cloak, a bloodstained bit of blue bordered in crescent moons. When his mother asked why her son was dead, he reflected bitterly, they would tell her he had fought to honor the King's Hand, Eddard Stark. "This was needless. War should not be a game." Ned turned to the woman beside the cart, shrouded in grey, face hidden but for her eyes. The silent sisters prepared men for the grave, and it was ill fortune to look on the face of death. "Send his armor home to the Vale. The mother will want to have it."

"It is worth a fair piece of silver," Ser Barristan said. "The boy had it forged special for the tourney. Plain work, but good. I do not know if he had finished paying the smith."

"He paid yesterday, my lord, and he paid dearly," Ned replied. And to the silent sister he said, "Send the mother the armor. I will deal with this smith." She bowed her head.

Afterward Ser Barristan walked with Ned to the king's pavilion. The camp was beginning to stir. Fat sausages sizzled and spit over firepits, spicing the air with the scents of garlic and pepper. Young squires hurried about on errands as their masters woke, yawning and stretching, to meet the day. A serving man with a goose under his arm bent his knee when he caught sight of them. "M'lords," he muttered as the goose honked and pecked at his fingers. The shields displayed outside each tent heralded its occupant: the silver eagle of Seagard, Bryce Caron's field of nightingales, a cluster of grapes for the Redwynes, brindled boar, red ox, burning tree, white ram, triple spiral, purple unicorn, dancing maiden, blackadder, twin towers, horned owl, and last the pure white blazons of the Kingsguard, shining like the dawn.

"The king means to fight in the melee today," Ser Barristan said as they were passing Ser Meryn's shield, its paint sullied by a deep gash where Loras Tyrell's lance had scarred the wood as he drove him from his saddle.

"Yes," Ned said grimly. Jory had woken him last night to bring him that news. Small wonder he had slept so badly.

Ser Barristan's look was troubled. "They say night's beauties fade at dawn, and the children of wine are oft disowned in the morning light."

"They say so," Ned agreed, "but not of Robert." Other men might reconsider words spoken in drunken bravado, but Robert Baratheon would remember and, remembering, would never back down.

The king's pavilion was close by the water, and the morning mists off the river had wreathed it in wisps of grey. It was all of golden silk, the largest and grandest structure in the camp. Outside the entrance, Robert's warhammer was displayed beside an immense iron shield blazoned with the crowned stag of House Baratheon.

Ned had hoped to discover the king still abed in a wine-soaked sleep, but luck was not with him. They found Robert drinking beer from a polished horn and roaring his displeasure at two young squires who were trying to buckle him into his armor. "Your Grace," one was saying, almost in tears, "it's made too small, it won't go." He fumbled, and the gorget he was trying to fit around Robert's thick neck tumbled to the ground.

"Seven hells!" Robert swore. "Do I have to do it myself? Piss on the both of you. Pick it up. Don't just stand there gaping, Lancel, *pick it up!"* The lad jumped, and the king noticed his company. "Look at these oafs, Ned. My wife insisted I take these two to squire for me, and they're worse than useless. Can't even put a man's armor on him properly. Squires, they say. *I* say they're swineherds dressed up in silk."

Ned only needed a glance to understand the difficulty. "The boys are not at fault," he told the king. "You're too fat for your armor, Robert."

Robert Baratheon took a long swallow of beer, tossed the empty horn onto his sleeping furs, wiped his mouth with the back of his hand, and said darkly, "Fat? *Fat,* is it? Is that how you speak to your king?" He let go his laughter, sudden as a storm. "Ah, damn you, Ned, why are you always right?"

The squires smiled nervously until the king turned on them. "You. Yes, both of you. You heard the Hand. The king is too fat for his armor. Go find Ser Aron Santagar. Tell him I need the breastplate stretcher. *Now! What are you waiting for?"*

The boys tripped over each other in their haste to be quit of the tent. Robert managed to keep a stern face until they were gone. Then he dropped back into a chair, shaking with laughter.

Ser Barristan Selmy chuckled with him. Even Eddard Stark managed a smile. Always, though, the graver thoughts crept in. He could not help taking note of the two squires: handsome boys, fair and well made. One was Sansa's age, with long golden curls; the other perhaps fifteen, sandy-haired, with a wisp of a mustache and the emerald-green eyes of the queen.

"Ah, I wish I could be there to see Santagar's face," Robert said. "I hope he'll have the wit to send them to someone else. We ought to keep them running all day!"

"Those boys," Ned asked him. "Lannisters?"

Robert nodded, wiping tears from his eyes. "Cousins. Sons of Lord Tywin's brother. One of the dead ones. Or perhaps the live one, now that I come to think on it. I don't recall. My wife comes from a very large family, Ned."

A very ambitious family, Ned thought. He had nothing against the squires, but it troubled him to see Robert surrounded by the queen's kin, waking and sleeping. The Lannister appetite for offices and honors seemed to know no bounds. "The talk is you and the queen had angry words last night."

The mirth curdled on Robert's face. "The woman tried to forbid me to fight in the melee. She's sulking in the castle now, damn her. Your sister would never have shamed me like that."

"You never knew Lyanna as I did, Robert," Ned told him. "You saw her beauty, but not the iron underneath. She would have told you that you have no business in the melee."

"You too?" The king frowned. "You are a sour man, Stark. Too long in the north, all the juices have frozen inside you. Well, *mine* are still running." He slapped his chest to prove it.

"You are the king," Ned reminded him.

"I sit on the damn iron seat when I must. Does that mean I don't have the same hungers as other men? A bit of wine now and again, a girl squealing in bed, the feel of a horse between my legs? Seven hells, Ned, I want to *hit* someone."

Ser Barristan Selmy spoke up. "Your Grace," he said,

"it is not seemly that the king should ride into the melee. It would not be a fair contest. Who would dare strike you?"

Robert seemed honestly taken aback. "Why, all of them, damn it. If they can. And the last man left standing . . ."

". . . will be you," Ned finished. He saw at once that Selmy had hit the mark. The dangers of the melee were only a savor to Robert, but this touched on his pride. "Ser Barristan is right. There's not a man in the Seven Kingdoms who would dare risk your displeasure by hurting you."

The king rose to his feet, his face flushed. "Are you telling me those prancing cravens will *let me win?*"

"For a certainty," Ned said, and Ser Barristan Selmy bowed his head in silent accord.

For a moment Robert was so angry he could not speak. He strode across the tent, whirled, strode back, his face dark and angry. He snatched up his breastplate from the ground and threw it at Barristan Selmy in a wordless fury. Selmy dodged. "Get out," the king said then, coldly. "Get out before I kill you."

Ser Barristan left quickly. Ned was about to follow when the king called out again. "Not you, Ned."

Ned turned back. Robert took up his horn again, filled it with beer from a barrel in the corner, and thrust it at Ned. "Drink," he said brusquely.

"I've no thirst—"

"*Drink.* Your king commands it."

Ned took the horn and drank. The beer was black and thick, so strong it stung the eyes.

Robert sat down again. "Damn you, Ned Stark. You and Jon Arryn, I loved you both. What have you done to me? You were the one should have been king, you or Jon."

"You had the better claim, Your Grace."

"I told you to drink, not to argue. You made me king, you could at least have the courtesy to listen when I talk, damn you. Look at me, Ned. Look at what kinging has done to me. Gods, too fat for my armor, how did it ever come to this?"

"Robert . . ."

"Drink and stay quiet, the king is talking. I swear to you, I was never so alive as when I was winning this throne, or so dead as now that I've won it. And Cersei . . . I have Jon Arryn to thank for her. I had no wish to marry after Lyanna was taken from me, but Jon said the realm needed an heir. Cersei Lannister would be a good match, he told me, she would bind Lord Tywin to me should Viserys Targaryen ever try to win back his father's throne." The king shook his head. "I loved that old man, I swear it, but now I think he was a bigger fool than Moon Boy. Oh, Cersei is lovely to look at, truly, but *cold* . . . the way she guards her cunt, you'd think she had all the gold of Casterly Rock between her legs. Here, give me that beer if you won't drink it." He took the horn, upended it, belched, wiped his mouth. "I am sorry for your girl, Ned. Truly. About the wolf, I mean. My son was lying, I'd stake my soul on it. My son . . . you love your children, don't you?"

"With all my heart," Ned said.

"Let me tell you a secret, Ned. More than once, I have dreamed of giving up the crown. Take ship for the Free Cities with my horse and my hammer, spend my time warring and whoring, that's what I was made for. The sellsword king, how the singers would love me. You know what stops me? The thought of Joffrey on the throne, with Cersei standing behind him whispering in his ear. My son. How could I have made a son like that, Ned?"

"He's only a boy," Ned said awkwardly. He had small liking for Prince Joffrey, but he could hear the pain in Robert's voice. "Have you forgotten how wild you were at his age?"

"It would not trouble me if the boy was wild, Ned. You don't know him as I do." He sighed and shook his head. "Ah, perhaps you are right. Jon despaired of me often enough, yet I grew into a good king." Robert looked at Ned and scowled at his silence. "You might speak up and agree now, you know."

"Your Grace . . ." Ned began, carefully.

Robert slapped Ned on the back. "Ah, say that I'm a better king than Aerys and be done with it. You never could lie for love nor honor, Ned Stark. I'm still young, and now that you're here with me, things will be different. We'll make this a reign to sing of, and damn the Lannisters to seven hells. I smell bacon. Who do you think our champion will be today? Have you seen Mace Tyrell's boy? The Knight of Flowers, they call him. Now there's a son any man would be proud to own to. Last tourney, he dumped the Kingslayer on his golden rump, you ought to have seen the look on Cersei's face. I laughed till my sides hurt. Renly says he has this sister, a maid of fourteen, lovely as a dawn . . ."

They broke their fast on black bread and boiled goose eggs and fish fried up with onions and bacon, at a trestle table by the river's edge. The king's melancholy melted away with the morning mist, and before long Robert was eating an orange and waxing fond about a morning at the Eyrie when they had been boys. ". . . had given Jon a barrel of oranges, remember? Only the things had gone rotten, so I flung mine across the table and hit Dacks right in the nose. You remember, Redfort's pock-faced squire? He tossed one back at me, and before Jon could so much as fart, there were oranges flying across the High Hall in every direction." He laughed uproariously, and even Ned smiled, remembering.

This was the boy he had grown up with, he thought; this was the Robert Baratheon he'd known and loved. If he could prove that the Lannisters were behind the attack on Bran, prove that they had murdered Jon Arryn, this man would listen. Then Cersei would fall, and the King-slayer with her, and if Lord Tywin dared to rouse the west, Robert would smash him as he had smashed Rhae-gar Targaryen on the Trident. He could see it all so clearly.

That breakfast tasted better than anything Eddard Stark had eaten in a long time, and afterward his smiles came easier and more often, until it was time for the tour-nament to resume.

Ned walked with the king to the jousting field. He had promised to watch the final tilts with Sansa; Septa Mordane was ill today, and his daughter was determined not to miss the end of the jousting. As he saw Robert to his place, he noted that Cersei Lannister had chosen not to appear; the place beside the king was empty. That too gave Ned cause to hope.

He shouldered his way to where his daughter was seated and found her as the horns blew for the day's first joust. Sansa was so engrossed she scarcely seemed to notice his arrival.

Sandor Clegane was the first rider to appear. He wore an olive-green cloak over his soot-grey armor. That, and his hound's-head helm, were his only concession to ornament.

"A hundred golden dragons on the Kingslayer," Littlefinger announced loudly as Jaime Lannister entered the lists, riding an elegant blood bay destrier. The horse wore a blanket of gilded ringmail, and Jaime glittered from head to heel. Even his lance was fashioned from the golden wood of the Summer Isles.

"Done," Lord Renly shouted back. "The Hound has a hungry look about him this morning."

"Even hungry dogs know better than to bite the hand that feeds them," Littlefinger called dryly.

Sandor Clegane dropped his visor with an audible *clang* and took up his position. Ser Jaime tossed a kiss to some woman in the commons, gently lowered his visor, and rode to the end of the lists. Both men couched their lances.

Ned Stark would have loved nothing so well as to see them both lose, but Sansa was watching it all moist-eyed and eager. The hastily erected gallery trembled as the horses broke into a gallop. The Hound leaned forward as he rode, his lance rock steady, but Jaime shifted his seat deftly in the instant before impact. Clegane's point was turned harmlessly against the golden shield with the lion blazon, while his own hit square. Wood shattered, and the Hound reeled, fighting to keep his seat. Sansa gasped. A ragged cheer went up from the commons.

"I wonder how I ought spend your money," Littlefinger called down to Lord Renly.

The Hound just managed to stay in his saddle. He jerked his mount around hard and rode back to the lists for the second pass. Jaime Lannister tossed down his broken lance and snatched up a fresh one, jesting with his squire. The Hound spurred forward at a hard gallop. Lannister rode to meet him. This time, when Jaime shifted his seat, Sandor Clegane shifted with him. Both lances exploded, and by the time the splinters had settled, a riderless blood bay was trotting off in search of grass while Ser Jaime Lannister rolled in the dirt, golden and dented.

Sansa said, "I knew the Hound would win."

Littlefinger overheard. "If you know who's going to win the second match, speak up now before Lord Renly plucks me clean," he called to her. Ned smiled.

"A pity the Imp is not here with us," Lord Renly said. "I should have won twice as much."

Jaime Lannister was back on his feet, but his ornate lion helmet had been twisted around and dented in his fall, and now he could not get it off. The commons were hooting and pointing, the lords and ladies were trying to stifle their chuckles, and failing, and over it all Ned could hear King Robert laughing, louder than anyone. Finally they had to lead the Lion of Lannister off to a blacksmith, blind and stumbling.

By then Ser Gregor Clegane was in position at the head of the lists. He was huge, the biggest man that Eddard Stark had ever seen. Robert Baratheon and his brothers were all big men, as was the Hound, and back at Winterfell there was a simpleminded stableboy named Hodor who dwarfed them all, but the knight they called the Mountain That Rides would have towered over Hodor. He was well over seven feet tall, closer to eight, with massive shoulders and arms thick as the trunks of small trees. His destrier seemed a pony in between his armored legs, and the lance he carried looked as small as a broom handle.

Unlike his brother, Ser Gregor did not live at court. He was a solitary man who seldom left his own lands, but for wars and tourneys. He had been with Lord Tywin when King's Landing fell, a new-made knight of seventeen years, even then distinguished by his size and his implacable ferocity. Some said it had been Gregor who'd dashed the skull of the infant prince Aegon Targaryen against a wall, and whispered that afterward he had raped the mother, the Dornish princess Elia, before putting her to the sword. These things were not said in Gregor's hearing.

Ned Stark could not recall ever speaking to the man, though Gregor had ridden with them during Balon Greyjoy's rebellion, one knight among thousands. He watched him with disquiet. Ned seldom put much stock in gossip, but the things said of Ser Gregor were more than ominous. He was soon to be married for the third time, and one heard dark whisperings about the deaths of his first two wives. It was said that his keep was a grim place where servants disappeared unaccountably and even the dogs were afraid to enter the hall. And there had been a sister who had died young under queer circumstances, and the fire that had disfigured his brother, and the hunting accident that had killed their father. Gregor had inherited the keep, the gold, and the family estates. His younger brother Sandor had left the same day to take service with the Lannisters as a sworn sword, and it was said that he had never returned, not even to visit.

When the Knight of Flowers made his entrance, a murmur ran through the crowd, and he heard Sansa's fervent whisper, "Oh, he's so *beautiful*." Ser Loras Tyrell was slender as a reed, dressed in a suit of fabulous silver armor polished to a blinding sheen and filigreed with twining black vines and tiny blue forget-me-nots. The commons realized in the same instant as Ned that the blue of the flowers came from sapphires; a gasp went up from a thousand throats. Across the boy's shoulders his cloak hung heavy. It was woven of forget-me-nots, real ones, hundreds of fresh blooms sewn to a heavy woolen cape.

His courser was as slim as her rider, a beautiful grey mare, built for speed. Ser Gregor's huge stallion trumpeted as he caught her scent. The boy from Highgarden did something with his legs, and his horse pranced sideways, nimble as a dancer. Sansa clutched at his arm. "Father, don't let Ser Gregor hurt him," she said. Ned saw she was wearing the rose that Ser Loras had given her yesterday. Jory had told him about that as well.

"These are tourney lances," he told his daughter. "They make them to splinter on impact, so no one is hurt." Yet he remembered the dead boy in the cart with his cloak of crescent moons, and the words were raw in his throat.

Ser Gregor was having trouble controlling his horse. The stallion was screaming and pawing the ground, shaking his head. The Mountain kicked at the animal savagely with an armored boot. The horse reared and almost threw him.

The Knight of Flowers saluted the king, rode to the far end of the list, and couched his lance, ready. Ser Gregor brought his animal to the line, fighting with the reins. And suddenly it began. The Mountain's stallion broke in a hard gallop, plunging forward wildly, while the mare charged as smooth as a flow of silk. Ser Gregor wrenched his shield into position, juggled with his lance, and all the while fought to hold his unruly mount on a straight line, and suddenly Loras Tyrell was on him, placing the point of his lance just *there*, and in an eye blink the Mountain was falling. He was so huge that he took his horse down with him in a tangle of steel and flesh.

Ned heard applause, cheers, whistles, shocked gasps, excited muttering, and over it all the rasping, raucous laughter of the Hound. The Knight of Flowers reined up at the end of the lists. His lance was not even broken. His sapphires winked in the sun as he raised his visor, smiling. The commons went mad for him.

In the middle of the field, Ser Gregor Clegane disentangled himself and came boiling to his feet. He wrenched off his helm and slammed it down onto the ground. His face was dark with fury and his hair fell down into his eyes. "My sword," he shouted to his squire, and the boy ran it out to him. By then his stallion was back on its feet as well.

Gregor Clegane killed the horse with a single blow of such ferocity that it half severed the animal's neck. Cheers turned to shrieks in a heartbeat. The stallion went to its knees, screaming as it died. By then Gregor was striding down the lists toward Ser Loras Tyrell, his bloody sword clutched in his fist. *"Stop him!"* Ned shouted, but his words were lost in the roar. Everyone else was yelling as well, and Sansa was crying.

It all happened so fast. The Knight of Flowers was shouting for his own sword as Ser Gregor knocked his squire aside and made a grab for the reins of his horse. The mare scented blood and reared. Loras Tyrell kept his seat, but barely. Ser Gregor swung his sword, a savage two-handed blow that took the boy in the chest and knocked him from the saddle. The courser dashed away in panic as Ser Loras lay stunned in the dirt. But as Gregor lifted his sword for the killing blow, a rasping voice warned, *"Leave him be,"* and a steel-clad hand wrenched him away from the boy.

The Mountain pivoted in wordless fury, swinging his longsword in a killing arc with all his massive strength behind it, but the Hound caught the blow and turned it, and for what seemed an eternity the two brothers stood hammering at each other as a dazed Loras Tyrell was helped to safety. Thrice Ned saw Ser Gregor aim savage blows at the hound's-head helmet, yet not once did Sandor send a cut at his brother's unprotected face.

It was the king's voice that put an end to it . . . the king's voice and twenty swords. Jon Arryn had told them that a commander needs a good battlefield voice, and Robert had proved the truth of that on the Trident. He used that voice now. *"STOP THIS MADNESS,"* he boomed, *"IN THE NAME OF YOUR KING!"*

The Hound went to one knee. Ser Gregor's blow cut air, and at last he came to his senses. He dropped his sword and glared at Robert, surrounded by his Kingsguard and a dozen other knights and guardsmen. Wordlessly, he turned and strode off, shoving past Barristan Selmy. "Let him go," Robert said, and as quickly as that, it was over.

"Is the Hound the champion now?" Sansa asked Ned.

"No," he told her. "There will be one final joust, between the Hound and the Knight of Flowers."

But Sansa had the right of it after all. A few moments later Ser Loras Tyrell walked back onto the field in a simple linen doublet and said to Sandor Clegane, "I owe you my life. The day is yours, ser."

"I am no *ser*," the Hound replied, but he took the victory, and the champion's purse, and, for perhaps the first time in his life, the love of the commons. They cheered him as he left the lists to return to his pavilion.

As Ned walked with Sansa to the archery field, Littlefinger and Lord Renly and some of the others fell in with them. "Tyrell had to know the mare was in heat," Littlefinger was saying. "I swear the boy planned the whole thing. Gregor has always favored huge, ill-tempered stallions with more spirit than sense." The notion seemed to amuse him.

It did not amuse Ser Barristan Selmy. "There is small honor in tricks," the old man said stiffly.

"Small honor and twenty thousand golds." Lord Renly smiled.

That afternoon a boy named Anguy, an unheralded commoner from the Dornish Marches, won the archery competition, outshooting Ser Balon Swann and Jalabhar Xho at a hundred paces after all the other bowmen had been eliminated at the shorter distances. Ned sent Alyn to seek him out and offer him a position with the Hand's guard, but the boy was flush with wine and victory and riches undreamed of, and he refused.

The melee went on for three hours. Near forty men took part, freeriders and hedge knights and new-made squires in search of a reputation. They fought with blunted weapons in a chaos of mud and blood, small troops fighting together and then turning on each other as alliances formed and fractured, until only one man was left standing. The victor was the red priest, Thoros of Myr, a madman who shaved his head and fought with a flaming sword. He had won melees before; the fire sword frightened the mounts of the other riders, and nothing frightened Thoros. The final tally was three broken limbs, a shattered collarbone, a dozen smashed fingers, two horses that had to be put down, and more cuts, sprains, and bruises than anyone cared to count. Ned was desperately pleased that Robert had not taken part.

That night at the feast, Eddard Stark was more hopeful than he had been in a great while. Robert was in high good humor, the Lannisters were nowhere to be seen, and even his daughters were behaving. Jory brought Arya down to join them, and Sansa spoke to her sister pleasantly. "The tournament was *magnificent*," she sighed. "You should have come. How was your dancing?"

"I'm sore all over," Arya reported happily, proudly displaying a huge purple bruise on her leg.

"You must be a terrible dancer," Sansa said doubtfully.

Later, while Sansa was off listening to a troupe of singers perform the complex round of interwoven ballads called the "Dance of the Dragons," Ned inspected the bruise himself. "I hope Forel is not being too hard on you," he said.

Arya stood on one leg. She was getting much better at that of late. "Syrio says that every hurt is a lesson, and every lesson makes you better."

Ned frowned. The man Syrio Forel had come with an excellent reputation, and his flamboyant Braavosi style was well suited to Arya's slender blade, yet still . . . a few days ago, she had been wandering around with a swatch of black silk tied over her eyes. Syrio was teaching her to see with her ears and her nose and her skin, she told him. Before that, he had her doing spins and back flips. "Arya, are you certain you want to persist in this?"

She nodded. "Tomorrow we're going to catch cats."

"Cats." Ned sighed. "Perhaps it was a mistake to hire this Braavosi. If you like, I will ask Jory to take over your lessons. Or I might have a quiet word with Ser Barristan. He was the finest sword in the Seven Kingdoms in his youth."

"I don't want them," Arya said. "I want Syrio."

Ned ran his fingers through his hair. Any decent master-at-arms could give Arya the rudiments of slash-and-parry without this nonsense of blindfolds, cartwheels, and hopping about on one leg, but he knew his youngest daughter well enough to know there was no arguing with that stubborn jut of jaw. "As you wish," he said. Surely she would grow tired of this soon. "Try to be careful."

"I will," she promised solemnly as she hopped smoothly from her right leg to her left.

Much later, after he had taken the girls back through the city and seen them both safe in bed, Sansa with her dreams and Arya with her bruises, Ned ascended to his own chambers atop the Tower of the Hand. The day had been warm and the room was close and stuffy. Ned went to the window and unfastened the heavy shutters to let in the cool night air. Across the Great Yard, he noticed the flickering glow of candlelight from Littlefinger's windows. The hour was well past midnight. Down by the river, the revels were only now beginning to dwindle and die.

He took out the dagger and studied it. Littlefinger's blade, won by Tyrion Lannister in a tourney wager, sent to slay Bran in his sleep. *Why?* Why would the dwarf want Bran dead? Why would *anyone* want Bran dead?

The dagger, Bran's fall, all of it was linked somehow to the murder of Jon Arryn, he could feel it in his gut, but the truth of Jon's death remained as clouded to him as when he had started. Lord Stannis had not returned to King's Landing for the tourney. Lysa Arryn held her silence behind the high walls of the Eyrie. The squire was dead, and Jory was still searching the whorehouses. What did he have but Robert's bastard?

That the armorer's sullen apprentice was the king's son, Ned had no doubt. The Baratheon look was stamped on his face, in his jaw, his eyes, that black hair. Renly was too young to have fathered a boy of that age, Stannis too cold and proud in his honor. Gendry had to be Robert's.

Yet knowing all that, what had he learned? The king had other baseborn children scattered throughout the Seven Kingdoms. He had openly acknowledged one of his bastards, a boy of Bran's age whose mother was highborn. The lad was being fostered by Lord Renly's castellan at Storm's End.

Ned remembered Robert's first child as well, a daughter born in the Vale when Robert was scarcely more than a boy himself. A sweet little girl; the young lord of Storm's End had doted on her. He used to make daily visits to play with the babe, long after he had lost interest in the mother. Ned was often dragged along for company, whether he willed it or not. The girl would be seventeen or eighteen now, he realized; older than Robert had been when he fathered her. A strange thought.

Cersei could not have been pleased by her lord husband's by-blows, yet in the end it mattered little whether the king had one bastard or a hundred. Law and custom gave the baseborn few rights. Gendry, the girl in the Vale, the boy at Storm's End, none of them could threaten Robert's trueborn children . . .

His musings were ended by a soft rap on his door. "A man to see you, my lord," Harwin called. "He will not give his name."

"Send him in," Ned said, wondering.

The visitor was a stout man in cracked, mud-caked boots and a heavy brown robe of the coarsest roughspun, his features hidden by a cowl, his hands drawn up into voluminous sleeves.

"Who are you?" Ned asked.

"A friend," the cowled man said in a strange, low voice. "We must speak alone, Lord Stark."

Curiosity was stronger than caution. "Harwin, leave us," he commanded. Not until they were alone behind closed doors did his visitor draw back his cowl.

"*Lord Varys?*" Ned said in astonishment.

"Lord Stark," Varys said politely, seating himself. "I wonder if I might trouble you for a drink?"

Ned filled two cups with summerwine and handed one to Varys. "I might have passed within a foot of you and never recognized you," he said, incredulous. He had never seen the eunuch dress in anything but silk and velvet and the richest damasks, and this man smelled of sweat instead of lilacs.

"That was my dearest hope," Varys said. "It would not do if certain people learned that we had spoken in private. The queen watches you closely. This wine is very choice. Thank you."

"How did you get past my other guards?" Ned asked. Porther and Cayn had been posted outside the tower, and Alyn on the stairs.

"The Red Keep has ways known only to ghosts and spiders." Varys smiled apologetically. "I will not keep you long, my lord. There are things you must know. You are the King's Hand, and the king is a fool." The eunuch's cloying tones were gone; now his voice was thin and sharp as a whip. "Your friend, I know, yet a fool nonetheless . . . and doomed, unless you save him. Today was a near thing. They had hoped to kill him during the melee."

For a moment Ned was speechless with shock. *"Who?"*

Varys sipped his wine. "If I truly need to tell you that, you are a bigger fool than Robert and I am on the wrong side."

"The Lannisters," Ned said. "The queen . . . no, I will not believe that, not even of Cersei. She asked him not to fight!"

"She *forbade* him to fight, in front of his brother, his knights, and half the court. Tell me truly, do you know any surer way to force King Robert into the melee? I ask you."

Ned had a sick feeling in his gut. The eunuch had hit upon a truth; tell Robert Baratheon he could not, should not, or must not do a thing, and it was as good as done. "Even if he'd fought, who would have dared to strike the king?"

Varys shrugged. "There were forty riders in the melee. The Lannisters have many friends. Amidst all that chaos, with horses screaming and bones breaking and Thoros of Myr waving that absurd firesword of his, who could name it murder if some chance blow felled His Grace?" He went to the flagon and refilled his cup. "After the deed was done, the slayer would be beside himself with grief. I can almost hear him weeping. So sad. Yet no doubt the gracious and compassionate widow would take pity, lift the poor unfortunate to his feet, and bless him with a gentle kiss of forgiveness. Good King Joffrey would have no choice but to pardon him." The eunuch stroked his cheek. "Or perhaps Cersei would let Ser Ilyn strike off his head. Less risk for the Lannisters that way, though quite an unpleasant surprise for their little friend."

Ned felt his anger rise. "You knew of this plot, and yet you did nothing."

"I command whisperers, not warriors."

"You might have come to me earlier."

"Oh, yes, I confess it. And you would have rushed straight to the king, yes? And when Robert heard of his peril, what would he have done? I wonder."

Ned considered that. "He would have damned them all, and fought anyway, to show he did not fear them."

Varys spread his hands. "I will make another confession, Lord Eddard. I was curious to see what you would do. *Why not come to me?* you ask, and I must answer, *Why, because I did not trust you, my lord.*"

"*You* did not trust *me?*" Ned was frankly astonished.

"The Red Keep shelters two sorts of people, Lord Eddard," Varys said. "Those who are loyal to the realm, and those who are loyal only to themselves. Until this morning, I could not say which you might be . . . so I waited to see . . . and now I know, for a certainty." He smiled a plump tight little smile, and for a moment his private face and public mask were one. "I begin to comprehend why the queen fears you so much. Oh, yes I do."

"You are the one she ought to fear," Ned said.

"No. I am what I am. The king makes use of me, but it shames him. A most puissant warrior is our Robert, and such a manly man has little love for sneaks and spies and eunuchs. If a day should come when Cersei whispers, 'Kill that man,' Ilyn Payne will snick my head off in a twinkling, and who will mourn poor Varys then? North or south, they sing no songs for spiders." He reached out and touched Ned with a soft hand. "But you, Lord Stark . . . I think . . . no, I *know* . . . he would not kill you, not even for his queen, and there may lie our salvation."

It was all too much. For a moment Eddard Stark wanted nothing so much as to return to Winterfell, to the clean simplicity of the north, where the enemies were winter and the wildlings beyond the Wall. "Surely Robert has other loyal friends," he protested. "His brothers, his—"

"—wife?" Varys finished, with a smile that cut. "His brothers hate the Lannisters, true enough, but hating the queen and loving the king are not quite the same thing, are they? Ser Barristan loves his honor, Grand Maester Pycelle loves his office, and Littlefinger loves Littlefinger."

"The Kingsguard—"

"A paper shield," the eunuch said. "*Try* not to look so shocked, Lord Stark. Jaime Lannister is himself a Sworn Brother of the White Swords, and we all know what *his* oath is worth. The days when men like Ryam Redwyne and Prince Aemon the Dragonknight wore the white cloak are gone to dust and song. Of these seven, only Ser Barristan Selmy is made of the true steel, and Selmy is *old*. Ser Boros and Ser Meryn are the queen's creatures to the bone, and I have deep suspicions of the others. No, my lord, when the swords come out in earnest, you will be the only true friend Robert Baratheon will have."

"Robert must be told," Ned said. "If what you say is true, if even a part of it is true, the king must hear it for himself."

"And what proof shall we lay before him? My words against theirs? My little birds against the queen and the Kingslayer, against his brothers and his council, against the Wardens of East and West, against all the might of Casterly Rock? Pray, send for Ser Ilyn directly, it will save us all some time. I know where that road ends."

"Yet if what you say is true, they will only bide their time and make another attempt."

"Indeed they will," said Varys, "and sooner rather than later, I do fear. You are making them most anxious, Lord Eddard. But my little birds will be listening, and together we may be able to forestall them, you and I." He rose and pulled up his cowl so his face was hidden once more. "Thank you for the wine. We will speak again. When you see me next at council, be certain to treat me with your accustomed contempt. You should not find it difficult."

He was at the door when Ned called, *"Varys."* The eunuch turned back. "How did Jon Arryn die?"

"I wondered when you would get around to that."

"Tell me."

"The tears of Lys, they call it. A rare and costly thing, clear and sweet as water, and it leaves no trace. I begged Lord Arryn to use a taster, in this very room I begged him, but he would not hear of it. Only one who was less than a man would even think of such a thing, he told me."

Ned had to know the rest. "Who gave him the poison?"

"Some dear sweet friend who often shared meat and mead with him, no doubt. Oh, but which one? There were many such. Lord Arryn was a kindly, trusting man." The eunuch sighed. "There *was* one boy. All he was, he owed Jon Arryn, but when the widow fled to the Eyrie with her household, he stayed in King's Landing and prospered. It always gladdens my heart to see the young rise in the world." The whip was in his voice again, every word a stroke. "He must have cut a gallant figure in the tourney, him in his bright new armor, with those crescent moons on his cloak. A pity he died so untimely, before you could talk to him . . ."

Ned felt half-poisoned himself. "The squire," he said. "Ser Hugh." Wheels within wheels within wheels. Ned's head was pounding. "*Why?* Why now? Jon Arryn had been Hand for fourteen years. What was he doing that they had to kill him?"

"Asking questions," Varys said, slipping out the door.

TYRION

As he stood in the predawn chill watching Chiggen butcher his horse, Tyrion Lannister chalked up one more debt owed the Starks. Steam rose from inside the carcass when the squat sellsword opened the belly with his skinning knife. His hands moved deftly, with never a wasted cut; the work had to be done quickly, before the stink of blood brought shadowcats down from the heights.

"None of us will go hungry tonight," Bronn said. He was near a shadow himself; bone thin and bone hard, with black eyes and black hair and a stubble of beard.

"Some of us may," Tyrion told him. "I am not fond of eating horse. Particularly *my* horse."

"Meat is meat," Bronn said with a shrug. "The Dothraki like horse more than beef or pork."

"Do you take me for a Dothraki?" Tyrion asked sourly. The Dothraki ate horse, in truth; they also left deformed children out for the feral dogs who ran behind their *khalasars*. Dothraki customs had scant appeal for him.

Chiggen sliced a thin strip of bloody meat off the carcass and held it up for inspection. "Want a taste, dwarf?"

"My brother Jaime gave me that mare for my twenty-third name day," Tyrion said in a flat voice.

"Thank him for us, then. If you ever see him again." Chiggen grinned, showing yellow teeth, and swallowed the raw meat in two bites. "Tastes well bred."

"Better if you fry it up with onions," Bronn put in.

Wordlessly, Tyrion limped away. The cold had settled deep in his bones, and his legs were so sore he could scarcely walk. Perhaps his dead mare was the lucky one. *He* had hours more riding ahead of him, followed by a few mouthfuls of food and a short, cold sleep on hard ground, and then another night of the same, and another, and another, and the gods only knew how it would end. "Damn her," he muttered as he struggled up the road to rejoin his captors, remembering, "damn her and all the Starks."

The memory was still bitter. One moment he'd been ordering supper, and an eye blink later he was facing a room of armed men, with Jyck reaching for a sword and the fat innkeep shrieking, "No swords, not *here*, please, m'lords."

Tyrion wrenched down Jyck's arm hurriedly, before he got them both hacked to pieces. "Where are your courtesies, Jyck? Our good hostess said no swords. Do as she asks." He forced a smile that must have looked as queasy as it felt. "You're making a sad mistake, Lady Stark. I had no part in any attack on your son. On my honor—"

"Lannister honor," was all she said. She held up her hands for all the room to see. "His dagger left these scars. The blade he sent to open my son's throat."

Tyrion felt the anger all around him, thick and smoky, fed by the deep cuts in the Stark woman's hands. "Kill him," hissed some drunken slattern from the back, and other voices took up the call, faster than he would have believed. Strangers all, friendly enough only a moment ago, and yet now they cried for his blood like hounds on a trail.

Tyrion spoke up loudly, trying to keep the quaver from his voice. "If Lady Stark believes I have some crime to answer for, I will go with her and answer for it."

It was the only possible course. Trying to cut their way out of this was a sure invitation to an early grave. A good dozen swords had responded to the Stark woman's plea for help: the Harrenhal man, the three Brackens, a pair of unsavory sellswords who looked as though they'd kill him as soon as spit, and some fool field hands who doubtless had no idea what they were doing. Against that, what did Tyrion have? A dagger at his belt, and two men. Jyck swung a fair enough sword, but Morrec scarcely counted; he was part groom, part cook, part body servant, and no soldier. As for Yoren, whatever his feelings might have been, the black brothers were sworn to take no part in the quarrels of the realm. Yoren would do nothing.

And indeed, the black brother stepped aside silently when the old knight by Catelyn Stark's side said, "Take their weapons," and the sellsword Bronn stepped forward to pull the sword from Jyck's fingers and relieve them all of their daggers. "Good," the old man said as the tension in the common room ebbed palpably, "excellent." Tyrion recognized the gruff voice; Winterfell's master-at-arms, shorn of his whiskers.

Scarlet-tinged spittle flew from the fat innkeep's mouth as she begged of Catelyn Stark, "Don't kill him here!"

"Don't kill him anywhere," Tyrion urged.

"Take him somewheres else, no blood here, m'lady, I wants no high lordlin's quarrels."

"We are taking him back to Winterfell," she said, and Tyrion thought, *Well, perhaps* . . . By then he'd had a moment to glance over the room and get a better idea of the situation. He was not altogether displeased by what he saw. Oh, the Stark woman had been clever, no doubt of it. Force them to make a public affirmation of the oaths sworn her father by the lords they served, and then call on them for succor, and her a woman, yes, that was sweet. Yet her success was not as complete as she might have liked. There were close to fifty in the common room by his rough count. Catelyn Stark's plea had roused a bare dozen; the others looked confused, or frightened, or sullen. Only two of the Freys had stirred, Tyrion noted, and they'd sat back down quick enough when their captain failed to move. He might have smiled if he'd dared.

"Winterfell it is, then," he said instead. That was a long ride, as he could well attest, having just ridden it the other way. So many things could happen along the way. "My father will wonder what has become of me," he added, catching the eye of the swordsman who'd offered to yield up his room. "He'll pay a handsome reward to any man who brings him word of what happened here today." Lord Tywin would do no such thing, of course, but Tyrion would make up for it if he won free.

Ser Rodrik glanced at his lady, his look worried, as well it might be. "His men come with him," the old knight announced. "And we'll thank the rest of you to stay quiet about what you've seen here."

It was all Tyrion could do not to laugh. *Quiet?* The old fool. Unless he took the whole inn, the word would begin to spread the instant they were gone. The freerider with the gold coin in his pocket would fly to Casterly Rock like an arrow. If not him, then someone else. Yoren would carry the story south. That fool singer might make a lay of it. The Freys would report back to their lord, and the gods only knew what he might do. Lord Walder Frey might be sworn to Riverrun, but he was a cautious man who had lived a long time by making certain he was always on the winning side. At the very least he would send his birds winging south to King's Landing, and he might well dare more than that.

Catelyn Stark wasted no time. "We must ride at once. We'll want fresh mounts, and provisions for the road. You men, know that you have the eternal gratitude of House Stark. If any of you choose to help us guard our captives and get them safe to Winterfell, I promise you shall be well rewarded." That was all it took; the fools came rushing forward. Tyrion studied their faces; they would indeed be well rewarded, he vowed to himself, but perhaps not quite as they imagined.

Yet even as they were bundling him outside, saddling the horses in the rain, and tying his hands with a length of coarse rope, Tyrion Lannister was not truly afraid. They would never get him to Winterfell, he would have given odds on that. Riders would be after them within the day, birds would take wing, and surely one of the river lords would want to curry favor with his father enough to take a hand. Tyrion was congratulating himself on his subtlety when someone pulled a hood down over his eyes and lifted him up onto a saddle.

They set out through the rain at a hard gallop, and before long Tyrion's thighs were cramped and aching and his butt throbbed with pain. Even when they were safely away from the inn, and Catelyn Stark slowed them to a trot, it was a miserable pounding journey over rough ground, made worse by his blindness. Every twist and turn put him in danger of falling off his horse. The hood muffled sound, so he could not make out what was being said around him, and the rain soaked through the cloth and made it cling to his face, until even breathing was a struggle. The rope chafed his wrists raw and seemed to grow tighter as the night wore on. *I was about to settle down to a warm fire and a roast fowl, and that wretched singer had to open his mouth,* he thought mournfully. The wretched singer had come along with them. "There is a great song to be made from this, and I'm the one to make it," he told Catelyn Stark when he announced his intention of riding with them to see how the "splendid adventure" turned out. Tyrion wondered whether the boy would think the adventure quite so splendid once the Lannister riders caught up with them.

The rain had finally stopped and dawn light was seeping through the wet cloth over his eyes when Catelyn Stark gave the command to dismount. Rough hands pulled him down from his horse, untied his wrists, and yanked the hood off his head. When he saw the narrow stony road, the foothills rising high and wild all around them, and the jagged snowcapped peaks on the distant horizon, all the hope went out of him in a rush. "This is the high road," he gasped, looking at Lady Stark with accusation. "The *eastern* road. You said we were riding for Winterfell!"

Catelyn Stark favored him with the faintest of smiles. "Often and loudly," she agreed. "No doubt your friends will ride that way when they come after us. I wish them good speed."

Even now, long days later, the memory filled him with a bitter rage. All his life Tyrion had prided himself on his cunning, the only gift the gods had seen fit to give him, and yet this seven-times-damned she-wolf Catelyn Stark had outwitted him at every turn. The knowledge was more galling than the bare fact of his abduction.

They stopped only as long as it took to feed and water the horses, and then they were off again. This time Tyrion was spared the hood. After the second night they no longer bound his hands, and once they had gained the heights they scarcely bothered to guard him at all. It seemed they did not fear his escape. And why should they? Up here the land was harsh and wild, and the high road little more than a stony track. If he did run, how far could he hope to go, alone and without provisions? The shadowcats would make a morsel of him, and the clans that dwelt in the mountain fastnesses were brigands and murderers who bowed to no law but the sword.

Yet still the Stark woman drove them forward relentlessly. He knew where they were bound. He had known it since the moment they pulled off his hood. These mountains were the domain of House Arryn, and the late Hand's widow was a Tully, Catelyn Stark's sister . . . and no friend to the Lannisters. Tyrion had known the Lady Lysa slightly during her years at King's Landing, and did not look forward to renewing the acquaintance.

His captors were clustered around a stream a short ways down the high road. The horses had drunk their fill of the icy cold water, and were grazing on clumps of brown grass that grew from clefts in the rock. Jyck and Morrec huddled close, sullen and miserable. Mohor stood over them, leaning on his spear and wearing a rounded iron cap that made him look as if he had a bowl on his head. Nearby, Marillion the singer sat oiling his woodharp, complaining of what the damp was doing to his strings.

"We must have some rest, my lady," the hedge knight Ser Willis Wode was saying to Catelyn Stark as Tyrion approached. He was Lady Whent's man, stiff-necked and stolid, and the first to rise to aid Catelyn Stark back at the inn.

"Ser Willis speaks truly, my lady," Ser Rodrik said. "This is the third horse we have lost—"

"We will lose more than horses if we're overtaken by the Lannisters," she reminded them. Her face was windburnt and gaunt, but it had lost none of its determination.

"Small chance of that here," Tyrion put in.

"The lady did not ask your views, dwarf," snapped Kurleket, a great fat oaf with short-cropped hair and a pig's face. He was one of the Brackens, a man-at-arms in the service of Lord Jonos. Tyrion had made a special effort to learn all their names, so he might thank them later for their tender treatment of him. A Lannister always paid his debts. Kurleket would learn that someday, as would his friends Lharys and Mohor, and the good Ser Willis, and the sellswords Bronn and Chiggen. He planned an especially sharp lesson for Marillion, him of the woodharp and the sweet tenor voice, who was struggling so manfully to rhyme *imp* with *gimp* and *limp* so he could make a song of this outrage.

"Let him speak," Lady Stark commanded.

Tyrion Lannister seated himself on a rock. "By now our pursuit is likely racing across the Neck, chasing your lie up the kingsroad . . . assuming there *is* a pursuit, which is by no means certain. Oh, no doubt the word has reached my father . . . but my father does not love me overmuch, and I am not at all sure that he will bother to bestir himself." It was only half a lie; Lord Tywin Lannister cared not a fig for his deformed son, but he tolerated no slights on the honor of his House. "This is a cruel land, Lady Stark. You'll find no succor until you reach the Vale, and each mount you lose burdens the others all the more. Worse, you risk losing *me*. I am small, and not strong, and if I die, then what's the point?" That was no lie at all; Tyrion did not know how much longer he could endure this pace.

"It might be said that your death *is* the point, Lannister," Catelyn Stark replied.

"I think not," Tyrion said. "If you wanted me dead, you had only to say the word, and one of these staunch friends of yours would gladly have given me a red smile." He looked at Kurleket, but the man was too dim to taste the mockery.

"The Starks do not murder men in their beds."

"Nor do I," he said. "I tell you again, I had no part in the attempt to kill your son."

"The assassin was armed with your dagger."

Tyrion felt the heat rise in him. "It was not my dagger," he insisted. "How many times must I swear to that? Lady Stark, whatever you may believe of me, I am not a stupid man. Only a fool would arm a common footpad with his own blade."

Just for a moment, he thought he saw a flicker of doubt in her eyes, but what she said was, "Why would Petyr lie to me?"

"Why does a bear shit in the woods?" he demanded. "Because it is his nature. Lying comes as easily as breathing to a man like Littlefinger. *You* ought to know that, you of all people."

She took a step toward him, her face tight. "And what does that mean, Lannister?"

Tyrion cocked his head. "Why, every man at court has heard him tell how he took your maidenhead, my lady."

"That is a lie!" Catelyn Stark said.

"Oh, wicked little imp," Marillion said, shocked.

Kurleket drew his dirk, a vicious piece of black iron. "At your word, m'lady, I'll toss his lying tongue at your feet." His pig eyes were wet with excitement at the prospect.

Catelyn Stark stared at Tyrion with a coldness on her face such as he had never seen. "Petyr Baelish loved me once. He was only a boy. His passion was a tragedy for all of us, but it was real, and pure, and nothing to be made mock of. He wanted my hand. That is the truth of the matter. You are truly an evil man, Lannister."

"And you are truly a fool, Lady Stark. Littlefinger has never loved anyone but Littlefinger, and I promise you that it is not your *hand* that he boasts of, it's those ripe breasts of yours, and that sweet mouth, and the heat between your legs."

Kurleket grabbed a handful of hair and yanked his head back in a hard jerk, baring his throat. Tyrion felt the cold kiss of steel beneath his chin. "Shall I bleed him, my lady?"

"Kill me and the truth dies with me," Tyrion gasped.

"Let him talk," Catelyn Stark commanded.

Kurleket let go of Tyrion's hair, reluctantly.

Tyrion took a deep breath. "How did Littlefinger tell you I came by this dagger of his? Answer me that."

"You won it from him in a wager, during the tourney on Prince Joffrey's name day."

"When my brother Jaime was unhorsed by the Knight of Flowers, that was his story, no?"

"It was," she admitted. A line creased her brow.

"Riders!"

The shriek came from the wind-carved ridge above them. Ser Rodrik had sent Lharys scrambling up the rock face to watch the road while they took their rest.

For a long second, no one moved. Catelyn Stark was the first to react. "Ser Rodrik, Ser Willis, to horse," she shouted. "Get the other mounts behind us. Mohor, guard the prisoners—"

"Arm us!" Tyrion sprang to his feet and seized her by the arm. "You will need every sword."

She knew he was right, Tyrion could see it. The mountain clans cared nothing for the enmities of the great houses; they would slaughter Stark and Lannister with equal fervor, as they slaughtered each other. They might spare Catelyn herself; she was still young enough to bear sons. Still, she hesitated.

"I hear them!" Ser Rodrik called out. Tyrion turned his head to listen, and there it was: hoofbeats, a dozen horses or more, coming nearer. Suddenly everyone was moving, reaching for weapons, running to their mounts.

Pebbles rained down around them as Lharys came springing and sliding down the ridge. He landed breathless in front of Catelyn Stark, an ungainly-looking man with wild tufts of rust-colored hair sticking out from under a conical steel cap. "Twenty men, maybe twenty-five," he said, breathless. "Milk Snakes or Moon Brothers, by my guess. They must have eyes out, m'lady . . . hidden watchers . . . they know we're here."

Ser Rodrik Cassel was already ahorse, a longsword in hand. Mohor crouched behind a boulder, both hands on his iron-tipped spear, a dagger between his teeth. "You, singer," Ser Willis Wode called out. "Help me with this breastplate." Marillion sat frozen, clutching his wood-harp, his face as pale as milk, but Tyrion's man Morrec bounded quickly to his feet and moved to help the knight with his armor.

Tyrion kept his grip on Catelyn Stark. "You have no choice," he told her. "Three of us, and a fourth man wasted guarding us . . . four men can be the difference between life and death up here."

"Give me your word that you will put down your swords again after the fight is done."

"My word?" The hoofbeats were louder now. Tyrion grinned crookedly. "Oh, that you have, my lady . . . on my honor as a Lannister."

For a moment he thought she would spit at him, but instead she snapped, "Arm them," and as quick as that she was pulling away. Ser Rodrik tossed Jyck his sword and scabbard, and wheeled to meet the foe. Morrec helped himself to a bow and quiver, and went to one knee beside the road. He was a better archer than swordsman. And Bronn rode up to offer Tyrion a double-bladed axe.

"I have never fought with an axe." The weapon felt awkward and unfamiliar in his hands. It had a short haft, a heavy head, a nasty spike on top.

"Pretend you're splitting logs," Bronn said, drawing his longsword from the scabbard across his back. He spat, and trotted off to form up beside Chiggen and Ser Rodrik. Ser Willis mounted up to join them, fumbling with his helmet, a metal pot with a thin slit for his eyes and a long black silk plume.

"Logs don't bleed," Tyrion said to no one in particular. He felt naked without armor. He looked around for a rock and ran over to where Marillion was hiding. "Move over."

"Go away!" the boy screamed back at him. "I'm a singer, I want no part of this fight!"

"What, lost your taste for adventure?" Tyrion kicked at the youth until he slid over, and not a moment too soon. A heartbeat later, the riders were on them.

There were no heralds, no banners, no horns nor drums, only the twang of bowstrings as Morrec and Lharys let fly, and suddenly the clansmen came thundering out of the dawn, lean dark men in boiled leather and mismatched armor, faces hidden behind barred halfhelms. In gloved hands were clutched all manner of weapons: longswords and lances and sharpened scythes, spiked clubs and daggers and heavy iron mauls. At their head rode a big man in a striped shadowskin cloak, armed with a two-handed greatsword.

Ser Rodrik shouted *"Winterfell!"* and rode to meet him, with Bronn and Chiggen beside him, screaming some wordless battle cry. Ser Willis Wode followed, swinging a spiked morningstar around his head. "Harrenhal! Harrenhal!" he sang. Tyrion felt a sudden urge to leap up, brandish his axe, and boom out, "Casterly Rock!" but the insanity passed quickly and he crouched down lower.

He heard the screams of frightened horses and the crash of metal on metal. Chiggen's sword raked across the naked face of a mailed rider, and Bronn plunged through the clansmen like a whirlwind, cutting down foes right and left. Ser Rodrik hammered at the big man in the shadowskin cloak, their horses dancing round each other as they traded blow for blow. Jyck vaulted onto a horse and galloped bareback into the fray. Tyrion saw an arrow sprout from the throat of the man in the shadowskin cloak. When he opened his mouth to scream, only blood came out. By the time he fell, Ser Rodrik was fighting someone else.

Suddenly Marillion shrieked, covering his head with his woodharp as a horse leapt over their rock. Tyrion scrambled to his feet as the rider turned to come back at them, hefting a spiked maul. Tyrion swung his axe with both hands. The blade caught the charging horse in the throat with a meaty *thunk*, angling upward, and Tyrion almost lost his grip as the animal screamed and collapsed. He managed to wrench the axe free and lurch clumsily out of the way. Marillion was less fortunate. Horse and rider crashed to the ground in a tangle on top of the singer. Tyrion danced back in while the brigand's leg was still pinned beneath his fallen mount, and buried the axe in the man's neck, just above the shoulder blades.

As he struggled to yank the blade loose, he heard Marillion moaning under the bodies. "Someone help me," the singer gasped. "Gods have mercy, I'm *bleeding*."

"I believe that's horse blood," Tyrion said. The singer's hand came crawling out from beneath the dead animal, scrabbling in the dirt like a spider with five legs. Tyrion put his heel on the grasping fingers and felt a satisfying crunch. "Close your eyes and pretend you're dead," he advised the singer before he hefted the axe and turned away.

After that, things ran together. The dawn was full of shouts and screams and heavy with the scent of blood, and the world had turned to chaos. Arrows hissed past his ear and clattered off the rocks. He saw Bronn unhorsed, fighting with a sword in each hand. Tyrion kept on the fringes of the fight, sliding from rock to rock and darting out of the shadows to hew at the legs of passing horses. He found a wounded clansman and left him dead, helping himself to the man's halfhelm. It fit too snugly, but Tyrion was glad of any protection at all. Jyck was cut down from behind while he sliced at a man in front of him, and later Tyrion stumbled over Kurleket's body. The pig face had been smashed in with a mace, but Tyrion recognized the dirk as he plucked it from the man's dead fingers. He was sliding it through his belt when he heard a woman's scream.

Catelyn Stark was trapped against the stone face of the mountain with three men around her, one still mounted and the other two on foot. She had a dagger clutched awkwardly in her maimed hands, but her back was to the rock now and they had penned her on three sides. *Let them have the bitch,* Tyrion thought, *and welcome to her,* yet somehow he was moving. He caught the first man in the back of the knee before they even knew he was there, and the heavy axehead split flesh and bone like rotten wood. *Logs that bleed,* Tyrion thought inanely as the second man came for him. Tyrion ducked under his sword, lashed out with the axe, the man reeled backward . . . and Catelyn Stark stepped up behind him and opened his throat. The horseman remembered an urgent engagement elsewhere and galloped off suddenly.

Tyrion looked around. The enemy were all vanquished or vanished. Somehow the fighting had ended when he wasn't looking. Dying horses and wounded men lay all around, screaming or moaning. To his vast astonishment, he was not one of them. He opened his fingers and let the axe *thunk* to the ground. His hands were sticky with blood. He could have sworn they had been fighting for half a day, but the sun seemed scarcely to have moved at all.

"Your first battle?" Bronn asked later as he bent over Jyck's body, pulling off his boots. They were good boots, as befit one of Lord Tywin's men; heavy leather, oiled and supple, much finer than what Bronn was wearing.

Tyrion nodded. "My father will be *so* proud," he said. His legs were cramping so badly he could scarcely stand. Odd, he had never once noticed the pain during the battle.

"You need a woman now," Bronn said with a glint in his black eyes. He shoved the boots into his saddlebag. "Nothing like a woman after a man's been blooded, take my word."

Chiggen stopped looting the corpses of the brigands long enough to snort and lick his lips.

Tyrion glanced over to where Lady Stark was dressing Ser Rodrik's wounds. "I'm willing if she is," he said. The freeriders broke into laughter, and Tyrion grinned and thought, *There's a start.*

Afterward he knelt by the stream and washed the blood off his face in water cold as ice. As he limped back to the others, he glanced again at the slain. The dead clansmen were thin, ragged men, their horses scrawny and undersized, with every rib showing. What weapons Bronn and Chiggen had left them were none too impressive. Mauls, clubs, a *scythe* . . . He remembered the big man in the shadowskin cloak who had dueled Ser Rodrik with a two-handed greatsword, but when he found his corpse sprawled on the stony ground, the man was not so big after all, the cloak was gone, and Tyrion saw that the blade was badly notched, its cheap steel spotted with rust. Small wonder the clansmen had left nine bodies on the ground.

They had only three dead; two of Lord Bracken's men-at-arms, Kurleket and Mohor, and his own man Jyck, who had made such a bold show with his bareback charge. *A fool to the end,* Tyrion thought.

"Lady Stark, I urge you to press on, with all haste," Ser Willis Wode said, his eyes scanning the ridgetops warily through the slit in his helm. "We drove them off for the moment, but they will not have gone far."

"We must bury our dead, Ser Willis," she said. "These were brave men. I will not leave them to the crows and shadowcats."

"This soil is too stony for digging," Ser Willis said.

"Then we shall gather stones for cairns."

"Gather all the stones you want," Bronn told her, "but do it without me or Chiggen. I've better things to do than pile rocks on dead men . . . breathing, for one." He looked over the rest of the survivors. "Any of you who hope to be alive come nightfall, ride with us."

"My lady, I fear he speaks the truth," Ser Rodrik said wearily. The old knight had been wounded in the fight, a deep gash in his left arm and a spear thrust that grazed his neck, and he sounded his age. "If we linger here, they will be on us again for a certainty, and we may not live through a second attack."

Tyrion could see the anger in Catelyn's face, but she

had no choice. "May the gods forgive us, then. We will ride at once."

There was no shortage of horses now. Tyrion moved his saddle to Jyck's spotted gelding, who looked strong enough to last another three or four days at least. He was about to mount when Lharys stepped up and said, "I'll take that dirk now, dwarf."

"Let him keep it." Catelyn Stark looked down from her horse. "And see that he has his axe back as well. We may have need of it if we are attacked again."

"You have my thanks, lady," Tyrion said, mounting up.

"Save them," she said curtly. "I trust you no more than I did before." She was gone before he could frame a reply.

Tyrion adjusted his stolen helm and took the axe from Bronn. He remembered how he had begun the journey, with his wrists bound and a hood pulled down over his head, and decided that this was a definite improvement. Lady Stark could keep her trust; so long as he could keep the axe, he would count himself ahead in the game.

Ser Willis Wode led them out. Bronn took the rear, with Lady Stark safely in the middle, Ser Rodrik a shadow beside her. Marillion kept throwing sullen looks back at Tyrion as they rode. The singer had broken several ribs, his woodharp, and all four fingers on his playing hand, yet the day had not been an utter loss to him; somewhere he had acquired a magnificent shadowskin cloak, thick black fur slashed by stripes of white. He huddled beneath its folds silently, and for once had nothing to say.

They heard the deep growls of shadowcats behind them before they had gone half a mile, and later the wild snarling of the beasts fighting over the corpses they had left behind. Marillion grew visibly pale. Tyrion trotted up beside him. *"Craven,"* he said, "rhymes nicely with *raven."* He kicked his horse and moved past the singer, up to Ser Rodrik and Catelyn Stark.

She looked at him, lips pressed tightly together.

"As I was saying before we were so rudely interrupted," Tyrion began, "there is a serious flaw in Littlefinger's fable. Whatever you may believe of me, Lady Stark, I promise you this—I *never* bet against my family."

ARYA

The one-eared black tom arched his back and hissed at her.

Arya padded down the alley, balanced lightly on the balls of her bare feet, listening to the flutter of her heart, breathing slow deep breaths. *Quiet as a shadow,* she told herself, *light as a feather.* The tomcat watched her come, his eyes wary.

Catching cats was hard. Her hands were covered with half-healed scratches, and both knees were scabbed over where she had scraped them raw in tumbles. At first even the cook's huge fat kitchen cat had been able to elude her, but Syrio had kept her at it day and night. When she'd run to him with her hands bleeding, he had said, "So slow? Be quicker, girl. Your enemies will give you more than scratches." He had dabbed her wounds with Myrish fire, which burned so bad she had had to bite her lip to keep from screaming. Then he sent her out after more cats.

The Red Keep was *full* of cats: lazy old cats dozing in the sun, cold-eyed mousers twitching their tails, quick little kittens with claws like needles, ladies' cats all combed and trusting, ragged shadows prowling the midden heaps. One by one Arya had chased them down and

snatched them up and brought them proudly to Syrio
Forel . . . all but this one, this one-eared black devil of a
tomcat. "That's the real king of this castle right there,"
one of the gold cloaks had told her. "Older than sin and
twice as mean. One time, the king was feasting the
queen's father, and that black bastard hopped up on the
table and snatched a roast quail right out of Lord Tywin's
fingers. Robert laughed so hard he like to burst. You stay
away from that one, child."

He had run her halfway across the castle; twice around
the Tower of the Hand, across the inner bailey, through
the stables, down the serpentine steps, past the small
kitchen and the pig yard and the barracks of the gold
cloaks, along the base of the river wall and up more steps
and back and forth over Traitor's Walk, and then down
again and through a gate and around a well and in and out
of strange buildings until Arya didn't know where she
was.

Now at last she had him. High walls pressed close on
either side, and ahead was a blank windowless mass of
stone. *Quiet as a shadow,* she repeated, sliding forward,
light as a feather.

When she was three steps away from him, the tomcat
bolted. Left, then right, he went; and right, then left, went
Arya, cutting off his escape. He hissed again and tried to
dart between her legs. *Quick as a snake,* she thought. Her
hands closed around him. She hugged him to her chest,
whirling and laughing aloud as his claws raked at the
front of her leather jerkin. Ever so fast, she kissed him
right between the eyes, and jerked her head back an instant before his claws would have found her face. The
tomcat yowled and spit.

"What's he doing to that cat?"

Startled, Arya dropped the cat and whirled toward the
voice. The tom bounded off in the blink of an eye. At the
end of the alley stood a girl with a mass of golden curls,
dressed as pretty as a doll in blue satin. Beside her was a
plump little blond boy with a prancing stag sewn in pearls
across the front of his doublet and a miniature sword at
his belt. *Princess Myrcella and Prince Tommen,* Arya
thought. A septa as large as a draft horse hovered over
them, and behind her two big men in crimson cloaks,
Lannister house guards.

"What were you doing to that cat, boy?" Myrcella asked again, sternly. To her brother she said, "He's a ragged boy, isn't he? Look at him." She giggled.

"A ragged dirty smelly boy," Tommen agreed.

They don't know me, Arya realized. *They don't even know I'm a girl.* Small wonder; she was barefoot and dirty, her hair tangled from the long run through the castle, clad in a jerkin ripped by cat claws and brown roughspun pants hacked off above her scabby knees. You don't wear skirts and silks when you're catching cats. Quickly she lowered her head and dropped to one knee. Maybe they *wouldn't* recognize her. If they did, she would never hear the end of it. Septa Mordane would be mortified, and Sansa would never speak to her again from the shame.

The old fat septa moved forward. "Boy, how did you come here? You have no business in this part of the castle."

"You can't keep this sort out," one of the red cloaks said. "Like trying to keep out rats."

"Who do you belong to, boy?" the septa demanded. "Answer me. What's wrong with you, are you mute?"

Arya's voice caught in her throat. If she answered, Tommen and Myrcella would know her for certain.

"Godwyn, bring him here," the septa said. The taller of the guardsmen started down the alley.

Panic gripped her throat like a giant's hand. Arya could not have spoken if her life had hung on it. *Calm as still water,* she mouthed silently.

As Godwyn reached for her, Arya moved. *Quick as a snake.* She leaned to her left, letting his fingers brush her arm, spinning around him. *Smooth as summer silk.* By the time he got himself turned, she was sprinting down the alley. *Swift as a deer.* The septa was screeching at her. Arya slid between legs as thick and white as marble columns, bounded to her feet, bowled into Prince Tommen and hopped over him when he sat down hard and said *"Oof,"* spun away from the second guard, and then she was past them all, running full out.

She heard shouts, then pounding footsteps, closing behind her. She dropped and rolled. The red cloak went careening past her, stumbling. Arya sprang back to her feet. She saw a window above her, high and narrow, scarcely more than an arrow slit. Arya leapt, caught the sill, pulled herself up. She held her breath as she wriggled through. *Slippery as an eel.* Dropping to the floor in front of a star- tled scrubwoman, she hopped up, brushed the rushes off her clothes, and was off again, out the door and along a long hall, down a stair, across a hidden courtyard, around a corner and over a wall and through a low narrow win- dow into a pitch-dark cellar. The sounds grew more and more distant behind her.

Arya was out of breath and quite thoroughly lost. She was in for it now if they had recognized her, but she didn't think they had. She'd moved too fast. *Swift as a deer.*

She hunkered down in the dark against a damp stone wall and listened for the pursuit, but the only sound was the beating of her own heart and a distant drip of water. *Quiet as a shadow,* she told herself. She wondered where she was. When they had first come to King's Landing, she used to have bad dreams about getting lost in the castle. Father said the Red Keep was smaller than Winterfell, but in her dreams it had been immense, an endless stone maze with walls that seemed to shift and change behind her. She would find herself wandering down gloomy halls past faded tapestries, descending endless circular stairs, darting through courtyards or over bridges, her shouts echoing unanswered. In some of the rooms the red stone walls would seem to drip blood, and nowhere could she find a window. Sometimes she would hear her father's voice, but always from a long way off, and no matter how hard she ran after it, it would grow fainter and fainter, until it faded to nothing and Arya was alone in the dark.

It was very dark right now, she realized. She hugged her bare knees tight against her chest and shivered. She would wait quietly and count to ten thousand. By then it would be safe for her to come creeping back out and find her way home.

By the time she had reached eighty-seven, the room had begun to lighten as her eyes adjusted to the blackness. Slowly the shapes around her took on form. Huge empty eyes stared at her hungrily through the gloom, and dimly she saw the jagged shadows of long teeth. She had lost the count. She closed her eyes and bit her lip and sent the fear away. When she looked again, the monsters would be gone. Would never have been. She pretended that Syrio was beside her in the dark, whispering in her ear. *Calm as still water,* she told herself. *Strong as a bear. Fierce as a wolverine.* She opened her eyes again.

The monsters were still there, but the fear was gone.

Arya got to her feet, moving warily. The heads were all around her. She touched one, curious, wondering if it was real. Her fingertips brushed a massive jaw. It *felt* real enough. The bone was smooth beneath her hand, cold and hard to the touch. She ran her fingers down a tooth, black and sharp, a dagger made of darkness. It made her shiver.

"It's dead," she said aloud. "It's just a skull, it can't hurt me." Yet somehow the monster seemed to know she was there. She could feel its empty eyes watching her through the gloom, and there was something in that dim, cavernous room that did not love her. She edged away from the skull and backed into a second, larger than the first. For an instant she could feel its teeth digging into her shoulder, as if it wanted a bite of her flesh. Arya whirled, felt leather catch and tear as a huge fang nipped at her jerkin, and then she was running. Another skull loomed ahead, the biggest monster of all, but Arya did not even slow. She leapt over a ridge of black teeth as tall as swords, dashed through hungry jaws, and threw herself against the door.

Her hands found a heavy iron ring set in the wood, and she yanked at it. The door resisted a moment, before it slowly began to swing inward, with a *creak* so loud Arya was certain it could be heard all through the city. She opened the door just far enough to slip through, into the hallway beyond.

If the room with the monsters had been dark, the hall was the blackest pit in the seven hells. *Calm as still water,* Arya told herself, but even when she gave her eyes a moment to adjust, there was nothing to see but the vague grey outline of the door she had come through. She wiggled her fingers in front of her face, felt the air move, saw nothing. She was blind. *A water dancer sees with all her senses,* she reminded herself. She closed her eyes and steadied her breathing one two three, drank in the quiet, reached out with her hands.

Her fingers brushed against rough unfinished stone to her left. She followed the wall, her hand skimming along the surface, taking small gliding steps through the darkness. *All halls lead somewhere. Where there is a way in, there is a way out. Fear cuts deeper than swords.* Arya would not be afraid. It seemed as if she had been walking a long ways when the wall ended abruptly and a draft of cold air blew past her cheek. Loose hairs stirred faintly against her skin.

From somewhere far below her, she heard noises. The scrape of boots, the distant sound of voices. A flickering light brushed the wall ever so faintly, and she saw that she stood at the top of a great black well, a shaft twenty feet across plunging deep into the earth. Huge stones had been set into the curving walls as steps, circling down and down, dark as the steps to hell that Old Nan used to tell them of. And *something* was coming up out of the darkness, out of the bowels of the earth . . .

Arya peered over the edge and felt the cold black breath on her face. Far below, she saw the light of a single torch, small as the flame of a candle. Two men, she made out. Their shadows writhed against the sides of the well, tall as giants. She could hear their voices, echoing up the shaft.

". . . found one bastard," one said. "The rest will come soon. A day, two days, a fortnight . . ."

"And when he learns the truth, what will he do?" a second voice asked in the liquid accents of the Free Cities.

"The gods alone know," the first voice said. Arya could see a wisp of grey smoke drifting up off the torch, writhing like a snake as it rose. "The fools tried to kill his son, and what's worse, they made a mummer's farce of it. He's not a man to put that aside. I warn you, the wolf and lion will soon be at each other's throats, whether we will it or no."

"Too soon, too soon," the voice with the accent complained. "What good is war *now*? We are not ready. Delay."

"As well bid me stop time. Do you take me for a wizard?"

The other chuckled. "No less." Flames licked at the cold air. The tall shadows were almost on top of her. An instant later the man holding the torch climbed into her sight, his companion beside him. Arya crept back away from the well, dropped to her stomach, and flattened herself against the wall. She held her breath as the men reached the top of the steps.

"What would you have me do?" asked the torchbearer, a stout man in a leather half cape. Even in heavy boots, his feet seemed to glide soundlessly over the ground. A round scarred face and a stubble of dark beard showed under his steel cap, and he wore mail over boiled leather, and a dirk and shortsword at his belt. It seemed to Arya there was something oddly familiar about him.

"If one Hand can die, why not a second?" replied the man with the accent and the forked yellow beard. "You have danced the dance before, my friend." He was no one Arya had ever seen before, she was certain of it. Grossly fat, yet he seemed to walk lightly, carrying his weight on the balls of his feet as a water dancer might. His rings glimmered in the torchlight, red-gold and pale silver, crusted with rubies, sapphires, slitted yellow tiger eyes. Every finger wore a ring; some had two.

"Before is not now, and this Hand is not the other," the scarred man said as they stepped out into the hall. *Still as stone,* Arya told herself, *quiet as a shadow.* Blinded by the blaze of their own torch, they did not see her pressed flat against the stone, only a few feet away.

"Perhaps so," the forked beard replied, pausing to catch his breath after the long climb. "Nonetheless, we must have time. The princess is with child. The *khal* will not bestir himself until his son is born. You know how they are, these savages."

The man with the torch pushed at something. Arya heard a deep rumbling. A huge slab of rock, red in the torchlight, slid down out of the ceiling with a resounding crash that almost made her cry out. Where the entry to the well had been was nothing but stone, solid and unbroken.

"If he does not bestir himself soon, it may be too late," the stout man in the steel cap said. "This is no longer a game for two players, if ever it was. Stannis Baratheon and Lysa Arryn have fled beyond my reach, and the whispers say they are gathering swords around them. The Knight of Flowers writes Highgarden, urging his lord father to send his sister to court. The girl is a maid of fourteen, sweet and beautiful and tractable, and Lord Renly and Ser Loras intend that Robert should bed her, wed her, and make a new queen. Littlefinger . . . the gods only know what game Littlefinger is playing. Yet Lord Stark's the one who troubles my sleep. He has the bastard, he has the book, and soon enough he'll have the truth. And now his wife has abducted Tyrion Lannister, thanks to Littlefinger's meddling. Lord Tywin will take that for an outrage, and Jaime has a queer affection for the Imp. If the Lannisters move north, that will bring the Tullys in as well. *Delay,* you say. *Make haste,* I reply. Even the finest of jugglers cannot keep a hundred balls in the air forever."

"You are more than a juggler, old friend. You are a true sorcerer. All I ask is that you work your magic awhile longer." They started down the hall in the direction Arya had come, past the room with the monsters.

"What I can do, I will," the one with the torch said softly. "I must have gold, and another fifty birds."

She let them get a long way ahead, then went creeping after them. *Quiet as a shadow.*

"So many?" The voices were fainter as the light dwindled ahead of her. "The ones you need are hard to find . . . so young, to know their letters . . . perhaps older . . . not die so easy . . ."

"No. The younger are safer . . . treat them gently . . ."

". . . if they kept their tongues . . ."

". . . the risk . . ."

Long after their voices had faded away, Arya could still see the light of the torch, a smoking star that bid her follow. Twice it seemed to disappear, but she kept on straight, and both times she found herself at the top of steep, narrow stairs, the torch glimmering far below her. She hurried after it, down and down. Once she stumbled over a rock and fell against the wall, and her hand found raw earth supported by timbers, whereas before the tunnel had been dressed stone.

She must have crept after them for miles. Finally they were gone, but there was no place to go but forward. She found the wall again and followed, blind and lost, pretending that Nymeria was padding along beside her in the darkness. At the end she was knee-deep in foul-smelling water, wishing she could dance upon it as Syrio might have, and wondering if she'd ever see light again. It was full dark when finally Arya emerged into the night air.

She found herself standing at the mouth of a sewer where it emptied into the river. She stank so badly that she stripped right there, dropping her soiled clothing on the riverbank as she dove into the deep black waters. She swam until she felt clean, and crawled out shivering. Some riders went past along the river road as Arya was washing her clothes, but if they saw the scrawny naked girl scrubbing her rags in the moonlight, they took no notice.

She was miles from the castle, but from anywhere in King's Landing you needed only to look up to see the Red Keep high on Aegon's Hill, so there was no danger of losing her way. Her clothes were almost dry by the time she reached the gatehouse. The portcullis was down and the gates barred, so she turned aside to a postern door. The gold cloaks who had the watch sneered when she told them to let her in. "Off with you," one said. "The kitchen scraps are gone, and we'll have no begging after dark."

"I'm not a beggar," she said. "I live here."

"I said, *off with you.* Do you need a clout on the ear to help your hearing?"

"I want to see my father."

The guards exchanged a glance. "I want to fuck the queen myself, for all the good it does me," the younger one said.

The older scowled. "Who's this father of yours, boy, the city ratcatcher?"

"The Hand of the King," Arya told him.

Both men laughed, but then the older one swung his fist at her, casually, as a man would swat a dog. Arya saw the blow coming even before it began. She danced back out of the way, untouched. "I'm not a boy," she spat at them. "I'm Arya Stark of Winterfell, and if you lay a hand on me my lord father will have both your heads on spikes. If you don't believe me, fetch Jory Cassel or Vayon Poole from the Tower of the Hand." She put her hands on her hips. "Now are you going to open the gate, or do you need a clout on the ear to help your hearing?"

Her father was alone in the solar when Harwin and Fat Tom marched her in, an oil lamp glowing softly at his elbow. He was bent over the biggest book Arya had ever seen, a great thick tome with cracked yellow pages of crabbed script, bound between faded leather covers, but he closed it to listen to Harwin's report. His face was stern as he sent the men away with thanks.

"You realize I had half my guard out searching for you?" Eddard Stark said when they were alone. "Septa Mordane is beside herself with fear. She's in the sept praying for your safe return. Arya, you *know* you are never to go beyond the castle gates without my leave."

"I didn't go out the gates," she blurted. "Well, I didn't mean to. I was down in the dungeons, only they turned into this tunnel. It was all dark, and I didn't have a torch or a candle to see by, so I had to follow. I couldn't go back the way I came on account of the monsters. Father, they were talking about *killing* you! Not the monsters, the two men. They didn't see me, I was being still as stone and quiet as a shadow, but I heard them. They said you had a book and a bastard and if one Hand could die, why not a second? Is that the book? Jon's the bastard, I bet."

"Jon? Arya, what are you talking about? Who said this?"

"*They* did," she told him. "There was a fat one with rings and a forked yellow beard, and another in mail and a steel cap, and the fat one said they had to delay but the other one told him he couldn't keep juggling and the wolf and the lion were going to eat each other and it was a mummer's farce." She tried to remember the rest. She hadn't quite understood everything she'd heard, and now it was all mixed up in her head. "The fat one said the princess was with child. The one in the steel cap, he had the torch, he said that they had to hurry. I think he was a wizard."

"A wizard," said Ned, unsmiling. "Did he have a long white beard and tall pointed hat speckled with stars?"

"No! It wasn't like Old Nan's stories. He didn't *look* like a wizard, but the fat one said he was."

"I warn you, Arya, if you're spinning this thread of air—"

"No, I *told* you, it was in the dungeons, by the place with the secret wall. I was chasing cats, and well . . ." She screwed up her face. If she admitted knocking over Prince Tommen, he would be *really* angry with her. ". . . well, I went in this window. That's where I found the monsters."

"Monsters *and* wizards," her father said. "It would

seem you've had quite an adventure. These men you heard, you say they spoke of juggling and mummery?"

"Yes," Arya admitted, "only—"

"Arya, they were mummers," her father told her. "There must be a dozen troupes in King's Landing right now, come to make some coin off the tourney crowds. I'm not certain what these two were doing in the castle, but perhaps the king has asked for a show."

"No." She shook her head stubbornly. "They weren't—"

"You shouldn't be following people about and spying on them in any case. Nor do I cherish the notion of my daughter climbing in strange windows after stray cats. Look at you, sweetling. Your arms are covered with scratches. This has gone on long enough. Tell Syrio Forel that I want a word with him—"

He was interrupted by a short, sudden knock. "Lord Eddard, pardons," Desmond called out, opening the door a crack, "but there's a black brother here begging audience. He says the matter is urgent. I thought you would want to know."

"My door is always open to the Night's Watch," Father said.

Desmond ushered the man inside. He was stooped and ugly, with an unkempt beard and unwashed clothes, yet Father greeted him pleasantly and asked his name.

"Yoren, as it please m'lord. My pardons for the hour." He bowed to Arya. "And this must be your son. He has your look."

"I'm a *girl*," Arya said, exasperated. If the old man was down from the Wall, he must have come by way of Winterfell. "Do you know my brothers?" she asked excitedly. "Robb and Bran are at Winterfell, and Jon's on the Wall. Jon Snow, he's in the Night's Watch too, you must know him, he has a direwolf, a white one with red eyes. Is Jon a ranger yet? I'm Arya Stark." The old man in his smelly black clothes was looking at her oddly, but Arya could not seem to stop talking. "When you ride back to the Wall, would you bring Jon a letter if I wrote one?" She wished Jon were here right now. *He'd* believe her about the dungeons and the fat man with the forked beard and the wizard in the steel cap.

"My daughter often forgets her courtesies," Eddard

Stark said with a faint smile that softened his words. "I beg your forgiveness, Yoren. Did my brother Benjen send you?"

"No one *sent* me, m'lord, saving old Mormont. I'm here to find men for the Wall, and when Robert next holds court, I'll bend the knee and cry our need, see if the king and his Hand have some scum in the dungeons they'd be well rid of. You might say as Benjen Stark is why we're talking, though. His blood ran black. Made him my brother as much as yours. It's for his sake I'm come. Rode hard, I did, near killed my horse the way I drove her, but I left the others well behind."

"The others?"

Yoren spat. "Sellswords and freeriders and like trash. That inn was full o' them, and I saw them take the scent. The scent of blood or the scent of gold, they smell the same in the end. Not all o' them made for King's Landing, either. Some went galloping for Casterly Rock, and the Rock lies closer. Lord Tywin will have gotten the word by now, you can count on it."

Father frowned. "What word is this?"

Yoren eyed Arya. "One best spoken in private, m'lord, begging your pardons."

"As you say. Desmond, see my daughter to her chambers." He kissed her on the brow. "We'll finish our talk on the morrow."

Arya stood rooted to the spot. "Nothing bad's happened to Jon, has it?" she asked Yoren. "Or Uncle Benjen?"

"Well, as to Stark, I can't say. The Snow boy was well enough when I left the Wall. It's not them as concerns me."

Desmond took her hand. "Come along, milady. You heard your lord father."

Arya had no choice but to go with him, wishing it had been Fat Tom. With Tom, she might have been able to linger at the door on some excuse and hear what Yoren was saying, but Desmond was too single-minded to trick. "How many guards does my father have?" she asked him as they descended to her bedchamber.

"Here at King's Landing? Fifty."

"You wouldn't let anyone kill him, would you?" she asked.

Desmond laughed. "No fear on that count, little lady. Lord Eddard's guarded night and day. He'll come to no harm."

"The Lannisters have more than fifty men," Arya pointed out.

"So they do, but every northerner is worth ten of these southron swords, so you can sleep easy."

"What if a wizard was sent to kill him?"

"Well, as to that," Desmond replied, drawing his long-sword, "wizards die the same as other men, once you cut their heads off."

EDDARD

"**R**obert, I beg of you," Ned pleaded, "hear what you are saying. You are talking of murdering a child."

"*The whore is pregnant!*" The king's fist slammed down on the council table loud as a thunderclap. "I warned you this would happen, Ned. Back in the barrowlands, I warned you, but you did not care to hear it. Well, you'll hear it now. I want them dead, mother and child both, and that fool Viserys as well. Is that plain enough for you? *I want them dead.*"

The other councillors were all doing their best to pretend that they were somewhere else. No doubt they were wiser than he was. Eddard Stark had seldom felt quite so alone. "You will dishonor yourself forever if you do this."

"Then let it be on my head, so long as it is done. I am not so blind that I cannot see the shadow of the axe when it is hanging over my own neck."

"There is no axe," Ned told his king. "Only the shadow of a shadow, twenty years removed . . . if it exists at all."

"*If?*" Varys asked softly, wringing powdered hands together. "My lord, you wrong me. Would I bring lies to king and council?"

Ned looked at the eunuch coldly. "You would bring us the whisperings of a traitor half a world away, my lord. Perhaps Mormont is wrong. Perhaps he is lying."

"Ser Jorah would not dare deceive me," Varys said with a sly smile. "Rely on it, my lord. The princess is with child."

"So you say. If you are wrong, we need not fear. If the girl miscarries, we need not fear. If she births a daughter in place of a son, we need not fear. If the babe dies in infancy, we need not fear."

"But if it *is* a boy?" Robert insisted. "If he lives?"

"The narrow sea would still lie between us. I shall fear the Dothraki the day they teach their horses to run on water."

The king took a swallow of wine and glowered at Ned across the council table. "So you would counsel me to do nothing until the dragonspawn has landed his army on my shores, is that it?"

"This 'dragonspawn' is in his mother's belly," Ned said. "Even Aegon did no conquering until after he was weaned."

"*Gods!* You are stubborn as an aurochs, Stark." The king looked around the council table. "Have the rest of you mislaid your tongues? Will no one talk sense to this frozen-faced fool?"

Varys gave the king an unctuous smile and laid a soft hand on Ned's sleeve. "I understand your qualms, Lord Eddard, truly I do. It gave me no joy to bring this grievous news to council. It is a terrible thing we contemplate, a *vile* thing. Yet we who presume to rule must do vile things for the good of the realm, howevermuch it pains us."

Lord Renly shrugged. "The matter seems simple enough to me. We ought to have had Viserys and his sister killed years ago, but His Grace my brother made the mistake of listening to Jon Arryn."

"Mercy is never a mistake, Lord Renly," Ned replied. "On the Trident, Ser Barristan here cut down a dozen good men, Robert's friends and mine. When they brought him to us, grievously wounded and near death, Roose Bolton urged us to cut his throat, but your brother said, 'I will not kill a man for loyalty, nor for fighting well,' and sent his own maester to tend Ser Barristan's wounds." He gave the king a long cool look. "Would that man were here today."

Robert had shame enough to blush. "It was not the same," he complained. "Ser Barristan was a knight of the Kingsguard."

"Whereas Daenerys is a fourteen-year-old girl." Ned knew he was pushing this well past the point of wisdom, yet he could not keep silent. "Robert, I ask you, what did we rise against Aerys Targaryen for, if not to put an end to the murder of children?"

"To put an end to *Targaryens*!" the king growled.

"Your Grace, I never knew you to fear Rhaegar." Ned fought to keep the scorn out of his voice, and failed. "Have the years so unmanned you that you tremble at the shadow of an unborn child?"

Robert purpled. "No more, Ned," he warned, pointing. "Not another word. Have you forgotten who is king here?"

"No, Your Grace," Ned replied. "Have you?"

"*Enough!*" the king bellowed. "I am sick of talk. I'll be done with this, or be damned. What say you all?"

"She must be killed," Lord Renly declared.

"We have no choice," murmured Varys. "Sadly, sadly . . ."

Ser Barristan Selmy raised his pale blue eyes from the table and said, "Your Grace, there is honor in facing an enemy on the battlefield, but none in killing him in his mother's womb. Forgive me, but I must stand with Lord Eddard."

Grand Maester Pycelle cleared his throat, a process that seemed to take some minutes. "My order serves the realm, not the ruler. Once I counseled King Aerys as loyally as I counsel King Robert now, so I bear this girl child of his no ill will. Yet I ask you this—should war come again, how many soldiers will die? How many towns will burn? How many children will be ripped from their mothers to perish on the end of a spear?" He stroked his luxuriant white beard, infinitely sad, infinitely weary. "Is it not wiser, even *kinder*, that Daenerys Targaryen should die now so that tens of thousands might live?"

"Kinder," Varys said. "Oh, well and truly spoken, Grand Maester. It is so true. Should the gods in their caprice grant Daenerys Targaryen a son, the realm must bleed."

Littlefinger was the last. As Ned looked to him, Lord Petyr stifled a yawn. "When you find yourself in bed with an ugly woman, the best thing to do is close your eyes and get on with it," he declared. "Waiting won't make the maid any prettier. Kiss her and be done with it."

"Kiss her?" Ser Barristan repeated, aghast.

"A steel kiss," said Littlefinger.

Robert turned to face his Hand. "Well, there it is, Ned. You and Selmy stand alone on this matter. The only question that remains is, who can we find to kill her?"

"Mormont craves a royal pardon," Lord Renly reminded them.

"Desperately," Varys said, "yet he craves life even more. By now, the princess nears Vaes Dothrak, where it is death to draw a blade. If I told you what the Dothraki would do to the poor man who used one on a *khaleesi*, none of you would sleep tonight." He stroked a powdered cheek. "Now, poison . . . the tears of Lys, let us say. Khal Drogo need never know it was not a natural death."

Grand Maester Pycelle's sleepy eyes flicked open. He squinted suspiciously at the eunuch.

"Poison is a coward's weapon," the king complained.

Ned had heard enough. "You send hired knives to kill a fourteen-year-old girl and still quibble about honor?" He pushed back his chair and stood. "Do it yourself, Robert. The man who passes the sentence should swing the sword. Look her in the eyes before you kill her. See her tears, hear her last words. You owe her that much at least."

"Gods," the king swore, the word exploding out of him as if he could barely contain his fury. "You mean it, damn you." He reached for the flagon of wine at his elbow, found it empty, and flung it away to shatter against the wall. "I am out of wine and out of patience. Enough of this. Just have it done."

"I will not be part of murder, Robert. Do as you will, but do not ask me to fix my seal to it."

For a moment Robert did not seem to understand what Ned was saying. Defiance was not a dish he tasted often. Slowly his face changed as comprehension came. His eyes narrowed and a flush crept up his neck past the velvet collar. He pointed an angry finger at Ned. "You are the King's Hand, Lord Stark. You will do as I command you, or I'll find me a Hand who will."

"I wish him every success." Ned unfastened the heavy clasp that clutched at the folds of his cloak, the ornate silver hand that was his badge of office. He laid it on the table in front of the king, saddened by the memory of the man who had pinned it on him, the friend he had loved. "I thought you a better man than this, Robert. I thought we had made a nobler king."

Robert's face was purple. *"Out,"* he croaked, choking on his rage. "Out, damn you, I'm done with you. What are you waiting for? Go, run back to Winterfell. And make certain I never look on your face again, or I swear, I'll have your head on a spike!"

Ned bowed, and turned on his heel without another word. He could feel Robert's eyes on his back. As he strode from the council chambers, the discussion resumed with scarcely a pause. "On Braavos there is a society called the Faceless Men," Grand Maester Pycelle offered.

"Do you have any idea how *costly* they are?" Littlefinger complained. "You could hire an army of common sellswords for half the price, and that's for a merchant. I don't dare think what they might ask for a princess."

The closing of the door behind him silenced the voices. Ser Boros Blount was stationed outside the chamber, wearing the long white cloak and armor of the Kingsguard. He gave Ned a quick, curious glance from the corner of his eye, but asked no questions.

The day felt heavy and oppressive as he crossed the bailey back to the Tower of the Hand. He could feel the threat of rain in the air. Ned would have welcomed it. It might have made him feel a trifle less unclean. When he reached his solar, he summoned Vayon Poole. The steward came at once. "You sent for me, my lord Hand?"

"Hand no longer," Ned told him. "The king and I have quarreled. We shall be returning to Winterfell."

"I shall begin making arrangements at once, my lord. We will need a fortnight to ready everything for the journey."

"We may not have a fortnight. We may not have a day. The king mentioned something about seeing my head on a spike." Ned frowned. He did not truly believe the king would harm him, not Robert. He was angry now, but once Ned was safely out of sight, his rage would cool as it always did.

Always? Suddenly, uncomfortably, he found himself recalling Rhaegar Targaryen. *Fifteen years dead, yet Robert hates him as much as ever.* It was a disturbing notion . . . and there was the other matter, the business with Catelyn and the dwarf that Yoren had warned him of last night. That would come to light soon, as sure as sunrise, and with the king in such a black fury . . . Robert might not care a fig for Tyrion Lannister, but it would touch on his pride, and there was no telling what the queen might do.

"It might be safest if I went on ahead," he told Poole. "I will take my daughters and a few guardsmen. The rest of you can follow when you are ready. Inform Jory, but tell no one else, and do nothing until the girls and I have gone. The castle is full of eyes and ears, and I would rather my plans were not known."

"As you command, my lord."

When he had gone, Eddard Stark went to the window and sat brooding. Robert had left him no choice that he could see. He ought to thank him. It would be good to return to Winterfell. He ought never have left. His sons were waiting there. Perhaps he and Catelyn would make a new son together when he returned, they were not so old yet. And of late he had often found himself dreaming of snow, of the deep quiet of the wolfswood at night.

And yet, the thought of leaving angered him as well. So much was still undone. Robert and his council of cravens and flatterers would beggar the realm if left unchecked . . . or, worse, sell it to the Lannisters in payment of their loans. And the truth of Jon Arryn's death still eluded him. Oh, he had found a few pieces, enough to convince him that Jon had indeed been murdered, but that was no more than the spoor of an animal on the forest floor. He had not sighted the beast itself yet, though he sensed it was there, lurking, hidden, treacherous.

It struck him suddenly that he might return to Winterfell by sea. Ned was no sailor, and ordinarily would have preferred the kingsroad, but if he took ship he could stop at Dragonstone and speak with Stannis Baratheon.

Pycelle had sent a raven off across the water, with a polite letter from Ned requesting Lord Stannis to return to his seat on the small council. As yet, there had been no reply, but the silence only deepened his suspicions. Lord Stannis shared the secret Jon Arryn had died for, he was certain of it. The truth he sought might very well be waiting for him on the ancient island fortress of House Targaryen.

And when you have it, what then? Some secrets are safer kept hidden. Some secrets are too dangerous to share, even with those you love and trust. Ned slid the dagger that Catelyn had brought him out of the sheath on his belt. The Imp's knife. Why would the dwarf want Bran dead? To silence him, surely. Another secret, or only a different strand of the same web?

Could *Robert* be part of it? He would not have thought so, but once he would not have thought Robert could command the murder of women and children either. Catelyn had tried to warn him. *You knew the man,* she had said. *The king is a stranger to you.* The sooner he was quit of King's Landing, the better. If there was a ship sailing north on the morrow, it would be well to be on it.

He summoned Vayon Poole again and sent him to the docks to make inquiries, quietly but quickly. "Find me a fast ship with a skilled captain," he told the steward. "I care nothing for the size of its cabins or the quality of its appointments, so long as it is swift and safe. I wish to leave at once."

Poole had no sooner taken his leave than Tomard announced a visitor. "Lord Baelish to see you, m'lord."

Ned was half-tempted to turn him away, but thought better of it. He was not free yet; until he was, he must play their games. "Show him in, Tom."

Lord Petyr sauntered into the solar as if nothing had gone amiss that morning. He wore a slashed velvet doublet in cream-and-silver, a grey silk cloak trimmed with black fox, and his customary mocking smile.

Ned greeted him coldly. "Might I ask the reason for this visit, Lord Baelish?"

"I won't detain you long, I'm on my way to dine with Lady Tanda. Lamprey pie and roast suckling pig. She has some thought to wed me to her younger daughter, so her table is always astonishing. If truth be told, I'd sooner marry the pig, but don't tell her. I do love lamprey pie."

"Don't let me keep you from your eels, my lord," Ned said with icy disdain. "At the moment, I cannot think of anyone whose company I desire less than yours."

"Oh, I'm certain if you put your mind to it, you could come up with a few names. Varys, say. Cersei. Or Robert. His Grace is most wroth with you. He went on about you at some length after you took your leave of us this morning. The words *insolence* and *ingratitude* came into it frequently, I seem to recall."

Ned did not honor that with a reply. Nor did he offer his guest a seat, but Littlefinger took one anyway. "After you stormed out, it was left to me to convince them not to hire the Faceless Men," he continued blithely. "Instead Varys will quietly let it be known that we'll make a lord of whoever does in the Targaryen girl."

Ned was disgusted. "So now we grant titles to assassins."

Littlefinger shrugged. "Titles are cheap. The Faceless Men are expensive. If truth be told, I did the Targaryen girl more good than you with all your talk of honor. *Let* some sellsword drunk on visions of lordship try to kill her. Likely he'll make a botch of it, and afterward the Dothraki will be on their guard. If we'd sent a Faceless Man after her, she'd be as good as buried."

Ned frowned. "You sit in council and talk of ugly women and steel kisses, and now you expect me to believe that you tried to protect the girl? How big a fool do you take me for?"

"Well, quite an enormous one, actually," said Littlefinger, laughing.

"Do you always find murder so amusing, Lord Baelish?"

"It's not murder I find amusing, Lord Stark, it's you. You rule like a man dancing on rotten ice. I daresay you will make a noble splash. I believe I heard the first crack this morning."

"The first and last," said Ned. "I've had my fill."

"When do you mean to return to Winterfell, my lord?"

"As soon as I can. What concern is that of yours?"

"None . . . but if perchance you're still here come evenfall, I'd be pleased to take you to this brothel your man Jory has been searching for so ineffectually." Littlefinger smiled. "And I won't even tell the Lady Catelyn."

CATELYN

"**M**y lady, you should have sent word of your coming," Ser Donnel Waynwood told her as their horses climbed the pass. "We would have sent an escort. The high road is not as safe as it once was, for a party as small as yours."

"We learned that to our sorrow, Ser Donnel," Catelyn said. Sometimes she felt as though her heart had turned to stone; six brave men had died to bring her this far, and she could not even find it in her to weep for them. Even their names were fading. "The clansmen harried us day and night. We lost three men in the first attack, and two more in the second, and Lannister's serving man died of a fever when his wounds festered. When we heard your men approaching, I thought us doomed for certain." They had drawn up for a last desperate fight, blades in hand and backs to the rock. The dwarf had been whetting the edge of his axe and making some mordant jest when Bronn spotted the banner the riders carried before them, the moon-and-falcon of House Arryn, sky-blue and white. Catelyn had never seen a more welcome sight.

"The clans have grown bolder since Lord Jon died," Ser Donnel said. He was a stocky youth of twenty years, earnest and homely, with a wide nose and a shock of thick brown hair. "If it were up to me, I would take a hundred men into the mountains, root them out of their fastnesses, and teach them some sharp lessons, but your sister has forbidden it. She would not even permit her knights to fight in the Hand's tourney. She wants all our swords kept close to home, to defend the Vale . . . against what, no one is certain. Shadows, some say." He looked at her anxiously, as if he had suddenly remembered who she was. "I hope I have not spoken out of turn, my lady. I meant no offense."

"Frank talk does not offend me, Ser Donnel." Catelyn knew what her sister feared. *Not shadows, Lannisters,* she thought to herself, glancing back to where the dwarf rode beside Bronn. The two of them had grown thick as thieves since Chiggen had died. The little man was more cunning than she liked. When they had entered the mountains, he had been her captive, bound and helpless. What was he now? Her captive still, yet he rode along with a dirk through his belt and an axe strapped to his saddle, wearing the shadowskin cloak he'd won dicing with the singer and the chainmail hauberk he'd taken off Chiggen's corpse. Two score men flanked the dwarf and the rest of her ragged band, knights and men-at-arms in service to her sister Lysa and Jon Arryn's young son, and yet Tyrion betrayed no hint of fear. *Could I be wrong?* Catelyn wondered, not for the first time. Could he be innocent after all, of Bran and Jon Arryn and all the rest? And if he was, what did that make her? Six men had died to bring him here.

Resolute, she pushed her doubts away. "When we reach your keep, I would take it kindly if you could send for Maester Colemon at once. Ser Rodrik is feverish from his wounds." More than once she had feared the gallant old knight would not survive the journey. Toward the end he could scarcely sit his horse, and Bronn had urged her to leave him to his fate, but Catelyn would not hear of it. They had tied him in the saddle instead, and she had commanded Marillion the singer to watch over him.

Ser Donnel hesitated before he answered. "The Lady Lysa has commanded the maester to remain at the Eyrie at all times, to care for Lord Robert," he said. "We have a septon at the gate who tends to our wounded. He can see to your man's hurts."

Catelyn had more faith in a maester's learning than a septon's prayers. She was about to say as much when she saw the battlements ahead, long parapets built into the very stone of the mountains on either side of them. Where the pass shrank to a narrow defile scarce wide enough for four men to ride abreast, twin watchtowers clung to the rocky slopes, joined by a covered bridge of weathered grey stone that arched above the road. Silent faces watched from arrow slits in tower, battlements, and bridge. When they had climbed almost to the top, a knight rode out to meet them. His horse and his armor were grey, but his cloak was the rippling blue-and-red of Riverrun, and a shiny black fish, wrought in gold and obsidian, pinned its folds against his shoulder. "Who would pass the Bloody Gate?" he called.

"Ser Donnel Waynwood, with the Lady Catelyn Stark and her companions," the young knight answered.

The Knight of the Gate lifted his visor. "I thought the lady looked familiar. You are far from home, little Cat."

"And you, Uncle," she said, smiling despite all she had been through. Hearing that hoarse, smoky voice again took her back twenty years, to the days of her childhood.

"My home is at my back," he said gruffly.

"Your home is in my heart," Catelyn told him. "Take off your helm. I would look on your face again."

"The years have not improved it, I fear," Brynden Tully said, but when he lifted off the helm, Catelyn saw that he lied. His features were lined and weathered, and time had stolen the auburn from his hair and left him only grey, but the smile was the same, and the bushy eyebrows fat as caterpillars, and the laughter in his deep blue eyes. "Did Lysa know you were coming?"

"There was no time to send word ahead," Catelyn told him. The others were coming up behind her. "I fear we ride before the storm, Uncle."

"May we enter the Vale?" Ser Donnel asked. The Waynwoods were ever ones for ceremony.

"In the name of Robert Arryn, Lord of the Eyrie, Defender of the Vale, True Warden of the East, I bid you enter freely, and charge you to keep his peace," Ser Brynden replied. "Come."

And so she rode behind him, beneath the shadow of the Bloody Gate where a dozen armies had dashed themselves to pieces in the Age of Heroes. On the far side of the stoneworks, the mountains opened up suddenly upon a vista of green fields, blue sky, and snowcapped mountains that took her breath away. The Vale of Arryn bathed in the morning light.

It stretched before them to the misty east, a tranquil land of rich black soil, wide slow-moving rivers, and hundreds of small lakes that shone like mirrors in the sun, protected on all sides by its sheltering peaks. Wheat and corn and barley grew high in its fields, and even in Highgarden the pumpkins were no larger nor the fruit any sweeter than here. They stood at the western end of the valley, where the high road crested the last pass and began its winding descent to the bottomlands two miles below. The Vale was narrow here, no more than a half day's ride across, and the northern mountains seemed so close that Catelyn could almost reach out and touch them. Looming over them all was the jagged peak called the Giant's Lance, a mountain that even mountains looked up to, its head lost in icy mists three and a half miles above the valley floor. Over its massive western shoulder flowed the ghost torrent of Alyssa's Tears. Even from this distance, Catelyn could make out the shining silver thread, bright against the dark stone.

When her uncle saw that she had stopped, he moved his horse closer and pointed. "It's there, beside Alyssa's Tears. All you can see from here is a flash of white every now and then, if you look hard and the sun hits the walls just right."

Seven towers, Ned had told her, *like white daggers thrust into the belly of the sky, so high you can stand on the parapets and look down on the clouds.* "How long a ride?" she asked.

"We can be at the mountain by evenfall," Uncle Brynden said, "but the climb will take another day."

Ser Rodrik Cassel spoke up from behind. "My lady," he said, "I fear I can go no farther today." His face sagged beneath his ragged, new-grown whiskers, and he looked so weary Catelyn feared he might fall off his horse.

"Nor should you," she said. "You have done all I could have asked of you, and a hundred times more. My uncle will see me the rest of the way to the Eyrie. Lannister must come with me, but there is no reason that you and the others should not rest here and recover your strength."

"We should be honored to have them to guest," Ser Donnel said with the grave courtesy of the young. Beside Ser Rodrik, only Bronn, Ser Willis Wode, and Marillion the singer remained of the party that had ridden with her from the inn by the crossroads.

"My lady," Marillion said, riding forward. "I beg you allow me to accompany you to the Eyrie, to see the end of the tale as I saw its beginnings." The boy sounded haggard, yet strangely determined; he had a fevered shine to his eyes.

Catelyn had never asked the singer to ride with them; that choice he had made himself, and how he had come to survive the journey when so many braver men lay dead and unburied behind them, she could never say. Yet here he was, with a scruff of beard that made him look almost a man. Perhaps she owed him something for having come this far. "Very well," she told him.

"I'll come as well," Bronn announced.

She liked that less well. Without Bronn she would never have reached the Vale, she knew; the sellsword was as fierce a fighter as she had ever seen, and his sword had helped cut them through to safety. Yet for all that, Catelyn misliked the man. Courage he had, and strength, but there was no kindness in him, and little loyalty. And she had seen him riding beside Lannister far too often, talking in low voices and laughing at some private joke. She would have preferred to separate him from the dwarf here and now, but having agreed that Marillion might continue to the Eyrie, she could see no gracious way to deny that same right to Bronn. "As you wish," she said, although she noted that he had not actually asked her permission.

Ser Willis Wode remained with Ser Rodrik, a soft-spoken septon fussing over their wounds. Their horses were left behind as well, poor ragged things. Ser Donnel promised to send birds ahead to the Eyrie and the Gates of the Moon with the word of their coming. Fresh mounts were brought forth from the stables, surefooted mountain stock with shaggy coats, and within the hour they set forth once again. Catelyn rode beside her uncle as they began the descent to the valley floor. Behind came Bronn, Tyrion Lannister, Marillion, and six of Brynden's men.

Not until they were a third of the way down the mountain path, well out of earshot of the others, did Brynden Tully turn to her and say, "So, child. Tell me about this storm of yours."

"I have not been a child in many years, Uncle," Catelyn said, but she told him nonetheless. It took longer than she would have believed to tell it all, Lysa's letter and Bran's fall, the assassin's dagger and Littlefinger and her chance meeting with Tyrion Lannister in the crossroads inn.

Her uncle listened silently, heavy brows shadowing his eyes as his frown grew deeper. Brynden Tully had always known how to listen . . . to anyone but her father. He was Lord Hoster's brother, younger by five years, but the two of them had been at war as far back as Catelyn could remember. During one of their louder quarrels, when Catelyn was eight, Lord Hoster had called Brynden "the black goat of the Tully flock." Laughing, Brynden had pointed out that the sigil of their house was a leaping trout, so he ought to be a black *fish* rather than a black goat, and from that day forward he had taken it as his personal emblem.

The war had not ended until the day she and Lysa had been wed. It was at their wedding feast that Brynden told his brother he was leaving Riverrun to serve Lysa and her new husband, the Lord of the Eyrie. Lord Hoster had not spoken his brother's name since, from what Edmure told her in his infrequent letters.

Nonetheless, during all those years of Catelyn's girlhood, it had been Brynden the Blackfish to whom Lord Hoster's children had run with their tears and their tales, when Father was too busy and Mother too ill. Catelyn, Lysa, Edmure . . . and yes, even Petyr Baelish, their father's ward . . . he had listened to them all patiently, as he listened now, laughing at their triumphs and sympathizing with their childish misfortunes.

When she was done, her uncle remained silent for a long time, as his horse negotiated the steep, rocky trail. "Your father must be told," he said at last. "If the Lannisters should march, Winterfell is remote and the Vale walled up behind its mountains, but Riverrun lies right in their path."

"I'd had the same fear," Catelyn admitted. "I shall ask Maester Colemon to send a bird when we reach the Eyrie." She had other messages to send as well; the commands that Ned had given her for his bannermen, to ready the defenses of the north. "What is the mood in the Vale?" she asked.

"Angry," Brynden Tully admitted. "Lord Jon was much loved, and the insult was keenly felt when the king named Jaime Lannister to an office the Arryns had held for near three hundred years. Lysa has commanded us to call her son the *True* Warden of the East, but no one is fooled. Nor is your sister alone in wondering at the manner of the Hand's death. None dare say Jon was murdered, not openly, but suspicion casts a long shadow." He gave Catelyn a look, his mouth tight. "And there is the boy."

"The boy? What of him?" She ducked her head as they passed under a low overhang of rock, and around a sharp turn.

Her uncle's voice was troubled. "Lord Robert," he sighed. "Six years old, sickly, and prone to weep if you take his dolls away. Jon Arryn's trueborn heir, by all the gods, yet there are some who say he is too weak to sit his father's seat. Nestor Royce has been high steward these past fourteen years, while Lord Jon served in King's Landing, and many whisper that he should rule until the boy comes of age. Others believe that Lysa must marry again, and soon. Already the suitors gather like crows on a battlefield. The Eyrie is full of them."

"I might have expected that," Catelyn said. Small wonder there; Lysa was still young, and the kingdom of Mountain and Vale made a handsome wedding gift. "Will Lysa take another husband?"

"She says yes, provided she finds a man who suits her," Brynden Tully said, "but she has already rejected Lord Nestor and a dozen other suitable men. She swears that this time *she* will choose her lord husband."

"You of all people can scarce fault her for that."

Ser Brynden snorted. "Nor do I, but . . . it seems to me Lysa is only playing at courtship. She enjoys the sport, but I believe your sister intends to rule herself until her boy is old enough to be Lord of the Eyrie in truth as well as name."

"A woman can rule as wisely as a man," Catelyn said.

"The *right* woman can," her uncle said with a sideways glance. "Make no mistake, Cat. Lysa is not you." He hesitated a moment. "If truth be told, I fear you may not find your sister as . . . helpful as you would like."

She was puzzled. "What do you mean?"

"The Lysa who came back from King's Landing is not the same girl who went south when her husband was named Hand. Those years were hard for her. You must know. Lord Arryn was a dutiful husband, but their marriage was made from politics, not passion."

"As was my own."

"They began the same, but your ending has been happier than your sister's. Two babes stillborn, twice as many miscarriages, Lord Arryn's death . . . Catelyn, the gods gave Lysa only the one child, and he is all your sister lives for now, poor boy. Small wonder she fled rather than see him handed over to the Lannisters. Your sister is *afraid*, child, and the Lannisters are what she fears most. She ran to the Vale, stealing away from the Red Keep like a thief in the night, and all to snatch her son out of the lion's mouth . . . and now you have brought the lion to her door."

"In chains," Catelyn said. A crevasse yawned on her right, falling away into darkness. She reined up her horse and picked her way along step by careful step.

"Oh?" Her uncle glanced back, to where Tyrion Lannister was making his slow descent behind them. "I see an axe on his saddle, a dirk at his belt, and a sellsword that trails after him like a hungry shadow. Where are the chains, sweet one?"

Catelyn shifted uneasily in her seat. "The dwarf is here, and not by choice. Chains or no, he is my prisoner. Lysa will want him to answer for his crimes no less than I. It was her own lord husband the Lannisters murdered, and her own letter that first warned us against them."

Brynden Blackfish gave her a weary smile. "I hope you are right, child," he sighed, in tones that said she was wrong.

The sun was well to the west by the time the slope began to flatten beneath the hooves of their horses. The road widened and grew straight, and for the first time Catelyn noticed wildflowers and grasses growing. Once they reached the valley floor, the going was faster and they made good time, cantering through verdant greenwoods and sleepy little hamlets, past orchards and golden wheat fields, splashing across a dozen sunlit streams. Her uncle sent a standard-bearer ahead of them, a double banner flying from his staff; the moon-and-falcon of House Arryn on high, and below it his own black fish. Farm wagons and merchants' carts and riders from lesser houses moved aside to let them pass.

Even so, it was full dark before they reached the stout castle that stood at the foot of the Giant's Lance. Torches flickered atop its ramparts, and the horned moon danced upon the dark waters of its moat. The drawbridge was up and the portcullis down, but Catelyn saw lights burning in the gatehouse and spilling from the windows of the square towers beyond.

"The Gates of the Moon," her uncle said as the party drew rein. His standard-bearer rode to the edge of the moat to hail the men in the gatehouse. "Lord Nestor's seat. He should be expecting us. Look up."

Catelyn raised her eyes, up and up and up. At first all she saw was stone and trees, the looming mass of the great mountain shrouded in night, as black as a starless sky. Then she noticed the glow of distant fires well above them; a tower keep, built upon the steep side of the mountain, its lights like orange eyes staring down from above. Above that was another, higher and more distant, and still higher a third, no more than a flickering spark in the sky. And finally, up where the falcons soared, a flash of white in the moonlight. Vertigo washed over her as she stared upward at the pale towers, so far above.

"The Eyrie," she heard Marillion murmur, awed.

The sharp voice of Tyrion Lannister broke in. "The Arryns must not be overfond of company. If you're planning to make us climb that mountain in the dark, I'd rather you kill me here."

"We'll spend the night here and make the ascent on the morrow," Brynden told him.

"I can scarcely wait," the dwarf replied. "How do we get up there? I've no experience at riding goats."

"Mules," Brynden said, smiling.

"There are steps carved into the mountain," Catelyn said. Ned had told her about them when he talked of his youth here with Robert Baratheon and Jon Arryn.

Her uncle nodded. "It is too dark to see them, but the steps are there. Too steep and narrow for horses, but mules can manage them most of the way. The path is guarded by three waycastles, Stone and Snow and Sky. The mules will take us as far up as Sky."

Tyrion Lannister glanced up doubtfully. "And beyond that?"

Brynden smiled. "Beyond that, the path is too steep even for mules. We ascend on foot the rest of the way. Or perchance you'd prefer to ride a basket. The Eyrie clings to the mountain directly above Sky, and in its cellars are six great winches with long iron chains to draw supplies up from below. If you prefer, my lord of Lannister, I can arrange for you to ride up with the bread and beer and apples."

The dwarf gave a bark of laughter. "Would that I were a pumpkin," he said. "Alas, my lord father would no doubt be most chagrined if his son of Lannister went to his fate like a load of turnips. If you ascend on foot, I fear I must do the same. We Lannisters do have a certain pride."

"Pride?" Catelyn snapped. His mocking tone and easy manner made her angry. "Arrogance, some might call it. Arrogance and avarice and lust for power."

"My brother is undoubtedly arrogant," Tyrion Lannister replied. "My father is the soul of avarice, and my sweet sister Cersei lusts for power with every waking breath. I, however, am innocent as a little lamb. Shall I bleat for you?" He grinned.

The drawbridge came creaking down before she could reply, and they heard the sound of oiled chains as the portcullis was drawn up. Men-at-arms carried burning brands out to light their way, and her uncle led them across the moat. Lord Nestor Royce, High Steward of the Vale and Keeper of the Gates of the Moon, was waiting in the yard to greet them, surrounded by his knights. "Lady Stark," he said, bowing. He was a massive, barrel-chested man, and his bow was clumsy.

Catelyn dismounted to stand before him. "Lord Nestor," she said. She knew the man only by reputation; Bronze Yohn's cousin, from a lesser branch of House

Royce, yet still a formidable lord in his own right. "We have had a long and tiring journey. I would beg the hospitality of your roof tonight, if I might."

"My roof is yours, my lady," Lord Nestor returned gruffly, "but your sister the Lady Lysa has sent down word from the Eyrie. She wishes to see you at once. The rest of your party will be housed here and sent up at first light."

Her uncle swung off his horse. "What madness is this?" he said bluntly. Brynden Tully had never been a man to blunt the edge of his words. "A night ascent, with the moon not even full? Even Lysa should know that's an invitation to a broken neck."

"The mules know the way, Ser Brynden." A wiry girl of seventeen or eighteen years stepped up beside Lord Nestor. Her dark hair was cropped short and straight around her head, and she wore riding leathers and a light shirt of silvered ringmail. She bowed to Catelyn, more gracefully than her lord. "I promise you, my lady, no harm will come to you. It would be my honor to take you up. I've made the dark climb a hundred times. Mychel says my father must have been a goat."

She sounded so cocky that Catelyn had to smile. "Do you have a name, child?"

"Mya Stone, if it please you, my lady," the girl said.

It did not please her; it was an effort for Catelyn to keep the smile on her face. *Stone* was a bastard's name in the Vale, as *Snow* was in the north, and *Flowers* in Highgarden; in each of the Seven Kingdoms, custom had fashioned a surname for children born with no names of their own. Catelyn had nothing against this girl, but suddenly she could not help but think of Ned's bastard on the Wall, and the thought made her angry and guilty, both at once. She struggled to find words for a reply.

Lord Nestor filled the silence. "Mya's a clever girl, and if she vows she will bring you safely to the Lady Lysa, I believe her. She has not failed me yet."

"Then I put myself in your hands, Mya Stone," Catelyn said. "Lord Nestor, I charge you to keep a close guard on my prisoner."

"And I charge you to bring the prisoner a cup of wine and a nicely crisped capon, before he dies of hunger," Lannister said. "A girl would be pleasant as well, but I suppose that's too much to ask of you." The sellsword Bronn laughed aloud.

Lord Nestor ignored the banter. "As you say, my lady, so it will be done." Only then did he look at the dwarf. "See our lord of Lannister to a tower cell, and bring him meat and mead."

Catelyn took her leave of her uncle and the others as Tyrion Lannister was led off, then followed the bastard girl through the castle. Two mules were waiting in the upper bailey, saddled and ready. Mya helped her mount one while a guardsman in a sky-blue cloak opened the narrow postern gate. Beyond was dense forest of pine and spruce, and the mountain like a black wall, but the steps were there, chiseled deep into the rock, ascending into the sky. "Some people find it easier if they close their eyes," Mya said as she led the mules through the gate into the dark wood. "When they get frightened or dizzy, sometimes they hold on to the mule too tight. They don't like that."

"I was born a Tully and wed to a Stark," Catelyn said. "I do not frighten easily. Do you plan to light a torch?" The steps were black as pitch.

The girl made a face. "Torches just blind you. On a clear night like this, the moon and the stars are enough. Mychel says I have the eyes of the owl." She mounted and urged her mule up the first step. Catelyn's animal followed of its own accord.

"You mentioned Mychel before," Catelyn said. The mules set the pace, slow but steady. She was perfectly content with that.

"Mychel's my love," Mya explained. "Mychel Redfort. He's squire to Ser Lyn Corbray. We're to wed as soon as he becomes a knight, next year or the year after."

She sounded so like Sansa, so happy and innocent with her dreams. Catelyn smiled, but the smile was tinged with sadness. The Redforts were an old name in the Vale, she knew, with the blood of the First Men in their veins. His love she might be, but no Redfort would ever wed a bastard. His family would arrange a more suitable match for him, to a Corbray or a Waynwood or a Royce, or perhaps a daughter of some greater house outside the Vale. If Mychel Redfort laid with this girl at all, it would be on the wrong side of the sheet.

The ascent was easier than Catelyn had dared hope. The trees pressed close, leaning over the path to make a rustling green roof that shut out even the moon, so it seemed as though they were moving up a long black tunnel. But the mules were surefooted and tireless, and Mya Stone did indeed seem blessed with night-eyes. They plodded upward, winding their way back and forth across the face of the mountain as the steps twisted and turned. A thick layer of fallen needles carpeted the path, so the shoes of their mules made only the softest sound on the rock. The quiet soothed her, and the gentle rocking motion set Catelyn to swaying in her saddle. Before long she was fighting sleep.

Perhaps she did doze for a moment, for suddenly a massive ironbound gate was looming before them. "Stone," Mya announced cheerily, dismounting. Iron spikes were set along the tops of formidable stone walls, and two fat round towers overtopped the keep. The gate swung open at Mya's shout. Inside, the portly knight who commanded the waycastle greeted Mya by name and offered them skewers of charred meat and onions still hot from the spit. Catelyn had not realized how hungry she was. She ate standing in the yard, as stablehands moved their saddles to fresh mules. The hot juices ran down her chin and dripped onto her cloak, but she was too famished to care.

Then it was up onto a new mule and out again into the starlight. The second part of the ascent seemed more treacherous to Catelyn. The trail was steeper, the steps more worn, and here and there littered with pebbles and broken stone. Mya had to dismount a half-dozen times to move fallen rocks from their path. "You don't want your mule to break a leg up here," she said. Catelyn was forced to agree. She could feel the altitude more now. The trees were sparser up here, and the wind blew more vigorously, sharp gusts that tugged at her clothing and pushed her hair into her eyes. From time to time the steps doubled back on themselves, and she could see Stone below them, and the Gates of the Moon farther down, its torches no brighter than candles.

Snow was smaller than Stone, a single fortified tower and a timber keep and stable hidden behind a low wall of unmortared rock. Yet it nestled against the Giant's Lance in such a way as to command the entire stone stair above the lower waycastle. An enemy intent on the Eyrie would have to fight his way from Stone step by step, while rocks and arrows rained down from Snow above. The commander, an anxious young knight with a pockmarked face, offered bread and cheese and the chance to warm themselves before his fire, but Mya declined. "We ought to keep going, my lady," she said. "If it please you." Catelyn nodded.

Again they were given fresh mules. Hers was white. Mya smiled when she saw him. "Whitey's a good one, my lady. Sure of foot, even on ice, but you need to be careful. He'll kick if he doesn't like you."

The white mule seemed to like Catelyn; there was no kicking, thank the gods. There was no ice either, and she was grateful for that as well. "My mother says that hundreds of years ago, this was where the snow began," Mya told her. "It was always white above here, and the ice never melted." She shrugged. "I can't remember ever seeing snow this far down the mountain, but maybe it was that way once, in the olden times."

So young, Catelyn thought, trying to remember if she had ever been like that. The girl had lived half her life in summer, and that was all she knew. *Winter is coming, child,* she wanted to tell her. The words were on her lips; she almost said them. Perhaps she was becoming a Stark at last.

Above Snow, the wind was a living thing, howling around them like a wolf in the waste, then falling off to nothing as if to lure them into complacency. The stars seemed brighter up here, so close that she could almost touch them, and the horned moon was huge in the clear black sky. As they climbed, Catelyn found it was better to look up than down. The steps were cracked and broken from centuries of freeze and thaw and the tread of countless mules, and even in the dark the heights put her heart in her throat. When they came to a high saddle between two spires of rock, Mya dismounted. "It's best to lead the mules over," she said. "The wind can be a little scary here, my lady."

Catelyn climbed stiffly from the shadows and looked at the path ahead; twenty feet long and close to three feet wide, but with a precipitous drop to either side. She could hear the wind shrieking. Mya stepped lightly out, her mule following as calmly as if they were crossing a bailey. It was her turn. Yet no sooner had she taken her first step than fear caught Catelyn in its jaws. She could *feel* the emptiness, the vast black gulfs of air that yawned around her. She stopped, trembling, afraid to move. The wind screamed at her and wrenched at her cloak, trying to pull her over the edge. Catelyn edged her foot backward, the most timid of steps, but the mule was behind her, and she could not retreat. *I am going to die here,* she thought. She could feel cold sweat trickling down her back.

"Lady Stark," Mya called across the gulf. The girl sounded a thousand leagues away. "Are you well?"

Catelyn Tully Stark swallowed what remained of her pride. "I . . . I cannot do this, child," she called out.

"Yes you can," the bastard girl said. "I know you can. Look how wide the path is."

"I don't want to look." The world seemed to be spinning around her, mountain and sky and mules, whirling like a child's top. Catelyn closed her eyes to steady her ragged breathing.

"I'll come back for you," Mya said. "Don't move, my lady."

Moving was about the last thing Catelyn was about to do. She listened to the skirling of the wind and the scuffling sound of leather on stone. Then Mya was there, taking her gently by the arm. "Keep your eyes closed if you like. Let go of the rope now, Whitey will take care of himself. Very good, my lady. I'll lead you over, it's easy, you'll see. Give me a step now. That's it, move your foot, just slide it forward. See. Now another. Easy. You could run across. Another one, go on. Yes." And so, foot by foot, step by step, the bastard girl led Catelyn across, blind and trembling, while the white mule followed placidly behind them.

The waycastle called Sky was no more than a high, crescent-shaped wall of unmortared stone raised against the side of the mountain, but even the topless towers of Valyria could not have looked more beautiful to Catelyn Stark. Here at last the snow crown began; Sky's weathered stones were rimed with frost, and long spears of ice hung from the slopes above.

Dawn was breaking in the east as Mya Stone *hallooed*

for the guards, and the gates opened before them. Inside the walls there was only a series of ramps and a great tumble of boulders and stones of all sizes. No doubt it would be the easiest thing in the world to begin an avalanche from here. A mouth yawned in the rock face in front of them. "The stables and barracks are in there," Mya said. "The last part is inside the mountain. It can be a little dark, but at least you're out of the wind. This is as far as the mules can go. Past here, well, it's a sort of chimney, more like a stone ladder than proper steps, but it's not too bad. Another hour and we'll be there."

Catelyn looked up. Directly overhead, pale in the dawn light, she could see the foundations of the Eyrie. It could not be more than six hundred feet above them. From below it looked like a small white honeycomb. She remembered what her uncle had said of baskets and winches. "The Lannisters may have their pride," she told Mya, "but the Tullys are born with better sense. I have ridden all day and the best part of a night. Tell them to lower a basket. I shall ride with the turnips."

The sun was well above the mountains by the time Catelyn Stark finally reached the Eyrie. A stocky, silver-haired man in a sky-blue cloak and hammered moon-and-falcon breastplate helped her from the basket; Ser Vardis Egen, captain of Jon Arryn's household guard. Beside him stood Maester Colemon, thin and nervous, with too little hair and too much neck. "Lady Stark," Ser Vardis said, "the pleasure is as great as it is unanticipated." Maester Colemon bobbed his head in agreement. "Indeed it is, my lady, indeed it is. I have sent word to your sister. She left orders to be awakened the instant you arrived."

"I hope she had a good night's rest," Catelyn said with a certain bite in her tone that seemed to go unnoticed.

The men escorted her from the winch room up a spiral stair. The Eyrie was a small castle by the standards of the great houses; seven slender white towers bunched as tightly as arrows in a quiver on a shoulder of the great mountain. It had no need of stables nor smithys nor kennels, but Ned said its granary was as large as Winterfell's, and its towers could house five hundred men. Yet it seemed strangely deserted to Catelyn as she passed through it, its pale stone halls echoing and empty.

Lysa was waiting alone in her solar, still clad in her bed

robes. Her long auburn hair tumbled unbound across bare white shoulders and down her back. A maid stood behind her, brushing out the night's tangles, but when Catelyn entered, her sister rose to her feet, smiling. "Cat," she said. "Oh, Cat, how good it is to see you. My sweet sister." She ran across the chamber and wrapped her sister in her arms. "How long it has been," Lysa murmured against her. "Oh, how very very long."

It had been five years, in truth; five cruel years, for Lysa. They had taken their toll. Her sister was two years the younger, yet she looked older now. Shorter than Catelyn, Lysa had grown thick of body, pale and puffy of face. She had the blue eyes of the Tullys, but hers were pale and watery, never still. Her small mouth had turned petulant. As Catelyn held her, she remembered the slender, high-breasted girl who'd waited beside her that day in the sept at Riverrun. How lovely and full of hope she had been. All that remained of her sister's beauty was the great fall of thick auburn hair that cascaded to her waist.

"You look well," Catelyn lied, "but . . . tired."

Her sister broke the embrace. "Tired. Yes. Oh, yes." She seemed to notice the others then; her maid, Maester Colemon, Ser Vardis. "Leave us," she told them. "I wish to speak to my sister alone." She held Catelyn's hand as they withdrew . . .

. . . and dropped it the instant the door closed. Catelyn saw her face change. It was as if the sun had gone behind a cloud. "Have you taken leave of your *senses*?" Lysa snapped at her. "To bring him *here*, without a word of permission, without so much as a warning, to drag us into your quarrels with the Lannisters . . ."

"*My* quarrels?" Catelyn could scarce believe what she was hearing. A great fire burned in the hearth, but there was no trace of warmth in Lysa's voice. "They were your quarrels first, sister. It was you who sent me that cursed letter, you who wrote that the Lannisters had murdered your husband."

"To warn you, so you could stay away from them! I never meant to *fight* them! Gods, Cat, do you know what you've *done*?"

"Mother?" a small voice said. Lysa whirled, her heavy robe swirling around her. Robert Arryn, Lord of the Eyrie, stood in the doorway, clutching a ragged cloth doll and looking at them with large eyes. He was a painfully thin child, small for his age and sickly all his days, and from time to time he trembled. The shaking sickness, the maesters called it. "I heard voices."

Small wonder, Catelyn thought; Lysa had almost been shouting. Still, her sister looked daggers at her. "This is your aunt Catelyn, baby. My sister, Lady Stark. Do you remember?"

The boy glanced at her blankly. "I think so," he said, blinking, though he had been less than a year old the last time Catelyn had seen him.

Lysa seated herself near the fire and said, "Come to Mother, my sweet one." She straightened his bedclothes and fussed with his fine brown hair. "Isn't he beautiful? And strong too, don't you believe the things you hear. Jon knew. *The seed is strong,* he told me. His last words. He kept saying Robert's name, and he grabbed my arm so hard he left marks. *Tell them, the seed is strong.* His seed. He wanted everyone to know what a good strong boy my baby was going to be."

"Lysa," Catelyn said, "if you're right about the Lannisters, all the more reason we must act quickly. We—"

"Not in front of the *baby,*" Lysa said. "He has a delicate temper, don't you, sweet one?"

"The boy is Lord of the Eyrie and Defender of the Vale," Catelyn reminded her, "and these are not times for delicacy. Ned thinks it may come to war."

"*Quiet!*" Lysa snapped at her. "You're scaring the boy." Little Robert took a quick peek over his shoulder at Catelyn and began to tremble. His doll fell to the rushes, and he pressed himself against his mother. "Don't be afraid, my sweet baby," Lysa whispered. "Mother's here, nothing will hurt you." She opened her robe and drew out a pale, heavy breast, tipped with red. The boy grabbed for it eagerly, buried his face against her chest, and began to suck. Lysa stroked his hair.

Catelyn was at a loss for words. *Jon Arryn's son,* she thought incredulously. She remembered her own baby, three-year-old Rickon, half the age of this boy and five times as fierce. Small wonder the lords of the Vale were restive. For the first time she understood why the king had tried to take the child away from his mother to foster with the Lannisters . . .

"We're safe here," Lysa was saying. Whether to her or to the boy, Catelyn was not sure.

"Don't be a fool," Catelyn said, the anger rising in her. "No one is safe. If you think hiding here will make the Lannisters forget you, you are sadly mistaken."

Lysa covered her boy's ear with her hand. "Even if they could bring an army through the mountains and past the Bloody Gate, the Eyrie is impregnable. You saw for yourself. No enemy could ever reach us up here."

Catelyn wanted to slap her. Uncle Brynden had tried to warn her, she realized. "No castle is impregnable."

"This one is," Lysa insisted. "Everyone says so. The only thing is, what am I to do with this Imp you have brought me?"

"Is he a bad man?" the Lord of the Eyrie asked, his mother's breast popping from his mouth, the nipple wet and red.

"A very bad man," Lysa told him as she covered herself, "but Mother won't let him harm my little baby."

"Make him fly," Robert said eagerly.

Lysa stroked her son's hair. "Perhaps we will," she murmured. "Perhaps that is just what we will do."

EDDARD

He found Littlefinger in the brothel's common room, chatting amiably with a tall, elegant woman who wore a feathered gown over skin as black as ink. By the hearth, Heward and a buxom wench were playing at forfeits. From the look of it, he'd lost his belt, his cloak, his mail shirt, and his right boot so far, while the girl had been forced to unbutton her shift to the waist. Jory Cassel stood beside a rain-streaked window with a wry smile on his face, watching Heward turn over tiles and enjoying the view.

Ned paused at the foot of the stair and pulled on his gloves. "It's time we took our leave. My business here is done."

Heward lurched to his feet, hurriedly gathering up his things. "As you will, my lord," Jory said. "I'll help Wyl bring round the horses." He strode to the door.

Littlefinger took his time saying his farewells. He kissed the black woman's hand, whispered some joke that made her laugh aloud, and sauntered over to Ned. "Your business," he said lightly, "or Robert's? They say the Hand dreams the king's dreams, speaks with the king's voice, and rules with the king's sword. Does that also mean you fuck with the king's—"

"Lord Baelish," Ned interrupted, "you presume too much. I am not ungrateful for your help. It might have taken us years to find this brothel without you. That does not mean I intend to endure your mockery. And I am no longer the King's Hand."

"The direwolf must be a prickly beast," said Littlefinger with a sharp twist of his mouth.

A warm rain was pelting down from a starless black sky as they walked to the stables. Ned drew up the hood of his cloak. Jory brought out his horse. Young Wyl came right behind him, leading Littlefinger's mare with one hand while the other fumbled with his belt and the lacings of his trousers. A barefoot whore leaned out of the stable door, giggling at him.

"Will we be going back to the castle now, my lord?" Jory asked. Ned nodded and swung into the saddle. Littlefinger mounted up beside him. Jory and the others followed.

"Chataya runs a choice establishment," Littlefinger said as they rode. "I've half a mind to buy it. Brothels are a much sounder investment than ships, I've found. Whores seldom sink, and when they are boarded by pirates, why, the pirates pay good coin like everyone else." Lord Petyr chuckled at his own wit.

Ned let him prattle on. After a time, he quieted and they rode in silence. The streets of King's Landing were dark and deserted. The rain had driven everyone under their roofs. It beat down on Ned's head, warm as blood and relentless as old guilts. Fat drops of water ran down his face.

"Robert will never keep to one bed," Lyanna had told him at Winterfell, on the night long ago when their father had promised her hand to the young Lord of Storm's End. "I hear he has gotten a child on some girl in the Vale." Ned had held the babe in his arms; he could scarcely deny her, nor would he lie to his sister, but he had assured her that what Robert did before their betrothal was of no matter, that he was a good man and true who would love her with all his heart. Lyanna had only smiled. "Love is sweet, dearest Ned, but it cannot change a man's nature."

The girl had been so young Ned had not dared to ask

her age. No doubt she'd been a virgin; the better brothels could always find a virgin, if the purse was fat enough. She had light red hair and a powdering of freckles across the bridge of her nose, and when she slipped free a breast to give her nipple to the babe, he saw that her bosom was freckled as well. "I named her Barra," she said as the child nursed. "She looks so like him, does she not, milord? She has his nose, and his hair . . ."

"She does." Eddard Stark had touched the baby's fine, dark hair. It flowed through his fingers like black silk. Robert's firstborn had had the same fine hair, he seemed to recall.

"Tell him that when you see him, milord, as it . . . as it please you. Tell him how beautiful she is."

"I will," Ned had promised her. That was his curse. Robert would swear undying love and forget them before evenfall, but Ned Stark kept his vows. He thought of the promises he'd made Lyanna as she lay dying, and the price he'd paid to keep them.

"And tell him I've not been with no one else. I swear it, milord, by the old gods and new. Chataya said I could have half a year, for the baby, and for hoping he'd come back. So you'll tell him I'm waiting, won't you? I don't want no jewels or nothing, just him. He was always good to me, truly."

Good to you, Ned thought hollowly. "I will tell him, child, and I promise you, Barra shall not go wanting."

She had smiled then, a smile so tremulous and sweet that it cut the heart out of him. Riding through the rainy night, Ned saw Jon Snow's face in front of him, so like a younger version of his own. If the gods frowned so on bastards, he thought dully, why did they fill men with such lusts? "Lord Baelish, what do you know of Robert's bastards?"

"Well, he has more than you, for a start."

"How many?"

Littlefinger shrugged. Rivulets of moisture twisted down the back of his cloak. "Does it matter? If you bed enough women, some will give you presents, and His Grace has never been shy on that count. I know he's acknowledged that boy at Storm's End, the one he fathered the night Lord Stannis wed. He could hardly do otherwise. The mother was a Florent, niece to the Lady Selyse, one of her bedmaids. Renly says that Robert carried the girl upstairs during the feast, and broke in the wedding bed while Stannis and his bride were still dancing. Lord Stannis seemed to think that was a blot on the honor of his wife's House, so when the boy was born, he shipped him off to Renly." He gave Ned a sideways glance. "I've also heard whispers that Robert got a pair of twins on a serving wench at Casterly Rock, three years ago when he went west for Lord Tywin's tourney. Cersei had the babes killed, and sold the mother to a passing slaver. Too much an affront to Lannister pride, that close to home."

Ned Stark grimaced. Ugly tales like that were told of every great lord in the realm. He could believe it of Cersei Lannister readily enough . . . but would the king stand by and let it happen? The Robert he had known would not have, but the Robert he had known had never been so practiced at shutting his eyes to things he did not wish to see. "Why would Jon Arryn take a sudden interest in the king's baseborn children?"

The short man gave a sodden shrug. "He was the King's Hand. Doubtless Robert asked him to see that they were provided for."

Ned was soaked through to the bone, and his soul had grown cold. "It had to be more than that, or why kill him?"

Littlefinger shook the rain from his hair and laughed. "Now I see. Lord Arryn learned that His Grace had filled the bellies of some whores and fishwives, and for that he had to be silenced. Small wonder. Allow a man like that to live, and next he's like to blurt out that the sun rises in the east."

There was no answer Ned Stark could give to that but a frown. For the first time in years, he found himself remembering Rhaegar Targaryen. He wondered if Rhaegar had frequented brothels; somehow he thought not.

The rain was falling harder now, stinging the eyes and drumming against the ground. Rivers of black water were running down the hill when Jory called out, "*My lord,*" his voice hoarse with alarm. And in an instant, the street was full of soldiers.

Ned glimpsed ringmail over leather, gauntlets and greaves, steel helms with golden lions on the crests. Their cloaks clung to their backs, sodden with rain. He had no time to count, but there were ten at least, a line of them, on foot, blocking the street, with longswords and iron-tipped spears. *"Behind!"* he heard Wyl cry, and when he turned his horse, there were more in back of them, cutting off their retreat. Jory's sword came singing from its scabbard. "Make way or die!"

"The wolves are howling," their leader said. Ned could see rain running down his face. "Such a small pack, though."

Littlefinger walked his horse forward, step by careful step. "What is the meaning of this? This is the Hand of the King."

"He *was* the Hand of the King." The mud muffled the hooves of the blood bay stallion. The line parted before him. On a golden breastplate, the lion of Lannister roared its defiance. "Now, if truth be told, I'm not sure what he is."

"Lannister, this is madness," Littlefinger said. "Let us pass. We are expected back at the castle. What do you think you're doing?"

"He knows what he's doing," Ned said calmly.

Jaime Lannister smiled. "Quite true. I'm looking for my brother. You remember my brother, don't you, Lord Stark? He was with us at Winterfell. Fair-haired, mismatched eyes, sharp of tongue. A short man."

"I remember him well," Ned replied.

"It would seem he has met some trouble on the road. My lord father is quite vexed. You would not perchance have any notion of who might have wished my brother ill, would you?"

"Your brother has been taken at my command, to answer for his crimes," Ned Stark said.

Littlefinger groaned in dismay. "My lords—"

Ser Jaime ripped his longsword from its sheath and urged his stallion forward. "Show me your steel, Lord Eddard. I'll butcher you like Aerys if I must, but I'd sooner you died with a blade in your hand." He gave Littlefinger a cool, contemptuous glance. "Lord Baelish, I'd leave here in some haste if I did not care to get bloodstains on my costly clothing."

Littlefinger did not need to be urged. "I will bring the City Watch," he promised Ned. The Lannister line parted to let him through, and closed behind him. Littlefinger put his heels to his mare and vanished around a corner.

Ned's men had drawn their swords, but they were three against twenty. Eyes watched from nearby windows and doors, but no one was about to intervene. His party was mounted, the Lannisters on foot save for Jaime himself. A charge might win them free, but it seemed to Eddard Stark that they had a surer, safer tactic. "Kill me," he warned the Kingslayer, "and Catelyn will most certainly slay Tyrion."

Jaime Lannister poked at Ned's chest with the gilded sword that had sipped the blood of the last of the Dragonkings. "Would she? The noble Catelyn Tully of Riverrun murder a hostage? I think . . . not." He sighed. "But I am not willing to chance my brother's life on a woman's honor." Jaime slid the golden sword into its sheath. "So I suppose I'll let you run back to Robert to tell him how I frightened you. I wonder if he'll care." Jaime pushed his wet hair back with his fingers and wheeled his horse around. When he was beyond the line of swordsmen, he glanced back at his captain. "Tregar, see that no harm comes to Lord Stark."

"As you say, m'lord."

"Still . . . we wouldn't want him to leave here *entirely* unchastened, so"—through the night and the rain, he glimpsed the white of Jaime's smile—"kill his men."

"No!" Ned Stark screamed, clawing for his sword. Jaime was already cantering off down the street as he heard Wyl shout. Men closed from both sides. Ned rode one down, cutting at phantoms in red cloaks who gave way before him. Jory Cassel put his heels into his mount and charged. A steel-shod hoof caught a Lannister guardsman in the face with a sickening *crunch*. A second man reeled away and for an instant Jory was free. Wyl cursed as they pulled him off his dying horse, swords slashing in the rain. Ned galloped to him, bringing his longsword down on Tregar's helm. The jolt of impact made him grit his teeth. Tregar stumbled to his knees, his lion crest sheared in half, blood running down his face. Heward was hacking at the hands that had seized his bridle when a spear caught him in the belly. Suddenly Jory was back among them, a red rain flying from his sword. *"No!"* Ned shouted. "Jory, *away!"* Ned's horse slipped under him

and came crashing down in the mud. There was a moment of blinding pain and the taste of blood in his mouth.

He saw them cut the legs from Jory's mount and drag him to the earth, swords rising and falling as they closed in around him. When Ned's horse lurched back to its feet, he tried to rise, only to fall again, choking on his scream. He could see the splintered bone poking through his calf. It was the last thing he saw for a time. The rain came down and down and down.

When he opened his eyes again, Lord Eddard Stark was alone with his dead. His horse moved closer, caught the rank scent of blood, and galloped away. Ned began to drag himself through the mud, gritting his teeth at the agony in his leg. It seemed to take years. Faces watched from candlelit windows, and people began to emerge from alleys and doors, but no one moved to help.

Littlefinger and the City Watch found him there in the street, cradling Jory Cassel's body in his arms.

Somewhere the gold cloaks found a litter, but the trip back to the castle was a blur of agony, and Ned lost consciousness more than once. He remembered seeing the Red Keep looming ahead of him in the first grey light of dawn. The rain had darkened the pale pink stone of the massive walls to the color of blood.

Then Grand Maester Pycelle was looming over him, holding a cup, whispering, "Drink, my lord. Here. The milk of the poppy, for your pain." He remembered swallowing, and Pycelle was telling someone to heat the wine to boiling and fetch him clean silk, and that was the last he knew.

DAENERYS

T he Horse Gate of Vaes Dothrak was made of two
gigantic bronze stallions, rearing, their hooves
meeting a hundred feet above the roadway to form
a pointed arch.

Dany could not have said why the city needed a gate
when it had no walls . . . and no *buildings* that she
could see. Yet there it stood, immense and beautiful, the
great horses framing the distant purple mountain beyond.
The bronze stallions threw long shadows across the waving grasses as Khal Drogo led the *khalasar* under their
hooves and down the godsway, his bloodriders beside
him.

Dany followed on her silver, escorted by Ser Jorah
Mormont and her brother Viserys, mounted once more.
After the day in the grass when she had left him to walk
back to the *khalasar*, the Dothraki had laughingly called
him *Khal Rhae Mhar*, the Sorefoot King. Khal Drogo had
offered him a place in a cart the next day, and Viserys had
accepted. In his stubborn ignorance, he had not even
known he was being mocked; the carts were for eunuchs,
cripples, women giving birth, the very young and the very
old. That won him yet another name: *Khal Rhaggat*, the

Cart King. Her brother had thought it was the *khal*'s way of apologizing for the wrong Dany had done him. She had begged Ser Jorah not to tell him the truth, lest he be shamed. The knight had replied that the king could well do with a bit of shame . . . yet he had done as she bid. It had taken much pleading, and all the pillow tricks Doreah had taught her, before Dany had been able to make Drogo relent and allow Viserys to rejoin them at the head of the column.

"Where is the *city*?" she asked as they passed beneath the bronze arch. There were no buildings to be seen, no people, only the grass and the road, lined with ancient monuments from all the lands the Dothraki had sacked over the centuries.

"Ahead," Ser Jorah answered. "Under the mountain."

Beyond the horse gate, plundered gods and stolen heroes loomed to either side of them. The forgotten deities of dead cities brandished their broken thunderbolts at the sky as Dany rode her silver past their feet. Stone kings looked down on her from their thrones, their faces chipped and stained, even their names lost in the mists of time. Lithe young maidens danced on marble plinths, draped only in flowers, or poured air from shattered jars. Monsters stood in the grass beside the road; black iron dragons with jewels for eyes, roaring griffins, manticores with their barbed tails poised to strike, and other beasts she could not name. Some of the statues were so lovely they took her breath away, others so misshapen and terrible that Dany could scarcely bear to look at them. Those, Ser Jorah said, had likely come from the Shadow Lands beyond Asshai.

"So many," she said as her silver stepped slowly onward, "and from so many lands."

Viserys was less impressed. "The trash of dead cities," he sneered. He was careful to speak in the Common Tongue, which few Dothraki could understand, yet even so Dany found herself glancing back at the men of her *khas*, to make certain he had not been overheard. He went on blithely. "All these savages know how to do is steal the things better men have built . . . and kill." He laughed. "They *do* know how to kill. Otherwise I'd have no use for them at all."

"They are my people now," Dany said. "You should not call them savages, brother."

"The dragon speaks as he likes," Viserys said . . . in the Common Tongue. He glanced over his shoulder at Aggo and Rakharo, riding behind them, and favored them with a mocking smile. "See, the savages lack the wit to understand the speech of civilized men." A moss-eaten stone monolith loomed over the road, fifty feet tall. Viserys gazed at it with boredom in his eyes. "How long must we linger amidst these ruins before Drogo gives me my army? I grow tired of waiting."

"The princess must be presented to the *dosh khaleen* . . ."

"The crones, yes," her brother interrupted, "and there's to be some mummer's show of a prophecy for the whelp in her belly, you told me. What is that to me? I'm tired of eating horsemeat and I'm sick of the stink of these savages." He sniffed at the wide, floppy sleeve of his tunic, where it was his custom to keep a sachet. It could not have helped much. The tunic was filthy. All the silk and heavy wools that Viserys had worn out of Pentos were stained by hard travel and rotted from sweat.

Ser Jorah Mormont said, "The Western Market will have food more to your taste, Your Grace. The traders from the Free Cities come there to sell their wares. The *khal* will honor his promise in his own time."

"He had better," Viserys said grimly. "I was promised a crown, and I mean to have it. The dragon is not mocked." Spying an obscene likeness of a woman with six breasts and a ferret's head, he rode off to inspect it more closely.

Dany was relieved, yet no less anxious. "I pray that my sun-and-stars will not keep him waiting too long," she told Ser Jorah when her brother was out of earshot.

The knight looked after Viserys doubtfully. "Your brother should have bided his time in Pentos. There is no place for him in a *khalasar*. Illyrio tried to warn him."

"He will go as soon as he has his ten thousand. My lord husband promised a golden crown."

Ser Jorah grunted. "Yes, *Khaleesi*, but . . . the Dothraki look on these things differently than we do in the west. I have told him as much, as Illyrio told him, but your brother does not listen. The horselords are no traders. Viserys thinks he sold you, and now he wants his price. Yet Khal Drogo would say he had you as a gift. He will give Viserys a gift in return, yes . . . in his own time. You do not *demand* a gift, not of a *khal*. You do not demand anything of a *khal*."

"It is not right to make him wait." Dany did not know why she was defending her brother, yet she was. "Viserys says he could sweep the Seven Kingdoms with ten thousand Dothraki screamers."

Ser Jorah snorted. "Viserys could not sweep a stable with ten thousand brooms."

Dany could not pretend to surprise at the disdain in his tone. "What . . . what if it were not Viserys?" she asked. "If it were someone else who led them? Someone stronger? Could the Dothraki truly conquer the Seven Kingdoms?"

Ser Jorah's face grew thoughtful as their horses trod together down the godsway. "When I first went into exile, I looked at the Dothraki and saw half-naked barbarians, as wild as their horses. If you had asked me then, Princess, I should have told you that a thousand good knights would have no trouble putting to flight a hundred times as many Dothraki."

"But if I asked you now?"

"Now," the knight said, "I am less certain. They are better riders than any knight, utterly fearless, and their bows outrange ours. In the Seven Kingdoms, most archers fight on foot, from behind a shieldwall or a barricade of sharpened stakes. The Dothraki fire from horseback, charging or retreating, it makes no matter, they are full as deadly . . . and there are so *many* of them, my lady. Your lord husband alone counts forty thousand mounted warriors in his *khalasar*."

"Is that truly so many?"

"Your brother Rhaegar brought as many men to the Trident," Ser Jorah admitted, "but of that number, no more than a tenth were knights. The rest were archers, freeriders, and foot soldiers armed with spears and pikes. When Rhaegar fell, many threw down their weapons and fled the field. How long do you imagine such a rabble would stand against the charge of forty thousand screamers howling for blood? How well would boiled leather jerkins and mailed shirts protect them when the arrows fall like rain?"

"Not long," she said, "not well."

He nodded. "Mind you, Princess, if the lords of the Seven Kingdoms have the wit the gods gave a goose, it will never come to that. The riders have no taste for siegecraft. I doubt they could take even the weakest castle in the Seven Kingdoms, but if Robert Baratheon were fool enough to give them battle . . ."

"Is he?" Dany asked. "A fool, I mean?"

Ser Jorah considered that for a moment. "Robert should have been born Dothraki," he said at last. "Your *khal* would tell you that only a coward hides behind stone walls instead of facing his enemy with a blade in hand. The Usurper would agree. He is a strong man, brave . . . and rash enough to meet a Dothraki horde in the open field. But the men around him, well, their pipers play a different tune. His brother Stannis, Lord Tywin Lannister, Eddard Stark . . ." He spat.

"You hate this Lord Stark," Dany said.

"He took from me all I loved, for the sake of a few lice-ridden poachers and his precious honor," Ser Jorah said bitterly. From his tone, she could tell the loss still pained him. He changed the subject quickly. "There," he announced, pointing. "Vaes Dothrak. The city of the horse-lords."

Khal Drogo and his bloodriders led them through the great bazaar of the Western Market, down the broad ways beyond. Dany followed close on her silver, staring at the strangeness about her. Vaes Dothrak was at once the largest city and the smallest that she had ever known. She thought it must be ten times as large as Pentos, a vastness without walls or limits, its broad windswept streets paved in grass and mud and carpeted with wildflowers. In the Free Cities of the west, towers and manses and hovels and bridges and shops and halls all crowded in on one another, but Vaes Dothrak sprawled languorously, baking in the warm sun, ancient, arrogant, and empty.

Even the buildings were so queer to her eyes. She saw carved stone pavilions, manses of woven grass as large as castles, rickety wooden towers, stepped pyramids faced with marble, log halls open to the sky. In place of walls, some palaces were surrounded by thorny hedges. "None of them are alike," she said.

"Your brother had part of the truth," Ser Jorah admitted. "The Dothraki do not build. A thousand years ago, to make a house, they would dig a hole in the earth and cover it with a woven grass roof. The buildings you see were made by slaves brought here from lands they've plundered, and they built each after the fashion of their own peoples."

Most of the halls, even the largest, seemed deserted. "Where are the people who live here?" Dany asked. The bazaar had been full of running children and men shouting, but elsewhere she had seen only a few eunuchs going about their business.

"Only the crones of the *dosh khaleen* dwell permanently in the sacred city, them and their slaves and servants," Ser Jorah replied, "yet Vaes Dothrak is large enough to house every man of every *khalasar*, should all the *khals* return to the Mother at once. The crones have prophesied that one day that will come to pass, and so Vaes Dothrak must be ready to embrace all its children."

Khal Drogo finally called a halt near the Eastern Market where the caravans from Yi Ti and Asshai and the Shadow Lands came to trade, with the Mother of Mountains looming overhead. Dany smiled as she recalled Magister Illyrio's slave girl and her talk of a palace with two hundred rooms and doors of solid silver. The "palace" was a cavernous wooden feasting hall, its rough-hewn timbered walls rising forty feet, its roof sewn silk, a vast billowing tent that could be raised to keep out the rare rains, or lowered to admit the endless sky. Around the hall were broad grassy horse yards fenced with high hedges, firepits, and hundreds of round earthen houses that bulged from the ground like miniature hills, covered with grass.

A small army of slaves had gone ahead to prepare for Khal Drogo's arrival. As each rider swung down from his saddle, he unbelted his *arakh* and handed it to a waiting slave, and any other weapons he carried as well. Even Khal Drogo himself was not exempt. Ser Jorah had explained that it was forbidden to carry a blade in Vaes Dothrak, or to shed a free man's blood. Even warring *khalasars* put aside their feuds and shared meat and mead together when they were in sight of the Mother of Mountains. In this place, the crones of the *dosh khaleen* had decreed, all Dothraki were one blood, one *khalasar*, one herd.

Cohollo came to Dany as Irri and Jhiqui were helping her down off her silver. He was the oldest of Drogo's three bloodriders, a squat bald man with a crooked nose and a mouth full of broken teeth, shattered by a mace twenty years before when he saved the young *khalakka* from sellswords who hoped to sell him to his father's enemies. His life had been bound to Drogo's the day her lord husband was born.

Every *khal* had his bloodriders. At first Dany had thought of them as a kind of Dothraki Kingsguard, sworn to protect their lord, but it went further than that. Jhiqui had taught her that a bloodrider was more than a guard; they were the *khal*'s brothers, his shadows, his fiercest friends. "Blood of my blood," Drogo called them, and so it was; they shared a single life. The ancient traditions of the horselords demanded that when the *khal* died, his bloodriders died with him, to ride at his side in the night lands. If the *khal* died at the hands of some enemy, they lived only long enough to avenge him, and then followed him joyfully into the grave. In some *khalasars*, Jhiqui said, the bloodriders shared the *khal*'s wine, his tent, and even his wives, though never his horses. A man's mount was his own.

Daenerys was glad that Khal Drogo did not hold to those ancient ways. She should not have liked being shared. And while old Cohollo treated her kindly enough, the others frightened her; Haggo, huge and silent, often glowered as if he had forgotten who she was, and Qotho had cruel eyes and quick hands that liked to hurt. He left bruises on Doreah's soft white skin whenever he touched her, and sometimes made Irri sob in the night. Even his horses seemed to fear him.

Yet they were bound to Drogo for life and death, so Daenerys had no choice but to accept them. And sometimes she found herself wishing her father had been protected by such men. In the songs, the white knights of the Kingsguard were ever noble, valiant, and true, and yet King Aerys had been murdered by one of them, the handsome boy they now called the Kingslayer, and a second, Ser Barristan the Bold, had gone over to the Usurper. She wondered if all men were as false in the Seven Kingdoms.

When her son sat the Iron Throne, she would see that he had bloodriders of his own to protect him against treachery in his Kingsguard.

"*Khaleesi,*" Cohollo said to her, in Dothraki. "Drogo, who is blood of my blood, commands me to tell you that he must ascend the Mother of Mountains this night, to sacrifice to the gods for his safe return."

Only men were allowed to set foot on the Mother, Dany knew. The *khal*'s bloodriders would go with him, and return at dawn. "Tell my sun-and-stars that I dream of him, and wait anxious for his return," she replied, thankful. Dany tired more easily as the child grew within her; in truth, a night of rest would be most welcome. Her pregnancy only seemed to have inflamed Drogo's desire for her, and of late his embraces left her exhausted.

Doreah led her to the hollow hill that had been prepared for her and her *khal*. It was cool and dim within, like a tent made of earth. "Jhiqui, a bath, please," she commanded, to wash the dust of travel from her skin and soak her weary bones. It was pleasant to know that they would linger here for a while, that she would not need to climb back on her silver on the morrow.

The water was scalding hot, as she liked it. "I will give my brother his gifts tonight," she decided as Jhiqui was washing her hair. "He should look a king in the sacred city. Doreah, run and find him and invite him to sup with me." Viserys was nicer to the Lysene girl than to her Dothraki handmaids, perhaps because Magister Illyrio had let him bed her back in Pentos. "Irri, go to the bazaar and buy fruit and meat. Anything but horseflesh."

"Horse is best," Irri said. "Horse makes a man strong."

"Viserys hates horsemeat."

"As you say, *Khaleesi.*"

She brought back a haunch of goat and a basket of fruits and vegetables. Jhiqui roasted the meat with sweetgrass and firepods, basting it with honey as it cooked, and there were melons and pomegranates and plums and some queer eastern fruit Dany did not know. While her handmaids prepared the meal, Dany laid out the clothing she'd had made to her brother's measure: a tunic and leggings of crisp white linen, leather sandals that laced up to the knee, a bronze medallion belt, a leather vest painted with fire-breathing dragons. The Dothraki would respect him more if he looked less a beggar, she hoped, and perhaps he would forgive her for shaming him that day in the grass. He was still her king, after all, and her brother. They were both blood of the dragon.

She was arranging the last of his gifts—a sandsilk cloak, green as grass, with a pale grey border that would bring out the silver in his hair—when Viserys arrived, dragging Doreah by the arm. Her eye was red where he'd hit her. "How *dare* you send this whore to give me commands," he said. He shoved the handmaid roughly to the carpet.

The anger took Dany utterly by surprise. "I only wanted . . . Doreah, what did you say?"

"*Khaleesi*, pardons, forgive me. I went to him, as you bid, and told him you commanded him to join you for supper."

"No one commands the dragon," Viserys snarled. "*I am your king!* I should have sent you back her head!"

The Lysene girl quailed, but Dany calmed her with a touch. "Don't be afraid, he won't hurt you. Sweet brother, please, forgive her, the girl misspoke herself, I told her to *ask* you to sup with me, if it pleases Your Grace." She took him by the hand and drew him across the room. "Look. These are for you."

Viserys frowned suspiciously. "What is all this?"

"New raiment. I had it made for you." Dany smiled shyly.

He looked at her and sneered. "Dothraki rags. Do you presume to dress me now?"

"Please . . . you'll be cooler and more comfortable, and I thought . . . maybe if you dressed like them, the Dothraki . . ." Dany did not know how to say it without waking his dragon.

"Next you'll want to braid my hair."

"I'd never . . ." Why was he always so cruel? She had only wanted to help. "You have no right to a braid, you have won no victories yet."

It was the wrong thing to say. Fury shone from his lilac eyes, yet he dared not strike her, not with her handmaids watching and the warriors of her *khas* outside. Viserys picked up the cloak and sniffed at it. "This stinks of manure. Perhaps I shall use it as a horse blanket."

"I had Doreah sew it specially for you," she told him, wounded. "These are garments fit for a *khal*."

"I am the Lord of the Seven Kingdoms, not some grass-stained savage with bells in his hair," Viserys spat back at her. He grabbed her arm. "You forget yourself, slut. Do you think that big belly will protect you if you wake the dragon?"

His fingers dug into her arm painfully and for an instant Dany felt like a child again, quailing in the face of his rage. She reached out with her other hand and grabbed the first thing she touched, the belt she'd hoped to give him, a heavy chain of ornate bronze medallions. She swung it with all her strength.

It caught him full in the face. Viserys let go of her. Blood ran down his cheek where the edge of one of the medallions had sliced it open. "You are the one who forgets himself," Dany said to him. "Didn't you learn *anything* that day in the grass? Leave me now, before I summon my *khas* to drag you out. And pray that Khal Drogo does not hear of this, or he will cut open your belly and feed you your own entrails."

Viserys scrambled back to his feet. "When I come into my kingdom, you will rue this day, slut." He walked off, holding his torn face, leaving her gifts behind him.

Drops of his blood had spattered the beautiful sandsilk cloak. Dany clutched the soft cloth to her cheek and sat cross-legged on her sleeping mats.

"Your supper is ready, *Khaleesi*," Jhiqui announced.

"I'm not hungry," Dany said sadly. She was suddenly very tired. "Share the food among yourselves, and send some to Ser Jorah, if you would." After a moment she added, "Please, bring me one of the dragon's eggs."

Irri fetched the egg with the deep green shell, bronze flecks shining amid its scales as she turned it in her small hands. Dany curled up on her side, pulling the sandsilk cloak across her and cradling the egg in the hollow between her swollen belly and small, tender breasts. She liked to hold them. They were so beautiful, and sometimes just being close to them made her feel stronger, braver, as if somehow she were drawing strength from the stone dragons locked inside.

She was lying there, holding the egg, when she felt the

child move within her . . . as if he were reaching out, brother to brother, blood to blood. "*You* are the dragon," Dany whispered to him, "the *true* dragon. I know it. I know it." And she smiled, and went to sleep dreaming of home.

BRAN

A light snow was falling. Bran could feel the flakes on his face, melting as they touched his skin like the gentlest of rains. He sat straight atop his horse, watching as the iron portcullis was winched upward. Try as he might to keep calm, his heart was fluttering in his chest.

"Are you ready?" Robb asked.

Bran nodded, trying not to let his fear show. He had not been outside Winterfell since his fall, but he was determined to ride out as proud as any knight.

"Let's ride, then." Robb put his heels into his big grey-and-white gelding, and the horse walked under the portcullis.

"Go," Bran whispered to his own horse. He touched her neck lightly, and the small chestnut filly started forward. Bran had named her Dancer. She was two years old, and Joseth said she was smarter than any horse had a right to be. They had trained her special, to respond to rein and voice and touch. Up to now, Bran had only ridden her around the yard. At first Joseth or Hodor would lead her, while Bran sat strapped to her back in the oversize saddle the Imp had drawn up for him, but for the past fortnight he had been riding her on his own, trotting her round and round, and growing bolder with every circuit.

They passed beneath the gatehouse, over the drawbridge, through the outer walls. Summer and Grey Wind came loping beside them, sniffing at the wind. Close behind came Theon Greyjoy, with his longbow and a quiver of broadheads; he had a mind to take a deer, he had told them. He was followed by four guardsmen in mailed shirts and coifs, and Joseth, a stick-thin stableman whom Robb had named master of horse while Hullen was away. Maester Luwin brought up the rear, riding on a donkey. Bran would have liked it better if he and Robb had gone off alone, just the two of them, but Hal Mollen would not hear of it, and Maester Luwin backed him. If Bran fell off his horse or injured himself, the maester was determined to be with him.

Beyond the castle lay the market square, its wooden stalls deserted now. They rode down the muddy streets of the village, past rows of small neat houses of log and undressed stone. Less than one in five were occupied, thin tendrils of woodsmoke curling up from their chimneys. The rest would fill up one by one as it grew colder. When the snow fell and the ice winds howled down out of the north, Old Nan said, farmers left their frozen fields and distant holdfasts, loaded up their wagons, and then the winter town came alive. Bran had never seen it happen, but Maester Luwin said the day was looming closer. The end of the long summer was near at hand. *Winter is coming.*

A few villagers eyed the direwolves anxiously as the riders went past, and one man dropped the wood he was carrying as he shrank away in fear, but most of the townfolk had grown used to the sight. They bent the knee when they saw the boys, and Robb greeted each of them with a lordly nod.

With his legs unable to grip, the swaying motion of the horse made Bran feel unsteady at first, but the huge saddle with its thick horn and high back cradled him comfortingly, and the straps around his chest and thighs would not allow him to fall. After a time the rhythm began to feel almost natural. His anxiety faded, and a tremulous smile crept across his face.

Two serving wenches stood beneath the sign of the

Smoking Log, the local alehouse. When Theon Greyjoy called out to them, the younger girl turned red and covered her face. Theon spurred his mount to move up beside Robb. "Sweet Kyra," he said with a laugh. "She squirms like a weasel in bed, but say a word to her on the street, and she blushes pink as a maid. Did I ever tell you about the night that she and Bessa—"

"Not where my brother can hear, Theon," Robb warned him with a glance at Bran.

Bran looked away and pretended not to have heard, but he could feel Greyjoy's eyes on him. No doubt he was smiling. He smiled a lot, as if the world were a secret joke that only he was clever enough to understand. Robb seemed to admire Theon and enjoy his company, but Bran had never warmed to his father's ward.

Robb rode closer. "You are doing well, Bran."

"I want to go faster," Bran replied.

Robb smiled. "As you will." He sent his gelding into a trot. The wolves raced after him. Bran snapped the reins sharply, and Dancer picked up her pace. He heard a shout from Theon Greyjoy, and the hoofbeats of the other horses behind him.

Bran's cloak billowed out, rippling in the wind, and the snow seemed to rush at his face. Robb was well ahead, glancing back over his shoulder from time to time to make sure Bran and the others were following. He snapped the reins again. Smooth as silk, Dancer slid into a gallop. The distance closed. By the time he caught Robb on the edge of the wolfswood, two miles beyond the winter town, they had left the others well behind. "I can *ride!*" Bran shouted, grinning. It felt almost as good as flying.

"I'd race you, but I fear you'd win." Robb's tone was light and joking, yet Bran could tell that something was troubling his brother underneath the smile.

"I don't want to race." Bran looked around for the direwolves. Both had vanished into the wood. "Did you hear Summer howling last night?"

"Grey Wind was restless too," Robb said. His auburn hair had grown shaggy and unkempt, and a reddish stubble covered his jaw, making him look older than his fifteen years. "Sometimes I think they know things . . .

sense things . . ." Robb sighed. "I never know how much to tell you, Bran. I wish you were older."

"I'm eight now!" Bran said. "Eight isn't so much younger than fifteen, and I'm the heir to Winterfell, after you."

"So you are." Robb sounded sad, and even a little scared. "Bran, I need to tell you something. There was a bird last night. From King's Landing. Maester Luwin woke me."

Bran felt a sudden dread. *Dark wings, dark words,* Old Nan always said, and of late the messenger ravens had been proving the truth of the proverb. When Robb wrote to the Lord Commander of the Night's Watch, the bird that came back brought word that Uncle Benjen was still missing. Then a message had arrived from the Eyrie, from Mother, but that had not been good news either. She did not say when she meant to return, only that she had taken the Imp as prisoner. Bran had sort of liked the little man, yet the name *Lannister* sent cold fingers creeping up his spine. There was something about the Lannisters, something he ought to remember, but when he tried to think what, he felt dizzy and his stomach clenched hard as a stone. Robb spent most of that day locked behind closed doors with Maester Luwin, Theon Greyjoy, and Hallis Mollen. Afterward, riders were sent out on fast horses, carrying Robb's commands throughout the north. Bran heard talk of Moat Cailin, the ancient stronghold the First Men had built at the top of the Neck. No one ever told him what was happening, yet he knew it was not good.

And now another raven, another message. Bran clung to hope. "Was the bird from Mother? Is she coming home?"

"The message was from Alyn in King's Landing. Jory Cassel is dead. And Wyl and Heward as well. Murdered by the Kingslayer." Robb lifted his face to the snow, and the flakes melted on his cheeks. "May the gods give them rest."

Bran did not know what to say. He felt as if he'd been punched. Jory had been captain of the household guard at Winterfell since before Bran was born. "They killed Jory?" He remembered all the times Jory had chased him over the roofs. He could picture him striding across the yard in mail and plate, or sitting at his accustomed place on the bench in the Great Hall, joking as he ate. "Why would anyone kill Jory?"

Robb shook his head numbly, the pain plain in his eyes. "I don't know, and . . . Bran, that's not the worst of it. Father was caught beneath a falling horse in the fight. Alyn says his leg was shattered, and . . . Maester Pycelle has given him the milk of the poppy, but they aren't sure when . . . when he . . ." The sound of hoofbeats made him glance down the road, to where Theon and the others were coming up. "When he will wake," Robb finished. He laid his hand on the pommel of his sword then, and went on in the solemn voice of Robb the Lord. "Bran, I promise you, whatever might happen, I will not let this be forgotten."

Something in his tone made Bran even more fearful. "What will you do?" he asked as Theon Greyjoy reined in beside them.

"Theon thinks I should call the banners," Robb said.

"Blood for blood." For once Greyjoy did not smile. His lean, dark face had a hungry look to it, and black hair fell down across his eyes.

"Only the lord can call the banners," Bran said as the snow drifted down around them.

"If your father dies," Theon said, "Robb will be Lord of Winterfell."

"He *won't* die!" Bran screamed at him.

Robb took his hand. "He won't die, not Father," he said calmly. "Still . . . the honor of the north is in my hands now. When our lord father took his leave of us, he told me to be strong for you and for Rickon. I'm almost a man grown, Bran."

Bran shivered. "I wish Mother was back," he said miserably. He looked around for Maester Luwin; his donkey was visible in the far distance, trotting over a rise. "Does Maester Luwin say to call the banners too?"

"The maester is timid as an old woman," said Theon.

"Father always listened to his counsel," Bran reminded his brother. "Mother too."

"I listen to him," Robb insisted. "I listen to everyone."

The joy Bran had felt at the ride was gone, melted away like the snowflakes on his face. Not so long ago, the thought of Robb calling the banners and riding off to war would have filled him with excitement, but now he felt only dread. "Can we go back now?" he asked. "I'm cold."

Robb glanced around. "We need to find the wolves. Can you stand to go a bit longer?"

"I can go as long as you can." Maester Luwin had warned him to keep the ride short, for fear of saddle sores, but Bran would not admit to weakness in front of his brother. He was sick of the way everyone was always fussing over him and asking how he was.

"Let's hunt down the hunters, then," Robb said. Side by side, they urged their mounts off the kingsroad and struck out into the wolfswood. Theon dropped back and followed well behind them, talking and joking with the guardsmen.

It was nice under the trees. Bran kept Dancer to a walk, holding the reins lightly and looking all around him as they went. He knew this wood, but he had been so long confined to Winterfell that he felt as though he were seeing it for the first time. The smells filled his nostrils; the sharp fresh tang of pine needles, the earthy odor of wet rotting leaves, the hints of animal musk and distant cooking fires. He caught a glimpse of a black squirrel moving through the snow-covered branches of an oak, and paused to study the silvery web of an empress spider.

Theon and the others fell farther and farther behind, until Bran could no longer hear their voices. From ahead came the faint sound of rushing waters. It grew louder until they reached the stream. Tears stung his eyes.

"Bran?" Robb asked. "What's wrong?"

Bran shook his head. "I was just remembering," he said. "Jory brought us here once, to fish for trout. You and me and Jon. Do you remember?"

"I remember," Robb said, his voice quiet and sad.

"I didn't catch anything," Bran said, "but Jon gave me his fish on the way back to Winterfell. Will we ever see Jon again?"

"We saw Uncle Benjen when the king came to visit," Robb pointed out. "Jon will visit too, you'll see."

The stream was running high and fast. Robb dismounted and led his gelding across the ford. In the deepest part of the crossing, the water came up to midthigh. He tied his horse to a tree on the far side, and waded back across for Bran and Dancer. The current foamed around rock and root, and Bran could feel the spray on his face as Robb led him over. It made him smile. For a moment he felt strong again, and whole. He looked up at the trees and dreamed of climbing them, right up to the very top, with the whole forest spread out beneath him.

They were on the far side when they heard the howl, a long rising wail that moved through the trees like a cold wind. Bran raised his head to listen. "Summer," he said. No sooner had he spoken than a second voice joined the first.

"They've made a kill," Robb said as he remounted. "I'd best go and bring them back. Wait here, Theon and the others should be along shortly."

"I want to go with you," Bran said.

"I'll find them faster by myself." Robb spurred his gelding and vanished into the trees.

Once he was gone, the woods seemed to close in around Bran. The snow was falling more heavily now. Where it touched the ground it melted, but all about him rock and root and branch wore a thin blanket of white. As he waited, he was conscious of how uncomfortable he felt. He could not feel his legs, hanging useless in the stirrups, but the strap around his chest was tight and chafing, and the melting snow had soaked through his gloves to chill his hands. He wondered what was keeping Theon and Maester Luwin and Joseth and the rest.

When he heard the rustle of leaves, Bran used the reins to make Dancer turn, expecting to see his friends, but the ragged men who stepped out onto the bank of the stream were strangers.

"Good day to you," he said nervously. One look, and Bran knew they were neither foresters nor farmers. He was suddenly conscious of how richly he was dressed. His surcoat was new, dark grey wool with silver buttons, and a heavy silver pin fastened his fur-trimmed cloak at the shoulders. His boots and gloves were lined with fur as well.

"All alone, are you?" said the biggest of them, a bald man with a raw windburnt face. "Lost in the wolfswood, poor lad."

"I'm not lost." Bran did not like the way the strangers were looking at him. He counted four, but when he turned his head, he saw two others behind him. "My brother rode off just a moment ago, and my guard will be here shortly."

"Your guard, is it?" a second man said. Grey stubble covered his gaunt face. "And what would they be guarding, my little lord? Is that a silver pin I see there on your cloak?"

"Pretty," said a woman's voice. She scarcely looked like a woman; tall and lean, with the same hard face as the others, her hair hidden beneath a bowl-shaped halfhelm. The spear she held was eight feet of black oak, tipped in rusted steel.

"Let's have a look," said the big bald man.

Bran watched him anxiously. The man's clothes were filthy, fallen almost to pieces, patched here with brown and here with blue and there with a dark green, and faded everywhere to grey, but once that cloak might have been black. The grey stubbly man wore black rags too, he saw with a sudden start. Suddenly Bran remembered the oathbreaker his father had beheaded, the day they had found the wolf pups; that man had worn black as well, and Father said he had been a deserter from the Night's Watch. *No man is more dangerous*, he remembered Lord Eddard saying. *The deserter knows his life is forfeit if he is taken, so he will not flinch from any crime, no matter how vile or cruel.*

"The pin, lad," the big man said. He held out his hand.

"We'll take the horse too," said another of them, a woman shorter than Robb, with a broad flat face and lank yellow hair. "Get down, and be quick about it." A knife slid from her sleeve into her hand, its edge jagged as a saw.

"No," Bran blurted. "I can't . . ."

The big man grabbed his reins before Bran could think to wheel Dancer around and gallop off. "You can, lordling . . . and will, if you know what's good for you."

"Stiv, look how he's strapped on." The tall woman pointed with her spear. "Might be it's the truth he's telling."

"Straps, is it?" Stiv said. He drew a dagger from a sheath at his belt. "There's ways to deal with straps."

"You some kind of cripple?" asked the short woman.

Bran flared. "I'm Brandon Stark of Winterfell, and you better let go of my horse, or I'll see you all dead."

The gaunt man with the grey stubbled face laughed. "The boy's a Stark, true enough. Only a Stark would be fool enough to threaten where smarter men would beg."

"Cut his little cock off and stuff it in his mouth," suggested the short woman. "That should shut him up."

"You're as stupid as you are ugly, Hali," said the tall woman. "The boy's worth nothing dead, but alive . . . gods be damned, think what Mance would give to have Benjen Stark's own blood to hostage!"

"Mance be damned," the big man cursed. "You want to go back there, Osha? More fool you. Think the white walkers will care if you have a hostage?" He turned back to Bran and slashed at the strap around his thigh. The leather parted with a sigh.

The stroke had been quick and careless, biting deep. Looking down, Bran glimpsed pale flesh where the wool of his leggings had parted. Then the blood began to flow. He watched the red stain spread, feeling light-headed, curiously apart; there had been no pain, not even a hint of feeling. The big man grunted in surprise.

"Put down your steel now, and I promise you shall have a quick and painless death," Robb called out.

Bran looked up in desperate hope, and there he was. The strength of the words were undercut by the way his voice cracked with strain. He was mounted, the bloody carcass of an elk slung across the back of his horse, his sword in a gloved hand.

"The brother," said the man with the grey stubbly face.

"He's a fierce one, he is," mocked the short woman. Hali, they called her. "You mean to fight us, boy?"

"Don't be a fool, lad. You're one against six." The tall woman, Osha, leveled her spear. "Off the horse, and throw down the sword. We'll thank you kindly for the mount and for the venison, and you and your brother can be on your way."

Robb whistled. They heard the faint sound of soft feet on wet leaves. The undergrowth parted, low-hanging branches giving up their accumulation of snow, and Grey Wind and Summer emerged from the green. Summer sniffed the air and growled.

"Wolves," gasped Hali.

"Direwolves," Bran said. Still half-grown, they were as

large as any wolf he had ever seen, but the differences were easy to spot, if you knew what to look for. Maester Luwin and Farlen the kennelmaster had taught him. A direwolf had a bigger head and longer legs in proportion to its body, and its snout and jaw were markedly leaner and more pronounced. There was something gaunt and terrible about them as they stood there amid the gently falling snow. Fresh blood spotted Grey Wind's muzzle.

"Dogs," the big bald man said contemptuously. "Yet I'm told there's nothing like a wolfskin cloak to warm a man by night." He made a sharp gesture. "Take them."

Robb shouted, *"Winterfell!"* and kicked his horse. The gelding plunged down the bank as the ragged men closed. A man with an axe rushed in, shouting and heedless. Robb's sword caught him full in the face with a sickening *crunch* and a spray of bright blood. The man with the gaunt stubbly face made a grab for the reins, and for half a second he had them . . . and then Grey Wind was on him, bearing him down. He fell back into the stream with a splash and a shout, flailing wildly with his knife as his head went under. The direwolf plunged in after him, and the white water turned red where they had vanished.

Robb and Osha matched blows in midstream. Her long spear was a steel-headed serpent, flashing out at his chest, once, twice, three times, but Robb parried every thrust with his longsword, turning the point aside. On the fourth or fifth thrust, the tall woman overextended herself and lost her balance, just for a second. Robb charged, riding her down.

A few feet away, Summer darted in and snapped at Hali. The knife bit at his flank. Summer slid away, snarling, and came rushing in again. This time his jaws closed around her calf. Holding the knife with both hands, the small woman stabbed down, but the direwolf seemed to sense the blade coming. He pulled free for an instant, his mouth full of leather and cloth and bloody flesh. When Hali stumbled and fell, he came at her again, slamming her backward, teeth tearing at her belly.

The sixth man ran from the carnage . . . but not far. As he went scrambling up the far side of the bank, Grey Wind emerged from the stream, dripping wet. He shook the water off and bounded after the running man, hamstringing him with a single snap of his teeth, and going for the throat as the screaming man slid back down toward the water.

And then there was no one left but the big man, Stiv. He slashed at Bran's chest strap, grabbed his arm, and yanked. Suddenly Bran was falling. He sprawled on the ground, his legs tangled under him, one foot in the stream. He could not feel the cold of the water, but he felt the steel when Stiv pressed his dagger to his throat. "Back away," the man warned, "or I'll open the boy's windpipe, I swear it."

Robb reined his horse in, breathing hard. The fury went out of his eyes, and his sword arm dropped.

In that moment Bran saw everything. Summer was savaging Hali, pulling glistening blue snakes from her belly. Her eyes were wide and staring. Bran could not tell whether she was alive or dead. The grey stubbly man and the one with the axe lay unmoving, but Osha was on her knees, crawling toward her fallen spear. Grey Wind padded toward her, dripping wet. "Call him off!" the big man shouted. "Call them both off, or the cripple boy dies now!"

"Grey Wind, Summer, to me," Robb said.

The direwolves stopped, turned their heads. Grey Wind loped back to Robb. Summer stayed where he was, his eyes on Bran and the man beside him. He growled. His muzzle was wet and red, but his eyes burned.

Osha used the butt end of her spear to lever herself back to her feet. Blood leaked from a wound on the upper arm where Robb had cut her. Bran could see sweat trickling down the big man's face. Stiv was as scared as he was, he realized. "Starks," the man muttered, "bloody Starks." He raised his voice. "Osha, kill the wolves and get his sword."

"Kill them yourself," she replied. "I'll not be getting near those monsters."

For a moment Stiv was at a loss. His hand trembled; Bran felt a trickle of blood where the knife pressed against his neck. The stench of the man filled his nose; he smelled of fear. "You," he called out to Robb. "You have a name?"

"I am Robb Stark, the heir to Winterfell."

"This is your brother?"

"Yes."

"You want him alive, you do what I say. Off the horse."

Robb hesitated a moment. Then, slowly and deliberately, he dismounted and stood with his sword in hand.

"Now kill the wolves."

Robb did not move.

"You do it. The wolves or the boy."

"*No!*" Bran screamed. If Robb did as they asked, Stiv would kill them both anyway, once the direwolves were dead.

The bald man took hold of his hair with his free hand and twisted it cruelly, till Bran sobbed in pain. "You shut your mouth, cripple, you hear me?" He twisted harder. "*You hear me!*"

A low *thrum* came from the woods behind them. Stiv gave a choked gasp as a half foot of razor-tipped broadhead suddenly exploded out of his chest. The arrow was bright red, as if it had been painted in blood.

The dagger fell away from Bran's throat. The big man swayed and collapsed, facedown in the stream. The arrow broke beneath him. Bran watched his life go swirling off in the water.

Osha glanced around as Father's guardsmen appeared from beneath the trees, steel in hand. She threw down her spear. "Mercy, m'lord," she called to Robb.

The guardsmen had a strange, pale look to their faces as they took in the scene of slaughter. They eyed the wolves uncertainly, and when Summer returned to Hali's corpse to feed, Joseth dropped his knife and scrambled for the bush, heaving. Even Maester Luwin seemed shocked as he stepped from behind a tree, but only for an instant. Then he shook his head and waded across the stream to Bran's side. "Are you hurt?"

"He cut my leg," Bran said, "but I couldn't feel it."

As the maester knelt to examine the wound, Bran turned his head. Theon Greyjoy stood beside a sentinel tree, his bow in hand. He was smiling. Ever smiling. A half-dozen arrows were thrust into the soft ground at his feet, but it had taken only one. "A dead enemy is a thing of beauty," he announced.

"Jon always said you were an ass, Greyjoy," Robb said loudly. "I ought to chain you up in the yard and let Bran take a few practice shots at *you*."

"You should be thanking me for saving your brother's life."

"What if you had missed the shot?" Robb said. "What if you'd only wounded him? What if you had made his hand jump, or hit Bran instead? For all you knew, the man might have been wearing a breastplate, all you could see was the back of his cloak. What would have happened to my brother then? Did you ever think of *that*, Greyjoy?"

Theon's smile was gone. He gave a sullen shrug and began to pull his arrows from the ground, one by one.

Robb glared at his guardsmen. "Where were you?" he demanded of them. "I was sure you were close behind us."

The men traded unhappy glances. "We were following, m'lord," said Quent, the youngest of them, his beard a soft brown fuzz. "Only first we waited for Maester Luwin and his ass, begging your pardons, and then, well, as it were . . ." He glanced over at Theon and quickly looked away, abashed.

"I spied a turkey," Theon said, annoyed by the question. "How was I to know that you'd leave the boy alone?"

Robb turned his head to look at Theon once more. Bran had never seen him so angry, yet he said nothing. Finally he knelt beside Maester Luwin. "How badly is my brother wounded?"

"No more than a scratch," the maester said. He wet a cloth in the stream to clean the cut. "Two of them wear the black," he told Robb as he worked.

Robb glanced over at where Stiv lay sprawled in the stream, his ragged black cloak moving fitfully as the rushing waters tugged at it. "Deserters from the Night's Watch," he said grimly. "They must have been fools, to come so close to Winterfell."

"Folly and desperation are ofttimes hard to tell apart," said Maester Luwin.

"Shall we bury them, m'lord?" asked Quent.

"They would not have buried us," Robb said. "Hack off their heads, we'll send them back to the Wall. Leave the rest for the carrion crows."

"And this one?" Quent jerked a thumb toward Osha.

Robb walked over to her. She was a head taller than he

was, but she dropped to her knees at his approach. "Give me my life, m'lord of Stark, and I am yours."

"Mine? What would I do with an oathbreaker?"

"I broke no oaths. Stiv and Wallen flew down off the Wall, not me. The black crows got no place for women."

Theon Greyjoy sauntered closer. "Give her to the wolves," he urged Robb. The woman's eyes went to what was left of Hali, and just as quickly away. She shuddered. Even the guardsmen looked queasy.

"She's a woman," Robb said.

"A wildling," Bran told him. "She said they should keep me alive so they could take me to Mance Rayder."

"Do you have a name?" Robb asked her.

"Osha, as it please the lord," she muttered sourly.

Maester Luwin stood. "We might do well to question her."

Bran could see the relief on his brother's face. "As you say, Maester. Wayn, bind her hands. She'll come back to Winterfell with us . . . and live or die by the truths she gives us."

TYRION

"**Y**ou want eat?" Mord asked, glowering. He had a plate of boiled beans in one thick, stub-fingered hand.

Tyrion Lannister was starved, but he refused to let this brute see him cringe. "A leg of lamb would be pleasant," he said, from the heap of soiled straw in the corner of his cell. "Perhaps a dish of peas and onions, some fresh baked bread with butter, and a flagon of mulled wine to wash it down. Or beer, if that's easier. I try not to be overly particular."

"Is beans," Mord said. "Here." He held out the plate.

Tyrion sighed. The turnkey was twenty stone of gross stupidity, with brown rotting teeth and small dark eyes. The left side of his face was slick with scar where an axe had cut off his ear and part of his cheek. He was as predictable as he was ugly, but Tyrion *was* hungry. He reached up for the plate.

Mord jerked it away, grinning. "Is here," he said, holding it out beyond Tyrion's reach.

The dwarf climbed stiffly to his feet, every joint aching. "Must we play the same fool's game with every meal?" He made another grab for the beans.

Mord shambled backward, grinning through his rotten teeth. "Is here, dwarf man." He held the plate out at arm's length, over the edge where the cell ended and the sky began. "You not want eat? Here. Come take."

Tyrion's arms were too short to reach the plate, and he was not about to step that close to the edge. All it would take would be a quick shove of Mord's heavy white belly, and he would end up a sickening red splotch on the stones of Sky, like so many other prisoners of the Eyrie over the centuries. "Come to think on it, I'm not hungry after all," he declared, retreating to the corner of his cell.

Mord grunted and opened his thick fingers. The wind took the plate, flipping it over as it fell. A handful of beans sprayed back at them as the food tumbled out of sight. The turnkey laughed, his gut shaking like a bowl of pudding.

Tyrion felt a pang of rage. "You fucking son of a pox-ridden ass," he spat. "I hope you die of a bloody flux."

For that, Mord gave him a kick, driving a steel-toed boot hard into Tyrion's ribs on the way out. "I take it back!" he gasped as he doubled over on the straw. "I'll kill you myself, I swear it!" The heavy iron-bound door slammed shut. Tyrion heard the rattle of keys.

For a small man, he had been cursed with a danger-ously big mouth, he reflected as he crawled back to his corner of what the Arryns laughably called their dungeon. He huddled beneath the thin blanket that was his only bedding, staring out at a blaze of empty blue sky and dis-tant mountains that seemed to go on forever, wishing he still had the shadowskin cloak he'd won from Marillion at dice, after the singer had stolen it off the body of that brigand chief. The skin had smelled of blood and mold, but it was warm and thick. Mord had taken it the mo-ment he laid eyes on it.

The wind tugged at his blanket with gusts sharp as talons. His cell was miserably small, even for a dwarf. Not five feet away, where a wall ought to have been, where a wall *would* be in a proper dungeon, the floor ended and the sky began. He had plenty of fresh air and sunshine, and the moon and stars by night, but Tyrion would have traded it all in an instant for the dankest, gloomiest pit in the bowels of the Casterly Rock.

"You fly," Mord had promised him, when he'd shoved

him into the cell. "Twenty day, thirty, fifty maybe. Then you fly."

The Arryns kept the only dungeon in the realm where the prisoners were welcome to escape at will. That first day, after girding up his courage for hours, Tyrion had lain flat on his stomach and squirmed to the edge, to poke out his head and look down. Sky was six hundred feet below, with nothing between but empty air. If he craned his neck out as far as it could go, he could see other cells to his right and left and above him. He was a bee in a stone honeycomb, and someone had torn off his wings.

It was cold in the cell, the wind screamed night and day, and worst of all, the floor *sloped.* Ever so slightly, yet it was enough. He was afraid to close his eyes, afraid that he might roll over in his sleep and wake in sudden terror as he went sliding off the edge. Small wonder the sky cells drove men mad.

Gods save me, some previous tenant had written on the wall in something that looked suspiciously like blood, *the blue is calling.* At first Tyrion wondered who he'd been, and what had become of him; later, he decided that he would rather not know.

If only he had shut his mouth . . .

The wretched boy had started it, looking down on him from a throne of carved weirwood beneath the moon-and-falcon banners of House Arryn. Tyrion Lannister had been looked down on all his life, but seldom by rheumy-eyed six-year-olds who needed to stuff fat cushions under their cheeks to lift them to the height of a man. "Is he the bad man?" the boy had asked, clutching his doll.

"He is," the Lady Lysa had said from the lesser throne beside him. She was all in blue, powdered and perfumed for the suitors who filled her court.

"He's so *small,*" the Lord of the Eyrie said, giggling.

"This is Tyrion the Imp, of House Lannister, who murdered your father." She raised her voice so it carried down the length of High Hall of the Eyrie, ringing off the milk-white walls and the slender pillars, so every man could hear it. *"He slew the Hand of the King!"*

"Oh, did I kill him too?" Tyrion had said, like a fool.

That would have been a very good time to have kept his mouth closed and his head bowed. He could see that now; seven hells, he had seen it then. The High Hall of the Arryns was long and austere, with a forbidding coldness to its walls of blue-veined white marble, but the faces around him had been colder by far. The power of Casterly Rock was far away, and there were no friends of the Lannisters in the Vale of Arryn. Submission and silence would have been his best defenses.

But Tyrion's mood had been too foul for sense. To his shame, he had faltered during the last leg of their day-long climb up to the Eyrie, his stunted legs unable to take him any higher. Bronn had carried him the rest of the way, and the humiliation poured oil on the flames of his anger. "It would seem I've been a busy little fellow," he said with bitter sarcasm. "I wonder when I found the time to do all this slaying and murdering."

He ought to have remembered who he was dealing with. Lysa Arryn and her half-sane weakling son had not been known at court for their love of wit, especially when it was directed at them.

"Imp," Lysa said coldly, "you will guard that mocking tongue of yours and speak to my son politely, or I promise you will have cause to regret it. Remember where you are. This is the Eyrie, and these are knights of the Vale you see around you, true men who loved Jon Arryn well. Every one of them would die for me."

"Lady Arryn, should any harm come to me, my brother Jaime will be pleased to see that they do." Even as he spat out the words, Tyrion knew they were folly.

"Can you fly, my lord of Lannister?" Lady Lysa asked. "Does a dwarf have wings? If not, you would be wiser to swallow the next threat that comes to mind."

"I made no threats," Tyrion said. "That was a promise."

Little Lord Robert hopped to his feet at that, so upset he dropped his doll. "You can't hurt us," he screamed. "No one can hurt us here. Tell him, Mother, tell him he can't hurt us here." The boy began to twitch.

"The Eyrie is impregnable," Lysa Arryn declared calmly. She drew her son close, holding him safe in the circle of her plump white arms. "The Imp is trying to frighten us, sweet baby. The Lannisters are all liars. No one will hurt my sweet boy."

The hell of it was, she was no doubt right. Having seen what it took to get here, Tyrion could well imagine how it would be for a knight trying to fight his way up in armor, while stones and arrows poured down from above and enemies contested with him for every step. *Nightmare* did not begin to describe it. Small wonder the Eyrie had never been taken.

Still, Tyrion had been unable to silence himself. "Not impregnable," he said, "merely inconvenient."

Young Robert pointed down, his hand trembling. "You're a *liar*. Mother, I want to see him fly." Two guardsmen in sky-blue cloaks seized Tyrion by the arms, lifting him off his floor.

The gods only know what might have happened then were it not for Catelyn Stark. "Sister," she called out from where she stood below the thrones, "I beg you to remember, this man is *my* prisoner. I will not have him harmed."

Lysa Arryn glanced at her sister coolly for a moment, then rose and swept down on Tyrion, her long skirts trailing after her. For an instant he feared she would strike him, but instead she commanded them to release him. Her men shoved him to the floor, his legs went out from under him, and Tyrion fell.

He must have made quite a sight as he struggled to his knees, only to feel his right leg spasm, sending him sprawling once more. Laughter boomed up and down the High Hall of the Arryns.

"My sister's little guest is too weary to stand," Lady Lysa announced. "Ser Vardis, take him down to the dungeon. A rest in one of our sky cells will do him much good."

The guardsmen jerked him upright. Tyrion Lannister dangled between them, kicking feebly, his face red with shame. "I will remember this," he told them all as they carried him off.

And so he did, for all the good it did him.

At first he had consoled himself that this imprisonment could not last long. Lysa Arryn wanted to humble him, that was all. She would send for him again, and soon. If not her, then Catelyn Stark would want to question him. This time he would guard his tongue more closely. They dare not kill him out of hand; he was still a Lannister of Casterly Rock, and if they shed his blood, it would mean war. Or so he had told himself.

Now he was not so certain.

Perhaps his captors only meant to let him rot here, but he feared he did not have the strength to rot for long. He was growing weaker every day, and it was only a matter of time until Mord's kicks and blows did him serious harm, provided the gaoler did not starve him to death first. A few more nights of cold and hunger, and the blue would start calling to him too.

He wondered what was happening beyond the walls (such as they were) of his cell. Lord Tywin would surely have sent out riders when the word reached him. Jaime might be leading a host through the Mountains of the Moon even now . . . unless he was riding north against Winterfell instead. Did anyone outside the Vale even suspect where Catelyn Stark had taken him? He wondered what Cersei would do when she heard. The king could order him freed, but would Robert listen to his queen or his Hand? Tyrion had no illusions about the king's love for his sister.

If Cersei kept her wits about her, she would insist the king sit in judgment of Tyrion himself. Even Ned Stark could scarcely object to that, not without impugning the honor of the king. And Tyrion would be only too glad to take his chances in a trial. Whatever murders they might lay at his door, the Starks had no proof of anything so far as he could see. Let them make their case before the Iron Throne and the lords of the land. It would be the end of them. If only Cersei were clever enough to see that . . .

Tyrion Lannister sighed. His sister was not without a certain low cunning, but her pride blinded her. She would see the insult in this, not the opportunity. And Jaime was even worse, rash and headstrong and quick to anger. His brother never untied a knot when he could slash it in two with his sword.

He wondered which of them had sent the footpad to silence the Stark boy, and whether they had truly conspired at the death of Lord Arryn. If the old Hand had been murdered, it was deftly and subtly done. Men of his age died of sudden illness all the time. In contrast, sending some oaf with a stolen knife after Brandon Stark struck him as unbelievably clumsy. And wasn't *that* peculiar, come to think on it . . .

Tyrion shivered. Now *there* was a nasty suspicion. Perhaps the direwolf and the lion were not the only beasts in the woods, and if that was true, someone was using him as a catspaw. Tyrion Lannister hated being used.

He would have to get out of here, and soon. His chances of overpowering Mord were small to none, and no one was about to smuggle him a six-hundred-foot-long rope, so he would have to talk himself free. His mouth had gotten him into this cell; it could damn well get him out.

Tyrion pushed himself to his feet, doing his best to ignore the slope of the floor beneath him, with its ever-so-subtle tug toward the edge. He hammered on the door with a fist. *"Mord!"* he shouted. *"Turnkey! Mord, I want you!"* He had to keep it up a good ten minutes before he heard footsteps. Tyrion stepped back an instant before the door opened with a crash.

"Making noise," Mord growled, with blood in his eyes. Dangling from one meaty hand was a leather strap, wide and thick, doubled over in his fist.

Never show them you're afraid, Tyrion reminded himself. "How would you like to be rich?" he asked.

Mord hit him. He swung the strap backhand, lazily, but the leather caught Tyrion high on the arm. The force of it staggered him, and the pain made him grit his teeth. "No mouth, dwarf man," Mord warned him.

"Gold," Tyrion said, miming a smile. "Casterly Rock is full of gold . . . *ahhhh* . . ." This time the blow was a forehand, and Mord put more of his arm into the swing, making the leather *crack* and jump. It caught Tyrion in the ribs and dropped him to his knees, wimpering. He forced himself to look up at the gaoler. "As rich as the Lannisters," he wheezed. "That's what they say, Mord—"

Mord grunted. The strap whistled through the air and smashed Tyrion full in the face. The pain was so bad he did not remember falling, but when he opened his eyes again he was on the floor of his cell. His ear was ringing, and his mouth was full of blood. He groped for purchase, to push himself up, and his fingers brushed against . . . nothing. Tyrion snatched his hand back as fast as if it had been scalded, and tried his best to stop breathing. He had fallen right on the edge, inches from the blue.

"More to say?" Mord held the strap between his fists

and gave it a sharp pull. The *snap* made Tyrion jump. The turnkey laughed.

He won't push me over, Tyrion told himself desperately as he crawled away from the edge. *Catelyn Stark wants me alive, he doesn't dare kill me.* He wiped the blood off his lips with the back of his hand, grinned, and said, "That was a stiff one, Mord." The gaoler squinted at him, trying to decide if he was being mocked. "I could make good use of a strong man like you." The strap flew at him, but this time Tyrion was able to cringe away from it. He took a glancing blow to the shoulder, nothing more. "Gold," he repeated, scrambling backward like a crab, "more gold than you'll see here in a lifetime. Enough to buy land, women, horses . . . you could be a lord. Lord Mord." Tyrion hawked up a glob of blood and phlegm and spat it out into the sky.

"Is no gold," Mord said.

He's listening! Tyrion thought. "They relieved me of my purse when they captured me, but the gold is still mine. Catelyn Stark might take a man prisoner, but she'd never stoop to rob him. That wouldn't be honorable. Help me, and all the gold is yours." Mord's strap licked out, but it was a halfhearted, desultory swing, slow and contemptuous. Tyrion caught the leather in his hand and held it prisoned. "There will be no risk to you. All you need do is deliver a message."

The gaoler yanked his leather strap free of Tyrion's grasp. "Message," he said, as if he had never heard the word before. His frown made deep creases in his brow.

"You heard me, my lord. Only carry my word to your lady. Tell her . . ." *What? What would possibly make Lysa Arryn relent?* The inspiration came to Tyrion Lannister suddenly. ". . . tell her that I wish to confess my crimes."

Mord raised his arm and Tyrion braced himself for another blow, but the turnkey hesitated. Suspicion and greed warred in his eyes. He wanted that gold, yet he feared a trick; he had the look of a man who had often been tricked. "Is lie," he muttered darkly. "Dwarf man cheat me."

"I will put my promise in writing," Tyrion vowed.

Some illiterates held writing in disdain; others seemed to have a superstitious reverence for the written word, as if it were some sort of magic. Fortunately, Mord was one of the latter. The turnkey lowered the strap. "Writing down gold. Much gold."

"Oh, *much* gold," Tyrion assured him. "The purse is just a taste, my friend. My brother wears armor of solid gold plate." In truth, Jaime's armor was gilded steel, but this oaf would never know the difference.

Mord fingered his strap thoughtfully, but in the end, he relented and went to fetch paper and ink. When the letter was written, the gaoler frowned at it suspiciously. "Now deliver my message," Tyrion urged.

He was shivering in his sleep when they came for him, late that night. Mord opened the door but kept his silence. Ser Vardis Egen woke Tyrion with the point of his boot. "On your feet, Imp. My lady wants to see you."

Tyrion rubbed the sleep from his eyes and put on a grimace he scarcely felt. "No doubt she does, but what makes you think I wish to see her?"

Ser Vardis frowned. Tyrion remembered him well from the years he had spent at King's Landing as the captain of the Hand's household guard. A square, plain face, silver hair, a heavy build, and no humor whatsoever. "Your wishes are not my concern. On your feet, or I'll have you carried."

Tyrion clambered awkwardly to his feet. "A cold night," he said casually, "and the High Hall is so drafty. I don't wish to catch a chill. Mord, if you would be so good, fetch my cloak."

The gaoler squinted at him, face dull with suspicion.

"My *cloak*," Tyrion repeated. "The shadowskin you took from me for safekeeping. You recall."

"Get him the damnable cloak," Ser Vardis said.

Mord did not dare grumble. He gave Tyrion a glare that promised future retribution, yet he went for the cloak. When he draped it around his prisoner's neck, Tyrion smiled. "My thanks. I shall think of you whenever I wear it." He flung the trailing end of the long fur over his right shoulder, and felt warm for the first time in days. "Lead on, Ser Vardis."

The High Hall of the Arryns was aglow with the light of fifty torches, burning in the sconces along the walls. The Lady Lysa wore black silk, with the moon-and-falcon sewn on her breast in pearls. Since she did not look the sort to join the Night's Watch, Tyrion could only imagine that she had decided mourning clothes were appropriate garb for a confession. Her long auburn hair, woven into an elaborate braid, fell across her left shoulder. The taller throne beside her was empty; no doubt the little Lord of the Eyrie was off shaking in his sleep. Tyrion was thankful for that much, at least.

He bowed deeply and took a moment to glance around the hall. Lady Arryn had summoned her knights and retainers to hear his confession, as he had hoped. He saw Ser Brynden Tully's craggy face and Lord Nestor Royce's bluff one. Beside Nestor stood a younger man with fierce black side-whiskers who could only be his heir, Ser Albar. Most of the principal houses of the Vale were represented. Tyrion noted Ser Lyn Corbray, slender as a sword, Lord Hunter with his gouty legs, the widowed Lady Waynwood surrounded by her sons. Others sported sigils he did not know; broken lance, green viper, burning tower, winged chalice.

Among the lords of the Vale were several of his companions from the high road; Ser Rodrik Cassel, pale from half-healed wounds, stood with Ser Willis Wode beside him. Marillion the singer had found a new woodharp. Tyrion smiled; whatever happened here tonight, he did not wish it to happen in secret, and there was no one like a singer for spreading a story near and far.

In the rear of the hall, Bronn lounged beneath a pillar. The freerider's black eyes were fixed on Tyrion, and his hand lay lightly on the pommel of his sword. Tyrion gave him a long look, wondering . . .

Catelyn Stark spoke first. "You wish to confess your crimes, we are told."

"I do, my lady," Tyrion answered.

Lysa Arryn smiled at her sister. "The sky cells always break them. The gods can see them there, and there is no darkness to hide in."

"He does not look broken to me," Lady Catelyn said.

Lady Lysa paid her no mind. "Say what you will," she commanded Tyrion.

And now to roll the dice, he thought with another quick glance back at Bronn. "Where to begin? I am a vile little man, I confess it. My crimes and sins are beyond counting, my lords and ladies. I have lain with whores, not once but hundreds of times. I have wished my own lord father dead, and my sister, our gracious queen, as well." Behind him, someone chuckled. "I have not always treated my servants with kindness. I have gambled. I have even cheated, I blush to admit. I have said many cruel and malicious things about the noble lords and ladies of the court." That drew outright laughter. "Once I—"

"*Silence!*" Lysa Arryn's pale round face had turned a burning pink. "What do you imagine you are doing, dwarf?"

Tyrion cocked his head to one side. "Why, confessing my crimes, my lady."

Catelyn Stark took a step forward. "You are accused of sending a hired knife to slay my son Bran in his bed, and of conspiring to murder Lord Jon Arryn, the Hand of the King."

Tyrion gave a helpless shrug. "*Those* crimes I cannot confess, I fear. I know nothing of any murders."

Lady Lysa rose from her weirwood throne. "I will *not* be made mock of. You have had your little jape, Imp. I trust you enjoyed it. Ser Vardis, take him back to the dungeon . . . but this time find him a smaller cell, with a floor more sharply sloped."

"Is *this* how justice is done in the Vale?" Tyrion roared, so loudly that Ser Vardis froze for an instant. "Does honor stop at the Bloody Gate? You accuse me of crimes, I deny them, so you throw me into an open cell to freeze and starve." He lifted his head, to give them all a good look at the bruises Mord had left on his face. "Where is the king's justice? Is the Eyrie not part of the Seven Kingdoms? I stand accused, you say. Very well. *I demand a trial!* Let me speak, and let my truth or falsehood be judged openly, in the sight of gods and men."

A low murmuring filled the High Hall. He had her, Tyrion knew. He was highborn, the son of the most powerful lord in the realm, the brother of the queen. He could not be denied a trial. Guardsmen in sky-blue cloaks had started toward Tyrion, but Ser Vardis bid them halt and looked to Lady Lysa.

Her small mouth twitched in a petulant smile. "If you are tried and found to be guilty of the crimes for which you stand accused, then by the king's own laws, you must pay with your life's blood. We keep no headsman in the Eyrie, my lord of Lannister. Open the Moon Door."

The press of spectators parted. A narrow weirwood door stood between two slender marble pillars, a crescent moon carved in the white wood. Those standing closest edged backward as a pair of guardsmen marched through. One man removed the heavy bronze bars; the second pulled the door inward. Their blue cloaks rose snapping from their shoulders, caught in the sudden gust of wind that came howling through the open door. Beyond was the emptiness of the night sky, speckled with cold uncaring stars.

"Behold the king's justice," Lysa Arryn said. Torch flames fluttered like pennons along the walls, and here and there the odd torch guttered out.

"Lysa, I think this unwise," Catelyn Stark said as the black wind swirled around the hall.

Her sister ignored her. "You want a trial, my lord of Lannister. Very well, a trial you shall have. My son will listen to whatever you care to say, and you shall hear his judgment. Then you may leave . . . by one door or the other."

She looked so pleased with herself, Tyrion thought, and small wonder. How could a trial threaten her, when her weakling son was the lord judge? Tyrion glanced at her Moon Door. *Mother, I want to see him fly!* the boy had said. How many men had the snot-nosed little wretch sent through that door already?

"I thank you, my good lady, but I see no need to trouble Lord Robert," Tyrion said politely. "The gods know the truth of my innocence. I will have their verdict, not the judgment of men. I demand trial by combat."

A storm of sudden laughter filled the High Hall of the Arryns. Lord Nestor Royce snorted, Ser Willis chuckled, Ser Lyn Corbray guffawed, and others threw back their heads and howled until tears ran down their faces. Marillion clumsily plucked a gay note on his new woodharp with the fingers of his broken hand. Even the wind seemed to whistle with derision as it came skirling through the Moon Door.

Lysa Arryn's watery blue eyes looked uncertain. He had caught her off balance. "You have that right, to be sure."

The young knight with the green viper embroidered on his surcoat stepped forward and went to one knee. "My lady, I beg the boon of championing your cause."

"The honor should be mine," old Lord Hunter said. "For the love I bore your lord husband, let me avenge his death."

"My father served Lord Jon faithfully as High Steward of the Vale," Ser Albar Royce boomed. "Let me serve his son in this."

"The gods favor the man with the just cause," said Ser Lyn Corbray, "yet often that turns out to be the man with the surest sword. We all know who that is." He smiled modestly.

A dozen other men all spoke at once, clamoring to be heard. Tyrion found it disheartening to realize so many strangers were eager to kill him. Perhaps this had not been such a clever plan after all.

Lady Lysa raised a hand for silence. "I thank you, my lords, as I know my son would thank you if he were among us. No men in the Seven Kingdoms are as bold and true as the knights of the Vale. Would that I could grant you all this honor. Yet I can choose only one." She gestured. "Ser Vardis Egen, you were ever my lord husband's good right hand. You shall be our champion."

Ser Vardis had been singularly silent. "My lady," he said gravely, sinking to one knee, "pray give this burden to another, I have no taste for it. The man is no warrior. Look at him. A dwarf, half my size and lame in the legs. It would be shameful to slaughter such a man and call it justice."

Oh, *excellent*, Tyrion thought. "I agree."

Lysa glared at him. "You demanded a trial by combat."

"And now I demand a champion, such as you have chosen for yourself. My brother Jaime will gladly take my part, I know."

"Your precious Kingslayer is hundreds of leagues from here," snapped Lysa Arryn.

"Send a bird for him. I will gladly await his arrival."

"You will face Ser Vardis on the morrow."

"Singer," Tyrion said, turning to Marillion, "when you make a ballad of this, be certain you tell them how Lady Arryn denied the dwarf the right to a champion, and sent him forth lame and bruised and hobbling to face her finest knight."

"I deny you *nothing!*" Lysa Arryn said, her voice peeved and shrill with irritation. "Name your champion, Imp . . . if you think you can find a man to die for you."

"If it is all the same to you, I'd sooner find one to kill for me." Tyrion looked over the long hall. No one moved. For a long moment he wondered if it had all been a colossal blunder.

Then there was a stirring in the rear of the chamber. "I'll stand for the dwarf," Bronn called out.

EDDARD

He dreamt an old dream, of three knights in white cloaks, and a tower long fallen, and Lyanna in her bed of blood.

In the dream his friends rode with him, as they had in life. Proud Martyn Cassel, Jory's father; faithful Theo Wull; Ethan Glover, who had been Brandon's squire; Ser Mark Ryswell, soft of speech and gentle of heart; the crannogman, Howland Reed; Lord Dustin on his great red stallion. Ned had known their faces as well as he knew his own once, but the years leech at a man's memories, even those he has vowed never to forget. In the dream they were only shadows, grey wraiths on horses made of mist.

They were seven, facing three. In the dream as it had been in life. Yet these were no ordinary three. They waited before the round tower, the red mountains of Dorne at their backs, their white cloaks blowing in the wind. And these were no shadows; their faces burned clear, even now. Ser Arthur Dayne, the Sword of the Morning, had a sad smile on his lips. The hilt of the greatsword Dawn poked up over his right shoulder. Ser Oswell Whent was on one knee, sharpening his blade with a whetstone. Across his white-enameled helm, the black bat of his House spread its wings. Between them stood fierce old Ser Gerold Hightower, the White Bull, Lord Commander of the Kingsguard.

"I looked for you on the Trident," Ned said to them.

"We were not there," Ser Gerold answered.

"Woe to the Usurper if we had been," said Ser Oswell.

"When King's Landing fell, Ser Jaime slew your king with a golden sword, and I wondered where you were."

"Far away," Ser Gerold said, "or Aerys would yet sit the Iron Throne, and our false brother would burn in seven hells."

"I came down on Storm's End to lift the siege," Ned told them, "and the Lords Tyrell and Redwyne dipped their banners, and all their knights bent the knee to pledge us fealty. I was certain you would be among them."

"Our knees do not bend easily," said Ser Arthur Dayne.

"Ser Willem Darry is fled to Dragonstone, with your queen and Prince Viserys. I thought you might have sailed with him."

"Ser Willem is a good man and true," said Ser Oswell.

"But not of the Kingsguard," Ser Gerold pointed out. "The Kingsguard does not flee."

"Then or now," said Ser Arthur. He donned his helm.

"We swore a vow," explained old Ser Gerold.

Ned's wraiths moved up beside him, with shadow swords in hand. They were seven against three.

"And now it begins," said Ser Arthur Dayne, the Sword of the Morning. He unsheathed Dawn and held it with both hands. The blade was pale as milkglass, alive with light.

"No," Ned said with sadness in his voice. "Now it ends." As they came together in a rush of steel and shadow, he could hear Lyanna screaming. *"Eddard!"* she called. A storm of rose petals blew across a blood-streaked sky, as blue as the eyes of death.

"Lord Eddard," Lyanna called again.

"I promise," he whispered. "Lya, I promise . . ."

"Lord Eddard," a man echoed from the dark.

Groaning, Eddard Stark opened his eyes. Moonlight streamed through the tall windows of the Tower of the Hand.

"Lord Eddard?" A shadow stood over the bed.

"How . . . how long?" The sheets were tangled, his leg splinted and plastered. A dull throb of pain shot up his side.

"Six days and seven nights." The voice was Vayon Poole's. The steward held a cup to Ned's lips. "Drink, my lord."

"What . . . ?"

"Only water. Maester Pycelle said you would be thirsty."

Ned drank. His lips were parched and cracked. The water tasted sweet as honey.

"The king left orders," Vayon Poole told him when the cup was empty. "He would speak with you, my lord."

"On the morrow," Ned said. "When I am stronger." He could not face Robert now. The dream had left him weak as a kitten.

"My lord," Poole said, "he commanded us to send you to him the moment you opened your eyes." The steward busied himself lighting a bedside candle.

Ned cursed softly. Robert was never known for his patience. "Tell him I'm too weak to come to him. If he wishes to speak with me, I should be pleased to receive him here. I hope you wake him from a sound sleep. And summon . . ." He was about to say *Jory* when he remembered. "Summon the captain of my guard."

Alyn stepped into the bedchamber a few moments after the steward had taken his leave. "My lord."

"Poole tells me it has been six days," Ned said. "I must know how things stand."

"The Kingslayer is fled the city," Alyn told him. "The talk is he's ridden back to Casterly Rock to join his father. The story of how Lady Catelyn took the Imp is on every lip. I have put on extra guards, if it please you."

"It does," Ned assured him. "My daughters?"

"They have been with you every day, my lord. Sansa prays quietly, but Arya . . ." He hesitated. "She has not said a word since they brought you back. She is a fierce little thing, my lord. I have never seen such anger in a girl."

"Whatever happens," Ned said, "I want my daughters kept safe. I fear this is only the beginning."

"No harm will come to them, Lord Eddard," Alyn said. "I stake my life on that."

"Jory and the others . . ."

"I gave them over to the silent sisters, to be sent north to Winterfell. Jory would want to lie beside his grandfather."

It would have to be his grandfather, for Jory's father was buried far to the south. Martyn Cassel had perished with the rest. Ned had pulled the tower down afterward, and used its bloody stones to build eight cairns upon the ridge. It was said that Rhaegar had named that place the tower of joy, but for Ned it was a bitter memory. They had been seven against three, yet only two had lived to ride away; Eddard Stark himself and the little crannogman, Howland Reed. He did not think it omened well that he should dream that dream again after so many years.

"You've done well, Alyn," Ned was saying when Vayon Poole returned. The steward bowed low. "His Grace is without, my lord, and the queen with him."

Ned pushed himself up higher, wincing as his leg trembled with pain. He had not expected Cersei to come. It did not bode well that she had. "Send them in, and leave us. What we have to say should not go beyond these walls." Poole withdrew quietly.

Robert had taken time to dress. He wore a black velvet doublet with the crowned stag of Baratheon worked upon the breast in golden thread, and a golden mantle with a cloak of black and gold squares. A flagon of wine was in his hand, his face already flushed from drink. Cersei Lannister entered behind him, a jeweled tiara in her hair.

"Your Grace," Ned said. "Your pardons. I cannot rise."

"No matter," the king said gruffly. "Some wine? From the Arbor. A good vintage."

"A small cup," Ned said. "My head is still heavy from the milk of the poppy."

"A man in your place should count himself fortunate that his head is still on his shoulders," the queen declared.

"Quiet, woman," Robert snapped. He brought Ned a cup of wine. "Does the leg still pain you?"

"Some," Ned said. His head was swimming, but it would not do to admit to weakness in front of the queen.

"Pycelle swears it will heal clean." Robert frowned. "I take it you know what Catelyn has done?"

"I do." Ned took a small swallow of wine. "My lady wife is blameless, Your Grace. All she did she did at my command."

"I am *not* pleased, Ned," Robert grumbled.

"By what right do you dare lay hands on my blood?" Cersei demanded. "Who do you think you are?"

"The Hand of the King," Ned told her with icy courtesy. "Charged by your own lord husband to keep the king's peace and enforce the king's justice."

"You *were* the Hand," Cersei began, "but now—"

"*Silence!*" the king roared. "You asked him a question and he answered it." Cersei subsided, cold with anger, and Robert turned back to Ned. "Keep the king's peace, you say. Is this how you keep my peace, Ned? Seven men are dead . . ."

"Eight," the queen corrected. "Tregar died this morning, of the blow Lord Stark gave him."

"Abductions on the kingsroad and drunken slaughter in my streets," the king said. "I will not have it, Ned."

"Catelyn had good reason for taking the Imp—"

"I said, I will *not* have it! To hell with her reasons. You will command her to release the dwarf at once, *and* you will make your peace with Jaime."

"Three of my men were butchered before my eyes, because Jaime Lannister wished to *chasten* me. Am I to forget that?"

"My brother was not the cause of this quarrel," Cersei told the king. "Lord Stark was returning drunk from a brothel. His men attacked Jaime and his guards, even as his wife attacked Tyrion on the kingsroad."

"You know me better than that, Robert," Ned said. "Ask Lord Baelish if you doubt me. He was there."

"I've talked to Littlefinger," Robert said. "He claims he rode off to bring the gold cloaks before the fighting began, but he admits you were returning from some whorehouse."

"*Some* whorehouse? Damn your eyes, Robert, I went there to have a look at your daughter! Her mother has named her Barra. She looks like that first girl you fathered, when we were boys together in the Vale." He watched the queen as he spoke; her face was a mask, still and pale, betraying nothing.

Robert flushed. "Barra," he grumbled. "Is that supposed to please me? Damn the girl. I thought she had more sense."

"She cannot be more than fifteen, and a whore, and you thought she had *sense?*" Ned said, incredulous. His leg was beginning to pain him sorely. It was hard to keep his temper. "The fool child is in love with you, Robert."

The king glanced at Cersei. "This is no fit subject for the queen's ears."

"Her Grace will have no liking for anything I have to say," Ned replied. "I am told the Kingslayer has fled the city. Give me leave to bring him back to justice."

The king swirled the wine in his cup, brooding. He took a swallow. "No," he said. "I want no more of this. Jaime slew three of your men, and you five of his. Now it ends."

"Is that your notion of justice?" Ned flared. "If so, I am pleased that I am no longer your Hand."

The queen looked to her husband. "If any man had dared speak to a Targaryen as he has spoken to you—"

"Do you take me for Aerys?" Robert interrupted.

"I took you for a *king*. Jaime and Tyrion are your own brothers, by all the laws of marriage and the bonds we share. The Starks have driven off the one and seized the other. This man dishonors you with every breath he takes, and yet you stand there meekly, asking if his leg pains him and would he like some wine."

Robert's face was dark with anger. "How many times must I tell you to hold your tongue, woman?"

Cersei's face was a study in contempt. "What a jape the gods have made of us two," she said. "By all rights, you ought to be in skirts and me in mail."

Purple with rage, the king lashed out, a vicious backhand blow to the side of the head. She stumbled against the table and fell hard, yet Cersei Lannister did not cry out. Her slender fingers brushed her cheek, where the pale smooth skin was already reddening. On the morrow the bruise would cover half her face. "I shall wear this as a badge of honor," she announced.

"Wear it in silence, or I'll honor you again," Robert vowed. He shouted for a guard. Ser Meryn Trant stepped into the room, tall and somber in his white armor. "The queen is tired. See her to her bedchamber." The knight helped Cersei to her feet and led her out without a word.

Robert reached for the flagon and refilled his cup. "You see what she does to me, Ned." The king seated himself, cradling his wine cup. "My loving wife. The mother of my children." The rage was gone from him now; in his eyes Ned saw something sad and scared. "I should not have hit her. That was not . . . that was not *kingly*." He stared down at his hands, as if he did not quite know what they were. "I was always strong . . . no one could stand before me, no one. How do you fight someone if you can't hit them?" Confused, the king shook his head. "Rhaegar . . . Rhaegar *won*, damn him. I killed him, Ned, I drove the spike right through that black armor into his black heart, and he died at my feet. They made up songs about it. Yet somehow he still won. He has Lyanna now, and I have *her*." The king drained his cup.

"Your Grace," Ned Stark said, "we must talk . . ."

Robert pressed his fingertips against his temples. "I am sick unto death of talk. On the morrow I'm going to the kingswood to hunt. Whatever you have to say can wait until I return."

"If the gods are good, I shall not be here on your return. You commanded me to return to Winterfell, remember?"

Robert stood up, grasping one of the bedposts to steady himself. "The gods are seldom good, Ned. Here, this is yours." He pulled the heavy silver hand clasp from a pocket in the lining of his cloak and tossed it on the bed. "Like it or not, you are my Hand, damn you. I forbid you to leave."

Ned picked up the silver clasp. He was being given no choice, it seemed. His leg throbbed, and he felt as helpless as a child. "The Targaryen girl—"

The king groaned. "Seven hells, don't start with her again. That's done, I'll hear no more of it."

"Why would you want me as your Hand, if you refuse to listen to my counsel?"

"Why?" Robert laughed. "Why not? Someone has to rule this damnable kingdom. Put on the badge, Ned. It suits you. And if you ever throw it in my face again, I swear to you, I'll pin the damned thing on Jaime Lannister."

CATELYN

The eastern sky was rose and gold as the sun broke over the Vale of Arryn. Catelyn Stark watched the light spread, her hands resting on the delicate carved stone of the balustrade outside her window. Below her the world turned from black to indigo to green as dawn crept across fields and forests. Pale white mists rose off Alyssa's Tears, where the ghost waters plunged over the shoulder of the mountain to begin their long tumble down the face of the Giant's Lance. Catelyn could feel the faint touch of spray on her face.

Alyssa Arryn had seen her husband, her brothers, and all her children slain, and yet in life she had never shed a tear. So in death, the gods had decreed that she would know no rest until her weeping watered the black earth of the Vale, where the men she had loved were buried. Alyssa had been dead six thousand years now, and still no drop of the torrent had ever reached the valley floor far below. Catelyn wondered how large a waterfall her own tears would make when she died. "Tell me the rest of it," she said.

"The Kingslayer is massing a host at Casterly Rock," Ser Rodrik Cassel answered from the room behind her.

"Your brother writes that he has sent riders to the Rock, demanding that Lord Tywin proclaim his intent, but he has had no answer. Edmure has commanded Lord Vance and Lord Piper to guard the pass below the Golden Tooth. He vows to you that he will yield no foot of Tully land without first watering it with Lannister blood."

Catelyn turned away from the sunrise. Its beauty did little to lighten her mood; it seemed cruel for a day to dawn so fair and end so foul as this one promised to. "Edmure has sent riders and made vows," she said, "but Edmure is not the Lord of Riverrun. What of my lord father?"

"The message made no mention of Lord Hoster, my lady." Ser Rodrik tugged at his whiskers. They had grown in white as snow and bristly as a thornbush while he was recovering from his wounds; he looked almost himself again.

"My father would not have given the defense of Riverrun over to Edmure unless he was very sick," she said, worried. "I should have been woken as soon as this bird arrived."

"Your lady sister thought it better to let you sleep, Maester Colemon told me."

"I should have been woken," she insisted.

"The maester tells me your sister planned to speak with you after the combat," Ser Rodrik said.

"Then she still plans to go through with this mummer's farce?" Catelyn grimaced. "The dwarf has played her like a set of pipes, and she is too deaf to hear the tune. Whatever happens this morning, Ser Rodrik, it is past time we took our leave. My place is at Winterfell with my sons. If you are strong enough to travel, I shall ask Lysa for an escort to see us to Gulltown. We can take ship from there."

"Another ship?" Ser Rodrik looked a shade green, yet he managed not to shudder. "As you say, my lady."

The old knight waited outside her door as Catelyn summoned the servants Lysa had given her. If she spoke to her sister before the duel, perhaps she could change her mind, she thought as they dressed her. Lysa's policies varied with her moods, and her moods changed hourly. The shy girl she had known at Riverrun had grown into a woman who was by turns proud, fearful, cruel, dreamy, reckless, timid, stubborn, vain, and, above all, *inconstant*.

When that vile turnkey of hers had come crawling to tell them that Tyrion Lannister wished to confess, Catelyn had urged Lysa to have the dwarf brought to them privately, but no, nothing would do but that her sister must make a show of him before half the Vale. And now this . . .

"Lannister is *my* prisoner," she told Ser Rodrik as they descended the tower stairs and made their way through the Eyrie's cold white halls. Catelyn wore plain grey wool with a silvered belt. "My sister must be reminded of that."

At the doors to Lysa's apartments, they met her uncle storming out. "Going to join the fool's festival?" Ser Brynden snapped. "I'd tell you to slap some sense into your sister, if I thought it would do any good, but you'd only bruise your hand."

"There was a bird from Riverrun," Catelyn began, "a letter from Edmure . . ."

"I know, child." The black fish that fastened his cloak was Brynden's only concession to ornament. "I had to hear it from Maester Colemon. I asked your sister for leave to take a thousand seasoned men and ride for Riverrun with all haste. Do you know what she told me? *The Vale cannot spare a thousand swords, nor even one, Uncle*, she said. *You are the Knight of the Gate. Your place is here.*" A gust of childish laughter drifted through the open doors behind him, and her uncle glanced darkly over his shoulder. "Well, I told her she could bloody well find herself a new Knight of the Gate. Black fish or no, I am still a Tully. I shall leave for Riverrun by evenfall."

Catelyn could not pretend to surprise. "Alone? You know as well as I that you will never survive the high road. Ser Rodrik and I are returning to Winterfell. Come with us, Uncle. I will give you your thousand men. Riverrun will not fight alone."

Brynden thought a moment, then nodded a brusque agreement. "As you say. It's the long way home, but I'm more like to get there. I'll wait for you below." He went striding off, his cloak swirling behind him.

Catelyn exchanged a look with Ser Rodrik. They went

through the doors to the high, nervous sound of a child's giggles.

Lysa's apartments opened over a small garden, a circle of dirt and grass planted with blue flowers and ringed on all sides by tall white towers. The builders had intended it as a godswood, but the Eyrie rested on the hard stone of the mountain, and no matter how much soil was hauled up from the Vale, they could not get a weirwood to take root here. So the Lords of the Eyrie planted grass and scattered statuary amidst low, flowering shrubs. It was there the two champions would meet to place their lives, and that of Tyrion Lannister, into the hands of the gods.

Lysa, freshly scrubbed and garbed in cream velvet with a rope of sapphires and moonstones around her milk-white neck, was holding court on the terrace overlooking the scene of the combat, surrounded by her knights, retainers, and lords high and low. Most of them still hoped to wed her, bed her, and rule the Vale of Arryn by her side. From what Catelyn had seen during her stay at the Eyrie, it was a vain hope.

A wooden platform had been built to elevate Robert's chair; there the Lord of the Eyrie sat, giggling and clapping his hands as a humpbacked puppeteer in blue-and-white motley made two wooden knights hack and slash at each other. Pitchers of thick cream and baskets of blackberries had been set out, and the guests were sipping a sweet orange-scented wine from engraved silver cups. *A fool's festival*, Brynden had called it, and small wonder.

Across the terrace, Lysa laughed gaily at some jest of Lord Hunter's, and nibbled a blackberry from the point of Ser Lyn Corbray's dagger. They were the suitors who stood highest in Lysa's favor . . . today, at least. Catelyn would have been hard-pressed to say which man was more unsuitable. Eon Hunter was even older than Jon Arryn had been, half-crippled by gout, and cursed with three quarrelsome sons, each more grasping than the last. Ser Lyn was a different sort of folly; lean and handsome, heir to an ancient but impoverished house, but vain, reckless, hot-tempered . . . and, it was whispered, notoriously uninterested in the intimate charms of women.

When Lysa espied Catelyn, she welcomed her with a sisterly embrace and a moist kiss on the cheek. "Isn't it a lovely morning? The gods are smiling on us. Do try a cup of the wine, sweet sister. Lord Hunter was kind enough to send for it, from his own cellars."

"Thank you, no. Lysa, we must talk."

"After," her sister promised, already beginning to turn away from her.

"Now." Catelyn spoke more loudly than she'd intended. Men were turning to look. "Lysa, you cannot mean to go ahead with this folly. Alive, the Imp has value. Dead, he is only food for crows. And if his champion should prevail here—"

"Small chance of that, my lady," Lord Hunter assured her, patting her shoulder with a liver-spotted hand. "Ser Vardis is a doughty fighter. He will make short work of the sellsword."

"Will he, my lord?" Catelyn said coolly. "I wonder." She had seen Bronn fight on the high road; it was no accident that he had survived the journey while other men had died. He moved like a panther, and that ugly sword of his seemed a part of his arm.

Lysa's suitors were gathering around them like bees round a blossom. "Women understand little of these things," Ser Morton Waynwood said. "Ser Vardis is a knight, sweet lady. This other fellow, well, his sort are all cowards at heart. Useful enough in a battle, with thousands of their fellows around them, but stand them up alone and the manhood leaks right out of them."

"Say you have the truth of it, then," Catelyn said with a courtesy that made her mouth ache. "What will we gain by the dwarf's death? Do you imagine that Jaime will care a fig that we gave his brother a *trial* before we flung him off a mountain?"

"Behead the man," Ser Lyn Corbray suggested. "When the Kingslayer receives the Imp's head, it will be a warning to him."

Lysa gave an impatient shake of her waist-long auburn hair. "Lord Robert wants to see him fly," she said, as if that settled the matter. "And the Imp has only himself to blame. It was he who demanded a trial by combat."

"Lady Lysa had no honorable way to deny him, even if she'd wished to," Lord Hunter intoned ponderously.

Ignoring them all, Catelyn turned all her force on her sister. "I remind you, Tyrion Lannister is *my* prisoner."

"And I remind *you*, the dwarf murdered my lord husband!" Her voice rose. "He poisoned the Hand of the King and left my sweet baby fatherless, and now I mean to see him pay!" Whirling, her skirts swinging around her, Lysa stalked across the terrace. Ser Lyn and Ser Morton and the other suitors excused themselves with cool nods and trailed after her.

"Do you think he did?" Ser Rodrik asked her quietly when they were alone again. "Murder Lord Jon, that is? The Imp still denies it, and most fiercely . . ."

"I believe the Lannisters murdered Lord Arryn," Catelyn replied, "but whether it was Tyrion, or Ser Jaime, or the queen, or all of them together, I could not begin to say." Lysa had named Cersei in the letter she had sent to Winterfell, but now she seemed certain that Tyrion was the killer . . . perhaps because the dwarf was here, while the queen was safe behind the walls of the Red Keep, hundreds of leagues to the south. Catelyn almost wished she had burned her sister's letter *before* reading it.

Ser Rodrik tugged at his whiskers. "Poison, well . . . that could be the dwarf's work, true enough. Or Cersei's. It's said poison is a woman's weapon, begging your pardons, my lady. The Kingslayer, now . . . I have no great liking for the man, but he's not the sort. Too fond of the sight of blood on that golden sword of his. *Was* it poison, my lady?"

Catelyn frowned, vaguely uneasy. "How else could they make it look a natural death?" Behind her, Lord Robert shrieked with delight as one of the puppet knights sliced the other in half, spilling a flood of red sawdust onto the terrace. She glanced at her nephew and sighed. "The boy is utterly without discipline. He will never be strong enough to rule unless he is taken away from his mother for a time."

"His lord father agreed with you," said a voice at her elbow. She turned to behold Maester Colemon, a cup of wine in his hand. "He was planning to send the boy to Dragonstone for fostering, you know . . . oh, but I'm speaking out of turn." The apple of his throat bobbed anxiously beneath the loose maester's chain. "I fear I've had too much of Lord Hunter's excellent wine. The prospect of bloodshed has my nerves all a-fray . . ."

"You are mistaken, Maester," Catelyn said. "It was Casterly Rock, not Dragonstone, and those arrangements were made after the Hand's death, without my sister's consent."

The maester's head jerked so vigorously at the end of his absurdly long neck that he looked half a puppet himself. "No, begging your forgiveness, my lady, but it was Lord Jon who—"

A bell tolled loudly below them. High lords and serving girls alike broke off what they were doing and moved to the balustrade. Below, two guardsmen in sky-blue cloaks led forth Tyrion Lannister. The Eyrie's plump septon escorted him to the statue in the center of the garden, a weeping woman carved in veined white marble, no doubt meant to be Alyssa.

"The bad little man," Lord Robert said, giggling. "Mother, can I make him fly? I want to see him fly."

"Later, my sweet baby," Lysa promised him.

"Trial first," drawled Ser Lyn Corbray, "*then* execution."

A moment later the two champions appeared from opposite sides of the garden. The knight was attended by two young squires, the sellsword by the Eyrie's master-at-arms.

Ser Vardis Egen was steel from head to heel, encased in heavy plate armor over mail and padded surcoat. Large circular rondels, enameled cream-and-blue in the moon-and-falcon sigil of House Arryn, protected the vulnerable juncture of arm and breast. A skirt of lobstered metal covered him from waist to midthigh, while a solid gorget encircled his throat. Falcon's wings sprouted from the temples of his helm, and his visor was a pointed metal beak with a narrow slit for vision.

Bronn was so lightly armored he looked almost naked beside the knight. He wore only a shirt of black oiled ringmail over boiled leather, a round steel halfhelm with a noseguard, and a mail coif. High leather boots with steel shinguards gave some protection to his legs, and discs of black iron were sewn into the fingers of his gloves. Yet Catelyn noted that the sellsword stood half a hand taller than his foe, with a longer reach . . . and Bronn was fifteen years younger, if she was any judge.

They knelt in the grass beneath the weeping woman, facing each other, with Lannister between them. The septon removed a faceted crystal sphere from the soft cloth bag at his waist. He lifted it high above his head, and the light shattered. Rainbows danced across the Imp's face. In a high, solemn, singsong voice, the septon asked the gods to look down and bear witness, to find the truth in this man's soul, to grant him life and freedom if he was innocent, death if he was guilty. His voice echoed off the surrounding towers.

When the last echo had died away, the septon lowered his crystal and made a hasty departure. Tyrion leaned over and whispered something in Bronn's ear before the guardsmen led him away. The sellsword rose laughing and brushed a blade of grass from his knee.

Robert Arryn, Lord of the Eyrie and Defender of the Vale, was fidgeting impatiently in his elevated chair. "When are they going to fight?" he asked plaintively.

Ser Vardis was helped back to his feet by one of his squires. The other brought him a triangular shield almost four feet tall, heavy oak dotted with iron studs. They strapped it to his left forearm. When Lysa's master-at-arms offered Bronn a similar shield, the sellsword spat and waved it away. Three days growth of coarse black beard covered his jaw and cheeks, but if he did not shave it was not for want of a razor; the edge of his sword had the dangerous glimmer of steel that had been honed every day for hours, until it was too sharp to touch.

Ser Vardis held out a gauntleted hand, and his squire placed a handsome double-edged longsword in his grasp. The blade was engraved with a delicate silver tracery of a mountain sky; its pommel was a falcon's head, its cross-guard fashioned into the shape of wings. "I had that sword crafted for Jon in King's Landing," Lysa told her guests proudly as they watched Ser Vardis try a practice cut. "He wore it whenever he sat the Iron Throne in King Robert's place. Isn't it a lovely thing? I thought it only fitting that our champion avenge Jon with his own blade."

The engraved silver blade was beautiful beyond a doubt, but it seemed to Catelyn that Ser Vardis might have been more comfortable with his own sword. Yet she said nothing; she was weary of futile arguments with her sister.

"Make them fight!" Lord Robert called out.

Ser Vardis faced the Lord of the Eyrie and lifted his sword in salute. "For the Eyrie and the Vale!"

Tyrion Lannister had been seated on a balcony across the garden, flanked by his guards. It was to him that Bronn turned with a cursory salute.

"They await your command," Lady Lysa said to her lord son.

"Fight!" the boy screamed, his arms trembling as they clutched at his chair.

Ser Vardis swiveled, bringing up his heavy shield. Bronn turned to face him. Their swords rang together, once, twice, a testing. The sellsword backed off a step. The knight came after, holding his shield before him. He tried a slash, but Bronn jerked back, just out of reach, and the silver blade cut only air. Bronn circled to his right. Ser Vardis turned to follow, keeping his shield between them. The knight pressed forward, placing each foot carefully on the uneven ground. The sellsword gave way, a faint smile playing over his lips. Ser Vardis attacked, slashing, but Bronn leapt away from him, hopping lightly over a low, moss-covered stone. Now the sellsword circled left, away from the shield, toward the knight's unprotected side. Ser Vardis tried a hack at his legs, but he did not have the reach. Bronn danced farther to his left. Ser Vardis turned in place.

"The man is craven," Lord Hunter declared. "Stand and fight, coward!" Other voices echoed the sentiment.

Catelyn looked to Ser Rodrik. Her master-at-arms gave a curt shake of his head. "He wants to make Ser Vardis chase him. The weight of armor and shield will tire even the strongest man."

She had seen men practice at their swordplay near every day of her life, had viewed half a hundred tourneys in her time, but this was something different and deadlier: a dance where the smallest misstep meant death. And as she watched, the memory of another duel in another time came back to Catelyn Stark, as vivid as if it had been yesterday.

They met in the lower bailey of Riverrun. When Brandon saw that Petyr wore only helm and breastplate and mail, he took off most of his armor. Petyr had begged her for a favor he might wear, but she had turned him away. Her lord father promised her to Brandon Stark, and so it was to him that she gave her token, a pale blue handscarf she had embroidered with the leaping trout of Riverrun.

As she pressed it into his hand, she pleaded with him. "He is only a foolish boy, but I have loved him like a brother. It would grieve me to see him die." And her betrothed looked at her with the cool grey eyes of a Stark and promised to spare the boy who loved her.

That fight was over almost as soon as it began. Brandon was a man grown, and he drove Littlefinger all the way across the bailey and down the water stair, raining steel on him with every step, until the boy was staggering and bleeding from a dozen wounds. "Yield!" he called, more than once, but Petyr would only shake his head and fight on, grimly. When the river was lapping at their ankles, Brandon finally ended it, with a brutal backhand cut that bit through Petyr's rings and leather into the soft flesh below the ribs, so deep that Catelyn was certain that the wound was mortal. He looked at her as he fell and murmured "Cat" as the bright blood came flowing out between his mailed fingers. She thought she had forgotten that.

That was the last time she had seen his face . . . until the day she was brought before him in King's Landing.

A fortnight passed before Littlefinger was strong enough to leave Riverrun, but her lord father forbade her to visit him in the tower where he lay abed. Lysa helped their maester nurse him; she had been softer and shyer in those days. Edmure had called on him as well, but Petyr had sent him away. Her brother had acted as Brandon's squire at the duel, and Littlefinger would not forgive that. As soon as he was strong enough to be moved, Lord Hoster Tully sent Petyr Baelish away in a closed litter, to finish his healing on the Fingers, upon the windswept jut of rock where he'd been born.

The ringing clash of steel on steel jarred Catelyn back to the present. Ser Vardis was coming hard at Bronn, driving into him with shield and sword. The sellsword scrambled backward, checking each blow, stepping lithely over rock and root, his eyes never leaving his foe. He was quicker, Catelyn saw; the knight's silvered sword never came near to touching him, but his own ugly grey blade hacked a notch from Ser Vardis's shoulder plate.

The brief flurry of fighting ended as swiftly as it had begun when Bronn sidestepped and slid behind the statue of the weeping woman. Ser Vardis lunged at where he had been, striking a spark off the pale marble of Alyssa's thigh.

"They're not fighting good, Mother," the Lord of the Eyrie complained. "I want them to *fight.*"

"They will, sweet baby," his mother soothed him. "The sellsword can't run all day."

Some of the lords on Lysa's terrace were making wry jests as they refilled their wine cups, but across the garden, Tyrion Lannister's mismatched eyes watched the champions dance as if there were nothing else in the world.

Bronn came out from behind the statue hard and fast, still moving left, aiming a two-handed cut at the knight's unshielded right side. Ser Vardis blocked, but clumsily, and the sellsword's blade flashed upward at his head. Metal rang, and a falcon's wing collapsed with a crunch. Ser Vardis took a half step back to brace himself, raised his shield. Oak chips flew as Bronn's sword hacked at the wooden wall. The sellsword stepped left again, away from the shield, and caught Ser Vardis across the stomach, the razor edge of his blade leaving a bright gash when it bit into the knight's plate.

Ser Vardis drove forward off his back foot, his own silver blade descending in a savage arc. Bronn slammed it aside and danced away. The knight crashed into the weeping woman, rocking her on her plinth. Staggered, he stepped backward, his head turning this way and that as he searched for his foe. The slit visor of his helm narrowed his vision.

"Behind you, ser!" Lord Hunter shouted, too late. Bronn brought his sword down with both hands, catching Ser Vardis in the elbow of his sword arm. The thin lobstered metal that protected the joint *crunched.* The knight grunted, turning, wrenching his weapon up. This time Bronn stood his ground. The swords flew at each other, and their steel song filled the garden and rang off the white towers of the Eyrie.

"Ser Vardis is hurt," Ser Rodrik said, his voice grave.

Catelyn did not need to be told; she had eyes, she could see the bright finger of blood running along the knight's forearm, the wetness inside the elbow joint. Every parry was a little slower and a little lower than the one before. Ser Vardis turned his side to his foe, trying to use his shield to block instead, but Bronn slid around him, quick as a cat. The sellsword seemed to be getting stronger. His cuts were leaving their marks now. Deep shiny gashes gleamed all over the knight's armor, on his right thigh, his beaked visor, crossing on his breastplate, a long one along the front of his gorget. The moon-and-falcon rondel over Ser Vardis's right arm was sheared clean in half, hanging by its strap. They could hear his labored breath, rattling through the air holes in his visor.

Blind with arrogance as they were, even the knights and lords of the Vale could see what was happening below them, yet her sister could not. "Enough, Ser Vardis!" Lady Lysa called down. "Finish him now, my baby is growing tired."

And it must be said of Ser Vardis Egen that he was true to his lady's command, even to the last. One moment he was reeling backward, half-crouched behind his scarred shield; the next he charged. The sudden bull rush caught Bronn off balance. Ser Vardis crashed into him and slammed the lip of his shield into the sellsword's face. Almost, *almost*, Bronn lost his feet . . . he staggered back, tripped over a rock, and caught hold of the weeping woman to keep his balance. Throwing aside his shield, Ser Vardis lurched after him, using both hands to raise his sword. His right arm was blood from elbow to fingers now, yet his last desperate blow would have opened Bronn from neck to navel . . . if the sellsword had stood to receive it.

But Bronn jerked back. Jon Arryn's beautiful engraved silver sword glanced off the marble elbow of the weeping woman and snapped clean a third of the way up the blade. Bronn put his shoulder into the statue's back. The weathered likeness of Alyssa Arryn tottered and fell with a great crash, and Ser Vardis Egen went down beneath her.

Bronn was on him in a heartbeat, kicking what was left of his shattered rondel aside to expose the weak spot between arm and breastplate. Ser Vardis was lying on his side, pinned beneath the broken torso of the weeping woman. Catelyn heard the knight groan as the sellsword lifted his blade with both hands and drove it down and in with all his weight behind it, under the arm and through the ribs. Ser Vardis Egen shuddered and lay still.

Silence hung over the Eyrie. Bronn yanked off his

halfhelm and let it fall to the grass. His lip was smashed and bloody where the shield had caught him, and his coal-black hair was soaked with sweat. He spit out a broken tooth.

"Is it over, Mother?" the Lord of the Eyrie asked.

No, Catelyn wanted to tell him, *it's only now beginning.*

"Yes," Lysa said glumly, her voice as cold and dead as the captain of her guard.

"Can I make the little man fly now?"

Across the garden, Tyrion Lannister got to his feet. "Not *this* little man," he said. "This little man is going down in the turnip hoist, thank you very much."

"You presume—" Lysa began.

"I presume that House Arryn remembers its own words," the Imp said. *"As High as Honor."*

"You promised I could make him fly," the Lord of the Eyrie screamed at his mother. He began to shake.

Lady Lysa's face was flushed with fury. "The gods have seen fit to proclaim him innocent, child. We have no choice but to free him." She lifted her voice. "Guards. Take my lord of Lannister and his . . . *creature* here out of my sight. Escort them to the Bloody Gate and set them free. See that they have horses and supplies sufficient to reach the Trident, and make certain all their goods and weapons are returned to them. They shall need them on the high road."

"The high road," Tyrion Lannister said. Lysa allowed herself a faint, satisfied smile. It was another sort of death sentence, Catelyn realized. Tyrion Lannister must know that as well. Yet the dwarf favored Lady Arryn with a mocking bow. "As you command, my lady," he said. "I believe we know the way."

JON

"**Y**ou are as hopeless as any boys I have ever trained," Ser Alliser Thorne announced when they had all assembled in the yard. "Your hands were made for manure shovels, not for swords, and if it were up to me, the lot of you would be set to herding swine. But last night I was told that Gueren is marching five new boys up the kingsroad. One or two may even be worth the price of piss. To make room for them, I have decided to pass eight of you on to the Lord Commander to do with as he will." He called out the names one by one. "Toad. Stone Head. Aurochs. Lover. Pimple. Monkey. Ser Loon." Last, he looked at Jon. "And the Bastard."

Pyp let fly a *whoop* and thrust his sword into the air. Ser Alliser fixed him with a reptile stare. "They will call you men of Night's Watch now, but you are bigger fools than the Mummer's Monkey here if you believe that. You are boys still, green and stinking of summer, and when the winter comes you will die like flies." And with that, Ser Alliser Thorne took his leave of them.

The other boys gathered round the eight who had been named, laughing and cursing and offering congratulations. Halder smacked Toad on the butt with the flat of his sword and shouted, "Toad, of the Night's Watch!" Yelling that a black brother needed a horse, Pyp leapt onto Grenn's shoulders, and they tumbled to the ground, rolling and punching and hooting. Dareon dashed inside the armory and returned with a skin of sour red. As they passed the wine from hand to hand, grinning like fools, Jon noticed Samwell Tarly standing by himself beneath a bare dead tree in the corner of the yard. Jon offered him the skin. "A swallow of wine?"

Sam shook his head. "No thank you, Jon."

"Are you well?"

"Very well, truly," the fat boy lied. "I am so happy for you all." His round face quivered as he forced a smile. "You will be First Ranger someday, just as your uncle was."

"*Is*," Jon corrected. He would not accept that Benjen Stark was dead. Before he could say more, Halder cried, "Here, you planning to drink that all yourself?" Pyp snatched the skin from his hand and danced away, laughing. While Grenn seized his arm, Pyp gave the skin a squeeze, and a thin stream of red squirted Jon in the face. Halder howled in protest at the waste of good wine. Jon sputtered and struggled. Matthar and Jeren climbed the wall and began pelting them all with snowballs.

By the time he wrenched free, with snow in his hair and wine stains on his surcoat, Samwell Tarly had gone.

That night, Three-Finger Hobb cooked the boys a special meal to mark the occasion. When Jon arrived at the common hall, the Lord Steward himself led him to the bench near the fire. The older men clapped him on the arm in passing. The eight soon-to-be brothers feasted on rack of lamb baked in a crust of garlic and herbs, garnished with sprigs of mint, and surrounded by mashed yellow turnips swimming in butter. "From the Lord Commander's own table," Bowen Marsh told them. There were salads of spinach and chickpeas and turnip greens, and afterward bowls of iced blueberries and sweet cream.

"Do you think they'll keep us together?" Pyp wondered as they gorged themselves happily.

Toad made a face. "I hope not. I'm sick of looking at those ears of yours."

"Ho," said Pyp. "Listen to the crow call the raven

black. You're certain to be a ranger, Toad. They'll want you as far from the castle as they can. If Mance Rayder attacks, lift your visor and show your face, and he'll run off screaming."

Everyone laughed but Grenn. "I hope I'm a ranger."

"You and everyone else," said Matthar. Every man who wore the black walked the Wall, and every man was expected to take up steel in its defense, but the rangers were the true fighting heart of the Night's Watch. It was they who dared ride beyond the Wall, sweeping through the haunted forest and the icy mountain heights west of the Shadow Tower, fighting wildlings and giants and monstrous snow bears.

"Not everyone," said Halder. "It's the builders for me. What use would rangers be if the Wall fell down?"

The order of builders provided the masons and carpenters to repair keeps and towers, the miners to dig tunnels and crush stone for roads and footpaths, the woodsmen to clear away new growth wherever the forest pressed too close to the Wall. Once, it was said, they had quarried immense blocks of ice from frozen lakes deep in the haunted forest, dragging them south on sledges so the Wall might be raised ever higher. Those days were centuries gone, however; now, it was all they could do to ride the Wall from Eastwatch to the Shadow Tower, watching for cracks or signs of melt and making what repairs they could.

"The Old Bear's no fool," Dareon observed. "You're certain to be a builder, and Jon's certain to be a ranger. He's the best sword and the best rider among us, and his uncle was the First before he . . ." His voice trailed off awkwardly as he realized what he had almost said.

"Benjen Stark is still First Ranger," Jon Snow told him, toying with his bowl of blueberries. The rest might have given up all hope of his uncle's safe return, but not him. He pushed away the berries, scarcely touched, and rose from the bench.

"Aren't you going to eat those?" Toad asked.

"They're yours." Jon had hardly tasted Hobb's great feast. "I could not eat another bite." He took his cloak from its hook near the door and shouldered his way out.

Pyp followed him. "Jon, what is it?"

"Sam," he admitted. "He was not at table tonight."

"It's not like him to miss a meal," Pyp said thoughtfully. "Do you suppose he's taken ill?"

"He's frightened. We're leaving him." He remembered the day he had left Winterfell, all the bittersweet farewells; Bran lying broken, Robb with snow in his hair, Arya raining kisses on him after he'd given her Needle. "Once we say our words, we'll all have duties to attend to. Some of us may be sent away, to Eastwatch or the Shadow Tower. Sam will remain in training, with the likes of Rast and Cuger and these new boys who are coming up the kingsroad. Gods only know what they'll be like, but you can bet Ser Alliser will send them against him, first chance he gets."

Pyp made a grimace. "You did all you could."

"All we could wasn't enough," Jon said.

A deep restlessness was on him as he went back to Hardin's Tower for Ghost. The direwolf walked beside him to the stables. Some of the more skittish horses kicked at their stalls and laid back their ears as they entered. Jon saddled his mare, mounted, and rode out from Castle Black, south across the moonlit night. Ghost raced ahead of him, flying over the ground, gone in the blink of an eye. Jon let him go. A wolf needed to hunt.

He had no destination in mind. He wanted only to ride. He followed the creek for a time, listening to the icy trickle of water over rock, then cut across the fields to the kingsroad. It stretched out before him, narrow and stony and pocked with weeds, a road of no particular promise, yet the sight of it filled Jon Snow with a vast longing. Winterfell was down that road, and beyond it Riverrun and King's Landing and the Eyrie and so many other places; Casterly Rock, the Isles of Faces, the red mountains of Dorne, the hundred islands of Braavos in the sea, the smoking ruins of old Valyria. All the places that Jon would never see. The world was down that road . . . and he was here.

Once he swore his vow, the Wall would be his home until he was old as Maester Aemon. "I have not sworn yet," he muttered. He was no outlaw, bound to take the black or pay the penalty for his crimes. He had come here freely, and he might leave freely . . . until he said the words. He need only ride on, and he could leave it all behind. By the time the moon was full again, he would be back in Winterfell with his brothers.

Your *half* brothers, a voice inside reminded him. *And Lady Stark, who will not welcome you.* There was no place for him in Winterfell, no place in King's Landing either. Even his own mother had not had a place for him. The thought of her made him sad. He wondered who she had been, what she had looked like, why his father had left her. *Because she was a whore or an adulteress, fool. Something dark and dishonorable, or else why was Lord Eddard too ashamed to speak of her?*

Jon Snow turned away from the kingsroad to look behind him. The fires of Castle Black were hidden behind a hill, but the Wall was there, pale beneath the moon, vast and cold, running from horizon to horizon.

He wheeled his horse around and started for home.

Ghost returned as he crested a rise and saw the distant glow of lamplight from the Lord Commander's Tower. The direwolf's muzzle was red with blood as he trotted beside the horse. Jon found himself thinking of Samwell Tarly again on the ride back. By the time he reached the stables, he knew what he must do.

Maester Aemon's apartments were in a stout wooden keep below the rookery. Aged and frail, the maester shared his chambers with two of the younger stewards, who tended to his needs and helped him in his duties. The brothers joked that he had been given the two ugliest men in the Night's Watch; being blind, he was spared having to look at them. Clydas was short, bald, and chinless, with small pink eyes like a mole. Chett had a wen on his neck the size of a pigeon's egg, and a face red with boils and pimples. Perhaps that was why he always seemed so angry.

It was Chett who answered Jon's knock. "I need to speak to Maester Aemon," Jon told him.

"The maester is abed, as you should be. Come back on the morrow and maybe he'll see you." He began to shut the door.

Jon jammed it open with his boot. "I need to speak to him now. The morning will be too late."

Chett scowled. "The maester is not accustomed to being woken in the night. Do you know how old he is?"

"Old enough to treat visitors with more courtesy than

you," Jon said. "Give him my pardons. I would not disturb his rest if it were not important."

"And if I refuse?"

Jon had his boot wedged solidly in the door. "I can stand here all night if I must."

The black brother made a disgusted noise and opened the door to admit him. "Wait in the library. There's wood. Start a fire. I won't have the maester catching a chill on account of you."

Jon had the logs crackling merrily by the time Chett led in Maester Aemon. The old man was clad in his bed robe, but around his throat was the chain collar of his order. A maester did not remove it even to sleep. "The chair beside the fire would be pleasant," he said when he felt the warmth on his face. When he was settled comfortably, Chett covered his legs with a fur and went to stand by the door.

"I am sorry to have woken you, Maester," Jon Snow said.

"You did not wake me," Maester Aemon replied. "I find I need less sleep as I grow older, and I am grown very old. I often spend half the night with ghosts, remembering times fifty years past as if they were yesterday. The mystery of a midnight visitor is a welcome diversion. So tell me, Jon Snow, why have you come calling at this strange hour?"

"To ask that Samwell Tarly be taken from training and accepted as a brother of the Night's Watch."

"This is no concern of Maester Aemon," Chett complained.

"Our Lord Commander has given the training of recruits into the hands of Ser Alliser Thorne," the maester said gently. "Only he may say when a boy is ready to swear his vow, as you surely know. Why then come to me?"

"The Lord Commander listens to you," Jon told him. "And the wounded and the sick of the Night's Watch are in your charge."

"And is your friend Samwell wounded or sick?"

"He will be," Jon promised, "unless you help."

He told them all of it, even the part where he'd set Ghost at Rast's throat. Maester Aemon listened silently, blind eyes fixed on the fire, but Chett's face darkened with each word. "Without us to keep him safe, Sam will have no chance," Jon finished. "He's *hopeless* with a sword. My sister Arya could tear him apart, and she's not yet ten. If Ser Alliser makes him fight, it's only a matter of time before he's hurt or killed."

Chett could stand no more. "I've seen this fat boy in the common hall," he said. "He *is* a pig, and a hopeless craven as well, if what you say is true."

"Maybe it is so," Maester Aemon said. "Tell me, Chett, what would you have us do with such a boy?"

"Leave him where he is," Chett said. "The Wall is no place for the weak. Let him train until he is ready, no matter how many years that takes. Ser Alliser shall make a man of him or kill him, as the gods will."

"That's *stupid*," Jon said. He took a deep breath to gather his thoughts. "I remember once I asked Maester Luwin why he wore a chain around his throat."

Maester Aemon touched his own collar lightly, his bony, wrinkled finger stroking the heavy metal links. "Go on."

"He told me that a maester's collar is made of chain to remind him that he is sworn to serve," Jon said, remembering. "I asked why each link was a different metal. A silver chain would look much finer with his grey robes, I said. Maester Luwin laughed. A maester forges his chain with study, he told me. The different metals are each a different kind of learning, gold for the study of money and accounts, silver for healing, iron for warcraft. And he said there were other meanings as well. The collar is supposed to remind a maester of the realm he serves, isn't that so? Lords are gold and knights steel, but two links can't make a chain. You also need silver and iron and lead, tin and copper and bronze and all the rest, and those are farmers and smiths and merchants and the like. A chain needs all sorts of metals, and a land needs all sorts of people."

Maester Aemon smiled. "And so?"

"The Night's Watch needs all sorts too. Why else have rangers and stewards and builders? Lord Randyll couldn't make Sam a warrior, and Ser Alliser won't either. You can't hammer tin into iron, no matter how hard you beat it, but that doesn't mean tin is useless. Why shouldn't Sam be a steward?"

Chett gave an angry scowl. "*I'm* a steward. You think

it's easy work, fit for cowards? The order of stewards keeps the Watch alive. We hunt and farm, tend the horses, milk the cows, gather firewood, cook the meals. Who do you think makes your clothing? Who brings up supplies from the south? The stewards."

Maester Aemon was gentler. "Is your friend a hunter?"

"He hates hunting," Jon had to admit.

"Can he plow a field?" the maester asked. "Can he drive a wagon or sail a ship? Could he butcher a cow?"

"No."

Chett gave a nasty laugh. "I've seen what happens to soft lordlings when they're put to work. Set them to churning butter and their hands blister and bleed. Give them an axe to split logs, and they cut off their own foot."

"I know one thing Sam could do better than anyone."

"Yes?" Maester Aemon prompted.

Jon glanced warily at Chett, standing beside the door, his boils red and angry. "He could help you," he said quickly. "He can do sums, and he knows how to read and write. I know Chett can't read, and Clydas has weak eyes. Sam read every book in his father's library. He'd be good with the ravens too. Animals seem to like him. Ghost took to him straight off. There's a lot he could do, besides fighting. The Night's Watch needs every man. Why kill one, to no end? Make use of him instead."

Maester Aemon closed his eyes, and for a brief moment Jon was afraid that he had gone to sleep. Finally he said, "Maester Luwin taught you well, Jon Snow. Your mind is as deft as your blade, it would seem."

"Does that mean . . . ?"

"It means I shall think on what you have said," the maester told him firmly. "And now, I believe I am ready to sleep. Chett, show our young brother to the door."

TYRION

They had taken shelter beneath a copse of aspens just off the high road. Tyrion was gathering deadwood while their horses took water from a mountain stream. He stooped to pick up a splintered branch and examined it critically. "Will this do? I am not practiced at starting fires. Morrec did that for me."

"A *fire?*" Bronn said, spitting. "Are you so hungry to die, dwarf? Or have you taken leave of your senses? A fire will bring the clansmen down on us from miles around. I mean to survive this journey, Lannister."

"And how do you hope to do that?" Tyrion asked. He tucked the branch under his arm and poked around through the sparse undergrowth, looking for more. His back ached from the effort of bending; they had been riding since daybreak, when a stone-faced Ser Lyn Corbray had ushered them through the Bloody Gate and commanded them never to return.

"We have no chance of fighting our way back," Bronn said, "but two can cover more ground than ten, and attract less notice. The fewer days we spend in these mountains, the more like we are to reach the riverlands. Ride hard and fast, I say. Travel by night and hole up by day, avoid the road where we can, make no noise and light no fires."

Tyrion Lannister sighed. "A splendid plan, Bronn. Try it, as you like . . . and forgive me if I do not linger to bury you."

"You think to outlive *me*, dwarf?" The sellsword grinned. He had a dark gap in his smile where the edge of Ser Vardis Egen's shield had cracked a tooth in half.

Tyrion shrugged. "Riding hard and fast by night is a sure way to tumble down a mountain and crack your skull. I prefer to make my crossing slow and easy. I know you love the taste of horse, Bronn, but if our mounts die under us this time, we'll be trying to saddle shadowcats . . . and if truth be told, I think the clans will find us no matter what we do. Their eyes are all around us." He swept a gloved hand over the high, wind-carved crags that surrounded them.

Bronn grimaced. "Then we're dead men, Lannister."

"If so, I prefer to die comfortable," Tyrion replied. "We need a fire. The nights are cold up here, and hot food will warm our bellies and lift our spirits. Do you suppose there's any game to be had? Lady Lysa has kindly provided us with a veritable feast of salt beef, hard cheese, and stale bread, but I would hate to break a tooth so far from the nearest maester."

"I can find meat." Beneath a fall of black hair, Bronn's dark eyes regarded Tyrion suspiciously. "I should leave you here with your fool's fire. If I took your horse, I'd have twice the chance to make it through. What would you do then, dwarf?"

"Die, most like." Tyrion stooped to get another stick.

"You don't think I'd do it?"

"You'd do it in an instant, if it meant your life. You were quick enough to silence your friend Chiggen when he caught that arrow in his belly." Bronn had yanked back the man's head by the hair and driven the point of his dirk in under the ear, and afterward told Catelyn Stark that the other sellsword had died of his wound.

"He was good as dead," Bronn said, "and his moaning was bringing them down on us. Chiggen would have done the same for me . . . and he was no friend, only a man I rode with. Make no mistake, dwarf. I fought for you, but I do not love you."

"It was your blade I needed," Tyrion said, "not your love." He dumped his armful of wood on the ground.

Bronn grinned. "You're bold as any sellsword, I'll give you that. How did you know I'd take your part?"

"Know?" Tyrion squatted awkwardly on his stunted legs to build the fire. "I tossed the dice. Back at the inn, you and Chiggen helped take me captive. Why? The others saw it as their duty, for the honor of the lords they served, but not you two. You had no lord, no duty, and precious little honor, so why trouble to involve yourselves?" He took out his knife and whittled some thin strips of bark off one of the sticks he'd gathered, to serve as kindling. "Well, why do sellswords do anything? For gold. You were thinking Lady Catelyn would reward you for your help, perhaps even take you into her service. Here, that should do, I hope. Do you have a flint?"

Bronn slid two fingers into the pouch at his belt and tossed down a flint. Tyrion caught it in the air.

"My thanks," he said. "The thing is, you did not know the Starks. Lord Eddard is a proud, honorable, and honest man, and his lady wife is worse. Oh, no doubt she would have found a coin or two for you when this was all over, and pressed it in your hand with a polite word and a look of distaste, but that's the most you could have hoped for. The Starks look for courage and loyalty and honor in the men they choose to serve them, and if truth be told, you and Chiggen were lowborn scum." Tyrion struck the flint against his dagger, trying for a spark. Nothing.

Bronn snorted. "You have a bold tongue, little man. One day someone is like to cut it out and make you eat it."

"Everyone tells me that." Tyrion glanced up at the sellsword. "Did I offend you? My pardons . . . but you *are* scum, Bronn, make no mistake. Duty, honor, friendship, what's that to you? No, don't trouble yourself, we both know the answer. Still, you're not stupid. Once we reached the Vale, Lady Stark had no more need of you . . . but I did, and the one thing the Lannisters have never lacked for is gold. When the moment came to toss the dice, I was counting on your being smart enough to know where your best interest lay. Happily for me, you did." He slammed stone and steel together again, fruitlessly.

"Here," said Bronn, squatting, "I'll do it." He took the knife and flint from Tyrion's hands and struck sparks on his first try. A curl of bark began to smolder.

"Well done," Tyrion said. "Scum you may be, but you're undeniably useful, and with a sword in your hand you're almost as good as my brother Jaime. What do you want, Bronn? Gold? Land? Women? Keep me alive, and you'll have it."

Bronn blew gently on the fire, and the flames leapt up higher. "And if you die?"

"Why then, I'll have one mourner whose grief is sincere," Tyrion said, grinning. "The gold ends when I do."

The fire was blazing up nicely. Bronn stood, tucked the flint back into his pouch, and tossed Tyrion his dagger. "Fair enough," he said. "My sword's yours, then . . . but don't go looking for me to bend the knee and *m'lord* you every time you take a shit. I'm no man's toady."

"Nor any man's friend," Tyrion said. "I've no doubt you'd betray me as quick as you did Lady Stark, if you saw a profit in it. If the day ever comes when you're tempted to sell me out, remember this, Bronn—I'll match their price, whatever it is. I *like* living. And now, do you think you could do something about finding us some supper?"

"Take care of the horses," Bronn said, unsheathing the long dirk he wore at his hip. He strode into the trees.

An hour later the horses had been rubbed down and fed, the fire was crackling away merrily, and a haunch of a young goat was turning above the flames, spitting and hissing. "All we lack now is some good wine to wash down our kid," Tyrion said.

"That, a woman, and another dozen swords," Bronn said. He sat cross-legged beside the fire, honing the edge of his longsword with an oilstone. There was something strangely reassuring about the rasping sound it made when he drew it down the steel. "It will be full dark soon," the sellsword pointed out. "I'll take first watch . . . for all the good it will do us. It might be kinder to let them kill us in our sleep."

"Oh, I imagine they'll be here long before it comes to sleep." The smell of the roasting meat made Tyrion's mouth water.

Bronn watched him across the fire. "You have a plan," he said flatly, with a scrape of steel on stone.

"A hope, call it," Tyrion said. "Another toss of the dice."

"With our lives as the stake?"

Tyrion shrugged. "What choice do we have?" He leaned over the fire and sawed a thin slice of meat from the kid. "Ahhhh," he sighed happily as he chewed. Grease ran down his chin. "A bit tougher than I'd like, and in want of spicing, but I'll not complain too loudly. If I were back at the Eyrie, I'd be dancing on a precipice in hopes of a boiled bean."

"And yet you gave the turnkey a purse of gold," Bronn said.

"A Lannister always pays his debts."

Even Mord had scarcely believed it when Tyrion tossed him the leather purse. The gaoler's eyes had gone big as boiled eggs as he yanked open the drawstring and beheld the glint of gold. "I kept the silver," Tyrion had told him with a crooked smile, "but you were promised the gold, and there it is." It was more than a man like Mord could hope to earn in a lifetime of abusing prisoners. "And remember what I said, this is only a taste. If you ever grow tired of Lady Arryn's service, present yourself at Casterly Rock, and I'll pay you the rest of what I owe you." With golden dragons spilling out of both hands, Mord had fallen to his knees and promised that he would do just that.

Bronn yanked out his dirk and pulled the meat from the fire. He began to carve thick chunks of charred meat off the bone as Tyrion hollowed out two heels of stale bread to serve as trenchers. "If we do reach the river, what will you do then?" the sellsword asked as he cut.

"Oh, a whore and a featherbed and a flagon of wine, for a start." Tyrion held out his trencher, and Bronn filled it with meat. "And then to Casterly Rock or King's Landing, I think. I have some questions that want answering, concerning a certain dagger."

The sellsword chewed and swallowed. "So you were telling it true? It was not your knife?"

Tyrion smiled thinly. "Do I look a liar to you?"

By the time their bellies were full, the stars had come out and a half-moon was rising over the mountains. Tyrion spread his shadowskin cloak on the ground and stretched out with his saddle for a pillow. "Our friends are taking their sweet time."

"If I were them, I'd fear a trap," Bronn said. "Why else would we be so open, if not to lure them in?"

Tyrion chuckled. "Then we ought to sing and send them fleeing in terror." He began to whistle a tune.

"You're mad, dwarf," Bronn said as he cleaned the grease out from under his nails with his dirk.

"Where's your love of music, Bronn?"

"If it was music you wanted, you should have gotten the singer to champion you."

Tyrion grinned. "That would have been amusing. I can just see him fending off Ser Vardis with his woodharp." He resumed his whistling. "Do you know this song?" he asked.

"You hear it here and there, in inns and whorehouses."

"Myrish. 'The Seasons of My Love.' Sweet and sad, if you understand the words. The first girl I ever bedded used to sing it, and I've never been able to put it out of my head." Tyrion gazed up at the sky. It was a clear cold night and the stars shone down upon the mountains as bright and merciless as truth. "I met her on a night like this," he heard himself saying. "Jaime and I were riding back from Lannisport when we heard a scream, and she came running out into the road with two men dogging her heels, shouting threats. My brother unsheathed his sword and went after them, while I dismounted to protect the girl. She was scarcely a year older than I was, dark-haired, slender, with a face that would break your heart. It certainly broke mine. Lowborn, half-starved, unwashed . . . yet lovely. They'd torn the rags she was wearing half off her back, so I wrapped her in my cloak while Jaime chased the men into the woods. By the time he came trotting back, I'd gotten a name out of her, and a story. She was a crofter's child, orphaned when her father died of fever, on her way to . . . well, nowhere, really.

"Jaime was all in a lather to hunt down the men. It was not often outlaws dared prey on travelers so near to Casterly Rock, and he took it as an insult. The girl was too frightened to send off by herself, though, so I offered to take her to the closest inn and feed her while my brother rode back to the Rock for help.

"She was hungrier than I would have believed. We finished two whole chickens and part of a third, and drank a flagon of wine, talking. I was only thirteen, and the wine went to my head, I fear. The next thing I knew, I was sharing her bed. If she was shy, I was shyer. I'll never know where I found the courage. When I broke her maidenhead, she wept, but afterward she kissed me and sang her little song, and by morning I was in love."

"You?" Bronn's voice was amused.

"Absurd, isn't it?" Tyrion began to whistle the song again. "I married her," he finally admitted.

"A Lannister of Casterly Rock wed to a crofter's daughter," Bronn said. "How did you manage that?"

"Oh, you'd be astonished at what a boy can make of a few lies, fifty pieces of silver, and a drunken septon. I dared not bring my bride home to Casterly Rock, so I set her up in a cottage of her own, and for a fortnight we played at being man and wife. And then the septon sobered and confessed all to my lord father." Tyrion was surprised at how desolate it made him feel to say it, even after all these years. Perhaps he was just tired. "That was the end of my marriage." He sat up and stared at the dying fire, blinking at the light.

"He sent the girl away?"

"He did better than that," Tyrion said. "First he made my brother tell me the truth. The girl was a whore, you see. Jaime arranged the whole affair, the road, the outlaws, all of it. He thought it was time I had a woman. He paid double for a maiden, knowing it would be my first time.

"After Jaime had made his confession, to drive home the lesson, Lord Tywin brought my wife in and gave her to his guards. They paid her fair enough. A silver for each man, how many whores command that high a price? He sat me down in the corner of the barracks and bade me watch, and at the end she had so many silvers the coins were slipping through her fingers and rolling on the floor, she . . ." The smoke was stinging his eyes. Tyrion cleared his throat and turned away from the fire, to gaze out into darkness. "Lord Tywin had me go last," he said in a quiet voice. "And he gave me a gold coin to pay her, because I was a Lannister, and worth more."

After a time he heard the noise again, the rasp of steel on stone as Bronn sharpened his sword. "Thirteen or thirty or three, I would have killed the man who did that to me."

Tyrion swung around to face him. "You may get that chance one day. Remember what I told you. A Lannister always pays his debts." He yawned. "I think I will try and sleep. Wake me if we're about to die."

He rolled himself up in the shadowskin and shut his eyes. The ground was stony and cold, but after a time Tyrion Lannister did sleep. He dreamt of the sky cell. This time he was the gaoler, not the prisoner, *big*, with a strap in his hand, and he was hitting his father, driving him back, toward the abyss . . .

"Tyrion." Bronn's warning was low and urgent.

Tyrion was awake in the blink of an eye. The fire had burned down to embers, and the shadows were creeping in all around them. Bronn had raised himself to one knee, his sword in one hand and his dirk in the other. Tyrion held up a hand: *stay still,* it said. "Come share our fire, the night is cold," he called out to the creeping shadows. "I fear we've no wine to offer you, but you're welcome to some of our goat."

All movement stopped. Tyrion saw the glint of moonlight on metal. "Our mountain," a voice called out from the trees, deep and hard and unfriendly. "Our goat."

"Your goat," Tyrion agreed. "Who are you?"

"When you meet your gods," a different voice replied, "say it was Gunthor son of Gurn of the Stone Crows who sent you to them." A branch cracked underfoot as he stepped into the light; a thin man in a horned helmet, armed with a long knife.

"And Shagga son of Dolf." That was the first voice, deep and deadly. A boulder shifted to their left, and stood, and became a man. Massive and slow and strong he seemed, dressed all in skins, with a club in his right hand and an axe in his left. He smashed them together as he lumbered closer.

Other voices called other names, Conn and Torrek and Jaggot and more that Tyrion forgot the instant he heard them; ten at least. A few had swords and knives; others brandished pitchforks and scythes and wooden spears. He waited until they were done shouting out their names before he gave them answer. "I am Tyrion son of Tywin, of the Clan Lannister, the Lions of the Rock. We will gladly pay you for the goat we ate."

"What do you have to give us, Tyrion son of Tywin?" asked the one who named himself Gunthor, who seemed to be their chief.

"There is silver in my purse," Tyrion told them. "This hauberk I wear is large for me, but it should fit Conn nicely, and the battle-axe I carry would suit Shagga's mighty hand far better than that wood-axe he holds."

"The halfman would pay us with our own coin," said Conn.

"Conn speaks truly," Gunthor said. "Your silver is ours. Your horses are ours. Your hauberk and your battle-axe and the knife at your belt, those are ours too. You have nothing to give us but your lives. How would you like to die, Tyrion son of Tywin?"

"In my own bed, with a belly full of wine and a maiden's mouth around my cock, at the age of eighty," he replied.

The huge one, Shagga, laughed first and loudest. The others seemed less amused. "Conn, take their horses," Gunthor commanded. "Kill the other and seize the halfman. He can milk the goats and make the mothers laugh."

Bronn sprang to his feet. "Who dies first?"

"*No!*" Tyrion said sharply. "Gunthor son of Gurn, hear me. My House is rich and powerful. If the Stone Crows will see us safely through these mountains, my lord father will shower you with gold."

"The gold of a lowland lord is as worthless as a halfman's promises," Gunthor said.

"Half a man I may be," Tyrion said, "yet I have the courage to face my enemies. What do the Stone Crows do, but hide behind rocks and shiver with fear as the knights of the Vale ride by?"

Shagga gave a roar of anger and clashed club against axe. Jaggot poked at Tyrion's face with the fire-hardened point of a long wooden spear. He did his best not to flinch. "Are these the best weapons you could steal?" he said. "Good enough for killing sheep, perhaps . . . if the sheep do not fight back. My father's smiths shit better steel."

"Little boyman," Shagga roared, "will you mock my

axe after I chop off your manhood and feed it to the goats?"

But Gunthor raised a hand. "No. I would hear his words. The mothers go hungry, and steel fills more mouths than gold. What would you give us for your lives, Tyrion son of Tywin? Swords? Lances? Mail?"

"All that, and more, Gunthor son of Gurn," Tyrion Lannister replied, smiling. "I will give you the Vale of Arryn."

EDDARD

Through the high narrow windows of the Red Keep's cavernous throne room, the light of sunset spilled across the floor, laying dark red stripes upon the walls where the heads of dragons had once hung. Now the stone was covered with hunting tapestries, vivid with greens and browns and blues, and yet still it seemed to Ned Stark that the only color in the hall was the red of blood.

He sat high upon the immense ancient seat of Aegon the Conqueror, an ironwork monstrosity of spikes and jagged edges and grotesquely twisted metal. It was, as Robert had warned him, a hellishly uncomfortable chair, and never more so than now, with his shattered leg throbbing more sharply every minute. The metal beneath him had grown harder by the hour, and the fanged steel behind made it impossible to lean back. *A king should never sit easy*, Aegon the Conqueror had said, when he commanded his armorers to forge a great seat from the swords laid down by his enemies. *Damn Aegon for his arrogance*, Ned thought sullenly, *and damn Robert and his hunting as well.*

"You are quite certain these were more than brigands?" Varys asked softly from the council table beneath the throne. Grand Maester Pycelle stirred uneasily beside him, while Littlefinger toyed with a pen. They were the only councillors in attendance. A white hart had been sighted in the kingswood, and Lord Renly and Ser Barristan had joined the king to hunt it, along with Prince Joffrey, Sandor Clegane, Balon Swann, and half the court. So Ned must needs sit the Iron Throne in his absence.

At least he *could* sit. Save the council, the rest must stand respectfully, or kneel. The petitioners clustered near the tall doors, the knights and high lords and ladies beneath the tapestries, the smallfolk in the gallery, the mailed guards in their cloaks, gold or grey: all stood.

The villagers were kneeling: men, women, and children, alike tattered and bloody, their faces drawn by fear. The three knights who had brought them here to bear witness stood behind them.

"*Brigands*, Lord Varys?" Ser Raymun Darry's voice dripped scorn. "Oh, they were brigands, beyond a doubt. Lannister brigands."

Ned could feel the unease in the hall, as high lords and servants alike strained to listen. He could not pretend to surprise. The west had been a tinderbox since Catelyn had seized Tyrion Lannister. Both Riverrun and Casterly Rock had called their banners, and armies were massing in the pass below the Golden Tooth. It had only been a matter of time until the blood began to flow. The sole question that remained was how best to stanch the wound.

Sad-eyed Ser Karyl Vance, who would have been handsome but for the winestain birthmark that discolored his face, gestured at the kneeling villagers. "This is all the remains of the holdfast of Sherrer, Lord Eddard. The rest are dead, along with the people of Wendish Town and the Mummer's Ford."

"Rise," Ned commanded the villagers. He never trusted what a man told him from his knees. "All of you, up."

In ones and twos, the holdfast of Sherrer struggled to its feet. One ancient needed to be helped, and a young girl in a bloody dress stayed on her knees, staring blankly at Ser Arys Oakheart, who stood by the foot of the throne in the white armor of the Kingsguard, ready to protect and defend the king . . . or, Ned supposed, the King's Hand.

"Joss," Ser Raymun Darry said to a plump balding man in a brewer's apron. "Tell the Hand what happened at Sherrer."

Joss nodded. "If it please His Grace—"

"His Grace is hunting across the Blackwater," Ned said, wondering how a man could live his whole life a few days ride from the Red Keep and still have no notion what his king looked like. Ned was clad in a white linen doublet with the direwolf of Stark on the breast; his black wool cloak was fastened at the collar by his silver hand of office. Black and white and grey, all the shades of truth. "I am Lord Eddard Stark, the King's Hand. Tell me who you are and what you know of these raiders."

"I keep . . . I *kept* . . . I kept an alehouse, m'lord, in Sherrer, by the stone bridge. The finest ale south of the Neck, everyone said so, begging your pardons, m'lord. It's gone now like all the rest, m'lord. They come and drank their fill and spilled the rest before they fired my roof, and they would of spilled my blood too, if they'd caught me. M'lord."

"They burnt us out," a farmer beside him said. "Come riding in the dark, up from the south, and fired the fields and the houses alike, killing them as tried to stop them. They weren't no raiders, though, m'lord. They had no mind to steal our stock, not these, they butchered my milk cow where she stood and left her for the flies and the crows."

"They rode down my 'prentice boy," said a squat man with a smith's muscles and a bandage around his head. He had put on his finest clothes to come to court, but his breeches were patched, his cloak travel-stained and dusty. "Chased him back and forth across the fields on their horses, poking at him with their lances like it was a game, them laughing and the boy stumbling and screaming till the big one pierced him clean through."

The girl on her knees craned her head up at Ned, high above her on the throne. "They killed my mother too, Your Grace. And they . . . they . . ." Her voice trailed off, as if she had forgotten what she had been about to say. She began to sob.

Ser Raymun Darry took up the tale. "At Wendish

Town, the people sought shelter in their holdfast, but the walls were timbered. The raiders piled straw against the wood and burnt them all alive. When the Wendish folk opened their gates to flee the fire, they shot them down with arrows as they came running out, even women with suckling babes."

"Oh, dreadful," murmured Varys. "How cruel can men be?"

"They would of done the same for us, but the Sherrer holdfast's made of stone," Joss said. "Some wanted to smoke us out, but the big one said there was riper fruit upriver, and they made for the Mummer's Ford."

Ned could feel cold steel against his fingers as he leaned forward. Between each finger was a blade, the points of twisted swords fanning out like talons from arms of the throne. Even after three centuries, some were still sharp enough to cut. The Iron Throne was full of traps for the unwary. The songs said it had taken a thousand blades to make it, heated white-hot in the furnace breath of Balerion the Black Dread. The hammering had taken fifty-nine days. The end of it was this hunched black beast made of razor edges and barbs and ribbons of sharp metal; a chair that could kill a man, and had, if the stories could be believed.

What Eddard Stark was doing sitting there he would never comprehend, yet there he sat, and these people looked to him for justice. "What proof do you have that these were Lannisters?" he asked, trying to keep his fury under control. "Did they wear crimson cloaks or fly a lion banner?"

"Even Lannisters are not so blind stupid as that," Ser Marq Piper snapped. He was a swaggering bantam rooster of a youth, too young and too hot-blooded for Ned's taste, though a fast friend of Catelyn's brother, Edmure Tully.

"Every man among them was mounted and mailed, my lord," Ser Karyl answered calmly. "They were armed with steel-tipped lances and longswords, with battle-axes for the butchering." He gestured toward one of the ragged survivors. "You. Yes, you, no one's going to hurt you. Tell the Hand what you told me."

The old man bobbed his head. "Concerning their horses," he said, "it were warhorses they rode. Many a year I worked in old Ser Willum's stables, so I knows the difference. Not a one of these ever pulled a plow, gods bear witness if I'm wrong."

"Well-mounted brigands," observed Littlefinger. "Perhaps they stole the horses from the last place they raided."

"How many men were there in this raiding party?" Ned asked.

"A hundred, at the least," Joss answered, in the same instant as the bandaged smith said, "Fifty," and the grandmother behind him, "Hunnerds and hunnerds, m'lord, an army they was."

"You are more right than you know, goodwoman," Lord Eddard told her. "You say they flew no banners. What of the armor they wore? Did any of you note ornaments or decorations, devices on shield or helm?"

The brewer, Joss, shook his head. "It grieves me, m'lord, but no, the armor they showed us was plain, only . . . the one who led them, he was armored like the rest, but there was no mistaking him all the same. It was the size of him, m'lord. Those as say the giants are all dead never saw this one, I swear. Big as an ox he was, and a voice like stone breaking."

"The Mountain!" Ser Marq said loudly. "Can any man doubt it? This was Gregor Clegane's work."

Ned heard muttering from beneath the windows and the far end of the hall. Even in the galley, nervous whispers were exchanged. High lords and smallfolk alike knew what it could mean if Ser Marq was proved right. Ser Gregor Clegane stood bannerman to Lord Tywin Lannister.

He studied the frightened faces of the villagers. Small wonder they had been so fearful; they had thought they were being dragged here to name Lord Tywin a red-handed butcher before a king who was his son by marriage. He wondered if the knights had given them a choice.

Grand Maester Pycelle rose ponderously from the council table, his chain of office clinking. "Ser Marq, with respect, you cannot know that this outlaw was Ser Gregor. There are many large men in the realm."

"As large as the Mountain That Rides?" Ser Karyl said. "I have never met one."

"Nor has any man here," Ser Raymun added hotly. "Even his brother is a pup beside him. My lords, open your eyes. Do you need to see his seal on the corpses? It was Gregor."

"Why should Ser Gregor turn brigand?" Pycelle asked. "By the grace of his liege lord, he holds a stout keep and lands of his own. The man is an anointed knight."

"A false knight!" Ser Marq said. "Lord Tywin's mad dog."

"My lord Hand," Pycelle declared in a stiff voice, "I urge you to remind this *good* knight that Lord Tywin Lannister is the father of our own gracious queen."

"Thank you, Grand Maester Pycelle," Ned said. "I fear we might have forgotten that if you had not pointed it out."

From his vantage point atop the throne, he could see men slipping out the door at the far end of the hall. Hares going to ground, he supposed . . . or rats off to nibble the queen's cheese. He caught a glimpse of Septa Mordane in the gallery, with his daughter Sansa beside her. Ned felt a flash of anger; this was no place for a girl. But the septa could not have known that today's court would be anything but the usual tedious business of hearing petitions, settling disputes between rival holdfasts, and adjudicating the placement of boundary stones.

At the council table below, Petyr Baelish lost interest in his quill and leaned forward. "Ser Marq, Ser Karyl, Ser Raymun—perhaps I might ask you a question? These holdfasts were under your protection. Where were you when all this slaughtering and burning was going on?"

Ser Karyl Vance answered. "I was attending my lord father in the pass below the Golden Tooth, as was Ser Marq. When the word of these outrages reached Ser Edmure Tully, he sent word that we should take a small force of men to find what survivors we could and bring them to the king."

Ser Raymun Darry spoke up. "Ser Edmure had summoned me to Riverrun with all my strength. I was camped across the river from his walls, awaiting his commands, when the word reached me. By the time I could return to my own lands, Clegane and his vermin were back across the Red Fork, riding for Lannister's hills."

Littlefinger stroked the point of his beard thoughtfully. "And if they come again, ser?"

"If they come again, we'll use their blood to water the fields they burnt," Ser Marq Piper declared hotly.

"Ser Edmure has sent men to every village and holdfast within a day's ride of the border," Ser Karyl explained. "The next raider will not have such an easy time of it."

And that may be precisely what Lord Tywin wants, Ned thought to himself, *to bleed off strength from Riverrun, goad the boy into scattering his swords.* His wife's brother was young, and more gallant than wise. He would try to hold every inch of his soil, to defend every man, woman, and child who named him lord, and Tywin Lannister was shrewd enough to know that.

"If your fields and holdfasts are safe from harm," Lord Petyr was saying, "what then do you ask of the throne?"

"The lords of the Trident keep the king's peace," Ser Raymun Darry said. "The Lannisters have broken it. We ask leave to answer them, steel for steel. We ask justice for the smallfolk of Sherrer and Wendish Town and the Mummer's Ford."

"Edmure agrees, we must pay Gregor Clegane back his bloody coin," Ser Marq declared, "but old Lord Hoster commanded us to come here and beg the king's leave before we strike."

Thank the gods for old Lord Hoster, then. Tywin Lannister was as much fox as lion. If indeed he'd sent Ser Gregor to burn and pillage—and Ned did not doubt that he had—he'd taken care to see that he rode under cover of night, without banners, in the guise of a common brigand. Should Riverrun strike back, Cersei and her father would insist that it had been the Tullys who broke the king's peace, not the Lannisters. The gods only knew what Robert would believe.

Grand Maester Pycelle was on his feet again. "My lord Hand, if these good folk believe that Ser Gregor has forsaken his holy vows for plunder and rape, let them go to his liege lord and make their complaint. These crimes are no concern of the throne. Let them seek Lord Tywin's justice."

"It is all the king's justice," Ned told him. "North, south, east, or west, all we do we do in Robert's name."

"The *king's* justice," Grand Maester Pycelle said. "So it is, and so we should defer this matter until the king—"

"The king is hunting across the river and may not return for days," Lord Eddard said. "Robert bid me to sit here in his place, to listen with his ears, and to speak with his voice. I mean to do just that . . . though I agree that he must be told." He saw a familiar face beneath the tapestries. "Ser Robar."

Ser Robar Royce stepped forward and bowed. "My lord."

"Your father is hunting with the king," Ned said. "Will you bring them word of what was said and done here today?"

"At once, my lord."

"Do we have your leave to take our vengeance against Ser Gregor, then?" Marq Piper asked the throne.

"Vengeance?" Ned said. "I thought we were speaking of justice. Burning Clegane's fields and slaughtering his people will not restore the king's peace, only your injured pride." He glanced away before the young knight could voice his outraged protest, and addressed the villagers. "People of Sherrer, I cannot give you back your homes or your crops, nor can I restore your dead to life. But perhaps I can give you some small measure of justice, in the name of our king, Robert."

Every eye in the hall was fixed on him, waiting. Slowly Ned struggled to his feet, pushing himself up from the throne with the strength of his arms, his shattered leg screaming inside its cast. He did his best to ignore the pain; it was no moment to let them see his weakness. "The First Men believed that the judge who called for death should wield the sword, and in the north we hold to that still. I mislike sending another to do my killing . . . yet it seems I have no choice." He gestured at his broken leg.

"*Lord Eddard!*" The shout came from the west side of the hall as a handsome stripling of a boy strode forth boldly. Out of his armor, Ser Loras Tyrell looked even younger than his sixteen years. He wore pale blue silk, his belt a linked chain of golden roses, the sigil of his House. "I beg you the honor of acting in your place. Give this task to me, my lord, and I swear I shall not fail you."

Littlefinger chuckled. "Ser Loras, if we send you off alone, Ser Gregor will send us back your head with a plum stuffed in that pretty mouth of yours. The Mountain is not the sort to bend his neck to any man's justice."

"I do not fear Gregor Clegane," Ser Loras said haughtily.

Ned eased himself slowly back onto the hard iron seat of Aegon's misshapen throne. His eyes searched the faces along the wall. "Lord Beric," he called out. "Thoros of Myr. Ser Gladden. Lord Lothar." The men named stepped forward one by one. "Each of you is to assemble twenty men, to bring my word to Gregor's keep. Twenty of my own guards shall go with you. Lord Beric Dondarrion, you shall have the command, as befits your rank."

The young lord with the red-gold hair bowed. "As you command, Lord Eddard."

Ned raised his voice, so it carried to the far end of the throne room. "In the name of Robert of the House Baratheon, the First of his Name, King of the Andals and the Rhoynar and the First Men, Lord of the Seven Kingdoms and Protector of the Realm, by the word of Eddard of the House Stark, his Hand, I charge you to ride to the westlands with all haste, to cross the Red Fork of the Trident under the king's flag, and there bring the king's justice to the false knight Gregor Clegane, and to all those who shared in his crimes. I denounce him, and attaint him, and strip him of all rank and titles, of all lands and incomes and holdings, and do sentence him to death. May the gods take pity on his soul."

When the echo of his words had died away, the Knight of Flowers seemed perplexed. "Lord Eddard, what of me?"

Ned looked down on him. From on high, Loras Tyrell seemed almost as young as Robb. "No one doubts your valor, Ser Loras, but we are about justice here, and what you seek is vengeance." He looked back to Lord Beric. "Ride at first light. These things are best done quickly." He held up a hand. "The throne will hear no more petitions today."

Alyn and Porther climbed the steep iron steps to help him back down. As they made their descent, he could feel Loras Tyrell's sullen stare, but the boy had stalked away before Ned reached the floor of the throne room.

At the base of the Iron Throne, Varys was gathering papers from the council table. Littlefinger and Grand Maester Pycelle had already taken their leave. "You are a bolder man than I, my lord," the eunuch said softly.

"How so, Lord Varys?" Ned asked brusquely. His leg was throbbing, and he was in no mood for word games.

"Had it been me up there, I should have sent Ser Loras. He *so* wanted to go . . . and a man who has the Lannisters for his enemies would do well to make the Tyrells his friends."

"Ser Loras is young," said Ned. "I daresay he will outgrow the disappointment."

"And Ser Ilyn?" The eunuch stroked a plump, powdered cheek. "He *is* the King's Justice, after all. Sending other men to do his office . . . some might construe that as a grave insult."

"No slight was intended." In truth, Ned did not trust the mute knight, though perhaps that was only because he misliked executioners. "I remind you, the Paynes are bannermen to House Lannister. I thought it best to choose men who owed Lord Tywin no fealty."

"Very prudent, no doubt," Varys said. "Still, I chanced to see Ser Ilyn in the back of the hall, staring at us with those pale eyes of his, and I must say, he did not look pleased, though to be sure it is hard to tell with our silent knight. I hope he outgrows his disappointment as well. He does so *love* his work . . ."

SANSA

"He wouldn't send Ser Loras," Sansa told Jeyne
Poole that night as they shared a cold supper by
lamplight. "I think it was because of his leg."

Lord Eddard had taken his supper in his bedchamber
with Alyn, Harwin, and Vayon Poole, the better to rest
his broken leg, and Septa Mordane had complained of sore
feet after standing in the gallery all day. Arya was supposed to join them, but she was late coming back from
her dancing lesson.

"His leg?" Jeyne said uncertainly. She was a pretty,
dark-haired girl of Sansa's own age. "Did Ser Loras hurt
his leg?"

"Not *his* leg," Sansa said, nibbling delicately at a
chicken leg. "*Father's* leg, silly. It hurts him ever so
much, it makes him cross. Otherwise I'm certain he
would have sent Ser Loras."

Her father's decision still bewildered her. When the
Knight of Flowers had spoken up, she'd been sure she was
about to see one of Old Nan's stories come to life. Ser
Gregor was the monster and Ser Loras the true hero who
would slay him. He even *looked* a true hero, so slim and
beautiful, with golden roses around his slender waist and

his rich brown hair tumbling down into his eyes. And then Father had *refused* him! It had upset her more than she could tell. She had said as much to Septa Mordane as they descended the stairs from the gallery, but the septa had only told her it was not her place to question her lord father's decisions.

That was when Lord Baelish had said, "Oh, I don't know, Septa. Some of her lord father's decisions could do with a bit of questioning. The young lady is as wise as she is lovely." He made a sweeping bow to Sansa, so deep she was not quite sure if she was being complimented or mocked.

Septa Mordane had been *very* upset to realize that Lord Baelish had overheard them. "The girl was just talking, my lord," she'd said. "Foolish chatter. She meant nothing by the comment."

Lord Baelish stroked his little pointed beard and said, "Nothing? Tell me, child, why would you have sent Ser Loras?"

Sansa had no choice but to explain about heroes and monsters. The king's councillor smiled. "Well, those are not the reasons I'd have given, but . . ." He had touched her cheek, his thumb lightly tracing the line of a cheekbone. "Life is not a song, sweetling. You may learn that one day to your sorrow."

Sansa did not feel like telling all that to Jeyne, however; it made her uneasy just to think back on it.

"Ser Ilyn's the King's Justice, not Ser Loras," Jeyne said. "Lord Eddard should have sent him."

Sansa shuddered. Every time she looked at Ser Ilyn Payne, she shivered. He made her feel as though something dead were slithering over her naked skin. "Ser Ilyn's almost like a *second* monster. I'm glad Father didn't pick him."

"Lord Beric is as much a hero as Ser Loras. He's ever so brave and gallant."

"I suppose," Sansa said doubtfully. Beric Dondarrion was handsome enough, but he was awfully *old*, almost twenty-two; the Knight of Flowers would have been much better. Of course, Jeyne had been in love with Lord Beric ever since she had first glimpsed him in the lists. Sansa thought she was being silly; Jeyne was only a steward's daughter, after all, and no matter how much she

mooned after him, Lord Beric would never look at someone so far beneath him, even if she hadn't been half his
age.

It would have been unkind to say so, however, so Sansa
took a sip of milk and changed the subject. "I had a dream
that Joffrey would be the one to take the white hart," she
said. It had been more of a wish, actually, but it sounded
better to call it a dream. Everyone knew that dreams were
prophetic. White harts were supposed to be very rare and
magical, and in her heart she knew her gallant prince was
worthier than his drunken father.

"A dream? Truly? Did Prince Joffrey just go up to it
and touch it with his bare hand and do it no harm?"

"No," Sansa said. "He shot it with a golden arrow and
brought it back for me." In the songs, the knights never
killed magical beasts, they just went up to them and
touched them and did them no harm, but she knew Joffrey liked hunting, especially the killing part. Only animals, though. Sansa was certain her prince had no part in
murdering Jory and those other poor men; that had been
his wicked uncle, the Kingslayer. She knew her father
was still angry about that, but it wasn't fair to blame Joff.
That would be like blaming her for something that Arya
had done.

"I saw your sister this afternoon," Jeyne blurted out, as
if she'd been reading Sansa's thoughts. "She was walking
through the stables on her hands. Why would she do a
thing like that?"

"I'm sure I don't know why Arya does anything."
Sansa hated stables, smelly places full of manure and
flies. Even when she went riding, she liked the boy to
saddle the horse and bring it to her in the yard. "Do you
want to hear about the court or not?"

"I do," Jeyne said.

"There was a black brother," Sansa said, "begging men
for the Wall, only he was kind of old and smelly." She
hadn't liked that at all. She had always imagined the
Night's Watch to be men like Uncle Benjen. In the songs,
they were called the black knights of the Wall. But this
man had been crookbacked and hideous, and he looked as
though he might have lice. If this was what the Night's
Watch was truly like, she felt sorry for her bastard half
brother, Jon. "Father asked if there were any knights in

the hall who would do honor to their houses by taking the black, but no one came forward, so he gave this Yoren his pick of the king's dungeons and sent him on his way. And later these two brothers came before him, freeriders from the Dornish Marches, and pledged their swords to the service of the king. Father accepted their oaths . . ."

Jeyne yawned. "Are there any lemon cakes?"

Sansa did not like being interrupted, but she had to admit, lemon cakes sounded more interesting than most of what had gone on in the throne room. "Let's see," she said.

The kitchen yielded no lemon cakes, but they did find half of a cold strawberry pie, and that was almost as good. They ate it on the tower steps, giggling and gossiping and sharing secrets, and Sansa went to bed that night feeling almost as wicked as Arya.

The next morning she woke before first light and crept sleepily to her window to watch Lord Beric form up his men. They rode out as dawn was breaking over the city, with three banners going before them; the crowned stag of the king flew from the high staff, the direwolf of Stark and Lord Beric's own forked lightning standard from shorter poles. It was all so exciting, a song come to life; the clatter of swords, the flicker of torchlight, banners dancing in the wind, horses snorting and whinnying, the golden glow of sunrise slanting through the bars of the portcullis as it jerked upward. The Winterfell men looked especially fine in their silvery mail and long grey cloaks.

Alyn carried the Stark banner. When she saw him rein in beside Lord Beric to exchange words, it made Sansa feel ever so proud. Alyn was handsomer than Jory had been; he was going to be a knight one day.

The Tower of the Hand seemed so empty after they left that Sansa was even pleased to see Arya when she went down to break her fast. "Where is everyone?" her sister wanted to know as she ripped the skin from a blood orange. "Did Father send them to hunt down Jaime Lannister?"

Sansa sighed. "They rode with Lord Beric, to behead Ser Gregor Clegane." She turned to Septa Mordane, who was eating porridge with a wooden spoon. "Septa, will Lord Beric spike Ser Gregor's head on his own gate or bring it back here for the king?" She and Jeyne Poole had been arguing over that last night.

The septa was horror-struck. "A lady does not discuss such things over her porridge. Where are your courtesies, Sansa? I swear, of late you've been near as bad as your sister."

"What did Gregor do?" Arya asked.

"He burned down a holdfast and murdered a lot of people, women and children too."

Arya screwed up her face in a scowl. "Jaime Lannister murdered Jory and Heward and Wyl, and the Hound murdered Mycah. Somebody should have beheaded *them*."

"It's not the same," Sansa said. "The Hound is Joffrey's sworn shield. Your butcher's boy attacked the prince."

"Liar," Arya said. Her hand clenched the blood orange so hard that red juice oozed between her fingers.

"Go ahead, call me all the names you want," Sansa said airily. "You won't dare when I'm married to Joffrey. You'll have to bow to me and call me Your Grace." She shrieked as Arya flung the orange across the table. It caught her in the middle of the forehead with a wet squish and plopped down into her lap.

"You have juice on your face, Your Grace," Arya said.

It was running down her nose and stinging her eyes. Sansa wiped it away with a napkin. When she saw what the fruit in her lap had done to her beautiful ivory silk dress, she shrieked again. "You're *horrible*," she screamed at her sister. "They should have killed *you* instead of Lady!"

Septa Mordane came lurching to her feet. "Your lord father will hear of this! Go to your chambers, at once. *At once!*"

"Me too?" Tears welled in Sansa's eyes. "That's not fair."

"The matter is not subject to discussion. Go!"

Sansa stalked away with her head up. She was to be a queen, and queens did not cry. At least not where people could see. When she reached her bedchamber, she barred the door and took off her dress. The blood orange had left a blotchy red stain on the silk. "I *hate* her!" she screamed. She balled up the dress and flung it into the cold hearth, on top of the ashes of last night's fire. When she saw that the stain had bled through onto her underskirt, she began to sob despite herself. She ripped off the rest of her clothes wildly, threw herself into bed, and cried herself back to sleep.

It was midday when Septa Mordane knocked upon her door. "Sansa. Your lord father will see you now."

Sansa sat up. "Lady," she whispered. For a moment it was as if the direwolf was there in the room, looking at her with those golden eyes, sad and knowing. She had been dreaming, she realized. Lady was with her, and they were running together, and . . . and . . . trying to remember was like trying to catch the rain with her fingers. The dream faded, and Lady was dead again.

"Sansa." The rap came again, sharply. "Do you hear me?"

"Yes, Septa," she called out. "Might I have a moment to dress, please?" Her eyes were red from crying, but she did her best to make herself beautiful.

Lord Eddard was bent over a huge leather-bound book when Septa Mordane marched her into the solar, his plaster-wrapped leg stiff beneath the table. "Come here, Sansa," he said, not unkindly, when the septa had gone for her sister. "Sit beside me." He closed the book.

Septa Mordane returned with Arya squirming in her grasp. Sansa had put on a lovely pale green damask gown and a look of remorse, but her sister was still wearing the ratty leathers and roughspun she'd worn at breakfast. "Here is the other one," the septa announced.

"My thanks, Septa Mordane. I would talk to my daughters alone, if you would be so kind." The septa bowed and left.

"Arya started it," Sansa said quickly, anxious to have the first word. "She called me a liar and threw an orange at me and spoiled my dress, the ivory silk, the one Queen Cersei gave me when I was betrothed to Prince Joffrey. She hates that I'm going to marry the prince. She tries to spoil *everything*, Father, she can't stand for anything to be beautiful or nice or splendid."

"*Enough*, Sansa." Lord Eddard's voice was sharp with impatience.

Arya raised her eyes. "I'm sorry, Father. I was wrong and I beg my sweet sister's forgiveness."

Sansa was so startled that for a moment she was

speechless. Finally she found her voice. "What about my dress?"

"Maybe . . . I could wash it," Arya said doubtfully.

"Washing won't do any good," Sansa said. "Not if you scrubbed all day and all night. The silk is *ruined.*"

"Then I'll . . . make you a new one," Arya said.

Sansa threw back her head in disdain. "*You!* You couldn't sew a dress fit to clean the pigsties."

Their father sighed. "I did not call you here to talk of dresses. I'm sending you both back to Winterfell."

For the second time Sansa found herself too stunned for words. She felt her eyes grow moist again.

"You *can't,*" Arya said.

"Please, Father," Sansa managed at last. "Please don't."

Eddard Stark favored his daughters with a tired smile. "At last we've found something you agree on."

"I didn't do anything wrong," Sansa pleaded with him. "I don't want to go back." She loved King's Landing; the pageantry of the court, the high lords and ladies in their velvets and silks and gemstones, the great city with all its people. The tournament had been the most magical time of her whole life, and there was so much she had not seen yet, harvest feasts and masked balls and mummer shows. She could not bear the thought of losing it all. "Send Arya away, she started it, Father, I swear it. I'll be good, you'll see, just let me stay and I promise to be as fine and noble and courteous as the queen."

Father's mouth twitched strangely. "Sansa, I'm not sending you away for fighting, though the gods know I'm sick of you two squabbling. I want you back in Winterfell for your own safety. Three of my men were cut down like dogs not a league from where we sit, and what does Robert do? He goes *hunting.*"

Arya was chewing at her lip in that disgusting way she had. "Can we take Syrio back with us?"

"Who cares about your stupid *dancing master?*" Sansa flared. "Father, I only just now remembered, I *can't* go away, I'm to marry Prince Joffrey." She tried to smile bravely for him. "I love him, Father, I truly truly do, I love him as much as Queen Naerys loved Prince Aemon the Dragonknight, as much as Jonquil loved Ser Florian. I want to be his queen and have his babies."

"Sweet one," her father said gently, "listen to me. When you're old enough, I will make you a match with a high lord who's worthy of you, someone brave and gentle and strong. This match with Joffrey was a terrible mistake. That boy is no Prince Aemon, you must believe me."

"He *is!*" Sansa insisted. "I don't want someone brave and gentle, I want *him*. We'll be ever so happy, just like in the songs, you'll see. I'll give him a son with golden hair, and one day he'll be the king of all the realm, the greatest king that ever was, as brave as the wolf and as proud as the lion."

Arya made a face. "Not if Joffrey's his father," she said. "He's a liar and a craven and anyhow he's a stag, not a lion."

Sansa felt tears in her eyes. "He is *not!* He's not the least bit like that old drunken king," she screamed at her sister, forgetting herself in her grief.

Father looked at her strangely. "*Gods*," he swore softly, "out of the mouth of babes . . ." He shouted for Septa Mordane. To the girls he said, "I am looking for a fast trading galley to take you home. These days, the sea is safer than the kingsroad. You will sail as soon as I can find a proper ship, with Septa Mordane and a complement of guards . . . and yes, with Syrio Forel, if he agrees to enter my service. But say nothing of this. It's better if no one knows of our plans. We'll talk again tomorrow."

Sansa cried as Septa Mordane marched them down the steps. They were going to take it all away; the tournaments and the court and her prince, everything, they were going to send her back to the bleak grey walls of Winterfell and lock her up forever. Her life was over before it had begun.

"Stop that weeping, child," Septa Mordane said sternly. "I am certain your lord father knows what is best for you."

"It won't be so bad, Sansa," Arya said. "We're going to sail on a galley. It will be an adventure, and then we'll be with Bran and Robb again, and Old Nan and Hodor and the rest." She touched her on the arm.

"*Hodor!*" Sansa yelled. "You ought to marry Hodor, you're just like him, stupid and hairy and ugly!" She wrenched away from her sister's hand, stormed into her bedchamber, and barred the door behind her.

EDDARD

"Pain is a gift from the gods, Lord Eddard," Grand Maester Pycelle told him. "It means the bone is knitting, the flesh healing itself. Be thankful."

"I will be thankful when my leg stops throbbing."

Pycelle set a stoppered flask on the table by the bed. "The milk of the poppy, for when the pain grows too onerous."

"I sleep too much already."

"Sleep is the great healer."

"I had hoped that was you."

Pycelle smiled wanly. "It is good to see you in such a fierce humor, my lord." He leaned close and lowered his voice. "There was a raven this morning, a letter for the queen from her lord father. I thought you had best know."

"Dark wings, dark words," Ned said grimly. "What of it?"

"Lord Tywin is greatly wroth about the men you sent after Ser Gregor Clegane," the maester confided. "I feared he would be. You will recall, I said as much in council."

"Let him be wroth," Ned said. Every time his leg throbbed, he remembered Jaime Lannister's smile, and Jory dead in his arms. "Let him write all the letters to the queen he likes. Lord Beric rides beneath the king's own banner. If Lord Tywin attempts to interfere with the king's justice, he will have Robert to answer to. The only thing His Grace enjoys more than hunting is making war on lords who defy him."

Pycelle pulled back, his maester's chain jangling. "As you say. I shall visit again on the morrow." The old man hurriedly gathered up his things and took his leave. Ned had little doubt that he was bound straight for the royal apartments, to whisper at the queen. *I thought you had best know, indeed . . .* as if Cersei had not instructed him to pass along her father's threats. He hoped his response rattled those perfect teeth of hers. Ned was not near as confident of Robert as he pretended, but there was no reason Cersei need know that.

When Pycelle was gone, Ned called for a cup of honeyed wine. That clouded the mind as well, yet not as badly. He needed to be able to think. A thousand times, he asked himself what Jon Arryn might have done, had he lived long enough to act on what he'd learned. Or perhaps he *had* acted, and died for it.

It was queer how sometimes a child's innocent eyes can see things that grown men are blind to. Someday, when Sansa was grown, he would have to tell her how she had made it all come clear for him. *He's not the least bit like that old drunken king,* she had declared, angry and unknowing, and the simple truth of it had twisted inside him, cold as death. *This was the sword that killed Jon Arryn,* Ned thought then, *and it will kill Robert as well, a slower death but full as certain.* Shattered legs may heal in time, but some betrayals fester and poison the soul.

Littlefinger came calling an hour after the Grand Maester had left, clad in a plum-colored doublet with a mockingbird embroidered on the breast in black thread, and a striped cloak of black and white. "I cannot visit long, my lord," he announced. "Lady Tanda expects me to lunch with her. No doubt she will roast me a fatted calf. If it's near as fatted as her daughter, I'm like to rupture and die. And how is your leg?"

"Inflamed and painful, with an itch that is driving me mad."

Littlefinger lifted an eyebrow. "In future, try not to let

any horses fall on it. I would urge you to heal quickly. The realm grows restive. Varys has heard ominous whispers from the west. Freeriders and sellswords have been flocking to Casterly Rock, and not for the thin pleasure of Lord Tywin's conversation."

"Is there word of the king?" Ned demanded. "Just how long does Robert intend to hunt?"

"Given his preferences, I believe he'd stay in the forest until you and the queen both die of old age," Lord Petyr replied with a faint smile. "Lacking that, I imagine he'll return as soon as he's killed something. They found the white hart, it seems . . . or rather, what remained of it. Some wolves found it first, and left His Grace scarcely more than a hoof and a horn. Robert was in a fury, until he heard talk of some monstrous boar deeper in the forest. Then nothing would do but he must have it. Prince Joffrey returned this morning, with the Royces, Ser Balon Swann, and some twenty others of the party. The rest are still with the king."

"The Hound?" Ned asked, frowning. Of all the Lannister party, Sandor Clegane was the one who concerned him the most, now that Ser Jaime had fled the city to join his father.

"Oh, returned with Joffrey, and went straight to the queen." Littlefinger smiled. "I would have given a hundred silver stags to have been a roach in the rushes when he learned that Lord Beric was off to behead his brother."

"Even a blind man could see the Hound loathed his brother."

"Ah, but Gregor was *his* to loathe, not yours to kill. Once Dondarrion lops the summit off our Mountain, the Clegane lands and incomes will pass to Sandor, but I wouldn't hold my water waiting for his thanks, not that one. And now you must forgive me. Lady Tanda awaits with her fatted calves."

On the way to the door, Lord Petyr spied Grand Maester Malleon's massive tome on the table and paused to idly flip open the cover. *"The Lineages and Histories of the Great Houses of the Seven Kingdoms, With Descriptions of Many High Lords and Noble Ladies and Their Children,"* he read. "Now there is tedious reading if ever I saw it. A sleeping potion, my lord?"

For a brief moment Ned considered telling him all of

it, but there was something in Littlefinger's japes that irked him. The man was too clever by half, a mocking smile never far from his lips. "Jon Arryn was studying this volume when he was taken sick," Ned said in a careful tone, to see how he might respond.

And he responded as he always did: with a quip. "In that case," he said, "death must have come as a blessed relief." Lord Petyr Baelish bowed and took his leave.

Eddard Stark allowed himself a curse. Aside from his own retainers, there was scarcely a man in this city he trusted. Littlefinger had concealed Catelyn and helped Ned in his inquiries, yet his haste to save his own skin when Jaime and his swords had come out of the rain still rankled. Varys was worse. For all his protestations of loyalty, the eunuch knew too much and did too little. Grand Maester Pycelle seemed more Cersei's creature with every passing day, and Ser Barristan was an old man, and rigid. He would tell Ned to do his duty.

Time was perilously short. The king would return from his hunt soon, and honor would require Ned to go to him with all he had learned. Vayon Poole had arranged for Sansa and Arya to sail on the *Wind Witch* out of Braavos, three days hence. They would be back at Winterfell before the harvest. Ned could no longer use his concern for their safety to excuse his delay.

Yet last night he had dreamt of Rhaegar's children. Lord Tywin had laid the bodies beneath the Iron Throne, wrapped in the crimson cloaks of his house guard. That was clever of him; the blood did not show so badly against the red cloth. The little princess had been barefoot, still dressed in her bed gown, and the boy . . . the boy . . .

Ned could not let that happen again. The realm could not withstand a second mad king, another dance of blood and vengeance. He must find some way to save the children.

Robert could be merciful. Ser Barristan was scarcely the only man he had pardoned. Grand Maester Pycelle, Varys the Spider, Lord Balon Greyjoy; each had been counted an enemy to Robert once, and each had been welcomed into friendship and allowed to retain honors and office for a pledge of fealty. So long as a man was brave and honest, Robert would treat him with all the honor and respect due a valiant enemy.

This was something else: poison in the dark, a knife thrust to the soul. This he could never forgive, no more than he had forgiven Rhaegar. *He will kill them all,* Ned realized.

And yet, he knew he could not keep silent. He had a duty to Robert, to the realm, to the shade of Jon Arryn . . . and to Bran, who surely must have stumbled on some part of the truth. Why else would they have tried to slay him?

Late that afternoon he summoned Tomard, the portly guardsman with the ginger-colored whiskers his children called Fat Tom. With Jory dead and Alyn gone, Fat Tom had command of his household guard. The thought filled Ned with vague disquiet. Tomard was a solid man; affable, loyal, tireless, capable in a limited way, but he was near fifty, and even in his youth he had never been energetic. Perhaps Ned should not have been so quick to send off half his guard, and all his best swords among them.

"I shall require your help," Ned said when Tomard appeared, looking faintly apprehensive, as he always did when called before his lord. "Take me to the godswood."

"Is that wise, Lord Eddard? With your leg and all?"

"Perhaps not. But necessary."

Tomard summoned Varly. With one arm around each man's shoulders, Ned managed to descend the steep tower steps and hobble across the bailey. "I want the guard doubled," he told Fat Tom. "No one enters or leaves the Tower of the Hand without my leave."

Tom blinked. "M'lord, with Alyn and the others away, we are hard-pressed already—"

"It will only be a short while. Lengthen the watches."

"As you say, m'lord," Tom answered. "Might I ask why—"

"Best not," Ned answered crisply.

The godswood was empty, as it always was here in this citadel of the southron gods. Ned's leg was screaming as they lowered him to the grass beside the heart tree. "Thank you." He drew a paper from his sleeve, sealed with the sigil of his House. "Kindly deliver this at once."

Tomard looked at the name Ned had written on the paper and licked his lips anxiously. "My lord . . ."

"Do as I bid you, Tom," Ned said.

How long he waited in the quiet of the godswood, he

could not say. It was peaceful here. The thick walls shut out the clamor of the castle, and he could hear birds singing, the murmur of crickets, leaves rustling in a gentle wind. The heart tree was an oak, brown and faceless, yet Ned Stark still felt the presence of his gods. His leg did not seem to hurt so much.

She came to him at sunset, as the clouds reddened above the walls and towers. She came alone, as he had bid her. For once she was dressed simply, in leather boots and hunting greens. When she drew back the hood of her brown cloak, he saw the bruise where the king had struck her. The angry plum color had faded to yellow, and the swelling was down, but there was no mistaking it for anything but what it was.

"Why here?" Cersei Lannister asked as she stood over him.

"So the gods can see."

She sat beside him on the grass. Her every move was graceful. Her curling blond hair moved in the wind, and her eyes were green as the leaves of summer. It had been a long time since Ned Stark had seen her beauty, but he saw it now. "I know the truth Jon Arryn died for," he told her.

"Do you?" The queen watched his face, wary as a cat. "Is that why you called me here, Lord Stark? To pose me riddles? Or is it your intent to seize me, as your wife seized my brother?"

"If you truly believed that, you would never have come." Ned touched her cheek gently. "Has he done this before?"

"Once or twice." She shied away from his hand. "Never on the face before. Jaime would have killed him, even if it meant his own life." Cersei looked at him defiantly. "My brother is worth a hundred of your friend."

"Your brother?" Ned said. "Or your lover?"

"Both." She did not flinch from the truth. "Since we were children together. And why not? The Targaryens wed brother to sister for three hundred years, to keep the bloodlines pure. And Jaime and I are more than brother and sister. We are one person in two bodies. We shared a womb together. He came into this world holding my foot, our old maester said. When he is in me, I feel . . . whole." The ghost of a smile flitted over her lips.

"My son Bran . . ."

To her credit, Cersei did not look away. "He saw us. You love your children, do you not?"

Robert had asked him the very same question, the morning of the melee. He gave her the same answer. "With all my heart."

"No less do I love mine."

Ned thought, *If it came to that, the life of some child I did not know, against Robb and Sansa and Arya and Bran and Rickon, what would I do? Even more so, what would* Catelyn *do, if it were Jon's life, against the children of her body?* He did not know. He prayed he never would.

"All three are Jaime's," he said. It was not a question.

"Thank the gods."

The seed is strong, Jon Arryn had cried on his deathbed, and so it was. All those bastards, all with hair as black as night. Grand Maester Malleon recorded the last mating between stag and lion, some ninety years ago, when Tya Lannister wed Gowen Baratheon, third son of the reigning lord. Their only issue, an unnamed boy described in Malleon's tome as a *large and lusty lad born with a full head of black hair,* died in infancy. Thirty years before that a male Lannister had taken a Baratheon maid to wife. She had given him three daughters and a son, each black-haired. No matter how far back Ned searched in the brittle yellowed pages, always he found the gold yielding before the coal.

"A dozen years," Ned said. "How is it that you have had no children by the king?"

She lifted her head, defiant. "Your Robert got me with child once," she said, her voice thick with contempt. "My brother found a woman to cleanse me. He never knew. If truth be told, I can scarcely bear for him to touch me, and I have not let him inside me for years. I know other ways to pleasure him, when he leaves his whores long enough to stagger up to my bedchamber. Whatever we do, the king is usually so drunk that he's forgotten it all by the next morning."

How could they have all been so blind? The truth was there in front of them all the time, written on the children's faces. Ned felt sick. "I remember Robert as he was the day he took the throne, every inch a king," he said quietly. "A thousand other women might have loved him with all their hearts. What did he do to make you hate him so?"

Her eyes burned, green fire in the dusk, like the lioness that was her sigil. "The night of our wedding feast, the first time we shared a bed, he called me by your sister's name. He was on top of me, *in* me, stinking of wine, and he whispered *Lyanna*."

Ned Stark thought of pale blue roses, and for a moment he wanted to weep. "I do not know which of you I pity most."

The queen seemed amused by that. "Save your pity for yourself, Lord Stark. I want none of it."

"You know what I must do."

"Must?" She put her hand on his good leg, just above the knee. "A true man does what he will, not what he must." Her fingers brushed lightly against his thigh, the gentlest of promises. "The realm needs a strong Hand. Joff will not come of age for years. No one wants war again, least of all me." Her hand touched his face, his hair. "If friends can turn to enemies, enemies can become friends. Your wife is a thousand leagues away, and my brother has fled. Be kind to me, Ned. I swear to you, you shall never regret it."

"Did you make the same offer to Jon Arryn?"

She slapped him.

"I shall wear that as a badge of honor," Ned said dryly.

"Honor," she spat. "How dare you play the noble lord with me! What do you take me for? You've a bastard of your own, I've seen him. Who was the mother, I wonder? Some Dornish peasant you raped while her holdfast burned? A whore? Or was it the grieving sister, the Lady Ashara? She threw herself into the sea, I'm told. Why was that? For the brother you slew, or the child you stole? Tell me, my *honorable* Lord Eddard, how are you any different from Robert, or me, or Jaime?"

"For a start," said Ned, "I do not kill children. You would do well to listen, my lady. I shall say this only once. When the king returns from his hunt, I intend to lay the truth before him. You must be gone by then. You and your children, all three, and not to Casterly Rock. If I were you, I should take ship for the Free Cities, or even farther, to the Summer Isles or the Port of Ibben. As far as the winds blow."

"Exile," she said. "A bitter cup to drink from."

"A sweeter cup than your father served Rhaegar's children," Ned said, "and kinder than you deserve. Your father and your brothers would do well to go with you. Lord Tywin's gold will buy you comfort and hire swords to keep you safe. You shall need them. I promise you, no matter where you flee, Robert's wrath will follow you, to the back of beyond if need be."

The queen stood. "And what of my wrath, Lord Stark?" she asked softly. Her eyes searched his face. "You should have taken the realm for yourself. It was there for the taking. Jaime told me how you found him on the Iron Throne the day King's Landing fell, and made him yield it up. That was your moment. All you needed to do was climb those steps, and sit. Such a sad mistake."

"I have made more mistakes than you can possibly imagine," Ned said, "but that was not one of them."

"Oh, but it was, my lord," Cersei insisted. "When you play the game of thrones, you win or you die. There is no middle ground."

She turned up her hood to hide her swollen face and left him there in the dark beneath the oak, amidst the quiet of the godswood, under a blue-black sky. The stars were coming out.

DAENERYS

The heart was steaming in the cool evening air when Khal Drogo set it before her, raw and bloody. His arms were red to the elbow. Behind him, his bloodriders knelt on the sand beside the corpse of the wild stallion, stone knives in their hands. The stallion's blood looked black in the flickering orange glare of the torches that ringed the high chalk walls of the pit.

Dany touched the soft swell of her belly. Sweat beaded her skin and trickled down her brow. She could feel the old women watching her, the ancient crones of Vaes Dothrak, with eyes that shone dark as polished flint in their wrinkled faces. She must not flinch or look afraid. *I am the blood of the dragon,* she told herself as she took the stallion's heart in both hands, lifted it to her mouth, and plunged her teeth into the tough, stringy flesh.

Warm blood filled her mouth and ran down over her chin. The taste threatened to gag her, but she made herself chew and swallow. The heart of a stallion would make her son strong and swift and fearless, or so the Dothraki believed, but only if the mother could eat it all. If she choked on the blood or retched up the flesh, the omens were less favorable; the child might be stillborn, or come forth weak, deformed, or female.

Her handmaids had helped her ready herself for the ceremony. Despite the tender mother's stomach that had afflicted her these past two moons, Dany had dined on bowls of half-clotted blood to accustom herself to the taste, and Irri made her chew strips of dried horseflesh until her jaws were aching. She had starved herself for a day and a night before the ceremony in the hopes that hunger would help her keep down the raw meat.

The wild stallion's heart was all muscle, and Dany had to worry it with her teeth and chew each mouthful a long time. No steel was permitted within the sacred confines of Vaes Dothrak, beneath the shadow of the Mother of Mountains; she had to rip the heart apart with teeth and nails. Her stomach roiled and heaved, yet she kept on, her face smeared with the heartsblood that sometimes seemed to explode against her lips.

Khal Drogo stood over her as she ate, his face as hard as a bronze shield. His long black braid was shiny with oil. He wore gold rings in his mustache, gold bells in his braid, and a heavy belt of solid gold medallions around his waist, but his chest was bare. She looked at him whenever she felt her strength failing; looked at him, and chewed and swallowed, chewed and swallowed, chewed and swallowed. Toward the end, Dany thought she glimpsed a fierce pride in his dark, almond-shaped eyes, but she could not be sure. The *khal's* face did not often betray the thoughts within.

And finally it was done. Her cheeks and fingers were sticky as she forced down the last of it. Only then did she turn her eyes back to the old women, the crones of the *dosh khaleen.*

"*Khalakka dothrae mr'anha!*" she proclaimed in her best Dothraki. *A prince rides inside me!* She had practiced the phrase for days with her handmaid Jhiqui.

The oldest of the crones, a bent and shriveled stick of a woman with a single black eye, raised her arms on high. "*Khalakka dothrae!*" she shrieked. *The prince is riding!*

"*He is riding!*" the other women answered. "*Rakh! Rakh! Rakh haj!*" they proclaimed. *A boy, a boy, a strong boy.*

Bells rang, a sudden clangor of bronze birds. A deep-throated warhorn sounded its long low note. The old women began to chant. Underneath their painted leather vests, their withered dugs swayed back and forth, shiny with oil and sweat. The eunuchs who served them threw bundles of dried grasses into a great bronze brazier, and clouds of fragrant smoke rose up toward the moon and the stars. The Dothraki believed the stars were horses made of fire, a great herd that galloped across the sky by night.

As the smoke ascended, the chanting died away and the ancient crone closed her single eye, the better to peer into the future. The silence that fell was complete. Dany could hear the distant call of night birds, the hiss and crackle of the torches, the gentle lapping of water from the lake. The Dothraki stared at her with eyes of night, waiting.

Khal Drogo laid his hand on Dany's arm. She could feel the tension in his fingers. Even a *khal* as mighty as Drogo could know fear when the *dosh khaleen* peered into smoke of the future. At her back, her handmaids fluttered anxiously.

Finally the crone opened her eye and lifted her arms. "I have seen his face, and heard the thunder of his hooves," she proclaimed in a thin, wavery voice.

"The thunder of his hooves!" the others chorused.

"As swift as the wind he rides, and behind him his *khalasar* covers the earth, men without number, with *arakhs* shining in their hands like blades of razor grass. Fierce as a storm this prince will be. His enemies will tremble before him, and their wives will weep tears of blood and rend their flesh in grief. The bells in his hair will sing his coming, and the milk men in the stone tents will fear his name." The old woman trembled and looked at Dany almost as if she were afraid. "The prince is riding, and he shall be the stallion who mounts the world."

"The stallion who mounts the world!" the onlookers cried in echo, until the night rang to the sound of their voices.

The one-eyed crone peered at Dany. "What shall he be called, the stallion who mounts the world?"

She stood to answer. "He shall be called Rhaego," she said, using the words that Jhiqui had taught her. Her hands touched the swell beneath her breasts protectively as a roar went up from the Dothraki. *"Rhaego,"* they screamed. *"Rhaego, Rhaego, Rhaego!"*

The name was still ringing in her ears as Khal Drogo led her from the pit. His bloodriders fell in behind them. A procession followed them out onto the godsway, the broad grassy road that ran through the heart of Vaes Dothrak, from the horse gate to the Mother of Mountains. The crones of the *dosh khaleen* came first, with their eunuchs and slaves. Some supported themselves with tall carved staffs as they struggled along on ancient, shaking legs, while others walked as proud as any horselord. Each of the old women had been a *khaleesi* once. When their lord husbands died and a new *khal* took his place at the front of his riders, with a new *khaleesi* mounted beside him, they were sent here, to reign over the vast Dothraki nation. Even the mightiest of *khals* bowed to the wisdom and authority of the *dosh khaleen.* Still, it gave Dany the shivers to think that one day she might be sent to join them, whether she willed it or no.

Behind the wise women came the others; Khal Ogo and his son, the *khalakka* Fogo, Khal Jommo and his wives, the chief men of Drogo's *khalasar*, Dany's handmaids, the *khal's* servants and slaves, and more. Bells rang and drums beat a stately cadence as they marched along the godsway. Stolen heroes and the gods of dead peoples brooded in the darkness beyond the road. Alongside the procession, slaves ran lightly through the grass with torches in their hands, and the flickering flames made the great monuments seem almost alive.

"What is meaning, name Rhaego?" Khal Drogo asked as they walked, using the Common Tongue of the Seven Kingdoms. She had been teaching him a few words when she could. Drogo was quick to learn when he put his mind to it, though his accent was so thick and barbarous that neither Ser Jorah nor Viserys could understand a word he said.

"My brother Rhaegar was a fierce warrior, my sun-and-stars," she told him. "He died before I was born. Ser Jorah says that he was the last of the dragons."

Khal Drogo looked down at her. His face was a copper mask, yet under the long black mustache, drooping beneath the weight of its gold rings, she thought she glimpsed the shadow of a smile. "Is good name, Dan Ares wife, moon of my life," he said.

They rode to the lake the Dothraki called the Womb of the World, surrounded by a fringe of reeds, its water still and calm. A thousand thousand years ago, Jhiqui told her, the first man had emerged from its depths, riding upon the back of the first horse.

The procession waited on the grassy shore as Dany stripped and let her soiled clothing fall to the ground. Naked, she stepped gingerly into the water. Irri said the lake had no bottom, but Dany felt soft mud squishing between her toes as she pushed through the tall reeds. The moon floated on the still black waters, shattering and re-forming as her ripples washed over it. Goose pimples rose on her pale skin as the coldness crept up her thighs and kissed her lower lips. The stallion's blood had dried on her hands and around her mouth. Dany cupped her fingers and lifted the sacred waters over her head, cleansing herself and the child inside her while the *khal* and the others looked on. She heard the old women of the *dosh khaleen* muttering to each other as they watched, and wondered what they were saying.

When she emerged from the lake, shivering and dripping, her handmaid Doreah hurried to her with a robe of painted sandsilk, but Khal Drogo waved her away. He was looking on her swollen breasts and the curve of her belly with approval, and Dany could see the shape of his manhood pressing through his horsehide trousers, below the heavy gold medallions of his belt. She went to him and helped him unlace. Then her huge *khal* took her by the hips and lifted her into the air, as he might lift a child. The bells in his hair rang softly.

Dany wrapped her arms around his shoulders and pressed her face against his neck as he thrust himself inside her. Three quick strokes and it was done. *"The stallion who mounts the world,"* Drogo whispered hoarsely. His hands still smelled of horse blood. He bit at her throat, hard, in the moment of his pleasure, and when he lifted her off, his seed filled her and trickled down the inside of her thighs. Only then was Doreah permitted to drape her in the scented sandsilk, and Irri to fit soft slippers to her feet.

Khal Drogo laced himself up and spoke a command,

and horses were brought to the lakeshore. Cohollo had the honor of helping the *khaleesi* onto her silver. Drogo spurred his stallion, and set off down the godsway beneath the moon and stars. On her silver, Dany easily kept pace.

The silk tenting that roofed Khal Drogo's hall had been rolled up tonight, and the moon followed them inside. Flames leapt ten feet in the air from three huge stone-lined firepits. The air was thick with the smells of roasting meat and curdled, fermented mare's milk. The hall was crowded and noisy when they entered, the cushions packed with those whose rank and name were not sufficient to allow them at the ceremony. As Dany rode beneath the arched entry and up the center aisle, every eye was on her. The Dothraki screamed out comments on her belly and her breasts, hailing the life within her. She could not understand all they shouted, but one phrase came clear. *"The stallion that mounts the world,"* she heard, bellowed in a thousand voices.

The sounds of drums and horns swirled up into the night. Half-clothed women spun and danced on the low tables, amid joints of meat and platters piled high with plums and dates and pomegranates. Many of the men were drunk on clotted mare's milk, yet Dany knew no *arakhs* would clash tonight, not here in the sacred city, where blades and bloodshed were forbidden.

Khal Drogo dismounted and took his place on the high bench. Khal Jommo and Khal Ogo, who had been in Vaes Dothrak with their *khalasars* when they arrived, were given seats of high honor to Drogo's right and left. The bloodriders of the three *khals* sat below them, and farther down Khal Jommo's four wives.

Dany climbed off her silver and gave the reins to one of the slaves. As Doreah and Irri arranged her cushions, she searched for her brother. Even across the length of the crowded hall, Viserys should have been conspicuous with his pale skin, silvery hair, and beggar's rags, but she did not see him anywhere.

Her glance roamed the crowded tables near the walls, where men whose braids were even shorter than their manhoods sat on frayed rugs and flat cushions around the low tables, but all the faces she saw had black eyes and copper skin. She spied Ser Jorah Mormont near the center of the hall, close to the middle firepit. It was a place of respect, if not high honor; the Dothraki esteemed the knight's prowess with a sword. Dany sent Jhiqui to bring him to her table. Mormont came at once, and went to one knee before her. *"Khaleesi,"* he said, "I am yours to command."

She patted the stuffed horsehide cushion beside her. "Sit and talk with me."

"You honor me." The knight seated himself cross-legged on the cushion. A slave knelt before him, offering a wooden platter full of ripe figs. Ser Jorah took one and bit it in half.

"Where is my brother?" Dany asked. "He ought to have come by now, for the feast."

"I saw His Grace this morning," he told her. "He told me he was going to the Western Market, in search of wine."

"Wine?" Dany said doubtfully. Viserys could not abide the taste of the fermented mare's milk the Dothraki drank, she knew that, and he was oft at the bazaars these days, drinking with the traders who came in the great caravans from east and west. He seemed to find their company more congenial than hers.

"Wine," Ser Jorah confirmed, "and he has some thought to recruit men for his army from the sellswords who guard the caravans." A serving girl laid a blood pie in front of him, and he attacked it with both hands.

"Is that wise?" she asked. "He has no gold to pay soldiers. What if he's betrayed?" Caravan guards were seldom troubled much by thoughts of honor, and the Usurper in King's Landing would pay well for her brother's head. "You ought to have gone with him, to keep him safe. You are his sworn sword."

"We are in Vaes Dothrak," he reminded her. "No one may carry a blade here or shed a man's blood."

"Yet men die," she said. "Jhogo told me. Some of the traders have eunuchs with them, huge men who strangle thieves with wisps of silk. That way no blood is shed and the gods are not angered."

"Then let us hope your brother will be wise enough not to steal anything." Ser Jorah wiped the grease off his mouth with the back of his hand and leaned close over the table. "He had planned to take your dragon's eggs, until I warned him that I'd cut off his hand if he so much as touched them."

For a moment Dany was so shocked she had no words. "My eggs . . . but they're *mine*, Magister Illyrio gave them to me, a bride gift, why would Viserys want . . . they're only stones . . ."

"The same could be said of rubies and diamonds and fire opals, Princess . . . and dragon's eggs are rarer by far. Those traders he's been drinking with would sell their own manhoods for even one of those *stones*, and with all three Viserys could buy as many sellswords as he might need."

Dany had not known, had not even suspected. "Then . . . he should have them. He does not need to steal them. He had only to ask. He is my brother . . . and my true king."

"He is your brother," Ser Jorah acknowledged.

"You do not understand, ser," she said. "My mother died giving me birth, and my father and my brother Rhaegar even before that. I would never have known so much as their names if Viserys had not been there to tell me. He was the only one left. The only one. He is all I have."

"Once," said Ser Jorah. "No longer, *Khaleesi*. You belong to the Dothraki now. In your womb rides the stallion who mounts the world." He held out his cup, and a slave filled it with fermented mare's milk, sour-smelling and thick with clots.

Dany waved her away. Even the smell of it made her feel ill, and she would take no chances of bringing up the horse heart she had forced herself to eat. "What does it mean?" she asked. "What is this stallion? Everyone was shouting it at me, but I don't understand."

"The stallion is the *khal* of *khals* promised in ancient prophecy, child. He will unite the Dothraki into a single *khalasar* and ride to the ends of the earth, or so it was promised. All the people of the world will be his herd."

"Oh," Dany said in a small voice. Her hand smoothed her robe down over the swell of her stomach. "I named him Rhaego."

"A name to make the Usurper's blood run cold."

Suddenly Doreah was tugging at her elbow. *"My lady,"* the handmaid whispered urgently, "your brother . . ."

Dany looked down the length of the long, roofless hall

and there he was, striding toward her. From the lurch in
his step, she could tell at once that Viserys had found his
wine . . . and something that passed for courage.

He was wearing his scarlet silks, soiled and travel-
stained. His cloak and gloves were black velvet, faded
from the sun. His boots were dry and cracked, his silver-
blond hair matted and tangled. A longsword swung from
his belt in a leather scabbard. The Dothraki eyed the
sword as he passed; Dany heard curses and threats and
angry muttering rising all around her, like a tide. The
music died away in a nervous stammering of drums.

A sense of dread closed around her heart. "Go to him,"
she commanded Ser Jorah. "Stop him. Bring him here.
Tell him he can have the dragon's eggs if that is what he
wants." The knight rose swiftly to his feet.

"Where is my sister?" Viserys shouted, his voice thick
with wine. "I've come for her feast. How dare you presume to eat without me? No one eats before the king.
Where is she? The whore can't hide from the dragon."

He stopped beside the largest of the three firepits, peering around at the faces of the Dothraki. There were five
thousand men in the hall, but only a handful who knew
the Common Tongue. Yet even if his words were incomprehensible, you had only to look at him to know that he
was drunk.

Ser Jorah went to him swiftly, whispered something in
his ear, and took him by the arm, but Viserys wrenched
free. "Keep your hands off me! No one touches the dragon
without leave."

Dany glanced anxiously up at the high bench. Khal
Drogo was saying something to the other *khals* beside
him. Khal Jommo grinned, and Khal Ogo began to guffaw
loudly.

The sound of laughter made Viserys lift his eyes. "Khal
Drogo," he said thickly, his voice almost polite. "I'm here
for the feast." He staggered away from Ser Jorah, making
to join the three *khals* on the high bench.

Khal Drogo rose, spat out a dozen words in Dothraki,
faster than Dany could understand, and pointed. "Khal
Drogo says your place is not on the high bench," Ser Jorah
translated for her brother. "Khal Drogo says your place is
there."

Viserys glanced where the *khal* was pointing. At the

back of the long hall, in a corner by the wall, deep in shadow so better men would not need to look on them, sat the lowest of the low; raw unblooded boys, old men with clouded eyes and stiff joints, the dim-witted and the maimed. Far from the meat, and farther from honor. "That is no place for a king," her brother declared.

"Is place," Khal Drogo answered, in the Common Tongue that Dany had taught him, "for Sorefoot King." He clapped his hands together. "A cart! Bring cart for *Khal Rhaggat!*"

Five thousand Dothraki began to laugh and shout. Ser Jorah was standing beside Viserys, screaming in his ear, but the roar in the hall was so thunderous that Dany could not hear what he was saying. Her brother shouted back and the two men grappled, until Mormont knocked Viserys bodily to the floor.

Her brother drew his sword.

The bared steel shone a fearful red in the glare from the firepits. *"Keep away from me!"* Viserys hissed. Ser Jorah backed off a step, and her brother climbed unsteadily to his feet. He waved the sword over his head, the borrowed blade that Magister Illyrio had given him to make him seem more kingly. Dothraki were shrieking at him from all sides, screaming vile curses.

Dany gave a wordless cry of terror. She knew what a drawn sword meant here, even if her brother did not.

Her voice made Viserys turn his head, and he saw her for the first time. "There she is," he said, smiling. He stalked toward her, slashing at the air as if to cut a path through a wall of enemies, though no one tried to bar his way.

"The blade . . . you must not," she begged him. "Please, Viserys. It is forbidden. Put down the sword and come share my cushions. There's drink, food . . . is it the dragon's eggs you want? You can have them, only throw away the sword."

"Do as she tells you, fool," Ser Jorah shouted, "before you get us all killed."

Viserys laughed. "They can't kill us. They can't shed blood here in the sacred city . . . but *I* can." He laid the point of his sword between Daenerys's breasts and slid it downward, over the curve of her belly. "I want what I came for," he told her. "I want the crown he promised me. He bought you, but he never paid for you. Tell him I want what I bargained for, or I'm taking you back. You and the eggs both. He can keep his bloody foal. I'll cut the bastard out and leave it for him." The sword point pushed through her silks and pricked at her navel. Viserys was weeping, she saw; weeping and laughing, both at the same time, this man who had once been her brother.

Distantly, as from far away, Dany heard her handmaid Jhiqui sobbing in fear, pleading that she dared not translate, that the *khal* would bind her and drag her behind his horse all the way up the Mother of Mountains. She put her arm around the girl. "Don't be afraid," she said. "I shall tell him."

She did not know if she had enough words, yet when she was done Khal Drogo spoke a few brusque sentences in Dothraki, and she knew he understood. The sun of her life stepped down from the high bench. "What did he say?" the man who had been her brother asked her, flinching.

It had grown so silent in the hall that she could hear the bells in Khal Drogo's hair, chiming softly with each step he took. His bloodriders followed him, like three copper shadows. Daenerys had gone cold all over. "He says you shall have a splendid golden crown that men shall tremble to behold."

Viserys smiled and lowered his sword. That was the saddest thing, the thing that tore at her afterward . . . the way he smiled. "That was all I wanted," he said. "What was promised."

When the sun of her life reached her, Dany slid an arm around his waist. The *khal* said a word, and his bloodriders leapt forward. Qotho seized the man who had been her brother by the arms. Haggo shattered his wrist with a single, sharp twist of his huge hands. Cohollo pulled the sword from his limp fingers. Even now Viserys did not understand. "No," he shouted, "you cannot touch me, I am the dragon, the *dragon*, and I will be *crowned!*"

Khal Drogo unfastened his belt. The medallions were pure gold, massive and ornate, each one as large as a man's hand. He shouted a command. Cook slaves pulled a heavy iron stew pot from the firepit, dumped the stew onto the ground, and returned the pot to the flames. Drogo tossed in the belt and watched without expression as the medallions turned red and began to lose their shape. She could see fires dancing in the onyx of his eyes. A slave handed him a pair of thick horsehair mittens, and he pulled them on, never so much as looking at the man.

Viserys began to scream the high, wordless scream of the coward facing death. He kicked and twisted, whimpered like a dog and wept like a child, but the Dothraki held him tight between them. Ser Jorah had made his way to Dany's side. He put a hand on her shoulder. "Turn away, my princess, I beg you."

"No." She folded her arms across the swell of her belly, protectively.

At the last, Viserys looked at her. "Sister, please . . . Dany, tell them . . . make them . . . sweet sister . . ."

When the gold was half-melted and starting to run, Drogo reached into the flames, snatched out the pot. "Crown!" he roared. "Here. A crown for Cart King!" And upended the pot over the head of the man who had been her brother.

The sound Viserys Targaryen made when that hideous iron helmet covered his face was like nothing human. His feet hammered a frantic beat against the dirt floor, slowed, stopped. Thick globs of molten gold dripped down onto his chest, setting the scarlet silk to smoldering . . . yet no drop of blood was spilled.

He was no dragon, Dany thought, curiously calm. *Fire cannot kill a dragon.*

EDDARD

He was walking through the crypts beneath Winterfell, as he had walked a thousand times before. The Kings of Winter watched him pass with eyes of ice, and the direwolves at their feet turned their great stone heads and snarled. Last of all, he came to the tomb where his father slept, with Brandon and Lyanna beside him. *"Promise me, Ned,"* Lyanna's statue whispered. She wore a garland of pale blue roses, and her eyes wept blood.

Eddard Stark jerked upright, his heart racing, the blankets tangled around him. The room was black as pitch, and someone was hammering on the door. "Lord Eddard," a voice called loudly.

"A moment." Groggy and naked, he stumbled his way across the darkened chamber. When he opened the door, he found Tomard with an upraised fist, and Cayn with a taper in hand. Between them stood the king's own steward.

The man's face might have been carved of stone, so little did it show. "My lord Hand," he intoned. "His Grace the King commands your presence. At once."

So Robert had returned from his hunt. It was long past

time. "I shall need a few moments to dress." Ned left the man waiting without. Cayn helped him with his clothes; white linen tunic and grey cloak, trousers cut open down his plaster-sheathed leg, his badge of office, and last of all a belt of heavy silver links. He sheathed the Valyrian dagger at his waist.

The Red Keep was dark and still as Cayn and Tomard escorted him across the inner bailey. The moon hung low over the walls, ripening toward full. On the ramparts, a guardsman in a gold cloak walked his rounds.

The royal apartments were in Maegor's Holdfast, a massive square fortress that nestled in the heart of the Red Keep behind walls twelve feet thick and a dry moat lined with iron spikes, a castle-within-a-castle. Ser Boros Blount guarded the far end of the bridge, white steel armor ghostly in the moonlight. Within, Ned passed two other knights of the Kingsguard; Ser Preston Greenfield stood at the bottom of the steps, and Ser Barristan Selmy waited at the door of the king's bedchamber. *Three men in white cloaks*, he thought, remembering, and a strange chill went through him. Ser Barristan's face was as pale as his armor. Ned had only to look at him to know that something was dreadfully wrong. The royal steward opened the door. "Lord Eddard Stark, the Hand of the King," he announced.

"Bring him here," Robert's voice called, strangely thick.

Fires blazed in the twin hearths at either end of the bedchamber, filling the room with a sullen red glare. The heat within was suffocating. Robert lay across the canopied bed. At the bedside hovered Grand Maester Pycelle, while Lord Renly paced restlessly before the shuttered windows. Servants moved back and forth, feeding logs to the fire and boiling wine. Cersei Lannister sat on the edge of the bed beside her husband. Her hair was tousled, as if from sleep, but there was nothing sleepy in her eyes. They followed Ned as Tomard and Cayn helped him cross the room. He seemed to move very slowly, as if he were still dreaming.

The king still wore his boots. Ned could see dried mud and blades of grass clinging to the leather where Robert's feet stuck out beneath the blanket that covered him. A green doublet lay on the floor, slashed open and discarded, the cloth crusted with red-brown stains. The room smelled of smoke and blood and death.

"Ned," the king whispered when he saw him. His face was pale as milk. "Come . . . closer."

His men brought him close. Ned steadied himself with a hand on the bedpost. He had only to look down at Robert to know how bad it was. "What . . . ?" he began, his throat clenched.

"A boar." Lord Renly was still in his hunting greens, his cloak spattered with blood.

"A devil," the king husked. "My own fault. Too much wine, damn me to hell. Missed my thrust."

"And where were the rest of you?" Ned demanded of Lord Renly. "Where was Ser Barristan and the Kingsguard?"

Renly's mouth twitched. "My brother commanded us to stand aside and let him take the boar alone."

Eddard Stark lifted the blanket.

They had done what they could to close him up, but it was nowhere near enough. The boar must have been a fearsome thing. It had ripped the king from groin to nipple with its tusks. The wine-soaked bandages that Grand Maester Pycelle had applied were already black with blood, and the smell off the wound was hideous. Ned's stomach turned. He let the blanket fall.

"Stinks," Robert said. "The stink of death, don't think I can't smell it. Bastard did me good, eh? But I . . . I paid him back in kind, Ned." The king's smile was as terrible as his wound, his teeth red. "Drove a knife right through his eye. Ask them if I didn't. Ask them."

"Truly," Lord Renly murmured. "We brought the carcass back with us, at my brother's command."

"For the feast," Robert whispered. "Now leave us. The lot of you. I need to speak with Ned."

"Robert, my sweet lord . . ." Cersei began.

"I said *leave*," Robert insisted with a hint of his old fierceness. "What part of that don't you understand, woman?"

Cersei gathered up her skirts and her dignity and led the way to the door. Lord Renly and the others followed. Grand Maester Pycelle lingered, his hands shaking as he offered the king a cup of thick white liquid. "The milk of the poppy, Your Grace," he said. "Drink. For your pain."

Robert knocked the cup away with the back of his hand. "Away with you. I'll sleep soon enough, old fool. Get out."

Grand Maester Pycelle gave Ned a stricken look as he shuffled from the room.

"Damn you, Robert," Ned said when they were alone. His leg was throbbing so badly he was almost blind with pain. Or perhaps it was grief that fogged his eyes. He lowered himself to the bed, beside his friend. "Why do you always have to be so headstrong?"

"Ah, fuck you, Ned," the king said hoarsely. "I killed the bastard, didn't I?" A lock of matted black hair fell across his eyes as he glared up at Ned. "Ought to do the same for you. Can't leave a man to hunt in peace. Ser Robar found me. Gregor's head. Ugly thought. Never told the Hound. Let Cersei surprise him." His laugh turned into a grunt as a spasm of pain hit him. "Gods have mercy," he muttered, swallowing his agony. "The girl. Daenerys. Only a child, you were right . . . that's why, the girl . . . the gods sent the boar . . . sent to punish me . . ." The king coughed, bringing up blood. "Wrong, it was wrong, I . . . only a girl . . . Varys, Littlefinger, even my brother . . . worthless . . . no one to tell me *no* but you, Ned . . . only you . . ." He lifted his hand, the gesture pained and feeble. "Paper and ink. There, on the table. Write what I tell you."

Ned smoothed the paper out across his knee and took up the quill. "At your command, Your Grace."

"This is the will and word of Robert of House Baratheon, the First of his Name, King of the Andals and all the rest—put in the damn titles, you know how it goes. I do hereby command Eddard of House Stark, Lord of Winterfell and Hand of the King, to serve as Lord Regent and Protector of the Realm upon my . . . upon my death . . . to rule in my . . . in my stead, until my son Joffrey does come of age . . ."

"Robert . . ." *Joffrey is not your son,* he wanted to say, but the words would not come. The agony was written too plainly across Robert's face; he could not hurt him more. So Ned bent his head and wrote, but where the king had said "my son Joffrey," he scrawled "my heir" instead. The deceit made him feel soiled. *The lies we tell for love,* he thought. *May the gods forgive me.* "What else would you have me say?"

"Say . . . whatever you need to. Protect and defend, gods old and new, you have the words. Write. I'll sign it. You give it to the council when I'm dead."

"Robert," Ned said in a voice thick with grief, "you must not do this. Don't die on me. The realm needs you."

Robert took his hand, fingers squeezing hard. "You are . . . such a bad liar, Ned Stark," he said through his pain. "The realm . . . the realm knows . . . what a wretched king I've been. Bad as Aerys, the gods spare me."

"No," Ned told his dying friend, "not so bad as Aerys, Your Grace. Not near so bad as Aerys."

Robert managed a weak red smile. "At the least, they will say . . . this last thing . . . this I did right. You won't fail me. You'll rule now. You'll hate it, worse than I did . . . but you'll do well. Are you done with the scribbling?"

"Yes, Your Grace." Ned offered Robert the paper. The king scrawled his signature blindly, leaving a smear of blood across the letter. "The seal should be witnessed."

"Serve the boar at my funeral feast," Robert rasped. "Apple in its mouth, skin seared crisp. Eat the bastard. Don't care if you choke on him. Promise me, Ned."

"I promise." *Promise me, Ned,* Lyanna's voice echoed.

"The girl," the king said. "Daenerys. Let her live. If you can, if it . . . not too late . . . talk to them . . . . Varys, Littlefinger . . . don't let them kill her. And help my son, Ned. Make him be . . . better than me." He winced. "Gods have mercy."

"They will, my friend," Ned said. "They will."

The king closed his eyes and seemed to relax. "Killed by a pig," he muttered. "Ought to laugh, but it hurts too much."

Ned was not laughing. "Shall I call them back?"

Robert gave a weak nod. "As you will. Gods, why is it so *cold* in here?"

The servants rushed back in and hurried to feed the fires. The queen had gone; that was some small relief, at least. If she had any sense, Cersei would take her children and fly before the break of day, Ned thought. She had lingered too long already.

King Robert did not seem to miss her. He bid his

brother Renly and Grand Maester Pycelle to stand in witness as he pressed his seal into the hot yellow wax that Ned had dripped upon his letter. "Now give me something for the pain and let me die."

Hurriedly Grand Maester Pycelle mixed him another draught of the milk of the poppy. This time the king drank deeply. His black beard was beaded with thick white droplets when he threw the empty cup aside. "Will I dream?"

Ned gave him his answer. "You will, my lord."

"Good," he said, smiling. "I will give Lyanna your love, Ned. Take care of my children for me."

The words twisted in Ned's belly like a knife. For a moment he was at a loss. He could not bring himself to lie. Then he remembered the bastards: little Barra at her mother's breast, Mya in the Vale, Gendry at his forge, and all the others. "I shall . . . guard your children as if they were my own," he said slowly.

Robert nodded and closed his eyes. Ned watched his old friend sag softly into the pillows as the milk of the poppy washed the pain from his face. Sleep took him.

Heavy chains jangled softly as Grand Maester Pycelle came up to Ned. "I will do all in my power, my lord, but the wound has mortified. It took them two days to get him back. By the time I saw him, it was too late. I can lessen His Grace's suffering, but only the gods can heal him now."

"How long?" Ned asked.

"By rights, he should be dead already. I have never seen a man cling to life so fiercely."

"My brother was always strong," Lord Renly said. "Not wise, perhaps, but strong." In the sweltering heat of the bedchamber, his brow was slick with sweat. He might have been Robert's ghost as he stood there, young and dark and handsome. "He slew the boar. His entrails were sliding from his belly, yet somehow he slew the boar." His voice was full of wonder.

"Robert was never a man to leave the battleground so long as a foe remained standing," Ned told him.

Outside the door, Ser Barristan Selmy still guarded the tower stairs. "Maester Pycelle has given Robert the milk of the poppy," Ned told him. "See that no one disturbs his rest without leave from me."

"It shall be as you command, my lord." Ser Barristan seemed old beyond his years. "I have failed my sacred trust."

"Even the truest knight cannot protect a king against himself," Ned said. "Robert loved to hunt boar. I have seen him take a thousand of them." He would stand his ground without flinching, his legs braced, the great spear in his hands, and as often as not he would curse the boar as it charged, and wait until the last possible second, until it was almost on him, before he killed it with a single sure and savage thrust. "No one could know this one would be his death."

"You are kind to say so, Lord Eddard."

"The king himself said as much. He blamed the wine."

The white-haired knight gave a weary nod. "His Grace was reeling in his saddle by the time we flushed the boar from his lair, yet he commanded us all to stand aside."

"I wonder, Ser Barristan," asked Varys, so quietly, "who gave the king this wine?"

Ned had not heard the eunuch approach, but when he looked around, there he stood. He wore a black velvet robe that brushed the floor, and his face was freshly powdered.

"The wine was from the king's own skin," Ser Barristan said.

"Only one skin? Hunting is such thirsty work."

"I did not keep count. More than one, for a certainty. His squire would fetch him a fresh skin whenever he required it."

"Such a dutiful boy," said Varys, "to make certain His Grace did not lack for refreshment."

Ned had a bitter taste in his mouth. He recalled the two fair-haired boys Robert had sent chasing after a breastplate stretcher. The king had told everyone the tale that night at the feast, laughing until he shook. "Which squire?"

"The elder," said Ser Barristan. "Lancel."

"I know the lad well," said Varys. "A stalwart boy, Ser Kevan Lannister's son, nephew to Lord Tywin and cousin to the queen. I hope the dear sweet lad does not blame himself. Children are so vulnerable in the innocence of their youth, how well do I remember."

Certainly Varys had once been young. Ned doubted

that he had ever been innocent. "You mention children. Robert had a change of heart concerning Daenerys Targaryen. Whatever arrangements you made, I want unmade. At once."

"Alas," said Varys. "At once may be too late. I fear those birds have flown. But I shall do what I can, my lord. With your leave." He bowed and vanished down the steps, his soft-soled slippers whispering against the stone as he made his descent.

Cayn and Tomard were helping Ned across the bridge when Lord Renly emerged from Maegor's Holdfast. "Lord Eddard," he called after Ned, "a moment, if you would be so kind."

Ned stopped. "As you wish."

Renly walked to his side. "Send your men away." They met in the center of the bridge, the dry moat beneath them. Moonlight silvered the cruel edges of the spikes that lined its bed.

Ned gestured. Tomard and Cayn bowed their heads and backed away respectfully. Lord Renly glanced warily at Ser Boros on the far end of the span, at Ser Preston in the doorway behind them. "That letter." He leaned close. "Was it the regency? Has my brother named you Protector?" He did not wait for a reply. "My lord, I have thirty men in my personal guard, and other friends beside, knights and lords. Give me an hour, and I can put a hundred swords in your hand."

"And what should I do with a hundred swords, my lord?"

"*Strike!* Now, while the castle sleeps." Renly looked back at Ser Boros again and dropped his voice to an urgent whisper. "We must get Joffrey away from his mother and take him in hand. Protector or no, the man who holds the king holds the kingdom. We should seize Myrcella and Tommen as well. Once we have her children, Cersei will not dare oppose us. The council will confirm you as Lord Protector and make Joffrey your ward."

Ned regarded him coldly. "Robert is not dead yet. The gods may spare him. If not, I shall convene the council to hear his final words and consider the matter of the succession, but I will not dishonor his last hours on earth by shedding blood in his halls and dragging frightened children from their beds."

Lord Renly took a step back, taut as a bowstring. "Every moment you delay gives Cersei another moment to prepare. By the time Robert dies, it may be too late . . . for both of us."

"Then we should pray that Robert does not die."

"Small chance of that," said Renly.

"Sometimes the gods are merciful."

"The Lannisters are not." Lord Renly turned away and went back across the moat, to the tower where his brother lay dying.

By the time Ned returned to his chambers, he felt weary and heartsick, yet there was no question of his going back to sleep, not now. *When you play the game of thrones, you win or you die,* Cersei Lannister had told him in the godswood. He found himself wondering if he had done the right thing by refusing Lord Renly's offer. He had no taste for these intrigues, and there was no honor in threatening children, and yet . . . if Cersei elected to fight rather than flee, he might well have need of Renly's hundred swords, and more besides.

"I want Littlefinger," he told Cayn. "If he's not in his chambers, take as many men as you need and search every winesink and whorehouse in King's Landing until you find him. Bring him to me before break of day." Cayn bowed and took his leave, and Ned turned to Tomard. "The *Wind Witch* sails on the evening tide. Have you chosen the escort?"

"Ten men, with Porther in command."

"Twenty, and you will command," Ned said. Porther was a brave man, but headstrong. He wanted someone more solid and sensible to keep watch over his daughters.

"As you wish, m'lord," Tom said. "Can't say I'll be sad to see the back of this place. I miss the wife."

"You will pass near Dragonstone when you turn north. I need you to deliver a letter for me."

Tom looked apprehensive. "To Dragonstone, m'lord?" The island fortress of House Targaryen had a sinister repute.

"Tell Captain Qos to hoist my banner as soon as he comes in sight of the island. They may be wary of unexpected visitors. If he is reluctant, offer him whatever it takes. I will give you a letter to place into the hand of Lord Stannis Baratheon. No one else. Not his steward, nor the captain of his guard, nor his lady wife, but only Lord Stannis himself."

"As you command, m'lord."

When Tomard had left him, Lord Eddard Stark sat staring at the flame of the candle that burned beside him on the table. For a moment his grief overwhelmed him. He wanted nothing so much as to seek out the godswood, to kneel before the heart tree and pray for the life of Robert Baratheon, who had been more than a brother to him. Men would whisper afterward that Eddard Stark had betrayed his king's friendship and disinherited his sons; he could only hope that the gods would know better, and that Robert would learn the truth of it in the land beyond the grave.

Ned took out the king's last letter. A roll of crisp white parchment sealed with golden wax, a few short words and a smear of blood. How small the difference between victory and defeat, between life and death.

He drew out a fresh sheet of paper and dipped his quill in the inkpot. *To His Grace, Stannis of the House Baratheon,* he wrote. *By the time you receive this letter, your brother Robert, our King these past fifteen years, will be dead. He was savaged by a boar whilst hunting in the kingswood . . .*

The letters seemed to writhe and twist on the paper as his hand trailed to a stop. Lord Tywin and Ser Jaime were not men to suffer disgrace meekly; they would fight rather than flee. No doubt Lord Stannis was wary, after the murder of Jon Arryn, but it was imperative that he sail for King's Landing at once with all his power, before the Lannisters could march.

Ned chose each word with care. When he was done, he signed the letter *Eddard Stark, Lord of Winterfell, Hand of the King, and Protector of the Realm,* blotted the paper, folded it twice, and melted the sealing wax over the candle flame.

His regency would be a short one, he reflected as the wax softened. The new king would choose his own Hand. Ned would be free to go home. The thought of Winterfell brought a wan smile to his face. He wanted to hear Bran's laughter once more, to go hawking with Robb, to watch Rickon at play. He wanted to drift off to a dreamless sleep in his own bed with his arms wrapped tight around his lady, Catelyn.

Cayn returned as he was pressing the direwolf seal down into the soft white wax. Desmond was with him, and between them Littlefinger. Ned thanked his guards and sent them away.

Lord Petyr was clad in a blue velvet tunic with puffed sleeves, his silvery cape patterned with mockingbirds. "I suppose congratulations are in order," he said as he seated himself.

Ned scowled. "The king lies wounded and near to death."

"I know," Littlefinger said. "I also know that Robert has named you Protector of the Realm."

Ned's eyes flicked to the king's letter on the table beside him, its seal unbroken. "And how is it you know that, my lord?"

"Varys hinted as much," Littlefinger said, "and you have just confirmed it."

Ned's mouth twisted in anger. "Damn Varys and his little birds. Catelyn spoke truly, the man has some black art. I do not trust him."

"Excellent. You're learning." Littlefinger leaned forward. "Yet I'll wager you did not drag me here in the black of night to discuss the eunuch."

"No," Ned admitted. "I know the secret Jon Arryn was murdered to protect. Robert will leave no trueborn son behind him. Joffrey and Tommen are Jaime Lannister's bastards, born of his incestuous union with the queen."

Littlefinger lifted an eyebrow. "Shocking," he said in a tone that suggested he was not shocked at all. "The girl as well? No doubt. So when the king dies . . ."

"The throne by rights passes to Lord Stannis, the elder of Robert's two brothers."

Lord Petyr stroked his pointed beard as he considered the matter. "So it would seem. Unless . . ."

"*Unless*, my lord? There is no *seeming* to this. Stannis is the heir. Nothing can change that."

"Stannis cannot take the throne without your help. If you're wise, you'll make certain Joffrey succeeds."

Ned gave him a stony stare. "Have you no shred of honor?"

"Oh, a *shred*, surely," Littlefinger replied negligently.

"Hear me out. Stannis is no friend of yours, nor of mine. Even his brothers can scarcely stomach him. The man is iron, hard and unyielding. He'll give us a new Hand and a new council, for a certainty. No doubt he'll thank you for handing him the crown, but he won't love you for it. And his ascent will mean war. Stannis cannot rest easy on the throne until Cersei and her bastards are dead. Do you think Lord Tywin will sit idly while his daughter's head is measured for a spike? Casterly Rock will rise, and not alone. Robert found it in him to pardon men who served King Aerys, so long as they did him fealty. Stannis is less forgiving. He will not have forgotten the siege of Storm's End, and the Lords Tyrell and Redwyne dare not. Every man who fought beneath the dragon banner or rose with Balon Greyjoy will have good cause to fear. Seat Stannis on the Iron Throne and I promise you, the realm will bleed.

"Now look at the other side of the coin. Joffrey is but twelve, and Robert gave *you* the regency, my lord. You are the Hand of the King and Protector of the Realm. The power is yours, Lord Stark. All you need do is reach out and take it. Make your peace with the Lannisters. Release the Imp. Wed Joffrey to your Sansa. Wed your younger girl to Prince Tommen, and your heir to Myrcella. It will be four years before Joffrey comes of age. By then he will look to you as a second father, and if not, well . . . four years is a good long while, my lord. Long enough to dispose of Lord Stannis. Then, should Joffrey prove troublesome, we can reveal his little secret and put Lord Renly on the throne."

"We?" Ned repeated.

Littlefinger gave a shrug. "You'll need someone to share your burdens. I assure you, my price would be modest."

"Your price." Ned's voice was ice. "Lord Baelish, what you suggest is treason."

"Only if we lose."

"You forget," Ned told him. "You forget Jon Arryn. You forget Jory Cassel. And you forget this." He drew the dagger and laid it on the table between them; a length of dragonbone and Valyrian steel, as sharp as the difference between right and wrong, between true and false, between life and death. "They sent a man to *cut my son's throat*, Lord Baelish."

Littlefinger sighed. "I fear I did forget, my lord. Pray forgive me. For a moment I did not remember that I was talking to a Stark." His mouth quirked. "So it will be Stannis, and war?"

"It is not a choice. Stannis is the heir."

"Far be it from me to dispute the Lord Protector. What would you have of me, then? Not my wisdom, for a certainty."

"I shall do my best to forget your . . . wisdom," Ned said with distaste. "I called you here to ask for the help you promised Catelyn. This is a perilous hour for all of us. Robert has named me Protector, true enough, but in the eyes of the world, Joffrey is still his son and heir. The queen has a dozen knights and a hundred men-at-arms who will do whatever she commands . . . enough to overwhelm what remains of my own household guard. And for all I know, her brother Jaime may be riding for King's Landing even as we speak, with a Lannister host at his back."

"And you without an army." Littlefinger toyed with the dagger on the table, turning it slowly with a finger. "There is small love lost between Lord Renly and the Lannisters. Bronze Yohn Royce, Ser Balon Swann, Ser Loras, Lady Tanda, the Redwyne twins . . . each of them has a retinue of knights and sworn swords here at court."

"Renly has thirty men in his personal guard, the rest even fewer. It is not enough, even if I could be certain that all of them will choose to give me their allegiance. I must have the gold cloaks. The City Watch is two thousand strong, sworn to defend the castle, the city, and the king's peace."

"Ah, but when the queen proclaims one king and the Hand another, whose peace do they protect?" Lord Petyr flicked at the dagger with his finger, setting it spinning in place. Round and round it went, wobbling as it turned. When at last it slowed to a stop, the blade pointed at Littlefinger. "Why, there's your answer," he said, smiling. "They follow the man who pays them." He leaned back and looked Ned full in the face, his grey-green eyes bright with mockery. "You wear your honor like a suit of armor, Stark. You think it keeps you safe, but all it does is weigh you down and make it hard for you to move. Look at you now. You know why you summoned me here. You know what you want to ask me to do. You know it has to be done . . . but it's not *honorable*, so the words stick in your throat."

Ned's neck was rigid with tension. For a moment he was so angry that he did not trust himself to speak.

Littlefinger laughed. "I ought to make you say it, but that would be cruel . . . so have no fear, my good lord. For the sake of the love I bear for Catelyn, I will go to Janos Slynt this very hour and make certain that the City Watch is yours. Six thousand gold pieces should do it. A third for the Commander, a third for the officers, a third for the men. We might be able to buy them for half that much, but I prefer not to take chances." Smiling, he plucked up the dagger and offered it to Ned, hilt first.

JON

Jon was breaking his fast on applecakes and blood sausage when Samwell Tarly plopped himself down on the bench. "I've been summoned to the sept," Sam said in an excited whisper. "They're passing me out of training. I'm to be made a brother with the rest of you. Can you believe it?"

"No, truly?"

"Truly. I'm to assist Maester Aemon with the library and the birds. He needs someone who can read and write letters."

"You'll do well at that," Jon said, smiling.

Sam glanced about anxiously. "Is it time to go? I shouldn't be late, they might change their minds." He was fairly bouncing as they crossed the weed-strewn courtyard. The day was warm and sunny. Rivulets of water trickled down the sides of the Wall, so the ice seemed to sparkle and shine.

Inside the sept, the great crystal caught the morning light as it streamed through the south-facing window and spread it in a rainbow on the altar. Pyp's mouth dropped open when he caught sight of Sam, and Toad poked Grenn in the ribs, but no one dared say a word. Septon Celladar was swinging a censer, filling the air with fragrant incense that reminded Jon of Lady Stark's little sept in Winterfell. For once the septon seemed sober.

The high officers arrived in a body; Maester Aemon leaning on Clydas, Ser Alliser cold-eyed and grim, Lord Commander Mormont resplendent in a black wool doublet with silvered bearclaw fastenings. Behind them came the senior members of the three orders: red-faced Bowen Marsh the Lord Steward, First Builder Othell Yarwyck, and Ser Jaremy Rykker, who commanded the rangers in the absence of Benjen Stark.

Mormont stood before the altar, the rainbow shining on his broad bald head. "You came to us outlaws," he began, "poachers, rapers, debtors, killers, and thieves. You came to us children. You came to us alone, in chains, with neither friends nor honor. You came to us rich, and you came to us poor. Some of you bear the names of proud houses. Others have only bastards' names, or no names at all. It makes no matter. All that is past now. On the Wall, we are all one house.

"At evenfall, as the sun sets and we face the gathering night, you shall take your vows. From that moment, you will be a Sworn Brother of the Night's Watch. Your crimes will be washed away, your debts forgiven. So too you must wash away your former loyalties, put aside your grudges, forget old wrongs and old loves alike. Here you begin anew.

"A man of the Night's Watch lives his life for the realm. Not for a king, nor a lord, nor the honor of this house or that house, neither for gold nor glory nor a woman's love, but for the *realm*, and all the people in it. A man of the Night's Watch takes no wife and fathers no sons. Our wife is duty. Our mistress is honor. And you are the only sons we shall ever know.

"You have learned the words of the vow. Think carefully before you say them, for once you have taken the black, there is no turning back. The penalty for desertion is death." The Old Bear paused for a moment before he said, "Are there any among you who wish to leave our company? If so, go now, and no one shall think the less of you."

No one moved.

"Well and good," said Mormont. "You may take your

vows here at evenfall, before Septon Celladar and the first of your order. Do any of you keep to the old gods?"

Jon stood. "I do, my lord."

"I expect you will want to say your words before a heart tree, as your uncle did," Mormont said.

"Yes, my lord," Jon said. The gods of the sept had nothing to do with him; the blood of the First Men flowed in the veins of the Starks.

He heard Grenn whispering behind him. "There's no godswood here. Is there? I never saw a godswood."

"You wouldn't see a herd of aurochs until they trampled you into the snow," Pyp whispered back.

"I would so," Grenn insisted. "I'd see them a long way off."

Mormont himself confirmed Grenn's doubts. "Castle Black has no need of a godswood. Beyond the Wall the haunted forest stands as it stood in the Dawn Age, long before the Andals brought the Seven across the narrow sea. You will find a grove of weirwoods half a league from this spot, and mayhap your gods as well."

"My lord." The voice made Jon glance back in surprise. Samwell Tarly was on his feet. The fat boy wiped his sweaty palms against his tunic. "Might I . . . might I go as well? To say my words at this heart tree?"

"Does House Tarly keep the old gods too?" Mormont asked.

"No, my lord," Sam replied in a thin, nervous voice. The high officers frightened him, Jon knew, the Old Bear most of all. "I was named in the light of the Seven at the sept on Horn Hill, as my father was, and his father, and all the Tarlys for a thousand years."

"Why would you forsake the gods of your father and your House?" wondered Ser Jaremy Rykker.

"The Night's Watch is my House now," Sam said. "The Seven have never answered my prayers. Perhaps the old gods will."

"As you wish, boy," Mormont said. Sam took his seat again, as did Jon. "We have placed each of you in an order, as befits our need and your own strengths and skills." Bowen Marsh stepped forward and handed him a paper. The Lord Commander unrolled it and began to read. "Halder, to the builders," he began. Halder gave a stiff nod of approval. "Grenn, to the rangers. Albett, to the builders.

Pypar, to the rangers." Pyp looked over at Jon and wiggled his ears. "Samwell, to the stewards." Sam sagged with relief, mopping at his brow with a scrap of silk. "Matthar, to the rangers. Dareon, to the stewards. Todder, to the rangers. Jon, to the stewards."

The *stewards?* For a moment Jon could not believe what he had heard. Mormont must have read it wrong. He started to rise, to open his mouth, to tell them there had been a mistake . . . and then he saw Ser Alliser studying him, eyes shiny as two flakes of obsidian, and he knew.

The Old Bear rolled up the paper. "Your firsts will instruct you in your duties. May all the gods preserve you, brothers." The Lord Commander favored them with a half bow, and took his leave. Ser Alliser went with him, a thin smile on his face. Jon had never seen the master-at-arms look quite so happy.

"Rangers with me," Ser Jaremy Rykker called when they were gone. Pyp was staring at Jon as he got slowly to his feet. His ears were red. Grenn, grinning broadly, did not seem to realize that anything was amiss. Matt and Toad fell in beside them, and they followed Ser Jaremy from the sept.

"Builders," announced lantern-jawed Othell Yarwyck. Halder and Albett trailed out after him.

Jon looked around him in sick disbelief. Maester Aemon's blind eyes were raised toward the light he could not see. The septon was arranging crystals on the altar. Only Sam and Dareon remained on the benches; a fat boy, a singer . . . and him.

Lord Steward Bowen Marsh rubbed his plump hands together. "Samwell, you will assist Maester Aemon in the rookery and library. Chett is going to the kennels, to help with the hounds. You shall have his cell, so as to be close to the maester night and day. I trust you will take good care of him. He is very old and very precious to us.

"Dareon, I am told that you sang at many a high lord's table and shared their meat and mead. We are sending you to Eastwatch. It may be your palate will be some help to Cotter Pyke when merchant galleys come trading. We are paying too dear for salt beef and pickled fish, and the quality of the olive oil we're getting has been frightful. Present yourself to Borcas when you arrive, he will keep you busy between ships."

Marsh turned his smile on Jon. "Lord Commander Mormont has requested you for his personal steward, Jon. You'll sleep in a cell beneath his chambers, in the Lord Commander's tower."

"And what will my duties be?" Jon asked sharply. "Will I serve the Lord Commander's meals, help him fasten his clothes, fetch hot water for his bath?"

"Certainly." Marsh frowned at Jon's tone. "And you will run his messages, keep a fire burning in his chambers, change his sheets and blankets daily, and do all else that the Lord Commander might require of you."

"Do you take me for a servant?"

"No," Maester Aemon said, from the back of the sept. Clydas helped him stand. "We took you for a man of Night's Watch . . . but perhaps we were wrong in that."

It was all Jon could do to stop himself from walking out. Was he supposed to churn butter and sew doublets like a girl for the rest of his days? "May I go?" he asked stiffly.

"As you wish," Bowen Marsh responded.

Dareon and Sam left with him. They descended to the yard in silence. Outside, Jon looked up at the Wall shining in the sun, the melting ice creeping down its side in a hundred thin fingers. Jon's rage was such that he would have smashed it all in an instant, and the world be damned.

"Jon," Samwell Tarly said excitedly. "Wait. Don't you see what they're doing?"

Jon turned on him in a fury. "I see Ser Alliser's bloody hand, that's all I see. He wanted to shame me, and he has."

Dareon gave him a look. "The stewards are fine for the likes of you and me, Sam, but not for Lord Snow."

"I'm a better swordsman and a better rider than any of you," Jon blazed back. "It's not *fair*!"

"Fair?" Dareon sneered. "The girl was waiting for me, naked as the day she was born. She pulled me through the window, and you talk to me of *fair*?" He walked off.

"There is no shame in being a steward," Sam said.

"Do you think I want to spend the rest of my life washing an old man's smallclothes?"

"The old man is Lord Commander of the Night's Watch," Sam reminded him. "You'll be with him day and night. Yes, you'll pour his wine and see that his bed linen is fresh, but you'll also take his letters, attend him at meetings, squire for him in battle. You'll be as close to him as his shadow. You'll know everything, be a part of everything . . . and the Lord Steward said Mormont asked for you *himself*!

"When I was little, my father used to insist that I attend him in the audience chamber whenever he held court. When he rode to Highgarden to bend his knee to Lord Tyrell, he made me come. Later, though, he started to take Dickon and leave me at home, and he no longer cared whether I sat through his audiences, so long as Dickon was there. He wanted his *heir* at his side, don't you see? To watch and listen and learn from all he did. I'll wager that's why Lord Mormont requested you, Jón. What else could it be? He wants to groom you for *command*!"

Jon was taken aback. It was true, Lord Eddard had often made Robb part of his councils back at Winterfell. Could Sam be right? Even a bastard could rise high in the Night's Watch, they said. "I never asked for this," he said stubbornly.

"None of us are here for *asking*," Sam reminded him.

And suddenly Jon Snow was ashamed.

Craven or not, Samwell Tarly had found the courage to accept his fate like a man. *On the Wall, a man gets only what he earns*, Benjen Stark had said the last night Jon had seen him alive. *You're no ranger, Jon, only a green boy with the smell of summer still on you.* He'd heard it said that bastards grow up faster than other children; on the Wall, you grew up or you died.

Jon let out a deep sigh. "You have the right of it. I was acting the boy."

"Then you'll stay and say your words with me?"

"The old gods will be expecting us." He made himself smile.

They set out late that afternoon. The Wall had no gates as such, neither here at Castle Black nor anywhere along its three hundred miles. They led their horses down a narrow tunnel cut through the ice, cold dark walls pressing in around them as the passage twisted and turned. Three times their way was blocked by iron bars, and they had to stop while Bowen Marsh drew out his keys and unlocked the massive chains that secured them. Jon could sense the vast weight pressing down on him as he waited behind the Lord Steward. The air was colder than a tomb, and more still. He felt a strange relief when they reemerged into the afternoon light on the north side of the Wall.

Sam blinked at the sudden glare and looked around apprehensively. "The wildlings . . . they wouldn't . . . they'd never dare come this close to the Wall. Would they?"

"They never have." Jon climbed into his saddle. When Bowen Marsh and their ranger escort had mounted, Jon put two fingers in his mouth and whistled. Ghost came loping out of the tunnel.

The Lord Steward's garron whickered and backed away from the direwolf. "Do you mean to take that beast?"

"Yes, my lord," Jon said. Ghost's head lifted. He seemed to taste the air. In the blink of an eye he was off, racing across the broad, weed-choked field to vanish in the trees.

Once they had entered the forest, they were in a different world. Jon had often hunted with his father and Jory and his brother Robb. He knew the wolfswood around Winterfell as well as any man. The haunted forest was much the same, and yet the feel of it was very different.

Perhaps it was all in the knowing. They had ridden past the end of the world; somehow that changed everything. Every shadow seemed darker, every sound more ominous. The trees pressed close and shut out the light of the setting sun. A thin crust of snow cracked beneath the hooves of their horses, with a sound like breaking bones. When the wind set the leaves to rustling, it was like a chilly finger tracing a path up Jon's spine. The Wall was at their backs, and only the gods knew what lay ahead.

The sun was sinking below the trees when they reached their destination, a small clearing in the deep of the wood where nine weirwoods grew in a rough circle. Jon drew in a breath, and he saw Sam Tarly staring. Even in the wolfswood, you never found more than two or three of the white trees growing together; a grove of nine was unheard of. The forest floor was carpeted with fallen leaves, bloodred on top, black rot beneath. The wide smooth trunks were bone pale, and nine faces stared inward. The dried sap that crusted in the eyes was red and hard as ruby. Bowen Marsh commanded them to leave their horses outside the circle. "This is a sacred place, we will not defile it."

When they entered the grove, Samwell Tarly turned slowly looking at each face in turn. No two were quite alike. "They're watching us," he whispered. "The old gods."

"Yes." Jon knelt, and Sam knelt beside him.

They said the words together, as the last light faded in the west and grey day became black night.

"Hear my words, and bear witness to my vow," they recited, their voices filling the twilit grove. "Night gathers, and now my watch begins. It shall not end until my death. I shall take no wife, hold no lands, father no children. I shall wear no crowns and win no glory. I shall live and die at my post. I am the sword in the darkness. I am the watcher on the walls. I am the fire that burns against the cold, the light that brings the dawn, the horn that wakes the sleepers, the shield that guards the realms of men. I pledge my life and honor to the Night's Watch, for this night and all the nights to come."

The woods fell silent. "You knelt as boys," Bowen Marsh intoned solemnly. "Rise now as men of the Night's Watch."

Jon held out a hand to pull Sam back to his feet. The rangers gathered round to offer smiles and congratulations, all but the gnarled old forester Dywen. "Best we be starting back, m'lord," he said to Bowen Marsh. "Dark's falling, and there's something in the smell o' the night that I mislike."

And suddenly Ghost was back, stalking softly between two weirwoods. *White fur and red eyes,* Jon realized, disquieted. *Like the trees . . .*

The wolf had something in his jaws. Something black. "What's he got there?" asked Bowen Marsh, frowning.

"To me, Ghost." Jon knelt. "Bring it here."

The direwolf trotted to him. Jon heard Samwell Tarly's sharp intake of breath.

"Gods be good," Dywen muttered. "That's a hand."

EDDARD

The grey light of dawn was streaming through his window when the thunder of hoofbeats awoke Eddard Stark from his brief, exhausted sleep. He lifted his head from the table to look down into the yard. Below, men in mail and leather and crimson cloaks were making the morning ring to the sound of swords, and riding down mock warriors stuffed with straw. Ned watched Sandor Clegane gallop across the hard-packed ground to drive an iron-tipped lance through a dummy's head. Canvas ripped and straw exploded as Lannister guardsmen joked and cursed.

Is this brave show for my benefit? he wondered. *If so, Cersei was a greater fool than he'd imagined.* Damn her, he thought, *why is the woman not fled? I have given her chance after chance . . .*

The morning was overcast and grim. Ned broke his fast with his daughters and Septa Mordane. Sansa, still disconsolate, stared sullenly at her food and refused to eat, but Arya wolfed down everything that was set in front of her. "Syrio says we have time for one last lesson before we take ship this evening," she said. "Can I, Father? All my things are packed."

"A short lesson, and make certain you leave yourself time to bathe and change. I want you ready to leave by midday, is that understood?"

"By midday," Arya said.

Sansa looked up from her food. "If she can have a dancing lesson, why won't you let me say farewell to Prince Joffrey?"

"I would gladly go with her, Lord Eddard," Septa Mordane offered. "There would be no question of her missing the ship."

"It would not be wise for you to go to Joffrey right now, Sansa. I'm sorry."

Sansa's eyes filled with tears. "But *why?*"

"Sansa, your lord father knows best," Septa Mordane said. "You are not to question his decisions."

"It's not *fair!*" Sansa pushed back from her table, knocked over her chair, and ran weeping from the solar.

Septa Mordane rose, but Ned gestured her back to her seat. "Let her go, Septa. I will try to make her understand when we are all safely back in Winterfell." The septa bowed her head and sat down to finish her breakfast.

It was an hour later when Grand Maester Pycelle came to Eddard Stark in his solar. His shoulders slumped, as if the weight of the great maester's chain around his neck had become too great to bear. "My lord," he said, "King Robert is gone. The gods give him rest."

"No," Ned answered. "He hated rest. The gods give him love and laughter, and the joy of righteous battle." It was strange how empty he felt. He had been expecting the visit, and yet with those words, something died within him. He would have given all his titles for the freedom to weep . . . but he was Robert's Hand, and the hour he dreaded had come. "Be so good as to summon the members of the council here to my solar," he told Pycelle. The Tower of the Hand was as secure as he and Tomard could make it; he could not say the same for the council chambers.

"My lord?" Pycelle blinked. "Surely the affairs of the kingdom will keep till the morrow, when our grief is not so fresh."

Ned was quiet but firm. "I fear we must convene at once."

Pycelle bowed. "As the Hand commands." He called

his servants and sent them running, then gratefully accepted Ned's offer of a chair and a cup of sweet beer.

Ser Barristan Selmy was the first to answer the summons, immaculate in white cloak and enameled scales. "My lords," he said, "my place is beside the young king now. Pray give me leave to attend him."

"Your place is here, Ser Barristan," Ned told him.

Littlefinger came next, still garbed in the blue velvets and silver mockingbird cape he had worn the night previous, his boots dusty from riding. "My lords," he said, smiling at nothing in particular before he turned to Ned. "That little task you set me is accomplished, Lord Eddard."

Varys entered in a wash of lavender, pink from his bath, his plump face scrubbed and freshly powdered, his soft slippers all but soundless. "The little birds sing a grievous song today," he said as he seated himself. "The realm weeps. Shall we begin?"

"When Lord Renly arrives," Ned said.

Varys gave him a sorrowful look. "I fear Lord Renly has left the city."

"Left the *city*?" Ned had counted on Renly's support.

"He took his leave through a postern gate an hour before dawn, accompanied by Ser Loras Tyrell and some fifty retainers," Varys told them. "When last seen, they were galloping south in some haste, no doubt bound for Storm's End or Highgarden."

So much for Renly and his hundred swords. Ned did not like the smell of that, but there was nothing to be done for it. He drew out Robert's last letter. "The king called me to his side last night and commanded me to record his final words. Lord Renly and Grand Maester Pycelle stood witness as Robert sealed the letter, to be opened by the council after his death. Ser Barristan, if you would be so kind?"

The Lord Commander of the Kingsguard examined the paper. "King Robert's seal, and unbroken." He opened the letter and read. "Lord Eddard Stark is herein named Protector of the Realm, to rule as regent until the heir comes of age."

And as it happens, he is of age, Ned reflected, but he did not give voice to the thought. He trusted neither Pycelle nor Varys, and Ser Barristan was honor-bound to protect and defend the boy he thought his new king. The old knight would not abandon Joffrey easily. The need for deceit was a bitter taste in his mouth, but Ned knew he must tread softly here, must keep his counsel and play the game until he was firmly established as regent. There would be time enough to deal with the succession when Arya and Sansa were safely back in Winterfell, and Lord Stannis had returned to King's Landing with all his power.

"I would ask this council to confirm me as Lord Protector, as Robert wished," Ned said, watching their faces, wondering what thoughts hid behind Pycelle's half-closed eyes, Littlefinger's lazy half-smile, and the nervous flutter of Varys's fingers.

The door opened. Fat Tom stepped into the solar. "Pardon, my lords, the king's steward insists . . ."

The royal steward entered and bowed. "Esteemed lords, the king demands the immediate presence of his small council in the throne room."

Ned had expected Cersei to strike quickly; the summons came as no surprise. "The king is dead," he said, "but we shall go with you nonetheless. Tom, assemble an escort, if you would."

Littlefinger gave Ned his arm to help him down the steps. Varys, Pycelle, and Ser Barristan followed close behind. A double column of men-at-arms in chainmail and steel helms was waiting outside the tower, eight strong. Grey cloaks snapped in the wind as the guardsmen marched them across the yard. There was no Lannister crimson to be seen, but Ned was reassured by the number of gold cloaks visible on the ramparts and at the gates.

Janos Slynt met them at the door to the throne room, armored in ornate black-and-gold plate, with a high-crested helm under one arm. The Commander bowed stiffly. His men pushed open the great oaken doors, twenty feet tall and banded with bronze.

The royal steward led them in. "All hail His Grace, Joffrey of the Houses Baratheon and Lannister, the First of his Name, King of the Andals and the Rhoynar and the First Men, Lord of the Seven Kingdoms and Protector of the Realm," he sang out.

It was a long walk to the far end of the hall, where Joffrey waited atop the Iron Throne. Supported by Littlefinger, Ned Stark slowly limped and hopped toward the boy who called himself king. The others followed. The first time he had come this way, he had been on horseback, sword in hand, and the Targaryen dragons had watched from the walls as he forced Jaime Lannister down from the throne. He wondered if Joffrey would step down quite so easily.

Five knights of the Kingsguard—all but Ser Jaime and Ser Barristan—were arrayed in a crescent around the base of the throne. They were in full armor, enameled steel from helm to heel, long pale cloaks over their shoulders, shining white shields strapped to their left arms. Cersei Lannister and her two younger children stood behind Ser Boros and Ser Meryn. The queen wore a gown of sea-green silk, trimmed with Myrish lace as pale as foam. On her finger was a golden ring with an emerald the size of a pigeon's egg, on her head a matching tiara.

Above them, Prince Joffrey sat amidst the barbs and spikes in a cloth-of-gold doublet and a red satin cape. Sandor Clegane was stationed at the foot of the throne's steep narrow stair. He wore mail and soot-grey plate and his snarling dog's-head helm.

Behind the throne, twenty Lannister guardsmen waited with longswords hanging from their belts. Crimson cloaks draped their shoulders and steel lions crested their helms. But Littlefinger had kept his promise; all along the walls, in front of Robert's tapestries with their scenes of hunt and battle, the gold-cloaked ranks of the City Watch stood stiffly to attention, each man's hand clasped around the haft of an eight-foot-long spear tipped in black iron. They outnumbered the Lannisters five to one.

Ned's leg was a blaze of pain by the time he stopped. He kept a hand on Littlefinger's shoulder to help support his weight.

Joffrey stood. His red satin cape was patterned in gold thread; fifty roaring lions to one side, fifty prancing stags to the other. "I command the council to make all the necessary arrangements for my coronation," the boy proclaimed. "I wish to be crowned within the fortnight. Today I shall accept oaths of fealty from my loyal councillors."

Ned produced Robert's letter. "Lord Varys, be so kind as to show this to my lady of Lannister."

The eunuch carried the letter to Cersei. The queen glanced at the words. "Protector of the Realm," she read. "Is this meant to be your shield, my lord? A piece of paper?" She ripped the letter in half, ripped the halves in quarters, and let the pieces flutter to the floor.

"Those were the king's words," Ser Barristan said, shocked.

"We have a new king now," Cersei Lannister replied. "Lord Eddard, when last we spoke, you gave me some counsel. Allow me to return the courtesy. Bend the knee, my lord. Bend the knee and swear fealty to my son, and we shall allow you to step down as Hand and live out your days in the grey waste you call home."

"Would that I could," Ned said grimly. If she was so determined to force the issue here and now, she left him no choice. "Your son has no claim to the throne he sits. Lord Stannis is Robert's true heir."

"*Liar!*" Joffrey screamed, his face reddening.

"Mother, what does he mean?" Princess Myrcella asked the queen plaintively. "Isn't Joff the king now?"

"You condemn yourself with your own mouth, Lord Stark," said Cersei Lannister. "Ser Barristan, seize this traitor."

The Lord Commander of the Kingsguard hesitated. In the blink of an eye he was surrounded by Stark guardsmen, bare steel in their mailed fists.

"And now the treason moves from words to deeds," Cersei said. "Do you think Ser Barristan stands alone, my lord?" With an ominous rasp of metal on metal, the Hound drew his longsword. The knights of the Kingsguard and twenty Lannister guardsmen in crimson cloaks moved to support him.

"*Kill him!*" the boy king screamed down from the Iron Throne. "*Kill all of them, I command it!*"

"You leave me no choice," Ned told Cersei Lannister. He called out to Janos Slynt. "Commander, take the queen and her children into custody. Do them no harm, but escort them back to the royal apartments and keep them there, under guard."

"Men of the Watch!" Janos Slynt shouted, donning his

helm. A hundred gold cloaks leveled their spears and closed.

"I want no bloodshed," Ned told the queen. "Tell your men to lay down their swords, and no one need—"

With a single sharp thrust, the nearest gold cloak drove his spear into Tomard's back. Fat Tom's blade dropped from nerveless fingers as the wet red point burst out through his ribs, piercing leather and mail. He was dead before his sword hit the floor.

Ned's shout came far too late. Janos Slynt himself slashed open Varly's throat. Cayn whirled, steel flashing, drove back the nearest spearman with a flurry of blows; for an instant it looked as though he might cut his way free. Then the Hound was on him. Sandor Clegane's first cut took off Cayn's sword hand at the wrist; his second drove him to his knees and opened him from shoulder to breastbone.

As his men died around him, Littlefinger slid Ned's dagger from its sheath and shoved it up under his chin. His smile was apologetic. "I *did* warn you not to trust me, you know."

ARYA

"**H**igh," Syrio Forel called out, slashing at her head. The stick swords *clack*ed as Arya parried. "Left," he shouted, and his blade came whistling. Hers darted to meet it. The *clack* made him click his teeth together.

"Right," he said, and "Low," and "Left," and "Left" again, faster and faster, moving forward. Arya retreated before him, checking each blow.

"Lunge," he warned, and when he thrust she side-stepped, swept his blade away, and slashed at his shoulder. She almost touched him, *almost*, so close it made her grin. A strand of hair dangled in her eyes, limp with sweat. She pushed it away with the back of her hand.

"Left," Syrio sang out. "Low." His sword was a blur, and the Small Hall echoed to the *clack clack clack*. "Left. Left. High. Left. Right. Left. Low. *Left!*"

The wooden blade caught her high in the breast, a sudden stinging blow that hurt all the more because it came from the wrong side. "*Ow*," she cried out. She would have a fresh bruise there by the time she went to sleep, somewhere out at sea. *A bruise is a lesson*, she told herself, *and each lesson makes us better*.

Syrio stepped back. "You are dead now."

Arya made a face. "You cheated," she said hotly. "You said left and you went right."

"Just so. And now you are a dead girl."

"But you *lied*!"

"My words lied. My eyes and my arm shouted out the truth, but you were not seeing."

"I was so," Arya said. "I watched you every second!"

"Watching is not seeing, dead girl. The water dancer sees. Come, put down the sword, it is time for listening now."

She followed him over to the wall, where he settled onto a bench. "Syrio Forel was first sword to the Sealord of Braavos, and are you knowing how that came to pass?"

"You were the finest swordsman in the city."

"Just so, but why? Other men were stronger, faster, younger, why was Syrio Forel the best? I will tell you now." He touched the tip of his little finger lightly to his eyelid. "The seeing, the true seeing, that is the heart of it.

"Hear me. The ships of Braavos sail as far as the winds blow, to lands strange and wonderful, and when they return their captains fetch queer animals to the Sealord's menagerie. Such animals as you have never seen, striped horses, great spotted things with necks as long as stilts, hairy mouse-pigs as big as cows, stinging manticores, tigers that carry their cubs in a pouch, terrible walking lizards with scythes for claws. Syrio Forel has seen these things.

"On the day I am speaking of, the first sword was newly dead, and the Sealord sent for me. Many bravos had come to him, and as many had been sent away, none could say why. When I came into his presence, he was seated, and in his lap was a fat yellow cat. He told me that one of his captains had brought the beast to him, from an island beyond the sunrise. 'Have you ever seen her like?' he asked of me.

"And to him I said, 'Each night in the alleys of Braavos I see a thousand like him,' and the Sealord laughed, and that day I was named the first sword."

Arya screwed up her face. "I don't understand."

Syrio clicked his teeth together. "The cat was an ordinary cat, no more. The others expected a fabulous beast, so that is what they saw. How large it was, they said. It was no larger than any other cat, only fat from indolence, for the Sealord fed it from his own table. What curious small ears, they said. Its ears had been chewed away in kitten fights. And it was plainly a tomcat, yet the Sealord said 'her,' and that is what the others saw. Are you hearing?"

Arya thought about it. "You saw what was there."

"Just so. Opening your eyes is all that is needing. The heart lies and the head plays tricks with us, but the eyes see true. Look with your eyes. Hear with your ears. Taste with your mouth. Smell with your nose. Feel with your skin. *Then* comes the thinking, afterward, and in that way knowing the truth."

"Just so," said Arya, grinning.

Syrio Forel allowed himself a smile. "I am thinking that when we are reaching this Winterfell of yours, it will be time to put this needle in your hand."

"Yes!" Arya said eagerly. "Wait till I show Jon—"

Behind her the great wooden doors of the Small Hall flew open with a resounding crash. Arya whirled.

A knight of the Kingsguard stood beneath the arch of the door with five Lannister guardsmen arrayed behind him. He was in full armor, but his visor was up. Arya remembered his droopy eyes and rust-colored whiskers from when he had come to Winterfell with the king: Ser Meryn Trant. The red cloaks wore mail shirts over boiled leather and steel caps with lion crests. "Arya Stark," the knight said, "come with us, child."

Arya chewed her lip uncertainly. "What do you want?"

"Your father wants to see you."

Arya took a step forward, but Syrio Forel held her by the arm. "And why is it that Lord Eddard is sending Lannister men in the place of his own? I am wondering."

"Mind your place, dancing master," Ser Meryn said. "This is no concern of yours."

"My father wouldn't send *you*," Arya said. She snatched up her stick sword. The Lannisters laughed.

"Put down the stick, girl," Ser Meryn told her. "I am a Sworn Brother of the Kingsguard, the White Swords."

"So was the Kingslayer when he killed the old king," Arya said. "I don't have to go with you if I don't want."

Ser Meryn Trant ran out of patience. "Take her," he said to his men. He lowered the visor of his helm.

Three of them started forward, chainmail clinking softly with each step. Arya was suddenly afraid. *Fear cuts deeper than swords,* she told herself, to slow the racing of her heart.

Syrio Forel stepped between them, tapping his wooden sword lightly against his boot. "You will be stopping there. Are you men or dogs that you would threaten a child?"

"Out of the way, old man," one of the red cloaks said.

Syrio's stick came whistling up and rang against his helm. "I am Syrio Forel, and you will now be speaking to me with more respect."

"Bald bastard." The man yanked free his longsword. The stick moved again, blindingly fast. Arya heard a loud *crack* as the sword went clattering to the stone floor. "My hand," the guardsman yelped, cradling his broken fingers.

"You are quick, for a dancing master," said Ser Meryn.

"You are slow, for a knight," Syrio replied.

"Kill the Braavosi and bring me the girl," the knight in the white armor commanded.

Four Lannister guardsmen unsheathed their swords. The fifth, with the broken fingers, spat and pulled free a dagger with his left hand.

Syrio Forel clicked his teeth together, sliding into his water dancer's stance, presenting only his side to the foe. "Arya child," he called out, never looking, never taking his eyes off the Lannisters, "we are done with dancing for the day. Best you are going now. Run to your father."

Arya did not want to leave him, but he had taught her to do as he said. *"Swift as a deer,"* she whispered.

"Just so," said Syrio Forel as the Lannisters closed.

Arya retreated, her own sword stick clutched tightly in her hand. Watching him now, she realized that Syrio had only been toying with her when they dueled. The red cloaks came at him from three sides with steel in their hands. They had chainmail over their chest and arms, and steel codpieces sewn into their pants, but only leather on their legs. Their hands were bare, and the caps they wore had noseguards, but no visor over the eyes.

Syrio did not wait for them to reach him, but spun to his left. Arya had never seen a man move as fast. He checked one sword with his stick and whirled away from a second. Off balance, the second man lurched into the first. Syrio put a boot to his back and the red cloaks went down together. The third guard came leaping over them, slashing at the water dancer's head. Syrio ducked under his blade and thrust upward. The guardsman fell screaming as blood welled from the wet red hole where his left eye had been.

The fallen men were getting up. Syrio kicked one in the face and snatched the steel cap off the other's head. The dagger man stabbed at him. Syrio caught the thrust in the helmet and shattered the man's kneecap with his stick. The last red cloak shouted a curse and charged, hacking down with both hands on his sword. Syrio rolled right, and the butcher's cut caught the helmetless man between neck and shoulder as he struggled to his knees. The longsword crunched through mail and leather and flesh. The man on his knees shrieked. Before his killer could wrench free his blade, Syrio jabbed him in the apple of his throat. The guardsman gave a choked cry and staggered back, clutching at his neck, his face blackening.

Five men were down, dead, or dying by the time Arya reached the back door that opened on the kitchen. She heard Ser Meryn Trant curse. "Bloody oafs," he swore, drawing his longsword from its scabbard.

Syrio Forel resumed his stance and clicked his teeth together. "Arya child," he called out, never looking at her, "be gone now."

Look with your eyes, he had said. She saw: the knight in his pale armor head to foot, legs, throat, and hands sheathed in metal, eyes hidden behind his high white helm, and in his hand cruel steel. Against that: Syrio, in a leather vest, with a wooden sword in his hand. "Syrio, *run,*" she screamed.

"The first sword of Braavos does not run," he sang as Ser Meryn slashed at him. Syrio danced away from his cut, his stick a blur. In a heartbeat, he had bounced blows off the knight's temple, elbow, and throat, the wood ringing against the metal of helm, gauntlet, and gorget. Arya stood frozen. Ser Meryn advanced; Syrio backed away. He checked the next blow, spun away from the second, deflected the third.

The fourth sliced his stick in two, splintering the wood and shearing through the lead core.

Sobbing, Arya spun and ran.

She plunged through the kitchens and buttery, blind with panic, weaving between cooks and potboys. A baker's helper stepped in front of her, holding a wooden tray. Arya bowled her over, scattering fragrant loaves of fresh-baked bread on the floor. She heard shouting behind her as she spun around a portly butcher who stood gaping at her with a cleaver in his hands. His arms were red to the elbow.

All that Syrio Forel had taught her went racing through her head. *Swift as a deer. Quiet as a shadow. Fear cuts deeper than swords. Quick as a snake. Calm as still water. Fear cuts deeper than swords. Strong as a bear. Fierce as a wolverine. Fear cuts deeper than swords. The man who fears losing has already lost. Fear cuts deeper than swords. Fear cuts deeper than swords. Fear cuts deeper than swords.* The grip of her wooden sword was slick with sweat, and Arya was breathing hard when she reached the turret stair. For an instant she froze. Up or down? Up would take her to the covered bridge that spanned the small court to the Tower of the Hand, but that would be the way they'd expect her to go, for certain. *Never do what they expect,* Syrio once said. Arya went down, around and around, leaping over the narrow stone steps two and three at a time. She emerged in a cavernous vaulted cellar, surrounded by casks of ale stacked twenty feet tall. The only light came through narrow slanting windows high in the wall.

The cellar was a dead end. There was no way out but the way she had come in. She dare not go back up those steps, but she couldn't stay here, either. She had to find her father and tell him what had happened. Her father would protect her.

Arya thrust her wooden sword through her belt and began to climb, leaping from cask to cask until she could reach the window. Grasping the stone with both hands, she pulled herself up. The wall was three feet thick, the window a tunnel slanting up and out. Arya wriggled toward daylight. When her head reached ground level, she peered across the bailey to the Tower of the Hand.

The stout wooden door hung splintered and broken, as if by axes. A dead man sprawled facedown on the steps, his cloak tangled beneath him, the back of his mailed shirt soaked red. The corpse's cloak was grey wool trimmed with white satin, she saw with sudden terror. She could not tell who he was.

"No," she whispered. What was happening? Where was her father? Why had the red cloaks come for her? She remembered what the man with the yellow beard had said, the day she had found the monsters. *If one Hand can die, why not a second?* Arya felt tears in her eyes. She held her breath to listen. She heard the sounds of fighting, shouts, screams, the clang of steel on steel, coming through the windows of the Tower of the Hand.

She could not go back. Her father . . .

Arya closed her eyes. For a moment she was too frightened to move. They had killed Jory and Wyl and Heward, and that guardsman on the step, whoever he had been. They could kill her father too, and her if they caught her. *"Fear cuts deeper than swords,"* she said aloud, but it was no good pretending to be a water dancer, Syrio had been a water dancer and the white knight had probably killed him, and anyhow she was only a little girl with a wooden stick, alone and afraid.

She squirmed out into the yard, glancing around warily as she climbed to her feet. The castle seemed deserted. The Red Keep was *never* deserted. All the people must be hiding inside, their doors barred. Arya glanced up longingly at her bedchamber, then moved away from the Tower of the Hand, keeping close to the wall as she slid from shadow to shadow. She pretended she was chasing cats . . . except she was the cat now, and if they caught her, they would kill her.

Moving between buildings and over walls, keeping stone to her back wherever possible so no one could surprise her, Arya reached the stables almost without incident. A dozen gold cloaks in mail and plate ran past as she was edging across the inner bailey, but without knowing whose side they were on, she hunched down low in the shadows and let them pass.

Hullen, who had been master of horse at Winterfell as long as Arya could remember, was slumped on the ground by the stable door. He had been stabbed so many times it looked as if his tunic was patterned with scarlet flowers. Arya was certain he was dead, but when she crept closer, his eyes opened. "Arya Underfoot," he whispered. "You must . . . warn your . . . your lord father . . ." Frothy red spittle bubbled from his mouth. The master of horse closed his eyes again and said no more.

Inside were more bodies; a groom she had played with, and three of her father's household guard. A wagon, laden with crates and chests, stood abandoned near the door of the stable. The dead men must have been loading it for the trip to the docks when they were attacked. Arya snuck closer. One of the corpses was Desmond, who'd shown her his longsword and promised to protect her father. He lay on his back, staring blindly at the ceiling as flies crawled across his eyes. Close to him was a dead man in the red cloak and lion-crest helm of the Lannisters. Only one, though. *Every northerner is worth ten of these southron swords,* Desmond had told her. "You liar!" she said, kicking his body in a sudden fury.

The animals were restless in their stalls, whickering and snorting at the scent of blood. Arya's only plan was to saddle a horse and flee, away from the castle and the city. All she had to do was stay on the kingsroad and it would take her back to Winterfell. She took a bridle and harness off the wall.

As she crossed in back of the wagon, a fallen chest caught her eye. It must have been knocked down in the fight or dropped as it was being loaded. The wood had split, the lid opening to spill the chest's contents across the ground. Arya recognized silks and satins and velvets she never wore. She might need warm clothes on the kingsroad, though . . . and besides . . .

Arya knelt in the dirt among the scattered clothes. She found a heavy woolen cloak, a velvet skirt and a silk tunic and some smallclothes, a dress her mother had embroidered for her, a silver baby bracelet she might sell. Shoving the broken lid out of the way, she groped inside the chest for Needle. She had hidden it way down at the bottom, under everything, but her stuff had all been jumbled around when the chest was dropped. For a moment Arya was afraid someone had found the sword and stolen it. Then her fingers felt the hardness of metal under a satin gown.

"*There* she is," a voice hissed close behind her.

Startled, Arya whirled. A stableboy stood behind her, a smirk on his face, his filthy white undertunic peeking out from beneath a soiled jerkin. His boots were covered with manure, and he had a pitchfork in one hand. "Who are you?" she asked.

"She don't know me," he said, "but I knows her, oh, yes. The wolf girl."

"Help me saddle a horse," Arya pleaded, reaching back into the chest, groping for Needle. "My father's the Hand of the King, he'll reward you."

"Father's *dead*," the boy said. He shuffled toward her. "It's the queen who'll be rewarding me. Come here, girl."

"*Stay away!*" Her fingers closed around Needle's hilt.

"I says, *come*." He grabbed her arm, hard.

Everything Syrio Forel had ever taught her vanished in a heartbeat. In that instant of sudden terror, the only lesson Arya could remember was the one Jon Snow had given her, the very first.

She stuck him with the pointy end, driving the blade upward with a wild, hysterical strength.

Needle went through his leather jerkin and the white flesh of his belly and came out between his shoulder blades. The boy dropped the pitchfork and made a soft noise, something between a gasp and a sigh. His hands closed around the blade. "Oh, gods," he moaned, as his undertunic began to redden. "Take it out."

When she took it out, he died.

The horses were screaming. Arya stood over the body, still and frightened in the face of death. Blood had gushed from the boy's mouth as he collapsed, and more was seeping from the slit in his belly, pooling beneath his body. His palms were cut where he'd grabbed at the blade. She backed away slowly, Needle red in her hand. She had to get away, someplace far from here, someplace safe away from the stableboy's accusing eyes.

She snatched up the bridle and harness again and ran to her mare, but as she lifted the saddle to the horse's back, Arya realized with a sudden sick dread that the castle gates would be closed. Even the postern doors would likely be guarded. Maybe the guards wouldn't recognize her. If they thought she was a boy, perhaps they'd let her . . . no, they'd have orders not to let *anyone* out, it wouldn't matter whether they knew her or not.

But there was another way out of the castle . . .

The saddle slipped from Arya's fingers and fell to the dirt with a thump and a puff of dust. Could she find the room with the monsters again? She wasn't certain, yet she knew she had to try.

She found the clothing she'd gathered and slipped into the cloak, concealing Needle beneath its folds. The rest of her things she tied in a roll. With the bundle under her arm, she crept to the far end of the stable. Unlatching the back door, she peeked out anxiously. She could hear the distant sound of swordplay, and the shivery wail of a man screaming in pain across the bailey. She would need to go down the serpentine steps, past the small kitchen and the pig yard, that was how she'd gone last time, chasing the black tomcat . . . only that would take her right past the barracks of the gold cloaks. She couldn't go that way. Arya tried to think of another way. If she crossed to the other side of the castle, she could creep along the river wall and through the little godswood . . . but first she'd have to cross the yard, in the plain view of the guards on the walls.

She had never seen so many men on the walls. Gold cloaks, most of them, armed with spears. Some of them knew her by sight. What would they do if they saw her running across the yard? She'd look so small from up there, would they be able to tell who she was? Would they care?

She had to leave *now,* she told herself, but when the moment came, she was too frightened to move.

Calm as still water, a small voice whispered in her ear. Arya was so startled she almost dropped her bundle. She looked around wildly, but there was no one in the stable but her, and the horses, and the dead men.

Quiet as a shadow, she heard. Was it her own voice, or Syrio's? She could not tell, yet somehow it calmed her fears.

She stepped out of the stable.

It was the scariest thing she'd ever done. She wanted to run and hide, but she made herself *walk* across the yard, slowly, putting one foot in front of the other as if she had all the time in the world and no reason to be afraid of anyone. She thought she could feel their eyes, like bugs crawling on her skin under her clothes. Arya never looked up. If she saw them watching, all her courage would desert her, she knew, and she would drop the bundle of clothes and run and cry like a baby, and then they would have her. She kept her gaze on the ground. By the time she reached the shadow of the royal sept on the far side of the yard, Arya was cold with sweat, but no one had raised the hue and cry.

The sept was open and empty. Inside, half a hundred prayer candles burned in a fragrant silence. Arya figured the gods would never miss two. She stuffed them up her sleeves, and left by a back window. Sneaking back to the alley where she had cornered the one-eared tom was easy, but after that she got lost. She crawled in and out of windows, hopped over walls, and felt her way through dark cellars, quiet as a shadow. Once she heard a woman weeping. It took her more than an hour to find the low narrow window that slanted down to the dungeon where the monsters waited.

She tossed her bundle through and doubled back to light her candle. That was chancy; the fire she'd remembered seeing had burnt down to embers, and she heard voices as she was blowing on the coals. Cupping her fingers around the flickering candle, she went out the window as they were coming in the door, without ever getting a glimpse of who it was.

This time the monsters did not frighten her. They seemed almost old friends. Arya held the candle over her head. With each step she took, the shadows moved against the walls, as if they were turning to watch her pass. *"Dragons,"* she whispered. She slid Needle out from under her cloak. The slender blade seemed very small and the dragons very big, yet somehow Arya felt better with steel in her hand.

The long windowless hall beyond the door was as black as she remembered. She held Needle in her left hand, her sword hand, the candle in her right fist. Hot wax ran down across her knuckles. The entrance to the well had been to the left, so Arya went right. Part of her wanted to run, but she was afraid of snuffing out her candle. She heard the faint squeaking of rats and glimpsed a pair of tiny glowing eyes on the edge of the light, but rats did not scare her. Other things did. It would be so easy to hide here, as she had hidden from the wizard and the man with the forked beard. She could almost see the stableboy standing against the wall, his hands curled into claws with the blood still dripping from the deep gashes in his palms where Needle had cut him. He might be waiting to grab her as she passed. He would see her candle coming a long way off. Maybe she would be better off without the light . . .

Fear cuts deeper than swords, the quiet voice inside her whispered. Suddenly Arya remembered the crypts at Winterfell. They were a lot scarier than this place, she told herself. She'd been just a little girl the first time she saw them. Her brother Robb had taken them down, her and Sansa and baby Bran, who'd been no bigger than Rickon was now. They'd only had one candle between them, and Bran's eyes had gotten as big as saucers as he stared at the stone faces of the Kings of Winter, with their wolves at their feet and their iron swords across their laps.

Robb took them all the way down to the end, past Grandfather and Brandon and Lyanna, to show them their own tombs. Sansa kept looking at the stubby little candle, anxious that it might go out. Old Nan had told her there were spiders down here, and rats as big as dogs. Robb smiled when she said that. "There are worse things than spiders and rats," he whispered. "This is where the dead walk." That was when they heard the sound, low and deep and shivery. Baby Bran had clutched at Arya's hand.

When the spirit stepped out of the open tomb, pale white and moaning for blood, Sansa ran shrieking for the stairs, and Bran wrapped himself around Robb's leg, sobbing. Arya stood her ground and gave the spirit a punch. It was only Jon, covered with flour. "You *stupid,*" she told him, "you scared the baby," but Jon and Robb just laughed and laughed, and pretty soon Bran and Arya were laughing too.

The memory made Arya smile, and after that the darkness held no more terrors for her. The stableboy was dead, she'd killed him, and if he jumped out at her she'd kill him again. She was going home. Everything would be better once she was home again, safe behind Winterfell's grey granite walls.

Her footsteps sent soft echoes hurrying ahead of her as Arya plunged deeper into the darkness.

SANSA

They came for Sansa on the third day.

She chose a simple dress of dark grey wool, plainly cut but richly embroidered around the collar and sleeves. Her fingers felt thick and clumsy as she struggled with the silver fastenings without the benefit of servants. Jeyne Poole had been confined with her, but Jeyne was useless. Her face was puffy from all her crying, and she could not seem to stop sobbing about her father.

"I'm certain your father is well," Sansa told her when she had finally gotten the dress buttoned right. "I'll ask the queen to let you see him." She thought that kindness might lift Jeyne's spirits, but the other girl just looked at her with red, swollen eyes and began to cry all the harder. She was such a *child*.

Sansa had wept too, the first day. Even within the stout walls of Maegor's Holdfast, with her door closed and barred, it was hard not to be terrified when the killing began. She had grown up to the sound of steel in the yard, and scarcely a day of her life had passed without hearing the clash of sword on sword, yet somehow knowing that the fighting was real made all the difference in the world. She heard it as she had never heard it before, and there were other sounds as well, grunts of pain, angry curses, shouts for help, and the moans of wounded and dying men. In the songs, the knights never screamed nor begged for mercy.

So she wept, pleading through her door for them to tell her what was happening, calling for her father, for Septa Mordane, for the king, for her gallant prince. If the men guarding her heard her pleas, they gave no answer. The only time the door opened was late that night, when they thrust Jeyne Poole inside, bruised and shaking. *"They're killing everyone,"* the steward's daughter had shrieked at her. She went on and on. The Hound had broken down her door with a warhammer, she said. There were bodies on the stair of the Tower of the Hand, and the steps were slick with blood. Sansa dried her own tears as she struggled to comfort her friend. They went to sleep in the same bed, cradled in each other's arms like sisters.

The second day was even worse. The room where Sansa had been confined was at the top of the highest tower of Maegor's Holdfast. From its window, she could see that the heavy iron portcullis in the gatehouse was down, and the drawbridge drawn up over the deep dry moat that separated the keep-within-a-keep from the larger castle that surrounded it. Lannister guardsmen prowled the walls with spears and crossbows to hand. The fighting was over, and the silence of the grave had settled over the Red Keep. The only sounds were Jeyne Poole's endless whimpers and sobs.

They were fed—hard cheese and fresh-baked bread and milk to break their fast, roast chicken and greens at midday, and a late supper of beef and barley stew—but the servants who brought the meals would not answer Sansa's questions. That evening, some women brought her clothes from the Tower of the Hand, and some of Jeyne's things as well, but they seemed nearly as frightened as Jeyne, and when she tried to talk to them, they fled from her as if she had the grey plague. The guards outside the door still refused to let them leave the room.

"Please, I need to speak to the queen again," Sansa told them, as she told everyone she saw that day. "She'll want to talk to me, I know she will. Tell her I want to see her, please. If not the queen, then Prince Joffrey, if you'd be so kind. We're to marry when we're older."

At sunset on the second day, a great bell began to ring. Its voice was deep and sonorous, and the long slow clanging filled Sansa with a sense of dread. The ringing went on and on, and after a while they heard other bells answering from the Great Sept of Baelor on Visenya's Hill. The sound rumbled across the city like thunder, warning of the storm to come.

"What is it?" Jeyne asked, covering her ears. "Why are they ringing the bells?"

"The king is dead." Sansa could not say how she knew it, yet she did. The slow, endless clanging filled their room, as mournful as a dirge. Had some enemy stormed the castle and murdered King Robert? Was that the meaning of the fighting they had heard?

She went to sleep wondering, restless, and fearful. Was her beautiful Joffrey the king now? Or had they killed him too? She was afraid for him, and for her father. If only they would tell her what was happening . . .

That night Sansa dreamt of Joffrey on the throne, with herself seated beside him in a gown of woven gold. She had a crown on her head, and everyone she had ever known came before her, to bend the knee and say their courtesies.

The next morning, the morning of the third day, Ser Boros Blount of the Kingsguard came to escort her to the queen.

Ser Boros was an ugly man with a broad chest and short, bandy legs. His nose was flat, his cheeks baggy with jowls, his hair grey and brittle. Today he wore white velvet, and his snowy cloak was fastened with a lion brooch. The beast had the soft sheen of gold, and his eyes were tiny rubies. "You look very handsome and splendid this morning, Ser Boros," Sansa told him. A lady remembered her courtesies, and she was resolved to be a lady no matter what.

"And you, my lady," Ser Boros said in a flat voice. "Her Grace awaits. Come with me."

There were guards outside her door, Lannister men-at-arms in crimson cloaks and lion-crested helms. Sansa made herself smile at them pleasantly and bid them a good morning as she passed. It was the first time she had been allowed outside the chamber since Ser Arys Oakheart had led her there two mornings past. "To keep you safe, my sweet one," Queen Cersei had told her. "Joffrey would never forgive me if anything happened to his precious."

Sansa had expected that Ser Boros would escort her to the royal apartments, but instead he led her out of Maegor's Holdfast. The bridge was down again. Some workmen were lowering a man on ropes into the depths of the dry moat. When Sansa peered down, she saw a body impaled on the huge iron spikes below. She averted her eyes quickly, afraid to ask, afraid to look too long, afraid he might be someone she knew.

They found Queen Cersei in the council chambers, seated at the head of a long table littered with papers, candles, and blocks of sealing wax. The room was as splendid as any that Sansa had ever seen. She stared in awe at the carved wooden screen and the twin sphinxes that sat beside the door.

"Your Grace," Ser Boros said when they were ushered inside by another of the Kingsguard, Ser Mandon of the curiously dead face, "I've brought the girl."

Sansa had hoped Joffrey might be with her. Her prince was not there, but three of the king's councillors were. Lord Petyr Baelish sat on the queen's left hand, Grand Maester Pycelle at the end of the table, while Lord Varys hovered over them, smelling flowery. All of them were clad in black, she realized with a feeling of dread. Mourning clothes . . .

The queen wore a high-collared black silk gown, with a hundred dark red rubies sewn into her bodice, covering her from neck to bosom. They were cut in the shape of teardrops, as if the queen were weeping blood. Cersei smiled to see her, and Sansa thought it was the sweetest and saddest smile she had ever seen. "Sansa, my sweet child," she said, "I know you've been asking for me. I'm sorry that I could not send for you sooner. Matters have been very unsettled, and I have not had a moment. I trust my people have been taking good care of you?"

"Everyone has been very sweet and pleasant, Your Grace, thank you ever so much for asking," Sansa said politely. "Only, well, no one will talk to us or tell us what's happened . . ."

"Us?" Cersei seemed puzzled.

"We put the steward's girl in with her," Ser Boros said. "We did not know what else to do with her."

The queen frowned. "Next time, you will ask," she said, her voice sharp. "The gods only know what sort of tales she's been filling Sansa's head with."

"Jeyne's scared," Sansa said. "She won't stop crying. I promised her I'd ask if she could see her father."

Old Grand Maester Pycelle lowered his eyes.

"Her father is well, isn't he?" Sansa said anxiously. She knew there had been fighting, but surely no one would harm a steward. Vayon Poole did not even wear a sword.

Queen Cersei looked at each of the councillors in turn. "I won't have Sansa fretting needlessly. What shall we do with this little friend of hers, my lords?"

Lord Petyr leaned forward. "I'll find a place for her."

"Not in the city," said the queen.

"Do you take me for a fool?"

The queen ignored that. "Ser Boros, escort this girl to Lord Petyr's apartments and instruct his people to keep her there until he comes for her. Tell her that Littlefinger will be taking her to see her father, that ought to calm her down. I want her gone before Sansa returns to her chamber."

"As you command, Your Grace," Ser Boros said. He bowed deeply, spun on his heel, and took his leave, his long white cloak stirring the air behind him.

Sansa was confused. "I don't understand," she said. "Where is Jeyne's father? Why can't Ser Boros take her to him instead of Lord Petyr having to do it?" She had promised herself she would be a lady, gentle as the queen and as strong as her mother, the Lady Catelyn, but all of a sudden she was scared again. For a second she thought she might cry. "Where are you sending her? She hasn't done anything wrong, she's a good girl."

"She's upset you," the queen said gently. "We can't be having that. Not another word, now. Lord Baelish will see that Jeyne's well taken care of, I promise you." She patted the chair beside her. "Sit down, Sansa. I want to talk to you."

Sansa seated herself beside the queen. Cersei smiled again, but that did not make her feel any less anxious. Varys was wringing his soft hands together, Grand

Maester Pycelle kept his sleepy eyes on the papers in front of him, but she could feel Littlefinger staring. Something about the way the small man looked at her made Sansa feel as though she had no clothes on. Goose bumps pimpled her skin.

"Sweet Sansa," Queen Cersei said, laying a soft hand on her wrist. "Such a beautiful child. I do hope you know how much Joffrey and I love you."

"You *do?*" Sansa said, breathless. Littlefinger was forgotten. Her prince loved her. Nothing else mattered.

The queen smiled. "I think of you almost as my own daughter. And I know the love you bear for Joffrey." She gave a weary shake of her head. "I am afraid we have some grave news about your lord father. You must be brave, child."

Her quiet words gave Sansa a chill. "What is it?"

"Your father is a traitor, dear," Lord Varys said.

Grand Maester Pycelle lifted his ancient head. "With my own ears, I heard Lord Eddard swear to our beloved King Robert that he would protect the young princes as if they were his own sons. And yet the moment the king was dead, he called the small council together to steal Prince Joffrey's rightful throne."

"No," Sansa blurted. "He wouldn't do that. He *wouldn't!*"

The queen picked up a letter. The paper was torn and stiff with dried blood, but the broken seal was her father's, the direwolf stamped in pale wax. "We found this on the captain of your household guard, Sansa. It is a letter to my late husband's brother Stannis, inviting him to take the crown."

"Please, Your Grace, there's been a mistake." Sudden panic made her dizzy and faint. "Please, send for my father, he'll tell you, he would never write such a letter, the king was his friend."

"Robert thought so," said the queen. "This betrayal would have broken his heart. The gods are kind, that he did not live to see it." She sighed. "Sansa, sweetling, you must see what a dreadful position this has left us in. You are innocent of any wrong, we all know that, and yet you are the daughter of a traitor. How can I allow you to marry my son?"

"But I *love* him," Sansa wailed, confused and frightened. What did they mean to do to her? What had they done to her father? It was not supposed to happen this way. She had to wed Joffrey, they were betrothed, he was promised to her, she had even dreamed about it. It wasn't fair to take him away from her on account of whatever her father might have done.

"How well I know that, child," Cersei said, her voice so kind and sweet. "Why else should you have come to me and told me of your father's plan to send you away from us, if not for love?"

"It *was* for love," Sansa said in a rush. "Father wouldn't even give me leave to say farewell." She was the good girl, the obedient girl, but she had felt as wicked as Arya that morning, sneaking away from Septa Mordane, defying her lord father. She had never done anything so willful before, and she would never have done it then if she hadn't loved Joffrey as much as she did. "He was going to take me back to Winterfell and marry me to some hedge knight, even though it was Joff I wanted. I told him, but he wouldn't listen." The king had been her last hope. The king could *command* Father to let her stay in King's Landing and marry Prince Joffrey, Sansa knew he could, but the king had always frightened her. He was loud and rough-voiced and drunk as often as not, and he would probably have just sent her back to Lord Eddard, if they even let her see him. So she went to the queen instead, and poured out her heart, and Cersei had listened and thanked her sweetly . . . only then Ser Arys had escorted her to the high room in Maegor's Holdfast and posted guards, and a few hours later, the fighting had begun outside. "Please," she finished, "you *have* to let me marry Joffrey, I'll be ever so good a wife to him, you'll see. I'll be a queen just like you, I promise."

Queen Cersei looked to the others. "My lords of the council, what do you say to her plea?"

"The poor child," murmured Varys. "A love so true and innocent, Your Grace, it would be cruel to deny it . . . and yet, what can we do? Her father stands condemned." His soft hands washed each other in a gesture of helpless distress.

"A child born of traitor's seed will find that betrayal comes naturally to her," said Grand Maester Pycelle.

"She is a sweet thing now, but in ten years, who can say what treasons she may hatch?"

"No," Sansa said, horrified. "I'm not, I'd never . . . I wouldn't betray Joffrey, I love him, I swear it, I do."

"Oh, so poignant," said Varys. "And yet, it is truly said that blood runs truer than oaths."

"She reminds me of the mother, not the father," Lord Petyr Baelish said quietly. "Look at her. The hair, the eyes. She is the very image of Cat at the same age."

The queen looked at her, troubled, and yet Sansa could see kindness in her clear green eyes. "Child," she said, "if I could truly believe that you were not like your father, why nothing should please me more than to see you wed to my Joffrey. I know he loves you with all his heart." She sighed. "And yet, I fear that Lord Varys and the Grand Maester have the right of it. The blood will tell. I have only to remember how your sister set her wolf on my son."

"I'm not like Arya," Sansa blurted. "She has the traitor's blood, not me. I'm *good,* ask Septa Mordane, she'll tell you, I only want to be Joffrey's loyal and loving wife."

She felt the weight of Cersei's eyes as the queen studied her face. "I believe you mean it, child." She turned to face the others. "My lords, it seems to me that if the rest of her kin were to remain loyal in this terrible time, that would go a long way toward laying our fears to rest."

Grand Maester Pycelle stroked his huge soft beard, his wide brow furrowed in thought. "Lord Eddard has three sons."

"Mere boys," Lord Petyr said with a shrug. "I should be more concerned with Lady Catelyn and the Tullys."

The queen took Sansa's hand in both of hers. "Child, do you know your letters?"

Sansa nodded nervously. She could read and write better than any of her brothers, although she was hopeless at sums.

"I am pleased to hear that. Perhaps there is hope for you and Joffrey still . . ."

"What do you want me to do?"

"You must write your lady mother, and your brother, the eldest . . . what is his name?"

"Robb," Sansa said.

"The word of your lord father's treason will no doubt

reach them soon. Better that it should come from you. You must tell them how Lord Eddard betrayed his king.''

Sansa wanted Joffrey desperately, but she did not think she had the courage to do as the queen was asking. "But he never . . . I don't . . . Your Grace, I wouldn't know what to say . . ."

The queen patted her hand. "We will tell you what to write, child. The important thing is that you urge Lady Catelyn and your brother to keep the king's peace."

"It will go hard for them if they don't," said Grand Maester Pycelle. "By the love you bear them, you must urge them to walk the path of wisdom."

"Your lady mother will no doubt fear for you dreadfully," the queen said. "You must tell her that you are well and in our care, that we are treating you gently and seeing to your every want. Bid them to come to King's Landing and pledge their fealty to Joffrey when he takes his throne. If they do that . . . why, then we shall know that there is no taint in your blood, and when you come into the flower of your womanhood, you shall wed the king in the Great Sept of Baelor, before the eyes of gods and men."

. . . *wed the king* . . . The words made her breath come faster, yet still Sansa hesitated. "Perhaps . . . if I might see my father, talk to him about . . ."

"Treason?" Lord Varys hinted.

"You disappoint me, Sansa," the queen said, with eyes gone hard as stones. "We've told you of your father's crimes. If you are truly as loyal as you say, why should you want to see him?"

"I . . . I only meant . . ." Sansa felt her eyes grow wet. "He's not . . . please, he hasn't been . . . hurt, or . . . or . . ."

"Lord Eddard has not been harmed," the queen said.

"But . . . what's to become of him?"

"That is a matter for the king to decide," Grand Maester Pycelle announced ponderously.

The *king!* Sansa blinked back her tears. Joffrey was the king now, she thought. Her gallant prince would never hurt her father, no matter what he might have done. If she went to him and pleaded for mercy, she was certain he'd listen. He *had* to listen, he loved her, even the queen said so. Joff would need to punish Father, the lords would expect it, but perhaps he could send him back to Winterfell, or exile him to one of the Free Cities across the narrow sea. It would only have to be for a few years. By then she and Joffrey would be married. Once she was queen, she could persuade Joff to bring Father back and grant him a pardon.

Only . . . if Mother or Robb did anything treasonous, called the banners or refused to swear fealty or *anything*, it would all go wrong. Her Joffrey was good and kind, she knew it in her heart, but a king had to be stern with rebels. She had to make them understand, she *had* to!

"I'll . . . I'll write the letters," Sansa told them.

With a smile as warm as the sunrise, Cersei Lannister leaned close and kissed her gently on the cheek. "I knew you would. Joffrey will be so proud when I tell him what courage and good sense you've shown here today."

In the end, she wrote four letters. To her mother, the Lady Catelyn Stark, and to her brothers at Winterfell, and to her aunt and her grandfather as well, Lady Lysa Arryn of the Eyrie, and Lord Hoster Tully of Riverrun. By the time she had done, her fingers were cramped and stiff and stained with ink. Varys had her father's seal. She warmed the pale white beeswax over a candle, poured it carefully, and watched as the eunuch stamped each letter with the direwolf of House Stark.

Jeyne Poole and all her things were gone when Ser Mandon Moore returned Sansa to the high tower of Maegor's Holdfast. No more weeping, she thought gratefully. Yet somehow it seemed colder with Jeyne gone, even after she'd built a fire. She pulled a chair close to the hearth, took down one of her favorite books, and lost herself in the stories of Florian and Jonquil, of Lady Shella and the Rainbow Knight, of valiant Prince Aemon and his doomed love for his brother's queen.

It was not until later that night, as she was drifting off to sleep, that Sansa realized she had forgotten to ask about her sister.

JON

"**O**thor," announced Ser Jaremy Rykker, "beyond a doubt. And this one was Jafer Flowers." He turned the corpse over with his foot, and the dead white face stared up at the overcast sky with blue, blue eyes. "They were Ben Stark's men, both of them."

My uncle's men, Jon thought numbly. He remembered how he'd pleaded to ride with them. *Gods, I was such a green boy. If he had taken me, it might be me lying here . . .*

Jafer's right wrist ended in the ruin of torn flesh and splintered bone left by Ghost's jaws. His right hand was floating in a jar of vinegar back in Maester Aemon's tower. His left hand, still at the end of his arm, was as black as his cloak.

"Gods have mercy," the Old Bear muttered. He swung down from his garron, handing his reins to Jon. The morning was unnaturally warm; beads of sweat dotted the Lord Commander's broad forehead like dew on a melon. His horse was nervous, rolling her eyes, backing away from the dead men as far as her lead would allow. Jon led her off a few paces, fighting to keep her from bolting. The horses did not like the feel of this place. For that matter, neither did Jon.

The dogs liked it least of all. Ghost had led the party here; the pack of hounds had been useless. When Bass the kennelmaster had tried to get them to take the scent from the severed hand, they had gone wild, yowling and barking, fighting to get away. Even now they were snarling and whimpering by turns, pulling at their leashes while Chett cursed them for curs.

It is only a wood, Jon told himself, *and they're only dead men.* He had seen dead men before . . .

Last night he had dreamt the Winterfell dream again. He was wandering the empty castle, searching for his father, descending into the crypts. Only this time the dream had gone further than before. In the dark he'd heard the scrape of stone on stone. When he turned he saw that the vaults were opening, one after the other. As the dead kings came stumbling from their cold black graves, Jon had woken in pitch-dark, his heart hammering. Even when Ghost leapt up on the bed to nuzzle at his face, he could not shake his deep sense of terror. He dared not go back to sleep. Instead he had climbed the Wall and walked, restless, until he saw the light of the dawn off to the east. *It was only a dream. I am a brother of the Night's Watch now, not a frightened boy.*

Samwell Tarly huddled beneath the trees, half-hidden behind the horses. His round fat face was the color of curdled milk. So far he had not lurched off to the woods to retch, but he had not so much as glanced at the dead men either. "I can't look," he whispered miserably.

"You have to look," Jon told him, keeping his voice low so the others would not hear. "Maester Aemon sent you to be his eyes, didn't he? What good are eyes if they're shut?"

"Yes, but . . . I'm such a coward, Jon."

Jon put a hand on Sam's shoulder. "We have a dozen rangers with us, and the dogs, even Ghost. No one will hurt you, Sam. Go ahead and look. The first look is the hardest."

Sam gave a tremulous nod, working up his courage with a visible effort. Slowly he swiveled his head. His eyes widened, but Jon held his arm so he could not turn away.

"Ser Jaremy," the Old Bear asked gruffly, "Ben Stark had six men with him when he rode from the Wall. Where are the others?"

Ser Jaremy shook his head. "Would that I knew."

Plainly Mormont was not pleased with that answer. "Two of our brothers butchered almost within sight of the Wall, yet your rangers heard nothing, saw nothing. Is this what the Night's Watch has fallen to? Do we still sweep these woods?"

"Yes, my lord, but—"

"Do we still mount watches?"

"We do, but—"

"This man wears a hunting horn." Mormont pointed at Othor. "Must I suppose that he died without sounding it? Or have your rangers all gone deaf as well as blind?"

Ser Jaremy bristled, his face taut with anger. "No horn was blown, my lord, or my rangers would have heard it. I do not have sufficient men to mount as many patrols as I should like . . . and since Benjen was lost, we have stayed closer to the Wall than we were wont to do before, by your own command."

The Old Bear grunted. "Yes. Well. Be that as it may." He made an impatient gesture. "Tell me how they died."

Squatting beside the dead man he had named Jafer Flowers, Ser Jaremy grasped his head by the scalp. The hair came out between his fingers, brittle as straw. The knight cursed and shoved at the face with the heel of his hand. A great gash in the side of the corpse's neck opened like a mouth, crusted with dried blood. Only a few ropes of pale tendon still attached the head to the neck. "This was done with an axe."

"Aye," muttered Dywen, the old forester. "Belike the axe that Othor carried, m'lord."

Jon could feel his breakfast churning in his belly, but he pressed his lips together and made himself look at the second body. Othor had been a big ugly man, and he made a big ugly corpse. No axe was in evidence. Jon remembered Othor; he had been the one bellowing the bawdy song as the rangers rode out. His singing days were done. His flesh was blanched white as milk, everywhere but his hands. His hands were black like Jafer's. Blossoms of hard cracked blood decorated the mortal wounds that covered him like a rash, breast and groin and throat. Yet his eyes were still open. They stared up at the sky, blue as sapphires.

Ser Jaremy stood. "The wildlings have axes too."

Mormont rounded on him. "So you believe this is Mance Rayder's work? This close to the Wall?"

"Who else, my lord?"

Jon could have told him. He knew, they all knew, yet no man of them would say the words. *The Others are only a story, a tale to make children shiver. If they ever lived at all, they are gone eight thousand years.* Even the thought made him feel foolish; he was a man grown now, a black brother of the Night's Watch, not the boy who'd once sat at Old Nan's feet with Bran and Robb and Arya.

Yet Lord Commander Mormont gave a snort. "If Ben Stark had come under wildling attack a half day's ride from Castle Black, he would have returned for more men, chased the killers through all seven hells and brought me back their heads."

"Unless he was slain as well," Ser Jaremy insisted.

The words hurt, even now. It had been so long, it seemed folly to cling to the hope that Ben Stark was still alive, but Jon Snow was nothing if not stubborn.

"It has been close on half a year since Benjen left us, my lord," Ser Jaremy went on. "The forest is vast. The wildlings might have fallen on him anywhere. I'd wager these two were the last survivors of his party, on their way back to us . . . but the enemy caught them before they could reach the safety of the Wall. The corpses are still fresh, these men cannot have been dead more than a day . . ."

"*No*," Samwell Tarly squeaked.

Jon was startled. Sam's nervous, high-pitched voice was the last he would have expected to hear. The fat boy was frightened of the officers, and Ser Jaremy was not known for his patience.

"I did not ask for your views, boy," Rykker said coldly.

"Let him speak, ser," Jon blurted.

Mormont's eyes flicked from Sam to Jon and back again. "If the lad has something to say, I'll hear him out. Come closer, boy. We can't see you behind those horses."

Sam edged past Jon and the garrons, sweating profusely. "My lord, it . . . it can't be a day or . . . look . . . the blood . . ."

"Yes?" Mormont growled impatiently. "Blood, what of it?"

"He soils his smallclothes at the sight of it," Chett shouted out, and the rangers laughed.

Sam mopped at the sweat on his brow. "You . . . you can see where Ghost . . . Jon's direwolf . . . you can see where he tore off that man's hand, and yet . . . the stump hasn't bled, look . . ." He waved a hand. "My father . . . L-lord Randyll, he, he made me watch him dress animals sometimes, when . . . after . . ." Sam shook his head from side to side, his chins quivering. Now that he had looked at the bodies, he could not seem to look away. "A fresh kill . . . the blood would still flow, my lords. Later . . . later it would be clotted, like a . . . a jelly, thick and . . . and . . ." He looked as though he was going to be sick. "This man . . . look at the wrist, it's all . . . *crusty* . . . dry . . . like . . ."

Jon saw at once what Sam meant. He could see the torn veins in the dead man's wrist, iron worms in the pale flesh. His blood was a black dust. Yet Jaremy Rykker was unconvinced. "If they'd been dead much longer than a day, they'd be ripe by now, boy. They don't even smell."

Dywen, the gnarled old forester who liked to boast that he could smell snow coming on, sidled closer to the corpses and took a whiff. "Well, they're no pansy flowers, but . . . m'lord has the truth of it. There's no corpse stink."

"They . . . they aren't rotting." Sam pointed, his fat finger shaking only a little. "Look, there's . . . there's no maggots or . . . or . . . worms or anything . . . they've been lying here in the woods, but they . . . they haven't been chewed or eaten by animals . . . only Ghost . . . otherwise they're . . . they're . . ."

"Untouched," Jon said softly. "And Ghost is different. The dogs and the horses won't go near them."

The rangers exchanged glances; they could see it was true, every man of them. Mormont frowned, glancing from the corpses to the dogs. "Chett, bring the hounds closer."

Chett tried, cursing, yanking on the leashes, giving one animal a lick of his boot. Most of the dogs just whimpered and planted their feet. He tried dragging one. The bitch resisted, growling and squirming as if to escape her collar.

Finally she lunged at him. Chett dropped the leash and stumbled backward. The dog leapt over him and bounded off into the trees.

"This . . . this is all wrong," Sam Tarly said earnestly. "The blood . . . there's bloodstains on their clothes, and . . . and their flesh, dry and hard, but . . . there's none on the ground, or . . . anywhere. With those . . . those . . . those . . ." Sam made himself swallow, took a deep breath. "With those *wounds* . . . terrible wounds . . . there should be blood all over. Shouldn't there?"

Dywen sucked at his wooden teeth. "Might be they didn't die here. Might be someone brought 'em and left 'em for us. A warning, as like." The old forester peered down suspiciously. "And might be I'm a fool, but I don't know that Othor never had no blue eyes afore."

Ser Jaremy looked startled. "Neither did Flowers," he blurted, turning to stare at the dead man.

A silence fell over the wood. For a moment all they heard was Sam's heavy breathing and the wet sound of Dywen sucking on his teeth. Jon squatted beside Ghost.

"Burn them," someone whispered. One of the rangers; Jon could not have said who. "Yes, burn them," a second voice urged.

The Old Bear gave a stubborn shake of his head. "Not yet. I want Maester Aemon to have a look at them. We'll bring them back to the Wall."

Some commands are more easily given than obeyed. They wrapped the dead men in cloaks, but when Hake and Dywen tried to tie one onto a horse, the animal went mad, screaming and rearing, lashing out with its hooves, even biting at Ketter when he ran to help. The rangers had no better luck with the other garrons; not even the most placid wanted any part of these burdens. In the end they were forced to hack off branches and fashion crude slings to carry the corpses back on foot. It was well past midday by the time they started back.

"I will have these woods searched," Mormont commanded Ser Jaremy as they set out. "Every tree, every rock, every bush, and every foot of muddy ground within ten leagues of here. Use all the men you have, and if you do not have enough, borrow hunters and foresters from the stewards. If Ben and the others are out here, dead or alive, I will have them found. And if there is anyone *else* in these woods, I will know of it. You are to track them and take them, alive if possible. Is that understood?"

"It is, my lord," Ser Jaremy said. "It will be done."

After that, Mormont rode in silence, brooding. Jon followed close behind him; as the Lord Commander's steward, that was his place. The day was grey, damp, overcast, the sort of day that made you wish for rain. No wind stirred the wood; the air hung humid and heavy, and Jon's clothes clung to his skin. It was warm. Too warm. The Wall was weeping copiously, had been weeping for days, and sometimes Jon even imagined it was shrinking.

The old men called this weather *spirit summer*, and said it meant the season was giving up its ghosts at last. After this the cold would come, they warned, and a long summer always meant a long winter. This summer had lasted ten years. Jon had been a babe in arms when it began.

Ghost ran with them for a time and then vanished among the trees. Without the direwolf, Jon felt almost naked. He found himself glancing at every shadow with unease. Unbidden, he thought back on the tales that Old Nan used to tell them, when he was a boy at Winterfell. He could almost hear her voice again, and the *click-click-click* of her needles. *In that darkness, the Others came riding,* she used to say, dropping her voice lower and lower. *Cold and dead they were, and they hated iron and fire and the touch of the sun, and every living creature with hot blood in its veins. Holdfasts and cities and kingdoms of men all fell before them, as they moved south on pale dead horses, leading hosts of the slain. They fed their dead servants on the flesh of human children . . .*

When he caught his first glimpse of the Wall looming above the tops of an ancient gnarled oak, Jon was vastly relieved. Mormont reined up suddenly and turned in his saddle. "Tarly," he barked, "come here."

Jon saw the start of fright on Sam's face as he lumbered up on his mare; doubtless he thought he was in trouble. "You're fat but you're not stupid, boy," the Old Bear said gruffly. "You did well back there. And you, Snow."

Sam blushed a vivid crimson and tripped over his own tongue as he tried to stammer out a courtesy. Jon had to smile.

When they emerged from under the trees, Mormont spurred his tough little garron to a trot. Ghost came streaking out from the woods to meet them, licking his chops, his muzzle red from prey. High above, the men on the Wall saw the column approaching. Jon heard the deep, throaty call of the watchman's great horn, calling out across the miles; a single long blast that shuddered through the trees and echoed off the ice.

UUUUUUUooooooooooooooooooooooooooooooooooo.

The sound faded slowly to silence. One blast meant rangers returning, and Jon thought, *I was a ranger for one day, at least. Whatever may come, they cannot take that away from me.*

Bowen Marsh was waiting at the first gate as they led their garrons through the icy tunnel. The Lord Steward was red-faced and agitated. "My lord," he blurted at Mormont as he swung open the iron bars, "there's been a bird, you must come at once."

"What is it, man?" Mormont said gruffly.

Curiously, Marsh glanced at Jon before he answered. "Maester Aemon has the letter. He's waiting in your solar."

"Very well. Jon, see to my horse, and tell Ser Jaremy to put the dead men in a storeroom until the maester is ready for them." Mormont strode away grumbling.

As they led their horses back to the stable, Jon was uncomfortably aware that people were watching him. Ser Alliser Thorne was drilling his boys in the yard, but he broke off to stare at Jon, a faint half smile on his lips. One-armed Donal Noye stood in the door of the armory. "The gods be with you, Snow," he called out.

Something's wrong, Jon thought. *Something's very wrong.*

The dead men were carried to one of the storerooms along the base of the Wall, a dark cold cell chiseled from the ice and used to keep meat and grain and sometimes even beer. Jon saw that Mormont's horse was fed and watered and groomed before he took care of his own. Afterward he sought out his friends. Grenn and Toad were on watch, but he found Pyp in the common hall. "What's happened?" he asked.

Pyp lowered his voice. "The king's dead."

Jon was stunned. Robert Baratheon had looked old and

fat when he visited Winterfell, yet he'd seemed hale enough, and there'd been no talk of illness. "How can you know?"

"One of the guards overheard Clydas reading the letter to Maester Aemon." Pyp leaned close. "Jon, I'm sorry. He was your father's friend, wasn't he?"

"They were as close as brothers, once." Jon wondered if Joffrey would keep his father as the King's Hand. It did not seem likely. That might mean Lord Eddard would return to Winterfell, and his sisters as well. He might even be allowed to visit them, with Lord Mormont's permission. It would be good to see Arya's grin again and to talk with his father. *I will ask him about my mother*, he resolved. *I am a man now, it is past time he told me. Even if she was a whore, I don't care, I want to know.*

"I heard Hake say the dead men were your uncle's," Pyp said.

"Yes," Jon replied. "Two of the six he took with him. They'd been dead a long time, only . . . the bodies are queer."

"Queer?" Pyp was all curiosity. "How queer?"

"Sam will tell you." Jon did not want to talk of it. "I should see if the Old Bear has need of me."

He walked to the Lord Commander's Tower alone, with a curious sense of apprehension. The brothers on guard eyed him solemnly as he approached. "The Old Bear's in his solar," one of them announced. "He was asking for you."

Jon nodded. He should have come straight from the stable. He climbed the tower steps briskly. *He wants wine or a fire in his hearth, that's all*, he told himself.

When he entered the solar, Mormont's raven screamed at him. *"Corn!"* the bird shrieked. *"Corn! Corn! Corn!"*

"Don't you believe it, I just fed him," the Old Bear growled. He was seated by the window, reading a letter. "Bring me a cup of wine, and pour one for yourself."

"For myself, my lord?"

Mormont lifted his eyes from the letter to stare at Jon. There was pity in that look; he could taste it. "You heard me."

Jon poured with exaggerated care, vaguely aware that he was drawing out the act. When the cups were filled, he would have no choice but to face whatever was in that letter. Yet all too soon, they were filled. "Sit, boy," Mormont commanded him. "Drink."

Jon remained standing. "It's my father, isn't it?"

The Old Bear tapped the letter with a finger. "Your father and the king," he rumbled. "I won't lie to you, it's grievous news. I never thought to see another king, not at my age, with Robert half my years and strong as a bull." He took a gulp of wine. "They say the king loved to hunt. The things we love destroy us every time, lad. Remember that. My son loved that young wife of his. Vain woman. If not for her, he would never have thought to sell those poachers."

Jon could scarcely follow what he was saying. "My lord, I don't understand. What's happened to my father?"

"I told you to sit," Mormont grumbled. "*Sit*," the raven screamed. "And have a drink, damn you. That's a command, Snow."

Jon sat, and took a sip of wine.

"Lord Eddard has been imprisoned. He is charged with treason. It is said he plotted with Robert's brothers to deny the throne to Prince Joffrey."

"No," Jon said at once. "That couldn't be. My father would never betray the king!"

"Be that as it may," said Mormont. "It is not for me to say. Nor for you."

"But it's a *lie*," Jon insisted. How could they think his father was a traitor, had they all gone mad? Lord Eddard Stark would never dishonor himself . . . would he?

He fathered a bastard, a small voice whispered inside him. *Where was the honor in that? And your mother, what of her? He will not even speak her name.*

"My lord, what will happen to him? Will they kill him?"

"As to that, I cannot say, lad. I mean to send a letter. I knew some of the king's councillors in my youth. Old Pycelle, Lord Stannis, Ser Barristan . . . Whatever your father has done, or hasn't done, he is a great lord. He must be allowed to take the black and join us here. Gods knows, we need men of Lord Eddard's ability."

Jon knew that other men accused of treason had been allowed to redeem their honor on the Wall in days past. Why not Lord Eddard? His father *here*. That was a strange thought, and strangely uncomfortable. It would be a monstrous injustice to strip him of Winterfell and force him to take the black, and yet if it meant his life . . .

And would Joffrey allow it? He remembered the prince at Winterfell, the way he'd mocked Robb and Ser Rodrik in the yard. Jon himself he had scarcely even noticed; bastards were beneath even his contempt. "My lord, will the king listen to you?"

The Old Bear shrugged. "A boy king . . . I imagine he'll listen to his mother. A pity the dwarf isn't with them. He's the lad's uncle, and he saw our need when he visited us. It was a bad thing, your lady mother taking him captive—"

"Lady Stark is not my mother," Jon reminded him sharply. Tyrion Lannister had been a friend to him. If Lord Eddard was killed, she would be as much to blame as the queen. "My lord, what of my sisters? Arya and Sansa, they were with my father, do you know—"

"Pycelle makes no mention of them, but doubtless they'll be treated gently. I will ask about them when I write." Mormont shook his head. "This could not have happened at a worse time. If ever the realm needed a strong king . . . there are dark days and cold nights ahead, I feel it in my bones . . ." He gave Jon a long shrewd look. "I hope you are not thinking of doing anything stupid, boy."

He's my father, Jon wanted to say, but he knew that Mormont would not want to hear it. His throat was dry. He made himself take another sip of wine.

"Your duty is here now," the Lord Commander reminded him. "Your old life ended when you took the black." His bird made a raucous echo. *"Black."* Mormont took no notice. "Whatever they do in King's Landing is none of our concern." When Jon did not answer, the old man finished his wine and said, "You're free to go. I'll have no further need of you today. On the morrow you can help me write that letter."

Jon did not remember standing or leaving the solar. The next he knew, he was descending the tower steps, thinking, *This is my father, my sisters, how can it be none of my concern!*

Outside, one of the guards looked at him and said, "Be strong, boy. The gods are cruel."

They know, Jon realized. "My father is no traitor," he

said hoarsely. Even the words stuck in his throat, as if to choke him. The wind was rising, and it seemed colder in the yard than it had when he'd gone in. Spirit summer was drawing to an end.

The rest of the afternoon passed as if in a dream. Jon could not have said where he walked, what he did, who he spoke with. Ghost was with him, he knew that much. The silent presence of the direwolf gave him comfort. *The girls do not even have that much*, he thought. *Their wolves might have kept them safe, but Lady is dead and Nymeria's lost, they're all alone.*

A north wind had begun to blow by the time the sun went down. Jon could hear it skirling against the Wall and over the icy battlements as he went to the common hall for the evening meal. Hobb had cooked up a venison stew, thick with barley, onions, and carrots. When he spooned an extra portion onto Jon's plate and gave him the crusty heel of the bread, he knew what it meant. *He knows.* He looked around the hall, saw heads turn quickly, eyes politely averted. *They all know.*

His friends rallied to him. "We asked the septon to light a candle for your father," Matthar told him. "It's a lie, we all know it's a lie, even *Grenn* knows it's a lie," Pyp chimed in. Grenn nodded, and Sam clasped Jon's hand, "You're my brother now, so he's my father too," the fat boy said. "If you want to go out to the weirwoods and pray to the old gods, I'll go with you."

The weirwoods were beyond the Wall, yet he knew Sam meant what he said. *They* are *my brothers*, he thought. *As much as Robb and Bran and Rickon . . .*

And then he heard the laughter, sharp and cruel as a whip, and the voice of Ser Alliser Thorne. "Not only a bastard, but a *traitor's* bastard," he was telling the men around him.

In the blink of an eye, Jon had vaulted onto the table, dagger in his hand. Pyp made a grab for him, but he wrenched his leg away, and then he was sprinting down the table and kicking the bowl from Ser Alliser's hand. Stew went flying everywhere, spattering the brothers. Thorne recoiled. People were shouting, but Jon Snow did not hear them. He lunged at Ser Alliser's face with the dagger, slashing at those cold onyx eyes, but Sam threw himself between them and before Jon could get around him, Pyp was on his back clinging like a monkey, and Grenn was grabbing his arm while Toad wrenched the knife from his fingers.

Later, much later, after they had marched him back to his sleeping cell, Mormont came down to see him, raven on his shoulder. "I told you not to do anything stupid, boy," the Old Bear said. *"Boy,"* the bird chorused. Mormont shook his head, disgusted. "And to think I had high hopes for you."

They took his knife and his sword and told him he was not to leave his cell until the high officers met to decide what was to be done with him. And then they placed a guard outside his door to make certain he obeyed. His friends were not allowed to see him, but the Old Bear did relent and permit him Ghost, so he was not utterly alone.

"My father is no traitor," he told the direwolf when the rest had gone. Ghost looked at him in silence. Jon slumped against the wall, hands around his knees, and stared at the candle on the table beside his narrow bed. The flame flickered and swayed, the shadows moved around him, the room seemed to grow darker and colder. *I will not sleep tonight,* Jon thought.

Yet he must have dozed. When he woke, his legs were stiff and cramped and the candle had long since burned out. Ghost stood on his hind legs, scrabbling at the door. Jon was startled to see how tall he'd grown. "Ghost, what is it?" he called softly. The direwolf turned his head and looked down at him, baring his fangs in a silent snarl. *Has he gone mad?* Jon wondered. "It's me, Ghost," he murmured, trying not to sound afraid. Yet he was trembling, violently. When had it gotten so cold?

Ghost backed away from the door. There were deep gouges where he'd raked the wood. Jon watched him with mounting disquiet. "There's someone out there, isn't there?" he whispered. Crouching, the direwolf crept backward, white fur rising on the back of his neck. *The guard,* he thought, *they left a man to guard my door, Ghost smells him through the door, that's all it is.*

Slowly, Jon pushed himself to his feet. He was shivering uncontrollably, wishing he still had a sword. Three quick steps brought him to the door. He grabbed the handle and pulled it inward. The *creak* of the hinges almost made him jump.

His guard was sprawled bonelessly across the narrow steps, looking up at him. Looking *up* at him, even though he was lying on his stomach. His head had been twisted completely around.

It can't be, Jon told himself. *This is the Lord Commander's Tower, it's guarded day and night, this couldn't happen, it's a dream, I'm having a nightmare.*

Ghost slid past him, out the door. The wolf started up the steps, stopped, looked back at Jon. That was when he heard it; the soft scrape of a boot on stone, the sound of a latch turning. The sounds came from above. From the Lord Commander's chambers.

A nightmare this might be, yet it was no dream.

The guard's sword was in its sheath. Jon knelt and worked it free. The heft of steel in his fist made him bolder. He moved up the steps, Ghost padding silently before him. Shadows lurked in every turn of the stair. Jon crept up warily, probing any suspicious darkness with the point of his sword.

Suddenly he heard the shriek of Mormont's raven. *"Corn,"* the bird was screaming. *"Corn, corn, corn, corn, corn, corn."* Ghost bounded ahead, and Jon came scrambling after. The door to Mormont's solar was wide open. The direwolf plunged through. Jon stopped in the doorway, blade in hand, giving his eyes a moment to adjust. Heavy drapes had been pulled across the windows, and the darkness was black as ink. *"Who's there?"* he called out.

Then he saw it, a shadow in the shadows, sliding toward the inner door that led to Mormont's sleeping cell, a man-shape all in black, cloaked and hooded . . . but beneath the hood, its eyes shone with an icy blue radiance . . .

Ghost leapt. Man and wolf went down together with neither scream nor snarl, rolling, smashing into a chair, knocking over a table laden with papers. Mormont's raven was flapping overhead, screaming, *"Corn, corn, corn, corn."* Jon felt as blind as Maester Aemon. Keeping the wall to his back, he slid toward the window and ripped down the curtain. Moonlight flooded the solar. He glimpsed black hands buried in white fur, swollen dark fingers tightening around his direwolf's throat. Ghost was twisting and snapping, legs flailing in the air, but he could not break free.

Jon had no time to be afraid. He threw himself forward, shouting, bringing down the longsword with all his weight behind it. Steel sheared through sleeve and skin and bone, yet the sound was *wrong* somehow. The smell that engulfed him was so queer and cold he almost gagged. He saw arm and hand on the floor, black fingers wriggling in a pool of moonlight. Ghost wrenched free of the other hand and crept away, red tongue lolling from his mouth.

The hooded man lifted his pale moon face, and Jon slashed at it without hesitation. The sword laid the intruder open to the bone, taking off half his nose and opening a gash cheek to cheek under those eyes, eyes, eyes like blue stars burning. Jon knew that face. *Othor*, he thought, reeling back. *Gods, he's dead, he's dead, I saw him dead.*

He felt something scrabble at his ankle. Black fingers clawed at his calf. The arm was crawling up his leg, ripping at wool and flesh. Shouting with revulsion, Jon pried the fingers off his leg with the point of his sword and flipped the thing away. It lay writhing, fingers opening and closing.

The corpse lurched forward. There was no blood. One-armed, face cut near in half, it seemed to feel nothing. Jon held the longsword before him. "Stay away!" he commanded, his voice gone shrill. *"Corn,"* screamed the raven, *"corn, corn."* The severed arm was wriggling out of its torn sleeve, a pale snake with a black five-fingered head. Ghost pounced and got it between his teeth. Finger bones crunched. Jon hacked at the corpse's neck, felt the steel bite deep and hard.

Dead Othor slammed into him, knocking him off his feet.

Jon's breath went out of him as the fallen table caught him between his shoulder blades. The sword, where was the sword? He'd lost the damned *sword*! When he opened his mouth to scream, the wight jammed its black corpse fingers into Jon's mouth. Gagging, he tried to shove it off, but the dead man was too heavy. Its hand forced itself farther down his throat, icy cold, choking him. Its face was against his own, filling the world. Frost covered its eyes, sparkling blue. Jon raked cold flesh with his nails and kicked at the thing's legs. He tried to bite, tried to punch, tried to breathe . . .

And suddenly the corpse's weight was gone, its fingers ripped from his throat. It was all Jon could do to roll over, retching and shaking. Ghost had it again. He watched as the direwolf buried his teeth in the wight's gut and began to rip and tear. He watched, only half conscious, for a long moment before he finally remembered to look for his sword . . .

. . . and saw Lord Mormont, naked and groggy from sleep, standing in the doorway with an oil lamp in hand. Gnawed and fingerless, the arm thrashed on the floor, wriggling toward him.

Jon tried to shout, but his voice was gone. Staggering to his feet, he kicked the arm away and snatched the lamp from the Old Bear's fingers. The flame flickered and almost died. *"Burn!"* the raven cawed. *"Burn, burn, burn!"*

Spinning, Jon saw the drapes he'd ripped from the window. He flung the lamp into the puddled cloth with both hands. Metal crunched, glass shattered, oil spewed, and the hangings went up in a great *whoosh* of flame. The heat of it on his face was sweeter than any kiss Jon had ever known. "Ghost!" he shouted.

The direwolf wrenched free and came to him as the wight struggled to rise, dark snakes spilling from the great wound in its belly. Jon plunged his hand into the flames, grabbed a fistful of the burning drapes, and whipped them at the dead man. *Let it burn,* he prayed as the cloth smothered the corpse, *gods, please, please, let it burn.*

BRAN

The Karstarks came in on a cold windy morning, bringing three hundred horsemen and near two thousand foot from their castle at Karhold. The steel points of their pikes winked in the pale sunlight as the column approached. A man went before them, pounding out a slow, deep-throated marching rhythm on a drum that was bigger than he was, *boom, boom, boom.*

Bran watched them come from a guard turret atop the outer wall, peering through Maester Luwin's bronze far-eye while perched on Hodor's shoulders. Lord Rickard himself led them, his sons Harrion and Eddard and Torrhen riding beside him beneath night-black banners emblazoned with the white sunburst of their House. Old Nan said they had Stark blood in them, going back hundreds of years, but they did not look like Starks to Bran. They were big men, and fierce, faces covered with thick beards, hair worn loose past the shoulders. Their cloaks were made of skins, the pelts of bear and seal and wolf.

They were the last, he knew. The other lords were already here, with their hosts. Bran yearned to ride out among them, to see the winter houses full to bursting, the jostling crowds in the market square every morning, the streets rutted and torn by wheel and hoof. But Robb had forbidden him to leave the castle. "We have no men to spare to guard you," his brother had explained.

"I'll take Summer," Bran argued.

"Don't act the boy with me, Bran," Robb said. "You know better than that. Only two days ago one of Lord Bolton's men knifed one of Lord Cerwyn's at the Smoking Log. Our lady mother would skin me for a pelt if I let you put yourself at risk." He was using the voice of Robb the Lord when he said it; Bran knew that meant there was no appeal.

It was because of what had happened in the wolfs-wood, he knew. The memory still gave him bad dreams. He had been as helpless as a baby, no more able to defend himself than Rickon would have been. Less, even . . . Rickon would have kicked them, at the least. It shamed him. He was only a few years younger than Robb; if his brother was almost a man grown, so was he. He should have been able to protect himself.

A year ago, *before*, he would have visited the town even if it meant climbing over the walls by himself. In those days he could run down stairs, get on and off his pony by himself, and wield a wooden sword good enough to knock Prince Tommen in the dirt. Now he could only watch, peering out through Maester Luwin's lens tube. The maester had taught him all the banners: the mailed fist of the Glovers, silver on scarlet; Lady Mormont's black bear; the hideous flayed man that went before Roose Bolton of the Dreadfort; a bull moose for the Hornwoods; a battle-axe for the Cerwyns; three sentinel trees for the Tallharts; and the fearsome sigil of House Umber, a roaring giant in shattered chains.

And soon enough he learned the faces too, when the lords and their sons and knights retainer came to Winterfell to feast. Even the Great Hall was not large enough to seat all of them at once, so Robb hosted each of the principal bannermen in turn. Bran was always given the place of honor at his brother's right hand. Some of the lords bannermen gave him queer hard stares as he sat there, as if they wondered by what right a green boy should be placed above them, and him a cripple too.

"How many is it now?" Bran asked Maester Luwin as

Lord Karstark and his sons rode through the gates in the outer wall.

"Twelve thousand men, or near enough as makes no matter."

"How many knights?"

"Few enough," the maester said with a touch of impatience. "To be a knight, you must stand your vigil in a sept, and be anointed with the seven oils to consecrate your vows. In the north, only a few of the great houses worship the Seven. The rest honor the old gods, and name no knights . . . but those lords and their sons and sworn swords are no less fierce or loyal or honorable. A man's worth is not marked by a *ser* before his name. As I have told you a hundred times before."

"Still," said Bran, "how many knights?"

Maester Luwin sighed. "Three hundred, perhaps four . . . among three thousand armored lances who are not knights."

"Lord Karstark is the last," Bran said thoughtfully. "Robb will feast him tonight."

"No doubt he will."

"How long before . . . before they go?"

"He must march soon, or not at all," Maester Luwin said. "The winter town is full to bursting, and this army of his will eat the countryside clean if it camps here much longer. Others are waiting to join him all along the kingsroad, barrow knights and crannogmen and the Lords Manderly and Flint. The fighting has begun in the riverlands, and your brother has many leagues to go."

"I know." Bran felt as miserable as he sounded. He handed the bronze tube back to the maester, and noticed how thin Luwin's hair had grown on top. He could see the pink of scalp showing through. It felt queer to look down on him this way, when he'd spent his whole life looking up at him, but when you sat on Hodor's back you looked down on everyone. "I don't want to watch anymore. Hodor, take me back to the keep."

"Hodor," said Hodor.

Maester Luwin tucked the tube up his sleeve. "Bran, your lord brother will not have time to see you now. He must greet Lord Karstark and his sons and make them welcome."

"I won't trouble Robb. I want to visit the godswood."
He put his hand on Hodor's shoulder. "Hodor."

A series of chisel-cut handholds made a ladder in the
granite of the tower's inner wall. Hodor hummed tunelessly as he went down hand under hand, Bran bouncing
against his back in the wicker seat that Maester Luwin
had fashioned for him. Luwin had gotten the idea from
the baskets the women used to carry firewood on their
backs; after that it had been a simple matter of cutting
legholes and attaching some new straps to spread Bran's
weight more evenly. It was not as good as riding Dancer,
but there were places Dancer could not go, and this did
not shame Bran the way it did when Hodor carried him in
his arms like a baby. Hodor seemed to like it too, though
with Hodor it was hard to tell. The only tricky part was
doors. Sometimes Hodor *forgot* that he had Bran on his
back, and that could be painful when he went through a
door.

For near a fortnight there had been so many comings
and goings that Robb ordered both portcullises kept up
and the drawbridge down between them, even in the dead
of night. A long column of armored lancers was crossing
the moat between the walls when Bran emerged from the
tower; Karstark men, following their lords into the castle.
They wore black iron halfhelms and black woolen cloaks
patterned with the white sunburst. Hodor trotted along
beside them, smiling to himself, his boots thudding
against the wood of the drawbridge. The riders gave them
queer looks as they went by, and once Bran heard someone guffaw. He refused to let it trouble him. "Men will
look at you," Maester Luwin had warned him the first
time they had strapped the wicker basket around Hodor's
chest. "They will look, and they will talk, and some will
mock you." *Let them mock*, Bran thought. No one
mocked him in his bedchamber, but he would not live his
life in bed.

As they passed beneath the gatehouse portcullis, Bran
put two fingers into his mouth and whistled. Summer
came loping across the yard. Suddenly the Karstark lancers were fighting for control, as their horses rolled their
eyes and whickered in dismay. One stallion reared,
screaming, his rider cursing and hanging on desperately.
The scent of the direwolves sent horses into a frenzy of

fear if they were not accustomed to it, but they'd quiet soon enough once Summer was gone. "The godswood," Bran reminded Hodor.

Even Winterfell itself was crowded. The yard rang to the sound of sword and axe, the rumble of wagons, and the barking of dogs. The armory doors were open, and Bran glimpsed Mikken at his forge, his hammer ringing as sweat dripped off his bare chest. Bran had never seen as many strangers in all his years, not even when King Robert had come to visit Father.

He tried not to flinch as Hodor ducked through a low door. They walked down a long dim hallway, Summer padding easily beside them. The wolf glanced up from time to time, eyes smoldering like liquid gold. Bran would have liked to touch him, but he was riding too high for his hand to reach.

The godswood was an island of peace in the sea of chaos that Winterfell had become. Hodor made his way through the dense stands of oak and ironwood and sentinels, to the still pool beside the heart tree. He stopped under the gnarled limbs of the weirwood, humming. Bran reached up over his head and pulled himself out of his seat, drawing the dead weight of his legs up through the holes in the wicker basket. He hung for a moment, dangling, the dark red leaves brushing against his face, until Hodor lifted him and lowered him to the smooth stone beside the water. "I want to be by myself for a while," he said. "You go soak. Go to the pools."

"Hodor." Hodor stomped through the trees and vanished. Across the godswood, beneath the windows of the Guest House, an underground hot spring fed three small ponds. Steam rose from the water day and night, and the wall that loomed above was thick with moss. Hodor hated cold water, and would fight like a treed wildcat when threatened with soap, but he would happily immerse himself in the hottest pool and sit for hours, giving a loud burp to echo the spring whenever a bubble rose from the murky green depths to break upon the surface.

Summer lapped at the water and settled down at Bran's side. He rubbed the wolf under the jaw, and for a moment boy and beast both felt at peace. Bran had always liked the godswood, even *before*, but of late he found himself drawn to it more and more. Even the heart tree no longer scared him the way it used to. The deep red eyes carved into the pale trunk still watched him, yet somehow he took comfort from that now. The gods were looking over him, he told himself; the old gods, gods of the Starks and the First Men and the children of the forest, his *father's* gods. He felt safe in their sight, and the deep silence of the trees helped him think. Bran had been thinking a lot since his fall; thinking, and dreaming, and talking with the gods.

"Please make it so Robb won't go away," he prayed softly. He moved his hand through the cold water, sending ripples across the pool. "Please make him stay. Or if he has to go, bring him home safe, with Mother and Father and the girls. And make it . . . make it so Rickon understands."

His baby brother had been wild as a winter storm since he learned Robb was riding off to war, weeping and angry by turns. He'd refused to eat, cried and screamed for most of a night, even punched Old Nan when she tried to sing him to sleep, and the next day he'd vanished. Robb had set half the castle searching for him, and when at last they'd found him down in the crypts, Rickon had slashed at them with a rusted iron sword he'd snatched from a dead king's hand, and Shaggydog had come slavering out of the darkness like a green-eyed demon. The wolf was near as wild as Rickon; he'd bitten Gage on the arm and torn a chunk of flesh from Mikken's thigh. It had taken Robb himself and Grey Wind to bring him to bay. Farlen had the black wolf chained up in the kennels now, and Rickon cried all the more for being without him.

Maester Luwin counseled Robb to remain at Winterfell, and Bran pleaded with him too, for his own sake as much as Rickon's, but his brother only shook his head stubbornly and said, "I don't want to go. I *have* to."

It was only half a lie. Someone had to go, to hold the Neck and help the Tullys against the Lannisters, Bran could understand that, but it did not *have* to be Robb. His brother might have given the command to Hal Mollen or Theon Greyjoy, or to one of his lords bannermen. Maester Luwin urged him to do just that, but Robb would not hear of it. "My lord father would never have sent men off to die while he huddled like a craven behind the walls of Winterfell," he said, all Robb the Lord.

Robb seemed half a stranger to Bran now, transformed, a lord in truth, though he had not yet seen his sixteenth name day. Even their father's bannermen seemed to sense it. Many tried to test him, each in his own way. Roose Bolton and Robett Glover both demanded the honor of battle command, the first brusquely, the second with a smile and a jest. Stout, grey-haired Maege Mormont, dressed in mail like a man, told Robb bluntly that he was young enough to be her grandson, and had no business giving her commands . . . but as it happened, she had a granddaughter she would be willing to have him marry. Soft-spoken Lord Cerwyn had actually brought his daughter with him, a plump, homely maid of thirty years who sat at her father's left hand and never lifted her eyes from her plate. Jovial Lord Hornwood had no daughters, but he did bring gifts, a horse one day, a haunch of venison the next, a silver-chased hunting horn the day after, and he asked nothing in return . . . nothing but a certain hold-fast taken from his grandfather, and hunting rights north of a certain ridge, and leave to dam the White Knife, if it please the lord.

Robb answered each of them with cool courtesy, much as Father might have, and somehow he bent them to his will.

And when Lord Umber, who was called the Greatjon by his men and stood as tall as Hodor and twice as wide, threatened to take his forces home if he was placed behind the Hornwoods or the Cerwyns in the order of march, Robb told him he was welcome to do so. "And when we are done with the Lannisters," he promised, scratching Grey Wind behind the ear, "we will march back north, root you out of your keep, and hang you for an oathbreaker." Cursing, the Greatjon flung a flagon of ale into the fire and bellowed that Robb was so green he must piss grass. When Hallis Mollen moved to restrain him, he knocked him to the floor, kicked over a table, and unsheathed the biggest, ugliest greatsword that Bran had ever seen. All along the benches, his sons and brothers and sworn swords leapt to their feet, grabbing for their steel.

Yet Robb only said a quiet word, and in a snarl and the blink of an eye Lord Umber was on his back, his sword spinning on the floor three feet away and his hand dripping blood where Grey Wind had bitten off two fingers. "My lord father taught me that it was death to bare steel against your liege lord," Robb said, "but doubtless you only meant to cut my meat." Bran's bowels went to water as the Greatjon struggled to rise, sucking at the red stumps of fingers . . . but then, astonishingly, the huge man *laughed*. "Your meat," he roared, "is bloody *tough*."

And somehow after that the Greatjon became Robb's right hand, his staunchest champion, loudly telling all and sundry that the boy lord was a Stark after all, and they'd damn well better bend their knees if they didn't fancy having them chewed off.

Yet that very night, his brother came to Bran's bedchamber pale and shaken, after the fires had burned low in the Great Hall. "I thought he was going to kill me," Robb confessed. "Did you see the way he threw down Hal, like he was no bigger than Rickon? Gods, I was so scared. And the Greatjon's not the worst of them, only the loudest. Lord Roose never says a word, he only looks at me, and all I can think of is that room they have in the Dreadfort, where the Boltons hang the skins of their enemies."

"That's just one of Old Nan's stories," Bran said. A note of doubt crept into his voice. "Isn't it?"

"I don't know." He gave a weary shake of his head. "Lord Cerwyn means to take his daughter south with us. To cook for him, he says. Theon is certain I'll find the girl in my bedroll one night. I wish . . . I wish Father was here . . ."

That was the one thing they could agree on, Bran and Rickon and Robb the Lord; they all wished Father was here. But Lord Eddard was a thousand leagues away, a captive in some dungeon, a hunted fugitive running for his life, or even dead. No one seemed to know for certain; every traveler told a different tale, each more terrifying than the last. The heads of Father's guardsmen were rotting on the walls of the Red Keep, impaled on spikes. King Robert was dead at Father's hands. The Baratheons had laid siege to King's Landing. Lord Eddard had fled south with the king's wicked brother Renly. Arya and Sansa had been murdered by the Hound. Mother had killed Tyrion the Imp and hung his body from the walls of Riverrun. Lord Tywin Lannister was marching on the Eyrie, burning and slaughtering as he went. One wine-sodden taleteller even claimed that Rhaegar Targaryen had returned from the dead and was marshaling a vast host of ancient heroes on Dragonstone to reclaim his father's throne.

When the raven came, bearing a letter marked with Father's own seal and written in Sansa's hand, the cruel truth seemed no less incredible. Bran would never forget the look on Robb's face as he stared at their sister's words. "She says Father conspired at treason with the king's brothers," he read. "King Robert is dead, and Mother and I are summoned to the Red Keep to swear fealty to Joffrey. She says we must be loyal, and when she marries Joffrey she will plead with him to spare our lord father's life." His fingers closed into a fist, crushing Sansa's letter between them. "And she says nothing of Arya, *nothing*, not so much as a word. Damn her! What's wrong with the girl?"

Bran felt all cold inside. "She lost her wolf," he said, weakly, remembering the day when four of his father's guardsmen had returned from the south with Lady's bones. Summer and Grey Wind and Shaggydog had begun to howl before they crossed the drawbridge, in voices drawn and desolate. Beneath the shadow of the First Keep was an ancient lichyard, its headstones spotted with pale lichen, where the old Kings of Winter had laid their faithful servants. It was there they buried Lady, while her brothers stalked between the graves like restless shadows. She had gone south, and only her bones had returned.

Their grandfather, old Lord Rickard, had gone as well, with his son Brandon who was Father's brother, and two hundred of his best men. None had ever returned. And Father had gone south, with Arya and Sansa, and Jory and Hullen and Fat Tom and the rest, and later Mother and Ser Rodrik had gone, and *they* hadn't come back either. And now Robb meant to go. Not to King's Landing and not to swear fealty, but to Riverrun, with a sword in his hand. And if their lord father were truly a prisoner, that could mean his death for a certainty. It frightened Bran more than he could say.

"If Robb has to go, watch over him," Bran entreated the old gods, as they watched him with the heart tree's red eyes, "and watch over his men, Hal and Quent and the rest, and Lord Umber and Lady Mormont and the other lords. And Theon too, I suppose. Watch them and keep them safe, if it please you, gods. Help them defeat the Lannisters and save Father and bring them home."

A faint wind sighed through the godswood and the red leaves stirred and whispered. Summer bared his teeth. "You hear them, boy?" a voice asked.

Bran lifted his head. Osha stood across the pool, beneath an ancient oak, her face shadowed by leaves. Even in irons, the wildling moved quiet as a cat. Summer circled the pool, sniffed at her. The tall woman flinched.

"Summer, to me," Bran called. The direwolf took one final sniff, spun, and bounded back. Bran wrapped his arms around him. "What are *you* doing here?" He had not seen Osha since they'd taken her captive in the wolfs-wood, though he knew she'd been set to working in the kitchens.

"They are my gods too," Osha said. "Beyond the Wall, they are the only gods." Her hair was growing out, brown and shaggy. It made her look more womanly, that and the simple dress of brown roughspun they'd given her when they took her mail and leather. "Gage lets me have my prayers from time to time, when I feel the need, and I let him do as he likes under my skirt, when he feels the need. It's nothing to me. I like the smell of flour on his hands, and he's gentler than Stiv." She gave an awkward bow. "I'll leave you. There's pots that want scouring."

"No, stay," Bran commanded her. "Tell me what you meant, about hearing the gods."

Osha studied him. "You asked them and they're answering. Open your ears, listen, you'll hear."

Bran listened. "It's only the wind," he said after a moment, uncertain. "The leaves are rustling."

"Who do you think sends the wind, if not the gods?" She seated herself across the pool from him, clinking faintly as she moved. Mikken had fixed iron manacles to her ankles, with a heavy chain between them; she could walk, so long as she kept her strides small, but there was no way for her to run, or climb, or mount a horse. "They see you, boy. They hear you talking. That rustling, that's them talking back."

"What are they saying?"

"They're sad. Your lord brother will get no help from them, not where he's going. The old gods have no power in the south. The weirwoods there were all cut down, thousands of years ago. How can they watch your brother when they have no eyes?"

Bran had not thought of that. It frightened him. If even the gods could not help his brother, what hope was there? Maybe Osha wasn't hearing them right. He cocked his head and tried to listen again. He thought he could hear the sadness now, but nothing more than that.

The rustling grew louder. Bran heard muffled footfalls and a low humming, and Hodor came blundering out of the trees, naked and smiling. "Hodor!"

"He must have heard our voices," Bran said. "Hodor, you forgot your clothes."

"Hodor," Hodor agreed. He was dripping wet from the neck down, steaming in the chill air. His body was covered with brown hair, thick as a pelt. Between his legs, his manhood swung long and heavy.

Osha eyed him with a sour smile. "Now there's a big man," she said. "He has giant's blood in him, or I'm the queen."

"Maester Luwin says there are no more giants. He says they're all dead, like the children of the forest. All that's left of them are old bones in the earth that men turn up with plows from time to time."

"Let Maester Luwin ride beyond the Wall," Osha said. "He'll find giants then, or they'll find him. My brother killed one. Ten foot tall she was, and stunted at that. They've been known to grow big as twelve and thirteen feet. Fierce things they are too, all hair and teeth, and the wives have beards like their husbands, so there's no telling them apart. The women take human men for lovers, and it's from them the half bloods come. It goes harder on the women they catch. The men are so big they'll rip a maid apart before they get her with child." She grinned at him. "But you don't know what I mean, do you, boy?"

"Yes I do," Bran insisted. He understood about mating; he had seen dogs in the yard, and watched a stallion mount a mare. But talking about it made him uncomfortable. He looked at Hodor. "Go back and bring your clothes, Hodor," he said. "Go dress."

"Hodor." He walked back the way he had come, ducking under a low-hanging tree limb.

He *was* awfully big, Bran thought as he watched him

go. "Are there truly giants beyond the Wall?" he asked Osha, uncertainly.

"Giants and worse than giants, Lordling. I tried to tell your brother when he asked his questions, him and your maester and that smiley boy Greyjoy. The cold winds are rising, and men go out from their fires and never come back . . . or if they do, they're not *men* no more, but only wights, with blue eyes and cold black hands. Why do you think I run south with Stiv and Hali and the rest of them fools? Mance thinks he'll fight, the brave sweet stubborn man, like the white walkers were no more than rangers, but what does he know? He can call himself King-beyond-the-Wall all he likes, but he's still just another old black crow who flew down from the Shadow Tower. He's never tasted winter. I was *born* up there, child, like my mother and her mother before her and *her* mother before her, born of the Free Folk. We remember." Osha stood, her chains rattling together. "I tried to tell your lordling brother. Only yesterday, when I saw him in the yard. 'M'lord Stark,' I called to him, respectful as you please, but he looked through me, and that sweaty oaf Greatjon Umber shoves me out of the path. So be it. I'll wear my irons and hold my tongue. A man who won't listen can't hear."

"Tell *me*. Robb will listen to me, I know he will."

"Will he now? We'll see. You tell him this, m'lord. You tell him he's bound on marching the wrong way. It's north he should be taking his swords. *North*, not south. You hear me?"

Bran nodded. "I'll tell him."

But that night, when they feasted in the Great Hall, Robb was not with them. He took his meal in the solar instead, with Lord Rickard and the Greatjon and the other lords bannermen, to make the final plans for the long march to come. It was left to Bran to fill his place at the head of the table, and act the host to Lord Karstark's sons and honored friends. They were already at their places when Hodor carried Bran into the hall on his back, and knelt beside the high seat. Two of the serving men helped lift him from his basket. Bran could feel the eyes of every stranger in the hall. It had grown quiet. "My lords," Hallis Mollen announced, "Brandon Stark, of Winterfell."

"I welcome you to our fires," Bran said stiffly, "and offer you meat and mead in honor of our friendship."

Harrion Karstark, the oldest of Lord Rickard's sons, bowed, and his brothers after him, yet as they settled back in their places he heard the younger two talking in low voices, over the clatter of wine cups. ". . . sooner die than live like that," muttered one, his father's namesake Eddard, and his brother Torrhen said likely the boy was broken inside as well as out, too craven to take his own life.

Broken, Bran thought bitterly as he clutched his knife. Is that what he was now? Bran the Broken? "I don't want to be broken," he whispered fiercely to Maester Luwin, who'd been seated to his right. "I want to be a knight."

"There are some who call my order the knights of the mind," Luwin replied. "You are a surpassing clever boy when you work at it, Bran. Have you ever thought that you might wear a maester's chain? There is no limit to what you might learn."

"I want to learn *magic,*" Bran told him. "The crow promised that I would fly."

Maester Luwin sighed. "I can teach you history, healing, herblore. I can teach you the speech of ravens, and how to build a castle, and the way a sailor steers his ship by the stars. I can teach you to measure the days and mark the seasons, and at the Citadel in Oldtown they can teach you a thousand things more. But, Bran, no man can teach you magic."

"The children could," Bran said. "The children of the forest." That reminded him of the promise he had made to Osha in the godswood, so he told Luwin what she had said.

The maester listened politely. "The wildling woman could give Old Nan lessons in telling tales, I think," he said when Bran was done. "I will talk with her again if you like, but it would be best if you did not trouble your brother with this folly. He has more than enough to concern him without fretting over giants and dead men in the woods. It's the Lannisters who hold your lord father, Bran, not the children of the forest." He put a gentle hand on Bran's arm. "Think on what I said, child."

And two days later, as a red dawn broke across a windswept sky, Bran found himself in the yard beneath the gatehouse, strapped atop Dancer as he said his farewells to his brother.

"You are the lord in Winterfell now," Robb told him. He was mounted on a shaggy grey stallion, his shield hung from the horse's side; wood banded with iron, white and grey, and on it the snarling face of a direwolf. His brother wore grey chainmail over bleached leathers, sword and dagger at his waist, a fur-trimmed cloak across his shoulders. "You must take my place, as I took Father's, until we come home."

"I know," Bran replied miserably. He had never felt so little or alone or scared. He did not know how to be a lord.

"Listen to Maester Luwin's counsel, and take care of Rickon. Tell him that I'll be back as soon as the fighting is done."

Rickon had refused to come down. He was up in his chamber, red-eyed and defiant. *No!* he'd screamed when Bran had asked if he didn't want to say farewell to Robb. *"NO farewell!"*

"I told him," Bran said. "He says no one ever comes back."

"He can't be a baby forever. He's a Stark, and near four." Robb sighed. "Well, Mother will be home soon. And I'll bring back Father, I promise."

He wheeled his courser around and trotted away. Grey Wind followed, loping beside the warhorse, lean and swift. Hallis Mollen went before them through the gate, carrying the rippling white banner of House Stark atop a high standard of grey ash. Theon Greyjoy and the Greatjon fell in on either side of Robb, and their knights formed up in a double column behind them, steel-tipped lances glinting in the sun.

Uncomfortably, he remembered Osha's words. *He's marching the wrong way,* he thought. For an instant he wanted to gallop after him and shout a warning, but when Robb vanished beneath the portcullis, the moment was gone.

Beyond the castle walls, a roar of sound went up. The foot soldiers and townsfolk were cheering Robb as he rode past, Bran knew; cheering for Lord Stark, for the Lord of Winterfell on his great stallion, with his cloak streaming and Grey Wind racing beside him. They would never cheer for him that way, he realized with a dull ache. He might be the lord in Winterfell while his brother and father were gone, but he was still Bran the Broken. He could not even get off his own horse, except to fall.

When the distant cheers had faded to silence and the yard was empty at last, Winterfell seemed deserted and dead. Bran looked around at the faces of those who remained, women and children and old men . . . and Hodor. The huge stableboy had a lost and frightened look to his face. "Hodor?" he said sadly.

"Hodor," Bran agreed, wondering what it meant.

DAENERYS

When he had taken his pleasure, Khal Drogo rose from their sleeping mats to tower above her. His skin shone dark as bronze in the ruddy light from the brazier, the faint lines of old scars visible on his broad chest. Ink-black hair, loose and unbound, cascaded over his shoulders and down his back, well past his waist. His manhood glistened wetly. The *khal*'s mouth twisted in a frown beneath the droop of his long mustachio. "The stallion who mounts the world has no need of iron chairs."

Dany propped herself on an elbow to look up at him, so tall and magnificent. She loved his hair especially. It had never been cut; he had never known defeat. "It was prophesied that the stallion will ride to the ends of the earth," she said.

"The earth ends at the black salt sea," Drogo answered at once. He wet a cloth in a basin of warm water to wipe the sweat and oil from his skin. "No horse can cross the poison water."

"In the Free Cities, there are ships by the thousand," Dany told him, as she had told him before. "Wooden horses with a hundred legs, that fly across the sea on wings full of wind."

Khal Drogo did not want to hear it. "We will speak no more of wooden horses and iron chairs." He dropped the cloth and began to dress. "This day I will go to the grass and hunt, woman wife," he announced as he shrugged into a painted vest and buckled on a wide belt with heavy medallions of silver, gold, and bronze.

"Yes, my sun-and-stars," Dany said. Drogo would take his bloodriders and ride in search of *hrakkar*, the great white lion of the plains. If they returned triumphant, her lord husband's joy would be fierce, and he might be willing to hear her out.

Savage beasts he did not fear, nor any man who had ever drawn breath, but the sea was a different matter. To the Dothraki, water that a horse could not drink was something foul; the heaving grey-green plains of the ocean filled them with superstitious loathing. Drogo was a bolder man than the other horselords in half a hundred ways, she had found . . . but not in this. If only she could get him onto a ship . . .

After the *khal* and his bloodriders had ridden off with their bows, Dany summoned her handmaids. Her body felt so fat and ungainly now that she welcomed the help of their strong arms and deft hands, whereas before she had often been uncomfortable with the way they fussed and fluttered about her. They scrubbed her clean and dressed her in sandsilk, loose and flowing. As Doreah combed out her hair, she sent Jhiqui to find Ser Jorah Mormont.

The knight came at once. He wore horsehair leggings and painted vest, like a rider. Coarse black hair covered his thick chest and muscular arms. "My princess. How may I serve you?"

"You must talk to my lord husband," Dany said. "Drogo says the stallion who mounts the world will have all the lands of the earth to rule, and no need to cross the poison water. He talks of leading his *khalasar* east after Rhaego is born, to plunder the lands around the Jade Sea."

The knight looked thoughtful. "The *khal* has never seen the Seven Kingdoms," he said. "They are nothing to him. If he thinks of them at all, no doubt he thinks of islands, a few small cities clinging to rocks in the manner of Lorath or Lys, surrounded by stormy seas. The riches of the east must seem a more tempting prospect."

"But he must ride *west*," Dany said, despairing. "Please, help me make him understand." She had never seen the Seven Kingdoms either, no more than Drogo, yet she felt as though she knew them from all the tales her brother had told her. Viserys had promised her a thousand times that he would take her back one day, but he was dead now and his promises had died with him.

"The Dothraki do things in their own time, for their own reasons," the knight answered. "Have patience, Princess. Do not make your brother's mistake. We will go home, I promise you."

Home? The word made her feel sad. Ser Jorah had his Bear Island, but what was home to her? A few tales, names recited as solemnly as the words of a prayer, the fading memory of a red door . . . was Vaes Dothrak to be her home forever? When she looked at the crones of the *dosh khaleen*, was she looking at her future?

Ser Jorah must have seen the sadness on her face. "A great caravan arrived during the night, *Khaleesi*. Four hundred horses, from Pentos by way of Norvos and Qohor, under the command of Merchant Captain Byan Votyris. Illyrio may have sent a letter. Would you care to visit the Western Market?"

Dany stirred. "Yes," she said. "I would like that." The markets came alive when a caravan had come in. You could never tell what treasures the traders might bring this time, and it would be good to hear men speaking Valyrian again, as they did in the Free Cities. "Irri, have them prepare a litter."

"I shall tell your *khas*," Ser Jorah said, withdrawing.

If Khal Drogo had been with her, Dany would have ridden her silver. Among the Dothraki, mothers stayed on horseback almost up to the moment of birth, and she did not want to seem weak in her husband's eyes. But with the *khal* off hunting, it was pleasant to lie back on soft cushions and be carried across Vaes Dothrak, with red silk curtains to shield her from the sun. Ser Jorah saddled up and rode beside her, with the four young men of her *khas* and her handmaids.

The day was warm and cloudless, the sky a deep blue. When the wind blew, she could smell the rich scents of grass and earth. As her litter passed beneath the stolen monuments, she went from sunlight to shadow and back again. Dany swayed along, studying the faces of dead heroes and forgotten kings. She wondered if the gods of burned cities could still answer prayers.

If I were not the blood of the dragon, she thought wistfully, *this could be my home.* She was *khaleesi,* she had a strong man and a swift horse, handmaids to serve her, warriors to keep her safe, an honored place in the *dosh khaleen* awaiting her when she grew old . . . and in her womb grew a son who would one day bestride the world. That should be enough for any woman . . . but not for the dragon. With Viserys gone, Daenerys was the last, the very last. She was the seed of kings and conquerors, and so too the child inside her. She must not forget.

The Western Market was a great square of beaten earth surrounded by warrens of mud-baked brick, animal pens, whitewashed drinking halls. Hummocks rose from the ground like the backs of great subterranean beasts breaking the surface, yawning black mouths leading down to cool and cavernous storerooms below. The interior of the square was a maze of stalls and crookback aisles, shaded by awnings of woven grass.

A hundred merchants and traders were unloading their goods and setting up in stalls when they arrived, yet even so the great market seemed hushed and deserted compared to the teeming bazaars that Dany remembered from Pentos and the other Free Cities. The caravans made their way to Vaes Dothrak from east and west not so much to sell to the Dothraki as to trade with each other, Ser Jorah had explained. The riders let them come and go unmolested, so long as they observed the peace of the sacred city, did not profane the Mother of Mountains or the Womb of the World, and honored the crones of the *dosh khaleen* with the traditional gifts of salt, silver, and seed. The Dothraki did not truly comprehend this business of buying and selling.

Dany liked the strangeness of the Eastern Market too, with all its queer sights and sounds and smells. She often spent her mornings there, nibbling tree eggs, locust pie, and green noodles, listening to the high ululating voices of the spellsingers, gaping at manticores in silver cages and immense grey elephants and the striped black-and-white horses of the Jogos Nhai. She enjoyed watching all the people too: dark solemn Asshai'i and tall pale Qartheen, the bright-eyed men of Yi Ti in monkey-tail hats, warrior maids from Bayasabhad, Shamyriana, and Kayakayanaya with iron rings in their nipples and rubies in their cheeks, even the dour and frightening Shadow Men, who covered their arms and legs and chests with tattoos and hid their faces behind masks. The Eastern Market was a place of wonder and magic for Dany.

But the Western Market smelled of home.

As Irri and Jhiqui helped her from her litter, she sniffed, and recognized the sharp odors of garlic and pepper, scents that reminded Dany of days long gone in the alleys of Tyrosh and Myr and brought a fond smile to her face. Under that she smelled the heady sweet perfumes of Lys. She saw slaves carrying bolts of intricate Myrish lace and fine wools in a dozen rich colors. Caravan guards wandered among the aisles in copper helmets and knee-length tunics of quilted yellow cotton, empty scabbards swinging from their woven leather belts. Behind one stall an armorer displayed steel breastplates worked with gold and silver in ornate patterns, and helms hammered in the shapes of fanciful beasts. Next to him was a pretty young woman selling Lannisport goldwork, rings and brooches and torcs and exquisitely wrought medallions suitable for belting. A huge eunuch guarded her stall, mute and hairless, dressed in sweat-stained velvets and scowling at anyone who came close. Across the aisle, a fat cloth trader from Yi Ti was haggling with a Pentoshi over the price of some green dye, the monkey tail on his hat swaying back and forth as he shook his head.

"When I was a little girl, I loved to play in the bazaar," Dany told Ser Jorah as they wandered down the shady aisle between the stalls. "It was so *alive* there, all the people shouting and laughing, so many wonderful things to look at . . . though we seldom had enough coin to buy anything . . . well, except for a sausage now and again, or honeyfingers . . . do they have honeyfingers in the Seven Kingdoms, the kind they bake in Tyrosh?"

"Cakes, are they? I could not say, Princess." The knight bowed. "If you would pardon me for a time, I will seek out the captain and see if he has letters for us."

"Very well. I'll help you find him."

"There is no need for you to trouble yourself." Ser Jorah glanced away impatiently. "Enjoy the market. I will rejoin you when my business is concluded."

Curious, Dany thought as she watched him stride off through the throngs. She didn't see why she should not go with him. Perhaps Ser Jorah meant to find a woman after he met with the merchant captain. Whores frequently traveled with the caravans, she knew, and some men were queerly shy about their couplings. She gave a shrug. "Come," she told the others.

Her handmaids trailed along as Dany resumed her stroll through the market. "Oh, look," she exclaimed to Doreah, "those are the kind of sausages I meant." She pointed to a stall where a wizened little woman was grilling meat and onions on a hot firestone. "They make them with lots of garlic and hot peppers." Delighted with her discovery, Dany insisted the others join her for a sausage. Her handmaids wolfed theirs down giggling and grinning, though the men of her *khas* sniffed at the grilled meat suspiciously. "They taste different than I remember," Dany said after her first few bites.

"In Pentos, I make them with pork," the old woman said, "but all my pigs died on the Dothraki sea. These are made of horsemeat, *Khaleesi,* but I spice them the same."

"Oh." Dany felt disappointed, but Quaro liked his sausage so well he decided to have another one, and Rakharo had to outdo him and eat three more, belching loudly. Dany giggled.

"You have not laughed since your brother the *Khal Rhaggat* was crowned by Drogo," said Irri. "It is good to see, *Khaleesi.*"

Dany smiled shyly. It *was* sweet to laugh. She felt half a girl again.

They wandered for half the morning. She saw a beautiful feathered cloak from the Summer Isles, and took it for a gift. In return, she gave the merchant a silver medallion from her belt. That was how it was done among the Dothraki. A birdseller taught a green-and-red parrot to say her name, and Dany laughed again, yet still refused to take him. What would she do with a green-and-red parrot in a *khalasar*? She did take a dozen flasks of scented oils, the perfumes of her childhood; she had only to close her eyes and sniff them and she could see the big house with the red door once more. When Doreah looked longingly at a fertility charm at a magician's booth, Dany took that too and gave it to the handmaid, thinking that now she should find something for Irri and Jhiqui as well.

Turning a corner, they came upon a wine merchant offering thimble-sized cups of his wares to the passersby. "Sweet reds," he cried in fluent Dothraki, "I have sweet reds, from Lys and Volantis and the Arbor. Whites from Lys, Tyroshi pear brandy, firewine, pepperwine, the pale green nectars of Myr. Smokeberry browns and Andalish sours, I have them, I have them." He was a small man, slender and handsome, his flaxen hair curled and perfumed after the fashion of Lys. When Dany paused before his stall, he bowed low. "A taste for the *khaleesi*? I have a sweet red from Dorne, my lady, it sings of plums and cherries and rich dark oak. A cask, a cup, a swallow? One taste, and you will name your child after me."

Dany smiled. "My son has his name, but I will try your summerwine," she said in Valyrian, Valyrian as they spoke it in the Free Cities. The words felt strange on her tongue, after so long. "Just a taste, if you would be so kind."

The merchant must have taken her for Dothraki, with her clothes and her oiled hair and sun-browned skin. When she spoke, he gaped at her in astonishment. "My lady, you are . . . Tyroshi? Can it be so?"

"My speech may be Tyroshi, and my garb Dothraki, but I am of Westeros, of the Sunset Kingdoms," Dany told him.

Doreah stepped up beside her. "You have the honor to address Daenerys of the House Targaryen, Daenerys Stormborn, *khaleesi* of the riding men and princess of the Seven Kingdoms."

The wine merchant dropped to his knees. "Princess," he said, bowing his head.

"Rise," Dany commanded him. "I would still like to taste that summerwine you spoke of."

The man bounded to his feet. "That? Dornish swill. It is not worthy of a princess. I have a dry red from the Arbor, crisp and delectable. Please, let me give you a cask."

Khal Drogo's visits to the Free Cities had given him a taste for good wine, and Dany knew that such a noble vintage would please him. "You honor me, ser," she murmured sweetly.

"The honor is mine." The merchant rummaged about in the back of his stall and produced a small oaken cask. Burned into the wood was a cluster of grapes. "The Redwyne sigil," he said, pointing, "for the Arbor. There is no finer drink."

"Khal Drogo and I will share it together. Aggo, take this back to my litter, if you'd be so kind." The wineseller beamed as the Dothraki hefted the cask.

She did not realize that Ser Jorah had returned until she heard the knight say, *"No."* His voice was strange, brusque. "Aggo, put down that cask."

Aggo looked at Dany. She gave a hesitant nod. "Ser Jorah, is something wrong?"

"I have a thirst. Open it, wineseller."

The merchant frowned. "The wine is for the *khaleesi*, not for the likes of you, ser."

Ser Jorah moved closer to the stall. "If you don't open it, I'll crack it open with your head." He carried no weapons here in the sacred city, save his hands—yet his hands were enough, big, hard, dangerous, his knuckles covered with coarse dark hairs. The wineseller hesitated a moment, then took up his hammer and knocked the plug from the cask.

"Pour," Ser Jorah commanded. The four young warriors of Dany's *khas* arrayed themselves behind him, frowning, watching with their dark, almond-shaped eyes.

"It would be a crime to drink this rich a wine without letting it breathe." The wineseller had not put his hammer down.

Jhogo reached for the whip coiled at his belt, but Dany stopped him with a light touch on the arm. "Do as Ser Jorah says," she said. People were stopping to watch.

The man gave her a quick, sullen glance. "As the princess commands." He had to set aside his hammer to lift the cask. He filled two thimble-sized tasting cups, pouring so deftly he did not spill a drop.

Ser Jorah lifted a cup and sniffed at the wine, frowning.

"Sweet, isn't it?" the wineseller said, smiling. "Can you smell the fruit, ser? The perfume of the Arbor. Taste it, my lord, and tell me it isn't the finest, richest wine that's ever touched your tongue."

Ser Jorah offered him the cup. "You taste it first."

"Me?" The man laughed. "I am not worthy of this vintage, my lord. And it's a poor wine merchant who drinks up his own wares." His smile was amiable, yet she could see the sheen of sweat on his brow.

"You *will* drink," Dany said, cold as ice. "Empty the cup, or I will tell them to hold you down while Ser Jorah pours the whole cask down your throat."

The wineseller shrugged, reached for the cup . . . and grabbed the cask instead, flinging it at her with both hands. Ser Jorah bulled into her, knocking her out of the way. The cask bounced off his shoulder and smashed open on the ground. Dany stumbled and lost her feet. *"No,"* she screamed, thrusting her hands out to break her fall . . . and Doreah caught her by the arm and wrenched her backward, so she landed on her legs and not her belly.

The trader vaulted over the stall, darting between Aggo and Rakharo. Quaro reached for an *arakh* that was not there as the blond man slammed him aside. He raced down the aisle. Dany heard the snap of Jhogo's whip, saw the leather lick out and coil around the wineseller's leg. The man sprawled face first in the dirt.

A dozen caravan guards had come running. With them was the master himself, Merchant Captain Byan Votyris, a diminutive Norvoshi with skin like old leather and a bristling blue mustachio that swept up to his ears. He seemed to know what had happened without a word being spoken. "Take this one away to await the pleasure of the *khal*," he commanded, gesturing at the man on the ground. Two guards hauled the wineseller to his feet. "His goods I gift to you as well, Princess," the merchant captain went on. "Small token of regret, that one of mine would do this thing."

Doreah and Jhiqui helped Dany back to her feet. The poisoned wine was leaking from the broken cask into the dirt. "How did you know?" she asked Ser Jorah, trembling. *"How?"*

"I did not know, *Khaleesi*, not until the man refused to drink, but once I read Magister Illyrio's letter, I feared." His dark eyes swept over the faces of the strangers in the market. "Come. Best not to talk of it here."

Dany was near tears as they carried her back. The taste in her mouth was one she had known before: fear. For years she had lived in terror of Viserys, afraid of waking the dragon. This was even worse. It was not just for herself that she feared now, but for her baby. He must have sensed her fright, for he moved restlessly inside her. Dany stroked the swell of her belly gently, wishing she could reach him, touch him, soothe him. "You are the blood of the dragon, little one," she whispered as her litter swayed along, curtains drawn tight. "You are the blood of the dragon, and the dragon does not fear."

Under the hollow hummock of earth that was her home in Vaes Dothrak, Dany ordered them to leave her—all but Ser Jorah. "Tell me," she commanded as she lowered herself onto her cushions. "Was it the Usurper?"

"Yes." The knight drew out a folded parchment. "A letter to Viserys, from Magister Illyrio. Robert Baratheon offers lands and lordships for your death, or your brother's."

"My brother?" Her sob was half a laugh. "He does not know yet, does he? The Usurper owes Drogo a lordship." This time her laugh was half a sob. She hugged herself protectively. "And me, you said. Only me?"

"You and the child," Ser Jorah said, grim.

"No. He cannot have my son." She would not weep, she decided. She would not shiver with fear. *The Usurper has woken the dragon now*, she told herself . . . and her eyes went to the dragon's eggs resting in their nest of dark velvet. The shifting lamplight limned their stony scales, and shimmering motes of jade and scarlet and gold swam in the air around them, like courtiers around a king.

Was it madness that seized her then, born of fear? Or some strange wisdom buried in her blood? Dany could not have said. She heard her own voice saying, "Ser Jorah, light the brazier."

"Khaleesi?" The knight looked at her strangely. "It is so hot. Are you certain?"

She had never been so certain. "Yes. I . . . I have a chill. Light the brazier."

He bowed. "As you command."

When the coals were afire, Dany sent Ser Jorah from her. She had to be alone to do what she must do. *This is madness*, she told herself as she lifted the black-and-scarlet egg from the velvet. *It will only crack and burn, and it's so beautiful, Ser Jorah will call me a fool if I ruin it,* and yet, and yet . . .

Cradling the egg with both hands, she carried it to the fire and pushed it down amongst the burning coals. The black scales seemed to glow as they drank the heat. Flames licked against the stone with small red tongues. Dany placed the other two eggs beside the black one in the fire. As she stepped back from the brazier, the breath trembled in her throat.

She watched until the coals had turned to ashes. Drifting sparks floated up and out of the smokehole. Heat shimmered in waves around the dragon's eggs. And that was all.

Your brother Rhaegar was the last dragon, Ser Jorah had said. Dany gazed at her eggs sadly. What had she expected? A thousand thousand years ago they had been alive, but now they were only pretty rocks. They could not make a dragon. A dragon was air and fire. Living flesh, not dead stone.

The brazier was cold again by the time Khal Drogo returned. Cohollo was leading a packhorse behind him, with the carcass of a great white lion slung across its back. Above, the stars were coming out. The *khal* laughed as he swung down off his stallion and showed her the scars on his leg where the *hrakkar* had raked him through his leggings. "I shall make you a cloak of its skin, moon of my life," he swore.

When Dany told him what had happened at the market, all laughter stopped, and Khal Drogo grew very quiet.

"This poisoner was the first," Ser Jorah Mormont warned him, "but he will not be the last. Men will risk much for a lordship."

Drogo was silent for a time. Finally he said, "This seller of poisons ran from the moon of my life. Better he should run after her. So he will. Jhogo, Jorah the Andal, to each of you I say, choose any horse you wish from my herds, and it is yours. Any horse save my red and the silver that was my bride gift to the moon of my life. I make this gift to you for what you did.

"And to Rhaego son of Drogo, the stallion who will mount the world, to him I also pledge a gift. To him I will give this iron chair his mother's father sat in. I will give him Seven Kingdoms. I, Drogo, *khal*, will do this thing."

His voice rose, and he lifted his fist to the sky. "I will take my *khalasar* west to where the world ends, and ride the wooden horses across the black salt water as no *khal* has done before. I will kill the men in the iron suits and tear down their stone houses. I will rape their women, take their children as slaves, and bring their broken gods back to Vaes Dothrak to bow down beneath the Mother of Mountains. This I vow, I, Drogo son of Bharbo. This I swear before the Mother of Mountains, as the stars look down in witness."

His *khalasar* left Vaes Dothrak two days later, striking south and west across the plains. Khal Drogo led them on his great red stallion, with Daenerys beside him on her silver. The wineseller hurried behind them, naked, on foot, chained at throat and wrists. His chains were fastened to the halter of Dany's silver. As she rode, he ran after her, barefoot and stumbling. No harm would come to him . . . so long as he kept up.

CATELYN

It was too far to make out the banners clearly, but even through the drifting fog she could see that they were white, with a dark smudge in their center that could only be the direwolf of Stark, grey upon its icy field. When she saw it with her own eyes, Catelyn reined up her horse and bowed her head in thanks. The gods were good. She was not too late.

"They await our coming, my lady," Ser Wylis Manderly said, "as my lord father swore they would."

"Let us not keep them waiting any longer, ser." Ser Brynden Tully put the spurs to his horse and trotted briskly toward the banners. Catelyn rode beside him.

Ser Wylis and his brother Ser Wendel followed, leading their levies, near fifteen hundred men: some twenty-odd knights and as many squires, two hundred mounted lances, swordsmen, and freeriders, and the rest foot, armed with spears, pikes and tridents. Lord Wyman had remained behind to see to the defenses of White Harbor. A man of near sixty years, he had grown too stout to sit a horse. "If I had thought to see war again in my lifetime, I should have eaten a few less eels," he'd told Catelyn when he met her ship, slapping his massive belly with both hands. His fingers were fat as sausages. "My boys will see you safe to your son, though, have no fear."

His "boys" were both older than Catelyn, and she might have wished that they did not take after their father quite so closely. Ser Wylis was only a few eels short of not being able to mount his own horse; she pitied the poor animal. Ser Wendel, the younger boy, would have been the fattest man she'd ever known, had she only neglected to meet his father and brother. Wylis was quiet and formal, Wendel loud and boisterous; both had ostentatious walrus mustaches and heads as bare as a baby's bottom; neither seemed to own a single garment that was not spotted with food stains. Yet she liked them well enough; they had gotten her to Robb, as their father had vowed, and nothing else mattered.

She was pleased to see that her son had sent eyes out, even to the east. The Lannisters would come from the south when they came, but it was good that Robb was being careful. *My son is leading a host to war,* she thought, still only half believing it. She was desperately afraid for him, and for Winterfell, yet she could not deny feeling a certain pride as well. A year ago he had been a boy. What was he now? she wondered.

Outriders spied the Manderly banners—the white merman with trident in hand, rising from a blue-green sea—and hailed them warmly. They were led to a spot of high ground dry enough for a camp. Ser Wylis called a halt there, and remained behind with his men to see the fires laid and the horses tended, while his brother Wendel rode on with Catelyn and her uncle to present their father's respects to their liege lord.

The ground under their horses' hooves was soft and wet. It fell away slowly beneath them as they rode past smoky peat fires, lines of horses, and wagons heavy-laden with hardbread and salt beef. On a stony outcrop of land higher than the surrounding country, they passed a lord's pavilion with walls of heavy sailcloth. Catelyn recognized the banner, the bull moose of the Hornwoods, brown on its dark orange field.

Just beyond, through the mists, she glimpsed the walls and towers of Moat Cailin . . . or what remained of them. Immense blocks of black basalt, each as large as a crofter's cottage, lay scattered and tumbled like a child's wooden blocks, half-sunk in the soft boggy soil. Nothing else remained of a curtain wall that had once stood as high as Winterfell's. The wooden keep was gone entirely, rotted away a thousand years past, with not so much as a timber to mark where it had stood. All that was left of the great stronghold of the First Men were three towers . . . three where there had once been twenty, if the taletellers could be believed.

The Gatehouse Tower looked sound enough, and even boasted a few feet of standing wall to either side of it. The Drunkard's Tower, off in the bog where the south and west walls had once met, leaned like a man about to spew a bellyful of wine into the gutter. And the tall, slender Children's Tower, where legend said the children of the forest had once called upon their nameless gods to send the hammer of the waters, had lost half its crown. It looked as if some great beast had taken a bite out of the crenellations along the tower top, and spit the rubble across the bog. All three towers were green with moss. A tree was growing out between the stones on the north side of the Gatehouse Tower, its gnarled limbs festooned with ropy white blankets of ghostskin.

"Gods have mercy," Ser Brynden exclaimed when he saw what lay before them. "*This* is Moat Cailin? It's no more than a—"

"—death trap," Catelyn finished. "I know how it looks, Uncle. I thought the same the first time I saw it, but Ned assured me that this *ruin* is more formidable than it seems. The three surviving towers command the causeway from all sides, and any enemy must pass between them. The bogs here are impenetrable, full of quicksands and suckholes and teeming with snakes. To assault any of the towers, an army would need to wade through waist-deep black muck, cross a moat full of lizard-lions, and scale walls slimy with moss, all the while exposing themselves to fire from archers in the other towers." She gave her uncle a grim smile. "And when night falls, there are said to be ghosts, cold vengeful spirits of the north who hunger for southron blood."

Ser Brynden chuckled. "Remind me not to linger here. Last I looked, I was southron myself."

Standards had been raised atop all three towers. The Karstark sunburst hung from the Drunkard's Tower, beneath the direwolf; on the Children's Tower it was the Greatjon's giant in shattered chains. But on the Gatehouse Tower, the Stark banner flew alone. That was where Robb had made his seat. Catelyn made for it, with Ser Brynden and Ser Wendel behind her, their horses stepping slowly down the log-and-plank road that had been laid across the green-and-black fields of mud.

She found her son surrounded by his father's lords bannermen, in a drafty hall with a peat fire smoking in a black hearth. He was seated at a massive stone table, a pile of maps and papers in front of him, talking intently with Roose Bolton and the Greatjon. At first he did not notice her . . . but his wolf did. The great grey beast was lying near the fire, but when Catelyn entered he lifted his head, and his golden eyes met hers. The lords fell silent one by one, and Robb looked up at the sudden quiet and saw her. *"Mother!"* he said, his voice thick with emotion.

Catelyn wanted to run to him, to kiss his sweet brow, to wrap him in her arms and hold him so tightly that he would never come to harm . . . but here in front of his lords, she dared not. He was playing a man's part now, and she would not take that away from him. So she held herself at the far end of the basalt slab they were using for a table. The direwolf got to his feet and padded across the room to where she stood. It seemed bigger than a wolf ought to be. "You've grown a beard," she said to Robb, while Grey Wind sniffed her hand.

He rubbed his stubbled jaw, suddenly awkward. "Yes." His chin hairs were redder than the ones on his head.

"I like it." Catelyn stroked the wolf's head, gently. "It makes you look like my brother Edmure." Grey Wind nipped at her fingers, playful, and trotted back to his place by the fire.

Ser Helman Tallhart was the first to follow the direwolf across the room to pay his respects, kneeling before her and pressing his brow to her hand. "Lady Catelyn," he said, "you are fair as ever, a welcome sight in troubled times." The Glovers followed, Galbart and Robett, and Greatjon Umber, and the rest, one by one. Theon Greyjoy was the last. "I had not looked to see you here, my lady," he said as he knelt.

"I had not thought to be here," Catelyn said, "until I came ashore at White Harbor, and Lord Wyman told me that Robb had called the banners. You know his son, Ser Wendel." Wendel Manderly stepped forward and bowed as low as his girth would allow. "And my uncle, Ser Brynden Tully, who has left my sister's service for mine."

"The Blackfish," Robb said. "Thank you for joining us, ser. We need men of your courage. And you, Ser Wendel, I am glad to have you here. Is Ser Rodrik with you as well, Mother? I've missed him."

"Ser Rodrik is on his way north from White Harbor. I have named him castellan and commanded him to hold Winterfell till our return. Maester Luwin is a wise counsellor, but unskilled in the arts of war."

"Have no fear on that count, Lady Stark," the Greatjon told her in his bass rumble. "Winterfell is safe. We'll shove our swords up Tywin Lannister's bunghole soon enough, begging your pardons, and then it's on to the Red Keep to free Ned."

"My lady, a question, as it please you." Roose Bolton, Lord of the Dreadfort, had a small voice, yet when he spoke larger men quieted to listen. His eyes were curiously pale, almost without color, and his look disturbing. "It is said that you hold Lord Tywin's dwarf son as captive. Have you brought him to us? I vow, we should make good use of such a hostage."

"I did hold Tyrion Lannister, but no longer," Catelyn was forced to admit. A chorus of consternation greeted the news. "I was no more pleased than you, my lords. The gods saw fit to free him, with some help from my fool of a sister." She ought not to be so open in her contempt, she knew, but her parting from the Eyrie had not been pleasant. She had offered to take Lord Robert with her, to foster him at Winterfell for a few years. The company of other boys would do him good, she had dared to suggest. Lysa's rage had been frightening to behold. "Sister or no," she had replied, "if you try to steal my son, you will leave by the Moon Door." After that there was no more to be said.

The lords were anxious to question her further, but Catelyn raised a hand. "No doubt we will have time for all this later, but my journey has fatigued me. I would speak with my son alone. I know you will forgive me, my lords." She gave them no choice; led by the ever-obliging Lord Hornwood, the bannermen bowed and took their leave. "And you, Theon," she added when Greyjoy lingered. He smiled and left them.

There was ale and cheese on the table. Catelyn filled a horn, sat, sipped, and studied her son. He seemed taller than when she'd left, and the wisps of beard did make him look older. "Edmure was sixteen when he grew his first whiskers."

"I will be sixteen soon enough," Robb said.

"And you are fifteen now. Fifteen, and leading a host to battle. Can you understand why I might fear, Robb?"

His look grew stubborn. "There was no one else."

"No one?" she said. "Pray, who were those men I saw here a moment ago? Roose Bolton, Rickard Karstark, Galbart and Robett Glover, the Greatjon, Helman Tallhart . . . you might have given the command to *any* of them. Gods be good, you might even have sent Theon, though he would not be my choice."

"They are not Starks," he said.

"They are *men*, Robb, seasoned in battle. You were fighting with wooden swords less than a year past."

She saw anger in his eyes at that, but it was gone as quick as it came, and suddenly he was a boy again. "I know," he said, abashed. "Are you . . . are you sending me back to Winterfell?"

Catelyn sighed. "I should. You ought never have left. Yet I dare not, not now. You have come too far. Someday these lords will look to you as their liege. If I pack you off now, like a child being sent to bed without his supper, they will remember, and laugh about it in their cups. The day will come when you need them to respect you, even fear you a little. Laughter is poison to fear. I will not do that to you, much as I might wish to keep you safe."

"You have my thanks, Mother," he said, his relief obvious beneath the formality.

She reached across his table and touched his hair. "You are my firstborn, Robb. I have only to look at you to remember the day you came into the world, red-faced and squalling."

He rose, clearly uncomfortable with her touch, and walked to the hearth. Grey Wind rubbed his head against his leg. "You know . . . about Father?"

"Yes." The reports of Robert's sudden death and Ned's fall had frightened Catelyn more than she could say, but she would not let her son see her fear. "Lord Manderly told me when I landed at White Harbor. Have you had any word of your sisters?"

"There was a letter," Robb said, scratching his direwolf under the jaw. "One for you as well, but it came to Winterfell with mine." He went to the table, rummaged among some maps and papers, and returned with a crumpled parchment. "This is the one she wrote me, I never thought to bring yours."

Something in Robb's tone troubled her. She smoothed out the paper and read. Concern gave way to disbelief, then to anger, and lastly to fear. "This is Cersei's letter, not your sister's," she said when she was done. "The real message is in what Sansa does not say. All this about how kindly and gently the Lannisters are treating her . . . I know the sound of a threat, even whispered. They have Sansa hostage, and they mean to keep her."

"There's no mention of Arya," Robb pointed out, miserable.

"No." Catelyn did not want to think what that might mean, not now, not here.

"I had hoped . . . if you still held the Imp, a trade of hostages . . ." He took Sansa's letter and crumpled it in his fist, and she could tell from the way he did it that it was not the first time. "Is there word from the Eyrie? I wrote to Aunt Lysa, asking help. Has she called Lord Arryn's banners, do you know? Will the knights of the Vale come join us?"

"Only one," she said, "the best of them, my uncle . . . but Brynden Blackfish was a Tully first. My sister is not about to stir beyond her Bloody Gate."

Robb took it hard. "Mother, what are we going to *do*? I brought this whole army together, eighteen thousand men, but I don't . . . I'm not certain . . ." He looked to her, his eyes shining, the proud young lord melted away in an instant, and quick as that he was a child again, a fifteen-year-old boy looking to his mother for answers.

It would not do.

"What are you so afraid of, Robb?" she asked gently.

"I . . ." He turned his head away, to hide the first tear. "If we march . . . even if we win . . . the Lannisters hold Sansa, and Father. They'll kill them, won't they?"

"They want us to think so."

"You mean they're lying?"

"I do not know, Robb. What I do know is that you have no choice. If you go to King's Landing and swear fealty, you will never be allowed to leave. If you turn your tail and retreat to Winterfell, your lords will lose all respect for you. Some may even go over to the Lannisters. Then the queen, with that much less to fear, can do as she likes with her prisoners. Our best hope, our *only* true hope, is that you can defeat the foe in the field. If you should chance to take Lord Tywin or the Kingslayer captive, why then a trade might very well be possible, but that is not the heart of it. So long as you have power enough that they must fear you, Ned and your sister should be safe. Cersei is wise enough to know that she may need them to make her peace, should the fighting go against her."

"What if the fighting *doesn't* go against her?" Robb asked. "What if it goes against us?"

Catelyn took his hand. "Robb, I will not soften the truth for you. If you lose, there is no hope for any of us. They say there is naught but stone at the heart of Casterly Rock. Remember the fate of Rhaegar's children."

She saw the fear in his young eyes then, but there was a strength as well. "Then I will not lose," he vowed.

"Tell me what you know of the fighting in the riverlands," she said. She had to learn if he was truly ready.

"Less than a fortnight past, they fought a battle in the hills below the Golden Tooth," Robb said. "Uncle Edmure had sent Lord Vance and Lord Piper to hold the pass, but the Kingslayer descended on them and put them to flight. Lord Vance was slain. The last word we had was that Lord Piper was falling back to join your brother and his other bannermen at Riverrun, with Jaime Lannister on his heels. That's not the worst of it, though. All the time they were battling in the pass, Lord Tywin was bringing a second Lannister army around from the south. It's said to be even larger than Jaime's host.

"Father must have known that, because he sent out some men to oppose them, under the king's own banner. He gave the command to some southron lordling, Lord Erik or Derik or something like that, but Ser Raymun Darry rode with him, and the letter said there were other knights as well, and a force of Father's own guardsmen. Only it was a trap. Lord Derik had no sooner crossed the

Red Fork than the Lannisters fell upon him, the king's banner be damned, and Gregor Clegane took them in the rear as they tried to pull back across the Mummer's Ford. This Lord Derik and a few others may have escaped, no one is certain, but Ser Raymun was killed, and most of our men from Winterfell. Lord Tywin has closed off the kingsroad, it's said, and now he's marching north toward Harrenhal, burning as he goes."

Grim and grimmer, thought Catelyn. It was worse than she'd imagined. "You mean to meet him here?" she asked.

"If he comes so far, but no one thinks he will," Robb said. "I've sent word to Howland Reed, Father's old friend at Greywater Watch. If the Lannisters come up the Neck, the crannogmen will bleed them every step of the way, but Galbart Glover says Lord Tywin is too smart for that, and Roose Bolton agrees. He'll stay close to the Trident, they believe, taking the castles of the river lords one by one, until Riverrun stands alone. We need to march south to meet him."

The very idea of it chilled Catelyn to the bone. What chance would a fifteen-year-old boy have against seasoned battle commanders like Jaime and Tywin Lannister? "Is that wise? You are strongly placed here. It's said that the old Kings in the North could stand at Moat Cailin and throw back hosts ten times the size of their own."

"Yes, but our food and supplies are running low, and this is not land we can live off easily. We've been waiting for Lord Manderly, but now that his sons have joined us, we need to march."

She was hearing the lords bannermen speaking with her son's voice, she realized. Over the years, she had hosted many of them at Winterfell, and been welcomed with Ned to their own hearths and tables. She knew what sorts of men they were, each one. She wondered if Robb did.

And yet there was sense in what they said. This host her son had assembled was not a standing army such as the Free Cities were accustomed to maintain, nor a force of guardsmen paid in coin. Most of them were smallfolk: crofters, fieldhands, fishermen, sheepherders, the sons of innkeeps and traders and tanners, leavened with a smattering of sellswords and freeriders hungry for plunder.

When their lords called, they came . . . but not forever. "Marching is all very well," she said to her son, "but *where*, and to what purpose? What do you mean to do?"

Robb hesitated. "The Greatjon thinks we should take the battle to Lord Tywin and surprise him," he said, "but the Glovers and the Karstarks feel we'd be wiser to go around his army and join up with Uncle Ser Edmure against the Kingslayer." He ran his fingers through his shaggy mane of auburn hair, looking unhappy. "Though by the time we reach Riverrun . . . I'm not certain . . ."

"*Be* certain," Catelyn told her son, "or go home and take up that wooden sword again. You cannot afford to seem indecisive in front of men like Roose Bolton and Rickard Karstark. Make no mistake, Robb—these are your bannermen, not your friends. You named yourself battle commander. *Command.*"

Her son looked at her, startled, as if he could not credit what he was hearing. "As you say, Mother."

"I'll ask you again. What do *you* mean to do?"

Robb drew a map across the table, a ragged piece of old leather covered with lines of faded paint. One end curled up from being rolled; he weighed it down with his dagger. "Both plans have virtues, but . . . look, if we try to swing around Lord Tywin's host, we take the risk of being caught between him and the Kingslayer, and if we attack him . . . by all reports, he has more men than I do, and a lot more armored horse. The Greatjon says that won't matter if we catch him with his breeches down, but it seems to me that a man who has fought as many battles as Tywin Lannister won't be so easily surprised."

"Good," she said. She could hear echoes of Ned in his voice, as he sat there, puzzling over the map. "Tell me more."

"I'd leave a small force here to hold Moat Cailin, archers mostly, and march the rest down the causeway," he said, "but once we're below the Neck, I'd split our host in two. The foot can continue down the kingsroad, while our horsemen cross the Green Fork at the Twins." He pointed. "When Lord Tywin gets word that we've come south, he'll march north to engage our main host, leaving our riders free to hurry down the west bank to Riverrun." Robb sat back, not quite daring to smile, but pleased with himself and hungry for her praise.

Catelyn frowned down at the map. "You'd put a river between the two parts of your army."

"*And* between Jaime and Lord Tywin," he said eagerly. The smile came at last. "There's no crossing on the Green Fork above the ruby ford, where Robert won his crown. Not until the Twins, all the way up here, and Lord Frey controls that bridge. He's your father's bannerman, isn't that so?"

The Late Lord Frey, Catelyn thought. "He is," she admitted, "but my father has never trusted him. Nor should you."

"I won't," Robb promised. "What do you think?"

She was impressed despite herself. *He looks like a Tully*, she thought, *yet he's still his father's son, and Ned taught him well.* "Which force would you command?"

"The horse," he answered at once. Again like his father; Ned would always take the more dangerous task himself.

"And the other?"

"The Greatjon is always saying that we should smash Lord Tywin. I thought I'd give him the honor."

It was his first misstep, but how to make him see it without wounding his fledgling confidence? "Your father once told me that the Greatjon was as fearless as any man he had ever known."

Robb grinned. "Grey Wind ate two of his fingers, and he *laughed* about it. So you agree, then?"

"Your father is not fearless," Catelyn pointed out. "He is brave, but that is very different."

Her son considered that for a moment. "The eastern host will be all that stands between Lord Tywin and Winterfell," he said thoughtfully. "Well, them and whatever few bowmen I leave here at the Moat. So I don't want someone fearless, do I?"

"No. You want cold cunning, I should think, not courage."

"Roose Bolton," Robb said at once. "That man scares me."

"Then let us pray he will scare Tywin Lannister as well."

Robb nodded and rolled up the map. "I'll give the commands, and assemble an escort to take you home to Winterfell."

Catelyn had fought to keep herself strong, for Ned's sake and for this stubborn brave son of theirs. She had put despair and fear aside, as if they were garments she did not choose to wear . . . but now she saw that she had donned them after all.

"I am not going to Winterfell," she heard herself say, surprised at the sudden rush of tears that blurred her vision. "My father may be dying behind the walls of Riverrun. My brother is surrounded by foes. I must go to them."

TYRION

Chella daughter of Cheyk of the Black Ears had gone ahead to scout, and it was she who brought back word of the army at the crossroads. "By their fires I call them twenty thousand strong," she said. "Their banners are red, with a golden lion."

"Your father?" Bronn asked.

"Or my brother Jaime," Tyrion said. "We shall know soon enough." He surveyed his ragged band of brigands: near three hundred Stone Crows, Moon Brothers, Black Ears, and Burned Men, and those just the seed of the army he hoped to grow. Gunthor son of Gurn was raising the other clans even now. He wondered what his lord father would make of them in their skins and bits of stolen steel. If truth be told, he did not know what to make of them himself. Was he their commander or their captive? Most of the time, it seemed to be a little of both. "It might be best if I rode down alone," he suggested.

"Best for Tyrion son of Tywin," said Ulf, who spoke for the Moon Brothers.

Shagga glowered, a fearsome sight to see. "Shagga son of Dolf likes this not. Shagga will go with the boyman, and if the boyman lies, Shagga will chop off his manhood—"

"—and feed it to the goats, yes," Tyrion said wearily. "Shagga, I give you my word as a Lannister, I will return."

"Why should we trust your word?" Chella was a small hard woman, flat as a boy, and no fool. "Lowland lords have lied to the clans before."

"You wound me, Chella," Tyrion said. "Here I thought we had become such friends. But as you will. You shall ride with me, and Shagga and Conn for the Stone Crows, Ulf for the Moon Brothers, and Timett son of Timett for the Burned Men." The clansmen exchanged wary looks as he named them. "The rest shall wait here until I send for you. *Try* not to kill and maim each other while I'm gone."

He put his heels to his horse and trotted off, giving them no choice but to follow or be left behind. Either was fine with him, so long as they did not sit down to *talk* for a day and a night. That was the trouble with the clans; they had an absurd notion that every man's voice should be heard in council, so they argued about *everything*, endlessly. Even their women were allowed to speak. Small wonder that it had been hundreds of years since they last threatened the Vale with anything beyond an occasional raid. Tyrion meant to change that.

Bronn rode with him. Behind them—after a quick bit of grumbling—the five clansmen followed on their undersize garrons, scrawny things that looked like ponies and scrambled up rock walls like goats.

The Stone Crows rode together, and Chella and Ulf stayed close as well, as the Moon Brothers and Black Ears had strong bonds between them. Timett son of Timett rode alone. Every clan in the Mountains of the Moon feared the Burned Men, who mortified their flesh with fire to prove their courage and (the others said) roasted babies at their feasts. And even the other Burned Men feared Timett, who had put out his own left eye with a white-hot knife when he reached the age of manhood. Tyrion gathered that it was more customary for a boy to burn off a nipple, a finger, or (if he was truly brave, or truly mad) an ear. Timett's fellow Burned Men were so awed by his choice of an eye that they promptly named him a red hand, which seemed to be some sort of a war chief.

"I wonder what their king burned off," Tyrion said to Bronn when he heard the tale. Grinning, the sellsword had tugged at his crotch . . . but even Bronn kept a respectful tongue around Timett. If a man was mad enough to put out his own eye, he was unlikely to be gentle to his enemies.

Distant watchers peered down from towers of unmortared stone as the party descended through the foothills, and once Tyrion saw a raven take wing. Where the high road twisted between two rocky outcrops, they came to the first strong point. A low earthen wall four feet high closed off the road, and a dozen crossbowmen manned the heights. Tyrion halted his followers out of range and rode to the wall alone. "Who commands here?" he shouted up.

The captain was quick to appear, and even quicker to give them an escort when he recognized his lord's son. They trotted past blackened fields and burned holdfasts, down to the riverlands and the Green Fork of the Trident. Tyrion saw no bodies, but the air was full of ravens and carrion crows; there had been fighting here, and recently.

Half a league from the crossroads, a barricade of sharpened stakes had been erected, manned by pikemen and archers. Behind the line, the camp spread out to the far distance. Thin fingers of smoke rose from hundreds of cookfires, mailed men sat under trees and honed their blades, and familiar banners fluttered from staffs thrust into the muddy ground.

A party of mounted horsemen rode forward to challenge them as they approached the stakes. The knight who led them wore silver armor inlaid with amethysts and a striped purple-and-silver cloak. His shield bore a unicorn sigil, and a spiral horn two feet long jutted up from the brow of his horsehead helm. Tyrion reined up to greet him. "Ser Flement."

Ser Flement Brax lifted his visor. "Tyrion," he said in astonishment. "My lord, we all feared you dead, or . . ." He looked at the clansmen uncertainly. "These . . . companions of yours . . ."

"Bosom friends and loyal retainers," Tyrion said. "Where will I find my lord father?"

"He has taken the inn at the crossroads for his quarters."

Tyrion laughed. The inn at the crossroads! Perhaps the gods were just after all. "I will see him at once."

"As you say, my lord." Ser Flement wheeled his horse about and shouted commands. Three rows of stakes were pulled from the ground to make a hole in the line. Tyrion led his party through.

Lord Tywin's camp spread over leagues. Chella's estimate of twenty thousand men could not be far wrong. The common men camped out in the open, but the knights had thrown up tents, and some of the high lords had erected pavilions as large as houses. Tyrion spied the red ox of the Presters, Lord Crakehall's brindled boar, the burning tree of Marbrand, the badger of Lydden. Knights called out to him as he cantered past, and men-at-arms gaped at the clansmen in open astonishment.

Shagga was gaping back; beyond a certainty, he had never seen so many men, horses, and weapons in all his days. The rest of the mountain brigands did a better job of guarding their faces, but Tyrion had no doubts that they were full as much in awe. Better and better. The more impressed they were with the power of the Lannisters, the easier they would be to command.

The inn and its stables were much as he remembered, though little more than tumbled stones and blackened foundations remained where the rest of the village had stood. A gibbet had been erected in the yard, and the body that swung there was covered with ravens. At Tyrion's approach they took to the air, squawking and flapping their black wings. He dismounted and glanced up at what remained of the corpse. The birds had eaten her lips and eyes and most of her cheeks, baring her stained red teeth in a hideous smile. "A room, a meal, and a flagon of wine, that was all I asked," he reminded her with a sigh of reproach.

Boys emerged hesitantly from the stables to see to their horses. Shagga did not want to give his up. "The lad won't steal your mare," Tyrion assured him. "He only wants to give her some oats and water and brush out her coat." Shagga's coat could have used a good brushing too, but it would have been less than tactful to mention it. "You have my word, the horse will not be harmed."

Glaring, Shagga let go his grip on the reins. "This is the horse of Shagga son of Dolf," he roared at the stableboy.

"If he doesn't give her back, chop off his manhood and feed it to the goats," Tyrion promised. "Provided you can find some."

A pair of house guards in crimson cloaks and lion-crested helms stood under the inn's sign, on either side of the door. Tyrion recognized their captain. "My father?"

"In the common room, m'lord."

"My men will want meat and mead," Tyrion told him. "See that they get it." He entered the inn, and there was Father.

Tywin Lannister, Lord of Casterly Rock and Warden of the West, was in his middle fifties, yet hard as a man of twenty. Even seated, he was tall, with long legs, broad shoulders, a flat stomach. His thin arms were corded with muscle. When his once-thick golden hair had begun to recede, he had commanded his barber to shave his head; Lord Tywin did not believe in half measures. He razored his lip and chin as well, but kept his side-whiskers, two great thickets of wiry golden hair that covered most of his cheeks from ear to jaw. His eyes were a pale green, flecked with gold. A fool more foolish than most had once jested that even Lord Tywin's shit was flecked with gold. Some said the man was still alive, deep in the bowels of Casterly Rock.

Ser Kevan Lannister, his father's only surviving brother, was sharing a flagon of ale with Lord Tywin when Tyrion entered the common room. His uncle was portly and balding, with a close-cropped yellow beard that followed the line of his massive jaw. Ser Kevan saw him first. "Tyrion," he said in surprise.

"Uncle," Tyrion said, bowing. "And my lord father. What a pleasure to find you here."

Lord Tywin did not stir from his chair, but he did give his dwarf son a long, searching look. "I see that the rumors of your demise were unfounded."

"Sorry to disappoint you, Father," Tyrion said. "No need to leap up and embrace me, I wouldn't want you to strain yourself." He crossed the room to their table, acutely conscious of the way his stunted legs made him waddle with every step. Whenever his father's eyes were on him, he became uncomfortably aware of all his deformities and shortcomings. "Kind of you to go to war for me," he said as he climbed into a chair and helped himself to a cup of his father's ale.

"By my lights, it was you who started this," Lord Tywin replied. "Your brother Jaime would never have meekly submitted to capture at the hands of a woman."

"That's one way we differ, Jaime and I. He's taller as well, you may have noticed."

His father ignored the sally. "The honor of our House was at stake. I had no choice but to ride. No man sheds Lannister blood with impunity."

"Hear Me Roar," Tyrion said, grinning. The Lannister words. "Truth be told, none of my blood was actually shed, although it was a close thing once or twice. Morrec and Jyck were killed."

"I suppose you will be wanting some new men."

"Don't trouble yourself, Father, I've acquired a few of my own." He tried a swallow of the ale. It was brown and yeasty, so thick you could almost chew it. Very fine, in truth. A pity his father had hanged the innkeep. "How is your war going?"

His uncle answered. "Well enough, for the nonce. Ser Edmure had scattered small troops of men along his borders to stop our raiding, and your lord father and I were able to destroy most of them piecemeal before they could regroup."

"Your brother has been covering himself with glory," his father said. "He smashed the Lords Vance and Piper at the Golden Tooth, and met the massed power of the Tullys under the walls of Riverrun. The lords of the Trident have been put to rout. Ser Edmure Tully was taken captive, with many of his knights and bannermen. Lord Blackwood led a few survivors back to Riverrun, where Jaime has them under siege. The rest fled to their own strongholds."

"Your father and I have been marching on each in turn," Ser Kevan said. "With Lord Blackwood gone, Raventree fell at once, and Lady Whent yielded Harrenhal for want of men to defend it. Ser Gregor burnt out the Pipers and the Brackens . . ."

"Leaving you unopposed?" Tyrion said.

"Not wholly," Ser Kevan said. "The Mallisters still hold Seagard and Walder Frey is marshaling his levies at the Twins."

"No matter," Lord Tywin said. "Frey only takes the field when the scent of victory is in the air, and all he smells now is ruin. And Jason Mallister lacks the strength to fight alone. Once Jaime takes Riverrun, they will both be quick enough to bend the knee. Unless the Starks and the Arryns come forth to oppose us, this war is good as won."

"I would not fret overmuch about the Arryns if I were you," Tyrion said. "The Starks are another matter. Lord Eddard—"

"—is our hostage," his father said. "He will lead no armies while he rots in a dungeon under the Red Keep."

"No," Ser Kevan agreed, "but his son has called the banners and sits at Moat Cailin with a strong host around him."

"No sword is strong until it's been tempered," Lord Tywin declared. "The Stark boy is a child. No doubt he likes the sound of warhorns well enough, and the sight of his banners fluttering in the wind, but in the end it comes down to butcher's work. I doubt he has the stomach for it."

Things *had* gotten interesting while he'd been away, Tyrion reflected. "And what is our fearless monarch doing whilst all this 'butcher's work' is being done?" he wondered. "How has my lovely and persuasive sister gotten Robert to agree to the imprisonment of his dear friend Ned?"

"Robert Baratheon is dead," his father told him. "Your nephew reigns in King's Landing."

That *did* take Tyrion aback. "My sister, you mean." He took another gulp of ale. The realm would be a much different place with Cersei ruling in place of her husband.

"If you have a mind to make yourself of use, I will give you a command," his father said. "Marq Piper and Karyl Vance are loose in our rear, raiding our lands across the Red Fork."

Tyrion made a *tsk*ing sound. "The gall of them, fighting back. Ordinarily I'd be glad to punish such rudeness, Father, but the truth is, I have pressing business elsewhere."

"Do you?" Lord Tywin did not seem awed. "We also

have a pair of Ned Stark's afterthoughts making a nuisance of themselves by harassing my foraging parties. Beric Dondarrion, some young lordling with delusions of valor. He has that fat jape of a priest with him, the one who likes to set his sword on fire. Do you think you might be able to deal with them as you scamper off? Without making too much a botch of it?"

Tyrion wiped his mouth with the back of his hand and smiled. "Father, it warms my heart to think that you might entrust me with . . . what, twenty men? Fifty? Are you sure you can spare so many? Well, no matter. If I should come across Thoros and Lord Beric, I shall spank them both." He climbed down from his chair and waddled to the sideboard, where a wheel of veined white cheese sat surrounded by fruit. "First, though, I have some promises of my own to keep," he said as he sliced off a wedge. "I shall require three thousand helms and as many hauberks, plus swords, pikes, steel spearheads, maces, battle-axes, gauntlets, gorgets, greaves, breastplates, wagons to carry all this—"

The door behind him opened with a crash, so violently that Tyrion almost dropped his cheese. Ser Kevan leapt up swearing as the captain of the guard went flying across the room to smash against the hearth. As he tumbled down into the cold ashes, his lion helm askew, Shagga snapped the man's sword in two over a knee thick as a tree trunk, threw down the pieces, and lumbered into the common room. He was preceded by his stench, riper than the cheese and overpowering in the closed space. "Little redcape," he snarled, "when next you bare steel on Shagga son of Dolf, I will chop off your manhood and roast it in the fire."

"What, no goats?" Tyrion said, taking a bite of cheese.

The other clansmen followed Shagga into the common room, Bronn with them. The sellsword gave Tyrion a rueful shrug.

"Who might you be?" Lord Tywin asked, cool as snow.

"They followed me home, Father," Tyrion explained. "May I keep them? They don't eat much."

No one was smiling. "By what right do you savages intrude on our councils?" demanded Ser Kevan.

"Savages, lowlander?" Conn might have been handsome if you washed him. "We are free men, and free men by rights sit on all war councils."

"Which one is the lion lord?" Chella asked.

"They are both old men," announced Timett son of Timett, who had yet to see his twentieth year.

Ser Kevan's hand went to his sword hilt, but his brother placed two fingers on his wrist and held him fast. Lord Tywin seemed unperturbed. "Tyrion, have you forgotten your courtesies? Kindly acquaint us with our . . . honored guests."

Tyrion licked his fingers. "With pleasure," he said. "The fair maid is Chella daughter of Cheyk of the Black Ears."

"I'm no maid," Chella protested. "My sons have taken fifty ears among them."

"May they take fifty more." Tyrion waddled away from her. "This is Conn son of Coratt. Shagga son of Dolf is the one who looks like Casterly Rock with hair. They are Stone Crows. Here is Ulf son of Umar of the Moon Brothers, and here Timett son of Timett, a red hand of the Burned Men. And this is Bronn, a sellsword of no particular allegiance. He has already changed sides twice in the short time I've known him, you and he ought to get on famously, Father." To Bronn and the clansmen he said, "May I present my lord father, Tywin son of Tytos of House Lannister, Lord of Casterly Rock, Warden of the West, Shield of Lannisport, and once and future Hand of the King."

Lord Tywin rose, dignified and correct. "Even in the west, we know the prowess of the warrior clans of the Mountains of the Moon. What brings you down from your strongholds, my lords?"

"Horses," said Shagga.

"A promise of silk and steel," said Timett son of Timett.

Tyrion was about to tell his lord father how he proposed to reduce the Vale of Arryn to a smoking wasteland, but he was never given the chance. The door banged open again. The messenger gave Tyrion's clansmen a quick, queer look as he dropped to one knee before Lord Tywin. "My lord," he said, "Ser Addam bid me tell you that the Stark host is moving down the causeway."

Lord Tywin Lannister did not smile. Lord Tywin *never*

smiled, but Tyrion had learned to read his father's pleasure all the same, and it was there on his face. "So the wolfling is leaving his den to play among the lions," he said in a voice of quiet satisfaction. "Splendid. Return to Ser Addam and tell him to fall back. He is not to engage the northerners until we arrive, but I want him to harass their flanks and draw them farther south."

"It will be as you command." The rider took his leave.

"We are well situated here," Ser Kevan pointed out. "Close to the ford and ringed by pits and spikes. If they are coming south, I say let them come, and break themselves against us."

"The boy may hang back or lose his courage when he sees our numbers," Lord Tywin replied. "The sooner the Starks are broken, the sooner I shall be free to deal with Stannis Baratheon. Tell the drummers to beat assembly, and send word to Jaime that I am marching against Robb Stark."

"As you will," Ser Kevan said.

Tyrion watched with a grim fascination as his lord father turned next to the half-wild clansmen. "It is said that the men of the mountain clans are warriors without fear."

"It is said truly," Conn of the Stone Crows answered.

"And the women," Chella added.

"Ride with me against my enemies, and you shall have all my son promised you, and more," Lord Tywin told them.

"Would you pay us with our own coin?" Ulf son of Umar said. "Why should we need the father's promise, when we have the son's?"

"I said nothing of *need*," Lord Tywin replied. "My words were courtesy, nothing more. You need not join us. The men of the winterlands are made of iron and ice, and even my boldest knights fear to face them."

Oh, deftly done, Tyrion thought, smiling crookedly.

"The Burned Men fear nothing. Timett son of Timett will ride with the lions."

"Wherever the Burned Men go, the Stone Crows have been there first," Conn declared hotly. "We ride as well."

"Shagga son of Dolf will chop off their manhoods and feed them to the crows."

"We will ride with you, lion lord," Chella daughter of

Cheyk agreed, "but only if your halfman son goes with us. He has bought his breath with promises. Until we hold the steel he has pledged us, his life is ours."

Lord Tywin turned his gold-flecked eyes on his son.

"Joy," Tyrion said with a resigned smile.

SANSA

The walls of the throne room had been stripped bare, the hunting tapestries that King Robert loved taken down and stacked in the corner in an untidy heap.

Ser Mandon Moore went to take his place under the throne beside two of his fellows of the Kingsguard. Sansa hovered by the door, for once unguarded. The queen had given her freedom of the castle as a reward for being good, yet even so, she was escorted everywhere she went. "Honor guards for my daughter-to-be," the queen called them, but they did not make Sansa feel honored.

"Freedom of the castle" meant that she could go wherever she chose within the Red Keep so long as she promised not to go beyond the walls, a promise Sansa had been more than willing to give. She couldn't have gone beyond the walls anyway. The gates were watched day and night by Janos Slynt's gold cloaks, and Lannister house guards were always about as well. Besides, even if she could leave the castle, where would she go? It was enough that she could walk in the yard, pick flowers in Myrcella's garden, and visit the sept to pray for her father. Some-

times she prayed in the godswood as well, since the
Starks kept the old gods.

This was the first court session of Joffrey's reign, so
Sansa looked about nervously. A line of Lannister house
guards stood beneath the western windows, a line of gold-
cloaked City Watchmen beneath the east. Of smallfolk
and commoners, she saw no sign, but under the gallery a
cluster of lords great and small milled restlessly. There
were no more than twenty, where a hundred had been
accustomed to wait upon King Robert.

Sansa slipped in among them, murmuring greetings as
she worked her way toward the front. She recognized
black-skinned Jalabhar Xho, gloomy Ser Aron Santagar,
the Redwyne twins Horror and Slobber . . . only none of
them seemed to recognize *her*. Or if they did, they shied
away as if she had the grey plague. Sickly Lord Gyles covered his face at her approach and feigned a fit of coughing,
and when funny drunken Ser Dontos started to hail her,
Ser Balon Swann whispered in his ear and he turned away.

And so many others were missing. Where had the rest
of them gone? Sansa wondered. Vainly, she searched for
friendly faces. Not one of them would meet her eyes. It
was as if she had become a ghost, dead before her time.

Grand Maester Pycelle was seated alone at the council
table, seemingly asleep, his hands clasped together atop
his beard. She saw Lord Varys hurry into the hall, his feet
making no sound. A moment later Lord Baelish entered
through the tall doors in the rear, smiling. He chatted
amiably with Ser Balon and Ser Dontos as he made his
way to the front. Butterflies fluttered nervously in Sansa's
stomach. *I shouldn't be afraid,* she told herself. *I have
nothing to be afraid of, it will all come out well, Joff loves
me and the queen does too, she said so.*

A herald's voice rang out. "All hail His Grace, Joffrey
of the Houses Baratheon and Lannister, the First of his
Name, King of the Andals, the Rhoynar, and the First
Men, and Lord of the Seven Kingdoms. All hail his lady
mother, Cersei of House Lannister, Queen Regent, Light
of the West, and Protector of the Realm."

Ser Barristan Selmy, resplendent in white plate, led
them in. Ser Arys Oakheart escorted the queen, while Ser
Boros Blount walked beside Joffrey, so six of the Kingsguard were now in the hall, all the White Swords save

Jaime Lannister alone. Her prince—no, her *king* now!—
took the steps of the Iron Throne two at a time, while his
mother was seated with the council. Joff wore plush black
velvets slashed with crimson, a shimmering cloth-of-gold
cape with a high collar, and on his head a golden crown
crusted with rubies and black diamonds.

When Joffrey turned to look out over the hall, his eye
caught Sansa's. He smiled, seated himself, and spoke. "It
is a king's duty to punish the disloyal and reward those
who are true. Grand Maester Pycelle, I command you to
read my decrees."

Pycelle pushed himself to his feet. He was clad in a
magnificent robe of thick red velvet, with an ermine collar and shiny gold fastenings. From a drooping sleeve,
heavy with gilded scrollwork, he drew a parchment, unrolled it, and began to read a long list of names, commanding each in the name of king and council to present
themselves and swear their fealty to Joffrey. Failing that,
they would be adjudged traitors, their lands and titles forfeit to the throne.

The names he read made Sansa hold her breath. Lord
Stannis Baratheon, his lady wife, his daughter. Lord Renly
Baratheon. Both Lord Royces and their sons. Ser Loras
Tyrell. Lord Mace Tyrell, his brothers, uncles, sons. The
red priest, Thoros of Myr. Lord Beric Dondarrion. Lady
Lysa Arryn and her son, the little Lord Robert. Lord
Hoster Tully, his brother Ser Brynden, his son Ser
Edmure. Lord Jason Mallister. Lord Bryce Caron of the
Marches. Lord Tytos Blackwood. Lord Walder Frey and his
heir Ser Stevron. Lord Karyl Vance. Lord Jonos Bracken.
Lady Shella Went. Doran Martell, Prince of Dorne, and
all his sons. *So many*, she thought as Pycelle read on and
on, *it will take a whole flock of ravens to send out these
commands.*

And at the end, near last, came the names Sansa had
been dreading. Lady Catelyn Stark. Robb Stark. Brandon
Stark, Rickon Stark, Arya Stark. Sansa stifled a gasp.
Arya. They wanted Arya to present herself and swear an
oath . . . it must mean her sister had fled on the galley,
she must be safe at Winterfell by now . . .

Grand Maester Pycelle rolled up the list, tucked it up
his left sleeve, and pulled another parchment from his
right. He cleared his throat and resumed. "In the place of

the traitor Eddard Stark, it is the wish of His Grace that Tywin Lannister, Lord of Casterly Rock and Warden of the West, take up the office of Hand of the King, to speak with his voice, lead his armies against his enemies, and carry out his royal will. So the king has decreed. The small council consents.

"In the place of the traitor Stannis Baratheon, it is the wish of His Grace that his lady mother, the Queen Regent Cersei Lannister, who has ever been his staunchest support, be seated upon his small council, that she may help him rule wisely and with justice. So the king has decreed. The small council consents."

Sansa heard a soft murmuring from the lords around her, but it was quickly stilled. Pycelle continued.

"It is also the wish of His Grace that his loyal servant, Janos Slynt, Commander of the City Watch of King's Landing, be at once raised to the rank of lord and granted the ancient seat of Harrenhal with all its attendant lands and incomes, and that his sons and grandsons shall hold these honors after him until the end of time. It is moreover his command that *Lord* Slynt be seated immediately upon his small council, to assist in the governance of the realm. So the king has decreed. The small council consents."

Sansa glimpsed motion from the corner of her eye as Janos Slynt made his entrance. This time the muttering was louder and angrier. Proud lords whose houses went back thousands of years made way reluctantly for the balding, frog-faced commoner as he marched past. Golden scales had been sewn onto the black velvet of his doublet and rang together softly with each step. His cloak was checked black-and-gold satin. Two ugly boys who must have been his sons went before him, struggling with the weight of a heavy metal shield as tall as they were. For his sigil he had taken a bloody spear, gold on a night-black field. The sight of it raised goose prickles up and down Sansa's arms.

As Lord Slynt took his place, Grand Maester Pycelle resumed. "Lastly, in these times of treason and turmoil, with our beloved Robert so lately dead, it is the view of the council that the life and safety of King Joffrey is of paramount importance . . ." He looked to the queen.

Cersei stood. "Ser Barristan Selmy, stand forth."

Ser Barristan had been standing at the foot of the Iron Throne, as still as any statue, but now he went to one knee and bowed his head. "Your Grace, I am yours to command."

"Rise, Ser Barristan," Cersei Lannister said. "You may remove your helm."

"My lady?" Standing, the old knight took off his high white helm, though he did not seem to understand why.

"You have served the realm long and faithfully, good ser, and every man and woman in the Seven Kingdoms owes you thanks. Yet now I fear your service is at an end. It is the wish of king and council that you lay down your heavy burden."

"My . . . burden? I fear I . . . I do not . . ."

The new-made lord, Janos Slynt, spoke up, his voice heavy and blunt. "Her Grace is trying to tell you that you are relieved as Lord Commander of the Kingsguard."

The tall, white-haired knight seemed to shrink as he stood there, scarcely breathing. "Your Grace," he said at last. "The Kingsguard is a Sworn Brotherhood. Our vows are taken for life. Only death may relieve the Lord Commander of his sacred trust."

"Whose death, Ser Barristan?" The queen's voice was soft as silk, but her words carried the whole length of the hall. "Yours, or your king's?"

"You let my father die," Joffrey said accusingly from atop the Iron Throne. "You're too old to protect anybody."

Sansa watched as the knight peered up at his new king. She had never seen him look his years before, yet now he did. "Your Grace," he said. "I was chosen for the White Swords in my twenty-third year. It was all I had ever dreamed, from the moment I first took sword in hand. I gave up all claim to my ancestral keep. The girl I was to wed married my cousin in my place, I had no need of land or sons, my life would be lived for the realm. Ser Gerold Hightower himself heard my vows . . . to ward the king with all my strength . . . to give my blood for his . . . I fought beside the White Bull and Prince Lewyn of Dorne . . . beside Ser Arthur Dayne, the Sword of the Morning. Before I served your father, I helped shield King Aerys, and his father Jaehaerys before him . . . three kings . . ."

"And all of them dead," Littlefinger pointed out.

"Your time is done," Cersei Lannister announced. "Joffrey requires men around him who are young and strong. The council has determined that Ser Jaime Lannister will take your place as the Lord Commander of Sworn Brothers of the White Swords."

"The Kingslayer," Ser Barristan said, his voice hard with contempt. "The false knight who profaned his blade with the blood of the king he had sworn to defend."

"Have a care for your words, ser," the queen warned. "You are speaking of our beloved brother, your king's own blood."

Lord Varys spoke, gentler than the others. "We are not unmindful of your service, good ser. Lord Tywin Lannister has generously agreed to grant you a handsome tract of land north of Lannisport, beside the sea, with gold and men sufficient to build you a stout keep, and servants to see to your every need."

Ser Barristan looked up sharply. "A hall to die in, and men to bury me. I thank you, my lords . . . but I spit upon your pity." He reached up and undid the clasps that held his cloak in place, and the heavy white garment slithered from his shoulders to fall in a heap on the floor. His helmet dropped with a *clang*. "I am a knight," he told them. He opened the silver fastenings of his breastplate and let that fall as well. "I shall die a knight."

"A naked knight, it would seem," quipped Littlefinger.

They all laughed then, Joffrey on his throne, and the lords standing attendance, Janos Slynt and Queen Cersei and Sandor Clegane and even the other men of the Kingsguard, the five who had been his brothers until a moment ago. *Surely that must have hurt the most*, Sansa thought. Her heart went out to the gallant old man as he stood shamed and red-faced, too angry to speak. Finally he drew his sword.

Sansa heard someone gasp. Ser Boros and Ser Meryn moved forward to confront him, but Ser Barristan froze them in place with a look that dripped contempt. "Have no fear, sers, your king is safe . . . no thanks to you. Even now, I could cut through the five of you as easy as a dagger cuts cheese. If you would serve under the King-slayer, not a one of you is fit to wear the white." He flung his sword at the foot of the Iron Throne. "Here, boy. Melt it down and add it to the others, if you like. It will do you more good than the swords in the hands of these five. Perhaps Lord Stannis will chance to sit on it when he takes your throne."

He took the long way out, his steps ringing loud against the floor and echoing off the bare stone walls. Lords and ladies parted to let him pass. Not until the pages had closed the great oak-and-bronze doors behind him did Sansa hear sounds again: soft voices, uneasy stirrings, the shuffle of papers from the council table. "He called me *boy*," Joffrey said peevishly, sounding younger than his years. "He talked about my uncle Stannis too."

"Idle talk," said Varys the eunuch. "Without meaning . . ."

"He could be making plots with my uncles. I want him seized and questioned." No one moved. Joffrey raised his voice. "I said, *I want him seized!*"

Janos Slynt rose from the council table. "My gold cloaks will see to it, Your Grace."

"Good," said King Joffrey. Lord Janos strode from the hall, his ugly sons double-stepping to keep up as they lugged the great metal shield with the arms of House Slynt.

"Your Grace," Littlefinger reminded the king. "If we might resume, the seven are now six. We find ourselves in need of a new sword for your Kingsguard."

Joffrey smiled. "Tell them, Mother."

"The king and council have determined that no man in the Seven Kingdoms is more fit to guard and protect His Grace than his sworn shield, Sandor Clegane."

"How do you like that, dog?" King Joffrey asked.

The Hound's scarred face was hard to read. He took a long moment to consider. "Why not? I have no lands nor wife to forsake, and who'd care if I did?" The burned side of his mouth twisted. "But I warn you, I'll say no knight's vows."

"The Sworn Brothers of the Kingsguard have always been knights," Ser Boros said firmly.

"Until now," the Hound said in his deep rasp, and Ser Boros fell silent.

When the king's herald moved forward, Sansa realized the moment was almost at hand. She smoothed down the cloth of her skirt nervously. She was dressed in mourning, as a sign of respect for the dead king, but she had taken special care to make herself beautiful. Her gown was the ivory silk that the queen had given her, the one Arya had ruined, but she'd had them dye it black and you couldn't see the stain at all. She had fretted over her jewelry for hours and finally decided upon the elegant simplicity of a plain silver chain.

The herald's voice boomed out. "If any man in this hall has other matters to set before His Grace, let him speak now or go forth and hold his silence."

Sansa quailed. *Now,* she told herself, *I must do it now. Gods give me courage.* She took one step, then another. Lords and knights stepped aside silently to let her pass, and she felt the weight of their eyes on her. *I must be as strong as my lady mother.* "Your Grace," she called out in a soft, tremulous voice.

The height of the Iron Throne gave Joffrey a better vantage point than anyone else in the hall. He was the first to see her. "Come forward, my lady," he called out, smiling.

His smile emboldened her, made her feel beautiful and strong. *He does love me, he does.* Sansa lifted her head and walked toward him, not too slow and not too fast. She must not let them see how nervous she was.

"The Lady Sansa, of House Stark," the herald cried.

She stopped under the throne, at the spot where Ser Barristan's white cloak lay puddled on the floor beside his helm and breastplate. "Do you have some business for king and council, Sansa?" the queen asked from the council table.

"I do." She knelt on the cloak, so as not to spoil her gown, and looked up at her prince on his fearsome black throne. "As it please Your Grace, I ask mercy for my father, Lord Eddard Stark, who was the Hand of the King." She had practiced the words a hundred times.

The queen sighed. "Sansa, you disappoint me. What did I tell you about traitor's blood?"

"Your father has committed grave and terrible crimes, my lady," Grand Maester Pycelle intoned.

"Ah, poor sad thing," sighed Varys. "She is only a babe, my lords, she does not know what she asks."

Sansa had eyes only for Joffrey. *He must listen to me, he must,* she thought. The king shifted on his seat. "Let her speak," he commanded. "I want to hear what she says."

"Thank you, Your Grace." Sansa smiled, a shy secret smile, just for him. He was listening. She knew he would.

"Treason is a noxious weed," Pycelle declared solemnly. "It must be torn up, root and stem and seed, lest new traitors sprout from every roadside."

"Do you deny your father's crime?" Lord Baelish asked.

"No, my lords." Sansa knew better than that. "I know he must be punished. All I ask is mercy. I know my lord father must regret what he did. He was King Robert's friend and he loved him, you all know he loved him. He never wanted to be Hand until the king asked him. They must have lied to him. Lord Renly or Lord Stannis or . . . or *somebody*, they must have lied, otherwise . . ."

King Joffrey leaned forward, hands grasping the arms of the throne. Broken sword points fanned out between his fingers. "He said I wasn't the king. Why did he say that?"

"His leg was broken," Sansa replied eagerly. "It hurt ever so much, Maester Pycelle was giving him milk of the poppy, and they say that milk of the poppy fills your head with clouds. Otherwise he would never have said it."

Varys said, "A child's faith . . . such sweet innocence . . . and yet, they say wisdom oft comes from the mouths of babes."

"Treason is treason," Pycelle replied at once.

Joffrey rocked restlessly on the throne. "Mother?"

Cersei Lannister considered Sansa thoughtfully. "If Lord Eddard were to confess his crime," she said at last, "we would know he had repented his folly."

Joffrey pushed himself to his feet. *Please,* Sansa thought, *please, please, be the king I know you are, good and kind and noble, please.* "Do you have any more to say?" he asked her.

"Only . . . that as you love me, you do me this kindness, my prince," Sansa said.

King Joffrey looked her up and down. "Your sweet words have moved me," he said gallantly, nodding, as if to say all would be well. "I shall do as you ask . . . but first your father has to confess. He has to confess and say that I'm the king, or there will be no mercy for him."

"He will," Sansa said, heart soaring. "Oh, I know he will."

EDDARD

The straw on the floor stank of urine. There was no window, no bed, not even a slop bucket. He remembered walls of pale red stone festooned with patches of nitre, a grey door of splintered wood, four inches thick and studded with iron. He had seen them, briefly, a quick glimpse as they shoved him inside. Once the door had slammed shut, he had seen no more. The dark was absolute. He had as well been blind.

Or dead. Buried with his king. "Ah, Robert," he murmured as his groping hand touched a cold stone wall, his leg throbbing with every motion. He remembered the jest the king had shared in the crypts of Winterfell, as the Kings of Winter looked on with cold stone eyes. *The king eats,* Robert had said, *and the Hand takes the shit.* How he had laughed. Yet he had gotten it wrong. *The king dies,* Ned Stark thought, *and the Hand is buried.*

The dungeon was under the Red Keep, deeper than he dared imagine. He remembered the old stories about Maegor the Cruel, who murdered all the masons who labored on his castle, so they might never reveal its secrets.

He damned them all: Littlefinger, Janos Slynt and his gold cloaks, the queen, the Kingslayer, Pycelle and Varys and Ser Barristan, even Lord Renly, Robert's own blood, who had run when he was needed most. Yet in the end he blamed himself. *"Fool,"* he cried to the darkness, "thrice-damned blind fool."

Cersei Lannister's face seemed to float before him in the darkness. Her hair was full of sunlight, but there was mockery in her smile. "When you play the game of thrones, you win or you die," she whispered. Ned had played and lost, and his men had paid the price of his folly with their life's blood.

When he thought of his daughters, he would have wept gladly, but the tears would not come. Even now, he was a Stark of Winterfell, and his grief and his rage froze hard inside him.

When he kept very still, his leg did not hurt so much, so he did his best to lie unmoving. For how long he could not say. There was no sun and no moon. He could not see to mark the walls. Ned closed his eyes and opened them; it made no difference. He slept and woke and slept again. He did not know which was more painful, the waking or the sleeping. When he slept, he dreamed: dark disturbing dreams of blood and broken promises. When he woke, there was nothing to do but think, and his waking thoughts were worse than nightmares. The thought of Cat was as painful as a bed of nettles. He wondered where she was, what she was doing. He wondered whether he would ever see her again.

Hours turned to days, or so it seemed. He could feel a dull ache in his shattered leg, an itch beneath the plaster. When he touched his thigh, the flesh was hot to his fingers. The only sound was his breathing. After a time, he began to talk aloud, just to hear a voice. He made plans to keep himself sane, built castles of hope in the dark. Robert's brothers were out in the world, raising armies at Dragonstone and Storm's End. Alyn and Harwin would return to King's Landing with the rest of his household guard once they had dealt with Ser Gregor. Catelyn would raise the north when the word reached her, and the lords of river and mountain and Vale would join her.

He found himself thinking of Robert more and more. He saw the king as he had been in the flower of his youth, tall and handsome, his great antlered helm on his head, his warhammer in hand, sitting his horse like a horned god. He heard his laughter in the dark, saw his eyes, blue and clear as mountain lakes. "Look at us, Ned," Robert said. "Gods, how did we come to this? You here, and me killed by a pig. We won a throne together . . ."

I failed you, Robert, Ned thought. He could not say the words. *I lied to you, hid the truth. I let them kill you.*

The king heard him. "You stiff-necked fool," he muttered, "too proud to listen. Can you eat pride, Stark? Will honor shield your children?" Cracks ran down his face, fissures opening in the flesh, and he reached up and ripped the mask away. It was not Robert at all; it was Littlefinger, grinning, mocking him. When he opened his mouth to speak, his lies turned to pale grey moths and took wing.

Ned was half-asleep when the footsteps came down the hall. At first he thought he dreamt them; it had been so long since he had heard anything but the sound of his own voice. Ned was feverish by then, his leg a dull agony, his lips parched and cracked. When the heavy wooden door creaked open, the sudden light was painful to his eyes.

A gaoler thrust a jug at him. The clay was cool and beaded with moisture. Ned grasped it with both hands and gulped eagerly. Water ran from his mouth and dripped down through his beard. He drank until he thought he would be sick. "How long . . . ?" he asked weakly when he could drink no more.

The gaoler was a scarecrow of a man with a rat's face and frayed beard, clad in a mail shirt and a leather half cape. "No talking," he said as he wrenched the jug from Ned's hands.

"Please," Ned said, "my daughters . . ." The door crashed shut. He blinked as the light vanished, lowered his head to his chest, and curled up on the straw. It no longer stank of urine and shit. It no longer smelled at all.

He could no longer tell the difference between waking and sleeping. The memory came creeping upon him in the darkness, as vivid as a dream. It was the year of false spring, and he was eighteen again, down from the Eyrie to the tourney at Harrenhal. He could see the deep green of the grass, and smell the pollen on the wind. Warm days and cool nights and the sweet taste of wine. He remembered Brandon's laughter, and Robert's berserk valor in the melee, the way he laughed as he unhorsed men left and right. He remembered Jaime Lannister, a golden youth in scaled white armor, kneeling on the grass in front of the king's pavilion and making his vows to protect and defend King Aerys. Afterward, Ser Oswell Whent helped Jaime to his feet, and the White Bull himself, Lord Commander Ser Gerold Hightower, fastened the snowy cloak of the Kingsguard about his shoulders. All six White Swords were there to welcome their newest brother.

Yet when the jousting began, the day belonged to Rhaegar Targaryen. The crown prince wore the armor he would die in: gleaming black plate with the three-headed dragon of his House wrought in rubies on the breast. A plume of scarlet silk streamed behind him when he rode, and it seemed no lance could touch him. Brandon fell to him, and Bronze Yohn Royce, and even the splendid Ser Arthur Dayne, the Sword of the Morning.

Robert had been jesting with Jon and old Lord Hunter as the prince circled the field after unhorsing Ser Barristan in the final tilt to claim the champion's crown. Ned remembered the moment when all the smiles died, when Prince Rhaegar Targaryen urged his horse past his own wife, the Dornish princess Elia Martell, to lay the queen of beauty's laurel in Lyanna's lap. He could see it still: a crown of winter roses, blue as frost.

Ned Stark reached out his hand to grasp the flowery crown, but beneath the pale blue petals the thorns lay hidden. He felt them clawing at his skin, sharp and cruel, saw the slow trickle of blood run down his fingers, and woke, trembling, in the dark.

Promise me, Ned, his sister had whispered from her bed of blood. She had loved the scent of winter roses.

"Gods save me," Ned wept. "I am going mad."

The gods did not deign to answer.

Each time the turnkey brought him water, he told himself another day had passed. At first he would beg the man for some word of his daughters and the world beyond his cell. Grunts and kicks were his only replies. Later, when the stomach cramps began, he begged for food instead. It made no matter; he was not fed. Perhaps the Lannisters meant for him to starve to death. "No," he told himself. If Cersei had wanted him dead, he would have been cut down in the throne room with his men. She wanted him alive. Weak, desperate, yet alive. Catelyn held her brother; she dare not kill him or the Imp's life would be forfeit as well.

From outside his cell came the rattle of iron chains. As the door creaked open, Ned put a hand to the damp wall and pushed himself toward the light. The glare of a torch made him squint. "Food," he croaked.

"Wine," a voice answered. It was not the rat-faced man; this gaoler was stouter, shorter, though he wore the same leather half cape and spiked steel cap. "Drink, Lord Eddard." He thrust a wineskin into Ned's hands.

The voice was strangely familiar, yet it took Ned Stark a moment to place it. *"Varys?"* he said groggily when it came. He touched the man's face. "I'm not . . . not dreaming this. You're here." The eunuch's plump cheeks were covered with a dark stubble of beard. Ned felt the coarse hair with his fingers. Varys had transformed himself into a grizzled turnkey, reeking of sweat and sour wine. "How did you . . . what sort of magician are you?"

"A thirsty one," Varys said. "Drink, my lord."

Ned's hands fumbled at the skin. "Is this the same poison they gave Robert?"

"You wrong me," Varys said sadly. "Truly, no one loves a eunuch. Give me the skin." He drank, a trickle of red leaking from the corner of his plump mouth. "Not the equal of the vintage you offered me the night of the tourney, but no more poisonous than most," he concluded, wiping his lips. "Here."

Ned tried a swallow. "Dregs." He felt as though he were about to bring the wine back up.

"All men must swallow the sour with the sweet. High lords and eunuchs alike. Your hour has come, my lord."

"My daughters . . ."

"The younger girl escaped Ser Meryn and fled," Varys told him. "I have not been able to find her. Nor have the Lannisters. A kindness, there. Our new king loves her not. Your older girl is still betrothed to Joffrey. Cersei keeps her close. She came to court a few days ago to plead that you be spared. A pity you couldn't have been there, you would have been touched." He leaned forward intently. "I trust you realize that you are a dead man, Lord Eddard?"

"The queen will not kill me," Ned said. His head swam; the wine was strong, and it had been too long since he'd eaten. "Cat . . . Cat holds her brother . . ."

"The *wrong* brother," Varys sighed. "And lost to her, in any case. She let the Imp slip through her fingers. I expect he is dead by now, somewhere in the Mountains of the Moon."

"If that is true, slit my throat and have done with it." He was dizzy from the wine, tired and heartsick.

"Your blood is the last thing I desire."

Ned frowned. "When they slaughtered my guard, you stood beside the queen and watched, and said not a word."

"And would again. I seem to recall that I was unarmed, unarmored, and surrounded by Lannister swords." The eunuch looked at him curiously, tilting his head. "When I was a young boy, before I was cut, I traveled with a troupe of mummers through the Free Cities. They taught me that each man has a role to play, in life as well as mummery. So it is at court. The King's Justice must be fearsome, the master of coin must be frugal, the Lord Commander of the Kingsguard must be valiant . . . and the master of whisperers must be sly and obsequious and without scruple. A courageous informer would be as useless as a cowardly knight." He took the wineskin back and drank.

Ned studied the eunuch's face, searching for truth beneath the mummer's scars and false stubble. He tried some more wine. This time it went down easier. "Can you free me from this pit?"

"I could . . . but *will* I? No. Questions would be asked, and the answers would lead back to me."

Ned had expected no more. "You are blunt."

"A eunuch has no honor, and a spider does not enjoy the luxury of scruples, my lord."

"Would you at least consent to carry a message out for me?"

"That would depend on the message. I will gladly provide you with paper and ink, if you like. And when you have written what you will, I will take the letter and read it, and deliver it or not, as best serves my own ends."

"Your own ends. What ends are those, Lord Varys?"

"Peace," Varys replied without hesitation. "If there

was one soul in King's Landing who was truly desperate to keep Robert Baratheon alive, it was me." He sighed. "For fifteen years I protected him from his enemies, but I could not protect him from his friends. What strange fit of madness led you to tell the queen that you had learned the truth of Joffrey's birth?"

"The madness of mercy," Ned admitted.

"Ah," said Varys. "To be sure. You are an honest and honorable man, Lord Eddard. Ofttimes I forget that. I have met so few of them in my life." He glanced around the cell. "When I see what honesty and honor have won you, I understand why."

Ned Stark laid his head back against the damp stone wall and closed his eyes. His leg was throbbing. "The king's wine . . . did you question Lancel?"

"Oh, indeed. Cersei gave him the wineskins, and told him it was Robert's favorite vintage." The eunuch shrugged. "A hunter lives a perilous life. If the boar had not done for Robert, it would have been a fall from a horse, the bite of a wood adder, an arrow gone astray . . . the forest is the abbatoir of the gods. It was not wine that killed the king. It was your *mercy*."

Ned had feared as much. "Gods forgive me."

"If there are gods," Varys said, "I expect they will. The queen would not have waited long in any case. Robert was becoming unruly, and she needed to be rid of him to free her hands to deal with his brothers. They are quite a pair, Stannis and Renly. The iron gauntlet and the silk glove." He wiped his mouth with the back of his hand. "You have been foolish, my lord. You ought to have heeded Littlefinger when he urged you to support Joffrey's succession."

"How . . . how could you know of that?"

Varys smiled. "I know, that's all that need concern you. I also know that on the morrow the queen will pay you a visit."

Slowly Ned raised his eyes. "Why?"

"Cersei is frightened of you, my lord . . . but she has other enemies she fears even more. Her beloved Jaime is fighting the river lords even now. Lysa Arryn sits in the Eyrie, ringed in stone and steel, and there is no love lost between her and the queen. In Dorne, the Martells still brood on the murder of Princess Elia and her babes. And now your son marches down the Neck with a northern host at his back."

"Robb is only a boy," Ned said, aghast.

"A boy with an army," Varys said. "Yet only a boy, as you say. The king's brothers are the ones giving Cersei sleepless nights . . . Lord Stannis in particular. His claim is the true one, he is known for his prowess as a battle commander, and he is utterly without mercy. There is no creature on earth half so terrifying as a truly just man. No one knows what Stannis has been doing on Dragonstone, but I will wager you that he's gathered more swords than seashells. So here is Cersei's nightmare: while her father and brother spend their power battling Starks and Tullys, Lord Stannis will land, proclaim himself king, and lop off her son's curly blond head . . . and her own in the bargain, though I truly believe she cares more about the boy."

"Stannis Baratheon is Robert's true heir," Ned said. "The throne is his by rights. I would welcome his ascent."

Varys *tsk*ed. "Cersei will not want to hear that, I promise you. Stannis may win the throne, but only your rotting head will remain to cheer unless you guard that tongue of yours. Sansa begged so sweetly, it would be a shame if you threw it all away. You are being given your life back, if you'll take it. Cersei is no fool. She knows a tame wolf is of more use than a dead one."

"You want me to *serve* the woman who murdered my king, butchered my men, and crippled my son?" Ned's voice was thick with disbelief.

"I want you to serve the realm," Varys said. "Tell the queen that you will confess your vile treason, command your son to lay down his sword, and proclaim Joffrey as the true heir. Offer to denounce Stannis and Renly as faithless usurpers. Our green-eyed lioness knows you are a man of honor. If you will give her the peace she needs and the time to deal with Stannis, and pledge to carry her secret to your grave, I believe she will allow you to take the black and live out the rest of your days on the Wall, with your brother and that baseborn son of yours."

The thought of Jon filled Ned with a sense of shame, and a sorrow too deep for words. If only he could see the boy again, sit and talk with him . . . pain shot through his broken leg, beneath the filthy grey plaster of his cast. He winced, his fingers opening and closing helplessly. "Is this your own scheme," he gasped out at Varys, "or are you in league with Littlefinger?"

That seemed to amuse the eunuch. "I would sooner wed the Black Goat of Qohor. Littlefinger is the second most devious man in the Seven Kingdoms. Oh, I feed him choice whispers, sufficient so that he *thinks* I am his . . . just as I allow Cersei to believe I am hers."

"And just as you let me believe that you were mine. Tell me, Lord Varys, who do you truly serve?"

Varys smiled thinly. "Why, the realm, my good lord, how ever could you doubt that? I swear it by my lost manhood. I serve the realm, and the realm needs peace." He finished the last swallow of wine, and tossed the empty skin aside. "So what is your answer, Lord Eddard? Give me your word that you'll tell the queen what she wants to hear when she comes calling."

"If I did, my word would be as hollow as an empty suit of armor. My life is not so precious to me as that."

"Pity." The eunuch stood. "And your daughter's life, my lord? How precious is that?"

A chill pierced Ned's heart. "My daughter . . ."

"Surely you did not think I'd forgotten about your sweet innocent, my lord? The queen most certainly has not."

"*No*," Ned pleaded, his voice cracking. "Varys, gods have mercy, do as you like with me, but leave my daughter out of your schemes. Sansa's no more than a child."

"Rhaenys was a child too. Prince Rhaegar's daughter. A precious little thing, younger than your girls. She had a small black kitten she called Balerion, did you know? I always wondered what happened to him. Rhaenys liked to pretend he was the true Balerion, the Black Dread of old, but I imagine the Lannisters taught her the difference between a kitten and a dragon quick enough, the day they broke down her door." Varys gave a long weary sigh, the sigh of a man who carried all the sadness of the world in a sack upon his shoulders. "The High Septon once told me that as we sin, so do we suffer. If that's true, Lord Eddard, tell me . . . why is it always the innocents who suffer most, when you high lords play your game of thrones? Ponder it, if you would, while you wait upon the queen.

And spare a thought for this as well: The next visitor who calls on you could bring you bread and cheese and the milk of the poppy for your pain . . . or he could bring you Sansa's head.

"The choice, my dear lord Hand, is *entirely* yours."

CATELYN

As the host trooped down the causeway through the black bogs of the Neck and spilled out into the riverlands beyond, Catelyn's apprehensions grew. She masked her fears behind a face kept still and stern, yet they were there all the same, growing with every league they crossed. Her days were anxious, her nights restless, and every raven that flew overhead made her clench her teeth.

She feared for her lord father, and wondered at his ominous silence. She feared for her brother Edmure, and prayed that the gods would watch over him if he must face the Kingslayer in battle. She feared for Ned and her girls, and for the sweet sons she had left behind at Winterfell. And yet there was nothing she could do for any of them, and so she made herself put all thought of them aside. *You must save your strength for Robb,* she told herself. *He is the only one you can help. You must be as fierce and hard as the north, Catelyn Tully. You must be a Stark for true now, like your son.*

Robb rode at the front of the column, beneath the flapping white banner of Winterfell. Each day he would ask one of his lords to join him, so they might confer as they marched; he honored every man in turn, showing no favorites, listening as his lord father had listened, weighing the words of one against the other. *He has learned so much from Ned*, she thought as she watched him, *but has he learned enough?*

The Blackfish had taken a hundred picked men and a hundred swift horses and raced ahead to screen their movements and scout the way. The reports Ser Brynden's riders brought back did little to reassure her. Lord Tywin's host was still many days to the south . . . but Walder Frey, Lord of the Crossing, had assembled a force of near four thousand men at his castles on the Green Fork.

"Late again," Catelyn murmured when she heard. It was the Trident all over, damn the man. Her brother Edmure had called the banners; by rights, Lord Frey should have gone to join the Tully host at Riverrun, yet here he sat.

"Four thousand men," Robb repeated, more perplexed than angry. "Lord Frey cannot hope to fight the Lannisters by himself. Surely he means to join his power to ours."

"Does he?" Catelyn asked. She had ridden forward to join Robb and Robett Glover, his companion of the day. The vanguard spread out behind them, a slow-moving forest of lances and banners and spears. "I wonder. Expect nothing of Walder Frey, and you will never be surprised."

"He's your father's bannerman."

"Some men take their oaths more seriously than others, Robb. And Lord Walder was always friendlier with Casterly Rock than my father would have liked. One of his sons is wed to Tywin Lannister's sister. That means little of itself, to be sure. Lord Walder has sired a great many children over the years, and they must needs marry someone. Still . . ."

"Do you think he means to betray us to the Lannisters, my lady?" Robett Glover asked gravely.

Catelyn sighed. "If truth be told, I doubt even Lord Frey knows what Lord Frey intends to do. He has an old man's caution and a young man's ambition, and has never lacked for cunning."

"We must have the Twins, Mother," Robb said heatedly. "There is no other way across the river. You know that."

"Yes. And so does Walder Frey, you can be sure of that."

That night they made camp on the southern edge of the bogs, halfway between the kingsroad and the river. It was there Theon Greyjoy brought them further word from her uncle. "Ser Brynden says to tell you he's crossed swords with the Lannisters. There are a dozen scouts who won't be reporting back to Lord Tywin anytime soon. Or ever." He grinned. "Ser Addam Marbrand commands their outriders, and he's pulling back south, burning as he goes. He knows where we are, more or less, but the Blackfish vows he will not know when we split."

"Unless Lord Frey tells him," Catelyn said sharply. "Theon, when you return to my uncle, tell him he is to place his best bowmen around the Twins, day and night, with orders to bring down any raven they see leaving the battlements. I want no birds bringing word of my son's movements to Lord Tywin."

"Ser Brynden has seen to it already, my lady," Theon replied with a cocky smile. "A few more blackbirds, and we should have enough to bake a pie. I'll save you their feathers for a hat."

She ought to have known that Brynden Blackfish would be well ahead of her. "What have the Freys been doing while the Lannisters burn their fields and plunder their holdfasts?"

"There's been some fighting between Ser Addam's men and Lord Walder's," Theon answered. "Not a day's ride from here, we found two Lannister scouts feeding the crows where the Freys had strung them up. Most of Lord Walder's strength remains massed at the Twins, though."

That bore Walder Frey's seal beyond a doubt, Catelyn thought bitterly; hold back, wait, watch, take no risk unless forced to it.

"If he's been fighting the Lannisters, perhaps he does mean to hold to his vows," Robb said.

Catelyn was less encouraged. "Defending his own lands is one thing, open battle against Lord Tywin quite another."

Robb turned back to Theon Greyjoy. "Has the Blackfish found any other way across the Green Fork?"

Theon shook his head. "The river's running high and

fast. Ser Brynden says it can't be forded, not this far north."

"I *must* have that crossing!" Robb declared, fuming. "Oh, our horses might be able to swim the river, I suppose, but not with armored men on their backs. We'd need to build rafts to pole our steel across, helms and mail and lances, and we don't have the trees for that. *Or* the time. Lord Tywin is marching north . . ." He balled his hand into a fist.

"Lord Frey would be a fool to try and bar our way," Theon Greyjoy said with his customary easy confidence. "We have five times his numbers. You can take the Twins if you need to, Robb."

"Not easily," Catelyn warned them, "and not in time. While you were mounting your siege, Tywin Lannister would bring up his host and assault you from the rear."

Robb glanced from her to Greyjoy, searching for an answer and finding none. For a moment he looked even younger than his fifteen years, despite his mail and sword and the stubble on his cheeks. "What would my lord father do?" he asked her.

"Find a way across," she told him. "Whatever it took."

The next morning it was Ser Brynden Tully himself who rode back to them. He had put aside the heavy plate and helm he'd worn as the Knight of the Gate for the lighter leather-and-mail of an outrider, but his obsidian fish still fastened his cloak.

Her uncle's face was grave as he swung down off his horse. "There has been a battle under the walls of Riverrun," he said, his mouth grim. "We had it from a Lannister outrider we took captive. The Kingslayer has destroyed Edmure's host and sent the lords of the Trident reeling in flight."

A cold hand clutched at Catelyn's heart. "And my brother?"

"Wounded and taken prisoner," Ser Brynden said. "Lord Blackwood and the other survivors are under siege inside Riverrun, surrounded by Jaime's host."

Robb looked fretful. "We must get across this accursed river if we're to have any hope of relieving them in time."

"That will not be easily done," her uncle cautioned. "Lord Frey has pulled his whole strength back inside his castles, and his gates are closed and barred."

"Damn the man," Robb swore. "If the old fool does not relent and let me cross, he'll leave me no choice but to storm his walls. I'll pull the Twins down around his ears if I have to, we'll see how well he likes that!"

"You sound like a sulky boy, Robb," Catelyn said sharply. "A child sees an obstacle, and his first thought is to run around it or knock it down. A lord must learn that sometimes words can accomplish what swords cannot."

Robb's neck reddened at the rebuke. "Tell me what you mean, Mother," he said meekly.

"The Freys have held the crossing for six hundred years, and for six hundred years they have never failed to exact their toll."

"What toll? What does he *want*?"

She smiled. "That is what we must discover."

"And what if I do not choose to pay this toll?"

"Then you had best retreat back to Moat Cailin, deploy to meet Lord Tywin in battle . . . or grow wings. I see no other choices." Catelyn put her heels to her horse and rode off, leaving her son to ponder her words. It would not do to make him feel as if his mother were usurping his place. *Did you teach him wisdom as well as valor, Ned?* she wondered. *Did you teach him how to kneel?* The graveyards of the Seven Kingdoms were full of brave men who had never learned that lesson.

It was near midday when their vanguard came in sight of the Twins, where the Lords of the Crossing had their seat.

The Green Fork ran swift and deep here, but the Freys had spanned it many centuries past and grown rich off the coin men paid them to cross. Their bridge was a massive arch of smooth grey rock, wide enough for two wagons to pass abreast; the Water Tower rose from the center of the span, commanding both road and river with its arrow slits, murder holes, and portcullises. It had taken the Freys three generations to complete their bridge; when they were done they'd thrown up stout timber keeps on either bank, so no one might cross without their leave.

The timber had long since given way to stone. The Twins—two squat, ugly, formidable castles, identical in every respect, with the bridge arching between—had guarded the crossing for centuries. High curtain walls, deep moats, and heavy oak-and-iron gates protected the approaches, the bridge footings rose from within stout inner keeps, there was a barbican and portcullis on either bank, and the Water Tower defended the span itself.

One glance was sufficient to tell Catelyn that the castle would not be taken by storm. The battlements bristled with spears and swords and scorpions, there was an archer at every crenel and arrow slit, the drawbridge was up, the portcullis down, the gates closed and barred.

The Greatjon began to curse and swear as soon as he saw what awaited them. Lord Rickard Karstark glowered in silence. "That cannot be assaulted, my lords," Roose Bolton announced.

"Nor can we take it by siege, without an army on the far bank to invest the other castle," Helman Tallhart said gloomily. Across the deep-running green waters, the western twin stood like a reflection of its eastern brother. "Even if we had the time. Which, to be sure, we do not."

As the northern lords studied the castle, a sally port opened, a plank bridge slid across the moat, and a dozen knights rode forth to confront them, led by four of Lord Walder's many sons. Their banner bore twin towers, dark blue on a field of pale silver-grey. Ser Stevron Frey, Lord Walder's heir, spoke for them. The Freys all looked like weasels; Ser Stevron, past sixty with grandchildren of his own, looked like an especially old and tired weasel, yet he was polite enough. "My lord father has sent me to greet you, and inquire as to who leads this mighty host."

"I do." Robb spurred his horse forward. He was in his armor, with the direwolf shield of Winterfell strapped to his saddle and Grey Wind padding by his side.

The old knight looked at her son with a faint flicker of amusement in his watery grey eyes, though his gelding whickered uneasily and sidled away from the direwolf. "My lord father would be most honored if you would share meat and mead with him in the castle and explain your purpose here."

His words crashed among the lords bannermen like a great stone from a catapult. Not one of them approved. They cursed, argued, shouted down each other.

"You must not do this, my lord," Galbart Glover pleaded with Robb. "Lord Walder is not to be trusted."

Roose Bolton nodded. "Go in there alone and you're

his. He can sell you to the Lannisters, throw you in a dungeon, or slit your throat, as he likes."

"If he wants to talk to us, let him open his gates, and we will *all* share his meat and mead," declared Ser Wendel Manderly.

"Or let him come out and treat with Robb here, in plain sight of his men and ours," suggested his brother, Ser Wylis.

Catelyn Stark shared all their doubts, but she had only to glance at Ser Stevron to see that he was not pleased by what he was hearing. A few more words and the chance would be lost. She had to act, and quickly. *"I will go,"* she said loudly.

"You, my lady?" The Greatjon furrowed his brow.

"Mother, are you certain?" Clearly, Robb was not.

"Never more," Catelyn lied glibly. "Lord Walder is my father's bannerman. I have known him since I was a girl. He would never offer me any harm." *Unless he saw some profit in it,* she added silently, but some truths did not bear saying, and some lies were necessary.

"I am certain my lord father would be pleased to speak to the Lady Catelyn," Ser Stevron said. "To vouchsafe for our good intentions, my brother Ser Perwyn will remain here until she is safely returned to you."

"He shall be our honored guest," said Robb. Ser Perwyn, the youngest of the four Freys in the party, dismounted and handed the reins of his horse to a brother. "I require my lady mother's return by evenfall, Ser Stevron," Robb went on. "It is not my intent to linger here long."

Ser Stevron Frey gave a polite nod. "As you say, my lord." Catelyn spurred her horse forward and did not look back. Lord Walder's sons and envoys fell in around her.

Her father had once said of Walder Frey that he was the only lord in the Seven Kingdoms who could field an army out of his breeches. When the Lord of the Crossing welcomed Catelyn in the great hall of the east castle, surrounded by twenty living sons (minus Ser Perwyn, who would have made twenty-one), thirty-six grandsons, nineteen great-grandsons, and numerous daughters, granddaughters, bastards, and grandbastards, she understood just what he had meant.

Lord Walder was ninety, a wizened pink weasel with a bald spotted head, too gouty to stand unassisted. His newest wife, a pale frail girl of sixteen years, walked beside his litter when they carried him in. She was the eighth Lady Frey.

"It is a great pleasure to see you again after so many years, my lord," Catelyn said.

The old man squinted at her suspiciously. "Is it? I doubt that. Spare me your sweet words, Lady Catelyn, I am too old. Why are you here? Is your boy too proud to come before me himself? What am I to do with *you*?"

Catelyn had been a girl the last time she had visited the Twins, but even then Lord Walder had been irascible, sharp of tongue, and blunt of manner. Age had made him worse than ever, it would seem. She would need to choose her words with care, and do her best to take no offense from his.

"Father," Ser Stevron said reproachfully, "you forget yourself. Lady Stark is here at your invitation."

"Did I ask *you*? You are not Lord Frey yet, not until I die. Do I look dead? I'll hear no instructions from you."

"This is no way to speak in front of our noble guest, Father," one of his younger sons said.

"Now my bastards presume to teach me courtesy," Lord Walder complained. "I'll speak any way I like, damn you. I've had three kings to guest in my life, and queens as well, do you think I require lessons from the likes of you, Ryger? Your mother was milking goats the first time I gave her my seed." He dismissed the red-faced youth with a flick of his fingers and gestured to two of his other sons. "Danwell, Whalen, help me to my chair."

They shifted Lord Walder from his litter and carried him to the high seat of the Freys, a tall chair of black oak whose back was carved in the shape of two towers linked by a bridge. His young wife crept up timidly and covered his legs with a blanket. When he was settled, the old man beckoned Catelyn forward and planted a papery dry kiss on her hand. "There," he announced. "Now that I have observed the courtesies, my lady, perhaps my sons will do me the honor of shutting their mouths. Why are you here?"

"To ask you to open your gates, my lord," Catelyn replied politely. "My son and his lords bannermen are most anxious to cross the river and be on their way."

"To Riverrun?" He sniggered. "Oh, no need to tell me,

no need. I'm not blind yet. The old man can still read a map."

"To Riverrun," Catelyn confirmed. She saw no reason to deny it. "Where I might have expected to find you, my lord. You are still my father's bannerman, are you not?"

"*Heh*," said Lord Walder, a noise halfway between a laugh and a grunt. "I called my swords, yes I did, here they are, you saw them on the walls. It was my intent to march as soon as all my strength was assembled. Well, to send my sons. I am well past marching myself, Lady Catelyn." He looked around for likely confirmation and pointed to a tall, stooped man of fifty years. "Tell her, Jared. Tell her that was my intent."

"It was, my lady," said Ser Jared Frey, one of his sons by his second wife. "On my honor."

"Is it my fault that your fool brother lost his battle before we could march?" He leaned back against his cushions and scowled at her, as if challenging her to dispute his version of events. "I am told the Kingslayer went through him like an axe through ripe cheese. Why should my boys hurry south to die? All those who did go south are running north again."

Catelyn would gladly have spitted the querulous old man and roasted him over a fire, but she had only till evenfall to open the bridge. Calmly, she said, "All the more reason that we must reach Riverrun, and soon. Where can we go to talk, my lord?"

"We're talking now," Lord Frey complained. The spotted pink head snapped around. "What are you all looking at?" he shouted at his kin. "Get out of here. Lady Stark wants to speak to me in private. Might be she has designs on my fidelity, *heh*. Go, all of you, find something useful to do. Yes, you too, woman. Out, out, *out*." As his sons and grandsons and daughters and bastards and nieces and nephews streamed from the hall, he leaned close to Catelyn and confessed, "They're all waiting for me to die. Stevron's been waiting for forty years, but I keep disappointing him. *Heh*. Why should I die just so he can be a lord? I ask you. I won't do it."

"I have every hope that you will live to be a hundred."

"*That* would boil them, to be sure. Oh, to be sure. Now, what do you want to say?"

"We want to cross," Catelyn told him.

"Oh, *do* you? That's blunt. Why should I let you?"

For a moment her anger flared. "If you were strong enough to climb your own battlements, Lord Frey, you would see that my son has twenty thousand men outside your walls."

"They'll be twenty thousand fresh corpses when Lord Tywin gets here," the old man shot back. "Don't you try and frighten me, my lady. Your husband's in some traitor's cell under the Red Keep, your father's sick, might be dying, and Jaime Lannister's got your brother in chains. What do you have that I should fear? That son of yours? I'll match you son for son, and I'll still have eighteen when yours are all dead."

"You swore an oath to my father," Catelyn reminded him.

He bobbed his head side to side, smiling. "Oh, yes, I said some words, but I swore oaths to the crown too, it seems to me. Joffrey's the king now, and that makes you and your boy and all those fools out there no better than rebels. If I had the sense the gods gave a fish, I'd help the Lannisters boil you all."

"Why don't you?" she challenged him.

Lord Walder snorted with disdain. "Lord Tywin the proud and splendid, Warden of the West, Hand of the King, oh, what a great man *that* one is, him and his gold this and gold that and lions here and lions there. I'll wager you, he eats too many beans, he breaks wind just like me, but you'll never hear *him* admit it, oh, no. What's *he* got to be so puffed up about anyway? Only two sons, and one of them's a twisted little monster. I'll match *him* son for son, and I'll still have nineteen and a *half* left when all of his are dead!" He cackled. "If Lord Tywin wants my help, he can bloody well *ask* for it."

That was all Catelyn needed to hear. "I am asking for your help, my lord," she said humbly. "And my father and my brother and my lord husband and my sons are asking with my voice."

Lord Walder jabbed a bony finger at her face. "Save your sweet words, my lady. Sweet words I get from my wife. Did you see her? Sixteen she is, a little flower, and her honey's only for me. I wager she gives me a son by this time next year. Perhaps I'll make *him* heir, wouldn't that boil the rest of them?"

"I'm certain she will give you many sons."

His head bobbed up and down. "Your lord father did not come to the wedding. An insult, as I see it. Even if he is dying. He never came to my last wedding either. He calls me the Late Lord Frey, you know. Does he think I'm dead? I'm not dead, and I promise you, I'll outlive him as I outlived his father. Your family has always pissed on me, don't deny it, don't lie, you know it's true. Years ago, I went to your father and suggested a match between his son and my daughter. Why not? I had a daughter in mind, sweet girl, only a few years older than Edmure, but if your brother didn't warm to her, I had others he might have had, young ones, old ones, virgins, widows, whatever he wanted. No, Lord Hoster would not hear of it. Sweet words he gave me, excuses, but what I *wanted* was to get rid of a daughter.

"And your sister, that one, she's full as bad. It was, oh, a year ago, no more, Jon Arryn was still the King's Hand, and I went to the city to see my sons ride in the tourney. Stevron and Jared are too old for the lists now, but Danwell and Hosteen rode, Perwyn as well, and a couple of my bastards tried the melee. If I'd known how they'd shame me, I would never have troubled myself to make the journey. Why did I need to ride all that way to see Hosteen knocked off his horse by that Tyrell whelp? I ask you. The boy's half his age, Ser Daisy they call him, something like that. And Danwell was unhorsed by a hedge knight! Some days I wonder if those two are truly mine. My third wife was a Crakehall, all of the Crakehall women are sluts. Well, never mind about that, she died before you were born, what do you care?

"I was speaking of your sister. I proposed that Lord and Lady Arryn foster two of my grandsons at court, and offered to take their own son to ward here at the Twins. Are my grandsons unworthy to be seen at the king's court? They are sweet boys, quiet and mannerly. Walder is Merrett's son, named after me, and the other one . . . *heh*, I don't recall . . . he might have been another Walder, they're always naming them Walder so I'll favor them, but his father . . . which one was his father now?" His face wrinkled up. "Well, whoever he was, Lord Arryn wouldn't have him, or the other one, and I blame your lady sister for that. She frosted up as if I'd suggested selling her boy to a mummer's show or making a eunuch out of him, and when Lord Arryn said the child was going to Dragonstone to foster with Stannis Baratheon, she stormed off without a word of regrets and all the Hand could give me was apologies. What good are apologies? I ask you."

Catelyn frowned, disquieted. "I had understood that Lysa's boy was to be fostered with Lord Tywin at Casterly Rock."

"No, it was Lord Stannis," Walder Frey said irritably. "Do you think I can't tell Lord Stannis from Lord Tywin? They're both bungholes who think they're too noble to shit, but never mind about that, I know the difference. Or do you think I'm so old I can't remember? I'm ninety and I remember very well. I remember what to do with a woman too. That wife of mine will give me a son before this time next year, I'll wager. Or a daughter, that can't be helped. Boy or girl, it will be red, wrinkled, and squalling, and like as not she'll want to name it Walder or Walda."

Catelyn was not concerned with what Lady Frey might choose to name her child. "Jon Arryn was going to foster his son with Lord Stannis, you are quite certain of that?"

"Yes, yes, yes," the old man said. "Only he died, so what does it matter? You say you want to cross the river?"

"We do."

"Well, you can't!" Lord Walder announced crisply. "Not unless I allow it, and why should I? The Tullys and the Starks have never been friends of mine." He pushed himself back in his chair and crossed his arms, smirking, waiting for her answer.

The rest was only haggling.

A swollen red sun hung low against the western hills when the gates of the castle opened. The drawbridge creaked down, the portcullis winched up, and Lady Catelyn Stark rode forth to rejoin her son and his lords bannermen. Behind her came Ser Jared Frey, Ser Hosteen Frey, Ser Danwell Frey, and Lord Walder's bastard son Ronel Rivers, leading a long column of pikemen, rank on rank of shuffling men in blue steel ringmail and silvery grey cloaks.

Robb galloped out to meet her, with Grey Wind racing beside his stallion. "It's done," she told him. "Lord

Walder will grant you your crossing. His swords are yours as well, less four hundred he means to keep back to hold the Twins. I suggest that you leave four hundred of your own, a mixed force of archers and swordsmen. He can scarcely object to an offer to augment his garrison . . . but make certain you give the command to a man you can trust. Lord Walder may need help keeping faith."

"As you say, Mother," Robb answered, gazing at the ranks of pikemen. "Perhaps . . . Ser Helman Tallhart, do you think?"

"A fine choice."

"What . . . what did he want of us?"

"If you can spare a few of your swords, I need some men to escort two of Lord Frey's grandsons north to Winterfell," she told him. "I have agreed to take them as wards. They are young boys, aged eight years and seven. It would seem they are both named Walder. Your brother Bran will welcome the companionship of lads near his own age, I should think."

"Is that all? Two fosterlings? That's a small enough price to—"

"Lord Frey's son Olyvar will be coming with us," she went on. "He is to serve as your personal squire. His father would like to see him knighted, in good time."

"A squire." He shrugged. "Fine, that's fine, if he's—"

"Also, if your sister Arya is returned to us safely, it is agreed that she will marry Lord Walder's youngest son, Elmar, when the two of them come of age."

Robb looked nonplussed. "Arya won't like that one bit."

"And you are to wed one of his daughters, once the fighting is done," she finished. "His lordship has graciously consented to allow you to choose whichever girl you prefer. He has a number he thinks might be suitable."

To his credit, Robb did not flinch. "I see."

"Do you consent?"

"Can I refuse?"

"Not if you wish to cross."

"I consent," Robb said solemnly. He had never seemed more manly to her than he did in that moment. Boys might play with swords, but it took a lord to make a marriage pact, knowing what it meant.

They crossed at evenfall as a horned moon floated

upon the river. The double column wound its way through the gate of the eastern twin like a great steel snake, slithering across the courtyard, into the keep and over the bridge, to issue forth once more from the second castle on the west bank.

Catelyn rode at the head of the serpent, with her son and her uncle Ser Brynden and Ser Stevron Frey. Behind followed nine tenths of their horse; knights, lancers, free-riders, and mounted bowmen. It took hours for them all to cross. Afterward, Catelyn would remember the clatter of countless hooves on the drawbridge, the sight of Lord Walder Frey in his litter watching them pass, the glitter of eyes peering down through the slats of the murder holes in the ceiling as they rode through the Water Tower.

The larger part of the northern host, pikes and archers and great masses of men-at-arms on foot, remained upon the east bank under the command of Roose Bolton. Robb had commanded him to continue the march south, to confront the huge Lannister army coming north under Lord Tywin.

For good or ill, her son had thrown the dice.

JON

"Are you well, Snow?" Lord Mormont asked, scowling.

"Well," his raven squawked. *"Well."*

"I am, my lord," Jon lied . . . loudly, as if that could make it true. "And you?"

Mormont frowned. "A dead man tried to kill me. How well could I be?" He scratched under his chin. His shaggy grey beard had been singed in the fire, and he'd hacked it off. The pale stubble of his new whiskers made him look old, disreputable, and grumpy. "You do not look well. How is your hand?"

"Healing." Jon flexed his bandaged fingers to show him. He had burned himself more badly than he knew throwing the flaming drapes, and his right hand was swathed in silk halfway to the elbow. At the time he'd felt nothing; the agony had come after. His cracked red skin oozed fluid, and fearsome blood blisters rose between his fingers, big as roaches. "The maester says I'll have scars, but otherwise the hand should be as good as it was before."

"A scarred hand is nothing. On the Wall, you'll be wearing gloves often as not."

"As you say, my lord." It was not the thought of scars that troubled Jon; it was the rest of it. Maester Aemon had given him milk of the poppy, yet even so, the pain had been hideous. At first it had felt as if his hand were still aflame, burning day and night. Only plunging it into basins of snow and shaved ice gave any relief at all. Jon thanked the gods that no one but Ghost saw him writhing on his bed, whimpering from the pain. And when at last he *did* sleep, he dreamt, and that was even worse. In the dream, the corpse he fought had blue eyes, black hands, and his father's face, but he dared not tell Mormont *that*.

"Dywen and Hake returned last night," the Old Bear said. "They found no sign of your uncle, no more than the others did."

"I know." Jon had dragged himself to the common hall to sup with his friends, and the failure of the rangers' search had been all the men had been talking of.

"You know," Mormont grumbled. "How is it that everyone knows everything around here?" He did not seem to expect an answer. "It would seem there were only the two of . . . of those *creatures*, whatever they were, I will not call them men. And thank the gods for that. Any more and . . . well, that doesn't bear thinking of. There will be more, though. I can feel it in these old bones of mine, and Maester Aemon agrees. The cold winds are rising. Summer is at an end, and a winter is coming such as this world has never seen."

Winter is coming. The Stark words had never sounded so grim or ominous to Jon as they did now. "My lord," he asked hesitantly, "it's said there was a bird last night . . ."

"There was. What of it?"

"I had hoped for some word of my father."

"Father," taunted the old raven, bobbing its head as it walked across Mormont's shoulders. *"Father."*

The Lord Commander reached up to pinch its beak shut, but the raven hopped up on his head, fluttered its wings, and flew across the chamber to light above a window. "Grief and noise," Mormont grumbled. "That's all they're good for, ravens. Why I put up with that pestilential bird . . . if there was news of Lord Eddard, don't you think I would have sent for you? Bastard or no, you're still his blood. The message concerned Ser Barristan Selmy. It seems he's been removed from the Kingsguard. They gave his place to that black dog Clegane, and now Selmy's wanted for treason. The fools sent some watchmen to seize him, but he slew two of them and escaped." Mormont snorted, leaving no doubt of his view of men who'd send gold cloaks against a knight as renowed as Barristan the Bold. "We have white shadows in the woods and unquiet dead stalking our halls, and a *boy* sits the Iron Throne," he said in disgust.

The raven laughed shrilly. *"Boy, boy, boy, boy."*

Ser Barristan had been the Old Bear's best hope, Jon remembered; if he had fallen, what chance was there that Mormont's letter would be heeded? He curled his hand into a fist. Pain shot through his burned fingers. "What of my sisters?"

"The message made no mention of Lord Eddard or the girls." He gave an irritated shrug. "Perhaps they never got my letter. Aemon sent two copies, with his best birds, but who can say? More like, Pycelle did not deign to reply. It would not be the first time, nor the last. I fear we count for less than nothing in King's Landing. They tell us what they want us to know, and that's little enough."

And you tell me *what you want* me *to know, and that's less,* Jon thought resentfully. His brother Robb had called the banners and ridden south to war, yet no word of that had been breathed to him . . . save by Samwell Tarly, who'd read the letter to Maester Aemon and whispered its contents to Jon that night in secret, all the time saying how he shouldn't. Doubtless they thought his brother's war was none of his concern. It troubled him more than he could say. Robb was marching and he was not. No matter how often Jon told himself that his place was here now, with his new brothers on the Wall, he still felt craven.

"Corn," the raven was crying. *"Corn, corn."*

"Oh, be quiet," the Old Bear told it. "Snow, how soon does Maester Aemon say you'll have use of that hand back?"

"Soon," Jon replied.

"Good." On the table between them, Lord Mormont laid a large sword in a black metal scabbard banded with silver. "Here. You'll be ready for this, then."

The raven flapped down and landed on the table, strutting toward the sword, head cocked curiously. Jon hesitated. He had no inkling what this meant. "My lord?"

"The fire melted the silver off the pommel and burnt the crossguard and grip. Well, dry leather and old wood, what could you expect? The blade, now . . . you'd need a fire a hundred times as hot to harm the blade." Mormont shoved the scabbard across the rough oak planks. "I had the rest made anew. Take it."

"*Take it,*" echoed his raven, preening. "*Take it, take it.*"

Awkwardly, Jon took the sword in hand. His *left* hand; his bandaged right was still too raw and clumsy. Carefully he pulled it from its scabbard and raised it level with his eyes.

The pommel was a hunk of pale stone weighted with lead to balance the long blade. It had been carved into the likeness of a snarling wolf's head, with chips of garnet set into the eyes. The grip was virgin leather, soft and black, as yet unstained by sweat or blood. The blade itself was a good half foot longer than those Jon was used to, tapered to thrust as well as slash, with three fullers deeply incised in the metal. Where Ice was a true two-handed greatsword, this was a hand-and-a-halfer, sometimes named a "bastard sword." Yet the wolf sword actually seemed lighter than the blades he had wielded before. When Jon turned it sideways, he could see the ripples in the dark steel where the metal had been folded back on itself again and again. "This is Valyrian steel, my lord," he said wonderingly. His father had let him handle Ice often enough; he knew the look, the feel.

"It is," the Old Bear told him. "It was my father's sword, and his father's before him. The Mormonts have carried it for five centuries. I wielded it in my day and passed it on to my son when I took the black."

He is giving me his son's sword. Jon could scarcely believe it. The blade was exquisitely balanced. The edges glimmered faintly as they kissed the light. "Your son—"

"My son brought dishonor to House Mormont, but at least he had the grace to leave the sword behind when he fled. My sister returned it to my keeping, but the very sight of it reminded me of Jorah's shame, so I put it aside and thought no more of it until we found it in the ashes of my bedchamber. The original pommel was a bear's head, silver, yet so worn its features were all but indistinguishable. For you, I thought a white wolf more apt. One of our builders is a fair stonecarver."

When Jon had been Bran's age, he had dreamed of doing great deeds, as boys always did. The details of his feats changed with every dreaming, but quite often he imagined saving his father's life. Afterward Lord Eddard would declare that Jon had proved himself a true Stark, and place Ice in his hand. Even then he had known it was only a child's folly; no bastard could ever hope to wield a father's sword. Even the memory shamed him. What kind of man stole his own brother's birthright? *I have no right to this,* he thought, *no more than to Ice.* He twitched his burned fingers, feeling a throb of pain deep under the skin. "My lord, you honor me, but—"

"Spare me your *but*'s, boy," Lord Mormont interrupted. "I would not be sitting here were it not for you and that beast of yours. You fought bravely . . . and more to the point, you thought quickly. *Fire!* Yes, damn it. We ought to have known. We ought to have *remembered.* The Long Night has come before. Oh, eight thousand years is a good while, to be sure . . . yet if the Night's Watch does not remember, who will?"

"Who will," chimed the talkative raven. *"Who will."*

Truly, the gods had heard Jon's prayer that night; the fire had caught in the dead man's clothing and consumed him as if his flesh were candle wax and his bones old dry wood. Jon had only to close his eyes to see the thing staggering across the solar, crashing against the furniture and flailing at the flames. It was the face that haunted him most; surrounded by a nimbus of fire, hair blazing like straw, the dead flesh melting away and sloughing off its skull to reveal the gleam of bone beneath.

Whatever demonic force moved Othor had been driven out by the flames; the twisted thing they had found in the ashes had been no more than cooked meat and charred bone. Yet in his nightmare he faced it again . . . and this time the burning corpse wore Lord Eddard's features. It was his father's skin that burst and blackened, his father's eyes that ran liquid down his cheeks like jellied tears. Jon did not understand why that should be or what it might mean, but it frightened him more than he could say.

"A sword's small payment for a life," Mormont concluded. "Take it, I'll hear no more of it, is that understood?"

"Yes, my lord." The soft leather gave beneath Jon's fingers, as if the sword were molding itself to his grip already. He knew he should be honored, and he was, and yet . . .

He is not my father. The thought leapt unbidden to Jon's mind. *Lord Eddard Stark is my father. I will not forget him, no matter how many swords they give me.* Yet he could scarcely tell Lord Mormont that it was another man's sword he dreamt of . . .

"I want no courtesies either," Mormont said, "so thank me no thanks. Honor the steel with deeds, not words."

Jon nodded. "Does it have a name, my lord?"

"It did, once. Longclaw, it was called."

"Claw," the raven cried. *"Claw."*

"Longclaw is an apt name." Jon tried a practice cut. He was clumsy and uncomfortable with his left hand, yet even so the steel seemed to flow through the air, as if it had a will of its own. "Wolves have claws, as much as bears."

The Old Bear seemed pleased by that. "I suppose they do. You'll want to wear that over the shoulder, I imagine. It's too long for the hip, at least until you've put on a few inches. And you'll need to work at your two-handed strikes as well. Ser Endrew can show you some moves, when your burns have healed."

"Ser Endrew?" Jon did not know the name.

"Ser Endrew Tarth, a good man. He's on his way from the Shadow Tower to assume the duties of master-at-arms. Ser Alliser Thorne left yestermorn for Eastwatch-by-the-Sea."

Jon lowered the sword. "Why?" he said, stupidly.

Mormont snorted. "Because I *sent* him, why do you think? He's bringing the hand your Ghost tore off the end of Jafer Flowers's wrist. I have commanded him to take ship to King's Landing and lay it before this boy king. *That* should get young Joffrey's attention, I'd think . . . and Ser Alliser's a knight, highborn, anointed, with old friends at court, altogether harder to ignore than a glorified crow."

"Crow." Jon thought the raven sounded faintly indignant.

"As well," the Lord Commander continued, ignoring the bird's protest, "it puts a thousand leagues twixt him and you without it seeming a rebuke." He jabbed a finger up at Jon's face. "And don't think this means I approve of that nonsense in the common hall. Valor makes up for a fair amount of folly, but you're not a boy anymore, however many years you've seen. That's a man's sword you have there, and it will take a man to wield her. I'll expect you to act the part, henceforth."

"Yes, my lord." Jon slid the sword back into the silver-banded scabbard. If not the blade he would have chosen, it was nonetheless a noble gift, and freeing him from Alliser Thorne's malignance was nobler still.

The Old Bear scratched at his chin. "I had forgotten how much a new beard itches," he said. "Well, no help for that. Is that hand of yours healed enough to resume your duties?"

"Yes, my lord."

"Good. The night will be cold, I'll want hot spice wine. Find me a flagon of red, not too sour, and don't skimp on the spices. And tell Hobb that if he sends me boiled mutton again I'm like to boil *him.* That last haunch was grey. Even the bird wouldn't touch it." He stroked the raven's head with his thumb, and the bird made a contented *quork*ing sound. "Away with you. I've work to do."

The guards smiled at him from their niches as he wound his way down the turret stair, carrying the sword in his good hand. "Sweet steel," one man said. "You earned that, Snow," another told him. Jon made himself smile back at them, but his heart was not in it. He knew he should be pleased, yet he did not feel it. His hand ached, and the taste of anger was in his mouth, though he could not have said who he was angry with or why.

A half dozen of his friends were lurking outside when he left the King's Tower, where Lord Commander Mormont now made his residence. They'd hung a target on the granary doors, so they could seem to be honing their skills as archers, but he knew lurkers when he saw them. No sooner did he emerge than Pyp called out, "Well, come about, let's have a look."

"At what?" Jon said.

Toad sidled close. "Your rosy butt cheeks, what else?"

"The sword," Grenn stated. "We want to see the sword."

Jon raked them with an accusing look. "You knew."

Pyp grinned. "We're not all as dumb as Grenn."

"You are so," insisted Grenn. "You're dumber."

Halder gave an apologetic shrug. "I helped Pate carve the stone for the pommel," the builder said, "and your friend Sam bought the garnets in Mole's Town."

"We knew even before that, though," Grenn said. "Rudge has been helping Donal Noye in the forge. He was there when the Old Bear brought him the burnt blade."

"The *sword*!" Matt insisted. The others took up the chant. "The *sword*, the *sword*, the *sword*."

Jon unsheathed Longclaw and showed it to them, turning it this way and that so they could admire it. The bastard blade glittered in the pale sunlight, dark and deadly. "Valyrian steel," he declared solemnly, trying to sound as pleased and proud as he ought to have felt.

"I heard of a man who had a razor made of Valyrian steel," declared Toad. "He cut his head off trying to shave."

Pyp grinned. "The Night's Watch is thousands of years old," he said, "but I'll wager Lord Snow's the first brother ever honored for burning down the Lord Commander's Tower."

The others laughed, and even Jon had to smile. The fire he'd started had not, in truth, burned down that formidable stone tower, but it had done a fair job of gutting the interior of the top two floors, where the Old Bear had his chambers. No one seemed to mind that very much, since it had also destroyed Othor's murderous corpse.

The other wight, the one-handed thing that had once been a ranger named Jafer Flowers, had also been destroyed, cut near to pieces by a dozen swords . . . but not before it had slain Ser Jaremy Rykker and four other men. Ser Jaremy had finished the job of hacking its head off, yet had died all the same when the headless corpse pulled his own dagger from its sheath and buried it in his bowels. Strength and courage did not avail much against foemen who would not fall because they were already dead; even arms and armor offered small protection.

That grim thought soured Jon's fragile mood. "I need

to see Hobb about the Old Bear's supper," he announced brusquely, sliding Longclaw back into its scabbard. His friends meant well, but they did not understand. It was not their fault, truly; they had not had to face Othor, they had not seen the pale glow of those dead blue eyes, had not felt the cold of those dead black fingers. Nor did they know of the fighting in the riverlands. How could they hope to comprehend? He turned away from them abruptly and strode off, sullen. Pyp called after him, but Jon paid him no mind.

They had moved him back to his old cell in tumbledown Hardin's Tower after the fire, and it was there he returned. Ghost was curled up asleep beside the door, but he lifted his head at the sound of Jon's boots. The direwolf's red eyes were darker than garnets and wiser than men. Jon knelt, scratched his ear, and showed him the pommel of the sword. "Look. It's you."

Ghost sniffed at his carved stone likeness and tried a lick. Jon smiled. "You're the one deserves an honor," he told the wolf . . . and suddenly he found himself remembering how he'd found him, that day in the late summer snow. They had been riding off with the other pups, but Jon had heard a noise and turned back, and there he was, white fur almost invisible against the drifts. *He was all alone,* he thought, *apart from the others in the litter. He was different, so they drove him out.*

"Jon?" He looked up. Samwell Tarly stood rocking nervously on his heels. His cheeks were red, and he was wrapped in a heavy fur cloak that made him look ready for hibernation.

"Sam." Jon stood. "What is it? Do you want to see the sword?" If the others had known, no doubt Sam did too.

The fat boy shook his head. "I was heir to my father's blade once," he said mournfully. "Heartsbane. Lord Randyll let me hold it a few times, but it always scared me. It was Valyrian steel, beautiful but so sharp I was afraid I'd hurt one of my sisters. Dickon will have it now." He wiped sweaty hands on his cloak. "I . . . ah . . . Maester Aemon wants to see you."

It was not time for his bandages to be changed. Jon frowned suspiciously. "Why?" he demanded. Sam looked miserable. That was answer enough. "You told him, didn't you?" Jon said angrily. "You told him that you told me."

"I . . . he . . . Jon, I didn't want to . . . he asked . . . I mean . . . I think he *knew*, he sees things no one else sees . . ."

"He's *blind*," Jon pointed out forcefully, disgusted. "I can find the way myself." He left Sam standing there, openmouthed and quivering.

He found Maester Aemon up in the rookery, feeding the ravens. Clydas was with him, carrying a bucket of chopped meat as they shuffled from cage to cage. "Sam said you wanted me?"

The maester nodded. "I did indeed. Clydas, give Jon the bucket. Perhaps he will be kind enough to assist me." The hunched, pink-eyed brother handed Jon the bucket and scurried down the ladder. "Toss the meat into the cages," Aemon instructed him. "The birds will do the rest."

Jon shifted the bucket to his right hand and thrust his left down into the bloody bits. The ravens began to scream noisily and fly at the bars, beating at the metal with night-black wings. The meat had been chopped into pieces no larger than a finger joint. He filled his fist and tossed the raw red morsels into the cage, and the squawking and squabbling grew hotter. Feathers flew as two of the larger birds fought over a choice piece. Quickly Jon grabbed a second handful and threw it in after the first. "Lord Mormont's raven likes fruit and corn."

"He is a rare bird," the maester said. "Most ravens will eat grain, but they prefer flesh. It makes them strong, and I fear they relish the taste of blood. In that they are like men . . . and like men, not all ravens are alike."

Jon had nothing to say to that. He threw meat, wondering why he'd been summoned. No doubt the old man would tell him, in his own good time. Maester Aemon was not a man to be hurried.

"Doves and pigeons can also be trained to carry messages," the maester went on, "though the raven is a stronger flyer, larger, bolder, far more clever, better able to defend itself against hawks . . . yet ravens are black, and they eat the dead, so some godly men abhor them. Baelor the Blessed tried to replace all the ravens with doves, did you know?" The maester turned his white eyes on Jon, smiling. "The Night's Watch prefers ravens."

Jon's fingers were in the bucket, blood up to the wrist. "Dywen says the wildlings call us crows," he said uncertainly.

"The crow is the raven's poor cousin. They are both beggars in black, hated and misunderstood."

Jon wished he understood what they were talking about, and why. What did he care about ravens and doves? If the old man had something to say to him, why couldn't he just say it?

"Jon, did you ever wonder *why* the men of the Night's Watch take no wives and father no children?" Maester Aemon asked.

Jon shrugged. "No." He scattered more meat. The fingers of his left hand were slimy with blood, and his right throbbed from the weight of the bucket.

"So they will not love," the old man answered, "for love is the bane of honor, the death of duty."

That did not sound right to Jon, yet he said nothing. The maester was a hundred years old, and a high officer of the Night's Watch; it was not his place to contradict him.

The old man seemed to sense his doubts. "Tell me, Jon, if the day should ever come when your lord father must needs choose between honor on the one hand and those he loves on the other, what would he do?"

Jon hesitated. He wanted to say that Lord Eddard would never dishonor himself, not even for love, yet inside a small sly voice whispered, *He fathered a bastard, where was the honor in that? And your mother, what of his duty to her, he will not even say her name.* "He would do whatever was right," he said . . . ringingly, to make up for his hesitation. "No matter what."

"Then Lord Eddard is a man in ten thousand. Most of us are not so strong. What is honor compared to a woman's love? What is duty against the feel of a newborn son in your arms . . . or the memory of a brother's smile? Wind and words. Wind and words. We are only human, and the gods have fashioned us for love. That is our great glory, and our great tragedy.

"The men who formed the Night's Watch knew that only their courage shielded the realm from the darkness to the north. They knew they must have no divided loyalties to weaken their resolve. So they vowed they would have no wives nor children.

"Yet brothers they had, and sisters. Mothers who gave them birth, fathers who gave them names. They came from a hundred quarrelsome kingdoms, and they knew times may change, but men do not. So they pledged as well that the Night's Watch would take no part in the battles of the realms it guarded.

"They kept their pledge. When Aegon slew Black Harren and claimed his kingdom, Harren's brother was Lord Commander on the Wall, with ten thousand swords to hand. He did not march. In the days when the Seven Kingdoms *were* seven kingdoms, not a generation passed that three or four of them were not at war. The Watch took no part. When the Andals crossed the narrow sea and swept away the kingdoms of the First Men, the sons of the fallen kings held true to their vows and remained at their posts. So it has always been, for years beyond counting. Such is the price of honor.

"A craven can be as brave as any man, when there is nothing to fear. And we all do our duty, when there is no cost to it. How easy it seems then, to walk the path of honor. Yet soon or late in every man's life comes a day when it is *not* easy, a day when he must choose."

Some of the ravens were still eating, long stringy bits of meat dangling from their beaks. The rest seemed to be watching him. Jon could feel the weight of all those tiny black eyes. "And this is my day . . . is that what you're saying?"

Maester Aemon turned his head and *looked* at him with those dead white eyes. It was as if he were seeing right into his heart. Jon felt naked and exposed. He took the bucket in both hands and flung the rest of the slops through the bars. Strings of meat and blood flew everywhere, scattering the ravens. They took to the air, shrieking wildly. The quicker birds snatched morsels on the wing and gulped them down greedily. Jon let the empty bucket clang to the floor.

The old man laid a withered, spotted hand on his shoulder. "It hurts, boy," he said softly. "Oh, yes. Choosing . . . it has always hurt. And always will. I know."

"You *don't* know," Jon said bitterly. "No one knows. Even if I am his bastard, he's still my *father* . . ."

Maester Aemon sighed. "Have you heard nothing I've told you, Jon? Do you think you are the first?" He shook his ancient head, a gesture weary beyond words. "Three times the gods saw fit to test my vows. Once when I was a boy, once in the fullness of my manhood, and once when I had grown old. By then my strength was fled, my eyes grown dim, yet that last choice was as cruel as the first. My ravens would bring the news from the south, words darker than their wings, the ruin of my House, the death of my kin, disgrace and desolation. What could I have done, old, blind, frail? I was helpless as a suckling babe, yet still it grieved me to sit forgotten as they cut down my brother's poor grandson, and *his* son, and even the little children . . ."

Jon was shocked to see the shine of tears in the old man's eyes. "Who are you?" he asked quietly, almost in dread.

A toothless smile quivered on the ancient lips. "Only a maester of the Citadel, bound in service to Castle Black and the Night's Watch. In my order, we put aside our house names when we take our vows and don the collar." The old man touched the maester's chain that hung loosely around his thin, fleshless neck. "My father was Maekar, the First of his Name, and my brother Aegon reigned after him in my stead. My grandfather named me for Prince Aemon the Dragonknight, who was his uncle, or his father, depending on which tale you believe. Aemon, he called me . . ."

"Aemon . . . *Targaryen?*" Jon could scarcely believe it.

"Once," the old man said. "Once. So you see, Jon, I *do* know . . . and knowing, I will not tell you *stay* or *go.* You must make that choice yourself, and live with it all the rest of your days. As I have." His voice fell to a whisper. "As I have . . ."

DAENERYS

When the battle was done, Dany rode her silver through the fields of the dead. Her handmaids and the men of her *khas* came after, smiling and jesting among themselves.

Dothraki hooves had torn the earth and trampled the rye and lentils into the ground, while *arakhs* and arrows had sown a terrible new crop and watered it with blood. Dying horses lifted their heads and screamed at her as she rode past. Wounded men moaned and prayed. *Jaqqa rhan* moved among them, the mercy men with their heavy axes, taking a harvest of heads from the dead and dying alike. After them would scurry a flock of small girls, pulling arrows from the corpses to fill their baskets. Last of all the dogs would come sniffing, lean and hungry, the feral pack that was never far behind the *khalasar*.

The sheep had been dead longest. There seemed to be thousands of them, black with flies, arrow shafts bristling from each carcass. Khal Ogo's riders had done that, Dany knew; no man of Drogo's *khalasar* would be such a fool as to waste his arrows on sheep when there were shepherds yet to kill.

The town was afire, black plumes of smoke roiling and

tumbling as they rose into a hard blue sky. Beneath broken walls of dried mud, riders galloped back and forth, swinging their long whips as they herded the survivors from the smoking rubble. The women and children of Ogo's *khalasar* walked with a sullen pride, even in defeat and bondage; they were slaves now, but they seemed not to fear it. It was different with the townsfolk. Dany pitied them; she remembered what terror felt like. Mothers stumbled along with blank, dead faces, pulling sobbing children by the hand. There were only a few men among them, cripples and cowards and grandfathers.

Ser Jorah said the people of this country named themselves the Lhazareen, but the Dothraki called them *haesh rakhi*, the Lamb Men. Once Dany might have taken them for Dothraki, for they had the same copper skin and almond-shaped eyes. Now they looked alien to her, squat and flat-faced, their black hair cropped unnaturally short. They were herders of sheep and eaters of vegetables, and Khal Drogo said they belonged south of the river bend. The grass of the Dothraki sea was not meant for sheep.

Dany saw one boy bolt and run for the river. A rider cut him off and turned him, and the others boxed him in, cracking their whips in his face, running him this way and that. One galloped behind him, lashing him across the buttocks until his thighs ran red with blood. Another snared his ankle with a lash and sent him sprawling. Finally, when the boy could only crawl, they grew bored of the sport and put an arrow through his back.

Ser Jorah met her outside the shattered gate. He wore a dark green surcoat over his mail. His gauntlets, greaves, and greathelm were dark grey steel. The Dothraki had mocked him for a coward when he donned his armor, but the knight had spit insults right back in their teeth, tempers had flared, longsword had clashed with *arakh*, and the rider whose taunts had been loudest had been left behind to bleed to death.

Ser Jorah lifted the visor of his flat-topped greathelm as he rode up. "Your lord husband awaits you within the town."

"Drogo took no harm?"

"A few cuts," Ser Jorah answered, "nothing of consequence. He slew two *khals* this day. Khal Ogo first, and then the son, Fogo, who became *khal* when Ogo fell. His bloodriders cut the bells from their hair, and now Khal Drogo's every step rings louder than before."

Ogo and his son had shared the high bench with her lord husband at the naming feast where Viserys had been crowned, but that was in Vaes Dothrak, beneath the Mother of Mountains, where every rider was a brother and all quarrels were put aside. It was different out in the grass. Ogo's *khalasar* had been attacking the town when Khal Drogo caught him. She wondered what the Lamb Men had thought, when they first saw the dust of their horses from atop those cracked-mud walls. Perhaps a few, the younger and more foolish who still believed that the gods heard the prayers of desperate men, took it for deliverance.

Across the road, a girl no older than Dany was sobbing in a high thin voice as a rider shoved her over a pile of corpses, facedown, and thrust himself inside her. Other riders dismounted to take their turns. That was the sort of deliverance the Dothraki brought the Lamb Men.

I am the blood of the dragon, Daenerys Targaryen reminded herself as she turned her face away. She pressed her lips together and hardened her heart and rode on toward the gate.

"Most of Ogo's riders fled," Ser Jorah was saying. "Still, there may be as many as ten thousand captives."

Slaves, Dany thought. Khal Drogo would drive them downriver to one of the towns on Slaver's Bay. She wanted to cry, but she told herself that she must be strong. *This is war, this is what it looks like, this is the price of the Iron Throne.*

"I've told the *khal* he ought to make for Meereen," Ser Jorah said. "They'll pay a better price than he'd get from a slaving caravan. Illyrio writes that they had a plague last year, so the brothels are paying double for healthy young girls, and triple for boys under ten. If enough children survive the journey, the gold will buy us all the ships we need, and hire men to sail them."

Behind them, the girl being raped made a heartrending sound, a long sobbing wail that went on and on and on. Dany's hand clenched hard around the reins, and she turned the silver's head. "Make them stop," she commanded Ser Jorah.

"*Khaleesi?*" The knight sounded perplexed.

"You heard my words," she said. "Stop them." She spoke to her *khas* in the harsh accents of Dothraki. "Jhogo, Quaro, you will aid Ser Jorah. I want no rape."

The warriors exchanged a baffled look.

Jorah Mormont spurred his horse closer. "Princess," he said, "you have a gentle heart, but you do not understand. This is how it has always been. Those men have shed blood for the *khal.* Now they claim their reward."

Across the road, the girl was still crying, her high sing-song tongue strange to Dany's ears. The first man was done with her now, and a second had taken his place.

"She is a lamb girl," Quaro said in Dothraki. "She is nothing, *Khaleesi.* The riders do her honor. The Lamb Men lay with sheep, it is known."

"It is known," her handmaid Irri echoed.

"It is known," agreed Jhogo, astride the tall grey stallion that Drogo had given him. "If her wailing offends your ears, *Khaleesi,* Jhogo will bring you her tongue." He drew his *arakh.*

"I will not have her harmed," Dany said. "I claim her. Do as I command you, or Khal Drogo will know the reason why."

"*Ai, Khaleesi,*" Jhogo replied, kicking his horse. Quaro and the others followed his lead, the bells in their hair chiming.

"Go with them," she commanded Ser Jorah.

"As you command." The knight gave her a curious look. "You are your brother's sister, in truth."

"Viserys?" She did not understand.

"No," he answered. "Rhaegar." He galloped off.

Dany heard Jhogo shout. The rapers laughed at him. One man shouted back. Jhogo's *arakh* flashed, and the man's head went tumbling from his shoulders. Laughter turned to curses as the horsemen reached for weapons, but by then Quaro and Aggo and Rakharo were there. She saw Aggo point across the road to where she sat upon her silver. The riders looked at her with cold black eyes. One spat. The others scattered to their mounts, muttering.

All the while the man atop the lamb girl continued to plunge in and out of her, so intent on his pleasure that he seemed unaware of what was going on around him. Ser Jorah dismounted and wrenched him off with a mailed hand. The Dothraki went sprawling in the mud, bounced up with a knife in hand, and died with Aggo's arrow through his throat. Mormont pulled the girl off the pile of corpses and wrapped her in his blood-spattered cloak. He led her across the road to Dany. "What do you want done with her?"

The girl was trembling, her eyes wide and vague. Her hair was matted with blood. "Doreah, see to her hurts. You do not have a rider's look, perhaps she will not fear you. The rest, with me." She urged the silver through the broken wooden gate.

It was worse inside the town. Many of the houses were afire, and the *jaqqa rhan* had been about their grisly work. Headless corpses filled the narrow, twisty lanes. They passed other women being raped. Each time Dany reined up, sent her *khas* to make an end to it, and claimed the victim as slave. One of them, a thick-bodied, flat-nosed woman of forty years, blessed Dany haltingly in the Common Tongue, but from the others she got only flat black stares. They were suspicious of her, she realized with sadness; afraid that she had saved them for some worse fate.

"You cannot claim them all, child," Ser Jorah said, the fourth time they stopped, while the warriors of her *khas* herded her new slaves behind her.

"I am *khaleesi*, heir to the Seven Kingdoms, the blood of the dragon," Dany reminded him. "It is not for you to tell me what I cannot do." Across the city, a building collapsed in a great gout of fire and smoke, and she heard distant screams and the wailing of frightened children.

They found Khal Drogo seated before a square window-less temple with thick mud walls and a bulbous dome like some immense brown onion. Beside him was a pile of heads taller than he was. One of the short arrows of the Lamb Men stuck through the meat of his upper arm, and blood covered the left side of his bare chest like a splash of paint. His three bloodriders were with him.

Jhiqui helped Dany dismount; she had grown clumsy as her belly grew larger and heavier. She knelt before the *khal*. "My sun-and-stars is wounded." The *arakh* cut was wide but shallow; his left nipple was gone, and a flap of bloody flesh and skin dangled from his chest like a wet rag.

"Is scratch, moon of life; from *arakh* of one bloodrider

to Khal Ogo," Khal Drogo said in the Common Tongue. "I kill him for it, and Ogo too." He turned his head, the bells in his braid ringing softly. "Is Ogo you hear, and Fogo his *khalakka*, who was *khal* when I slew him."

"No man can stand before the sun of my life," Dany said, "the father of the stallion who mounts the world."

A mounted warrior rode up and vaulted from his saddle. He spoke to Haggo, a stream of angry Dothraki too fast for Dany to understand. The huge bloodrider gave her a heavy look before he turned to his *khal.* "This one is Mago, who rides in the *khas* of Ko Jhaqo. He says the *khaleesi* has taken his spoils, a daughter of the lambs who was his to mount."

Khal Drogo's face was still and hard, but his black eyes were curious as they went to Dany. "Tell me the truth of this, moon of my life," he commanded in Dothraki.

Dany told him what she had done, in his own tongue so the *khal* would understand her better, her words simple and direct.

When she was done, Drogo was frowning. "This is the way of war. These women are our slaves now, to do with as we please."

"It pleases me to hold them safe," Dany said, wondering if she had dared too much. "If your warriors would mount these women, let them take them gently and keep them for wives. Give them places in the *khalasar* and let them bear you sons."

Qotho was ever the cruelest of the bloodriders. It was he who laughed. "Does the horse breed with the sheep?"

Something in his tone reminded her of Viserys. Dany turned on him angrily. "The dragon feeds on horse and sheep alike."

Khal Drogo smiled. "See how fierce she grows!" he said. "It is my son inside her, the stallion who mounts the world, filling her with his fire. Ride slowly, Qotho . . . if the mother does not burn you where you sit, the son will trample you into the mud. And you, Mago, hold your tongue and find another lamb to mount. These belong to my *khaleesi*." He started to reach out a hand to Daenerys, but as he lifted his arm Drogo grimaced in sudden pain and turned his head.

Dany could almost feel his agony. The wounds were worse than Ser Jorah had led her to believe. "Where are the healers?" she demanded. The *khalasar* had two sorts: barren women and eunuch slaves. The herbwomen dealt in potions and spells, the eunuchs in knife, needle, and fire. "Why do they not attend the *khal*?"

"The *khal* sent the hairless men away, *Khaleesi*," old Cohollo assured her. Dany saw the bloodrider had taken a wound himself; a deep gash in his left shoulder.

"Many riders are hurt," Khal Drogo said stubbornly. "Let them be healed first. This arrow is no more than the bite of a fly, this little cut only a new scar to boast of to my son."

Dany could see the muscles in his chest where the skin had been cut away. A trickle of blood ran from the arrow that pierced his arm. "It is not for Khal Drogo to wait," she proclaimed. "Jhogo, seek out these eunuchs and bring them here at once."

"Silver Lady," a woman's voice said behind her, "I can help the Great Rider with his hurts."

Dany turned her head. The speaker was one of the slaves she had claimed, the heavy, flat-nosed woman who had blessed her.

"The *khal* needs no help from women who lie with sheep," barked Qotho. "Aggo, cut out her tongue."

Aggo grabbed her hair and pressed a knife to her throat. Dany lifted a hand. "No. She is mine. Let her speak."

Aggo looked from her to Qotho. He lowered his knife.

"I meant no wrong, fierce riders." The woman spoke Dothraki well. The robes she wore had once been the lightest and finest of woolens, rich with embroidery, but now they were mud-caked and bloody and ripped. She clutched the torn cloth of her bodice to her heavy breasts. "I have some small skill in the healing arts."

"Who are you?" Dany asked her.

"I am named Mirri Maz Duur. I am godswife of this temple."

"*Maegi*," grunted Haggo, fingering his *arakh*. His look was dark. Dany remembered the word from a terrifying story that Jhiqui had told her one night by the cookfire. A *maegi* was a woman who lay with demons and practiced the blackest of sorceries, a vile thing, evil and soulless, who came to men in the dark of night and sucked life and strength from their bodies.

"I am a healer," Mirri Maz Duur said.

"A healer of sheeps," sneered Qotho. "Blood of my blood, I say kill this *maegi* and wait for the hairless men."

Dany ignored the bloodrider's outburst. This old, homely, thick-bodied woman did not look like a *maegi* to her. "Where did you learn your healing, Mirri Maz Duur?"

"My mother was godswife before me, and taught me all the songs and spells most pleasing to the Great Shepherd, and how to make the sacred smokes and ointments from leaf and root and berry. When I was younger and more fair, I went in caravan to Asshai by the Shadow, to learn from their mages. Ships from many lands come to Asshai, so I lingered long to study the healing ways of distant peoples. A moonsinger of the Jogos Nhai gifted me with her birthing songs, a woman of your own riding people taught me the magics of grass and corn and horse, and a maester from the Sunset Lands opened a body for me and showed me all the secrets that hide beneath the skin."

Ser Jorah Mormont spoke up. "A maester?"

"Marwyn, he named himself," the woman replied in the Common Tongue. "From the sea. Beyond the sea. The Seven Lands, he said. Sunset Lands. Where men are iron and dragons rule. He taught me this speech."

"A maester in Asshai," Ser Jorah mused. "Tell me, Godswife, what did this Marwyn wear about his neck?"

"A chain so tight it was like to choke him, Iron Lord, with links of many metals."

The knight looked at Dany. "Only a man trained in the Citadel of Oldtown wears such a chain," he said, "and such men do know much of healing."

"Why should you want to help my *khal*?"

"All men are one flock, or so we are taught," replied Mirri Maz Duur. "The Great Shepherd sent me to earth to heal his lambs, wherever I might find them."

Qotho gave her a stinging slap. "We are no sheep, *maegi*."

"Stop it," Dany said angrily. "She is mine. I will not have her harmed."

Khal Drogo grunted. "The arrow must come out, Qotho."

"Yes, Great Rider," Mirri Maz Duur answered, touching her bruised face. "And your breast must be washed and sewn, lest the wound fester."

"Do it, then," Khal Drogo commanded.

"Great Rider," the woman said, "my tools and potions are inside the god's house, where the healing powers are strongest."

"I will carry you, blood of my blood," Haggo offered.

Khal Drogo waved him away. "I need no man's help," he said, in a voice proud and hard. He stood, unaided, towering over them all. A fresh wave of blood ran down his breast, from where Ogo's *arakh* had cut off his nipple. Dany moved quickly to his side. "I am no man," she whispered, "so you may lean on me." Drogo put a huge hand on her shoulder. She took some of his weight as they walked toward the great mud temple. The three blood-riders followed. Dany commanded Ser Jorah and the warriors of her *khas* to guard the entrance and make certain no one set the building afire while they were still inside.

They passed through a series of anterooms, into the high central chamber under the onion. Faint light shone down through hidden windows above. A few torches burnt smokily from sconces on the walls. Sheepskins were scattered across the mud floor. "There," Mirri Maz Duur said, pointing to the altar, a massive blue-veined stone carved with images of shepherds and their flocks. Khal Drogo lay upon it. The old woman threw a handful of dried leaves onto a brazier, filling the chamber with fragrant smoke. "Best if you wait outside," she told the rest of them.

"We are blood of his blood," Cohollo said. "Here we wait."

Qotho stepped close to Mirri Maz Duur. "Know this, wife of the Lamb God. Harm the *khal* and you suffer the same." He drew his skinning knife and showed her the blade.

"She will do no harm." Dany felt she could trust this old, plain-faced woman with her flat nose; she had saved her from the hard hands of her rapers, after all.

"If you must stay, then help," Mirri told the blood-riders. "The Great Rider is too strong for me. Hold him still while I draw the arrow from his flesh." She let the rags of her gown fall to her waist as she opened a carved chest, and busied herself with bottles and boxes, knives

and needles. When she was ready, she broke off the barbed
arrowhead and pulled out the shaft, chanting in the sing-
song tongue of the Lhazareen. She heated a flagon of wine
to boiling on the brazier, and poured it over his wounds.
Khal Drogo cursed her, but he did not move. She bound
the arrow wound with a plaster of wet leaves and turned
to the gash on his breast, smearing it with a pale green
paste before she pulled the flap of skin back in place. The
khal ground his teeth together and swallowed a scream.
The godswife took out a silver needle and a bobbin of silk
thread and began to close the flesh. When she was done
she painted the skin with red ointment, covered it with
more leaves, and bound the breast in a ragged piece of
lambskin. "You must say the prayers I give you and keep
the lambskin in place for ten days and ten nights," she
said. "There will be fever, and itching, and a great scar
when the healing is done."

Khal Drogo sat, bells ringing. "I sing of my scars, sheep
woman." He flexed his arm and scowled.

"Drink neither wine nor the milk of the poppy," she
cautioned him. "Pain you will have, but you must keep
your body strong to fight the poison spirits."

"I am *khal*," Drogo said. "I spit on pain and drink what
I like. Cohollo, bring my vest." The older man hastened
off.

"Before," Dany said to the ugly Lhazareen woman, "I
heard you speak of birthing songs . . ."

"I know every secret of the bloody bed, Silver Lady,
nor have I ever lost a babe," Mirri Maz Duur replied.

"My time is near," Dany said. "I would have you attend me when he comes, if you would."

Khal Drogo laughed. "Moon of my life, you do not ask
a slave, you tell her. She will do as you command." He
jumped down from the altar. "Come, my blood. The stallions call, this place is ashes. It is time to ride."

Haggo followed the *khal* from the temple, but Qotho
lingered long enough to favor Mirri Maz Duur with a
stare. "Remember, *maegi*, as the *khal* fares, so shall you."

"As you say, rider," the woman answered him, gathering up her jars and bottles. "The Great Shepherd guards
the flock."

TYRION

On a hill overlooking the kingsroad, a long trestle table of rough-hewn pine had been erected beneath an elm tree and covered with a golden cloth. There, beside his pavilion, Lord Tywin took his evening meal with his chief knights and lords bannermen, his great crimson-and-gold standard waving overhead from a lofty pike.

Tyrion arrived late, saddlesore, and sour, all too vividly aware of how amusing he must look as he waddled up the slope to his father. The day's march had been long and tiring. He thought he might get quite drunk tonight. It was twilight, and the air was alive with drifting fireflies.

The cooks were serving the meat course: five suckling pigs, skin seared and crackling, a different fruit in every mouth. The smell made his mouth water. "My pardons," he began, taking his place on the bench beside his uncle.

"Perhaps I'd best charge you with burying our dead, Tyrion," Lord Tywin said. "If you are as late to battle as you are to table, the fighting will all be done by the time you arrive."

"Oh, surely you can save me a peasant or two, Father," Tyrion replied. "Not too many, I wouldn't want to be greedy." He filled his wine cup and watched a serving man carve into the pig. The crisp skin crackled under his knife, and hot juice ran from the meat. It was the loveliest sight Tyrion had seen in ages.

"Ser Addam's outriders say the Stark host has moved south from the Twins," his father reported as his trencher was filled with slices of pork. "Lord Frey's levies have joined them. They are likely no more than a day's march north of us."

"Please, Father," Tyrion said. "I'm about to eat."

"Does the thought of facing the Stark boy unman you, Tyrion? Your brother Jaime would be eager to come to grips with him."

"I'd sooner come to grips with that pig. Robb Stark is not half so tender, and he never smelled as good."

Lord Lefford, the sour bird who had charge of their stores and supplies, leaned forward. "I hope your savages do not share your reluctance, else we've wasted our good steel on them."

"My savages will put your steel to excellent use, my lord," Tyrion replied. When he had told Lefford he needed arms and armor to equip the three hundred men Ulf had fetched down out of the foothills, you would have thought he'd asked the man to turn his virgin daughters over to their pleasure.

Lord Lefford frowned. "I saw that great hairy one today, the one who insisted that he must have *two* battle-axes, the heavy black steel ones with twin crescent blades."

"Shagga likes to kill with either hand," Tyrion said as a trencher of steaming pork was laid in front of him.

"He still had that wood-axe of his strapped to his back."

"Shagga is of the opinion that three axes are even better than two." Tyrion reached a thumb and forefinger into the salt dish, and sprinkled a healthy pinch over his meat.

Ser Kevan leaned forward. "We had a thought to put you and your wildlings in the vanguard when we come to battle."

Ser Kevan seldom "had a thought" that Lord Tywin had not had first. Tyrion had skewered a chunk of meat on the point of his dagger and brought it to his mouth. Now he lowered it. "The vanguard?" he repeated dubiously. Either his lord father had a new respect for Tyrion's abilities, or he'd decided to rid himself of his embarrassing get for good. Tyrion had the gloomy feeling he knew which.

"They seem ferocious enough," Ser Kevan said.

"Ferocious?" Tyrion realized he was echoing his uncle like a trained bird. His father watched, judging him, weighing every word. "Let me tell you how ferocious they are. Last night, a Moon Brother stabbed a Stone Crow over a sausage. So today as we made camp three Stone Crows seized the man and opened his throat for him. Perhaps they were hoping to get the sausage back, I couldn't say. Bronn managed to keep Shagga from chopping off the dead man's cock, which was fortunate, but even so Ulf is demanding blood money, which Conn and Shagga refuse to pay."

"When soldiers lack discipline, the fault lies with their lord commander," his father said.

His brother Jaime had always been able to make men follow him eagerly, and die for him if need be. Tyrion lacked that gift. He bought loyalty with gold, and compelled obedience with his name. "A *bigger* man would be able to put the fear in them, is that what you're saying, my lord?"

Lord Tywin Lannister turned to his brother. "If my son's men will not obey his commands, perhaps the vanguard is not the place for him. No doubt he would be more comfortable in the rear, guarding our baggage train."

"Do me no kindnesses, Father," he said angrily. "If you have no other command to offer me, I'll lead your van."

Lord Tywin studied his dwarf son. "I said nothing about command. You will serve under Ser Gregor."

Tyrion took one bite of pork, chewed a moment, and spit it out angrily. "I find I am not hungry after all," he said, climbing awkwardly off the bench. "Pray excuse me, my lords."

Lord Tywin inclined his head, dismissing him. Tyrion turned and walked away. He was conscious of their eyes on his back as he waddled down the hill. A great gust of laughter went up from behind him, but he did not look back. He hoped they all choked on their suckling pigs.

Dusk had settled, turning all the banners black. The Lannister camp sprawled for miles between the river and the kingsroad. In amongst the men and the horses and the trees, it was easy to get lost, and Tyrion did. He passed a dozen great pavilions and a hundred cookfires. Fireflies drifted amongst the tents like wandering stars. He caught the scent of garlic sausage, spiced and savory, so tempting it made his empty stomach growl. Away in the distance, he heard voices raised in some bawdy song. A giggling woman raced past him, naked beneath a dark cloak, her drunken pursuer stumbling over tree roots. Farther on, two spearmen faced each other across a little trickle of a stream, practicing their thrust-and-parry in the fading light, their chests bare and slick with sweat.

No one looked at him. No one spoke to him. No one paid him any mind. He was surrounded by men sworn to House Lannister, a vast host twenty thousand strong, and yet he was alone.

When he heard the deep rumble of Shagga's laughter booming through the dark, he followed it to the Stone Crows in their small corner of the night. Conn son of Coratt waved a tankard of ale. "Tyrion Halfman! Come, sit by our fire, share meat with the Stone Crows. We have an ox."

"I can see that, Conn son of Coratt." The huge red carcass was suspended over a roaring fire, skewered on a spit the size of a small tree. No doubt it *was* a small tree. Blood and grease dripped down into the flames as two Stone Crows turned the meat. "I thank you. Send for me when the ox is cooked." From the look of it, that might even be before the battle. He walked on.

Each clan had its own cookfire; Black Ears did not eat with Stone Crows, Stone Crows did not eat with Moon Brothers, and no one ate with Burned Men. The modest tent he had coaxed out of Lord Lefford's stores had been erected in the center of the four fires. Tyrion found Bronn sharing a skin of wine with the new servants. Lord Tywin had sent him a groom and a body servant to see to his needs, and even insisted he take a squire. They were seated around the embers of a small cookfire. A girl was with them; slim, dark-haired, no more than eighteen by the look of her. Tyrion studied her face for a moment, before he spied fishbones in the ashes. "What did you eat?"

"Trout, m'lord," said his groom. "Bronn caught them."

Trout, he thought. *Suckling pig. Damn my father.* He stared mournfully at the bones, his belly rumbling.

His squire, a boy with the unfortunate name of Podrick Payne, swallowed whatever he had been about to say. The lad was a distant cousin to Ser Ilyn Payne, the king's headsman . . . and almost as quiet, although not for want of a tongue. Tyrion had made him stick it out once, just to be certain. "Definitely a tongue," he had said. "Someday you must learn to use it."

At the moment, he did not have the patience to try and coax a thought out of the lad, whom he suspected had been inflicted on him as a cruel jape. Tyrion turned his attention back to the girl. "Is this her?" he asked Bronn.

She rose gracefully and looked down at him from the lofty height of five feet or more. "It is, m'lord, and she can speak for herself, if it please you."

He cocked his head to one side. "I am Tyrion, of House Lannister. Men call me the Imp."

"My mother named me Shae. Men call me . . . often."

Bronn laughed, and Tyrion had to smile. "Into the tent, Shae, if you would be so kind." He lifted the flap and held it for her. Inside, he knelt to light a candle.

The life of a soldier was not without certain compensations. Wherever you have a camp, you are certain to have camp followers. At the end of the day's march, Tyrion had sent Bronn back to find him a likely whore. "I would prefer one who is reasonably young, with as pretty a face as you can find," he had said. "If she has washed sometime this year, I shall be glad. If she hasn't, wash her. Be certain that you tell her who I am, and warn her of *what* I am." Jyck had not always troubled to do that. There was a look the girls got in their eyes sometimes when they first beheld the lordling they'd been hired to pleasure . . . a look that Tyrion Lannister did not ever care to see again.

He lifted the candle and looked her over. Bronn had done well enough; she was doe-eyed and slim, with small firm breasts and a smile that was by turns shy, insolent, and wicked. He liked that. "Shall I take my gown off, m'lord?" she asked.

"In good time. Are you a maiden, Shae?"

"If it please you, m'lord," she said demurely.

"What would please me would be the truth of you, girl."

"Aye, but that will cost you double."

Tyrion decided they would get along splendidly. "I am a Lannister. Gold I have in plenty, and you'll find me generous . . . but I'll want more from you than what you've got between your legs, though I'll want that too. You'll share my tent, pour my wine, laugh at my jests, rub the ache from my legs after each day's ride . . . and whether I keep you a day or a year, for so long as we are together you will take no other men into your bed."

"Fair enough." She reached down to the hem of her thin roughspun gown and pulled it up over her head in one smooth motion, tossing it aside. There was nothing underneath but Shae. "If he don't put down that candle, m'lord will burn his fingers."

Tyrion put down the candle, took her hand in his, and pulled her gently to him. She bent to kiss him. Her mouth tasted of honey and cloves, and her fingers were deft and practiced as they found the fastenings of his clothes.

When he entered her, she welcomed him with whispered endearments and small, shuddering gasps of pleasure. Tyrion suspected her delight was feigned, but she did it so well that it did not matter. *That* much truth he did not crave.

He had needed her, Tyrion realized afterward, as she lay quietly in his arms. Her or someone like her. It had been nigh on a year since he'd lain with a woman, since before he had set out for Winterfell in company with his brother and King Robert. He could well die on the morrow or the day after, and if he did, he would sooner go to his grave thinking of Shae than of his lord father, Lysa Arryn, or the Lady Catelyn Stark.

He could feel the softness of her breasts pressed against his arm as she lay beside him. That was a good feeling. A song filled his head. Softly, quietly, he began to whistle.

"What's that, m'lord?" Shae murmured against him.

"Nothing," he told her. "A song I learned as a boy, that's all. Go to sleep, sweetling."

When her eyes were closed and her breathing deep and steady, Tyrion slid out from beneath her, gently, so as not to disturb her sleep. Naked, he crawled outside, stepped over his squire, and walked around behind his tent to make water.

Bronn was seated cross-legged under a chestnut tree, near where they'd tied the horses. He was honing the edge of his sword, wide awake; the sellsword did not seem to sleep like other men. "Where did you find her?" Tyrion asked him as he pissed.

"I took her from a knight. The man was loath to give her up, but your name changed his thinking somewhat . . . that, and my dirk at his throat."

"Splendid," Tyrion said dryly, shaking off the last drops. "I seem to recall saying *find me a whore*, not *make me an enemy*."

"The pretty ones were all claimed," Bronn said. "I'll be pleased to take her back if you'd prefer a toothless drab."

Tyrion limped closer to where he sat. "My lord father would call that insolence, and send you to the mines for impertinence."

"Good for me you're not your father," Bronn replied. "I saw one with boils all over her nose. Would you like her?"

"What, and break your heart?" Tyrion shot back. "I shall keep Shae. Did you perchance note the *name* of this knight you took her from? I'd rather not have him beside me in the battle."

Bronn rose, cat-quick and cat-graceful, turning his sword in his hand. "You'll have me beside you in the battle, dwarf."

Tyrion nodded. The night air was warm on his bare skin. "See that I survive this battle, and you can name your reward."

Bronn tossed the longsword from his right hand to his left, and tried a cut. "Who'd want to kill the likes of you?"

"My lord father, for one. He's put me in the van."

"I'd do the same. A small man with a big shield. You'll give the archers fits."

"I find you oddly cheering," Tyrion said. "I must be mad."

Bronn sheathed his sword. "Beyond a doubt."

When Tyrion returned to his tent, Shae rolled onto her elbow and murmured sleepily, "I woke and m'lord was gone."

"M'lord is back now." He slid in beside her.

Her hand went between his stunted legs, and found him hard. "Yes he is," she whispered, stroking him.

He asked her about the man Bronn had taken her from, and she named the minor retainer of an insignificant lordling. "You need not fear his like, m'lord," the girl said, her fingers busy at his cock. "He is a small man."

"And what am I, pray?" Tyrion asked her. "A giant?"

"Oh, yes," she purred, "my giant of Lannister." She mounted him then, and for a time, she almost made him believe it. Tyrion went to sleep smiling . . .

. . . and woke in darkness to the blare of trumpets. Shae was shaking him by the shoulder. "M'lord," she whispered. "Wake up, m'lord. I'm frightened."

Groggy, he sat up and threw back the blanket. The horns called through the night, wild and urgent, a cry that said *hurry hurry hurry.* He heard shouts, the clatter of spears, the whicker of horses, though nothing yet that spoke to him of fighting. "My lord father's trumpets," he said. "Battle assembly. I thought Stark was yet a day's march away."

Shae shook her head, lost. Her eyes were wide and white.

Groaning, Tyrion lurched to his feet and pushed his way outside, shouting for his squire. Wisps of pale fog drifted through the night, long white fingers off the river. Men and horses blundered through the predawn chill; saddles were being cinched, wagons loaded, fires extinguished. The trumpets blew again: *hurry hurry hurry.* Knights vaulted onto snorting coursers while men-at-arms buckled their sword belts as they ran. When he found Pod, the boy was snoring softly. Tyrion gave him a sharp poke in the ribs with his toe. "My armor," he said, "and be quick about it." Bronn came trotting out of the mists, already armored and ahorse, wearing his battered halfhelm. "Do you know what's happened?" Tyrion asked him.

"The Stark boy stole a march on us," Bronn said. "He crept down the kingsroad in the night, and now his host is less than a mile north of here, forming up in battle array."

Hurry, the trumpets called, *hurry hurry hurry.*

"See that the clansmen are ready to ride." Tyrion ducked back inside his tent. "Where are my clothes?" he barked at Shae. "There. No, the leather, damn it. Yes. Bring me my boots."

By the time he was dressed, his squire had laid out his armor, such that it was. Tyrion owned a fine suit of heavy plate, expertly crafted to fit his misshapen body. Alas, it was safe at Casterly Rock, and he was not. He had to make do with oddments assembled from Lord Lefford's wagons: mail hauberk and coif, a dead knight's gorget, lobstered greaves and gauntlets and pointed steel boots. Some of it was ornate, some plain; not a bit of it matched, or fit as it should. His breastplate was meant for a bigger man; for his oversize head, they found a huge bucket-shaped greathelm topped with a foot-long triangular spike.

Shae helped Pod with the buckles and clasps. "If I die, weep for me," Tyrion told the whore.

"How will you know? You'll be dead."

"I'll know."

"I believe you would." Shae lowered the greathelm down over his head, and Pod fastened it to his gorget. Tyrion buckled on his belt, heavy with the weight of shortsword and dirk. By then his groom had brought up his mount, a formidable brown courser armored as heavily as he was. He needed help to mount; he felt as though he weighed a thousand stone. Pod handed him up his shield, a massive slab of heavy ironwood banded with steel. Lastly they gave him his battle-axe. Shae stepped back and looked him over. "M'lord looks fearsome."

"M'lord looks a dwarf in mismatched armor," Tyrion answered sourly, "but I thank you for the kindness. Podrick, should the battle go against us, see the lady safely home." He saluted her with his axe, wheeled his horse about, and trotted off. His stomach was a hard knot, so tight it pained him. Behind, his servants hurriedly began to strike his tent. Pale crimson fingers fanned out to the east as the first rays of the sun broke over the horizon. The western sky was a deep purple, speckled with stars. Tyrion wondered whether this was the last sunrise he would ever see . . . and whether wondering was a mark of cowardice. Did his brother Jaime ever contemplate death before a battle?

A warhorn sounded in the far distance, a deep mournful note that chilled the soul. The clansmen climbed onto their scrawny mountain horses, shouting curses and rude jokes. Several appeared to be drunk. The rising sun was burning off the drifting tendrils of fog as Tyrion led them off. What grass the horses had left was heavy with dew, as if some passing god had scattered a bag of diamonds over the earth. The mountain men fell in behind him, each clan arrayed behind its own leaders.

In the dawn light, the army of Lord Tywin Lannister unfolded like an iron rose, thorns gleaming.

His uncle would lead the center. Ser Kevan had raised his standards above the kingsroad. Quivers hanging from their belts, the foot archers arrayed themselves into three long lines, to east and west of the road, and stood calmly stringing their bows. Between them, pikemen formed squares; behind were rank on rank of men-at-arms with spear and sword and axe. Three hundred heavy horse surrounded Ser Kevan and the lords bannermen Lefford, Lydden, and Serrett with all their sworn retainers.

The right wing was all cavalry, some four thousand men, heavy with the weight of their armor. More than three quarters of the knights were there, massed together like a great steel fist. Ser Addam Marbrand had the command. Tyrion saw his banner unfurl as his standard-bearer shook it out; a burning tree, orange and smoke. Behind him flew Ser Flement's purple unicorn, the brindled boar of Crakehall, the bantam rooster of Swyft, and more.

His lord father took his place on the hill where he had slept. Around him, the reserve assembled; a huge force, half mounted and half foot, five thousand strong. Lord Tywin almost always chose to command the reserve; he would take the high ground and watch the battle unfold below him, committing his forces when and where they were needed most.

Even from afar, his lord father was resplendent. Tywin Lannister's battle armor put his son Jaime's gilded suit to shame. His greatcloak was sewn from countless layers of cloth-of-gold, so heavy that it barely stirred even when he charged, so large that its drape covered most of his stallion's hindquarters when he took the saddle. No ordinary clasp would suffice for such a weight, so the greatcloak was held in place by a matched pair of miniature lionesses crouching on his shoulders, as if poised to spring. Their mate, a male with a magnificent mane, reclined atop Lord

Tywin's greathelm, one paw raking the air as he roared. All three lions were wrought in gold, with ruby eyes. His armor was heavy steel plate, enameled in a dark crimson, greaves and gauntlets inlaid with ornate gold scrollwork. His rondels were golden sunbursts, all his fastenings were gilded, and the red steel was burnished to such a high sheen that it shone like fire in the light of the rising sun.

Tyrion could hear the rumble of the foemen's drums now. He remembered Robb Stark as he had last seen him, in his father's high seat in the Great Hall of Winterfell, a sword naked and shining in his hands. He remembered how the direwolves had come at him out of the shadows, and suddenly he could see them again, snarling and snapping, teeth bared in his face. Would the boy bring his wolves to war with him? The thought made him uneasy.

The northerners would be exhausted after their long sleepless march. Tyrion wondered what the boy had been thinking. Did he think to take them unawares while they slept? Small chance of that; whatever else might be said of him, Tywin Lannister was no man's fool.

The van was massing on the left. He saw the standard first, three black dogs on a yellow field. Ser Gregor sat beneath it, mounted on the biggest horse Tyrion had ever seen. Bronn took one look at him and grinned. "Always follow a big man into battle."

Tyrion threw him a hard look. "And why is that?"

"They make such splendid targets. That one, he'll draw the eyes of every bowman on the field."

Laughing, Tyrion regarded the Mountain with fresh eyes. "I confess, I had not considered it in that light."

Clegane had no splendor about him; his armor was steel plate, dull grey, scarred by hard use and showing neither sigil nor ornament. He was pointing men into position with his blade, a two-handed greatsword that Ser Gregor waved about with one hand as a lesser man might wave a dagger. "Any man runs, I'll cut him down myself," he was roaring when he caught sight of Tyrion. "Imp! Take the left. Hold the river. If you can."

The left of the left. To turn their flank, the Starks would need horses that could run on water. Tyrion led his men toward the riverbank. "Look," he shouted, pointing with his axe. "The river." A blanket of pale mist still clung to the surface of the water, the murky green current swirling past underneath. The shallows were muddy and choked with reeds. "That river is ours. Whatever happens, keep close to the water. Never lose sight of it. Let no enemy come between us and our river. If they dirty our waters, hack off their cocks and feed them to the fishes."

Shagga had an axe in either hand. He smashed them together and made them ring. *"Halfman!"* he shouted. Other Stone Crows picked up the cry, and the Black Ears and Moon Brothers as well. The Burned Men did not shout, but they rattled their swords and spears. *"Halfman! Halfman! Halfman!"*

Tyrion turned his courser in a circle to look over the field. The ground was rolling and uneven here; soft and muddy near the river, rising in a gentle slope toward the kingsroad, stony and broken beyond it, to the east. A few trees spotted the hillsides, but most of the land had been cleared and planted. His heart pounded in his chest in time to the drums, and under his layers of leather and steel his brow was cold with sweat. He watched Ser Gregor as the Mountain rode up and down the line, shouting and gesticulating. This wing too was all cavalry, but where the right was a mailed fist of knights and heavy lancers, the vanguard was made up of the sweepings of the west: mounted archers in leather jerkins, a swarming mass of undisciplined freeriders and sellswords, field-hands on plow horses armed with scythes and their fathers' rusted swords, half-trained boys from the stews of Lannisport . . . and Tyrion and his mountain clansmen.

"Crow food," Bronn muttered beside him, giving voice to what Tyrion had left unsaid. He could only nod. Had his lord father taken leave of his senses? No pikes, too few bowmen, a bare handful of knights, the ill-armed and unarmored, commanded by an unthinking brute who led with his rage . . . how could his father expect this travesty of a battle to hold his left?

He had no time to think about it. The drums were so near that the beat crept under his skin and set his hands to twitching. Bronn drew his longsword, and suddenly the enemy was there before them, boiling over the tops of the hills, advancing with measured tread behind a wall of shields and pikes.

Gods be damned, look at them all, Tyrion thought, though he knew his father had more men on the field.

Their captains led them on armored warhorses, standard-bearers riding alongside with their banners. He glimpsed the bull moose of the Hornwoods, the Karstark sunburst, Lord Cerwyn's battle-axe, and the mailed fist of the Glovers . . . *and* the twin towers of Frey, blue on grey. So much for his father's certainty that Lord Walder would not bestir himself. The white of House Stark was seen everywhere, the grey direwolves seeming to run and leap as the banners swirled and streamed from the high staffs. *Where is the boy?* Tyrion wondered.

A warhorn blew. *Haroooooooooooooooooooooooooo,* it cried, its voice as long and low and chilling as a cold wind from the north. The Lannister trumpets answered, *da-DA da-DA da-DAAAAAAAAA,* brazen and defiant, yet it seemed to Tyrion that they sounded somehow smaller, more anxious. He could feel a fluttering in his bowels, a queasy liquid feeling; he hoped he was not going to die sick.

As the horns died away, a hissing filled the air; a vast flight of arrows arched up from his right, where the archers stood flanking the road. The northerners broke into a run, shouting as they came, but the Lannister arrows fell on them like hail, hundreds of arrows, thousands, and shouts turned to screams as men stumbled and went down. By then a second flight was in the air, and the archers were fitting a third arrow to their bowstrings.

The trumpets blared again, *da-DAAA da-DAAA da-DA da-DA da-DAAAAAAA.* Ser Gregor waved his huge sword and bellowed a command, and a thousand other voices screamed back at him. Tyrion put his spurs to his horse and added one more voice to the cacophony, and the van surged forward. "The river!" he shouted at his clansmen as they rode. "Remember, hew to the river." He was still leading when they broke a canter, until Chella gave a bloodcurdling shriek and galloped past him, and Shagga howled and followed. The clansmen charged after them, leaving Tyrion in their dust.

A crescent of enemy spearmen had formed ahead, a double hedgehog bristling with steel, waiting behind tall oaken shields marked with the sunburst of Karstark. Gregor Clegane was the first to reach them, leading a wedge of armored veterans. Half the horses shied at the last second, breaking their charge before the row of spears. The others died, sharp steel points ripping through their chests. Tyrion saw a dozen men go down. The Mountain's stallion reared, lashing out with iron-shod hooves as a barbed spearhead raked across his neck. Maddened, the beast lunged into the ranks. Spears thrust at him from every side, but the shield wall broke beneath his weight. The northerners stumbled away from the animal's death throes. As his horse fell, snorting blood and biting with his last red breath, the Mountain rose untouched, laying about him with his two-handed greatsword.

Shagga went bursting through the gap before the shields could close, other Stone Crows hard behind him. Tyrion shouted, "Burned Men! Moon Brothers! After me!" but most of them were *ahead* of him. He glimpsed Timett son of Timett vault free as his mount died under him in full stride, saw a Moon Brother impaled on a Karstark spear, watched Conn's horse shatter a man's ribs with a kick. A flight of arrows descended on them; where they came from he could not say, but they fell on Stark and Lannister alike, rattling off armor or finding flesh. Tyrion lifted his shield and hid beneath it.

The hedgehog was crumbling, the northerners reeling back under the impact of the mounted assault. Tyrion saw Shagga catch a spearman full in the chest as the fool came on at a run, saw his axe shear through mail and leather and muscle and lungs. The man was dead on his feet, the axehead lodged in his breast, yet Shagga rode on, cleaving a shield in two with his left-hand battle-axe while the corpse was bouncing and stumbling bonelessly along on his right. Finally the dead man slid off. Shagga smashed the two axes together and roared.

By then the enemy was on him, and Tyrion's battle shrunk to the few feet of ground around his horse. A man-at-arms thrust at his chest and his axe lashed out, knocking the spear aside. The man danced back for another try, but Tyrion spurred his horse and rode right over him. Bronn was surrounded by three foes, but he lopped the head off the first spear that came at him, and raked his blade across a second man's face on his backslash.

A thrown spear came hurtling at Tyrion from the left and lodged in his shield with a woody *chunk*. He wheeled and raced after the thrower, but the man raised his own shield over his head. Tyrion circled around him, raining axe blows down on the wood. Chips of oak went flying, until the northerner lost his feet and slipped, falling flat on his back with his shield on top of him. He was below the reach of Tyrion's axe and it was too much bother to dismount, so he left him there and rode after another man, taking him from behind with a sweeping downcut that sent a jolt of impact up his arm. That won him a moment's respite. Reining up, he looked for the river. There it was, off to the right. Somehow he had gotten turned around.

A Burned Man rode past, slumped against his horse. A spear had entered his belly and come out through his back. He was past any help, but when Tyrion saw one of the northerners run up and make a grab for his reins, he charged.

His quarry met him sword in hand. He was tall and spare, wearing a long chainmail hauberk and gauntlets of lobstered steel, but he'd lost his helm and blood ran down into his eyes from a gash across his forehead. Tyrion aimed a swipe at his face, but the tall man slammed it aside. "Dwarf," he screamed. "Die." He turned in a circle as Tyrion rode around him, hacking at his head and shoulders. Steel rang on steel, and Tyrion soon realized that the tall man was quicker and stronger than he was. Where in the seven hells was Bronn? "Die," the man grunted, chopping at him savagely. Tyrion barely got his shield up in time, and the wood seemed to explode inward under the force of the blow. The shattered pieces fell away from his arm. *"Die!"* the swordsman bellowed, shoving in close and whanging Tyrion across the temple so hard his head rang. The blade made a hideous scraping sound as he drew it back over the steel. The tall man grinned . . . until Tyrion's destrier bit, quick as a snake, laying his cheek bare to the bone. Then he screamed. Tyrion buried his axe in his head. *"You die,"* he told him, and he did.

As he wrenched the blade free, he heard a shout. *"Eddard!"* a voice rang out. *"For Eddard and Winterfell!"* The knight came thundering down on him, swinging the spiked ball of a morningstar around his head. Their warhorses slammed together before Tyrion could so much as open his mouth to shout for Bronn. His right elbow exploded with pain as the spikes punched through the thin metal around the joint. His axe was gone, as fast as that. He clawed for his sword, but the morningstar was circling again, coming at his face. A sickening *crunch*, and he was falling. He did not recall hitting the ground, but when he looked up there was only sky above him. He rolled onto his side and tried to find his feet, but pain shuddered through him and the world throbbed. The knight who had felled him drew up above him. "Tyrion the Imp," he boomed down. "You are mine. Do you yield, Lannister?"

Yes, Tyrion thought, but the word caught in his throat. He made a croaking sound and fought his way to his knees, fumbling for a weapon. His sword, his dirk, anything . . .

"Do you yield?" The knight loomed overhead on his armored warhorse. Man and horse both seemed immense. The spiked ball swung in a lazy circle. Tyrion's hands were numb, his vision blurred, his scabbard empty. "Yield or die," the knight declared, his flail whirling faster and faster.

Tyrion lurched to his feet, driving his head into the horse's belly. The animal gave a hideous scream and reared. It tried to twist away from the agony, a shower of blood and viscera poured down over Tyrion's face, and the horse fell like an avalanche. The next he knew, his visor was packed with mud and something was crushing his foot. He wriggled free, his throat so tight he could scarce talk. ". . . yield . . ." he managed to croak faintly.

"Yes," a voice moaned, thick with pain.

Tyrion scraped the mud off his helm so he could see again. The horse had fallen away from him, onto its rider. The knight's leg was trapped, the arm he'd used to break his fall twisted at a grotesque angle. "Yield," he repeated. Fumbling at his belt with his good hand, he drew a sword and flung it at Tyrion's feet. "I yield, my lord."

Dazed, the dwarf knelt and lifted the blade. Pain hammered through his elbow when he moved his arm. The battle seemed to have moved beyond him. No one remained on his part of the field save a large number of corpses. Ravens were already circling and landing to feed. He saw that Ser Kevan had brought up his center in support of the van; his huge mass of pikemen had pushed the northerners back against the hills. They were struggling on the slopes, pikes thrusting against another wall of shields, these oval and reinforced with iron studs. As he watched, the air filled with arrows again, and the men behind the oak wall crumbled beneath the murderous fire. "I believe you are losing, ser," he told the knight under the horse. The man made no reply.

The sound of hooves coming up behind him made him whirl, though he could scarcely lift the sword he held for the agony in his elbow. Bronn reined up and looked down on him.

"Small use you turned out to be," Tyrion told him.

"It would seem you did well enough on your own," Bronn answered. "You've lost the spike off your helm, though."

Tyrion groped at the top of the greathelm. The spike had snapped off clean. "I haven't lost it. I know just where it is. Do you see my horse?"

By the time they found it, the trumpets had sounded again and Lord Tywin's reserve came sweeping up along the river. Tyrion watched his father fly past, the crimson-and-gold banner of Lannister rippling over his head as he thundered across the field. Five hundred knights surrounded him, sunlight flashing off the points of their lances. The remnants of the Stark lines shattered like glass beneath the hammer of their charge.

With his elbow swollen and throbbing inside his armor, Tyrion made no attempt to join the slaughter. He and Bronn went looking for his men. Many he found among the dead. Ulf son of Umar lay in a pool of congealing blood, his arm gone at the elbow, a dozen of his Moon Brothers sprawled around him. Shagga was slumped beneath a tree, riddled with arrows, Conn's head in his lap. Tyrion thought they were both dead, but as he dismounted, Shagga opened his eyes and said, "They have killed Conn son of Coratt." Handsome Conn had no mark but for the red stain over his breast, where the spear thrust had killed him. When Bronn pulled Shagga to his feet, the big man seemed to notice the arrows for the first time. He plucked them out one by one, cursing the holes they had made in his layers of mail and leather, and yowling like a babe at the few that had buried themselves in his flesh. Chella daughter of Cheyk rode up as they were yanking arrows out of Shagga, and showed them four ears she had taken. Timett they discovered looting the bodies

of the slain with his Burned Men. Of the three hundred
clansmen who had ridden to battle behind Tyrion Lannister, perhaps half had survived.

He left the living to look after the dead, sent Bronn to
take charge of his captive knight, and went alone in
search of his father. Lord Tywin was seated by the river,
sipping wine from a jeweled cup as his squire undid the
fastenings on his breastplate. "A fine victory," Ser Kevan
said when he saw Tyrion. "Your wild men fought well."

His father's eyes were on him, pale green flecked with
gold, so cool they gave Tyrion a chill. "Did that surprise
you, Father?" he asked. "Did it upset your plans? We were
supposed to be butchered, were we not?"

Lord Tywin drained his cup, his face expressionless. "I
put the least disciplined men on the left, yes. I anticipated
that they would break. Robb Stark is a green boy, more
like to be brave than wise. I'd hoped that if he saw our left
collapse, he might plunge into the gap, eager for a rout.
Once he was fully committed, Ser Kevan's pikes would
wheel and take him in the flank, driving him into the
river while I brought up the reserve."

"And you thought it best to place me in the midst of
this carnage, yet keep me ignorant of your plans."

"A feigned rout is less convincing," his father said,
"and I am not inclined to trust my plans to a man who
consorts with sellswords and savages."

"A pity my savages ruined your dance." Tyrion pulled
off his steel gauntlet and let it fall to the ground, wincing
at the pain that stabbed up his arm.

"The Stark boy proved more cautious than I expected
for one of his years," Lord Tywin admitted, "but a victory
is a victory. You appear to be wounded."

Tyrion's right arm was soaked with blood. "Good of
you to notice, Father," he said through clenched teeth.
"Might I trouble you to send for your maesters? Unless
you relish the notion of having a *one-armed* dwarf for a
son . . ."

An urgent shout of *"Lord Tywin!"* turned his father's
head before he could reply. Tywin Lannister rose to his
feet as Ser Addam Marbrand leapt down off his courser.
The horse was lathered and bleeding from the mouth. Ser
Addam dropped to one knee, a rangy man with dark copper hair that fell to his shoulders, armored in burnished

bronzed steel with the fiery tree of his House etched black on his breastplate. "My liege, we have taken some of their commanders. Lord Cerwyn, Ser Wylis Manderly, Harrion Karstark, four Freys. Lord Hornwood is dead, and I fear Roose Bolton has escaped us."

"And the boy?" Lord Tywin asked.

Ser Addam hesitated. "The Stark boy was not with them, my lord. They say he crossed at the Twins with the great part of his horse, riding hard for Riverrun."

A green boy, Tyrion remembered, *more like to be brave than wise.* He would have laughed, if he hadn't hurt so much.

CATELYN

The woods were full of whispers.

Moonlight winked on the tumbling waters of the stream below as it wound its rocky way along the floor of the valley. Beneath the trees, warhorses whickered softly and pawed at the moist, leafy ground, while men made nervous jests in hushed voices. Now and again, she heard the chink of spears, the faint metallic slither of chain mail, but even those sounds were muffled.

"It should not be long now, my lady," Hallis Mollen said. He had asked for the honor of protecting her in the battle to come; it was his right, as Winterfell's captain of guards, and Robb had not refused it to him. She had thirty men around her, charged to keep her unharmed and see her safely home to Winterfell if the fighting went against them. Robb had wanted fifty; Catelyn had insisted that ten would be enough, that he would need every sword for the fight. They made their peace at thirty, neither happy with it.

"It will come when it comes," Catelyn told him. When it came, she knew it would mean death. Hal's death perhaps . . . or hers, or Robb's. No one was safe. No life was certain. Catelyn was content to wait, to listen to the whispers in the woods and the faint music of the brook, to feel the warm wind in her hair.

She was no stranger to waiting, after all. Her men had always made her wait. "Watch for me, little cat," her father would always tell her, when he rode off to court or fair or battle. And she would, standing patiently on the battlements of Riverrun as the waters of the Red Fork and the Tumblestone flowed by. He did not always come when he said he would, and days would ofttimes pass as Catelyn stood her vigil, peering out between crenels and through arrow loops until she caught a glimpse of Lord Hoster on his old brown gelding, trotting along the rivershore toward the landing. "Did you watch for me?" he'd ask when he bent to hug her. "Did you, little cat?"

Brandon Stark had bid her wait as well. "I shall not be long, my lady," he had vowed. "We will be wed on my return." Yet when the day came at last, it was his brother Eddard who stood beside her in the sept.

Ned had lingered scarcely a fortnight with his new bride before he too had ridden off to war with promises on his lips. At least he had left her with more than words; he had given her a son. Nine moons had waxed and waned, and Robb had been born in Riverrun while his father still warred in the south. She had brought him forth in blood and pain, not knowing whether Ned would ever see him. Her son. He had been so small . . .

And now it was for Robb that she waited . . . for Robb, and for Jaime Lannister, the gilded knight who men said had never learned to wait at all. "The Kingslayer is restless, and quick to anger," her uncle Brynden had told Robb. And he had wagered their lives and their best hope of victory on the truth of what he said.

If Robb was frightened, he gave no sign of it. Catelyn watched her son as he moved among the men, touching one on the shoulder, sharing a jest with another, helping a third to gentle an anxious horse. His armor clinked softly when he moved. Only his head was bare. Catelyn watched a breeze stir his auburn hair, so like her own, and wondered when her son had grown so big. Fifteen, and near as tall as she was.

Let him grow taller, she asked the gods. *Let him know sixteen, and twenty, and fifty. Let him grow as tall as his father, and hold his own son in his arms. Please, please,*

please. As she watched him, this tall young man with the new beard and the direwolf prowling at his heels, all she could see was the babe they had laid at her breast at Riverrun, so long ago.

The night was warm, but the thought of Riverrun was enough to make her shiver. *Where are they?* she wondered. Could her uncle have been wrong? So much rested on the truth of what he had told them. Robb had given the Blackfish three hundred picked men, and sent them ahead to screen his march. "Jaime does not know," Ser Brynden said when he rode back. "I'll stake my life on that. No bird has reached him, my archers have seen to that. We've seen a few of his outriders, but those that saw us did not live to tell of it. He ought to have sent out more. He does not know."

"How large is his host?" her son asked.

"Twelve thousand foot, scattered around the castle in three separate camps, with the rivers between," her uncle said, with the craggy smile she remembered so well. "There is no other way to besiege Riverrun, yet still, that will be their undoing. Two or three thousand horse."

"The Kingslayer has us three to one," said Galbart Glover.

"True enough," Ser Brynden said, "yet there is one thing Ser Jaime lacks."

"Yes?" Robb asked.

"Patience."

Their host was greater than it had been when they left the Twins. Lord Jason Mallister had brought his power out from Seagard to join them as they swept around the headwaters of the Blue Fork and galloped south, and others had crept forth as well, hedge knights and small lords and masterless men-at-arms who had fled north when her brother Edmure's army was shattered beneath the walls of Riverrun. They had driven their horses as hard as they dared to reach this place before Jaime Lannister had word of their coming, and now the hour was at hand.

Catelyn watched her son mount up. Olyvar Frey held his horse for him, Lord Walder's son, two years older than Robb, and ten years younger and more anxious. He strapped Robb's shield in place and handed up his helm. When he lowered it over the face she loved so well, a tall young knight sat on his grey stallion where her son had been. It was dark among the trees, where the moon did not reach. When Robb turned his head to look at her, she could see only black inside his visor. "I must ride down the line, Mother," he told her. "Father says you should let the men see you before a battle."

"Go, then," she said. "Let them see you."

"It will give them courage," Robb said.

And who will give me courage? she wondered, yet she kept her silence and made herself smile for him. Robb turned the big grey stallion and walked him slowly away from her, Grey Wind shadowing his steps. Behind him his battle guard formed up. When he'd forced Catelyn to accept her protectors, she had insisted that he be guarded as well, and the lords bannermen had agreed. Many of their sons had clamored for the honor of riding with the Young Wolf, as they had taken to calling him. Torrhen Karstark and his brother Eddard were among his thirty, and Patrek Mallister, Smalljon Umber, Daryn Hornwood, Theon Greyjoy, no less than five of Walder Frey's vast brood, along with older men like Ser Wendel Manderly and Robin Flint. One of his companions was even a woman: Dacey Mormont, Lady Maege's eldest daughter and heir to Bear Island, a lanky six-footer who had been given a morningstar at an age when most girls were given dolls. Some of the other lords muttered about that, but Catelyn would not listen to their complaints. "This is not about the honor of your houses," she told them. "This is about keeping my son alive and whole."

And if it comes to that, she wondered, *will thirty be enough? Will six thousand be enough?*

A bird called faintly in the distance, a high sharp trill that felt like an icy hand on Catelyn's neck. Another bird answered; a third, a fourth. She knew their call well enough, from her years at Winterfell. Snow shrikes. Sometimes you saw them in the deep of winter, when the godswood was white and still. They were northern birds.

They are coming, Catelyn thought.

"They're coming, my lady," Hal Mollen whispered. He was always a man for stating the obvious. "Gods be with us."

She nodded as the woods grew still around them. In the quiet she could hear them, far off yet moving closer; the tread of many horses, the rattle of swords and spears and armor, the murmur of human voices, with here a laugh, and there a curse.

Eons seemed to come and go. The sounds grew louder. She heard more laughter, a shouted command, splashing as they crossed and recrossed the little stream. A horse snorted. A man swore. And then at last she saw him . . . only for an instant, framed between the branches of the trees as she looked down at the valley floor, yet she knew it was him. Even at a distance, Ser Jaime Lannister was unmistakable. The moonlight had silvered his armor and the gold of his hair, and turned his crimson cloak to black. He was not wearing a helm.

He was there and he was gone again, his silvery armor obscured by the trees once more. Others came behind him, long columns of them, knights and sworn swords and freeriders, three quarters of the Lannister horse.

"He is no man for sitting in a tent while his carpenters build siege towers," Ser Brynden had promised. "He has ridden out with his knights thrice already, to chase down raiders or storm a stubborn holdfast."

Nodding, Robb had studied the map her uncle had drawn him. Ned had taught him to read maps. "Raid him *here*," he said, pointing. "A few hundred men, no more. Tully banners. When he comes after you, we will be waiting"—his finger moved an inch to the left—"*here*."

Here was a hush in the night, moonlight and shadows, a thick carpet of dead leaves underfoot, densely wooded ridges sloping gently down to the streambed, the underbrush thinning as the ground fell away.

Here was her son on his stallion, glancing back at her one last time and lifting his sword in salute.

Here was the call of Maege Mormont's warhorn, a long low blast that rolled down the valley from the east, to tell them that the last of Jaime's riders had entered the trap.

And Grey Wind threw back his head and howled.

The sound seemed to go right through Catelyn Stark, and she found herself shivering. It was a terrible sound, a frightening sound, yet there was music in it too. For a second she felt something like pity for the Lannisters below. *So this is what death sounds like*, she thought.

HAArooooooooooooooooooooooooo came the answer from the far ridge as the Greatjon winded his own horn. To east and west, the trumpets of the Mallisters and Freys blew vengeance. North, where the valley narrowed and bent like a cocked elbow, Lord Karstark's warhorns added their own deep, mournful voices to the dark chorus. Men were shouting and horses rearing in the stream below.

The whispering wood let out its breath all at once, as the bowmen Robb had hidden in the branches of the trees let fly their arrows and the night erupted with the screams of men and horses. All around her, the riders raised their lances, and the dirt and leaves that had buried the cruel bright points fell away to reveal the gleam of sharpened steel. *"Winterfell!"* she heard Robb shout as the arrows sighed again. He moved away from her at a trot, leading his men downhill.

Catelyn sat on her horse, unmoving, with Hal Mollen and her guard around her, and she waited as she had waited before, for Brandon and Ned and her father. She was high on the ridge, and the trees hid most of what was going on beneath her. A heartbeat, two, four, and suddenly it was as if she and her protectors were alone in the wood. The rest were melted away into the green.

Yet when she looked across the valley to the far ridge, she saw the Greatjon's riders emerge from the darkness beneath the trees. They were in a long line, an endless line, and as they burst from the wood there was an instant, the smallest part of a heartbeat, when all Catelyn saw was the moonlight on the points of their lances, as if a thousand willowisps were coming down the ridge, wreathed in silver flame.

Then she blinked, and they were only men, rushing down to kill or die.

Afterward, she could not claim she had seen the battle. Yet she could hear, and the valley rang with echoes. The *crack* of a broken lance, the clash of swords, the cries of "Lannister" and "Winterfell" and "Tully! Riverrun and Tully!" When she realized there was no more to see, she closed her eyes and listened. The battle came alive around her. She heard hoofbeats, iron boots splashing in shallow water, the woody sound of swords on oaken shields and the scrape of steel against steel, the hiss of arrows, the thunder of drums, the terrified screaming of a thousand horses. Men shouted curses and begged for mercy, and got it (or not), and lived (or died). The ridges seemed to play queer tricks with sound. Once she heard Robb's voice, as clear as if he'd been standing at her side, calling, "To me! To me!" And she heard his direwolf, snarling and growling, heard the snap of those long teeth, the tearing of flesh, shrieks of fear and pain from man and horse alike. Was there only one wolf? It was hard to be certain.

Little by little, the sounds dwindled and died, until at last there was only the wolf. As a red dawn broke in the east, Grey Wind began to howl again.

Robb came back to her on a different horse, riding a piebald gelding in the place of the grey stallion he had taken down into the valley. The wolf's head on his shield was slashed half to pieces, raw wood showing where deep gouges had been hacked in the oak, but Robb himself seemed unhurt. Yet when he came closer, Catelyn saw that his mailed glove and the sleeve of his surcoat were black with blood. "You're hurt," she said.

Robb lifted his hand, opened and closed his fingers. "No," he said. "This is . . . Torrhen's blood, perhaps, or . . ." He shook his head. "I do not know."

A mob of men followed him up the slope, dirty and dented and grinning, with Theon and the Greatjon at their head. Between them they dragged Ser Jaime Lannister. They threw him down in front of her horse. "The Kingslayer," Hal announced, unnecessarily.

Lannister raised his head. "Lady Stark," he said from his knees. Blood ran down one cheek from a gash across his scalp, but the pale light of dawn had put the glint of gold back in his hair. "I would offer you my sword, but I seem to have mislaid it."

"It is not your sword I want, ser," she told him. "Give me my father and my brother Edmure. Give me my daughters. Give me my lord husband."

"I have mislaid them as well, I fear."

"A pity," Catelyn said coldly.

"Kill him, Robb," Theon Greyjoy urged. "Take his head off."

"No," her son answered, peeling off his bloody glove. "He's more use alive than dead. And my lord father never condoned the murder of prisoners after a battle."

"A wise man," Jaime Lannister said, "and honorable."

"Take him away and put him in irons," Catelyn said.

"Do as my lady mother says," Robb commanded, "and

make certain there's a strong guard around him. Lord Karstark will want his head on a pike."

"That he will," the Greatjon agreed, gesturing. Lannister was led away to be bandaged and chained.

"Why should Lord Karstark want him dead?" Catelyn asked.

Robb looked away into the woods, with the same brooding look that Ned often got. "He . . . he killed them . . ."

"Lord Karstark's sons," Galbart Glover explained.

"Both of them," said Robb. "Torrhen and Eddard. And Daryn Hornwood as well."

"No one can fault Lannister on his courage," Glover said. "When he saw that he was lost, he rallied his retainers and fought his way up the valley, hoping to reach Lord Robb and cut him down. And almost did."

"He *mislaid* his sword in Eddard Karstark's neck, after he took Torrhen's hand off and split Daryn Hornwood's skull open," Robb said. "All the time he was shouting for me. If they hadn't tried to stop him—"

"—I should then be mourning in place of Lord Karstark," Catelyn said. "Your men did what they were sworn to do, Robb. They died protecting their liege lord. Grieve for them. Honor them for their valor. But not now. You have no time for grief. You may have lopped the head off the snake, but three quarters of the body is still coiled around my father's castle. We have won a battle, not a war."

"But *such* a battle!" said Theon Greyjoy eagerly. "My lady, the realm has not seen such a victory since the Field of Fire. I vow, the Lannisters lost ten men for every one of ours that fell. We've taken close to a hundred knights captive, and a dozen lords bannermen. Lord Westerling, Lord Banefort, Ser Garth Greenfield, Lord Estren, Ser Tytos Brax, Mallor the Dornishman . . . *and* three Lannisters besides Jaime, Lord Tywin's own nephews, two of his sister's sons and one of his dead brother's . . ."

"And Lord Tywin?" Catelyn interrupted. "Have you perchance taken Lord Tywin, Theon?"

"No," Greyjoy answered, brought up short.

"Until you do, this war is far from done."

Robb raised his head and pushed his hair back out of his eyes. "My mother is right. We still have Riverrun."

DAENERYS

The flies circled Khal Drogo slowly, their wings buzzing, a low thrum at the edge of hearing that filled Dany with dread.

The sun was high and pitiless. Heat shimmered in waves off the stony outcrops of low hills. A thin finger of sweat trickled slowly between Dany's swollen breasts. The only sounds were the steady clop of their horses' hooves, the rhythmic tingle of the bells in Drogo's hair, and the distant voices behind them.

Dany watched the flies.

They were as large as bees, gross, purplish, glistening. The Dothraki called them *bloodflies*. They lived in marshes and stagnant pools, sucked blood from man and horse alike, and laid their eggs in the dead and dying. Drogo hated them. Whenever one came near him, his hand would shoot out quick as a striking snake to close around it. She had never seen him miss. He would hold the fly inside his huge fist long enough to hear its frantic buzzing. Then his fingers would tighten, and when he opened his hand again, the fly would be only a red smear on his palm.

Now one crept across the rump of his stallion, and the

horse gave an angry flick of its tail to brush it away. The others flitted about Drogo, closer and closer. The *khal* did not react. His eyes were fixed on distant brown hills, the reins loose in his hands. Beneath his painted vest, a plaster of fig leaves and caked blue mud covered the wound on his breast. The herbwomen had made it for him. Mirri Maz Duur's poultice had itched and burned, and he had torn it off six days ago, cursing her for a *maegi*. The mud plaster was more soothing, and the herbwomen made him poppy wine as well. He'd been drinking it heavily these past three days; when it was not poppy wine, it was fermented mare's milk or pepper beer.

Yet he scarcely touched his food, and he thrashed and groaned in the night. Dany could see how drawn his face had become. Rhaego was restless in her belly, kicking like a stallion, yet even that did not stir Drogo's interest as it had. Every morning her eyes found fresh lines of pain on his face when he woke from his troubled sleep. And now this silence. It was making her afraid. Since they had mounted up at dawn, he had said not a word. When she spoke, she got no answer but a grunt, and not even that much since midday.

One of the bloodflies landed on the bare skin of the *khal*'s shoulder. Another, circling, touched down on his neck and crept up toward his mouth. Khal Drogo swayed in the saddle, bells ringing, as his stallion kept onward at a steady walking pace.

Dany pressed her heels into her silver and rode closer. "My lord," she said softly. "Drogo. My sun-and-stars."

He did not seem to hear. The bloodfly crawled up under his drooping mustache and settled on his cheek, in the crease beside his nose. Dany gasped, "*Drogo*." Clumsily she reached over and touched his arm.

Khal Drogo reeled in the saddle, tilted slowly, and fell heavily from his horse. The flies scattered for a heartbeat, and then circled back to settle on him where he lay.

"No," Dany said, reining up. Heedless of her belly for once, she scrambled off her silver and ran to him.

The grass beneath him was brown and dry. Drogo cried out in pain as Dany knelt beside him. His breath rattled harshly in his throat, and he looked at her without recognition. "My horse," he gasped. Dany brushed the flies off his chest, smashing one as he would have. His skin burned beneath her fingers.

The *khal*'s bloodriders had been following just behind them. She heard Haggo shout as they galloped up. Cohollo vaulted from his horse. "Blood of my blood," he said as he dropped to his knees. The other two kept to their mounts.

"No," Khal Drogo groaned, struggling in Dany's arms. "Must ride. Ride. No."

"He fell from his horse," Haggo said, staring down. His broad face was impassive, but his voice was leaden.

"You must not say that," Dany told him. "We have ridden far enough today. We will camp here."

"Here?" Haggo looked around them. The land was brown and sere, inhospitable. "This is no camping ground."

"It is not for a woman to bid us halt," said Qotho, "not even a *khaleesi*."

"We camp here," Dany repeated. "Haggo, tell them Khal Drogo commanded the halt. If any ask why, say to them that my time is near and I could not continue. Cohollo, bring up the slaves, they must put up the *khal*'s tent at once. Qotho—"

"You do not command me, *Khaleesi*," Qotho said.

"Find Mirri Maz Duur," she told him. The godswife would be walking among the other Lamb Men, in the long column of slaves. "Bring her to me, with her chest."

Qotho glared down at her, his eyes hard as flint. "The *maegi*." He spat. "This I will not do."

"You will," Dany said, "or when Drogo wakes, he will hear why you defied me."

Furious, Qotho wheeled his stallion around and galloped off in anger . . . but Dany knew he would return with Mirri Maz Duur, however little he might like it. The slaves erected Khal Drogo's tent beneath a jagged outcrop of black rock whose shadow gave some relief from the heat of the afternoon sun. Even so, it was stifling under the sandsilk as Irri and Doreah helped Dany walk Drogo inside. Thick patterned carpets had been laid down over the ground, and pillows scattered in the corners. Eroeh, the timid girl Dany had rescued outside the mud walls of the Lamb Men, set up a brazier. They stretched Drogo out on a woven mat. "No," he muttered in the Common

Tongue. "No, no." It was all he said, all he seemed capable of saying.

Doreah unhooked his medallion belt and stripped off his vest and leggings, while Jhiqui knelt by his feet to undo the laces of his riding sandals. Irri wanted to leave the tent flaps open to let in the breeze, but Dany forbade it. She would not have any see Drogo this way, in delirium and weakness. When her *khas* came up, she posted them outside at guard. "Admit no one without my leave," she told Jhogo. "No one."

Eroeh stared fearfully at Drogo where he lay. "He dies," she whispered.

Dany slapped her. "The *khal* cannot die. He is the father of the stallion who mounts the world. His hair has never been cut. He still wears the bells his father gave him."

"*Khaleesi*," Jhiqui said, "he fell from his horse."

Trembling, her eyes full of sudden tears, Dany turned away from them. *He fell from his horse!* It was so, she had seen it, and the bloodriders, and no doubt her handmaids and the men of her *khas* as well. And how many more? They could not keep it secret, and Dany knew what that meant. A *khal* who could not ride could not rule, and Drogo had fallen from his horse.

"We must bathe him," she said stubbornly. She must not allow herself to despair. "Irri, have the tub brought at once. Doreah, Eroeh, find water, cool water, he's so hot." He was a fire in human skin.

The slaves set up the heavy copper tub in the corner of the tent. When Doreah brought the first jar of water, Dany wet a length of silk to lay across Drogo's brow, over the burning skin. His eyes looked at her, but he did not see. When his lips opened, no words escaped them, only a moan. "Where is Mirri Maz Duur?" she demanded, her patience rubbed raw with fear.

"Qotho will find her," Irri said.

Her handmaids filled the tub with tepid water that stank of sulfur, sweetening it with jars of bitter oil and handfuls of crushed mint leaves. While the bath was being prepared, Dany knelt awkwardly beside her lord husband, her belly great with their child within. She undid his braid with anxious fingers, as she had on the night he'd taken her for the first time, beneath the stars. His bells she laid aside carefully, one by one. He would want them again when he was well, she told herself.

A breath of air entered the tent as Aggo poked his head through the silk. *"Khaleesi,"* he said, "the Andal is come, and begs leave to enter."

"The Andal" was what the Dothraki called Ser Jorah. "Yes," she said, rising clumsily, "send him in." She trusted the knight. He would know what to do if anyone did.

Ser Jorah Mormont ducked through the door flap and waited a moment for his eyes to adjust to the dimness. In the fierce heat of the south, he wore loose trousers of mottled sandsilk and open-toed riding sandals that laced up to his knee. His scabbard hung from a twisted horse-hair belt. Under a bleached white vest, he was bare-chested, skin reddened by the sun. "Talk goes from mouth to ear, all over the *khalasar,*" he said. "It is said Khal Drogo fell from his horse."

"Help him," Dany pleaded. "For the love you say you bear me, help him now."

The knight knelt beside her. He looked at Drogo long and hard, and then at Dany. "Send your maids away."

Wordlessly, her throat tight with fear, Dany made a gesture. Irri herded the other girls from the tent.

When they were alone, Ser Jorah drew his dagger. Deftly, with a delicacy surprising in such a big man, he began to scrape away the black leaves and dried blue mud from Drogo's chest. The plaster had caked hard as the mud walls of the Lamb Men, and like those walls it cracked easily. Ser Jorah broke the dry mud with his knife, pried the chunks from the flesh, peeled off the leaves one by one. A foul, sweet smell rose from the wound, so thick it almost choked her. The leaves were crusted with blood and pus, Drogo's breast black and glistening with corruption.

"No," Dany whispered as tears ran down her cheeks. "No, please, gods hear me, *no.*"

Khal Drogo thrashed, fighting some unseen enemy. Black blood ran slow and thick from his open wound.

"Your *khal* is good as dead, Princess."

"No, he can't die, he *mustn't,* it was only a cut." Dany took his large callused hand in her own small ones, and held it tight between them. "I will not let him die . . ."

Ser Jorah gave a bitter laugh. "*Khaleesi* or queen, that command is beyond your power. Save your tears, child. Weep for him tomorrow, or a year from now. We do not have time for grief. We must go, and quickly, before he dies."

Dany was lost. "Go? Where should we go?"

"Asshai, I would say. It lies far to the south, at the end of the known world, yet men say it is a great port. We will find a ship to take us back to Pentos. It will be a hard journey, make no mistake. Do you trust your *khas*? Will they come with us?"

"Khal Drogo commanded them to keep me safe," Dany replied uncertainly, "but if he dies . . ." She touched the swell of her belly. "I don't understand. Why should we flee? I am *khaleesi*. I carry Drogo's heir. He will be *khal* after Drogo . . ."

Ser Jorah frowned. "Princess, hear me. The Dothraki will not follow a suckling babe. Drogo's strength was what they bowed to, and only that. When he is gone, Jhaqo and Pono and the other *kos* will fight for his place, and this *khalasar* will devour itself. The winner will want no more rivals. The boy will be taken from your breast the moment he is born. They will give him to the dogs . . ."

Dany hugged herself. "But *why*?" she cried plaintively. "Why should they kill a little baby?"

"He is Drogo's son, and the crones say he will be the stallion who mounts the world. It was prophesied. Better to kill the child than to risk his fury when he grows to manhood."

The child kicked inside her, as if he had heard. Dany remembered the story Viserys had told her, of what the Usurper's dogs had done to Rhaegar's children. His son had been a babe as well, yet they had ripped him from his mother's breast and dashed his head against a wall. That was the way of men. "They must not hurt my son!" she cried. "I will order my *khas* to keep him safe, and Drogo's bloodriders will—"

Ser Jorah held her by the shoulders. "A bloodrider dies with his *khal*. You know that, child. They will take you to Vaes Dothrak, to the crones, that is the last duty they owe him in life . . . when it is done, they will join Drogo in the night lands."

Dany did not want to go back to Vaes Dothrak and live the rest of her life among those terrible old women, yet she knew that the knight spoke the truth. Drogo had been more than her sun-and-stars; he had been the shield that kept her safe. "I will not leave him," she said stubbornly, miserably. She took his hand again. "I will not."

A stirring at the tent flap made Dany turn her head. Mirri Maz Duur entered, bowing low. Days on the march, trailing behind the *khalasar*, had left her limping and haggard, with blistered and bleeding feet and hollows under her eyes. Behind her came Qotho and Haggo, carrying the godswife's chest between them. When the bloodriders caught sight of Drogo's wound, the chest slipped from Haggo's fingers and crashed to the floor of the tent, and Qotho swore an oath so foul it seared the air.

Mirri Maz Duur studied Drogo, her face still and dead. "The wound has festered."

"This is your work, *maegi*," Qotho said. Haggo laid his fist across Mirri's cheek with a meaty *smack* that drove her to the ground. Then he kicked her where she lay.

"Stop it!" Dany screamed.

Qotho pulled Haggo away, saying, "Kicks are too merciful for a *maegi*. Take her outside. We will stake her to the earth, to be the mount of every passing man. And when they are done with her, the dogs will use her as well. Weasels will tear out her entrails and carrion crows feast upon her eyes. The flies off the river shall lay their eggs in her womb and drink pus from the ruins of her breasts . . ." He dug iron-hard fingers into the soft, wobbly flesh under the godswife's arm and hauled her to her feet.

"No," Dany said. "I will not have her harmed."

Qotho's lips skinned back from his crooked brown teeth in a terrible mockery of a smile. "No? You say me *no*? Better you should pray that we do not stake you out beside your *maegi*. You did this, as much as the other."

Ser Jorah stepped between them, loosening his long-sword in its scabbard. "Rein in your tongue, bloodrider. The princess is still your *khaleesi*."

"Only while the blood-of-my-blood still lives," Qotho told the knight. "When he dies, she is nothing."

Dany felt a tightness inside her. "Before I was *khaleesi*,

I was the blood of the dragon. Ser Jorah, summon my *khas*."

"No," said Qotho. "We will go. For now . . . *Khaleesi*." Haggo followed him from the tent, scowling.

"That one means you no good, Princess," Mormont said. "The Dothraki say a man and his bloodriders share one life, and Qotho sees it ending. A dead man is beyond fear."

"No one has died," Dany said. "Ser Jorah, I may have need of your blade. Best go don your armor." She was more frightened than she dared admit, even to herself.

The knight bowed. "As you say." He strode from the tent.

Dany turned back to Mirri Maz Duur. The woman's eyes were wary. "So you have saved me once more."

"And now you must save him," Dany said. "Please . . ."

"You do not ask a slave," Mirri replied sharply, "you tell her." She went to Drogo burning on his mat, and gazed long at his wound. "Ask or tell, it makes no matter. He is beyond a healer's skills." The *khal*'s eyes were closed. She opened one with her fingers. "He has been dulling the hurt with milk of the poppy."

"Yes," Dany admitted.

"I made him a poultice of firepod and sting-me-not and bound it in a lambskin."

"It burned, he said. He tore it off. The herbwomen made him a new one, wet and soothing."

"It burned, yes. There is great healing magic in fire, even your hairless men know that."

"Make him another poultice," Dany begged. "This time I will make certain he wears it."

"The time for that is past, my lady," Mirri said. "All I can do now is ease the dark road before him, so he might ride painless to the night lands. He will be gone by morning."

Her words were a knife through Dany's breast. What had she ever done to make the gods so cruel? She had finally found a safe place, had finally tasted love and hope. She was finally going home. And now to lose it all . . . "No," she pleaded. "Save him, and I will free you, I swear it. You must know a way . . . some magic, some . . ."

Mirri Maz Duur sat back on her heels and studied Daenerys through eyes as black as night. "There is a spell." Her voice was quiet, scarcely more than a whisper. "But it is hard, lady, and dark. Some would say that death is cleaner. I learned the way in Asshai, and paid dear for the lesson. My teacher was a bloodmage from the Shadow Lands."

Dany went cold all over. "Then you truly are a *maegi . . .*"

"Am I?" Mirri Maz Duur smiled. "Only a *maegi* can save your rider now, Silver Lady."

"Is there no other way?"

"No other."

Khal Drogo gave a shuddering gasp.

"Do it," Dany blurted. She must not be afraid; she was the blood of the dragon. "Save him."

"There is a price," the godswife warned her.

"You'll have gold, horses, whatever you like."

"It is not a matter of gold or horses. This is blood-magic, lady. Only death may pay for life."

"Death?" Dany wrapped her arms around herself protectively, rocked back and forth on her heels. "My death?" She told herself she would die for him, if she must. She was the blood of the dragon, she would not be afraid. Her brother Rhaegar had died for the woman he loved.

"No," Mirri Maz Duur promised. "Not your death, *Khaleesi.*"

Dany trembled with relief. "Do it."

The *maegi* nodded solemnly. "As you speak, so it shall be done. Call your servants."

Khal Drogo writhed feebly as Rakharo and Quaro lowered him into the bath. "No," he muttered, "no. Must ride." Once in the water, all the strength seemed to leak out of him.

"Bring his horse," Mirri Maz Duur commanded, and so it was done. Jhogo led the great red stallion into the tent. When the animal caught the scent of death, he screamed and reared, rolling his eyes. It took three men to subdue him.

"What do you mean to do?" Dany asked her.

"We need the blood," Mirri answered. "That is the way."

Jhogo edged back, his hand on his *arakh*. He was a youth of sixteen years, whip-thin, fearless, quick to laugh, with the faint shadow of his first mustachio on his upper lip. He fell to his knees before her. *"Khaleesi,"* he pleaded, "you must not do this thing. Let me kill this *maegi."*

"Kill her and you kill your *khal*," Dany said.

"This is bloodmagic," he said. "It is forbidden."

"I am *khaleesi*, and I say it is not forbidden. In Vaes Dothrak, Khal Drogo slew a stallion and I ate his heart, to give our son strength and courage. This is the same. The *same."*

The stallion kicked and reared as Rakharo, Quaro, and Aggo pulled him close to the tub where the *khal* floated like one already dead, pus and blood seeping from his wound to stain the bathwaters. Mirri Maz Duur chanted words in a tongue that Dany did not know, and a knife appeared in her hand. Dany never saw where it came from. It looked old; hammered red bronze, leaf-shaped, its blade covered with ancient glyphs. The *maegi* drew it across the stallion's throat, under the noble head, and the horse screamed and shuddered as the blood poured out of him in a red rush. He would have collapsed, but the men of her *khas* held him up. "Strength of the mount, go into the rider," Mirri sang as horse blood swirled into the waters of Drogo's bath. "Strength of the beast, go into the man."

Jhogo looked terrified as he struggled with the stallion's weight, afraid to touch the dead flesh, yet afraid to let go as well. *Only a horse*, Dany thought. If she could buy Drogo's life with the death of a horse, she would pay a thousand times over.

When they let the stallion fall, the bath was a dark red, and nothing showed of Drogo but his face. Mirri Maz Duur had no use for the carcass. "Burn it," Dany told them. It was what they did, she knew. When a man died, his mount was killed and placed beneath him on the funeral pyre, to carry him to the night lands. The men of her *khas* dragged the carcass from the tent. The blood had gone everywhere. Even the sandsilk walls were spotted with red, and the rugs underfoot were black and wet.

Braziers were lit. Mirri Maz Duur tossed a red powder onto the coals. It gave the smoke a spicy scent, a pleasant enough smell, yet Eroeh fled sobbing, and Dany was filled with fear. But she had gone too far to turn back now. She sent her handmaids away. "Go with them, Silver Lady," Mirri Maz Duur told her.

"I will stay," Dany said. "The man took me under the stars and gave life to the child inside me. I will not leave him."

"You must. Once I begin to sing, no one must enter this tent. My song will wake powers old and dark. The dead will dance here this night. No living man must look on them."

Dany bowed her head, helpless. "No one will enter." She bent over the tub, over Drogo in his bath of blood, and kissed him lightly on the brow. *"Bring him back to me,"* she whispered to Mirri Maz Duur before she fled.

Outside, the sun was low on the horizon, the sky a bruised red. The *khalasar* had made camp. Tents and sleeping mats were scattered as far as the eye could see. A hot wind blew. Jhogo and Aggo were digging a firepit to burn the dead stallion. A crowd had gathered to stare at Dany with hard black eyes, their faces like masks of beaten copper. She saw Ser Jorah Mormont, wearing mail and leather now, sweat beading on his broad, balding forehead. He pushed his way through the Dothraki to Dany's side. When he saw the scarlet footprints her boots had left on the ground, the color seemed to drain from his face. "What have you done, you little fool?" he asked hoarsely.

"I had to save him."

"We could have fled," he said. "I would have seen you safe to Asshai, Princess. There was no need . . ."

"Am I truly your princess?" she asked him.

"You know you are, gods save us both."

"Then help me now."

Ser Jorah grimaced. "Would that I knew how."

Mirri Maz Duur's voice rose to a high, ululating wail that sent a shiver down Dany's back. Some of the Dothraki began to mutter and back away. The tent was aglow with the light of braziers within. Through the blood-spattered sandsilk, she glimpsed shadows moving.

Mirri Maz Duur was dancing, and not alone.

Dany saw naked fear on the faces of the Dothraki. "This *must not be*," Qotho thundered.

She had not seen the bloodrider return. Haggo and

Cohollo were with him. They had brought the hairless men, the eunuchs who healed with knife and needle and fire.

"This *will* be," Dany replied.

"Maegi," Haggo growled. And old Cohollo—Cohollo who had bound his life to Drogo's on the day of his birth, Cohollo who had always been kind to her—Cohollo spat full in her face.

"You will die, *maegi,"* Qotho promised, "but the other must die first." He drew his *arakh* and made for the tent.

"No," she shouted, "you *mustn't."* She caught him by the shoulder, but Qotho shoved her aside. Dany fell to her knees, crossing her arms over her belly to protect the child within. "Stop him," she commanded her *khas,* "kill him."

Rakharo and Quaro stood beside the tent flap. Quaro took a step forward, reaching for the handle of his whip, but Qotho spun graceful as a dancer, the curved *arakh* rising. It caught Quaro low under the arm, the bright sharp steel biting up through leather and skin, through muscle and rib bone. Blood fountained as the young rider reeled backward, gasping.

Qotho wrenched the blade free. *"Horselord,"* Ser Jorah Mormont called. "Try me." His longsword slid from its scabbard.

Qotho whirled, cursing. The *arakh* moved so fast that Quaro's blood flew from it in a fine spray, like rain in a hot wind. The longsword caught it a foot from Ser Jorah's face, and held it quivering for an instant as Qotho howled in fury. The knight was clad in chainmail, with gauntlets and greaves of lobstered steel and a heavy gorget around his throat, but he had not thought to don his helm.

Qotho danced backward, *arakh* whirling around his head in a shining blur, flickering out like lightning as the knight came on in a rush. Ser Jorah parried as best he could, but the slashes came so fast that it seemed to Dany that Qotho had four *arakhs* and as many arms. She heard the crunch of sword on mail, saw sparks fly as the long curved blade glanced off a gauntlet. Suddenly it was Mormont stumbling backward, and Qotho leaping to the attack. The left side of the knight's face ran red with blood, and a cut to the hip opened a gash in his mail and left him limping. Qotho screamed taunts at him, calling him a craven, a milk man, a eunuch in an iron suit. "You die now!" he promised, *arakh* shivering through the red twilight. Inside Dany's womb, her son kicked wildly. The curved blade slipped past the straight one and bit deep into the knight's hip where the mail gaped open.

Mormont grunted, stumbled. Dany felt a sharp pain in her belly, a wetness on her thighs. Qotho shrieked triumph, but his *arakh* had found bone, and for half a heartbeat it caught.

It was enough. Ser Jorah brought his longsword down with all the strength left him, through flesh and muscle and bone, and Qotho's forearm dangled loose, flopping on a thin cord of skin and sinew. The knight's next cut was at the Dothraki's ear, so savage that Qotho's face seemed almost to explode.

The Dothraki were shouting, Mirri Maz Duur wailing inside the tent like nothing human, Quaro pleading for water as he died. Dany cried out for help, but no one heard. Rakharo was fighting Haggo, *arakh* dancing with *arakh* until Jhogo's whip cracked, loud as thunder, the lash coiling around Haggo's throat. A yank, and the bloodrider stumbled backward, losing his feet and his sword. Rakharo sprang forward, howling, swinging his *arakh* down with both hands through the top of Haggo's head. The point caught between his eyes, red and quivering. Someone threw a stone, and when Dany looked, her shoulder was torn and bloody. "No," she wept, "no, please, stop it, it's too high, the price is too high." More stones came flying. She tried to crawl toward the tent, but Cohollo caught her. Fingers in her hair, he pulled her head back and she felt the cold touch of his knife at her throat. "My baby," she screamed, and perhaps the gods heard, for as quick as that, Cohollo was dead. Aggo's arrow took him under the arm, to pierce his lungs and heart.

When at last Daenerys found the strength to raise her head, she saw the crowd dispersing, the Dothraki stealing silently back to their tents and sleeping mats. Some were saddling horses and riding off. The sun had set. Fires burned throughout the *khalasar*, great orange blazes that crackled with fury and spit embers at the sky. She tried to rise, and agony seized her and squeezed her like a giant's fist. The breath went out of her; it was all she could do to gasp. The sound of Mirri Maz Duur's voice was like a funeral dirge. Inside the tent, the shadows whirled.

An arm went under her waist, and then Ser Jorah was lifting her off her feet. His face was sticky with blood, and Dany saw that half his ear was gone. She convulsed in his arms as the pain took her again, and heard the knight shouting for her handmaids to help him. *Are they all so afraid?* She knew the answer. Another pain grasped her, and Dany bit back a scream. It felt as if her son had a knife in each hand, as if he were hacking at her to cut his way out. "Doreah, curse you," Ser Jorah roared. "Come here. Fetch the birthing women."

"They will not come. They say she is accursed."

"They'll come or I'll have their heads."

Doreah wept. "They are gone, my lord."

"The *maegi*," someone else said. Was that Aggo? "Take her to the *maegi*."

No, Dany wanted to say, *no, not that, you mustn't*, but when she opened her mouth, a long wail of pain escaped, and the sweat broke over her skin. *What was wrong with them, couldn't they see?* Inside the tent the shapes were dancing, circling the brazier and the bloody bath, dark against the sandsilk, and some did not look human. She glimpsed the shadow of a great wolf, and another like a man wreathed in flames.

"The Lamb Woman knows the secrets of the birthing bed," Irri said. "She said so, I heard her."

"Yes," Doreah agreed, "I heard her too."

No, she shouted, or perhaps she only thought it, for no whisper of sound escaped her lips. She was being carried. Her eyes opened to gaze up at a flat dead sky, black and bleak and starless. *Please, no.* The sound of Mirri Maz Duur's voice grew louder, until it filled the world. *The shapes!* she screamed. *The dancers!*

Ser Jorah carried her inside the tent.

ARYA

The scent of hot bread drifting from the shops along the Street of Flour was sweeter than any perfume Arya had ever smelled. She took a deep breath and stepped closer to the pigeon. It was a plump one, speckled brown, busily pecking at a crust that had fallen between two cobblestones, but when Arya's shadow touched it, it took to the air.

Her stick sword whistled out and caught it two feet off the ground, and it went down in a flurry of brown feathers. She was on it in the blink of an eye, grabbing a wing as the pigeon flapped and fluttered. It pecked at her hand. She grabbed its neck and twisted until she felt the bone snap.

Compared with catching cats, pigeons were *easy*.

A passing septon was looking at her askance. "Here's the best place to find pigeon," Arya told him as she brushed herself off and picked up her fallen stick sword. "They come for the crumbs." He hurried away.

She tied the pigeon to her belt and started down the street. A man was pushing a load of tarts by on a two-wheeled cart; the smells sang of blueberries and lemons and apricots. Her stomach made a hollow rumbly noise.

"Could I have one?" she heard herself say. "A lemon, or . . . or any kind."

The pushcart man looked her up and down. Plainly he did not like what he saw. "Three coppers."

Arya tapped her wooden sword against the side of her boot. "I'll trade you a fat pigeon," she said.

"The Others take your pigeon," the pushcart man said. The tarts were still warm from the oven. The smells were making her mouth water, but she did not have three coppers . . . or one. She gave the pushcart man a look, remembering what Syrio had told her about *seeing*. He was short, with a little round belly, and when he moved he seemed to favor his left leg a little. She was just thinking that if she snatched a tart and ran he would never be able to catch her when he said, "You be keepin' your filthy hands off. The gold cloaks know how to deal with thieving little gutter rats, that they do."

Arya glanced warily behind her. Two of the City Watch were standing at the mouth of an alley. Their cloaks hung almost to the ground, the heavy wool dyed a rich gold; their mail and boots and gloves were black. One wore a longsword at his hip, the other an iron cudgel. With a last wistful glance at the tarts, Arya edged back from the cart and hurried off. The gold cloaks had not been paying her any special attention, but the sight of them tied her stomach in knots. Arya had been staying as far from the castle as she could get, yet even from a distance she could see the heads rotting atop the high red walls. Flocks of crows squabbled noisily over each head, thick as flies. The talk in Flea Bottom was that the gold cloaks had thrown in with the Lannisters, their commander raised to a lord, with lands on the Trident and a seat on the king's council.

She had also heard other things, scary things, things that made no sense to her. Some said her father had murdered King Robert and been slain in turn by Lord Renly. Others insisted that *Renly* had killed the king in a drunken quarrel between brothers. Why else should he have fled in the night like a common thief? One story said the king had been killed by a boar while hunting, another that he'd died *eating* a boar, stuffing himself so full that he'd ruptured at the table. No, the king had died at table, others said, but only because Varys the Spider poisoned him. No, it had been *the queen* who poisoned him. No, he had died of a pox. No, he had choked on a fish bone.

One thing all the stories agreed on: King Robert was dead. The bells in the seven towers of the Great Sept of Baelor had tolled for a day and a night, the thunder of their grief rolling across the city in a bronze tide. They only rang the bells like that for the death of a king, a tanner's boy told Arya.

All she wanted was to go home, but leaving King's Landing was not so easy as she had hoped. Talk of war was on every lip, and gold cloaks were as thick on the city walls as fleas on . . . well, her, for one. She had been sleeping in Flea Bottom, on rooftops and in stables, wherever she could find a place to lie down, and it hadn't taken her long to learn that the district was well named.

Every day since her escape from the Red Keep, Arya had visited each of the seven city gates in turn. The Dragon Gate, the Lion Gate, and the Old Gate were closed and barred. The Mud Gate and the Gate of the Gods were open, but only to those who wanted to enter the city; the guards let no one out. Those who were allowed to leave left by the King's Gate or the Iron Gate, but Lannister men-at-arms in crimson cloaks and lion-crested helms manned the guard posts there. Spying down from the roof of an inn by the King's Gate, Arya saw them searching wagons and carriages, forcing riders to open their saddlebags, and questioning everyone who tried to pass on foot.

Sometimes she thought about swimming the river, but the Blackwater Rush was wide and deep, and everyone agreed that its currents were wicked and treacherous. She had no coin to pay a ferryman or take passage on a ship.

Her lord father had taught her never to steal, but it was growing harder to remember why. If she did not get out soon, she would have to take her chances with the gold cloaks. She hadn't gone hungry much since she learned to knock down birds with her stick sword, but she feared so much pigeon was making her sick. A couple she'd eaten raw, before she found Flea Bottom.

In the Bottom there were pot-shops along the alleys where huge tubs of stew had been simmering for years, and you could trade half your bird for a heel of yesterday's bread and a "bowl o' brown," and they'd even stick the other half in the fire and crisp it up for you, so long as you plucked the feathers yourself. Arya would have given anything for a cup of milk and a lemon cake, but the brown wasn't so bad. It usually had barley in it, and chunks of carrot and onion and turnip, and sometimes even apple, with a film of grease swimming on top. Mostly she tried not to think about the meat. Once she had gotten a piece of fish.

The only thing was, the pot-shops were never empty, and even as she bolted down her food, Arya could feel them watching. Some of them stared at her boots or her cloak, and she knew what they were thinking. With others, she could almost feel their eyes crawling under her leathers; she *didn't* know what they were thinking, and that scared her even more. A couple times, she was followed out into the alleys and chased, but so far no one had been able to catch her.

The silver bracelet she'd hoped to sell had been stolen her first night out of the castle, along with her bundle of good clothes, snatched while she slept in a burnt-out house off Pig Alley. All they left her was the cloak she had been huddled in, the leathers on her back, her wooden practice sword . . . and Needle. She'd been lying on top of Needle, or else it would have been gone too; it was worth more than all the rest together. Since then Arya had taken to walking around with her cloak draped over her right arm, to conceal the blade at her hip. The wooden sword she carried in her left hand, out where everybody could see it, to scare off robbers, but there were men in the pot-shops who wouldn't have been scared off if she'd had a battle-axe. It was enough to make her lose her taste for pigeon and stale bread. Often as not, she went to bed hungry rather than risk the stares.

Once she was outside the city, she would find berries to pick, or orchards she might raid for apples and cherries. Arya remembered seeing some from the kingsroad on the journey south. And she could dig for roots in the forest, even run down some rabbits. In the city, the only things to run down were rats and cats and scrawny dogs. The pot-shops would give you a fistful of coppers for a litter of pups, she'd heard, but she didn't like to think about that.

Down below the Street of Flour was a maze of twisting alleys and cross streets. Arya scrambled through the crowds, trying to put distance between her and the gold cloaks. She had learned to keep to the center of the street. Sometimes she had to dodge wagons and horses, but at least you could see them coming. If you walked near the buildings, people grabbed you. In some alleys you couldn't help but brush against the walls; the buildings leaned in so close they almost met.

A whooping gang of small children went running past, chasing a rolling hoop. Arya stared at them with resentment, remembering the times she'd played at hoops with Bran and Jon and their baby brother Rickon. She wondered how big Rickon had grown, and whether Bran was sad. She would have given anything if Jon had been here to call her "little sister" and muss her hair. Not that it needed mussing. She'd seen her reflection in puddles, and she didn't think hair got any more mussed than hers.

She had tried talking to the children she saw in the street, hoping to make a friend who would give her a place to sleep, but she must have talked wrong or something. The little ones only looked at her with quick, wary eyes and ran away if she came too close. Their big brothers and sisters asked questions Arya couldn't answer, called her names, and tried to steal from her. Only yesterday, a scrawny barefoot girl twice her age had knocked her down and tried to pull the boots off her feet, but Arya gave her a *crack* on her ear with her stick sword that sent her off sobbing and bleeding.

A gull wheeled overhead as she made her way down the hill toward Flea Bottom. Arya glanced at it thoughtfully, but it was well beyond the reach of her stick. It made her think of the sea. Maybe *that* was the way out. Old Nan used to tell stories of boys who stowed away on trading galleys and sailed off into all kinds of adventures. Maybe Arya could do that too. She decided to visit the riverfront. It was on the way to the Mud Gate anyway, and she hadn't checked that one today.

The wharfs were oddly quiet when Arya got there. She spied another pair of gold cloaks, walking side by side through the fish market, but they never so much as looked at her. Half the stalls were empty, and it seemed to her that there were fewer ships at dock than she remembered. Out on the Blackwater, three of the king's war galleys moved in formation, gold-painted hulls splitting the water as their oars rose and fell. Arya watched them for a bit, then began to make her way along the river.

When she saw the guardsmen on the third pier, in grey woolen cloaks trimmed with white satin, her heart almost stopped in her chest. The sight of Winterfell's colors brought tears to her eyes. Behind them, a sleek three-banked trading galley rocked at her moorings. Arya could not read the name painted on the hull; the words were strange, Myrish, Braavosi, perhaps even High Valyrian. She grabbed a passing longshoreman by the sleeve. "Please," she said, "what ship is this?"

"She's the *Wind Witch*, out of Myr," the man said.

"She's *still here*," Arya blurted. The longshoreman gave her a queer look, shrugged, and walked away. Arya ran toward the pier. The *Wind Witch* was the ship Father had hired to take her home . . . still waiting! She'd imagined it had sailed ages ago.

Two of the guardsmen were dicing together while the third walked rounds, his hand on the pommel of his sword. Ashamed to let them see her crying like a baby, she stopped to rub at her eyes. Her eyes her eyes her eyes, why did . . .

Look with your eyes, she heard Syrio whisper.

Arya looked. She knew all of her father's men. The three in the grey cloaks were strangers. "You," the one walking rounds called out. "What do you want here, boy?" The other two looked up from their dice.

It was all Arya could do not to bolt and run, but she knew that if she did, they would be after her at once. She made herself walk closer. They were looking for a girl, but he thought she was a boy. She'd *be* a boy, then. "Want to buy a pigeon?" She showed him the dead bird.

"Get out of here," the guardsman said.

Arya did as he told her. She did not have to pretend to be frightened. Behind her, the men went back to their dice.

She could not have said how she got back to Flea Bottom, but she was breathing hard by the time she reached the narrow crooked unpaved streets between the hills. The Bottom had a stench to it, a stink of pigsties and stables and tanner's sheds, mixed in with the sour smell of winesinks and cheap whorehouses. Arya wound her way through the maze dully. It was not until she caught a whiff of bubbling brown coming through a pot-shop door that she realized her pigeon was gone. It must have slipped from her belt as she ran, or someone had stolen it and she'd never noticed. For a moment she wanted to cry again. She'd have to walk all the way back to the Street of Flour to find another one that plump.

Far across the city, bells began to ring.

Arya glanced up, listening, wondering what the ringing meant this time.

"What's this now?" a fat man called from the pot-shop.

"The bells again, gods ha'mercy," wailed an old woman.

A red-haired whore in a wisp of painted silk pushed open a second-story window. "Is it the boy king that's died now?" she shouted down, leaning out over the street. "Ah, that's a boy for you, they never last long." As she laughed, a naked man slid his arms around her from behind, biting her neck and rubbing the heavy white breasts that hung loose beneath her shift.

"Stupid slut," the fat man shouted up. "The king's not dead, that's only summoning bells. One tower tolling. When the king dies, they ring every bell in the city."

"Here, quit your biting, or I'll ring *your* bells," the woman in the window said to the man behind her, pushing him off with an elbow. "So who is it died, if not the king?"

"It's a summoning," the fat man repeated.

Two boys close to Arya's age scampered past, splashing through a puddle. The old woman cursed them, but they kept right on going. Other people were moving too, heading up the hill to see what the noise was about. Arya ran after the slower boy. "Where you going?" she shouted when she was right behind him. "What's happening?"

He glanced back without slowing. "The gold cloaks is carryin' him to the sept."

"Who?" she yelled, running hard.

"The *Hand*! They'll be taking his head off, Buu says."

A passing wagon had left a deep rut in the street. The boy leapt over, but Arya never saw it. She tripped and fell, face first, scraping her knee open on a stone and smashing her fingers when her hands hit the hard-packed earth. Needle tangled between her legs. She sobbed as she struggled to her knees. The thumb of her left hand was covered with blood. When she sucked on it, she saw that half the thumbnail was gone, ripped off in her fall. Her hands throbbed, and her knee was all bloody too.

"Make way!" someone shouted from the cross street. *"Make way for my lords of Redwyne!"* It was all Arya could do to get out of the road before they ran her down, four guardsmen on huge horses, pounding past at a gallop. They wore checked cloaks, blue-and-burgundy. Behind them, two young lordlings rode side by side on a pair of chestnut mares alike as peas in a pod. Arya had seen them in the bailey a hundred times; the Redwyne twins, Ser Horas and Ser Hobber, homely youths with orange hair and square, freckled faces. Sansa and Jeyne Poole used to call them Ser Horror and Ser Slobber, and giggle whenever they caught sight of them. They did not look funny now.

Everyone was moving in the same direction, all in a hurry to see what the ringing was all about. The bells seemed louder now, clanging, calling. Arya joined the stream of people. Her thumb hurt so bad where the nail had broken that it was all she could do not to cry. She bit her lip as she limped along, listening to the excited voices around her.

"—the King's Hand, Lord Stark. They're carrying him up to Baelor's Sept."

"I heard he was dead."

"Soon enough, soon enough. Here, I got me a silver stag says they lop his head off."

"Past time, the traitor." The man spat.

Arya struggled to find a voice. "He *never*—" she started, but she was only a child and they talked right over her.

"*Fool!* They ain't neither going to lop him. Since when do they knick traitors on the steps of the Great Sept?"

"Well, they don't mean to anoint him no knight. I heard it was Stark killed old King Robert. Slit his throat in the woods, and when they found him, he stood there cool as you please and said it was some old boar did for His Grace."

"Ah, that's not true, it was his own brother did him, that Renly, him with his gold antlers."

"You shut your lying mouth, woman. You don't know what you're saying, his lordship's a fine true man."

By the time they reached the Street of the Sisters, they

were packed in shoulder to shoulder. Arya let the human current carry her along, up to the top of Visenya's Hill. The white marble plaza was a solid mass of people, all yammering excitedly at each other and straining to get closer to the Great Sept of Baelor. The bells were very loud here.

Arya squirmed through the press, ducking between the legs of horses and clutching tight to her sword stick. From the middle of the crowd, all she could see were arms and legs and stomachs, and the seven slender towers of the sept looming overhead. She spotted a wood wagon and thought to climb up on the back where she might be able to see, but others had the same idea. The teamster cursed at them and drove them off with a crack of his whip.

Arya grew frantic. Forcing her way to the front of the crowd, she was shoved up against the stone of a plinth. She looked up at Baelor the Blessed, the septon king. Sliding her stick sword through her belt, Arya began to climb. Her broken thumbnail left smears of blood on the painted marble, but she made it up, and wedged herself in between the king's feet.

That was when she saw her father.

Lord Eddard stood on the High Septon's pulpit outside the doors of the sept, supported between two of the gold cloaks. He was dressed in a rich grey velvet doublet with a white wolf sewn on the front in beads, and a grey wool cloak trimmed with fur, but he was thinner than Arya had ever seen him, his long face drawn with pain. He was not standing so much as being held up; the cast over his broken leg was grey and rotten.

The High Septon himself stood behind him, a squat man, grey with age and ponderously fat, wearing long white robes and an immense crown of spun gold and crystal that wreathed his head with rainbows whenever he moved.

Clustered around the doors of the sept, in front of the raised marble pulpit, were a knot of knights and high lords. Joffrey was prominent among them, his raiment all crimson, silk and satin patterned with prancing stags and roaring lions, a gold crown on his head. His queen mother stood beside him in a black mourning gown slashed with crimson, a veil of black diamonds in her hair. Arya recognized the Hound, wearing a snowy white cloak over his dark grey armor, with four of the Kingsguard around him. She saw Varys the eunuch gliding among the lords in soft slippers and a patterned damask robe, and she thought the short man with the silvery cape and pointed beard might be the one who had once fought a duel for Mother.

And there in their midst was Sansa, dressed in sky-blue silk, with her long auburn hair washed and curled and silver bracelets on her wrists. Arya scowled, wondering what her sister was doing here, why she looked so happy.

A long line of gold-cloaked spearmen held back the crowd, commanded by a stout man in elaborate armor, all black lacquer and gold filigree. His cloak had the metallic shimmer of true cloth-of-gold.

When the bell ceased to toll, a quiet slowly settled across the great plaza, and her father lifted his head and began to speak, his voice so thin and weak she could scarcely make him out. People behind her began to shout out, *"What?"* and *"Louder!"* The man in the black-and-gold armor stepped up behind Father and prodded him sharply. *You leave him alone!* Arya wanted to shout, but she knew no one would listen. She chewed her lip.

Her father raised his voice and began again. "I am Eddard Stark, Lord of Winterfell and Hand of the King," he said more loudly, his voice carrying across the plaza, "and I come before you to confess my treason in the sight of gods and men."

"No," Arya whimpered. Below her, the crowd began to scream and shout. Taunts and obscenities filled the air. Sansa had hidden her face in her hands.

Her father raised his voice still higher, straining to be heard. "I betrayed the faith of my king and the trust of my friend, Robert," he shouted. "I swore to defend and protect his children, yet before his blood was cold, I plotted to depose and murder his son and seize the throne for myself. Let the High Septon and Baelor the Beloved and the Seven bear witness to the truth of what I say: Joffrey Baratheon is the one true heir to the Iron Throne, and by the grace of all the gods, Lord of the Seven Kingdoms and Protector of the Realm."

A stone came sailing out of the crowd. Arya cried out as she saw her father hit. The gold cloaks kept him from falling. Blood ran down his face from a deep gash across his forehead. More stones followed. One struck the guard to Father's left. Another went clanging off the breastplate of the knight in the black-and-gold armor. Two of the Kingsguard stepped in front of Joffrey and the queen, protecting them with their shields.

Her hand slid beneath her cloak and found Needle in its sheath. She tightened her fingers around the grip, squeezing as hard as she had ever squeezed anything. *Please, gods, keep him safe,* she prayed. *Don't let them hurt my father.*

The High Septon knelt before Joffrey and his mother. "As we sin, so do we suffer," he intoned, in a deep swelling voice much louder than Father's. "This man has confessed his crimes in the sight of gods and men, here in this holy place." Rainbows danced around his head as he lifted his hands in entreaty. "The gods are just, yet Blessed Baelor taught us that they are also merciful. What shall be done with this traitor, Your Grace?"

A thousand voices were screaming, but Arya never heard them. Prince Joffrey . . . no, *King* Joffrey . . . stepped out from behind the shields of his Kingsguard. "My mother bids me let Lord Eddard take the black, and Lady Sansa has begged mercy for her father." He looked straight at Sansa then, and *smiled*, and for a moment Arya thought that the gods had heard her prayer, until Joffrey turned back to the crowd and said, "But they have the soft hearts of women. So long as I am your king, treason shall never go unpunished. Ser Ilyn, bring me his head!"

The crowd roared, and Arya felt the statue of Baelor rock as they surged against it. The High Septon clutched at the king's cape, and Varys came rushing over waving his arms, and even the queen was saying something to him, but Joffrey shook his head. Lords and knights moved aside as *he* stepped through, tall and fleshless, a skeleton in iron mail, the King's Justice. Dimly, as if from far off, Arya heard her sister scream. Sansa had fallen to her knees, sobbing hysterically. Ser Ilyn Payne climbed the steps of the pulpit.

Arya wriggled between Baelor's feet and threw herself into the crowd, drawing Needle. She landed on a man in a butcher's apron, knocking him to the ground. Immediately someone slammed into her back and she almost went down herself. Bodies closed in around her, stumbling and pushing, trampling on the poor butcher. Arya slashed at them with Needle.

High atop the pulpit, Ser Ilyn Payne gestured and the knight in black-and-gold gave a command. The gold cloaks flung Lord Eddard to the marble, with his head and chest out over the edge.

"Here, you!" an angry voice shouted at Arya, but she bowled past, shoving people aside, squirming between them, slamming into anyone in her way. A hand fumbled at her leg and she hacked at it, kicked at shins. A woman stumbled and Arya ran up her back, cutting to both sides, but it was no good, *no good*, there were too many people, no sooner did she make a hole than it closed again. Someone buffeted her aside. She could still hear Sansa screaming.

Ser Ilyn drew a two-handed greatsword from the scabbard on his back. As he lifted the blade above his head, sunlight seemed to ripple and dance down the dark metal, glinting off an edge sharper than any razor. *Ice,* she thought, *he has Ice!* Her tears streamed down her face, blinding her.

And then a hand shot out of the press and closed round her arm like a wolf trap, so hard that Needle went flying from her hand. Arya was wrenched off her feet. She would have fallen if he hadn't held her up, as easy as if she were a doll. A face pressed close to hers, long black hair and tangled beard and rotten teeth. *"Don't look!"* a thick voice snarled at her.

"I . . . I . . . I . . ." Arya sobbed.

The old man shook her so hard her teeth rattled. "Shut your mouth and close your eyes, *boy*." Dimly, as if from far away, she heard a . . . a *noise* . . . a soft sighing sound, as if a million people had let out their breath at once. The old man's fingers dug into her arm, stiff as iron. "Look at me. Yes, that's the way of it, at *me*." Sour wine perfumed his breath. "Remember, *boy*?"

It was the smell that did it. Arya saw the matted greasy hair, the patched, dusty black cloak that covered his twisted shoulders, the hard black eyes squinting at her. And she remembered the black brother who had come to visit her father.

"Know me now, do you? There's a bright boy." He

spat. "They're done here. You'll be coming with me, and you'll be keeping your mouth shut." When she started to reply, he shook her again, even harder. "*Shut,* I said."

The plaza was beginning to empty. The press dissolved around them as people drifted back to their lives. But Arya's life was gone. Numb, she trailed along beside . . . *Yoren, yes, his name is Yoren.* She did not recall him finding Needle, until he handed the sword back to her. "Hope you can use that, boy."

"I'm not—" she started.

He shoved her into a doorway, thrust dirty fingers through her hair, and gave it a twist, yanking her head back. "—not a smart *boy,* that what you mean to say?"

He had a knife in his other hand.

As the blade flashed toward her face, Arya threw herself backward, kicking wildly, wrenching her head from side to side, but he had her by the hair, so *strong,* she could feel her scalp tearing, and on her lips the salt taste of tears.

BRAN

The oldest were men grown, seventeen and eighteen years from the day of their naming. One was past twenty. Most were younger, sixteen or less.

Bran watched them from the balcony of Maester Luwin's turret, listening to them grunt and strain and curse as they swung their staves and wooden swords. The yard was alive to the *clack* of wood on wood, punctuated all too often by *thwacks* and yowls of pain when a blow struck leather or flesh. Ser Rodrik strode among the boys, face reddening beneath his white whiskers, muttering at them one and all. Bran had never seen the old knight look so fierce. "No," he kept saying. "No. No. No."

"They don't fight very well," Bran said dubiously. He scratched Summer idly behind the ears as the direwolf tore at a haunch of meat. Bones crunched between his teeth.

"For a certainty," Maester Luwin agreed with a deep sigh. The maester was peering through his big Myrish lens tube, measuring shadows and noting the position of the comet that hung low in the morning sky. "Yet given time . . . Ser Rodrik has the truth of it, we need men to walk the walls. Your lord father took the cream of his guard to King's Landing, and your brother took the rest, along with all the likely lads for leagues around. Many will not come back to us, and we must needs find the men to take their places."

Bran stared resentfully at the sweating boys below. "If I still had my legs, I could beat them all." He remembered the last time he'd held a sword in his hand, when the king had come to Winterfell. It was only a wooden sword, yet he'd knocked Prince Tommen down half a hundred times. "Ser Rodrik should teach me to use a poleaxe. If I had a poleaxe with a big long haft, Hodor could be my legs. We could be a knight together."

"I think that . . . unlikely," Maester Luwin said. "Bran, when a man fights, his arms and legs and thoughts must be as one."

Below in the yard, Ser Rodrik was yelling. "You fight like a goose. He pecks you and you peck him harder. *Parry!* Block the blow. Goose fighting will not suffice. If those were real swords, the first peck would take your arm off!" One of the other boys laughed, and the old knight rounded on him. "You laugh. You. Now that is gall. *You* fight like a hedgehog . . ."

"There was a knight once who couldn't see," Bran said stubbornly, as Ser Rodrik went on below. "Old Nan told me about him. He had a long staff with blades at both ends and he could spin it in his hands and chop two men at once."

"Symeon Star-Eyes," Luwin said as he marked numbers in a book. "When he lost his eyes, he put star sapphires in the empty sockets, or so the singers claim. Bran, that is only a story, like the tales of Florian the Fool. A fable from the Age of Heroes." The maester *tsk*ed. "You must put these dreams aside, they will only break your heart."

The mention of dreams reminded him. "I dreamed about the crow again last night. The one with three eyes. He flew into my bedchamber and told me to come with him, so I did. We went down to the crypts. Father was there, and we talked. He was sad."

"And why was that?" Luwin peered through his tube.

"It was something to do about Jon, I think." The dream had been deeply disturbing, more so than any of the other crow dreams. "Hodor won't go down into the crypts."

The maester had only been half listening, Bran could tell. He lifted his eye from the tube, blinking. "Hodor won't . . . ?"

"Go down into the crypts. When I woke, I told him to take me down, to see if Father was truly there. At first he didn't know what I was saying, but I got him to the steps by telling him to go here and go there, only then he wouldn't go down. He just stood on the top step and said 'Hodor,' like he was scared of the dark, but I *had* a torch. It made me so mad I almost gave him a swat in the head, like Old Nan is always doing." He saw the way the maester was frowning and hurriedly added, "I didn't, though."

"Good. Hodor is a man, not a mule to be beaten."

"In the dream I flew down with the crow, but I can't do that when I'm awake," Bran explained.

"Why would you want to go down to the crypts?"

"I told you. To look for Father."

The maester tugged at the chain around his neck, as he often did when he was uncomfortable. "Bran, sweet child, one day Lord Eddard will sit below in stone, beside his father and his father's father and all the Starks back to the old Kings in the North . . . but that will not be for many years, gods be good. Your father is a prisoner of the queen in King's Landing. You will not find him in the crypts."

"He was there last night. I talked to him."

"Stubborn boy," the maester sighed, setting his book aside. "Would you like to go see?"

"I can't. Hodor won't go, and the steps are too narrow and twisty for Dancer."

"I believe I can solve that difficulty."

In place of Hodor, the wildling woman Osha was summoned. She was tall and tough and uncomplaining, willing to go wherever she was commanded. "I lived my life beyond the Wall, a hole in the ground won't fret me none, m'lords," she said.

"Summer, come," Bran called as she lifted him in wiry-strong arms. The direwolf left his bone and followed as Osha carried Bran across the yard and down the spiral steps to the cold vault under the earth. Maester Luwin went ahead with a torch. Bran did not even mind—*too* badly—that she carried him in her arms and not on her back. Ser Rodrik had ordered Osha's chain struck off, since she had served faithfully and well since she had been at Winterfell. She still wore the heavy iron shackles around her ankles—a sign that she was not yet wholly trusted—but they did not hinder her sure strides down the steps.

Bran could not recall the last time he had been in the crypts. It had been *before*, for certain. When he was little, he used to play down here with Robb and Jon and his sisters.

He wished they were here now; the vault might not have seemed so dark and scary. Summer stalked out in the echoing gloom, then stopped, lifted his head, and sniffed the chill dead air. He bared his teeth and crept backward, eyes glowing golden in the light of the maester's torch. Even Osha, hard as old iron, seemed uncomfortable. "Grim folk, by the look of them," she said as she eyed the long row of granite Starks on their stone thrones.

"They were the Kings of Winter," Bran whispered. Somehow it felt wrong to talk too loudly in this place.

Osha smiled. "Winter's got no king. If you'd seen it, you'd know that, summer boy."

"They were the Kings in the North for thousands of years," Maester Luwin said, lifting the torch high so the light shone on the stone faces. Some were hairy and bearded, shaggy men fierce as the wolves that crouched by their feet. Others were shaved clean, their features gaunt and sharp-edged as the iron longswords across their laps. "Hard men for a hard time. Come." He strode briskly down the vault, past the procession of stone pillars and the endless carved figures. A tongue of flame trailed back from the upraised torch as he went.

The vault was cavernous, longer than Winterfell itself, and Jon had told him once that there were other levels underneath, vaults even deeper and darker where the older kings were buried. It would not do to lose the light. Summer refused to move from the steps, even when Osha followed the torch, Bran in her arms.

"Do you recall your history, Bran?" the maester said as they walked. "Tell Osha who they were and what they did, if you can."

He looked at the passing faces and the tales came back to him. The maester had told him the stories, and Old

Nan had made them come alive. "That one is Jon Stark. When the sea raiders landed in the east, he drove them out and built the castle at White Harbor. His son was Rickard Stark, not my father's father but another Rickard, he took the Neck away from the Marsh King and married his daughter. Theon Stark's the real thin one with the long hair and the skinny beard. They called him the 'Hungry Wolf,' because he was always at war. That's a Brandon, the tall one with the dreamy face, he was Brandon the Shipwright, because he loved the sea. His tomb is empty. He tried to sail west across the Sunset Sea and was never seen again. His son was Brandon the Burner, because he put the torch to all his father's ships in grief. There's Rodrik Stark, who won Bear Island in a wrestling match and gave it to the Mormonts. And that's Torrhen Stark, the King Who Knelt. He was the last King in the North and the first Lord of Winterfell, after he yielded to Aegon the Conqueror. Oh, there, he's Cregan Stark. He fought with Prince Aemon once, and the Dragonknight said he'd never faced a finer swordsman." They were almost at the end now, and Bran felt a sadness creeping over him. "And there's my grandfather, Lord Rickard, who was beheaded by Mad King Aerys. His daughter Lyanna and his son Brandon are in the tombs beside him. Not me, another Brandon, my father's brother. They're not supposed to have statues, that's only for the lords and the kings, but my father loved them so much he had them done."

"The maid's a fair one," Osha said.

"Robert was betrothed to marry her, but Prince Rhaegar carried her off and raped her," Bran explained. "Robert fought a war to win her back. He killed Rhaegar on the Trident with his hammer, but Lyanna died and he never got her back at all."

"A sad tale," said Osha, "but those empty holes are sadder."

"Lord Eddard's tomb, for when his time comes," Maester Luwin said. "Is this where you saw your father in your dream, Bran?"

"Yes." The memory made him shiver. He looked around the vault uneasily, the hairs on the back of his neck bristling. Had he heard a noise? Was there someone here?

Maester Luwin stepped toward the open sepulchre, torch in hand. "As you see, he's not here. Nor will he be, for many a year. Dreams are only dreams, child." He thrust his arm into the blackness inside the tomb, as into the mouth of some great beast. "Do you see? It's quite empt—"

The darkness sprang at him, snarling.

Bran saw eyes like green fire, a flash of teeth, fur as black as the pit around them. Maester Luwin yelled and threw up his hands. The torch went flying from his fingers, caromed off the stone face of Brandon Stark, and tumbled to the statue's feet, the flames licking up his legs. In the drunken shifting torchlight, they saw Luwin struggling with the direwolf, beating at his muzzle with one hand while the jaws closed on the other.

"Summer!" Bran screamed.

And Summer came, shooting from the dimness behind them, a leaping shadow. He slammed into Shaggydog and knocked him back, and the two direwolves rolled over and over in a tangle of grey and black fur, snapping and biting at each other, while Maester Luwin struggled to his knees, his arm torn and bloody. Osha propped Bran up against Lord Rickard's stone wolf as she hurried to assist the maester. In the light of the guttering torch, shadow wolves twenty feet tall fought on the wall and roof.

"Shaggy," a small voice called. When Bran looked up, his little brother was standing in the mouth of Father's tomb. With one final snap at Summer's face, Shaggydog broke off and bounded to Rickon's side. "You let my father be," Rickon warned Luwin. "You let him be."

"Rickon," Bran said softly. "Father's not here."

"Yes he is. I saw him." Tears glistened on Rickon's face. "I saw him last night."

"In your dream . . . ?"

Rickon nodded. "You leave him. You leave him be. He's coming home now, like he promised. He's coming home."

Bran had never seen Maester Luwin look so uncertain before. Blood dripped down his arm where Shaggydog had shredded the wool of his sleeve and the flesh beneath. "Osha, the torch," he said, biting through his pain, and she snatched it up before it went out. Soot stains blackened both legs of his uncle's likeness. "That . . . that *beast,"* Luwin went on, "is supposed to be chained up in the kennels."

Rickon patted Shaggydog's muzzle, damp with blood. "I let him loose. He doesn't like chains." He licked at his fingers.

"Rickon," Bran said, "would you like to come with me?"

"No. I like it here."

"It's dark here. And cold."

"I'm not afraid. I have to wait for Father."

"You can wait with me," Bran said. "We'll wait together, you and me and our wolves." Both of the direwolves were licking wounds now, and would bear close watching.

"Bran," the maester said firmly, "I know you mean well, but Shaggydog is too wild to run loose. I'm the third man he's savaged. Give him the freedom of the castle and it's only a question of time before he kills someone. The truth is hard, but the wolf has to be chained, or . . ." He hesitated.

. . . or killed, Bran thought, but what he said was, "He was not made for chains. We will wait in your tower, all of us."

"That is quite impossible," Maester Luwin said.

Osha grinned. "The boy's the lordling here, as I recall." She handed Luwin back his torch and scooped Bran up into her arms again. "The maester's tower it is."

"Will you come, Rickon?"

His brother nodded. "If Shaggy comes too," he said, running after Osha and Bran, and there was nothing Maester Luwin could do but follow, keeping a wary eye on the wolves.

Maester Luwin's turret was so cluttered that it seemed to Bran a wonder that he ever found anything. Tottering piles of books covered tables and chairs, rows of stoppered jars lined the shelves, candle stubs and puddles of dried wax dotted the furniture, the bronze Myrish lens tube sat on a tripod by the terrace door, star charts hung from the walls, shadow maps lay scattered among the rushes, papers, quills, and pots of inks were everywhere, and all of it was spotted with droppings from the ravens in the rafters. Their strident *quorks* drifted down from above as Osha washed and cleaned and bandaged the maester's wounds, under Luwin's terse instruction. "This is folly," the small grey man said while she dabbed at the wolf bites with a stinging ointment. "I agree that it is odd that both you boys dreamed the same dream, yet when you stop to consider it, it's only natural. You miss your lord father, and you know that he is a captive. Fear can fever a man's mind and give him queer thoughts. Rickon is too young to comprehend—"

"I'm four now," Rickon said. He was peeking through the lens tube at the gargoyles on the First Keep. The direwolves sat on opposite sides of the large round room, licking their wounds and gnawing on bones.

"—too young, and—*ooh*, seven hells, that burns, no, don't stop, more. Too young, as I say, but you, Bran, you're old enough to know that dreams are only dreams."

"Some are, some aren't." Osha poured pale red firemilk into a long gash. Luwin gasped. "The children of the forest could tell you a thing or two about dreaming."

Tears were streaming down the maester's face, yet he shook his head doggedly. "The children . . . live only in dreams. Now. Dead and gone. Enough, that's enough. Now the bandages. Pads and then wrap, and make it tight, I'll be bleeding."

"Old Nan says the children knew the songs of the trees, that they could fly like birds and swim like fish and talk to the animals," Bran said. "She says that they made music so beautiful that it made you cry like a little baby just to hear it."

"And all this they did with magic," Maester Luwin said, distracted. "I wish they were here now. A spell would heal my arm less painfully, and they could talk to Shaggydog and tell him not to bite." He gave the big black wolf an angry glance out of the corner of his eye. "Take a lesson, Bran. The man who trusts in spells is dueling with a glass sword. As the children did. Here, let me show you something." He stood abruptly, crossed the room, and returned with a green jar in his good hand. "Have a look at these," he said as he pulled the stopper and shook out a handful of shiny black arrowheads.

Bran picked one up. "It's made of glass." Curious, Rickon drifted closer to peer over the table.

"Dragonglass," Osha named it as she sat down beside Luwin, bandagings in hand.

"Obsidian," Maester Luwin insisted, holding out his wounded arm. "Forged in the fires of the gods, far below the earth. The children of the forest hunted with that, thousands of years ago. The children worked no metal. In place of mail, they wore long shirts of woven leaves and bound their legs in bark, so they seemed to melt into the wood. In place of swords, they carried blades of obsidian."

"And still do." Osha placed soft pads over the bites on the maester's forearm and bound them tight with long strips of linen.

Bran held the arrowhead up close. The black glass was slick and shiny. He thought it beautiful. "Can I keep one?"

"As you wish," the maester said.

"I want one too," Rickon said. "I want four. *I'm* four."

Luwin made him count them out. "Careful, they're still sharp. Don't cut yourself."

"Tell me about the children," Bran said. It was important.

"What do you wish to know?"

"Everything."

Maester Luwin tugged at his chain collar where it chafed against his neck. "They were people of the Dawn Age, the very first, before kings and kingdoms," he said. "In those days, there were no castles or holdfasts, no cities, not so much as a market town to be found between here and the sea of Dorne. There were no men at all. Only the children of the forest dwelt in the lands we now call the Seven Kingdoms.

"They were a people dark and beautiful, small of stature, no taller than children even when grown to manhood. They lived in the depths of the wood, in caves and crannogs and secret tree towns. Slight as they were, the children were quick and graceful. Male and female hunted together, with weirwood bows and flying snares. Their gods were the gods of the forest, stream, and stone, the old gods whose names are secret. Their wise men were called *greenseers*, and carved strange faces in the weirwoods to keep watch on the woods. How long the children reigned here or where they came from, no man can know.

"But some twelve thousand years ago, the First Men appeared from the east, crossing the Broken Arm of Dorne before it was broken. They came with bronze swords and great leathern shields, riding horses. No horse had ever been seen on this side of the narrow sea. No doubt the children were as frightened by the horses as the First Men were by the faces in the trees. As the First Men carved out holdfasts and farms, they cut down the faces and gave them to the fire. Horror-struck, the children went to war. The old songs say that the greenseers used dark magics to make the seas rise and sweep away the land, shattering the Arm, but it was too late to close the door. The wars went on until the earth ran red with blood of men and children both, but more children than men, for men were bigger and stronger, and wood and stone and obsidian make a poor match for bronze. Finally the wise of both races prevailed, and the chiefs and heroes of the First Men met the greenseers and wood dancers amidst the weirwood groves of a small island in the great lake called Gods Eye.

"There they forged the Pact. The First Men were given the coastlands, the high plains and bright meadows, the mountains and bogs, but the deep woods were to remain forever the children's, and no more weirwoods were to be put to the axe anywhere in the realm. So the gods might bear witness to the signing, every tree on the island was given a face, and afterward, the sacred order of green men was formed to keep watch over the Isle of Faces.

"The Pact began four thousand years of friendship between men and children. In time, the First Men even put aside the gods they had brought with them, and took up the worship of the secret gods of the wood. The signing of the Pact ended the Dawn Age, and began the Age of Heroes."

Bran's fist curled around the shiny black arrowhead. "But the children of the forest are all gone now, you said."

"Here, they are," said Osha, as she bit off the end of the last bandage with her teeth. "North of the Wall, things are different. That's where the children went, and the giants, and the other old races."

Maester Luwin sighed. "Woman, by rights you ought to be dead or in chains. The Starks have treated you more gently than you deserve. It is unkind to repay them for their kindness by filling the boys' heads with folly."

"Tell me where they went," Bran said. "I want to know."

"Me too," Rickon echoed.

"Oh, very well," Luwin muttered. "So long as the kingdoms of the First Men held sway, the Pact endured, all through the Age of Heroes and the Long Night and the birth of the Seven Kingdoms, yet finally there came a time, many centuries later, when other peoples crossed the narrow sea.

"The Andals were the first, a race of tall, fair-haired warriors who came with steel and fire and the seven-pointed star of the new gods painted on their chests. The wars lasted hundreds of years, but in the end the six southron kingdoms all fell before them. Only here, where the King in the North threw back every army that tried to cross the Neck, did the rule of the First Men endure. The Andals burnt out the weirwood groves, hacked down the faces, slaughtered the children where they found them, and everywhere proclaimed the triumph of the Seven over the old gods. So the children fled north—"

Summer began to howl.

Maester Luwin broke off, startled. When Shaggydog bounded to his feet and added his voice to his brother's, dread clutched at Bran's heart. *"It's coming,"* he whispered, with the certainty of despair. He had known it since last night, he realized, since the crow had led him down into the crypts to say farewell. He had known it, but he had not believed. He had wanted Maester Luwin to be right. *The crow,* he thought, *the three-eyed crow . . .*

The howling stopped as suddenly as it had begun. Summer padded across the tower floor to Shaggydog, and began to lick at a mat of bloody fur on the back of his brother's neck. From the window came a flutter of wings.

A raven landed on the grey stone sill, opened its beak, and gave a harsh, raucous rattle of distress.

Rickon began to cry. His arrowheads fell from his hand one by one and clattered on the floor. Bran pulled him close and hugged him.

Maester Luwin stared at the black bird as if it were a scorpion with feathers. He rose, slow as a sleepwalker, and moved to the window. When he whistled, the raven hopped onto his bandaged forearm. There was dried blood on its wings. "A hawk," Luwin murmured, "perhaps an owl. Poor thing, a wonder it got through." He took the letter from its leg.

Bran found himself shivering as the maester unrolled the paper. "What is it?" he said, holding his brother all the harder.

"You know what it is, boy," Osha said, not unkindly. She put her hand on his head.

Maester Luwin looked up at them numbly, a small grey man with blood on the sleeve of his grey wool robe and tears in his bright grey eyes. "My lords," he said to the sons, in a voice gone hoarse and shrunken, "we . . . we shall need to find a stonecarver who knew his likeness well . . ."

SANSA

I n the tower room at the heart of Maegor's Holdfast, Sansa gave herself to the darkness.

She drew the curtains around her bed, slept, woke weeping, and slept again. When she could not sleep she lay under her blankets shivering with grief. Servants came and went, bringing meals, but the sight of food was more than she could bear. The dishes piled up on the table beneath her window, untouched and spoiling, until the servants took them away again.

Sometimes her sleep was leaden and dreamless, and she woke from it more tired than when she had closed her eyes. Yet those were the best times, for when she dreamed, she dreamed of Father. Waking or sleeping, she saw him, saw the gold cloaks fling him down, saw Ser Ilyn striding forward, unsheathing Ice from the scabbard on his back, saw the moment . . . the moment when . . . she had wanted to look away, she had *wanted* to, her legs had gone out from under her and she had fallen to her knees, yet somehow she could not turn her head, and all the people were screaming and shouting, and her prince had smiled at her, he'd *smiled* and she'd felt safe, but only for a heartbeat, until he said those words, and her father's legs . . . that was what she remembered, his legs, the way they'd *jerked* when Ser Ilyn . . . when the sword . . .

Perhaps I will die too, she told herself, and the thought did not seem so terrible to her. If she flung herself from the window, she could put an end to her suffering, and in the years to come the singers would write songs of her grief. Her body would lie on the stones below, broken and innocent, shaming all those who had betrayed her. Sansa went so far as to cross the bedchamber and throw open the shutters . . . but then her courage left her, and she ran back to her bed, sobbing.

The serving girls tried to talk to her when they brought her meals, but she never answered them. Once Grand Maester Pycelle came with a box of flasks and bottles, to ask if she was ill. He felt her brow, made her undress, and touched her all over while her bedmaid held her down. When he left he gave her a potion of honeywater and herbs and told her to drink a swallow every night. She drank it all right then and went back to sleep.

She dreamt of footsteps on the tower stair, an ominous scraping of leather on stone as a man climbed slowly toward her bedchamber, step by step. All she could do was huddle behind her door and listen, trembling, as he came closer and closer. It was Ser Ilyn Payne, she knew, coming for her with Ice in his hand, coming to take her head. There was no place to run, no place to hide, no way to bar the door. Finally the footsteps stopped and she knew he was just outside, standing there silent with his dead eyes and his long pocked face. That was when she realized she was naked. She crouched down, trying to cover herself with her hands, as her door began to swing open, creaking, the point of the greatsword poking through . . .

She woke murmuring, "Please, please, I'll be good, I'll be *good*, please don't," but there was no one to hear.

When they finally came for her in truth, Sansa never heard their footsteps. It was Joffrey who opened her door, not Ser Ilyn but the boy who had been her prince. She was in bed, curled up tight, her curtains drawn, and she could not have said if it was noon or midnight. The first thing she heard was the slam of the door. Then her bed hangings were yanked back, and she threw up a hand against the sudden light and saw them standing over her.

"You will attend me in court this afternoon," Joffrey said. "See that you bathe and dress as befits my betrothed." Sandor Clegane stood at his shoulder in a plain brown doublet and green mantle, his burned face hideous in the morning light. Behind them were two knights of the Kingsguard in long white satin cloaks.

Sansa drew her blanket up to her chin to cover herself. "No," she whimpered, "please . . . leave me be."

"If you won't rise and dress yourself, my Hound will do it for you," Joffrey said.

"I beg of you, my prince . . ."

"I'm king now. Dog, get her out of bed."

Sandor Clegane scooped her up around the waist and lifted her off the featherbed as she struggled feebly. Her blanket fell to the floor. Underneath she had only a thin bedgown to cover her nakedness. "Do as you're bid, child," Clegane said. "Dress." He pushed her toward her wardrobe, almost gently.

Sansa backed away from them. "I did as the queen asked, I wrote the letters, I wrote what she told me. You promised you'd be merciful. Please, let me go home. I won't do any treason, I'll be good, I swear it, I don't have traitor's blood, I *don't*. I only want to go home." Remembering her courtesies, she lowered her head. "As it please you," she finished weakly.

"It does *not* please me," Joffrey said. "Mother says I'm still to marry you, so you'll stay here, and you'll obey."

"I don't *want* to marry you," Sansa wailed. "You chopped off my father's *head*!"

"He was a traitor. I never promised to spare him, only that I'd be merciful, and I was. If he hadn't been your father, I would have had him torn or flayed, but I gave him a clean death."

Sansa stared at him, seeing him for the first time. He was wearing a padded crimson doublet patterned with lions and a cloth-of-gold cape with a high collar that framed his face. She wondered how she could ever have thought him handsome. His lips were as soft and red as the worms you found after a rain, and his eyes were vain and cruel. "I hate you," she whispered.

King Joffrey's face hardened. "My mother tells me that

it isn't fitting that a king should strike his wife. Ser Meryn."

The knight was on her before she could think, yanking back her hand as she tried to shield her face and back-handing her across the ear with a gloved fist. Sansa did not remember falling, yet the next she knew she was sprawled on one knee amongst the rushes. Her head was ringing. Ser Meryn Trant stood over her, with blood on the knuckles of his white silk glove.

"Will you obey now, or shall I have him chastise you again?"

Sansa's ear felt numb. She touched it, and her finger-tips came away wet and red. "I . . . as . . . as you command, my lord."

"*Your Grace*," Joffrey corrected her. "I shall look for you in court." He turned and left.

Ser Meryn and Ser Arys followed him out, but Sandor Clegane lingered long enough to yank her roughly to her feet. "Save yourself some pain, girl, and give him what he wants."

"What . . . what does he want? Please, tell me."

"He wants you to smile and smell sweet and be his lady love," the Hound rasped. "He wants to hear you re-cite all your pretty little words the way the septa taught you. He wants you to love him . . . and fear him."

After he was gone, Sansa sank back onto the rushes, staring at the wall until two of her bedmaids crept timidly into the chamber. "I will need hot water for my bath, please," she told them, "and perfume, and some powder to hide this bruise." The right side of her face was swollen and beginning to ache, but she knew Joffrey would want her to be beautiful.

The hot water made her think of Winterfell, and she took strength from that. She had not washed since the day her father died, and she was startled at how filthy the water became. Her maids sluiced the blood off her face, scrubbed the dirt from her back, washed her hair and brushed it out until it sprang back in thick auburn curls. Sansa did not speak to them, except to give them com-mands; they were Lannister servants, not her own, and she did not trust them. When the time came to dress, she chose the green silk gown that she had worn to the tour-ney. She recalled how gallant Joff had been to her that night at the feast. Perhaps it would make him remember as well, and treat her more gently.

She drank a glass of buttermilk and nibbled at some sweet biscuits as she waited, to settle her stomach. It was midday when Ser Meryn returned. He had donned his white armor; a shirt of enameled scales chased with gold, a tall helm with a golden sunburst crest, greaves and gorget and gauntlet and boots of gleaming plate, a heavy wool cloak clasped with a golden lion. His visor had been removed from his helm, to better show his dour face; pouchy bags under his eyes, a wide sour mouth, rusty hair spotted with grey. "My lady," he said, bowing, as if he had not beaten her bloody only three hours past. "His Grace has instructed me to escort you to the throne room."

"Did he instruct you to hit me if I refused to come?"

"Are you refusing to come, my lady?" The look he gave her was without expression. He did not so much as glance at the bruise he had left her.

He did not hate her, Sansa realized; neither did he love her. He felt nothing for her at all. She was only a . . . a *thing* to him. "No," she said, rising. She wanted to rage, to hurt him as he'd hurt her, to warn him that when she was queen she would have him exiled if he ever dared strike her again . . . but she remembered what the Hound had told her, so all she said was, "I shall do whatever His Grace commands."

"As I do," he replied.

"Yes . . . but you are no true knight, Ser Meryn."

Sandor Clegane would have laughed at that, Sansa knew. Other men might have cursed her, warned her to keep silent, even begged for her forgiveness. Ser Meryn Trant did none of these. Ser Meryn Trant simply did not care.

The balcony was deserted save for Sansa. She stood with her head bowed, fighting to hold back her tears, while below Joffrey sat on his Iron Throne and dispensed what it pleased him to call justice. Nine cases out of ten seemed to bore him; those he allowed his council to handle, squirming restlessly while Lord Baelish, Grand Maester Pycelle, or Queen Cersei resolved the matter. When he did choose to make a ruling, though, not even his queen mother could sway him.

A thief was brought before him and he had Ser Ilyn chop his hand off, right there in court. Two knights came to him with a dispute about some land, and he decreed that they should duel for it on the morrow. "To the *death*," he added. A woman fell to her knees to plead for the head of a man executed as a traitor. She had loved him, she said, and she wanted to see him decently buried. "If you loved a traitor, you must be a traitor too," Joffrey said. Two gold cloaks dragged her off to the dungeons.

Frog-faced Lord Slynt sat at the end of the council table wearing a black velvet doublet and a shiny cloth-of-gold cape, nodding with approval every time the king pronounced a sentence. Sansa stared hard at his ugly face, remembering how he had thrown down her father for Ser Ilyn to behead, wishing she could hurt him, wishing that some hero would throw *him* down and cut off his head. But a voice inside her whispered, *There are no heroes,* and she remembered what Lord Petyr had said to her, here in this very hall. "Life is not a song, sweetling," he'd told her. "You may learn that one day to your sorrow." *In life, the monsters win,* she told herself, and now it was the Hound's voice she heard, a cold rasp, metal on stone. "Save yourself some pain, girl, and give him what he wants."

The last case was a plump tavern singer, accused of making a song that ridiculed the late King Robert. Joff commanded them to fetch his woodharp and ordered him to perform the song for the court. The singer wept and swore he would never sing that song again, but the king insisted. It was sort of a funny song, all about Robert fighting with a pig. The pig was the boar who'd killed him, Sansa knew, but in some verses it almost sounded as if he were singing about the queen. When the song was done, Joffrey announced that he'd decided to be merciful. The singer could keep either his fingers or his tongue. He would have a day to make his choice. Janos Slynt nodded.

That was the final business of the afternoon, Sansa saw with relief, but her ordeal was not yet done. When the herald's voice dismissed the court, she fled the balcony, only to find Joffrey waiting for her at the base of the curving stairs. The Hound was with him, and Ser Meryn as well. The young king examined her critically, top to bottom. "You look much better than you did."

"Thank you, Your Grace," Sansa said. Hollow words, but they made him nod and smile.

"Walk with me," Joffrey commanded, offering her his arm. She had no choice but to take it. The touch of his hand would have thrilled her once; now it made her flesh crawl. "My name day will be here soon," Joffrey said as they slipped out the rear of the throne room. "There will be a great feast, and gifts. What are you going to give me?"

"I . . . I had not thought, my lord."

"*Your Grace*," he said sharply. "You truly are a stupid girl, aren't you? My mother says so."

"She does?" After all that had happened, his words should have lost their power to hurt her, yet somehow they had not. The queen had always been so kind to her.

"Oh, yes. She worries about our children, whether they'll be stupid like you, but I told her not to trouble herself." The king gestured, and Ser Meryn opened a door for them.

"Thank you, Your Grace," she murmured. *The Hound was right*, she thought, *I am only a little bird, repeating the words they taught me*. The sun had fallen below the western wall, and the stones of the Red Keep glowed dark as blood.

"I'll get you with child as soon as you're able," Joffrey said as he escorted her across the practice yard. "If the first one is stupid, I'll chop off your head and find a smarter wife. When do you think you'll be able to have children?"

Sansa could not look at him, he shamed her so. "Septa Mordane says most . . . most highborn girls have their flowering at twelve or thirteen."

Joffrey nodded. "This way." He led her into the gatehouse, to the base of the steps that led up to the battlements.

Sansa jerked back away from him, trembling. Suddenly she knew where they were going. "*No*," she said, her voice a frightened gasp. "Please, no, don't make me, I beg you . . ."

Joffrey pressed his lips together. "I want to show you what happens to traitors."

Sansa shook her head wildly. "I won't. I *won't*."

"I can have Ser Meryn drag you up," he said. "You won't like that. You had better do what I say." Joffrey reached for her, and Sansa cringed away from him, backing into the Hound.

"Do it, girl," Sandor Clegane told her, pushing her back toward the king. His mouth twitched on the burned side of his face and Sansa could almost hear the rest of it. *He'll have you up there no matter what, so give him what he wants.*

She forced herself to take King Joffrey's hand. The climb was something out of a nightmare; every step was a struggle, as if she were pulling her feet out of ankle-deep mud, and there were more steps than she would have believed, a thousand thousand steps, and horror waiting on the ramparts.

From the high battlements of the gatehouse, the whole world spread out below them. Sansa could see the Great Sept of Baelor on Visenya's hill, where her father had died. At the other end of the Street of the Sisters stood the fire-blackened ruins of the Dragonpit. To the west, the swollen red sun was half-hidden behind the Gate of the Gods. The salt sea was at her back, and to the south was the fish market and the docks and the swirling torrent of the Blackwater Rush. And to the north . . .

She turned that way, and saw only the city, streets and alleys and hills and bottoms and more streets and more alleys and the stone of distant walls. Yet she knew that beyond them was open country, farms and fields and forests, and beyond that, north and north and north again, stood Winterfell.

"What are you looking at?" Joffrey said. "This is what I wanted you to see, right here."

A thick stone parapet protected the outer edge of the rampart, reaching as high as Sansa's chin, with crenellations cut into it every five feet for archers. The heads were mounted between the crenels, along the top of the wall, impaled on iron spikes so they faced out over the city. Sansa had noted them the moment she'd stepped out onto the wallwalk, but the river and the bustling streets and the setting sun were ever so much prettier. *He can make me look at the heads,* she told herself, *but he can't make me see them.*

"This one is your father," he said. "This one here. Dog, turn it around so she can see him."

Sandor Clegane took the head by the hair and turned

it. The severed head had been dipped in tar to preserve it longer. Sansa looked at it calmly, not seeing it at all. It did not really look like Lord Eddard, she thought; it did not even look *real*. "How long do I have to look?"

Joffrey seemed disappointed. "Do you want to see the rest?" There was a long row of them.

"If it please Your Grace."

Joffrey marched her down the wallwalk, past a dozen more heads and two empty spikes. "I'm saving those for my uncle Stannis and my uncle Renly," he explained. The other heads had been dead and mounted much longer than her father. Despite the tar, most were long past being recognizable. The king pointed to one and said, "That's your septa there," but Sansa could not even have told that it was a woman. The jaw had rotted off her face, and birds had eaten one ear and most of a cheek.

Sansa had wondered what had happened to Septa Mordane, although she supposed she had known all along. "Why did you kill *her*?" she asked. "She was god-sworn . . ."

"She was a traitor." Joffrey looked pouty; somehow she was upsetting him. "You haven't said what you mean to give me for my name day. Maybe I should give you something instead, would you like that?"

"If it please you, my lord," Sansa said.

When he smiled, she knew he was mocking her. "Your brother is a traitor too, you know." He turned Septa Mordane's head back around. "I remember your brother from Winterfell. My dog called him the lord of the wooden sword. Didn't you, dog?"

"Did I?" the Hound replied. "I don't recall."

Joffrey gave a petulant shrug. "Your brother defeated my uncle Jaime. My mother says it was treachery and deceit. She wept when she heard. Women are all weak, even her, though she pretends she isn't. She says we need to stay in King's Landing in case my other uncles attack, but I don't care. After my name day feast, I'm going to raise a host and kill your brother myself. That's what I'll give you, Lady Sansa. Your brother's head."

A kind of madness took over her then, and she heard herself say, "Maybe my brother will give me *your* head."

Joffrey scowled. "You must never mock me like that.

A true wife does not mock her lord. Ser Meryn, teach her."

This time the knight grasped her beneath the jaw and held her head still as he struck her. He hit her twice, left to right, and harder, right to left. Her lip split and blood ran down her chin, to mingle with the salt of her tears.

"You shouldn't be crying all the time," Joffrey told her. "You're more pretty when you smile and laugh."

Sansa made herself smile, afraid that he would have Ser Meryn hit her again if she did not, but it was no good, the king still shook his head. "Wipe off the blood, you're all messy."

The outer parapet came up to her chin, but along the inner edge of the walk was nothing, nothing but a long plunge to the bailey seventy or eighty feet below. All it would take was a shove, she told herself. He was standing right there, right *there*, smirking at her with those fat wormlips. *You could do it*, she told herself. *You could. Do it right now.* It wouldn't even matter if she went over with him. It wouldn't matter at all.

"Here, girl." Sandor Clegane knelt before her, *between* her and Joffrey. With a delicacy surprising in such a big man, he dabbed at the blood welling from her broken lip.

The moment was gone. Sansa lowered her eyes. "Thank you," she said when he was done. She was a good girl, and always remembered her courtesies.

DAENERYS

Wings shadowed her fever dreams.

"You don't want to wake the dragon, do you!"

She was walking down a long hall beneath high stone arches. She could not look behind her, *must* not look behind her. There was a door ahead of her, tiny with distance, but even from afar, she saw that it was painted red. She walked faster, and her bare feet left bloody footprints on the stone.

"You don't want to wake the dragon, do you!"

She saw sunlight on the Dothraki sea, the living plain, rich with the smells of earth and death. Wind stirred the grasses, and they rippled like water. Drogo held her in strong arms, and his hand stroked her sex and opened her and woke that sweet wetness that was his alone, and the stars smiled down on them, stars in a daylight sky. "Home," she whispered as he entered her and filled her with his seed, but suddenly the stars were gone, and across the blue sky swept the great wings, and the world took flame.

". . . don't want to wake the dragon, do you!"

Ser Jorah's face was drawn and sorrowful. "Rhaegar

was the last dragon," he told her. He warmed translucent hands over a glowing brazier where stone eggs smouldered red as coals. One moment he was there and the next he was fading, his flesh colorless, less substantial than the wind. "The last dragon," he whispered, thin as a wisp, and was gone. She felt the dark behind her, and the red door seemed farther away than ever.

". . . don't want to wake the dragon, do you?"

Viserys stood before her, screaming. "The dragon does not beg, slut. You do not command the dragon. I am the dragon, and I will be crowned." The molten gold trickled down his face like wax, burning deep channels in his flesh. *"I am the dragon and I will be crowned!"* he shrieked, and his fingers snapped like snakes, biting at her nipples, pinching, twisting, even as his eyes burst and ran like jelly down seared and blackened cheeks.

". . . don't want to wake the dragon . . ."

The red door was so far ahead of her, and she could feel the icy breath behind, sweeping up on her. If it caught her she would die a death that was more than death, howling forever alone in the darkness. She began to run.

". . . don't want to wake the dragon . . ."

She could feel the heat inside her, a terrible burning in her womb. Her son was tall and proud, with Drogo's copper skin and her own silver-gold hair, violet eyes shaped like almonds. And he smiled for her and began to lift his hand toward hers, but when he opened his mouth the fire poured out. She saw his heart burning through his chest, and in an instant he was gone, consumed like a moth by a candle, turned to ash. She wept for her child, the promise of a sweet mouth on her breast, but her tears turned to steam as they touched her skin.

". . . want to wake the dragon . . ."

Ghosts lined the hallway, dressed in the faded raiment of kings. In their hands were swords of pale fire. They had hair of silver and hair of gold and hair of platinum white, and their eyes were opal and amethyst, tourmaline and jade. "Faster," they cried, "faster, faster." She raced, her feet melting the stone wherever they touched. *"Faster!"* the ghosts cried as one, and she screamed and threw herself forward. A great knife of pain ripped down her back, and she felt her skin tear open and smelled the stench of burning blood and saw the shadow of wings. And Daenerys Targaryen flew.

"*. . . wake the dragon . . .*"

The door loomed before her, the red door, so close, so close, the hall was a blur around her, the cold receding behind. And now the stone was gone and she flew across the Dothraki sea, high and higher, the green rippling beneath, and all that lived and breathed fled in terror from the shadow of her wings. She could smell home, she could see it, there, just beyond that door, green fields and great stone houses and arms to keep her warm, *there*. She threw open the door.

"*. . . the dragon . . .*"

And saw her brother Rhaegar, mounted on a stallion as black as his armor. Fire glimmered red through the narrow eye slit of his helm. "The last dragon," Ser Jorah's voice whispered faintly. "The last, the last." Dany lifted his polished black visor. The face within was her own.

After that, for a long time, there was only the pain, the fire within her, and the whisperings of stars.

She woke to the taste of ashes.

"No," she moaned, "no, please."

"*Khaleesi?*" Jhiqui hovered over her, a frightened doe. The tent was drenched in shadow, still and close. Flakes of ash drifted upward from a brazier, and Dany followed them with her eyes through the smoke hole above. *Flying*, she thought. *I had wings, I was flying.* But it was only a dream. "Help me," she whispered, struggling to rise. "Bring me . . ." Her voice was raw as a wound, and she could not think what she wanted. Why did she hurt so much? It was as if her body had been torn to pieces and remade from the scraps. "I want . . ."

"Yes, *Khaleesi*." Quick as that Jhiqui was gone, bolting from the tent, shouting. Dany needed . . . something . . . someone . . . what? It was important, she knew. It was the only thing in the world that mattered. She rolled onto her side and got an elbow under her, fighting the blanket tangled about her legs. It was so hard to move. The world swam dizzily. *I have to . . .*

They found her on the carpet, crawling toward her dragon eggs. Ser Jorah Mormont lifted her in his arms and carried her back to her sleeping silks, while she struggled feebly against him. Over his shoulder she saw her three handmaids, Jhogo with his little wisp of mustache, and the flat broad face of Mirri Maz Duur. "I must," she tried to tell them, "I have to . . ."

". . . sleep, Princess," Ser Jorah said.

"No," Dany said. "Please. Please."

"Yes." He covered her with silk, though she was burning. "Sleep and grow strong again, *Khaleesi*. Come back to us." And then Mirri Maz Duur was there, the *maegi*, tipping a cup against her lips. She tasted sour milk, and something else, something thick and bitter. Warm liquid ran down her chin. Somehow she swallowed. The tent grew dimmer, and sleep took her again. This time she did not dream. She floated, serene and at peace, on a black sea that knew no shore.

After a time—a night, a day, a year, she could not say— she woke again. The tent was dark, its silken walls flapping like wings when the wind gusted outside. This time Dany did not attempt to rise. "Irri," she called, "Jhiqui. Doreah." They were there at once. "My throat is dry," she said, "so dry," and they brought her water. It was warm and flat, yet Dany drank it eagerly, and sent Jhiqui for more. Irri dampened a soft cloth and stroked her brow. "I have been sick," Dany said. The Dothraki girl nodded. "How long?" The cloth was soothing, but Irri seemed so sad, it frightened her. *"Long,"* she whispered. When Jhiqui returned with more water, Mirri Maz Duur came with her, eyes heavy from sleep. "Drink," she said, lifting Dany's head to the cup once more, but this time it was only wine. Sweet, sweet wine. Dany drank, and lay back, listening to the soft sound of her own breathing. She could feel the heaviness in her limbs, as sleep crept in to fill her up once more. "Bring me . . ." she murmured, her voice slurred and drowsy. "Bring . . . I want to hold . . ."

"Yes?" the *maegi* asked. "What is it you wish, *Khaleesi*?"

"Bring me . . . egg . . . dragon's egg . . . please . . ." Her lashes turned to lead, and she was too weary to hold them up.

When she woke the third time, a shaft of golden sunlight was pouring through the smoke hole of the tent, and her arms were wrapped around a dragon's egg. It was the pale one, its scales the color of butter cream, veined with whorls of gold and bronze, and Dany could feel the heat of it. Beneath her bedsilks, a fine sheen of perspiration covered her bare skin. *Dragondew*, she thought. Her fingers trailed lightly across the surface of the shell, tracing the wisps of gold, and deep in the stone she felt something twist and stretch in response. It did not frighten her. All her fear was gone, burned away.

Dany touched her brow. Under the film of sweat, her skin was cool to the touch, her fever gone. She made herself sit. There was a moment of dizziness, and the deep ache between her thighs. Yet she felt strong. Her maids came running at the sound of her voice. "Water," she told them, "a flagon of water, cold as you can find it. And fruit, I think. Dates."

"As you say, *Khaleesi*."

"I want Ser Jorah," she said, standing. Jhiqui brought a sandsilk robe and draped it over her shoulders. "And a warm bath, and Mirri Maz Duur, and . . ." Memory came back to her all at once, and she faltered. "Khal Drogo," she forced herself to say, watching their faces with dread. "Is he—?"

"The *khal* lives," Irri answered quietly . . . yet Dany saw a darkness in her eyes when she said the words, and no sooner had she spoken than she rushed away to fetch water.

She turned to Doreah. "Tell me."

"I . . . I shall bring Ser Jorah," the Lysene girl said, bowing her head and fleeing the tent.

Jhiqui would have run as well, but Dany caught her by the wrist and held her captive. "What is it? I must know. Drogo . . . and my child." Why had she not remembered the child until now? "My son . . . Rhaego . . . where is he? I want him."

Her handmaid lowered her eyes. "The boy . . . he did not live, *Khaleesi*." Her voice was a frightened whisper.

Dany released her wrist. *My son is dead*, she thought as Jhiqui left the tent. She had known somehow. She had known since she woke the first time to Jhiqui's tears. No, she had known *before* she woke. Her dream came back to her, sudden and vivid, and she remembered the tall man with the copper skin and long silver-gold braid, bursting into flame.

She should weep, she knew, yet her eyes were dry as

ash. She had wept in her dream, and the tears had turned to steam on her cheeks. *All the grief has been burned out of me,* she told herself. She felt sad, and yet . . . she could feel Rhaego receding from her, as if he had never been.

Ser Jorah and Mirri Maz Duur entered a few moments later, and found Dany standing over the other dragon's eggs, the two still in their chest. It seemed to her that they felt as hot as the one she had slept with, which was passing strange. "Ser Jorah, come here," she said. She took his hand and placed it on the black egg with the scarlet swirls. "What do you feel?"

"Shell, hard as rock." The knight was wary. "Scales."

"Heat?"

"No. Cold stone." He took his hand away. "Princess, are you well? Should you be up, weak as you are?"

"Weak? I am strong, Jorah." To please him, she reclined on a pile of cushions. "Tell me how my child died."

"He never lived, my princess. The women say . . ." He faltered, and Dany saw how the flesh hung loose on him, and the way he limped when he moved.

"Tell me. Tell me what the women say."

He turned his face away. His eyes were haunted. "They say the child was . . ."

She waited, but Ser Jorah could not say it. His face grew dark with shame. He looked half a corpse himself.

"Monstrous," Mirri Maz Duur finished for him. The knight was a powerful man, yet Dany understood in that moment that the *maegi* was stronger, and crueler, and infinitely more dangerous. "Twisted. I drew him forth myself. He was scaled like a lizard, blind, with the stub of a tail and small leather wings like the wings of a bat. When I touched him, the flesh sloughed off the bone, and inside he was full of graveworms and the stink of corruption. He had been dead for years."

Darkness, Dany thought. The terrible darkness sweeping up behind to devour her. If she looked back she was lost. "My son was alive and strong when Ser Jorah carried me into this tent," she said. "I could feel him kicking, fighting to be born."

"That may be as it may be," answered Mirri Maz

Duur, "yet the creature that came forth from your womb was as I said. Death was in that tent, *Khaleesi*."

"Only shadows," Ser Jorah husked, but Dany could hear the doubt in his voice. "I saw, *maegi*. I saw you, alone, dancing with the shadows."

"The grave casts long shadows, Iron Lord," Mirri said. "Long and dark, and in the end no light can hold them back."

Ser Jorah had killed her son, Dany knew. He had done what he did for love and loyalty, yet he had carried her into a place no living man should go and fed her baby to the darkness. He knew it too; the grey face, the hollow eyes, the limp. "The shadows have touched you too, Ser Jorah," she told him. The knight made no reply. Dany turned to the godswife. "You warned me that only death could pay for life. I thought you meant the horse."

"No," Mirri Maz Duur said. "That was a lie you told yourself. You knew the price."

Had she? Had she? *If I look back I am lost.* "The price was paid," Dany said. "The horse, my child, Quaro and Qotho, Haggo and Cohollo. The price was paid and paid and paid." She rose from her cushions. "Where is Khal Drogo? Show him to me, godswife, *maegi*, bloodmage, whatever you are. Show me Khal Drogo. Show me what I bought with my son's life."

"As you command, *Khaleesi*," the old woman said. "Come, I will take you to him."

Dany was weaker than she knew. Ser Jorah slipped an arm around her and helped her stand. "Time enough for this later, my princess," he said quietly.

"I would see him now, Ser Jorah."

After the dimness of the tent, the world outside was blinding bright. The sun burned like molten gold, and the land was seared and empty. Her handmaids waited with fruit and wine and water, and Jhogo moved close to help Ser Jorah support her. Aggo and Rakharo stood behind. The glare of sun on sand made it hard to see more, until Dany raised her hand to shade her eyes. She saw the ashes of a fire, a few score horses milling listlessly and searching for a bite of grass, a scattering of tents and bedrolls. A small crowd of children had gathered to watch her, and beyond she glimpsed women going about their work, and withered old men staring at the flat blue sky with tired eyes, swatting feebly at bloodflies. A count might show a hundred people, no more. Where the other forty thousand had made their camp, only the wind and dust lived now.

"Drogo's *khalasar* is gone," she said.

"A *khal* who cannot ride is no *khal*," said Jhogo.

"The Dothraki follow only the strong," Ser Jorah said. "I am sorry, my princess. There was no way to hold them. Ko Pono left first, naming himself Khal Pono, and many followed him. Jhaqo was not long to do the same. The rest slipped away night by night, in large bands and small. There are a dozen new *khalasars* on the Dothraki sea, where once there was only Drogo's."

"The old remain," said Aggo. "The frightened, the weak, and the sick. And we who swore. We remain."

"They took Khal Drogo's herds, *Khaleesi*," Rakharo said. "We were too few to stop them. It is the right of the strong to take from the weak. They took many slaves as well, the *khal's* and yours, yet they left some few."

"Eroeh?" asked Dany, remembering the frightened child she had saved outside the city of the Lamb Men.

"Mago seized her, who is Khal Jhaqo's bloodrider now," said Jhogo. "He mounted her high and low and gave her to his *khal*, and Jhaqo gave her to his other bloodriders. They were six. When they were done with her, they cut her throat."

"It was her fate, *Khaleesi*," said Aggo.

If I look back I am lost. "It was a cruel fate," Dany said, "yet not so cruel as Mago's will be. I promise you that, by the old gods and the new, by the lamb god and the horse god and every god that lives. I swear it by the Mother of Mountains and the Womb of the World. Before I am done with them, Mago and Ko Jhaqo will plead for the mercy they showed Eroeh."

The Dothraki exchanged uncertain glances. "*Khaleesi*," the handmaid Irri explained, as if to a child, "Jhaqo is a *khal* now, with twenty thousand riders at his back."

She lifted her head. "And I am Daenerys Stormborn, Daenerys of House Targaryen, of the blood of Aegon the Conqueror and Maegor the Cruel and old Valyria before them. I am the dragon's daughter, and I swear to you, these men will die screaming. Now bring me to Khal Drogo."

He was lying on the bare red earth, staring up at the sun.

A dozen bloodflies had settled on his body, though he did not seem to feel them. Dany brushed them away and knelt beside him. His eyes were wide open but did not see, and she knew at once that he was blind. When she whispered his name, he did not seem to hear. The wound on his breast was as healed as it would ever be, the scar that covered it grey and red and hideous.

"Why is he out here alone, in the sun?" she asked them.

"He seems to like the warmth, Princess," Ser Jorah said. "His eyes follow the sun, though he does not see it. He can walk after a fashion. He will go where you lead him, but no farther. He will eat if you put food in his mouth, drink if you dribble water on his lips."

Dany kissed her sun-and-stars gently on the brow, and stood to face Mirri Maz Duur. "Your spells are costly, *maegi*."

"He lives," said Mirri Maz Duur. "You asked for life. You paid for life."

"This is not life, for one who was as Drogo was. His life was laughter, and meat roasting over a firepit, and a horse between his legs. His life was an *arakh* in his hand and his bells ringing in his hair as he rode to meet an enemy. His life was his bloodriders, and me, and the son I was to give him."

Mirri Maz Duur made no reply.

"When will he be as he was?" Dany demanded.

"When the sun rises in the west and sets in the east," said Mirri Maz Duur. "When the seas go dry and mountains blow in the wind like leaves. When your womb quickens again, and you bear a living child. Then he will return, and not before."

Dany gestured at Ser Jorah and the others. "Leave us. I would speak with this *maegi* alone." Mormont and the Dothraki withdrew. "You *knew*," Dany said when they were gone. She ached, inside and out, but her fury gave her strength. "You knew what I was buying, and you knew the price, and yet you let me pay it."

"It was wrong of them to burn my temple," the heavy, flat-nosed woman said placidly. "That angered the Great Shepherd."

"This was no god's work," Dany said coldly. *If I look back I am lost.* "You cheated me. You murdered my child within me."

"The stallion who mounts the world will burn no cities now. His *khalasar* shall trample no nations into dust."

"I spoke for you," she said, anguished. "I saved you."

"*Saved* me?" The Lhazareen woman spat. "Three riders had taken me, not as a man takes a woman but from behind, as a dog takes a bitch. The fourth was in me when you rode past. How then did you save me? I saw my god's house burn, where I had healed good men beyond counting. My home they burned as well, and in the street I saw piles of heads. I saw the head of a baker who made my bread. I saw the head of a boy I had saved from deadeye fever, only three moons past. I heard children crying as the riders drove them off with their whips. Tell me again what you saved."

"Your life."

Mirri Maz Duur laughed cruelly. "Look to your *khal* and see what life is worth, when all the rest is gone."

Dany called out for the men of her *khas* and bid them take Mirri Maz Duur and bind her hand and foot, but the *maegi* smiled at her as they carried her off, as if they shared a secret. A word, and Dany could have her head off . . . yet then what would she have? A head? If life was worthless, what was death?

They led Khal Drogo back to her tent, and Dany commanded them to fill a tub, and this time there was no blood in the water. She bathed him herself, washing the dirt and the dust from his arms and chest, cleaning his face with a soft cloth, soaping his long black hair and combing the knots and tangles from it till it shone again as she remembered. It was well past dark before she was done, and Dany was exhausted. She stopped for drink and food, but it was all she could do to nibble at a fig and keep down a mouthful of water. Sleep would have been a release, but she had slept enough . . . too long, in truth. She owed this night to Drogo, for all the nights that had been, and yet might be.

The memory of their first ride was with her when she led him out into the darkness, for the Dothraki believed that all things of importance in a man's life must be done beneath the open sky. She told herself that there were powers stronger than hatred, and spells older and truer than any the *maegi* had learned in Asshai. The night was black and moonless, but overhead a million stars burned bright. She took that for an omen.

No soft blanket of grass welcomed them here, only the hard dusty ground, bare and strewn with stones. No trees stirred in the wind, and there was no stream to soothe her fears with the gentle music of water. Dany told herself that the stars would be enough. "Remember, Drogo," she whispered. "Remember our first ride together, the day we wed. Remember the night we made Rhaego, with the *khalasar* all around us and your eyes on my face. Remember how cool and clean the water was in the Womb of the World. Remember, my sun-and-stars. Remember, and come back to me."

The birth had left her too raw and torn to take him inside of her, as she would have wanted, but Doreah had taught her other ways. Dany used her hands, her mouth, her breasts. She raked him with her nails and covered him with kisses and whispered and prayed and told him stories, and by the end she had bathed him with her tears. Yet Drogo did not feel, or speak, or rise.

And when the bleak dawn broke over an empty horizon, Dany knew that he was truly lost to her. "When the sun rises in the west and sets in the east," she said sadly. "When the seas go dry and mountains blow in the wind like leaves. When my womb quickens again, and I bear a living child. Then you will return, my sun-and-stars, and not before."

Never, the darkness cried, *never never never*.

Inside the tent Dany found a cushion, soft silk stuffed with feathers. She clutched it to her breasts as she walked back out to Drogo, to her sun-and-stars. *If I look back I am lost.* It hurt even to walk, and she wanted to sleep, to sleep and not to dream.

She knelt, kissed Drogo on the lips, and pressed the cushion down across his face.

TYRION

"They have my son," Tywin Lannister said.

"They do, my lord." The messenger's voice was dulled by exhaustion. On the breast of his torn surcoat, the brindled boar of Crakehall was half-obscured by dried blood.

One of your sons, Tyrion thought. He took a sip of wine and said not a word, thinking of Jaime. When he lifted his arm, pain shot through his elbow, reminding him of his own brief taste of battle. He loved his brother, but he would not have wanted to be with him in the Whispering Wood for all the gold in Casterly Rock.

His lord father's assembled captains and bannermen had fallen very quiet as the courier told his tale. The only sound was the crackle and hiss of the log burning in the hearth at the end of the long, drafty common room.

After the hardships of the long relentless drive south, the prospect of even a single night in an inn had cheered Tyrion mightily . . . though he rather wished it had not been *this* inn again, with all its memories. His father had set a grueling pace, and it had taken its toll. Men wounded in the battle kept up as best they could or were abandoned to fend for themselves. Every morning they left a few more by the roadside, men who went to sleep never to wake. Every afternoon a few more collapsed along the way. And every evening a few more deserted, stealing off into the dusk. Tyrion had been half-tempted to go with them.

He had been upstairs, enjoying the comfort of a featherbed and the warmth of Shae's body beside him, when his squire had woken him to say that a rider had arrived with dire news of Riverrun. So it had all been for nothing. The rush south, the endless forced marches, the bodies left beside the road . . . all for naught. Robb Stark had reached Riverrun days and days ago.

"How could this happen?" Ser Harys Swyft moaned. "*How!* Even after the Whispering Wood, you had Riverrun ringed in iron, surrounded by a great host . . . what madness made Ser Jaime decide to split his men into three separate camps? Surely he knew how vulnerable that would leave them?"

Better than you, you chinless craven, Tyrion thought. Jaime might have lost Riverrun, but it angered him to hear his brother slandered by the likes of Swyft, a shameless lickspittle whose greatest accomplishment was marrying his equally chinless daughter to Ser Kevan, and thereby attaching himself to the Lannisters.

"I would have done the same," his uncle responded, a good deal more calmly than Tyrion might have. "You have never seen Riverrun, Ser Harys, or you would know that Jaime had little choice in the matter. The castle is situated at the end of the point of land where the Tumblestone flows into the Red Fork of the Trident. The rivers form two sides of a triangle, and when danger threatens, the Tullys open their sluice gates upstream to create a wide moat on the third side, turning Riverrun into an island. The walls rise sheer from the water, and from their towers the defenders have a commanding view of the opposite shores for many leagues around. To cut off all the approaches, a besieger must needs place one camp north of the Tumblestone, one south of the Red Fork, and a third between the rivers, west of the moat. There is no other way, none."

"Ser Kevan speaks truly, my lords," the courier said. "We'd built palisades of sharpened stakes around the camps, yet it was not enough, not with no warning and the rivers cutting us off from each other. They came down on the north camp first. No one was expecting an attack. Marq Piper had been raiding our supply trains, but he had no more than fifty men. Ser Jaime had gone out to deal with them the night before . . . well, with what we *thought* was them. We were told the Stark host was east of the Green Fork, marching south . . ."

"And your outriders?" Ser Gregor Clegane's face might have been hewn from rock. The fire in the hearth gave a somber orange cast to his skin and put deep shadows in the hollows of his eyes. "They saw nothing? They gave you no warning?"

The bloodstained messenger shook his head. "Our outriders had been vanishing. Marq Piper's work, we thought. The ones who did come back had seen nothing."

"A man who sees nothing has no use for his eyes," the Mountain declared. "Cut them out and give them to your next outrider. Tell him you hope that four eyes might see better than two . . . and if not, the man after him will have six."

Lord Tywin Lannister turned his face to study Ser Gregor. Tyrion saw a glimmer of gold as the light shone off his father's pupils, but he could not have said whether the look was one of approval or disgust. Lord Tywin was oft quiet in council, preferring to listen before he spoke, a habit Tyrion himself tried to emulate. Yet this silence was uncharacteristic even for him, and his wine was untouched.

"You said they came at night," Ser Kevan prompted.

The man gave a weary nod. "The Blackfish led the van, cutting down our sentries and clearing away the palisades for the main assault. By the time our men knew what was happening, riders were pouring over the ditch banks and galloping through the camp with swords and torches in hand. I was sleeping in the west camp, between the rivers. When we heard the fighting and saw the tents being fired, Lord Brax led us to the rafts and we tried to pole across, but the current pushed us downstream and the Tullys started flinging rocks at us with the catapults on their walls. I saw one raft smashed to kindling and three others overturned, men swept into the river and drowned . . . and those who did make it across found the Starks waiting for them on the riverbanks."

Ser Flement Brax wore a silver-and-purple tabard and the look of a man who cannot comprehend what he has just heard. "My lord father—"

"Sorry, my lord," the messenger said. "Lord Brax was clad in plate-and-mail when his raft overturned. He was very gallant."

He was a fool, Tyrion thought, swirling his cup and staring down into the winy depths. Crossing a river at night on a crude raft, wearing armor, with an enemy waiting on the other side—if that was gallantry, he would take cowardice every time. He wondered if Lord Brax had felt especially gallant as the weight of his steel pulled him under the black water.

"The camp between the rivers was overrun as well," the messenger was saying. "While we were trying to cross, more Starks swept in from the west, two columns of armored horse. I saw Lord Umber's giant-in-chains and the Mallister eagle, but it was the boy who led them, with a monstrous wolf running at his side. I wasn't there to see, but it's said the beast killed four men and ripped apart a dozen horses. Our spearmen formed up a shieldwall and held against their first charge, but when the Tullys saw them engaged, they opened the gates of Riverrun and Tytos Blackwood led a sortie across the drawbridge and took them in the rear."

"Gods save us," Lord Lefford swore.

"Greatjon Umber fired the siege towers we were building, and Lord Blackwood found Ser Edmure Tully in chains among the other captives, and made off with them all. Our south camp was under the command of Ser Forley Prester. He retreated in good order when he saw that the other camps were lost, with two thousand spears and as many bowmen, but the Tyroshi sellsword who led his freeriders struck his banners and went over to the foe."

"Curse the man." His uncle Kevan sounded more angry than surprised. "I warned Jaime not to trust that one. A man who fights for coin is loyal only to his purse."

Lord Tywin wove his fingers together under his chin. Only his eyes moved as he listened. His bristling golden side-whiskers framed a face so still it might have been a mask, but Tyrion could see tiny beads of sweat dappling his father's shaven head.

"How could it *happen*?" Ser Harys Swyft wailed again.

"Ser Jaime taken, the siege broken . . . this is a *catastrophe!*"

Ser Addam Marbrand said, "I am sure we are all grateful to you for pointing out the obvious, Ser Harys. The question is, what shall we do about it?"

"What *can* we do? Jaime's host is all slaughtered or taken or put to flight, and the Starks and the Tullys sit squarely across our line of supply. We are cut off from the west! They can march on Casterly Rock if they so choose, and what's to stop them? My lords, we are beaten. We must sue for peace."

"Peace?" Tyrion swirled his wine thoughtfully, took a deep draft, and hurled his empty cup to the floor, where it shattered into a thousand pieces. "There's your peace, Ser Harys. My sweet nephew broke it for good and all when he decided to ornament the Red Keep with Lord Eddard's head. You'll have an easier time drinking wine from that cup than you will convincing Robb Stark to make peace *now*. He's *winning* . . . or hadn't you noticed?"

"Two battles do not make a war," Ser Addam insisted. "We are far from lost. I should welcome the chance to try my own steel against this Stark boy."

"Perhaps they would consent to a truce, and allow us to trade our prisoners for theirs," offered Lord Lefford.

"Unless they trade three-for-one, we still come out light on those scales," Tyrion said acidly. "And what are we to offer for my brother? Lord Eddard's rotting head?"

"I had heard that Queen Cersei has the Hand's daughters," Lefford said hopefully. "If we give the lad his sisters back . . ."

Ser Addam snorted disdainfully. "He would have to be an utter ass to trade Jaime Lannister's life for two girls."

"Then we must ransom Ser Jaime, whatever it costs," Lord Lefford said.

Tyrion rolled his eyes. "If the Starks feel the need for gold, they can melt down Jaime's armor."

"If we ask for a truce, they will think us weak," Ser Addam argued. "We should march on them at once."

"Surely our friends at court could be prevailed upon to join us with fresh troops," said Ser Harys. "And someone might return to Casterly Rock to raise a new host."

Lord Tywin Lannister rose to his feet. "*They have my*

son," he said once more, in a voice that cut through the babble like a sword through suet. "Leave me. All of you."

Ever the soul of obedience, Tyrion rose to depart with the rest, but his father gave him a look. "Not you, Tyrion. Remain. And you as well, Kevan. The rest of you, out."

Tyrion eased himself back onto the bench, startled into speechlessness. Ser Kevan crossed the room to the wine casks. "Uncle," Tyrion called, "if you would be so kind—"

"Here." His father offered him his cup, the wine untouched.

Now Tyrion truly *was* nonplussed. He drank.

Lord Tywin seated himself. "You have the right of it about Stark. Alive, we might have used Lord Eddard to forge a peace with Winterfell and Riverrun, a peace that would have given us the time we need to deal with Robert's brothers. Dead . . ." His hand curled into a fist. "Madness. Rank madness."

"Joff's only a boy," Tyrion pointed out. "At his age, I committed a few follies of my own."

His father gave him a sharp look. "I suppose we ought to be grateful that he has not yet married a whore."

Tyrion sipped at his wine, wondering how Lord Tywin would look if he flung the cup in his face.

"Our position is worse than you know," his father went on. "It would seem we have a new king."

Ser Kevan looked poleaxed. "A new—*who?* What have they done to Joffrey?"

The faintest flicker of distaste played across Lord Tywin's thin lips. "Nothing . . . yet. My grandson still sits the Iron Throne, but the eunuch has heard whispers from the south. Renly Baratheon wed Margaery Tyrell at Highgarden this fortnight past, and now he has claimed the crown. The bride's father and brothers have bent the knee and sworn him their swords."

"Those are grave tidings." When Ser Kevan frowned, the furrows in his brow grew deep as canyons.

"My daughter commands us to ride for King's Landing at once, to defend the Red Keep against King Renly and the Knight of Flowers." His mouth tightened. "*Commands* us, mind you. In the name of the king and council."

"How is King Joffrey taking the news?" Tyrion asked with a certain black amusement.

"Cersei has not seen fit to tell him yet," Lord Tywin said. "She fears he might insist on marching against Renly himself."

"With what army?" Tyrion asked. "You don't plan to give him *this* one, I hope?"

"He talks of leading the City Watch," Lord Tywin said.

"If he takes the Watch, he'll leave the city undefended," Ser Kevan said. "And with Lord Stannis on Dragonstone . . ."

"Yes." Lord Tywin looked down at his son. "I had thought you were the one made for motley, Tyrion, but it would appear that I was wrong."

"Why, Father," said Tyrion, "that almost sounds like praise." He leaned forward intently. "What of Stannis? He's the elder, not Renly. How does he feel about his brother's claim?"

His father frowned. "I have felt from the beginning that Stannis was a greater danger than all the others combined. Yet he does nothing. Oh, Varys hears his whispers. Stannis is building ships, Stannis is hiring sellswords, Stannis is bringing a shadowbinder from Asshai. What does it mean? Is any of it true?" He gave an irritated shrug. "Kevan, bring us the map."

Ser Kevan did as he was bid. Lord Tywin unrolled the leather, smoothing it flat. "Jaime has left us in a bad way. Roose Bolton and the remnants of his host are north of us. Our enemies hold the Twins and Moat Cailin. Robb Stark sits to the west, so we cannot retreat to Lannisport and the Rock unless we choose to give battle. Jaime is taken, and his army for all purposes has ceased to exist. Thoros of Myr and Beric Dondarrion continue to plague our foraging parties. To our east we have the Arryns, Stannis Baratheon sits on Dragonstone, and in the south Highgarden and Storm's End are calling their banners."

Tyrion smiled crookedly. "Take heart, Father. At least Rhaegar Targaryen is still dead."

"I had hoped you might have more to offer us than japes, Tyrion," Lord Tywin Lannister said.

Ser Kevan frowned over the map, forehead creasing. "Robb Stark will have Edmure Tully and the lords of the Trident with him now. Their combined power may ex-

ceed our own. And with Roose Bolton behind us . . .
Tywin, if we remain here, I fear we might be caught between three armies."

"I have no intention of remaining here. We must finish
our business with young Lord Stark before Renly
Baratheon can march from Highgarden. Bolton does not
concern me. He is a wary man, and we made him warier
on the Green Fork. He will be slow to give pursuit. So
. . . on the morrow, we make for Harrenhal. Kevan, I
want Ser Addam's outriders to screen our movements.
Give him as many men as he requires, and send them out
in groups of four. I will have no vanishings."

"As you say, my lord, but . . . why Harrenhal? That
is a grim, unlucky place. Some call it cursed."

"Let them," Lord Tywin said. "Unleash Ser Gregor and
send him before us with his reavers. Send forth Vargo
Hoat and his freeriders as well, and Ser Amory Lorch.
Each is to have three hundred horse. Tell them I want to
see the riverlands afire from the Gods Eye to the Red
Fork."

"They will burn, my lord," Ser Kevan said, rising. "I
shall give the commands." He bowed and made for the
door.

When they were alone, Lord Tywin glanced at Tyrion.
"Your savages might relish a bit of rapine. Tell them they
may ride with Vargo Hoat and plunder as they like—
goods, stock, women, they may take what they want and
burn the rest."

"Telling Shagga and Timett how to pillage is like telling a rooster how to crow," Tyrion commented, "but I
should prefer to keep them with me." Uncouth and unruly they might be, yet the wildlings were *his*, and he
trusted them more than any of his father's men. He was
not about to hand them over.

"Then you had best learn to control them. I will not
have the city plundered."

"The city?" Tyrion was lost. "What city would that
be?"

"King's Landing. I am sending you to court."

It was the last thing Tyrion Lannister would ever have
anticipated. He reached for his wine, and considered for a
moment as he sipped. "And what am I to do there?"

"Rule," his father said curtly.

Tyrion hooted with laughter. "My sweet sister might have a word or two to say about that!"

"Let her say what she likes. Her son needs to be taken in hand before he ruins us all. I blame those jackanapes on the council—our friend Petyr, the venerable Grand Maester, and that cockless wonder Lord Varys. What sort of counsel are they giving Joffrey when he lurches from one folly to the next? Whose notion was it to make this Janos Slynt a lord? The man's father was a *butcher*, and they grant him Harrenhal. *Harrenhal*, that was the seat of kings! Not that he will ever set foot inside it, if I have a say. I am told he took a bloody spear for his sigil. A bloody cleaver would have been my choice." His father had not raised his voice, yet Tyrion could see the anger in the gold of his eyes. "And dismissing Selmy, where was the sense in that? Yes, the man was old, but the name of Barristan the Bold still has meaning in the realm. He lent honor to any man he served. Can anyone say the same of the Hound? You feed your dog bones under the table, you do not seat him beside you on the high bench." He pointed a finger at Tyrion's face. "If Cersei cannot curb the boy, you must. And if these councillors are playing us false . . ."

Tyrion knew. "Spikes," he sighed. "Heads. Walls."

"I see you have taken a few lessons from me."

"More than you know, Father," Tyrion answered quietly. He finished his wine and set the cup aside, thoughtful. A part of him was more pleased than he cared to admit. Another part was remembering the battle upriver, and wondering if he was being sent to hold the left again. "Why me?" he asked, cocking his head to one side. "Why not my uncle? Why not Ser Addam or Ser Flement or Lord Serrett? Why not a . . . *bigger* man?"

Lord Tywin rose abruptly. "You are my son."

That was when he knew. *You have given him up for lost*, he thought. *You bloody bastard, you think Jaime's good as dead, so I'm all you have left*. Tyrion wanted to slap him, to spit in his face, to draw his dagger and cut the heart out of him and see if it was made of old hard gold, the way the smallfolks said. Yet he sat there, silent and still.

The shards of the broken cup crunched beneath his father's heels as Lord Tywin crossed the room. "One last thing," he said at the door. "You will not take the whore to court."

Tyrion sat alone in the common room for a long while after his father was gone. Finally he climbed the steps to his cozy garret beneath the bell tower. The ceiling was low, but that was scarcely a drawback for a dwarf. From the window, he could see the gibbet his father had erected in the yard. The innkeep's body turned slowly on its rope whenever the night wind gusted. Her flesh had grown as thin and ragged as Lannister hopes.

Shae murmured sleepily and rolled toward him when he sat on the edge of the featherbed. He slid his hand under the blanket and cupped a soft breast, and her eyes opened. "M'lord," she said with a drowsy smile.

When he felt her nipple stiffen, Tyrion kissed her. "I have a mind to take you to King's Landing, sweetling," he whispered.

JON

The mare whickered softly as Jon Snow tightened the cinch. "Easy, sweet lady," he said in a soft voice, quieting her with a touch. Wind whispered through the stable, a cold dead breath on his face, but Jon paid it no mind. He strapped his roll to the saddle, his scarred fingers stiff and clumsy. "Ghost," he called softly, "to me." And the wolf was there, eyes like embers.

"Jon, please. You must not do this."

He mounted, the reins in his hand, and wheeled the horse around to face the night. Samwell Tarly stood in the stable door, a full moon peering over his shoulder. He threw a giant's shadow, immense and black. "Get out of my way, Sam."

"Jon, you *can't*," Sam said. "I won't let you."

"I would sooner not hurt you," Jon told him. "Move aside, Sam, or I'll ride you down."

"You won't. You have to listen to me. Please . . ."

Jon put his spurs to horseflesh, and the mare bolted for the door. For an instant Sam stood his ground, his face as round and pale as the moon behind him, his mouth a widening O of surprise. At the last moment, when they were almost on him, he jumped aside as Jon had known he would, stumbled, and fell. The mare leapt over him, out into the night.

Jon raised the hood of his heavy cloak and gave the horse her head. Castle Black was silent and still as he rode out, with Ghost racing at his side. Men watched from the Wall behind him, he knew, but their eyes were turned north, not south. No one would see him go, no one but Sam Tarly, struggling back to his feet in the dust of the old stables. He hoped Sam hadn't hurt himself, falling like that. He was so heavy and so ungainly, it would be just like him to break a wrist or twist his ankle getting out of the way. "I warned him," Jon said aloud. "It was nothing to do with him, anyway." He flexed his burned hand as he rode, opening and closing the scarred fingers. They still pained him, but it felt good to have the wrappings off.

Moonlight silvered the hills as he followed the twisting ribbon of the kingsroad. He needed to get as far from the Wall as he could before they realized he was gone. On the morrow he would leave the road and strike out overland through field and bush and stream to throw off pursuit, but for the moment speed was more important than deception. It was not as though they would not guess where he was going.

The Old Bear was accustomed to rise at first light, so Jon had until dawn to put as many leagues as he could between him and the Wall . . . *if* Sam Tarly did not betray him. The fat boy was dutiful and easily frightened, but he loved Jon like a brother. If questioned, Sam would doubtless tell them the truth, but Jon could not imagine him braving the guards in front of the King's Tower to wake Mormont from sleep.

When Jon did not appear to fetch the Old Bear's breakfast from the kitchen, they'd look in his cell and find Longclaw on the bed. It had been hard to abandon it, but Jon was not so lost to honor as to take it with him. Even Jorah Mormont had not done that, when he fled in disgrace. Doubtless Lord Mormont would find someone more worthy of the blade. Jon felt bad when he thought of the old man. He knew his desertion would be salt in the still-raw wound of his son's disgrace. That seemed a poor way to repay him for his trust, but it couldn't be helped.

No matter what he did, Jon felt as though he were betraying someone.

Even now, he did not know if he was doing the honorable thing. The southron had it easier. They had their septons to talk to, someone to tell them the gods' will and help sort out right from wrong. But the Starks worshiped the old gods, the nameless gods, and if the heart trees heard, they did not speak.

When the last lights of Castle Black vanished behind him, Jon slowed his mare to a walk. He had a long journey ahead and only the one horse to see him through. There were holdfasts and farming villages along the road south where he might be able to trade the mare for a fresh mount when he needed one, but not if she were injured or blown.

He would need to find new clothes soon; most like, he'd need to steal them. He was clad in black from head to heel; high leather riding boots, roughspun breeches and tunic, sleeveless leather jerkin, and heavy wool cloak. His longsword and dagger were sheathed in black moleskin, and the hauberk and coif in his saddlebag were black ringmail. Any bit of it could mean his death if he were taken. A stranger wearing black was viewed with cold suspicion in every village and holdfast north of the Neck, and men would soon be watching for him. Once Maester Aemon's ravens took flight, Jon knew he would find no safe haven. Not even at Winterfell. Bran might want to let him in, but Maester Luwin had better sense. He would bar the gates and send Jon away, as he should. Better not to call there at all.

Yet he saw the castle clear in his mind's eye, as if he had left it only yesterday; the towering granite walls, the Great Hall with its smells of smoke and dog and roasting meat, his father's solar, the turret room where he had slept. Part of him wanted nothing so much as to hear Bran laugh again, to sup on one of Gage's beef-and-bacon pies, to listen to Old Nan tell her tales of the children of the forest and Florian the Fool.

But he had not left the Wall for that; he had left because he was after all his father's son, and Robb's brother. The gift of a sword, even a sword as fine as Longclaw, did not make him a Mormont. Nor was he Aemon Targaryen. Three times the old man had chosen, and three times he had chosen honor, but that was him. Even now, Jon could not decide whether the maester had stayed because he was weak and craven, or because he was strong and true. Yet he understood what the old man had meant, about the pain of choosing; he understood that all too well.

Tyrion Lannister had claimed that most men would rather deny a hard truth than face it, but Jon was done with denials. He was who he was; Jon Snow, bastard and oathbreaker, motherless, friendless, and damned. For the rest of his life—however long that might be—he would be condemned to be an outsider, the silent man standing in the shadows who dares not speak his true name. Wherever he might go throughout the Seven Kingdoms, he would need to live a lie, lest every man's hand be raised against him. But it made no matter, so long as he lived long enough to take his place by his brother's side and help avenge his father.

He remembered Robb as he had last seen him, standing in the yard with snow melting in his auburn hair. Jon would have to come to him in secret, disguised. He tried to imagine the look on Robb's face when he revealed himself. His brother would shake his head and smile, and he'd say . . . he'd say . . .

He could not see the smile. Hard as he tried, he could not see it. He found himself thinking of the deserter his father had beheaded the day they'd found the direwolves. "You said the words," Lord Eddard had told him. "You took a vow, before your brothers, before the old gods and the new." Desmond and Fat Tom had dragged the man to the stump. Bran's eyes had been wide as saucers, and Jon had to remind him to keep his pony in hand. He remembered the look on Father's face when Theon Greyjoy brought forth Ice, the spray of blood on the snow, the way Theon had kicked the head when it came rolling at his feet.

He wondered what Lord Eddard might have done if the deserter had been his brother Benjen instead of that ragged stranger. Would it have been any different? It must, surely, *surely* . . . and Robb would welcome him, for a certainty. He *had* to, or else . . .

It did not bear thinking about. Pain throbbed, deep in his fingers, as he clutched the reins. Jon put his heels into his horse and broke into a gallop, racing down the kingsroad, as if to outrun his doubts. Jon was not afraid of death, but he did not want to die like that, trussed and bound and beheaded like a common brigand. If he must perish, let it be with a sword in his hand, fighting his father's killers. He was no true Stark, had never been one . . . but he could die like one. Let them say that Eddard Stark had fathered four sons, not three.

Ghost kept pace with them for almost half a mile, red tongue lolling from his mouth. Man and horse alike lowered their heads as he asked the mare for more speed. The wolf slowed, stopped, watching, his eyes glowing red in the moonlight. He vanished behind, but Jon knew he would follow, at his own pace.

Scattered lights flickered through the trees ahead of him, on both sides of the road: Mole's Town. A dog barked as he rode through, and he heard a mule's raucous *haw* from the stable, but otherwise the village was still. Here and there the glow of hearth fires shone through shuttered windows, leaking between wooden slats, but only a few.

Mole's Town was bigger than it seemed, but three quarters of it was under the ground, in deep warm cellars connected by a maze of tunnels. Even the whorehouse was down there, nothing on the surface but a wooden shack no bigger than a privy, with a red lantern hung over the door. On the Wall, he'd heard men call the whores "buried treasures." He wondered whether any of his brothers in black were down there tonight, mining. That was oathbreaking too, yet no one seemed to care.

Not until he was well beyond the village did Jon slow again. By then both he and the mare were damp with sweat. He dismounted, shivering, his burned hand aching. A bank of melting snow lay under the trees, bright in the moonlight, water trickling off to form small shallow pools. Jon squatted and brought his hands together, cupping the runoff between his fingers. The snowmelt was icy cold. He drank, and splashed some on his face, until his cheeks tingled. His fingers were throbbing worse than they had in days, and his head was pounding too. *I am doing the right thing*, he told himself, *so why do I feel so bad?*

The horse was well lathered, so Jon took the lead and walked her for a while. The road was scarcely wide enough for two riders to pass abreast, its surface cut by tiny streams and littered with stone. That run had been truly stupid, an invitation to a broken neck. Jon wondered what had gotten into him. Was he in such a great rush to die?

Off in the trees, the distant scream of some frightened animal made him look up. His mare whinnied nervously. Had his wolf found some prey? He cupped his hands around his mouth. *"Ghost!"* he shouted. "Ghost, to me." The only answer was a rush of wings behind him as an owl took flight.

Frowning, Jon continued on his way. He led the mare for half an hour, until she was dry. Ghost did not appear. Jon wanted to mount up and ride again, but he was concerned about his missing wolf. *"Ghost,"* he called again. "Where are you? To me! *Ghost!"* Nothing in these woods could trouble a direwolf, even a half-grown direwolf, unless . . . no, Ghost was too smart to attack a bear, and if there was a wolf pack anywhere close Jon would have surely heard them howling.

He should eat, he decided. Food would settle his stomach and give Ghost the chance to catch up. There was no danger yet; Castle Black still slept. In his saddlebag, he found a biscuit, a piece of cheese, and a small withered brown apple. He'd brought salt beef as well, and a rasher of bacon he'd filched from the kitchens, but he would save the meat for the morrow. After it was gone he'd need to hunt, and that would slow him.

Jon sat under the trees and ate his biscuit and cheese while his mare grazed along the kingsroad. He kept the apple for last. It had gone a little soft, but the flesh was still tart and juicy. He was down to the core when he heard the sounds: horses, and from the north. Quickly Jon leapt up and strode to his mare. Could he outrun them? No, they were too close, they'd hear him for a certainty, and if they were from Castle Black . . .

He led the mare off the road, behind a thick stand of grey-green sentinels. "Quiet now," he said in a hushed voice, crouching down to peer through the branches. If the gods were kind, the riders would pass by. Likely as not, they were only smallfolk from Mole's Town, farmers on their way to their fields, although what they were doing out in the middle of the night . . .

He listened to the sound of hooves growing steadily louder as they trotted briskly down the kingsroad. From the sound, there were five or six of them at the least. Their voices drifted through the trees.

". . . certain he came this way?"

"We *can't* be certain."

"He could have ridden east, for all you know. Or left the road to cut through the woods. That's what I'd do."

"In the dark? Stupid. If you didn't fall off your horse and break your neck, you'd get lost and wind up back at the Wall when the sun came up."

"I would not." Grenn sounded peeved. "I'd just ride south, you can tell south by the stars."

"What if the sky was cloudy?" Pyp asked.

"Then I wouldn't go."

Another voice broke in. "You know where *I'd* be if it was me? I'd be in Mole's Town, digging for buried treasure." Toad's shrill laughter boomed through the trees. Jon's mare snorted.

"Keep quiet, all of you," Halder said. "I thought I heard something."

"Where? I didn't hear anything." The horses stopped.

"*You* can't hear yourself fart."

"I can too," Grenn insisted.

"*Quiet!*"

They all fell silent, listening. Jon found himself holding his breath. *Sam,* he thought. He hadn't gone to the Old Bear, but he hadn't gone to bed either, he'd woken the other boys. Damn them all. Come dawn, if they were not in their beds, they'd be named deserters too. What did they think they were doing?

The hushed silence seemed to stretch on and on. From where Jon crouched, he could see the legs of their horses through the branches. Finally Pyp spoke up. "What did you hear?"

"I don't know," Halder admitted. "A sound, I thought it might have been a horse but . . ."

"There's nothing here."

Out of the corner of his eye, Jon glimpsed a pale shape moving through the trees. Leaves rustled, and Ghost came bounding out of the shadows, so suddenly that Jon's mare started and gave a whinny. "*There!*" Halder shouted.

"I heard it too!"

"Traitor," Jon told the direwolf as he swung up into the saddle. He turned the mare's head to slide off through the trees, but they were on him before he had gone ten feet.

"Jon!" Pyp shouted after him.

"Pull up," Grenn said. "You can't outrun us all."

Jon wheeled around to face them, drawing his sword. "Get back. I don't wish to hurt you, but I will if I have to."

"One against seven?" Halder gave a signal. The boys spread out, surrounding him.

"What do you want with me?" Jon demanded.

"We want to take you back where you belong," Pyp said.

"I belong with my brother."

"We're your brothers now," Grenn said.

"They'll cut off your head if they catch you, you know," Toad put in with a nervous laugh. "This is so stupid, it's like something the Aurochs would do."

"I would not," Grenn said. "I'm no oathbreaker. I said the words and I meant them."

"So did I," Jon told them. "Don't you understand? They murdered my *father*. It's war, my brother Robb is fighting in the riverlands—"

"We know," said Pyp solemnly. "Sam told us everything."

"We're sorry about your father," Grenn said, "but it doesn't matter. Once you say the words, you can't leave, no matter what."

"I *have* to," Jon said fervently.

"You said the words," Pyp reminded him. *"Now my watch begins,* you said it. *It shall not end until my death."*

"I shall live and die at my post," Grenn added, nodding.

"You don't have to tell me the words, I know them as well as you do." He was angry now. Why couldn't they let him go in peace? They were only making it harder.

"I am the sword in the darkness," Halder intoned.

"The watcher on the walls," piped Toad.

Jon cursed them all to their faces. They took no notice. Pyp spurred his horse closer, reciting, *"I am the fire that burns against the cold, the light that brings the dawn, the horn that wakes the sleepers, the shield that guards the realms of men."*

"Stay back," Jon warned him, brandishing his sword. "I mean it, Pyp." They weren't even wearing armor, he could cut them to pieces if he had to.

Matthar had circled behind him. He joined the chorus. *"I pledge my life and honor to the Night's Watch."*

Jon kicked his mare, spinning her in a circle. The boys were all around him now, closing from every side.

"For this night . . ." Halder trotted in from the left.

". . . and all the nights to come," finished Pyp. He reached over for Jon's reins. "So here are your choices. Kill me, or come back with me."

Jon lifted his sword . . . and lowered it, helpless. "Damn you," he said. "Damn you all."

"Do we have to bind your hands, or will you give us your word you'll ride back peaceful?" asked Halder.

"I won't run, if that's what you mean." Ghost moved out from under the trees and Jon glared at him. "Small help you were," he said. The deep red eyes looked at him knowingly.

"We had best hurry," Pyp said. "If we're not back before first light, the Old Bear will have *all* our heads."

Of the ride back, Jon Snow remembered little. It seemed shorter than the journey south, perhaps because his mind was elsewhere. Pyp set the pace, galloping, walking, trotting, and then breaking into another gallop. Mole's Town came and went, the red lantern over the brothel long extinguished. They made good time. Dawn was still an hour off when Jon glimpsed the towers of Castle Black ahead of them, dark against the pale immensity of the Wall. It did not seem like home this time.

They could take him back, Jon told himself, but they could not make him stay. The war would not end on the morrow, or the day after, and his friends could not watch him day and night. He would bide his time, make them think he was content to remain here . . . and then, when they had grown lax, he would be off again. Next time he would avoid the kingsroad. He could follow the Wall east, perhaps all the way to the sea, a longer route but a safer one. Or even west, to the mountains, and then south over the high passes. That was the wildling's way, hard and perilous, but at least no one would follow him. He wouldn't stray within a hundred leagues of Winterfell or the kingsroad.

Samwell Tarly awaited them in the old stables, slumped on the ground against a bale of hay, too anxious to sleep. He rose and brushed himself off. "I . . . I'm glad they found you, Jon."

"I'm not," Jon said, dismounting.

Pyp hopped off his horse and looked at the lightening sky with disgust. "Give us a hand bedding down the horses, Sam," the small boy said. "We have a long day before us, and no sleep to face it on, thanks to Lord Snow."

When day broke, Jon walked to the kitchens as he did every dawn. Three-Finger Hobb said nothing as he gave him the Old Bear's breakfast. Today it was three brown eggs boiled hard, with fried bread and ham steak and a bowl of wrinkled plums. Jon carried the food back to the King's Tower. He found Mormont at the window seat, writing. His raven was walking back and forth across his shoulders, muttering, *"Corn, corn, corn."* The bird shrieked when Jon entered. "Put the food on the table," the Old Bear said, glancing up. "I'll have some beer."

Jon opened a shuttered window, took the flagon of beer off the outside ledge, and filled a horn. Hobb had given him a lemon, still cold from the Wall. Jon crushed it in his fist. The juice trickled through his fingers. Mormont drank lemon in his beer every day, and claimed that was why he still had his own teeth.

"Doubtless you loved your father," Mormont said when Jon brought him his horn. "The things we love destroy us every time, lad. Remember when I told you that?"

"I remember," Jon said sullenly. He did not care to talk of his father's death, not even to Mormont.

"See that you never forget it. The hard truths are the ones to hold tight. Fetch me my plate. Is it ham again? So be it. You look weary. Was your moonlight ride so tiring?"

Jon's throat was dry. "You know?"

"Know," the raven echoed from Mormont's shoulder. *"Know."*

The Old Bear snorted. "Do you think they chose me

Lord Commander of the Night's Watch because I'm dumb as a stump, Snow? Aemon told me you'd go. I told him you'd be back. I know my men . . . and my *boys* too. Honor set you on the kingsroad . . . and honor brought you back."

"My friends brought me back," Jon said.

"Did I say it was *your* honor?" Mormont inspected his plate.

"They killed my father. Did you expect me to do nothing?"

"If truth be told, we expected you to do just as you did." Mormont tried a plum, spit out the pit. "I ordered a watch kept over you. You were seen leaving. If your brothers had not fetched you back, you would have been taken along the way, and not by friends. Unless you have a horse with wings like a raven. Do you?"

"No." Jon felt like a fool.

"Pity, we could use a horse like that."

Jon stood tall. He told himself that he would die well; that much he could do, at the least. "I know the penalty for desertion, my lord. I'm not afraid to die."

"*Die!*" the raven cried.

"Nor live, I hope," Mormont said, cutting his ham with a dagger and feeding a bite to the bird. "You have not deserted—yet. Here you stand. If we beheaded every boy who rode to Mole's Town in the night, only ghosts would guard the Wall. Yet maybe you mean to flee again on the morrow, or a fortnight from now. Is that it? Is that your hope, boy?"

Jon kept silent.

"I thought so." Mormont peeled the shell off a boiled egg. "Your father is dead, lad. Do you think you can bring him back?"

"No," he answered, sullen.

"Good," Mormont said. "We've seen the dead come back, you and me, and it's not something I care to see again." He ate the egg in two bites and flicked a bit of shell out from between his teeth. "Your brother is in the field with all the power of the north behind him. Any one of his lords bannermen commands more swords than you'll find in all the Night's Watch. Why do you imagine that they need *your* help? Are you such a mighty warrior, or do you carry a grumkin in your pocket to magic up your sword?"

Jon had no answer for him. The raven was pecking at an egg, breaking the shell. Pushing his beak through the hole, he pulled out morsels of white and yoke.

The Old Bear sighed. "You are not the only one touched by this war. Like as not, my sister is marching in your brother's host, her and those daughters of hers, dressed in men's mail. Maege is a hoary old snark, stubborn, short-tempered, and willful. Truth be told, I can hardly stand to be around the wretched woman, but that does not mean my love for her is any less than the love you bear your half sisters." Frowning, Mormont took his last egg and squeezed it in his fist until the shell crunched. "Or perhaps it does. Be that as it may, I'd still grieve if she were slain, yet you don't see me running off. I said the words, just as you did. My place is here . . . where is yours, boy?"

I have no place, Jon wanted to say, *I'm a bastard, I have no rights, no name, no mother, and now not even a father.* The words would not come. "I don't know."

"I do," said Lord Commander Mormont. "The cold winds are rising, Snow. Beyond the Wall, the shadows lengthen. Cotter Pyke writes of vast herds of elk, streaming south and east toward the sea, and mammoths as well. He says one of his men discovered huge, misshapen footprints not three leagues from Eastwatch. Rangers from the Shadow Tower have found whole villages abandoned, and at night Ser Denys says they see fires in the mountains, huge blazes that burn from dusk till dawn. Quorin Halfhand took a captive in the depths of the Gorge, and the man swears that Mance Rayder is massing all his people in some new, secret stronghold he's found, to what end the gods only know. Do you think your uncle Benjen was the only ranger we've lost this past year?"

"*Ben Jen*," the raven squawked, bobbing its head, bits of egg dribbling from its beak. "*Ben Jen. Ben Jen.*"

"No," Jon said. There had been others. Too many.

"Do you think your brother's war is more important than ours?" the old man barked.

Jon chewed his lip. The raven flapped its wings at him. "*War, war, war, war,*" it sang.

"It's not," Mormont told him. "Gods save us, boy,

you're not blind and you're not stupid. When dead men come hunting in the night, do you think it matters who sits the Iron Throne?"

"No." Jon had not thought of it that way.

"Your lord father sent you to us, Jon. Why, who can say?"

"Why? Why? Why?" the raven called.

"All I know is that the blood of the First Men flows in the veins of the Starks. The First Men built the Wall, and it's said they remember things otherwise forgotten. And that beast of yours . . . he led us to the wights, warned you of the dead man on the steps. Ser Jaremy would doubtless call that happenstance, yet Ser Jaremy is dead and I'm not." Lord Mormont stabbed a chunk of ham with the point of his dagger. "I think you were meant to be here, and I want you and that wolf of yours with us when we go beyond the Wall."

His words sent a chill of excitement down Jon's back. "Beyond the Wall?"

"You heard me. I mean to find Ben Stark, alive or dead." He chewed and swallowed. "I will not sit here meekly and wait for the snows and the ice winds. We must know what is happening. This time the Night's Watch will ride in force, against the King-beyond-the-Wall, the Others, and anything else that may be out there. I mean to command them myself." He pointed his dagger at Jon's chest. "By custom, the Lord Commander's steward is his squire as well . . . but I do not care to wake every dawn wondering if you've run off again. So I will have an answer from you, Lord Snow, and I will have it now. Are you a brother of the Night's Watch . . . or only a bastard boy who wants to play at war?"

Jon Snow straightened himself and took a long deep breath. *Forgive me, Father. Robb, Arya, Bran . . . forgive me, I cannot help you. He has the truth of it. This is my place.* "I am . . . yours, my lord. Your man. I swear it. I will not run again."

The Old Bear snorted. "Good. Now go put on your sword."

CATELYN

It seemed a thousand years ago that Catelyn Stark had carried her infant son out of Riverrun, crossing the Tumblestone in a small boat to begin their journey north to Winterfell. And it was across the Tumblestone that they came home now, though the boy wore plate and mail in place of swaddling clothes.

Robb sat in the bow with Grey Wind, his hand resting on his direwolf's head as the rowers pulled at their oars. Theon Greyjoy was with him. Her uncle Brynden would come behind in the second boat, with the Greatjon and Lord Karstark.

Catelyn took a place toward the stern. They shot down the Tumblestone, letting the strong current push them past the looming Wheel Tower. The splash and rumble of the great waterwheel within was a sound from her girlhood that brought a sad smile to Catelyn's face. From the sandstone walls of the castle, soldiers and servants shouted down her name, and Robb's, and "Winterfell!" From every rampart waved the banner of House Tully: a leaping trout, silver, against a rippling blue-and-red field. It was a stirring sight, yet it did not lift her heart. She wondered if indeed her heart would ever lift again. *Oh, Ned . . .*

Below the Wheel Tower, they made a wide turn and knifed through the churning water. The men put their backs into it. The wide arch of the Water Gate came into view, and she heard the creak of heavy chains as the great iron portcullis was winched upward. It rose slowly as they approached, and Catelyn saw that the lower half of it was red with rust. The bottom foot dripped brown mud on them as they passed underneath, the barbed spikes mere inches above their heads. Catelyn gazed up at the bars and wondered how deep the rust went and how well the portcullis would stand up to a ram and whether it ought to be replaced. Thoughts like that were seldom far from her mind these days.

They passed beneath the arch and under the walls, moving from sunlight to shadow and back into sunlight. Boats large and small were tied up all around them, secured to iron rings set in the stone. Her father's guards waited on the water stair with her brother. Ser Edmure Tully was a stocky young man with a shaggy head of auburn hair and a fiery beard. His breastplate was scratched and dented from battle, his blue-and-red cloak stained by blood and smoke. At his side stood the Lord Tytos Blackwood, a hard pike of a man with close-cropped salt-and-pepper whiskers and a hook nose. His bright yellow armor was inlaid with jet in elaborate vine-and-leaf patterns, and a cloak sewn from raven feathers draped his thin shoulders. It had been Lord Tytos who led the sortie that plucked her brother from the Lannister camp.

"Bring them in," Ser Edmure commanded. Three men scrambled down the stairs knee-deep in the water and pulled the boat close with long hooks. When Grey Wind bounded out, one of them dropped his pole and lurched back, stumbling and sitting down abruptly in the river. The others laughed, and the man got a sheepish look on his face. Theon Greyjoy vaulted over the side of the boat and lifted Catelyn by the waist, setting her on a dry step above him as water lapped around his boots.

Edmure came down the steps to embrace her. "Sweet sister," he murmured hoarsely. He had deep blue eyes and a mouth made for smiles, but he was not smiling now. He looked worn and tired, battered by battle and haggard from strain. His neck was bandaged where he had taken a wound. Catelyn hugged him fiercely.

"Your grief is mine, Cat," he said when they broke apart. "When we heard about Lord Eddard . . . the Lannisters will pay, I swear it, you will have your vengeance."

"Will that bring Ned back to me?" she said sharply. The wound was still too fresh for softer words. She could not think about Ned now. She would not. It would not do. She had to be strong. "All that will keep. I must see Father."

"He awaits you in his solar," Edmure said.

"Lord Hoster is bedridden, my lady," her father's steward explained. When had that good man grown so old and grey? "He instructed me to bring you to him at once."

"I'll take her." Edmure escorted her up the water stair and across the lower bailey, where Petyr Baelish and Brandon Stark had once crossed swords for her favor. The massive sandstone walls of the keep loomed above them. As they pushed through a door between two guardsmen in fish-crest helms, she asked, "How bad is he?" dreading the answer even as she said the words.

Edmure's look was somber. "He will not be with us long, the maesters say. The pain is . . . constant, and grievous."

A blind rage filled her, a rage at all the world; at her brother Edmure and her sister Lysa, at the Lannisters, at the maesters, at Ned and her father and the monstrous gods who would take them both away from her. "You should have told me," she said. "You should have sent word as soon as you knew."

"He forbade it. He did not want his enemies to know that he was dying. With the realm so troubled, he feared that if the Lannisters suspected how frail he was . . ."

". . . they might attack?" Catelyn finished, hard. *It was your doing, yours,* a voice whispered inside her. *If you had not taken it upon yourself to seize the dwarf . . .*

They climbed the spiral stair in silence.

The keep was three-sided, like Riverrun itself, and Lord Hoster's solar was triangular as well, with a stone balcony that jutted out to the east like the prow of some great sandstone ship. From there the lord of the castle could look down on his walls and battlements, and beyond, to where the waters met. They had moved her father's bed out onto the balcony. "He likes to sit in the sun and watch the rivers," Edmure explained. "Father, see who I've brought. Cat has come to see you . . ."

Hoster Tully had always been a big man; tall and broad in his youth, portly as he grew older. Now he seemed shrunken, the muscle and meat melted off his bones. Even his face sagged. The last time Catelyn had seen him, his hair and beard had been brown, well streaked with grey. Now they had gone white as snow.

His eyes opened to the sound of Edmure's voice. "Little cat," he murmured in a voice thin and wispy and wracked by pain. "My little cat." A tremulous smile touched his face as his hand groped for hers. "I watched for you . . ."

"I shall leave you to talk," her brother said, kissing their lord father gently on the brow before he withdrew.

Catelyn knelt and took her father's hand in hers. It was a big hand, but fleshless now, the bones moving loosely under the skin, all the strength gone from it. "You should have told me," she said. "A rider, a raven . . ."

"Riders are taken, questioned," he answered. "Ravens are brought down . . ." A spasm of pain took him, and his fingers clutched hers hard. "The crabs are in my belly . . . pinching, always pinching. Day and night. They have fierce claws, the crabs. Maester Vyman makes me dreamwine, milk of the poppy . . . I sleep a lot . . . but I wanted to be awake to see you, when you came. I was afraid . . . when the Lannisters took your brother, the camps all around us . . . I was afraid I would go, before I could see you again . . . I was afraid . . ."

"I'm here, Father," she said. "With Robb, my son. He'll want to see you too."

"Your boy," he whispered. "He had my eyes, I remember . . ."

"He did, and does. And we've brought you Jaime Lannister, in irons. Riverrun is free again, Father."

Lord Hoster smiled. "I saw. Last night, when it began, I told them . . . had to see. They carried me to the gatehouse . . . watched from the battlements. Ah, that was beautiful . . . the torches came in a wave, I could hear the cries floating across the river . . . sweet cries . . .

when that siege tower went up, gods . . . would have died then, and glad, if only I could have seen you children first. Was it your boy who did it? Was it your Robb?"

"Yes," Catelyn said, fiercely proud. "It was Robb . . . and Brynden. Your brother is here as well, my lord."

"Him." Her father's voice was a faint whisper. "The Blackfish . . . came back? From the Vale?"

"Yes."

"And Lysa?" A cool wind moved through his thin white hair. "Gods be good, your sister . . . did she come as well?"

He sounded so full of hope and yearning that it was hard to tell the truth. "No. I'm sorry . . ."

"Oh." His face fell, and some light went out of his eyes. "I'd hoped . . . I would have liked to see her, before . . ."

"She's with her son, in the Eyrie."

Lord Hoster gave a weary nod. "Lord Robert now, poor Arryn's gone . . . I remember . . . why did she not come with you?"

"She is frightened, my lord. In the Eyrie she feels safe." She kissed his wrinkled brow. "Robb will be waiting. Will you see him? And Brynden?"

"Your son," he whispered. "Yes. Cat's child . . . he had my eyes, I remember. When he was born. Bring him . . . yes."

"And your brother?"

Her father glanced out over the rivers. "Blackfish," he said. "Has he wed yet? Taken some . . . girl to wife?"

Even on his deathbed, Catelyn thought sadly. "He has not wed. You know that, Father. Nor will he ever."

"I told him . . . *commanded* him. Marry! I was his lord. He knows. My right, to make his match. A good match. A Redwyne. Old House. Sweet girl, pretty . . . freckles . . . Bethany, yes. Poor child. Still waiting. Yes. Still . . ."

"Bethany Redwyne wed Lord Rowan years ago," Catelyn reminded him. "She has three children by him."

"Even so," Lord Hoster muttered. "Even so. Spit on the girl. The Redwynes. Spit on *me.* His lord, his brother . . . that Blackfish. I had other offers. Lord Bracken's girl. Walder Frey . . . any of three, he said . . . Has he wed? Anyone? Anyone?"

"No one," Catelyn said, "yet he has come many leagues to see you, fighting his way back to Riverrun. I would not be here now, if Ser Brynden had not helped us."

"He was ever a warrior," her father husked. "That he could do. Knight of the Gate, yes." He leaned back and closed his eyes, inutterably weary. "Send him. Later. I'll sleep now. Too sick to fight. Send him up later, the Blackfish . . . ."

Catelyn kissed him gently, smoothed his hair, and left him there in the shade of his keep, with his rivers flowing beneath. He was asleep before she left the solar.

When she returned to the lower bailey, Ser Brynden Tully stood on the water stairs with wet boots, talking with the captain of Riverrun's guards. He came to her at once. "Is he—?"

"Dying," she said. "As we feared."

Her uncle's craggy face showed his pain plain. He ran his fingers through his thick grey hair. "Will he see me?"

She nodded. "He says he is too sick to fight."

Brynden Blackfish chuckled. "I am too old a soldier to believe that. Hoster will be chiding me about the Redwyne girl even as we light his funeral pyre, damn his bones."

Catelyn smiled, knowing it was true. "I do not see Robb."

"He went with Greyjoy to the hall, I believe."

Theon Greyjoy was seated on a bench in Riverrun's Great Hall, enjoying a horn of ale and regaling her father's garrison with an account of the slaughter in the Whispering Wood. "Some tried to flee, but we'd pinched the valley shut at both ends, and we rode out of the darkness with sword and lance. The Lannisters must have thought the Others themselves were on them when that wolf of Robb's got in among them. I saw him tear one man's arm from his shoulder, and their horses went mad at the scent of him. I couldn't tell you how many men were thrown—"

"Theon," she interrupted, "where might I find my son?"

"Lord Robb went to visit the godswood, my lady."

It was what Ned would have done. *He is his father's son as much as mine, I must remember. Oh, gods, Ned . . .*

She found Robb beneath the green canopy of leaves, surrounded by tall redwoods and great old elms, kneeling before the heart tree, a slender weirwood with a face more sad than fierce. His longsword was before him, the point thrust in the earth, his gloved hands clasped around the hilt. Around him others knelt: Greatjon Umber, Rickard Karstark, Maege Mormont, Galbart Glover, and more. Even Tytos Blackwood was among them, the great raven cloak fanned out behind him. *These are the ones who keep the old gods,* she realized. She asked herself what gods she kept these days, and could not find an answer.

It would not do to disturb them at their prayers. The gods must have their due . . . even cruel gods who would take Ned from her, and her lord father as well. So Catelyn waited. The river wind moved through the high branches, and she could see the Wheel Tower to her right, ivy crawling up its side. As she stood there, all the memories came flooding back to her. Her father had taught her to ride amongst these trees, and that was the elm that Edmure had fallen from when he broke his arm, and over there, beneath that bower, she and Lysa had played at kissing with Petyr.

She had not thought of that in years. How young they all had been—she no older than Sansa, Lysa younger than Arya, and Petyr younger still, yet eager. The girls had traded him between them, serious and giggling by turns. It came back to her so vividly she could almost feel his sweaty fingers on her shoulders and taste the mint on his breath. There was always mint growing in the godswood, and Petyr had liked to chew it. He had been such a bold little boy, always in trouble. "He tried to put his tongue in my mouth," Catelyn had confessed to her sister afterward, when they were alone. "He did with me too," Lysa had whispered, shy and breathless. "I liked it."

Robb got to his feet slowly and sheathed his sword, and Catelyn found herself wondering whether her son had ever kissed a girl in the godswood. Surely he must have. She had seen Jeyne Poole giving him moist-eyed glances, and some of the serving girls, even ones as old as eighteen . . . he had ridden in battle and killed men with a sword, surely he had been kissed. There were tears in her eyes. She wiped them away angrily.

"Mother," Robb said when he saw her standing there. "We must call a council. There are things to be decided."

"Your grandfather would like to see you," she said. "Robb, he's very sick."

"Ser Edmure told me. I am sorry, Mother . . . for Lord Hoster and for you. Yet first we must meet. We've had word from the south. Renly Baratheon has claimed his brother's crown."

"Renly?" she said, shocked. "I had thought, surely it would be Lord Stannis . . ."

"So did we all, my lady," Galbart Glover said.

The war council convened in the Great Hall, at four long trestle tables arranged in a broken square. Lord Hoster was too weak to attend, asleep on his balcony, dreaming of the sun on the rivers of his youth. Edmure sat in the high seat of the Tullys, with Brynden Blackfish at his side, and his father's bannermen arrayed to right and left and along the side tables. Word of the victory at River-run had spread to the fugitive lords of the Trident, drawing them back. Karyl Vance came in, a lord now, his father dead beneath the Golden Tooth. Ser Marq Piper was with him, and they brought a Darry, Ser Raymun's son, a lad no older than Bran. Lord Jonos Bracken arrived from the ruins of Stone Hedge, glowering and blustering, and took a seat as far from Tytos Blackwood as the tables would permit.

The northern lords sat opposite, with Catelyn and Robb facing her brother across the tables. They were fewer. The Greatjon sat at Robb's left hand, and then Theon Greyjoy; Galbart Glover and Lady Mormont were to the right of Catelyn. Lord Rickard Karstark, gaunt and hollow-eyed in his grief, took his seat like a man in a nightmare, his long beard uncombed and unwashed. He had left two sons dead in the Whispering Wood, and there was no word of the third, his eldest, who had led the Karstark spears against Tywin Lannister on the Green Fork.

The arguing raged on late into the night. Each lord had a right to speak, and speak they did . . . and shout, and curse, and reason, and cajole, and jest, and bargain, and slam tankards on the table, and threaten, and walk out, and return sullen or smiling. Catelyn sat and listened to it all.

Roose Bolton had re-formed the battered remnants of their other host at the mouth of the causeway. Ser Helman Tallhart and Walder Frey still held the Twins. Lord Tywin's army had crossed the Trident, and was making for Harrenhal. And there were two kings in the realm. Two kings, and no agreement.

Many of the lords bannermen wanted to march on Harrenhal at once, to meet Lord Tywin and end Lannister power for all time. Young, hot-tempered Marq Piper urged a strike west at Casterly Rock instead. Still others counseled patience. Riverrun sat athwart the Lannister supply lines, Jason Mallister pointed out; let them bide their time, denying Lord Tywin fresh levies and provisions while they strengthened their defenses and rested their weary troops. Lord Blackwood would have none of it. They should finish the work they began in the Whispering Wood. March to Harrenhal and bring Roose Bolton's army down as well. What Blackwood urged, Bracken opposed, as ever; Lord Jonos Bracken rose to insist they ought pledge their fealty to King Renly, and move south to join their might to his.

"Renly is not the king," Robb said. It was the first time her son had spoken. Like his father, he knew how to listen.

"You cannot mean to hold to Joffrey, my lord," Galbart Glover said. "He put your father to death."

"That makes him evil," Robb replied. "I do not know that it makes Renly king. Joffrey is still Robert's eldest trueborn son, so the throne is rightfully his by all the laws of the realm. Were he to die, and I mean to see that he does, he has a younger brother. Tommen is next in line after Joffrey."

"Tommen is no less a Lannister," Ser Marq Piper snapped.

"As you say," said Robb, troubled. "Yet if neither one is king, still, how could it be Lord Renly? He's Robert's *younger* brother. Bran can't be Lord of Winterfell before me, and Renly can't be king before Lord Stannis."

Lady Mormont agreed. "Lord Stannis has the better claim."

"Renly is *crowned*," said Marq Piper. "Highgarden and Storm's End support his claim, and the Dornishmen will not be laggardly. If Winterfell and Riverrun add their strength to his, he will have five of the seven great houses behind him. *Six,* if the Arryns bestir themselves! Six against the Rock! My lords, within the year, we will have all their heads on pikes, the queen and the boy king, Lord Tywin, the Imp, the Kingslayer, Ser Kevan, *all* of them! That is what we shall win if we join with King Renly. What does Lord Stannis have against that, that we should cast it all aside?"

"The right," said Robb stubbornly. Catelyn thought he sounded eerily like his father as he said it.

"So you mean us to declare for Stannis?" asked Edmure.

"I don't know," said Robb. "I prayed to know what to do, but the gods did not answer. The Lannisters killed my father for a traitor, and we know that was a lie, but if Joffrey is the lawful king and we fight against him, we *will* be traitors."

"My lord father would urge caution," aged Ser Stevron said, with the weaselly smile of a Frey. "Wait, let these two kings play their game of thrones. When they are done fighting, we can bend our knees to the victor, or oppose him, as we choose. With Renly arming, likely Lord Tywin would welcome a truce . . . and the safe return of his son. Noble lords, allow me to go to him at Harrenhal and arrange good terms and ransoms . . ."

A roar of outrage drowned out his voice. *"Craven!"* the Greatjon thundered. "Begging for a truce will make us seem weak," declared Lady Mormont. "Ransoms be damned, we must *not* give up the Kingslayer," shouted Rickard Karstark.

"Why not a peace?" Catelyn asked.

The lords looked at her, but it was Robb's eyes she felt, his and his alone. "My lady, they murdered my lord father, your husband," he said grimly. He unsheathed his longsword and laid it on the table before him, the bright steel on the rough wood. "This is the only peace I have for Lannisters."

The Greatjon bellowed his approval, and other men added their voices, shouting and drawing swords and pounding their fists on the table. Catelyn waited until they had quieted. "My lords," she said then, "Lord Eddard was your liege, but I shared his bed and bore his children. Do you think I love him any less than you?" Her voice almost broke with her grief, but Catelyn took a long breath and steadied herself. "Robb, if that sword could bring him back, I should never let you sheathe it until Ned stood at my side once more . . . but he is gone, and a hundred Whispering Woods will not change that. Ned is gone, and Daryn Hornwood, and Lord Karstark's valiant sons, and many other good men besides, and none of them will return to us. Must we have more deaths still?"

"You are a woman, my lady," the Greatjon rumbled in his deep voice. "Women do not understand these things."

"You are the gentle sex," said Lord Karstark, with the lines of grief fresh on his face. "A man has a need for vengeance."

"Give me Cersei Lannister, Lord Karstark, and you would see how *gentle* a woman can be," Catelyn replied. "Perhaps I do not understand tactics and strategy . . . but I understand futility. We went to war when Lannister armies were ravaging the riverlands, and Ned was a prisoner, falsely accused of treason. We fought to defend ourselves, and to win my lord's freedom.

"Well, the one is done, and the other forever beyond our reach. I will mourn for Ned until the end of my days, but I must think of the living. I want my daughters back, and the queen holds them still. If I must trade our four Lannisters for their two Starks, I will call that a bargain and thank the gods. I want you safe, Robb, ruling at Winterfell from your father's seat. I want you to live your life, to kiss a girl and wed a woman and father a son. I want to write an end to this. I want to go home, my lords, and weep for my husband."

The hall was very quiet when Catelyn finished speaking.

"Peace," said her uncle Brynden. "Peace is sweet, my lady . . . but on what terms? It is no good hammering your sword into a plowshare if you must forge it again on the morrow."

"What did Torrhen and my Eddard die for, if I am to return to Karhold with nothing but their bones?" asked Rickard Karstark.

"Aye," said Lord Bracken. "Gregor Clegane laid waste to my fields, slaughtered my smallfolk, and left Stone Hedge a smoking ruin. Am I now to bend the knee to the ones who sent him? What have we fought for, if we are to put all back as it was before?"

Lord Blackwood agreed, to Catelyn's surprise and dismay. "And if we do make peace with King Joffrey, are we not then traitors to King Renly? What if the stag should prevail against the lion, where would that leave us?"

"Whatever you may decide for yourselves, I shall never call a Lannister my king," declared Marq Piper.

"Nor I!" yelled the little Darry boy. "I never will!"

Again the shouting began. Catelyn sat despairing. She had come so close, she thought. They had almost listened, *almost* . . . but the moment was gone. There would be no peace, no chance to heal, no safety. She looked at her son, watched him as he listened to the lords debate, frowning, troubled, yet wedded to his war. He had pledged himself to marry a daughter of Walder Frey, but she saw his true bride plain before her now: the sword he had laid on the table.

Catelyn was thinking of her girls, wondering if she would ever see them again, when the Greatjon lurched to his feet.

"MY LORDS!" he shouted, his voice booming off the rafters. "Here is what I say to these two kings!" He spat. "Renly Baratheon is nothing to me, nor Stannis neither. Why should they rule over me and mine, from some flowery seat in Highgarden or Dorne? What do they know of the Wall or the wolfswood or the barrows of the First Men? Even their *gods* are wrong. The Others take the Lannisters too, I've had a bellyful of them." He reached back over his shoulder and drew his immense two-handed greatsword. "Why shouldn't we rule ourselves again? It was the dragons we married, and the dragons are all dead!" He pointed at Robb with the blade. "*There* sits the only king I mean to bow *my* knee to, m'lords," he thundered. "The King in the North!"

And he knelt, and laid his sword at her son's feet.

"I'll have peace on *those* terms," Lord Karstark said. "They can keep their red castle and their iron chair as well." He eased his longsword from its scabbard. "The King in the North!" he said, kneeling beside the Greatjon.

Maege Mormont stood. "The King of Winter!" she declared, and laid her spiked mace beside the swords. And the river lords were rising too, Blackwood and Bracken and Mallister, houses who had never been ruled from Winterfell, yet Catelyn watched them rise and draw their blades, bending their knees and shouting the old words that had not been heard in the realm for more than three hundred years, since Aegon the Dragon had come to make the Seven Kingdoms one . . . yet now were heard again, ringing from the timbers of her father's hall:

"The King in the North!"

"The King in the North!"

"THE KING IN THE NORTH!"

DAENERYS

The land was red and dead and parched, and good wood was hard to come by. Her foragers returned with gnarled cottonwoods, purple brush, sheaves of brown grass. They took the two straightest trees, hacked the limbs and branches from them, skinned off their bark, and split them, laying the logs in a square. Its center they filled with straw, brush, bark shavings, and bundles of dry grass. Rakharo chose a stallion from the small herd that remained to them; he was not the equal of Khal Drogo's red, but few horses were. In the center of the square, Aggo fed him a withered apple and dropped him in an instant with an axe blow between the eyes.

Bound hand and foot, Mirri Maz Duur watched from the dust with disquiet in her black eyes. "It is not enough to kill a horse," she told Dany. "By itself, the blood is nothing. You do not have the words to make a spell, nor the wisdom to find them. Do you think bloodmagic is a game for children? You call me *maegi* as if it were a curse, but all it means is *wise*. You are a child, with a child's ignorance. Whatever you mean to do, it will not work. Loose me from these bonds and I will help you."

"I am tired of the *maegi*'s braying," Dany told Jhogo.

He took his whip to her, and after that the godswife kept silent.

Over the carcass of the horse, they built a platform of hewn logs; trunks of smaller trees and limbs from the greater, and the thickest straightest branches they could find. They laid the wood east to west, from sunrise to sunset. On the platform they piled Khal Drogo's treasures: his great tent, his painted vests, his saddles and harness, the whip his father had given him when he came to manhood, the *arakh* he had used to slay Khal Ogo and his son, a mighty dragonbone bow. Aggo would have added the weapons Drogo's bloodriders had given Dany for bride gifts as well, but she forbade it. "Those are mine," she told him, "and I mean to keep them." Another layer of brush was piled about the *khal's* treasures, and bundles of dried grass scattered over them.

Ser Jorah Mormont drew her aside as the sun was creeping toward its zenith. "Princess . . ." he began.

"Why do you call me that?" Dany challenged him. "My brother Viserys was your king, was he not?"

"He was, my lady."

"Viserys is dead. I am his heir, the last blood of House Targaryen. Whatever was his is mine now."

"My . . . queen," Ser Jorah said, going to one knee. "My sword that was his is yours, Daenerys. And my heart as well, that never belonged to your brother. I am only a knight, and I have nothing to offer you but exile, but I beg you, hear me. Let Khal Drogo go. You shall not be alone. I promise you, no man shall take you to Vaes Dothrak unless you wish to go. You need not join the *dosh khaleen.* Come east with me. Yi Ti, Qarth, the Jade Sea, Asshai by the Shadow. We will see all the wonders yet unseen, and drink what wines the gods see fit to serve us. Please, *Khaleesi.* I know what you intend. Do not. *Do not.*"

"I must," Dany told him. She touched his face, fondly, sadly. "You do not understand."

"I understand that you loved him," Ser Jorah said in a voice thick with despair. "I loved my lady wife once, yet I did not die with her. You are my queen, my sword is yours, but do not ask me to stand aside as you climb on Drogo's pyre. I will not watch you burn."

"Is that what you fear?" Dany kissed him lightly on

his broad forehead. "I am not such a child as that, sweet ser."

"You do not mean to die with him? You swear it, my queen?"

"I swear it," she said in the Common Tongue of the Seven Kingdoms that by rights were hers.

The third level of the platform was woven of branches no thicker than a finger, and covered with dry leaves and twigs. They laid them north to south, from ice to fire, and piled them high with soft cushions and sleeping silks. The sun had begun to lower toward the west by the time they were done. Dany called the Dothraki around her. Fewer than a hundred were left. How many had Aegon started with? she wondered. It did not matter.

"You will be my *khalasar*," she told them. "I see the faces of slaves. I free you. Take off your collars. Go if you wish, no one shall harm you. If you stay, it will be as brothers and sisters, husbands and wives." The black eyes watched her, wary, expressionless. "I see the children, women, the wrinkled faces of the aged. I was a child yesterday. Today I am a woman. Tomorrow I will be old. To each of you I say, give me your hands and your hearts, and there will always be a place for you." She turned to the three young warriors of her *khas*. "Jhogo, to you I give the silver-handled whip that was my bride gift, and name you *ko*, and ask your oath, that you will live and die as blood of my blood, riding at my side to keep me safe from harm."

Jhogo took the whip from her hands, but his face was confused. "*Khaleesi*," he said hesitantly, "this is not done. It would shame me, to be bloodrider to a woman."

"Aggo," Dany called, paying no heed to Jhogo's words. *If I look back I am lost.* "To you I give the dragonbone bow that was my bride gift." It was double-curved, shiny black and exquisite, taller than she was. "I name you *ko*, and ask your oath, that you should live and die as blood of my blood, riding at my side to keep me safe from harm."

Aggo accepted the bow with lowered eyes. "I cannot say these words. Only a man can lead a *khalasar* or name a *ko*."

"Rakharo," Dany said, turning away from the refusal, "you shall have the great *arakh* that was my bride gift, with hilt and blade chased in gold. And you too I name my *ko*, and ask that you live and die as blood of my blood, riding at my side to keep me safe from harm."

"You are *khaleesi*," Rakharo said, taking the *arakh*. "I shall ride at your side to Vaes Dothrak beneath the Mother of Mountains, and keep you safe from harm until you take your place with the crones of the *dosh khaleen*. No more can I promise."

She nodded, as calmly as if she had not heard his answer, and turned to the last of her champions. "Ser Jorah Mormont," she said, "first and greatest of my knights, I have no bride gift to give you, but I swear to you, one day you shall have from my hands a longsword like none the world has ever seen, dragon-forged and made of Valyrian steel. And I would ask for your oath as well."

"You have it, my queen," Ser Jorah said, kneeling to lay his sword at her feet. "I vow to serve you, to obey you, to die for you if need be."

"Whatever may come?"

"Whatever may come."

"I shall hold you to that oath. I pray you never regret the giving of it." Dany lifted him to his feet. Stretching on her toes to reach his lips, she kissed the knight gently and said, "You are the first of my Queensguard."

She could feel the eyes of the *khalasar* on her as she entered her tent. The Dothraki were muttering and giving her strange sideways looks from the corners of their dark almond eyes. They thought her mad, Dany realized. Perhaps she was. She would know soon enough. *If I look back I am lost.*

Her bath was scalding hot when Irri helped her into the tub, but Dany did not flinch or cry aloud. She liked the heat. It made her feel clean. Jhiqui had scented the water with the oils she had found in the market in Vaes Dothrak; the steam rose moist and fragrant. Doreah washed her hair and combed it out, working loose the mats and tangles. Irri scrubbed her back. Dany closed her eyes and let the smell and the warmth enfold her. She could feel the heat soaking through the soreness between her thighs. She shuddered when it entered her, and her pain and stiffness seemed to dissolve. She floated.

When she was clean, her handmaids helped her from

the water. Irri and Jhiqui fanned her dry, while Doreah brushed her hair until it fell like a river of liquid silver down her back. They scented her with spiceflower and cinnamon; a touch on each wrist, behind her ears, on the tips of her milk-heavy breasts. The last dab was for her sex. Irri's finger felt as light and cool as a lover's kiss as it slid softly up between her lips.

Afterward, Dany sent them all away, so she might prepare Khal Drogo for his final ride into the night lands. She washed his body clean and brushed and oiled his hair, running her fingers through it for the last time, feeling the weight of it, remembering the first time she had touched it, the night of their wedding ride. His hair had never been cut. How many men could die with their hair uncut? She buried her face in it and inhaled the dark fragrance of the oils. He smelled like grass and warm earth, like smoke and semen and horses. He smelled like Drogo. *Forgive me, sun of my life*, she thought. *Forgive me for all I have done and all I must do. I paid the price, my star, but it was too high, too high . . .*

Dany braided his hair and slid the silver rings onto his mustache and hung his bells one by one. So many bells, gold and silver and bronze. Bells so his enemies would hear him coming and grow weak with fear. She dressed him in horsehair leggings and high boots, buckling a belt heavy with gold and silver medallions about his waist. Over his scarred chest she slipped a painted vest, old and faded, the one Drogo had loved best. For herself she chose loose sandsilk trousers, sandals that laced halfway up her legs, and a vest like Drogo's.

The sun was going down when she called them back to carry his body to the pyre. The Dothraki watched in silence as Jhogo and Aggo bore him from the tent. Dany walked behind them. They laid him down on his cushions and silks, his head toward the Mother of Mountains far to the northeast.

"Oil," she commanded, and they brought forth the jars and poured them over the pyre, soaking the silks and the brush and the bundles of dry grass, until the oil trickled from beneath the logs and the air was rich with fragrance. "Bring my eggs," Dany commanded her handmaids. Something in her voice made them run.

Ser Jorah took her arm. "My queen, Drogo will have no use for dragon's eggs in the night lands. Better to sell them in Asshai. Sell one and we can buy a ship to take us back to the Free Cities. Sell all three and you will be a wealthy woman all your days."

"They were not given to me to sell," Dany told him.

She climbed the pyre herself to place the eggs around her sun-and-stars. The black beside his heart, under his arm. The green beside his head, his braid coiled around it. The cream-and-gold down between his legs. When she kissed him for the last time, Dany could taste the sweetness of the oil on his lips.

As she climbed down off the pyre, she noticed Mirri Maz Duur watching her. "You are mad," the godswife said hoarsely.

"Is it so far from madness to wisdom?" Dany asked. "Ser Jorah, take this *maegi* and bind her to the pyre."

"To the . . . my queen, no, hear me . . ."

"Do as I say." Still he hesitated, until her anger flared. "You swore to obey me, whatever might come. Rakharo, help him."

The godswife did not cry out as they dragged her to Khal Drogo's pyre and staked her down amidst his treasures. Dany poured the oil over the woman's head herself. "I thank you, Mirri Maz Duur," she said, "for the lessons you have taught me."

"You will not hear me scream," Mirri responded as the oil dripped from her hair and soaked her clothing.

"I will," Dany said, "but it is not your screams I want, only your life. I remember what you told me. Only death can pay for life." Mirri Maz Duur opened her mouth, but made no reply. As she stepped away, Dany saw that the contempt was gone from the *maegi*'s flat black eyes; in its place was something that might have been fear. Then there was nothing to be done but watch the sun and look for the first star.

When a horselord dies, his horse is slain with him, so he might ride proud into the night lands. The bodies are burned beneath the open sky, and the *khal* rises on his fiery steed to take his place among the stars. The more fiercely the man burned in life, the brighter his star will shine in the darkness.

Jhogo spied it first. *"There,"* he said in a hushed voice. Dany looked and saw it, low in the east. The first star was a comet, burning red. Bloodred; fire red; the dragon's tail. She could not have asked for a stronger sign.

Dany took the torch from Aggo's hand and thrust it between the logs. The oil took the fire at once, the brush and dried grass a heartbeat later. Tiny flames went darting up the wood like swift red mice, skating over the oil and leaping from bark to branch to leaf. A rising heat puffed at her face, soft and sudden as a lover's breath, but in seconds it had grown too hot to bear. Dany stepped backward. The wood crackled, louder and louder. Mirri Maz Duur began to sing in a shrill, ululating voice. The flames whirled and writhed, racing each other up the platform. The dusk shimmered as the air itself seemed to liquefy from the heat. Dany heard logs spit and crack. The fires swept over Mirri Maz Duur. Her song grew louder, shriller . . . then she gasped, again and again, and her song became a shuddering wail, thin and high and full of agony.

And now the flames reached her Drogo, and now they were all around him. His clothing took fire, and for an instant the *khal* was clad in wisps of floating orange silk and tendrils of curling smoke, grey and greasy. Dany's lips parted and she found herself holding her breath. Part of her wanted to go to him as Ser Jorah had feared, to rush into the flames to beg for his forgiveness and take him inside her one last time, the fire melting the flesh from their bones until they were as one, forever.

She could smell the odor of burning flesh, no different than horseflesh roasting in a firepit. The pyre roared in the deepening dusk like some great beast, drowning out the fainter sound of Mirri Maz Duur's screaming and sending up long tongues of flame to lick at the belly of the night. As the smoke grew thicker, the Dothraki backed away, coughing. Huge orange gouts of fire unfurled their banners in that hellish wind, the logs hissing and cracking, glowing cinders rising on the smoke to float away into the dark like so many newborn fireflies. The heat beat at the air with great red wings, driving the Dothraki back, driving off even Mormont, but Dany stood her ground. She was the blood of the dragon, and the fire was in her.

She had sensed the truth of it long ago, Dany thought as she took a step closer to the conflagration, but the brazier had not been hot enough. The flames writhed before her like the women who had danced at her wedding, whirling and singing and spinning their yellow and orange and crimson veils, fearsome to behold, yet lovely, so lovely, alive with heat. Dany opened her arms to them, her skin flushed and glowing. *This is a wedding, too,* she thought. Mirri Maz Duur had fallen silent. The godswife thought her a child, but children grow, and children learn.

Another step, and Dany could feel the heat of the sand on the soles of her feet, even through her sandals. Sweat ran down her thighs and between her breasts and in rivulets over her cheeks, where tears had once run. Ser Jorah was shouting behind her, but he did not matter anymore, only the fire mattered. The flames were so beautiful, the loveliest things she had ever seen, each one a sorcerer robed in yellow and orange and scarlet, swirling long smoky cloaks. She saw crimson firelions and great yellow serpents and unicorns made of pale blue flame; she saw fish and foxes and monsters, wolves and bright birds and flowering trees, each more beautiful than the last. She saw a horse, a great grey stallion limned in smoke, its flowing mane a nimbus of blue flame. *Yes, my love, my sun-and-stars, yes, mount now, ride now.*

Her vest had begun to smolder, so Dany shrugged it off and let it fall to the ground. The painted leather burst into sudden flame as she skipped closer to the fire, her breasts bare to the blaze, streams of milk flowing from her red and swollen nipples. *Now,* she thought, *now,* and for an instant she glimpsed Khal Drogo before her, mounted on his smoky stallion, a flaming lash in his hand. He smiled, and the whip snaked down at the pyre, hissing.

She heard a *crack,* the sound of shattering stone. The platform of wood and brush and grass began to shift and collapse in upon itself. Bits of burning wood slid down at her, and Dany was showered with ash and cinders. And something else came crashing down, bouncing and rolling, to land at her feet; a chunk of curved rock, pale and veined with gold, broken and smoking. The roaring filled the world, yet dimly through the firefall Dany heard women shriek and children cry out in wonder.

Only death can pay for life.

And there came a second *crack*, loud and sharp as thunder, and the smoke stirred and whirled around her and the pyre shifted, the logs exploding as the fire touched their secret hearts. She heard the screams of frightened horses, and the voices of the Dothraki raised in shouts of fear and terror, and Ser Jorah calling her name and cursing. *No*, she wanted to shout to him, *no, my good knight, do not fear for me. The fire is mine. I am Daenerys Stormborn, daughter of dragons, bride of dragons, mother of dragons, don't you see? Don't you SEE?* With a belch of flame and smoke that reached thirty feet into the sky, the pyre collapsed and came down around her. Unafraid, Dany stepped forward into the firestorm, calling to her children.

The third *crack* was as loud and sharp as the breaking of the world.

When the fire died at last and the ground became cool enough to walk upon, Ser Jorah Mormont found her amidst the ashes, surrounded by blackened logs and bits of glowing ember and the burnt bones of man and woman and stallion. She was naked, covered with soot, her clothes turned to ash, her beautiful hair all crisped away . . . yet she was unhurt.

The cream-and-gold dragon was suckling at her left breast, the green-and-bronze at the right. Her arms cradled them close. The black-and-scarlet beast was draped across her shoulders, its long sinuous neck coiled under her chin. When it saw Jorah, it raised its head and looked at him with eyes as red as coals.

Wordless, the knight fell to his knees. The men of her *khas* came up behind him. Jhogo was the first to lay his *arakh* at her feet. "Blood of my blood," he murmured, pushing his face to the smoking earth. "Blood of my blood," she heard Aggo echo. "Blood of my blood," Rakharo shouted.

And after them came her handmaids, and then the others, all the Dothraki, men and women and children, and Dany had only to look at their eyes to know that they were hers now, today and tomorrow and forever, hers as they had never been Drogo's.

As Daenerys Targaryen rose to her feet, her black

hissed, pale smoke venting from its mouth and nostrils. The other two pulled away from her breasts and added their voices to the call, translucent wings unfolding and stirring the air, and for the first time in hundreds of years, the night came alive with the music of dragons.

APPENDIX

HOUSE BARATHEON

The youngest of the Great Houses, born during the Wars of Conquest. Its founder, Orys Baratheon, was rumored to be Aegon the Dragon's bastard brother. Orys rose through the ranks to become one of Aegon's fiercest commanders. When he defeated and slew Argilac the Arrogant, the last Storm King, Aegon rewarded him with Argilac's castle, lands, and daughter. Orys took the girl to bride, and adopted the banner, honors, and words of her line. The Baratheon sigil is a crowned stag, black, on a golden field. Their words are *Ours is the Fury*.

KING ROBERT BARATHEON, the First of His Name,
— his wife, QUEEN CERSEI, of House Lannister,
— their children:
— PRINCE JOFFREY, heir to the Iron Throne, twelve,
— PRINCESS MYRCELLA, a girl of eight,
— PRINCE TOMMEN, a boy of seven,

— his brothers:
  — STANNIS BARATHEON, Lord of
    Dragonstone,
      — his wife, LADY SELYSE of House
        Florent,
      — their daughter, SHIREEN, a girl of
        nine,
  — RENLY BARATHEON, Lord of Storm's
    End,
— his small council:
  — GRAND MAESTER PYCELLE,
  — LORD PETYR BAELISH, called
    LITTLEFINGER, master of coin,
  — LORD STANNIS BARATHEON, master
    of ships,
  — LORD RENLY BARATHEON, master of
    laws,
  — SER BARRISTAN SELMY, Lord
    Commander of the Kingsguard,
  — VARYS, a eunuch, called the Spider,
    master of whisperers,
— his court and retainers:
  — SER ILYN PAYNE, the King's Justice, a
    headsman,
  — SANDOR CLEGANE, called the Hound,
    sworn shield to Prince Joffrey,
  — JANOS SLYNT, a commoner,
commander of the City Watch of King's
Landing,
    — JALABHAR XHO, an exile prince from
      the Summer Isles,
    — MOON BOY, a jester and fool,

— LANCEL and TYREK LANNISTER,
   squires to the king, the queen's cousins,
— SER ARON SANTAGAR, master-at-
   arms,
— his Kingsguard:
— SER BARRISTAN SELMY, Lord
   Commander,
— SER JAIME LANNISTER, called the
   Kingslayer,
— SER BOROS BLOUNT,
— SER MERYN TRANT,
— SER ARYS OAKHEART,
— SER PRESTON GREENFIELD,
— SER MANDON MOORE,

The principal houses sworn to Storm's End are
Selmy, Wylde, Trant, Penrose, Errol, Estermont,
Tarth, Swann, Dondarrion, Caron.

The principal houses sworn to Dragonstone are Cel-
tigar, Velaryon, Seaworth, Bar Emmon, and Sun-
glass.

HOUSE STARK

The Starks trace their descent from Brandon the Builder and the ancient Kings of Winter. For thousands of years, they ruled from Winterfell as Kings in the North, until Torrhen Stark, the King Who Knelt, chose to swear fealty to Aegon the Dragon rather than give battle. Their blazon is a grey direwolf on an ice-white field. The Stark words are *Winter Is Coming*.

EDDARD STARK, Lord of Winterfell, Warden of the North,
— his wife, LADY CATELYN, of House Tully,
— their children:
— ROBB, the heir to Winterfell, fourteen years of age,
— SANSA, the eldest daughter, eleven,
— ARYA, the younger daughter, a girl of nine,
— BRANDON, called Bran, seven,
— RICKON, a boy of three,

— his bastard son, JON SNOW, a boy of
fourteen,

— his ward, THEON GREYJOY, heir to the
Iron Islands,

— his siblings:

— {BRANDON}, his elder brother,
murdered by the command of Aerys II
Targaryen,

— {LYANNA}, his younger sister, died in
the mountains of Dorne,

— BENJEN, his younger brother, a man of
the Night's Watch,

— his household:

— MAESTER LUWIN, counselor, healer,
and tutor,

— VAYON POOLE, steward of Winterfell,

— JEYNE, his daughter, Sansa's closest
friend,

— JORY CASSEL, captain of the guard,

— HALLIS MOLLEN, DESMOND,
JACKS, PORTHER, QUENT, ALYN,
TOMARD, VARLY, HEWARD,
CAYN, WYL, guardsmen,

— SER RODRIK CASSEL, master-at-arms,
Jory's uncle,

— BETH, his young daughter,

— SEPTA MORDANE, tutor to Lord
Eddard's daughters,

— SEPTON CHAYLE, keeper of the castle
sept and library,

— HULLEN, master of horse,

— his son, HARWIN, a guardsman,

- JOSETH, a stableman and horse trainer,
- FARLEN, kennelmaster,
- OLD NAN, storyteller, once a wet nurse,
  - HODOR, her great-grandson, a simpleminded stableboy,
- GAGE, the cook,
- MIKKEN, smith and armorer,
- his principal lords bannermen:
  - SER HELMAN TALLHART,
  - RICKARD KARSTARK, Lord of Karhold,
  - ROOSE BOLTON, Lord of the Dreadfort,
  - JON UMBER, called the Greatjon,
  - GALBART and ROBETT GLOVER,
  - WYMAN MANDERLY, Lord of White Harbor,
  - MAEGE MORMONT, the Lady of Bear Island,

The principal houses sworn to Winterfell are Karstark, Umber, Flint, Mormont, Hornwood, Cerwyn, Reed, Manderly, Glover, Tallhart, Bolton.

HOUSE LANNISTER

Fair-haired, tall, and handsome, the Lannisters are the blood of Andal adventurers who carved out a mighty kingdom in the western hills and valleys. Through the female line they boast of descent from Lann the Clever, the legendary trickster of the Age of Heroes. The gold of Casterly Rock and the Golden Tooth has made them the wealthiest of the Great Houses. Their sigil is a golden lion upon a crimson field. The Lannister words are *Hear Me Roar!*

TYWIN LANNISTER, Lord of Casterly Rock, Warden of the West, Shield of Lannisport,
— his wife, {LADY JOANNA}, a cousin, died in childbed,
— their children:
— SER JAIME, called the Kingslayer, heir to Casterly Rock, a twin to Cersei,
— QUEEN CERSEI, wife of King Robert I Baratheon, a twin to Jaime,
— TYRION, called the Imp, a dwarf,

— his siblings:
  — SER KEVAN, his eldest brother,
    — his wife, DORNA, of House Swyft,
    — their eldest son, LANCEL, squire to
      the king,
    — their twin sons, WILLEM and
      MARTYN,
    — their infant daughter, JANEI,
  — GENNA, his sister, wed to Ser Emmon
    Frey,
    — their son, SER CLEOS FREY,
    — their son, TION FREY, a squire,
  — {SER TYGETT}, his second brother, died
    of a pox,
    — his widow, DARLESSA, of House
      Marbrand,
    — their son, TYREK, squire to the king,
  — {GERION}, his youngest brother, lost at
    sea,
    — his bastard daughter, JOY, a girl of
      ten,
— their cousin, SER STAFFORD
  LANNISTER, brother to the late Lady
  Joanna,
  — his daughters, CERENNA and
    MYRIELLE,
  — his son, SER DAVEN LANNISTER,
— his counselor, MAESTER CREYLEN,
— his chief knights and lords bannermen:
  — LORD LEO LEFFORD,
  — SER ADDAM MARBRAND,
  — SER GREGOR CLEGANE, the
    Mountain That Rides,

— SER HARYS SWYFT, father by marriage
to Ser Kevan,
— LORD ANDROS BRAX,
— SER FORLEY PRESTER,
— SER AMORY LORCH,
— VARGO HOAT, of the Free City of
Qohor, a sellsword,

Principal houses sworn to Casterly Rock are Payne,
Swyft, Marbrand, Lydden, Banefort, Lefford,
Crakehall, Serrett, Broom, Clegane, Prester, and
Westerling.

HOUSE ARRYN

The Arryns are descended from the Kings of Mountain and Vale, one of the oldest and purest lines of Andal nobility. Their sigil is the moon-and-falcon, white, upon a sky blue field. The Arryn words are *As High As Honor.*

{JON ARRYN}, Lord of the Eyrie, Defender of the Vale, Warden of the East, Hand of the King, recently deceased,
— his first wife, {LADY JEYNE, of House Royce}, died in childbed, her daughter stillborn,
— his second wife, {LADY ROWENA, of House Arryn}, his cousin, died of a winter chill, childless,
— his third wife and widow, LADY LYSA, of House Tully,
— their son:
— ROBERT ARRYN, a sickly boy of six years, now Lord of the Eyrie and Defender of the Vale,

— their retainers and household:
—MAESTER COLEMON, counselor,
healer, and tutor,
—SER VARDIS EGEN, captain of the
guard,
—SER BRYNDEN TULLY, called the
Blackfish, Knight of the Gate and uncle
to the Lady Lysa,
—LORD NESTOR ROYCE, High Steward
of the Vale,
—SER ALBAR ROYCE, his son,
—MYA STONE, a bastard girl in his
service,
—LORD EON HUNTER, suitor to Lady
Lysa,
—SER LYN CORBRAY, suitor to Lady
Lysa,
—MYCHEL REDFORT, his squire,
—LADY ANYA WAYNWOOD, a widow,
—SER MORTON WAYNWOOD, her
son, suitor to Lady Lysa,
—SER DONNEL WAYNWOOD, her
son,
—MORD, a brutal gaoler,

The principal houses sworn to the Eyrie are Royce,
Baelish, Egen, Waynwood, Hunter, Redfort, Corbray, Belmore, Melcolm, and Hersy.

HOUSE TULLY

The Tullys never reigned as kings, though they held rich lands and the great castle at Riverrun for a thousand years. During the Wars of Conquest, the riverlands belonged to Harren the Black, King of the Isles. Harren's grandfather, King Harwyn Hardhand, had taken the Trident from Arrec the Storm King, whose ancestors had conquered all the way to the Neck three hundred years earlier, slaying the last of the old River Kings. A vain and bloody tyrant, Harren the Black was little loved by those he ruled, and many of the river lords deserted him to join Aegon's host. First among them was Edmyn Tully of Riverrun. When Harren and his line perished in the burning of Harrenhal, Aegon rewarded House Tully by raising Lord Edmyn to dominion over the lands of the Trident and requiring the other river lords to swear him fealty. The Tully sigil is a leaping trout, silver, on a field of rippling blue and red. The Tully words are *Family, Duty, Honor.*

HOSTER TULLY, Lord of Riverrun,

— his wife, {LADY MINISA, of House Whent}, died in childbed,
— their children:
  — CATELYN, the eldest daughter, wed to Lord Eddard Stark,
  — LYSA, the younger daughter, wed to Lord Jon Arryn,
  — SER EDMURE, heir to Riverrun,
— his brother, SER BRYNDEN, called the Blackfish,
— his household:
  — MAESTER VYMAN, counselor, healer, and tutor,
  — SER DESMOND GRELL, master-at-arms,
  — SER ROBIN RYGER, captain of the guard,
  — UTHERYDES WAYN, steward of Riverrun,
— his knights and lords bannermen:
  — JASON MALLISTER, Lord of Seagard,
    — PATREK MALLISTER, his son and heir,
  — WALDER FREY, Lord of the Crossing,
    — his numerous sons, grandsons, and bastards,
  — JONOS BRACKEN, Lord of the Stone Hedge,
  — TYTOS BLACKWOOD, Lord of Raventree,
  — SER RAYMUN DARRY,
  — SER KARYL VANCE,
  — SER MARQ PIPER,

— SHELLA WHENT, Lady of Harrenhal,
— SER WILLIS WODE, a knight in her
service,

Lesser houses sworn to Riverrun include Darry,
Frey, Mallister, Bracken, Blackwood, Whent, Ryger,
Piper, Vance.

HOUSE TYRELL

The Tyrells rose to power as stewards to the Kings of the Reach, whose domain included the fertile plains of the southwest from the Dornish marches and Blackwater Rush to the shores of the Sunset Sea. Through the female line, they claim descent from Garth Greenhand, gardener king of the First Men, who wore a crown of vines and flowers and made the land bloom. When King Mern, last of the old line, perished on the Field of Fire, his steward Harlen Tyrell surrendered Highgarden to Aegon Targaryen, pledging fealty. Aegon granted him the castle and dominion over the Reach. The Tyrell sigil is a golden rose on a grass-green field. Their words are *Growing Strong*.

MACE TYRELL, Lord of Highgarden, Warden of the South, Defender of the Marches, High Marshal of the Reach,
— his wife, LADY ALERIE, of House Hightower of Oldtown,
— their children:

— WILLAS, their eldest son, heir to Highgarden,
— SER GARLAN, called the Gallant, their second son,
— SER LORAS, the Knight of Flowers, their youngest son,
— MARGAERY, their daughter, a maid of fourteen years,
— his widowed mother, LADY OLENNA of House Redwyne, called the Queen of Thorns,
— his sisters:
— MINA, wed to Lord Paxter Redwyne,
— JANNA, wed to Ser Jon Fossoway,
— his uncles:
— GARTH, called the Gross, Lord Seneschal of Highgarden,
— his bastard sons, GARSE and GARRETT FLOWERS,
— SER MORYN, Lord Commander of the City Watch of Oldtown,
— MAESTER GORMON, a scholar of the Citadel,
— his household:
— MAESTER LOMYS, counselor, healer, and tutor,
— IGON VYRWEL, captain of the guard,
— SER VORTIMER CRANE, master-at-arms,
— his knights and lord bannermen:
— PAXTER REDWYNE, Lord of the Arbor,
— his wife, LADY MINA, of House Tyrell,

— their children:
  — SER HORAS, mocked as Horror,
    twin to Hobber,
  — SER HOBBER, mocked as Slobber,
    twin to Horas,
  — DESMERA, a maid of fifteen,
— RANDYLL TARLY, Lord of Horn Hill,
  — SAMWELL, his elder son, of the
    Night's Watch,
  — DICKON, his younger son, heir to
    Horn Hill,
— ARWYN OAKHEART, Lady of Old Oak,
— MATHIS ROWAN, Lord of Goldengrove,
— LEYTON HIGHTOWER, Voice of
  Oldtown, Lord of the Port,
— SER JON FOSSOWAY,

Principal houses sworn to Highgarden are Vyrwel,
Florent, Oakheart, Hightower, Crane, Tarly,
Redwyne, Rowan, Fossoway, and Mullendore.

HOUSE GREYJOY

The Greyjoys of Pyke claim descent from the Grey King of the Age of Heroes. Legend says the Grey King ruled not only the western isles but the sea itself, and took a mermaid to wife.

For thousands of years, raiders from the Iron Islands —called "ironmen" by those they plundered—were the terrors of the seas, sailing as far as the Port of Ibben and the Summer Isles. They prided themselves on their fierceness in battle and their sacred freedoms. Each island had its own "salt king" and "rock king." The High King of the Isles was chosen from among their number, until King Urron made the throne hereditary by murdering the other kings when they assembled for a choosing. Urron's own line was extinguished a thousand years later when the Andals swept over the islands. The Greyjoys, like other island lords, intermarried with the conquerers.

The Iron Kings extended their rule far beyond the isles themselves, carving kingdoms out of the mainland with fire and sword. King Qhored could truthfully boast that his writ ran "wherever men can smell salt water or hear the crash of waves." In later centuries, Qhored's descendents lost the Arbor, Oldtown, Bear Island, and much of the western shore. Still, come the Wars of Conquest, King Harren the Black ruled all the lands between the mountains, from the Neck to the Blackwater Rush. When Harren and his sons perished in the fall of Harrenhal, Aegon Targaryen granted the riverlands to House Tully, and allowed the surviving lords of the Iron Islands to revive their ancient custom and chose who should have the primacy among them. They chose Lord Vickon Greyjoy of Pyke.

The Greyjoy sigil is a golden kraken upon a black field. Their words are *We Do Not Sow.*

BALON GREYJOY, Lord of the Iron Islands, King of Salt and Rock, Son of the Sea Wind, Lord Reaper of Pyke,
— his wife, LADY ALANNYS, of House Harlaw,
— their children:
— {RODRIK}, their eldest son, slain at Seagard during Greyjoy's Rebellion,
— {MARON}, their second son, slain on the walls of Pyke during Greyjoy's Rebellion,
— ASHA, their daughter, captain of the *Black Wind*,
— THEON, their sole surviving son, heir to Pyke, a ward of Lord Eddard Stark,

—his brothers:
  —EURON, called Crow's Eye, captain of the *Silence*, an outlaw, pirate, and raider,
  —VICTARION, Lord Captain of the Iron Fleet,
  —AERON, called Damphair, a priest of the Drowned God,

Lesser houses sworn to Pyke include Harlaw, Stonehouse, Merlyn, Sunderly, Botley, Tawney, Wynch, Goodbrother.

HOUSE MARTELL

Nymeria, the warrior queen of the Rhoyne, brought her ten thousand ships to land in Dorne, the southernmost of the Seven Kingdoms, and took Lord Mors Martell to husband. With her help, he vanquished his rivals to rule all Dorne. The Rhoynar influence remains strong. Thus Dornish rulers style themselves "Prince" rather than "King." Under Dornish law, lands and titles pass to the eldest child, not the eldest male. Dorne, alone of the Seven Kingdoms, was never conquered by Aegon the Dragon. It was not permanently joined to the realm until two hundred years later, and then by marriage and treaty, not the sword. Peaceable King Daeron II succeeded where the warriors had failed by wedding the Dornish princess Myriah and giving his own sister in marriage to the reigning Prince of Dorne. The Martell banner is a red sun pierced by a golden spear. Their words are *Unbowed, Unbent, Unbroken.*

DORAN NYMEROS MARTELL, Lord of
Sunspear, Prince of Dorne,

— his wife, MELLARIO, of the Free City of Norvos,

— their children:

— PRINCESS ARIANNE, their eldest daughter, heir to Sunspear,

— PRINCE QUENTYN, their elder son,

— PRINCE TRYSTANE, their younger son,

— his siblings:

— his sister, {PRINCESS ELIA}, wed to Prince Rhaegar Targaryen, slain during the Sack of King's Landing,

— their children:

— {PRINCESS RHAENYS}, a young girl, slain during the Sack of King's Landing,

— {PRINCE AEGON}, a babe, slain during the Sack of King's Landing,

— his brother, PRINCE OBERYN, the Red Viper,

— his household:

— AREO HOTAH, a Norvoshi sellsword, captain of guards,

— MAESTER CALEOTTE, counselor, healer, and tutor,

— his knights and lord bannermen:

— EDRIC DAYNE, Lord of Starfall,

The principal houses sworn to Sunspear include Jordayne, Santagar, Allyrion, Toland, Yronwood, Wyl, Fowler, and Dayne.

The Old Dynasty
HOUSE TARGARYEN

The Targaryens are the blood of the dragon, descended from the high lords of the ancient Freehold of Valyria, their heritage proclaimed in a striking (some say inhuman) beauty, with lilac or indigo or violet eyes and hair of silver-gold or platinum white.

Aegon the Dragon's ancestors escaped the Doom of Valyria and the chaos and slaughter that followed to settle on Dragonstone, a rocky island in the narrow sea. It was from there that Aegon and his sisters Visenya and Rhaenys sailed to conquer the Seven Kingdoms. To preserve the blood royal and keep it pure, House Targaryen has often followed the Valyrian custom of wedding brother to sister. Aegon himself took both his sisters to wife, and fathered sons on each. The Targaryen banner is a three-headed dragon, red on black, the three heads representing Aegon and his sisters. The Targaryen words are *Fire and Blood*.

THE TARGARYEN SUCCESSION
dated by years after Aegon's Landing

1–37	Aegon I	Aegon the Conquerer, Aegon the Dragon,
37–42	Aenys I	son of Aegon and Rhaenys,
42–48	Maegor I	Maegor the Cruel, son of Aegon and Visenya,
48–103	Jaehaerys I	the Old King, the Conciliator, Aenys' son,
103–129	Viserys I	grandson to Jaehaerys,
129–131	Aegon II	eldest son of Viserys, [Aegon II's ascent was disputed by his sister Rhaenyra, a year his elder. Both perished in the war between them, called by singers the Dance of the Dragons.]
131–157	Aegon III	the Dragonbane, Rhaenyra's son, [The last of the Targaryen dragons died during the reign of Aegon III.]
157–161	Daeron I	the Young Dragon, the Boy King, eldest son of Aegon III, [Daeron conquered Dorne, but was unable to hold it, and died young.]
161–171	Baelor I	the Beloved, the Blessed, septon and king, second son of Aegon III,
171–172	Viserys II	younger brother of Aegon III,
172–184	Aegon IV	the Unworthy, eldest son of Viserys, [His younger brother, Prince Aemon the Dragonknight, was champion and some say lover to Queen Naerys.]

184–209	Daeron II	Queen Naerys' son, by Aegon or Aemon, [Daeron brought Dorne into the realm by wedding the Dornish princess Myriah.]
209–221	Aerys I	second son to Daeron II (left no issue),
221–233	Maekar I	fourth son of Daeron II,
233–259	Aegon V	the Unlikely, Maekar's fourth son,
259–262	Jaehaerys II	second son of Aegon the Unlikely,
262–283	Aerys II	the Mad King, only son to Jaehaerys,

Therein the line of the dragon kings ended, when Aerys II was dethroned and killed, along with his heir, the crown prince Rhaegar Targaryen, slain by Robert Baratheon on the Trident.

THE LAST TARGARYENS

{KING AERYS TARGARYEN}, the Second of His Name, slain by Jaime Lannister during the Sack of King's Landing,
— his sister and wife, {QUEEN RHAELLA} of House Targaryen, died in childbed on Dragonstone,
— their children:
— {PRINCE RHAEGAR}, heir to the Iron Throne, slain by Robert Baratheon on the Trident,
— his wife, {PRINCESS ELIA} of House Martell, slain during the Sack of King's Landing,
— their children:
— {PRINCESS RHAENYS}, a young girl, slain during the Sack of King's Landing,

— {PRINCE AEGON}, a babe, slain during the Sack of King's Landing,

— PRINCE VISERYS, styling himself Viserys, the Third of His Name, Lord of the Seven Kingdoms, called the Beggar King,

— PRINCESS DAENERYS, called Daenerys Stormborn, a maid of thirteen years.

ACKNOWLEDGMENTS

The devil is in the details, they say.

A book this size has a *lot* of devils, any one of which will bite you if you don't watch out. Fortunately, I know a lot of angels.

Thanks and appreciation, therefore, to all those good folks who so kindly lent me their ears and their expertise (and in some cases their books) so I could get all those little details right—to Sage Walker, Martin Wright, Melinda Snodgrass, Carl Keim, Bruce Baugh, Tim O'Brien, Roger Zelazny, Jane Lindskold, and Laura J. Mixon, and of course to Parris.

And a special thanks to Jennifer Hershey, for labors above and beyond the call . . .

ABOUT THE AUTHOR

GEORGE R. R. MARTIN is the award-winning author of six novels, including *Fevre Dream* and *The Armageddon Rag*. For the last ten years, he has been a screenwriter for feature films and television and was a writer-producer of the TV series *Beauty and the Beast* as well as story editor for *The Twilight Zone*. After a ten-year hiatus, he has now returned to writing novels full-time and is presently at work on *A Dance With Dragons*, the fifth book of *A Song of Ice and Fire*.

George R. R. Martin's
epic fantasy saga
A Song of Ice and Fire

begins with

A GAME OF THRONES

and continues in

A CLASH OF KINGS

and

A STORM OF SWORDS

And coming in fall 2005

A FEAST FOR CROWS

The long-awaited next volume
in the series!

Now, here's a special preview of
the next book in

George R. R. Martin's

landmark series

A CLASH OF KINGS

the riveting sequel to

A GAME OF THRONES

On sale now

THEON

There was no safe anchorage at Pyke, but Theon Greyjoy wished to look on his father's castle from the sea, to see it as he had seen it last, ten years before, when Robert Baratheon's war galley had borne him from the island to be a ward of Eddard Stark. On that day he had stood beside the rail, listening to the stroke of the oars and the pounding of the master's drum while he watched Pyke grow smaller and smaller in the distance, until it vanished beneath a green horizon. Now he wanted to see it grow larger, to rise from the sea before him.

Obedient to his wishes, the *Myraham* beat her way past the point with her sails snapping and her captain cursing the wind and his crew and the follies of highborn lordlings. Theon drew the hood of his cloak up against the spray, and looked for home.

The shore was all sharp rocks and glowering cliffs, and the castle seemed one with the rest, its towers and walls and bridges quarried from the same grey-black stone, wet by the same salt waves, festooned with the same spreading patches of dark green moss, speckled by the droppings of the same sea birds. The point of land on which the Greyjoys had raised their fortress had once thrust like a sword into the bowels of the ocean, but the great waves had hammered at it day and night until the land broke and shattered, thousands of years past. All that remained were three bare and barren islands and a dozen towering stacks of rock that rose from the water like the pillars of some sea god's temple, while the angry waves foamed and crashed around them.

Drear, dark, forbidding, Pyke stood atop those islands and pillars, almost a part of them, its curtain walls closing off the headland to guard the foot of the great stone bridge that leapt from the clifftop to the largest islet, dominated by massive bulk of the Great Keep, whose walls still bore the scars of Robert Baratheon's assault. Further out were the Kitchen Keep and the Bloody Keep, each on its own stony island at the end of a high, vaulting bridge. Towers and outbuildings clung to the stacks beyond, linked to each other by covered archways when the pillars stood close, by long swaying walks of wood and rope when they did not. The Sea Tower rose from the outmost island at the point of the broken sword, the oldest part of the castle, round and tall, the sheer-sided pillar on which it stood half eaten through by the end-less battering of the waves. The base of the tower was white from centuries of salt spray, the upper stories green from the moss that crawled over it like a thick blanket, the jagged crown black with soot from its nightly watchfire.

Above the Sea Tower snapped his father's sigil on a long banner with three tails. The *Myraham* was too far off for Theon to see more than the cloth itself, but he knew the device it bore: the golden kraken of House Greyjoy, arms writhing and reaching against the black field. The banner streamed from an iron mast, shivering and twisting as the wind gusted, like a bird struggling to take flight. Best of all, the direwolf of Stark did not fly above, casting its shadow down upon the Greyjoy kraken.

Theon had never seen a more stirring sight. In the sky behind the castle, the fine red tail of the comet was visible through thin, scuttling clouds. All the way from Riverrun to Seagard, the Mallisters had argued about its meaning. *It is my comet*, Theon told himself, sliding a hand into his fur-lined cloak to touch the oilskin pouch snug in its pocket. Inside was the letter Robb Stark had given him, paper as good as a crown.

"Does the castle look as you remember it, milord?" the captain's daughter asked as she pressed herself against his arm.

"It looks smaller," Theon confessed, "though perhaps that is only the distance." The *Myraham* was a fat-bellied southron merchanter up from Oldtown, carrying wine and spice and seed to trade for iron ore. Her captain was a fat-bellied southron merchanter as well, and the stony sea that foamed at the feet of the castle made his plump lips quiver, so he stayed well out, further than Theon would have liked. An ironborn captain in a longship would have taken them along the cliffs and under the high bridge that spanned the gap between the gatehouse and the Great Keep, but this plump Oldtowner had neither the craft, the crew, nor the courage to attempt such a thing. So they sailed past at a safe distance, and Theon must content himself with seeing Pyke from afar. Even so, the *Myraham* had to struggle mightily to keep itself off those rocks.

"It must be windy there," the captain's daughter observed.

He laughed. "Windy and cold and damp. A miserable hard place, in truth . . . but my lord father once told me that hard places breed hard men, and hard men rule the world."

The captain's face was as green as the sea when he came bowing up to Theon and asked, "May we make for port now, milord?"

"You may," Theon said, a faint smile playing about his lips. The promise of gold had turned the Oldtowner into a shameless lickspittle. It would have been a much different voyage if a longship from the islands had been waiting at Seagard, as he'd hoped. Ironborn captains were proud and wilful, and did not go in awe of a man's blood. The islands were too small for awe, and a longship smaller still. If every captain was a king aboard his own ship, as was often said, it was small wonder they named the islands the land of ten thousand kings. And when you have seen your kings shit over the rail and turn green in a storm, it was hard to bend the knee and pretend they were a god. "The Drowned God makes men," old King Urron Redhand had once said, thousands of years ago, "but it's men who make crowns."

The *Myraham* was rounding a wooded point. Below the pine-clad bluffs, a dozen fishing boats were pulling in their nets. The big merchanter stayed well out from them, tacking. Theon moved to the bow for a better view. He saw the castle first, the stronghold of the Botleys, a lesser house sworn to his father. When he was a boy it had been timber and wattle, but Robert Baratheon had razed that structure to the ground. Lord Sawane had rebuilt in stone, for now a small square keep crowned the hill. Pale green flags drooped from the squat corner towers; the Botley banner, he knew, emblazoned with a shoal of silvery fish.

Beneath the dubious protection of the fish-ridden little castle lay the village of Lordsport, its harbor aswarm with ships. When last he'd seen Lordsport, it had been a smoking wasteland, the skeletons of burnt galleys lying black on the stony shore like the bones of dead leviathans, the houses no more than broken walls and cold ashes. After ten years, few traces of the war remained. The smallfolk had built new hovels with the stones of the old, and cut fresh sod for their roofs. A new inn had risen beside the landing, twice the size of the old one, with a lower story of cut stone and two upper stories of timber. The sept beyond had never been rebuilt, though; only a seven-sided foundation remained to show where it had stood. Robert Baratheon's fury had soured the ironmen's taste for the new gods, it would seem.

Theon was more interested in ships than gods. Among the masts of countless fishing boats, he spied a Tyroshi trading galley offloading beside a lumbering Ibbanese cog with her black-tarred hull. A great number of longships, fifty or sixty at the least, stood out to sea or lay beached on the pebbled shore to the north. *So many*, he thought, uneasy. Theon could not recall ever seeing this many longships in Lordsport before, save on the eve of his father's ill-fated rebellion. And some of the sails bore devices from the other islands; the blood moon of Wynch, Lord Goodbrother's banded black warhorn, Harlaw's silver scythe. He searched for a glimpse of his uncle Euron's *Silence*. Of that lean and terrible red ship he saw no sign, but his father's *Great Kraken* was there, looming over the lesser craft, her bow ornamented with a grey iron ram in the shape of its namesake.

Had Lord Balon anticipated him and called the Greyjoy banners when he received Robb's message from Riverrun? His hand went inside his cloak again, to the oilskin pouch. No one knew of his letter but Robb Stark; they were no fools, and only a fool entrusted his secrets to a bird. Still, Lord Balon was no fool either. He might well have guessed why his son was coming home at long last, and acted accordingly.

The thought did not please him. His father's war was long done, and lost. This was Theon's hour—his plan, his glory, and in time, his crown. *Yet if the longships are hosting . . .*

It might be only a caution, now that he thought on it. A defensive move, lest the war spill out across the sea. Old men were cautious by nature. His father was old now, and so too his uncle Victarion, who commanded the Iron Fleet. His uncle Euron was a different song, to be sure, but the *Silence* did not seem to be in port. *It is for the good*, Theon told himself. *This way, I shall be able to strike all the more quickly.*

As the *Myraham* made her way landward, Theon paced the deck restlessly, scanning the shore. He had not thought to find Lord Balon himself waiting at quayside, but surely his father would have sent someone to meet him. Old Sylas Sourmouth the steward, or perhaps Lord Botley or Dagmer Cleftjaw. They knew he was coming. Robb had sent word before Theon left Riverrun, and when they'd found no long-ship waiting at Seagard, Lord Jason Mallister had sent his own birds to Pyke, supposing that Robb's were lost.

Yet he saw no familiar faces on the landing, no honor guard of riders to escort him from Lordsport to Pyke, only smallfolk going about their small business. Shorehands rolled casks of wine off the Tyroshi trader, fisherfolk cried the day's catch, children ran and played. A priest in the sea-water robes of the Drowned God was leading a pair of horses along the pebbled shore, while above him a slattern leaned out a window in the inn, calling out to some passing Ib-banese sailors.

A handful of Lordsport merchants had gathered to meet the ship. They shouted up questions as the *Myraham* was tying up. "We're out of Oldtown," the captain called down in reply, "bearing apples and oranges, wines from the Arbor, feathers from the Summer Isles. I have pepper, woven leathers, a bolt of Myrish lace, mirrors for milady, a pair of Oldtown woodharps sweet as any you ever heard." The gang-plank descended with a creak and a thud. "And I've brought your heir back to you."

The Lordsport men gazed on Theon with blank, bovine eyes, and he realized that they did not know who he was. It made him angry. He pressed a golden dragon into the captain's palm. "Have your men bring my things." Without waiting for a reply, he strode down the gangplank. "Innkeep," he barked, "I require a horse."

"As you say, m'lord," the man responded, without so much as a bow. He had forgotten how bold the ironborn could be. "Happens as I have one might do. Where would you be riding, m'lord?"

"Pyke," Theon snapped curtly. The fool *still* did not know him. He should have worn his good doublet, with the kraken embroidered on the breast, that would have left no question.

"You'll want to be off soon, to reach Pyke afore dark," the innkeep said. "My boy will go with you and show you the way."

"Your boy will not be needed," a deep voice called, "nor your horse. I shall see my nephew back to his father's house."

The speaker was the priest he had seen leading the horses along the shoreline. As the man approached, the smallfolk bent the knee, and Theon heard the innkeep murmur, "Damphair."

Tall and thin, with fierce black eyes and a beak of a nose, the priest was garbed in mottled robes of green and grey and blue, the swirling colors of the Drowned God. A waterskin hung under his arm on a leather strap, and ropes of dried seaweed were braided through his waist-long black hair and untrimmed beard.

Theon frowned at the prod of memory. In one of his few curt letters, Lord Balon had written of his youngest brother going down in a storm, and turning holy when he washed up safe on shore. "Uncle Aeron?" he said, doubtfully.

"Nephew Theon," the priest replied. "Your lord father bid me fetch you. Come."

"In a moment, uncle." He turned back to the *Myraham.* "My things," he commanded the captain.

A sailor fetched him down his tall yew bow and quiver of arrows, but it was the captain's daughter who brought the pack with his good clothing. "Milord." Her eyes were red. When he took the pack, she made as if to embrace him, there in front of her own father and his priestly uncle and half the island.

Theon turned deftly aside. "You have my thanks."

"Please," she said, "I do love you well, milord."

"I must go." He hurried after his uncle, who was already well down the pier. Theon caught him with a dozen long strides. "I had not looked for you, uncle. After ten years, I thought perhaps my lord father and lady mother might come themselves, or send Dagmer with an honor guard."

"It is not for you to question the commands of the Lord Reaper of Pyke." The priest's manner was chilly, most unlike the man Theon remembered. Aeron Greyjoy had been the most amiable of his uncles, feckless and quick to laugh, fond of songs, ale, and women. "As to Dagmer, the Cleftjaw is gone to Old Wyk at your father's behest, to roust the Stonehouses and the Drumms."

"To what purpose?" Theon asked sharply. "Why are the longships hosting?"

"Why have longships ever hosted?" His uncle had left the horses tied up in front of the waterside inn. When they reached them, he turned to Theon. "Tell me true, nephew. Do you pray to the wolf gods now?"

Theon seldom prayed at all, but that was not something you confessed to a priest, even your father's own brother. "Ned Stark prayed to a tree. No, I care nothing for Stark's gods."

"Good. Kneel."

The ground was all stones and mud. "Uncle, I—"

"*Kneel*. Or are you too proud now, a lordling of the green lands come among us?"

Scowling, Theon knelt. He had a purpose here, and might need Aeron's help to achieve it. A crown was worth a little mud and horseshit on his breeches, he supposed.

"Bow your head." Lifting the skin, his uncle pulled the cork and directed a thin stream of seawater down upon Theon's head. It drenched his hair and ran over his forehead into his eyes. Sheets washed down his cheeks, and a finger crept under his cloak and doublet and down his back, a cold rivulet along his spine. The salt made his eyes burn, until it was all he could do not to cry out. He could taste the ocean on his lips. "Let Theon your servant be born again from the sea, as you were," Aeron Greyjoy intoned. "Bless him with salt, bless him with stone, bless him with steel. Nephew, do you still know the words?"

"What is dead may never die," Theon said, remembering.

"What is dead may never die," his uncle echoed, "but rises again, harder and stronger. Stand."

Theon stood, blinking back tears from the salt in his eyes. Wordless, his uncle corked the waterskin, untied his horse, and mounted. Theon did the same. They set off together, leaving the inn and the harbor behind them, up past the castle of Lord Botley into the stony hills. The priest ventured no further word.

"I have been half my life away from home," Theon ventured at last. "Will I find the islands changed?"

"Men fish the sea, dig in the earth, and die. Women birth children in blood and pain, and die. Night follows day. The winds and tides remain. The islands are as our god made them."

Gods, he has grown grim, Theon thought. "Will I find my sister and my lady mother at Pyke?"

"You will not. Your mother dwells on Harlaw, with her own sister. It is less raw there, and her cough troubles her. Your sister has taken *Black Wind* to Great Wyk, with messages from your lord father. She will return e'er long, you may be sure."

Theon did not need to be told that *Black Wind* was Asha's longship. He had not seen his sister in ten years, but that much he knew of her. Odd that she would call it that, when Robb Stark had a wolf named Grey Wind. "Stark is grey and Greyjoy's black," he murmured, smiling, "but it seems we're both windy."

The priest had nothing to say to that.

"And what of you, uncle?" Theon asked. "You were no priest when I was taken from Pyke. I remember how you would sing the old reaving songs standing on the table with a horn of ale in hand."

"Young I was, and vain," Aeron Greyjoy said, "but the sea washed my follies and my vanities away. That man drowned, nephew. His lungs filled with seawater, and the fish ate the scales off his eyes. When I rose again, I saw clearly."

He is mad as he is sour, Theon thought, saddened. He had liked what he remembered of the old Aeron Greyjoy. "Uncle, why has my father called his swords and sails?"

"Doubtless he will tell you at Pyke."

"I would know his plans now," Theon said.

"From me, you shall not. We are commanded not to speak of this to any man."

"Even to *me*!" Theon's anger flared. He'd led men in war, hunted with a king, won honor in tourney melees, ridden with Brynden Blackfish and Greatjon Umber, fought in the Whispering Wood, bedded more girls than he could name, and yet this uncle was treating him as though he were still a child of ten. "If my father makes plans for war, I must know of them. I am not '*any man*,' I am heir to Pyke and the Iron Islands."

"As to that," his uncle said, "we shall see."

The words were a slap in the face. "What does that mean, *we shall see?*" Theon said scornfully. "My brothers are both dead. I am my lord father's only living son."

"Your sister lives." Aeron gave Theon not so much as the courtesy of a glance.

Asha, he thought, confounded. She was three years older than Theon, yet still . . . "A woman may inherit only if there is no male heir in the direct line," he insisted loudly. "I will not be cheated of my rights, I warn you."

His uncle grunted. "You *warn* a servant of the Drowned God, boy? You have forgotten more than you know. And you are a great fool if you believe your lord father will ever hand these holy islands over to a Stark. Now be silent. The ride is long enough without your magpie chatterings."

Theon held his tongue, though not without struggle. *So that is the way of it*, he thought. He almost laughed. As if ten years in Winterfell could make a Stark. Lord Eddard may have raised him among his own children, but Theon had never truly felt one of them. The whole castle, from Ned Stark himself to the lowliest kitchen scullion, knew he was there as hostage to his father's good behavior, and treated him accordingly. Even the bastard Jon Snow had been accorded more honor than he had.

Lord Eddard had tried to play the father to him from time to time, but to Theon he had always remained the man who'd brought blood and fire to Pyke and taken him from his home. As a boy, he had lived in fear of Stark's stern face and great dark sword. His lady wife was, if anything, even more distant and suspicious.

As for their children, the younger ones had been mewling babes for most of his years at Winterfell. Only Robb and his baseborn half-brother Jon Snow had been old enough to be worth his notice. The bastard was a sullen boy, quick to sense a slight, jealous of Theon's high birth and Robb's regard for him. For Robb himself, Theon did have a certain affection, as for a younger brother . . . but it would be best not to mention that. In Pyke, it would seem, the old wars were still being fought. That ought not surprise him. The Iron Islands lived in the past; the present was too hard and bitter to be borne. Besides, his father and uncles were old, and the old lords were like that; they took their dusty feuds to the grave, forgetting nothing and forgiving less.

The path they rode wound up and up, into bare and stony hills. Soon they were out of sight of the sea, though the smell of salt still hung sharp in the damp air. They kept a steady plodding pace, past a shepherd's croft and the abandoned workings of a mine. This new, holy Aeron Greyjoy was not much for talk. They rode in a gloom of silence. Finally Theon could suffer it no longer. "Robb Stark is Lord of Winterfell now," he said.

Aeron rode on. "One wolf is much like the other."

"Robb has broken fealty with the Iron Throne and crowned himself King in the North. There's war."

"The maester's ravens fly over salt as soon as rock. This news is old and cold."

"It means a new day, uncle," Theon promised.

"Every morning brings a new day, much like the old."

"In Riverrun, they would tell you different," he said. "I've heard it said that the red comet is a herald of a new age. A messenger from the gods, they say."

"A sign it is," the priest agreed, "but from our god, not theirs. A burning brand it is, such as our people carried of old. It is the flame the Drowned God brought from the sea, and it proclaims a rising tide. It is time to hoist our sails and go forth into the world with fire and sword, as he did."

Theon smiled. "I could not agree more."

"A man agrees with god as a raindrop with the storm."

This raindrop will one day be a king, old man. Theon had suffered quite enough of his uncle's gloom. He put his spurs into his horse and trotted on ahead, smiling.

It was nigh on sunset when they reached the walls of Pyke, a crescent of dark stone that ran from cliff to cliff, with the gatehouse in the center and three square towers to either side. Theon could still make out the scars left by the stones of Robert Baratheon's catapults. A new south tower had risen from the ruins of the old, its stone a paler shade of grey, and as yet unmarred by patches of lichen. That was where Robert had made his breach, swarming in over the rubble and corpses with his warhammer in hand and Ned Stark at his side. Theon had watched from the safety of the Sea Tower, and sometimes he still saw the torches in his dreams, and heard the dull thunder of the collapse.

The gates stood open to him, the rusted iron portcullis drawn up. The guards atop the battlements watched with strangers' eyes as Theon Greyjoy came home at last.

Beyond the curtain wall were half a hundred acres of headland hard against the sky and the sea. The stables were here, and the kennels, and a scatter of other outbuildings. Sheep and swine huddled in their pens, and the castle dogs ran free. To the south were the cliffs, and the wide stone bridge to the Great Keep. Theon could hear the crashing of waves as he swung down from his saddle. A stableman came to take his horse. A pair of gaunt children and some serving men stared at him with dull eyes, but there was no sign of his lord father, nor anyone else he recalled from boyhood. *A bleak and bitter homecoming,* he thought.

The priest had not dismounted. "Will you not stay the night and share our meat and mead, uncle?"

"Bring you, I was told. You are brought. Now I return to our god's business." Aeron Greyjoy turned his horse and rode slowly out beneath the muddy spikes of the portcullis.

A bentback old crone in a shapeless grey dress approached him warily. "M'lord," she said, "I am sent to make you welcome and show you to chambers."

"By whose bidding?"

"Your lord father, m'lord."

Theon pulled off his gloves. "So you *do* know who I am. Why is my father not here to greet me?"

"He awaits you in the Sea Tower, m'lord. When you are rested from your trip."

And I thought Ned Stark cold. "And who are you?"

"Helya, who keeps this castle for your lord father."

"Sylas was steward here. They called him Sourmouth." Even now, Theon could recall the winey stench of the old man's breath.

"Dead these five years, m'lord."

"And what of Maester Qalen, where is he?"

"He sleeps in the sea. Wendamyr keeps the ravens now, but he is gone south to Oldtown on some maester's business."

It is as if I were a stranger here, Theon thought. *Nothing has changed, and yet everything has changed.* "Show me to my chambers, woman," he commanded. Bowing stiffly, she led him across the headland to the bridge. That at least was as he remembered; the ancient stones slick with spray and spotted by lichen and moss, the sea foaming under their feet like some great wild beast, the salt wind clutching at their clothes.

When he had imagined his homecoming, he had always pictured himself returning to the snug bedchamber in the Sea Tower where he'd slept as a child. Instead the old woman led him to the Bloody Keep. The halls were larger and better furnished, if no less cold nor damp. Theon was given a suite of chilly rooms with ceilings so high that they were lost in gloom. He might have been more impressed if he had not known that these were the very chambers that had given the Bloody Keep its name. A thousand years before, the sons of the River King had been slaughtered here, hacked to bits in their beds so the pieces of their bodies might be sent back to their father on the mainland.

But Theon was a Greyjoy, and Greyjoys were not murdered in Pyke, except once in a great while by their brothers, and his brothers were both mercifully dead. It was not the memories of ancient murders that made him glance about with distaste. The wall hangings were green with mildew, the mattress musty-smelling and sagging, and rushes old and brittle. It had been years since these chambers had last been opened. The damp went bone deep.

"I'll have a basin of hot water, and a fire in this hearth," he told the crone. "See that they light braziers in the other rooms to drive out some of the chill. And gods be good, get someone in here at once to change these rushes."

"Yes, m'lord. As you command." She fled.

After some time, they brought the hot water he had asked for. It was only tepid, and soon cold, and seawater in the bargain, but it served to wash the dust of the long ride from his face and hair and hands. As bondservants scurried about lighting braziers, Theon stripped off his travel-stained clothing and dressed to meet his father. He chose boots of supple black leather, soft lambswool breeches of silvery-grey, a black velvet doublet with the golden kraken of the Greyjoys embroidered on the breast. Around his throat he fastened a slender gold chain, around his waist a belt of bleached white leather. He hung a dirk at one hip and a longsword at the other, in scabbards striped black-and-gold. Drawing the dirk, he tested its edge with his thumb, pulled a whetstone from his belt pouch, and gave it a few licks. He prided himself on keeping his weapons sharp. "When I return, I shall expect a warm room and clean rushes," he warned the bondservants as he drew on a pair of black gloves, the silk decorated with a delicate scrollwork tracery in golden thread.

Theon returned to the Great Keep through a covered stone walkway, the echoes of his footsteps mingling with the ceaseless rumble of the sea below. To get to the Sea Tower on its crooked pillar, he must needs cross three further bridges, each narrower than the one before. The last was made of rope and wood, and the wet salt wind made it sway underfoot like a living thing. Theon's heart was in his mouth by the time he was halfway across. A long way below, the waves threw up tall plumes of spray as they crashed against the rock. As a boy, he used to run across this bridge, even in the black of night. *Boys believe nothing can hurt them*, his doubt whispered. *Grown men know better.*

The door was narrow, made of grey wood studded with iron, and Theon found it barred from the inside. He hammered on it with a fist, and cursed when a splinter snagged the fine silk of his glove. The wood was damp and moldy, the iron studs rusted.

After a moment the door was opened from within by a guard in a black iron breastplate and pothelm. "You are the son?"

"Out of my way, or you'll learn who I am, to your sorrow." The man stood aside. Theon climbed the twisting steps to the solar. He found his father seated beside a brazier, beneath a robe of musty sealskins that covered him foot to chin. At the sound of boots on stone, the Lord of the Iron Islands lifted his eyes to behold his last living son. He was smaller than Theon remembered him. And so gaunt. Balon

Greyjoy had always been thin, but now he looked as though the gods had put him in a cauldron and boiled every spare ounce of flesh from his bones, until nothing remained but hair and skin. Bone thin and bone hard he was, with a face that might have been chipped from flint. His eyes were flinty too, black and sharp, but the years and the salt winds had turned his hair the grey of a winter sea, flecked with white-caps. Unbound, it hung past the small of the back.

"Nine years, is it?" Lord Balon said at last.

"Ten," Theon answered, pulling off his torn gloves.

"A boy they took," his father said. "What are you now?"

"A man," Theon answered. "Your blood and your heir."

Lord Balon grunted. "We shall see."

"You shall," Theon promised.

"Ten years, you say. Stark had you as long as I. And now you come as his envoy."

"Not his," Theon said. "Lord Eddard is dead, beheaded by the Lannister queen."

"They are both dead," Lord Balon said. "Stark, and that Robert who took broke my walls with his stones. Once I vowed I'd live to see them both in their graves, and now I have." He grimaced. "Yet the cold and the damp still make my joints ache, as when they were alive. So what does it serve?"

"It serves." Theon moved closer. "I bring a letter—"

"Did Ned Stark dress you like that?" his father interrupted, squinting up from beneath his robe. "Was it his plea-sure to garb you in velvets and silks and make you his own sweet daughter?"

Theon felt the blood rising to his face. "I am no man's daughter. If you mislike my garb, I will change it."

"You will," Lord Balon agreed brusquely. Throwing off the fur robe, he pushed himself to his feet. He was not so tall as Theon remembered. "That bauble around your neck—did you buy it with gold or iron?"

Theon touched the gold chain, at a loss for words. He had forgotten. *It has been so long . . .* In the Old Way, only women decorated themselves with ornaments bought with coin. A warrior wore only the jewelry he took off the corpses of enemies slain by his own hand. *Paying the iron price*, it was called.

"You blush red as a maid, Theon," his father said. "A question was asked. Is it the gold price you paid, or the iron?"

"The gold," Theon admitted.

His father slid his fingers under the necklace and gave it a yank so hard it was like to take Theon's head off, had the chain not snapped first. "My daughter has taken an axe for a lover," Lord Balon said. "I will not have my son bedeck himself like a whore." He dropped the broken chain onto the brazier, where it slid down among the coals. "It is as I feared. The green lands have made you soft, and the Starks have made you theirs."

"You're wrong," Theon said. "Ned Stark was my gaoler, but my blood is still salt and iron."

Lord Balon turned away and warmed his boney hands over the brazier. "Yet the Stark pup sends you to me like a well-trained raven, clutching his little message."

"There is nothing small about the letter I bear," Theon said, "and the offer he makes is one I suggested to him."

"This wolf king heeds your counsel, does he?" The notion seemed to amuse Lord Balon.

"He heeds me, yes. I've hunted with him, trained with him, shared meat and mead with him, warred at his side. I have earned his trust. He looks on me as an older brother, he—"

"No." His father jabbed a finger at his face. "Not here, not in Pyke, not in my hearing, you will not name him brother, this son of the man who put your true brothers to the sword. Or have you forgotten Rodrik and Maron, who were your own blood?"

"I forget nothing." Theon might have reminded his father that Ned Stark had killed neither of his sons, in truth. Rodrik had been slain by Lord Jason Mallister at Seagard, Maron crushed in the collapse of the old south tower . . . but Stark would have done for them just as quick had the tide of battle chanced to sweep them together. "I remember my brothers very well," he said instead. Chiefly he remembered Rodrik's drunken cuffs and Maron's cruel japes and endless lies. "I remember when my father was a king, too." He took out the letter Robb had given him, and thrust it forward. "Here. Read it . . . Your Grace."

Lord Balon broke the seal and unfolded the parchment. His black eyes flicked back and forth. "So the boy would give me a crown again," he said, "and all I need do is destroy his enemies." His thin lips twisted in a smile.

"By now Robb is likely besieging the Golden Tooth," Theon said. "Once it falls, he'll be through the hills in a day. Lord Tywin and his host are at Harrenhal, cut off from the west. The Kingslayer is a captive at Riverrun. Only Ser Stafford Lannister and the raw green levies he's been gathering remain to oppose Robb in the west. Ser Stafford will have no choice but to put himself between Robb's army and Lannisport . . . which means the city will be undefended when we descend on it by sea. If the gods are with us, even Casterly Rock itself may fall before the Lannisters so much as realize that we are upon them."

Lord Balon grunted. "Casterly Rock has never fallen."

"Until now." Theon smiled. *And how sweet that will be.*

His father did not return the smile. "So this is why Robb Stark sends you back to me, after so long? So you might win my consent to this plan of his?"

"It is my plan, not Robb's," Theon said proudly. *Mine, as the victory will be mine, and in time the crown.* "I will lead the attack myself, if it please you. As my reward I would ask that you grant me Casterly Rock for my own seat, once we have taken it from the Lannisters." With the Rock, he could hold Lannisport and the green lands of the west, and the gold-rich hills that surrounded them. It would mean wealth and power such as House Greyjoy had never known.

"You reward yourself handsomely for a notion and a few lines of scribbling." His father read the letter again. "The pup says nothing about a reward. Only that you speak for him, and I am to listen, and give him my sails and swords, and in return he will give me a crown." His flinty eyes lifted to meet his son's. "He will *give* me a crown," he repeated, his voice growing sharp.

"A poor choice of words, what is meant is—"

"What is meant is what is said. The boy will *give* me a crown. And what is given can be taken away." Lord Balon tossed the letter onto the brazier, atop the necklace. The parchment curled, blackened, and took flame.

Theon was aghast. "Have you gone mad?"

His father laid a stinging backhand across his cheek. "Mind your tongue. You are not in Winterfell now, and I am not Robb the Boy, that you should speak to me so. I am the Greyjoy, Lord Reaper of Pyke, King of Salt and Rock, Son of the Sea Wind, and no man gives me a crown. I pay the iron price. I will *take* my crown, as Urron Redhand did five thousand years ago."

A GAME OF THRONES

Collectible Card Game

Take control of one of the
Great Houses of Westeros
and pit your favorite
characters against
each other.

George R.R. Martin's
A Song of Ice and Fire series
comes to life in this
collectible card game of conquest,
battle, intrigue, and betrayal.

FANTASY FLIGHT GAMES

A Game of Thrones
collectible card game is
available at hobby game stores
everywhere, and online at:

www.fantasyflightgames.com

© 2005 George R. R. Martin. © 2005 FFG

A GAME OF THRONES

THE BOARDGAME

In the world of George R.R. Martin's *A Song of Ice and Fire*, winter is coming.
The king lies dead and the Great Houses vie for control of the Seven Kingdoms.

Take control of House Stark, Lannister, Baratheon, Greyjoy, or Tyrell. Battle,
outmaneuver and outwit your opponents as you struggle to gain the Iron Throne.
Because in the game of thrones, you either win or you die.

A Game of Thrones is a board
game for
2-5 players.

Also available:
A Clash of Kings
expansion
A Storm of Swords
expansion (coming
November 2005)

FANTASY
FLIGHT
GAMES

www.fantasyflightgames.com   2005 George R. R. Martin. © 2005 FFG